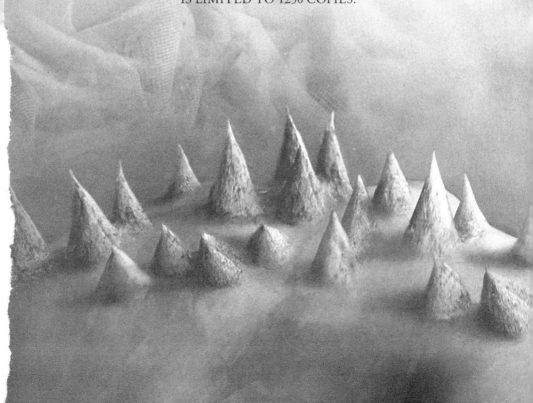

CAITLÍN R. KIERNAN

THIS SPECIAL SIGNED EDITION
IS LIMITED TO 1250 COPIES.

Houses Under the Sea:
Mythos Tales

Houses Under the Sea:
Mythos Tales

CAITLÍN R. KIERNAN

Subterranean Press • 2019

Signed, Trade Hardcover

ISBN
978-1-59606-920-6

Subterranean Press
PO Box 190106
Burton, MI 48519

subterraneanpress.com
www.caitlinrkiernan.com
greygirlbeast.livejournal.com
Twitter: @auntbeast

Manufactured in the United States of America

This book is dedicated to the four brilliant people who have made it possible for me to do paleontology again – Jun Ebersole (McWane Science Center, University of Alabama at Birmingham), Andrew Gentry (UAB, McWane Science Center), Mary Beth Prondzinski (University of Alabama Museums), and Andrew K. Rindsberg (University of West Alabama). Thank you all very much.

Table of Contents

We seem to move on a thin crust which may at any moment be rent by the subterranean forces slumbering below.

Sir James Frazer, *The Golden Bough* (1890)

Lovecraft and I

(Delivered as the keynote address, 15th Annual HPL Film Festival, Portland, Oregon, October 2, 2010)

Oh, where to start.

First off, I think that when you're a Guest of Honor it means you're *being* honored. But, truthfully, I feel very much the other way around about this turn of events, having been invited to appear as a Guest of Honor at the Lovecraft Film Festival. *I'm* honored to have been *asked* and honored that the Festival has gone to considerable trouble and expense to get me here. I certainly couldn't have managed it otherwise. It doesn't help that I'm a bit of a recluse and not much given to travel. Just getting me out of the house can be a chore. Getting me to cross the country and back, well, that's something I've not done in more than a decade. But when I was asked to be here, I couldn't very well say no. Lovecraft's work has been too great an influence on my own writing to have possibly said no, and, as I've stated, it is an honor.

Then, when I was asked to speak at the opening ceremonies, I said yes. After all, it was *another* honor, being asked, and so again I couldn't exactly say no. Still, I had no clue whatsoever as to what I was going to say up here at the podium. I'm truly not good at this sort of thing. I'm never sure where to begin or where to end. I ramble. I lose my train of thought. But I pondered and pondered *and* pondered, and finally at the last minute – which was Wednesday afternoon – I figured it out.

I'll begin here, with the day I first encountered H. P. Lovecraft. Oddly, I found him in Trussville, Alabama on a yellow school bus. I was seventeen years old. It was a rainy morning in the spring of 1981, and Lovecraft was lying all alone on an empty seat, in the form of a library book from the Birmingham Public Library that someone had accidentally left behind when they got off. It was, in fact, the original 1965 Arkham House edition of *Dagon and Other Macabre Tales.* The black-and-white cover, by Lee Brown Coye (1907–1981), depicts a decrepit, bug-eyed man clad all in rags, a monstrous figure that reminded me at once of Captain Ahab Ceely. The bug-eyed man is wielding a harpoon, which, as one might expect from a decrepit sort of Captain Ahab Ceely, has impaled an albino sperm whale. Turns out, Coye had something of an obsession with *Moby Dick,* and whales are a recurring motif in his artwork. But the man on the book's cover was a giant, by comparison to the whale, which, I'd soon learn, echoes a passage from "Dagon." Lovecraft writes:

> It was the pictorial carving, however, that did most to hold me spellbound. Plainly visible across the intervening water on account of their enormous size, were an array of bas-reliefs whose subjects would have excited the envy of a Doré. I think that these things were supposed to depict men – at least, a certain sort of men; though the creatures were shewn disporting like fishes in the waters of some marine grotto, or paying homage at some monolithic shrine which appeared to be under the waves as well. Of their faces and forms I dare not speak in detail; for the mere remembrance makes me grow faint. Grotesque beyond the imagination of a Poe or a Bulwer, they were damnably human in general outline despite webbed hands and feet, shockingly wide and flabby lips, glassy, bulging eyes, and other features less pleasant to recall. Curiously enough, they seemed to have been chiselled badly out of proportion with their scenic background; for one of the creatures was shewn in the act of killing a whale represented as but little larger than himself. I remarked, as I say, their grotesqueness and strange size; but in a moment decided that they were merely the imaginary gods of some primitive fishing or seafaring tribe; some tribe whose last descendant had perished eras before the first ancestor of the Piltdown or Neanderthal Man was born. Awestruck at this unexpected glimpse into a past beyond the conception of the most daring anthropologist, I stood musing whilst the moon cast queer reflections on the silent channel before me.

Of course, the figures in the bas-relief are *not* imaginary, and the proportions are likely *not* that far off.

But anyway, for me that's how the love affair with Lovecraft began – a stark black-and-white cover, with the name *Dagon* emblazoned in crimson. As a teenager, I admit that I had the somewhat reprehensible habit of judging a book by its cover. I was even worse about this as a child. Fortunately, I fell in love with Coye's cover at once. And it was just lying there on the seat of the school bus, with no one in sight to lay claim to it. I checked to see if anyone were watching. Nobody was. I felt a distinct thrill in picking it up and hurrying away with it clutched in my arms. I suppose I should have given it to the bus driver or taken it to the lost and found…or something. But I was too intrigued. I had to know what was inside. So I spent several days and nights devouring *Dagon and Other Macabre Tales*. I sat up late when I ought to have been asleep. I hid it inside my algebra textbook during class. These things sound horridly cliché, I know, but they're true. And as I read, I fell for the author of these stories, just as I'd fallen for Lee Brown Coye's cover art.

After reading the collection, I'd realize how effectively that cover art evoked the mood of the stories, their atmosphere, the overall *frisson*. And any admirer of HPL's knows that, to him, the success or failure of any weird or macabre tale hinges on whether or not the author has managed to evoke *mood*, first and foremost. No amount of rotting New England seaports or arcane texts or slithering tentacles can ever take the place of expertly crafted mood. You get the mood right, or you give it up. So, in that sense, Coye's cover is spot on. It drew me in, and I discovered not only the title story, but such dark gems as "The Hound," "The Strange High House in the Mist," "The Lurking Fear," "The Doom That Came to Sarnath," and, perhaps, most importantly, the essay "Supernatural Horror in Literature." I read *Dagon and Other Macabre Tales* cover to cover, and some of the stories I read more than once. Then I reluctantly dropped the book into the return bin at the Trussville branch of the library. I have often regretted not keeping it. It's not like I was the one who carelessly left it lying on the school bus. It's not like I was the one who'd be in trouble for losing it. But I didn't keep it. I returned it back into the world.

So, that was my initiation, my introduction to Lovecraft. A left-behind library book with an odd, grotesque, eye-catching cover created by a man who, by coincidence, died that same year.

Now, at the time, I had no idea that these were far from Lovecraft's best stories, and it would be several years yet before I'd figure that out, before I'd discover the wonders of *At the Mountains of Madness,* and "The

Colour Out of Space," and "The Shadow Over Innsmouth." I was a voracious reader, but it wasn't easy finding Lovecraft in Alabama in 1981, and I was very busy with high school, and then college, and many other authors, besides. My life became consumed with my studies in paleontology, geology, and biology, and I didn't find my way back to Lovecraft until 1988 or so. In part, it was reading T.E.D. Klein's sublime novel *The Ceremonies* and then his collection *Dark Gods* that reminded me of that rainy day on the school bus and what I found there. While at the University of Colorado in Boulder, I found the other Arkham House volumes in the college library, and I devoured them immediately.

I think it's no coincidence that my fondness for Lovecraft was cinched about this time. I was working as a paleontologist, and continuing my education in that subject. For me, conceiving of vast gulfs of time and space had become part of my everyday life, though I was aware it was something most people seemed never to pause to consider. Here we are, an infinitesimal speck in a largely unknowable and entirely indifferent universe. Here we are, only a momentary incarnation of matter and energy. Eternity and infinity stretch away all around us. We see it in the stars, and in quantum mechanics, in rocks that were already ancient before the evolution of multicellular life, and we see it in the profusion of plants and animals that inhabited this world before us, preserved now as fossils. We see it in the coming of our own species, and all the ages of human history. For me, this awareness of what geologists call "deep time" was both mundane and marvelous. Still, I wasn't that accustomed to finding it in literature. But here it was in Lovecraft, and here it was in spades.

Few other speculative fiction writers, and certainly very few prior to Lovecraft, seem to have so thoroughly comprehended the profundity of deep time and its consequences for humanity. Lovecraft not only comprehended it, he spent his life writing stories that, among other things, sought to convey the truth of our place in the cosmos. Sure, the monsters were great, and the disintegrating ancestral castles, and the mutant fish people – but for me, it was his appreciation for time and his ability to convey a cosmic perspective in fiction. He knew, instinctively, the power of these revelations. Time and space – spacetime – is scary shit. If it weren't, Galileo wouldn't have been forced to recant, and we wouldn't still have creationists yammering about Biblical myths more than a century and a half after Darwin published his great book. Lovecraft didn't just write creepy stories. In his own way, he subverted religious dogma and said, "Look, we're so tiny, and we'll be gone before you know it. And nothing and no one cares. And this is terrifying, but it's also grand."

I should wrap this. I've already mentioned the trouble I have finding endings. But here we are, twenty-nine years and a couple of odd lifetimes after that day on the school bus. I now live in Providence, Rhode Island, Lovecraft's city, the city he declared himself to exemplify. I certainly never planned for things to work out that way, but fate's an odd and wondrous and disquieting thing. I regularly walk the same redbrick sidewalks he walked, past houses where he lived, and I visit libraries and museums he visited. On a regular basis, I pass the observatory where a young Lovecraft watched the stars. And I sometimes leave tokens of appreciation on his modest headstone at Swan Point Cemetery.

My own fiction has been receiving comparisons to his since my second novel, *Threshold,* was published in 2001. I've never quite known what to make of these comparisons, except that I find them flattering. Indeed, I find, when I read them, that I am honored. And humbled.

Thank you.

Valentia
(1994)

All night tossing and turning on the flight from JFK to Shannon, interminable jet drone and the whole autumn-long night spent sailing through ice-crystal clouds far above the black roil and churn of the Atlantic. Finally, the ragged west coast of Ireland appearing outside her window like a grey-green gem, uncut, unpolished, and then the plane was on the ground. Routinely suspicious glances at her passport from the customs agent – her short hair still blonde in the photograph, but now it's red, auburn – and Anne was grateful when she spotted one of Morris' grad students waiting for her with a cardboard sign, DR. CAMPBELL printed neatly in blue marker on brown cardboard. She dozed on the long drive down to Kerry, nodding off while the student talked and the crooked patchwork of villages and farms rolled by outside.

"It's so terrible," the student says, has said that more than once, apologized more than once, like any of this might have been her fault somehow. Máire, pale, coal-haired girl from Dublin with her tourist-brochure eyes, green eyes that never leave the road, never glance at Anne as the car rolls on south and west, the slate-dark waters of Dingle Bay stretching away to the north and all the way down to the sea. Past Killorglin now, and there's a tall signpost, black letters on whitewashed wood, a white arrow pointing the way on to Cahirciveen, still forty kilometers ahead of them, and so Anne closes her eyes again.

"Do you have any idea how it happened?" she asks, and "Ah, Christ. I'm so sorry, Dr. Campbell," the girl says, her voice like she might be close to tears, and so Anne doesn't ask again.

Two hours later, and the blue and white car ferry from Renard Point is pulling away from the dock, plowing across the harbor towards the big island of Valentia. Only a five-minute crossing, but the water just rough enough that Anne wishes there was a bottle of Dramamine tablets packed somewhere in her Army surplus duffel in the rental car's trunk. She stands at the railing because she figures it's more polite to puke over the side than on the decks, stands with nervous, green-eyed Máire on her left, emerald eyes and wringing hands.

None of this feels real, Anne thinks. *None of this feels the least bit real.*

The girl is clutching a rosary now, something shiny from a sweater pocket, silver crucifix and black beads. Anne turns away, watching the horizon, the indefinite confluence of the grey island and greyer sea. The air smells like saltwater and fish and coming rain, and she concentrates on the questions she's carried with her all the way from New York, unpleasant thoughts to drown her old dread of seasickness. The questions that began two days earlier with the first news of Morris Whitney's death, with Dr. Randall's Sunday afternoon phone call. "Can you come in this evening, Anne?" he said, sounding tired, sleepless, sounding like all his sixty years had finally, suddenly, caught up with him.

"It's Morris. Something's happened. There's been an accident," but she didn't want to hear the rest, said so, made him stop there, no more until she took the subway from her Tribeca apartment uptown to the museum. No more until she was sitting in her tiny, fifth-floor office, listening to Arthur Randall talk. Everything he knew, scant and ugly details, and at first none of it seeming to add up – the phone call from the police in Cahirciveen, Morris' body hauled from the sea by a fishing boat out of Knightstown, the vandalized excavation. But Anne listened silently, the old man's shaky voice and her eyes lingering safely on the cover of a back issue of the *Journal of Vertebrate Paleontology* lying on her desk – the glossy orange and white cover, black print, the precise line drawing of an Eocene percopsid, all safe and sensible things so she wouldn't have to see the look on Arthur's face.

"Do you have any idea what he was doing out there after dark?" she asks, almost whispering, and Máire turns her head slightly, her eyes still on the rosary in her hands.

"No," the girl says. "None of us do."

Anne glances back at the mainland, growing smaller as the little ferry chugs diligently across the harbor, and she knows now that she shouldn't have come, that Arthur was right, and there are probably no more answers here than would have found her in Manhattan. Not if this skittish girl at her side is any indication, and there's something else, besides, a quiet anxiety beneath the lead-weight ache of her loss, beneath the disorientation. A vague unease as the shores of Valentia grow nearer; but *He would have come for you,* she thinks, and then Máire is talking again.

"Dr. Whitney had us back in Knightstown, you know. Me and Billy both. He said he was worried about whether or not the grants would be renewed. Said he needed the solitude to write at night, to work on the progress report for the *National Geographic* people, but we knew he was havin' bad dreams."

"So you weren't at the field house Friday night?" and Máire shakes her head, no, "This last week, we've been riding out on our bicycles every mornin', an' ridin' back again in the evenings. It's only half an hour, maybe..."

And then the ferry whistle blows, shrill and steam-throat bellow to smother whatever Máire might have said next, and the girl slips the rosary back into the pocket of her sweater.

Valentia Island, seven miles by three, rocky exile cut off from the Irish mainland long ago by the restless Atlantic and the thin, encircling finger of the Portmagee Channel. Sheep and cattle, and a century ago strong men mined slate from a huge quarry near the island's northeast corner, mined stone for roofing tiles in London and railroad pavement in Nottingham and Leicester. A small but sturdy white lighthouse where Valentia Harbor meets the ocean proper, once upon a time a fortress for Cromwell's men, its beacon automated years ago. Farther west, the land rises abruptly to Reenadrolaun Point more than a hundred feet above the sea, a rocky precipice where the rollers have carved away the world; from there, the raw charcoal and ash periphery of the island stretches from Fogher Cliff to Beennakryraka Head. And on these weathered ledges Morris Whitney found the Valentia trackway in 1993; two months in Ireland on an NSF grant to study a poorly-curated collection of Devonian lobe-finned and placoderm fishes at the Cork Geology Museum, but he was led astray to Valentia by persistent rumors of footprints in stone. First, a local farmer's stories of "dinosaur tracks" and then a letter to the curator of the museum from a birders club, and so he finally took a day off and made the drive from Cork. And not believing his eyes when the old man led him across a pasture to the ledges, the farmer's gap-toothed pride at the expression on the paleontologist's astonished face when he saw the perfect, single trail, winding across the slate towards the sea, all the tracks exposed on a single bedding plane.

"Didn't I tell you? Are they not dinosaurs, then?" the old man asked, and Morris could only shake his head, his own grin grown almost as wide as the old man's, clambering down to get a better look as the waves slammed loud against the rocks.

"No, Mr. O'Shea, these are definitely *not* dinosaur tracks. Whatever made these tracks lived…" and he paused, doing the math in his head, calculating the age of rocks and the duration of geological periods. "Whatever made them was walking around a hundred and forty million years before the first dinosaurs. These are something much, much *better* than dinosaur tracks." The old man's eyes went wide and doubtful, then, and he sat down on the grass and dangled his short legs over the edge of the little cliff.

"Ah," he said, "Well, now that *is* a bloody wonder, wouldn't ye say?"

And Morris on his knees, a cheap black plastic Instamatic camera from his backpack, and he was staring at the fossils though the viewfinder. "Yes sir, it is. It certainly is that," and he snapped away a whole roll of film before following the old man back across the field.

Two hours after dawn and Anne Campbell, jetlagged and shivering in the October gales, stands beside the tracks, a single bedding plane exposed along the thirty-foot ledge, narrow, an almost horizontal rind of bare stone to mark this place where the island is slowly being reclaimed by the Atlantic. Overhead gulls and kittiwakes wheel and cry like lost and hungry children. Behind her, Máire is still talking to the constable, the red-cheeked, pot-bellied man who escorted them from Kingstown; they speak in hushed voices, as if they're saying things they don't want Anne to hear.

There are still traces of Morris' chalk marks, despite the tides and salt spray, despite everything his killers did to the site. White chalk lines to measure the width of manual and pedal strides, faint reference numbers for his photographs; another day or two, and the sea will have swept the ledge clean again. Tears in her eyes and she isn't sure how much of that's for Morris, how much for the ruined treasures, and how much is merely the stinging, icy fingers of the wind.

There were a hundred tracks to begin with, according to Morris' notes, a hundred already exposed when he first saw the ledge and another fifty or sixty uncovered as he and Máire and Billy followed the prints back into the cliff's face, sledges and pry bars to clear away the heavy blocks of Valentia slate. And now, only five or six that haven't been damaged or obliterated altogether. *Desecrated,* Anne thinks. *This place has been desecrated.* As surely as any church that was ever burned or any shrine that was ever looted, and she sits down beside one of the few tracks that hasn't been chipped or scraped or smashed beyond recognition. The gently-rippled surface of the rock shimmers faintly, glitter-dull interplay of mica crystals and the sun, and she puts her fingers into the shallow depression on the ledge, touches the clear imprint left by something that passed this way three hundred and eighty-five million years ago. She looks up, past the trackway, at the rest of the ledge; patches of algal scum the unhealthy color of an infection and small accumulations of brown sand, bright against the slate, a few stingy pools of water stranded in the low places, waiting for the next high tide.

"He got everythin' on film," Máire says behind her, trying to sound reassuring, trying to sound responsible. "And we have the casts. Dr. Whitney sent a set of them off to Cork just last week, and another to the Survey in Dublin."

"I want to see the photographs, Máire. Everything that's been developed. As soon as possible, okay?"

"Aye," the girl says. "They're all back in town. It didn't seem safe to leave anythin' in the field house."

"No," Anne says, as much to herself as Máire, "No, I guess not." And then Máire's talking with the constable again, and Anne stares past the ledge at the wide, cold ocean.

Her room in Kingstown, dingy plaster walls and faded Catholic icons, the faint, oily smell of fish, but it's some place warm and dry against the rain that started falling an hour after sunset. Cold drops that pepper the windowpane, and she sat there for awhile, waiting for Dr. Randall to return her call, stared down at the drenched and narrow streets, a pub across from the hotel and its windows glowing yellow orange through the downpour, soft and welcoming glow, and she wished she'd asked Máire to stay. She could have thought of an excuse if she tried – help with Morris' records, questions about the sediment samples sent to Dublin for radiometric tests, anything against the sound of the storm and her loneliness. But the girl made her uncomfortable, nothing she could quite put her finger on, and on the way back from the site, Máire leaned close and asked if it was true, that Anne and Morris were lovers, a whispered question so Constable Bryce wouldn't overhear. Anne blushed, confused, embarrassed, and "That was a long time ago," she replied, nothing else, though, her surprise turning quick to anger and unasked questions as to what this girl might know about her, what she might *think* she knows.

So relief when the phone rang, the voice at the other end sounding far away, distance strained, cable filtered, but relief anyway. The familiarity something to push away her homesickness for a few minutes, at least, and Arthur Randall asked if she were okay, if she were holding up. "Yeah," she said, "Sure," an unconvincing lie, and he sighed loudly; she could hear him lighting a cigarette, exhaling, before he asked her about the trackway, if there was anything at all that might be salvaged.

"Only if it's still beneath the overburden. You absolutely would not *believe* this shit, Arthur. I've never seen a site so completely...so..." and that word from the ledge coming back to her again, *...so completely desecrated,* but it was nothing she wanted to say aloud, so "They trashed everything," she said instead, and then added "It just doesn't make sense."

"Then you *don't* think it was someone after the tracks?"

"No. If this was someone trying to steal fossils, it's the worst botched attempt I could imagine. And there's no sign they actually tried to remove anything. Nothing at all. Whoever it was, they wanted to *erase* the tracks, Arthur, not steal them."

And now she sits on her bed listening to the rain on the roof, the rain at the window, and all Morris' photographs are spread out in front of her, glossy 8"×10" documents of his month on Valentia, every inch of the trackway painstakingly recorded, these photos to back up Máire's maps and diagrams of the ledge, carefully-gridded sketches recording the relative position and size of every footprint. So at least the data has been saved, the fossils themselves gone but not the information. Enough that she can finish what he began, a description of some of the very oldest known tetrapod ichnofossils, among the earliest evidence of the ancestors of all terrestrial vertebrates, left here by something a little more than a meter in length, no longer precisely a fish, but still a long way from terrestrial. Only one other set of tracks this old was known, fossils from the Genoa River in Australia, described in 1972.

Anne puts down one of the photographs and picks up another. There are no tracks in this shot, the fossilized ripple marks from the bed of an ancient stream, and for a moment she thinks that's all. Silt and sand shaped by the currents of warm Paleozoic waters and then that pattern frozen here for almost four hundred thousand millennia, and she's about to put this picture down, too, when she notices something small in the lower left-hand corner. Something embedded in the slate, glinting in the sun like metal, and she holds it under the lamp beside her bed for a better look.

Her first impression is that Morris has placed a coin in the shot for scale, one of the seven-sided Irish fifty-pence pieces, maybe. She leans closer to the photograph, squints, her nose almost touching the paper now, and she can see that the surface of the thing is smooth, so it's no coin, and there's no doubt that it's actually embedded in the stone, not merely lying on the surface. She chews at her bottom lip, turns the print upside down, and at this angle she can see that it isn't perfectly smooth after all, that there's the faintest suggestion of a raised pattern on its surface, ridges and dimples worn almost away by years of exposure to the wind and sea. A single crinoid plate perhaps, broken away from the calyx, or some other echinoderm fossil, only a heptagonal bit of silica and a trick of light and shadow to make it *look* metallic.

No, not a crinoid, she thinks. *Not a crinoid or a cystoid, and not a plate from a primitive sea urchin, either, because these beds were laid down in fresh water.* Maybe it's a bit of bony armor from one of the placoderm fishes. And didn't she see a note somewhere in Morris' papers, or something Máire mentioned in passing, that they'd found remains of the placoderm *Bothriolepis* in nearby strata? But under the dim lamp light the thing certainly *looks* metallic, and her first impression, that she was seeing a coin, lingers stubbornly in her mind; Anne rubs at her tired eyes.

"Jesus," she whispers, still too exhausted from the flight and then the long day out at the site, and it's no wonder she can't think straight. The reality of Morris' death hasn't even sunk in yet; she gathers up the photographs and slips them all back into the big manila envelope, the mystery shot lying on top. In the morning, she'll ask Máire about the odd fossil, or Billy if he's at breakfast. But it can wait until then. The clock on her nightstand reads ten twenty-five, and Anne switches off the lamp and sits for a moment in the darkness, thinking of home as the wind buffets and rattles at the window.

In the dream, she's back in Manhattan, standing on the marble steps of the American Museum's Central Park West entrance, steps smoothed by fifty-eight years of footfalls. There are pigeons perched irreverently on the bronze statue of Teddy Roosevelt; bronze gone to verdigris, and the Great White Chief proud atop his horse, noble tarnished savages on his left and right as he leads them away to civilization and extinction. But where the street ought to be there's a shallow brook with sandy sidewalk banks, restless water sparkling bright in the New York sun. Anne looks past the stream, expecting the autumn fire of the park, all the familiar, innumerable shades of orange and gold and ruddy browns, but instead – a green so dense, so primeval, the inviolable green of the world's first forests. Eden past a Fallen World, and as she descends the steps, bare feet silent on stone and discarded hot dog wrappers, she cannot take her eyes off the strange plants rooted on the far side of the stream, the mad bloom of foliage sprouting from the cracked and weathered cement; a towering canopy of alien "trees" – *Wattieza, Archaeopteris, Lepidosigillaria, Pseudosporochnus* – and the sun slanting in cathedral shafts between the impossible branches, falling across scale bark and the impenetrable underbrush of horsetails and ferns. Only a dozen yards in, and that forest's already so dense the green has faded black.

Anything might live in there, she thinks, *anything at all.*

Beyond Roosevelt and the Indians and a man selling Snapple and hot pretzels, she stands at the shore, the concrete and sand and there's no rude blat of taxi horns here, no ceaseless background drone of human voices; an always-summer wind through the trees, the cool murmur and purl of the water between avenue-straight banks and the buzz of dragonflies the size of ravens. Earth turned back, past man and ice ages, past the time of terrible lizards and screeching, kite-winged pterodactyls; continents torn apart and reconfigured for these long, last days before all the world will be squeezed together into the supercontinent Pangaea.

This is not a new dream. Her entire adult life has been spent chasing these ghosts, her unconscious always resurrecting and refining this wilderness. But the dream was never half this real. These sounds and smells never half so alive, the quality of sunlight never this brilliant, and she kneels beside the stream, staring down at the logs jammed together just below the surface, the water plants she knows no names for. Tiny fish dart away into the submerged jumble of shattered limbs and trunks. The water isn't deep here, and there are tracks on the muddy bottom, prints left by fins that will be toes some day, toes that haven't yet forgotten fins, and her eyes follow the tracks upstream to the place where there's something big slipping off this shoal into deeper water. A frog-wide head breaks the surface, wary black eyes watching her, and then it's gone, one flick of its tail and the sinuous thing glides away in an obscuring cloud of silt.

Anne Campbell knows *where* she is this time, not just *when,* this wilderness that will be a rocky Irish coast someday, and she glances back at the forest. The forest darker and deeper than all the tangled dreams of humanity, and she closes her eyes, can hear the cold rain falling on the hotel's roof eons and eons away. "Not yet, Anne," someone says close behind her, someone speaking with Morris' voice. She opens her eyes again, but there's no one back there but the pretzel vendor, and he hasn't even seemed to notice her. She stands up and brushes the sand from the knees of jeans.

And that's when she spots the silver thing shining up at her from the water's edge, a seven-sided disc that isn't a coin; she knows that now, and she knows that it isn't part of anything that ever lived, either. Something shaped from metal, something fashioned, and she bends down and picks it up; it's ice cold to the touch, cold enough it burns the palm of her hand. But she has to hold it, has to *see* the markings worked into the thing, the symbols she doesn't recognize and cannot read, runes or an unknown cuneiform set around the image at the disc's center – the tentacled face, its parrot beak, the dragon wings – and then there's a deafening clap of thunder from the clear sky, and Anne drops the thing. It falls into the water with a small but definite splash, sinking between the dead branches where the little fish disappeared. She almost reaches for it, but then thinks of the jointed, razor jaws of arthrodires, the serrate claws of scuttling, scorpion-legged eurypterids and, instead, looks up at the infinite blue vault of Heaven overhead.

"What was I supposed to see?" she dreams herself asking the unclouded sky, no clouds but there is thunder anyway, just as there was Morris Whitney's voice without his body. And she's scared for the first time, wants to wake up now, because there's something moving about in the ferns on the other side of the stream, something huge, and that sound that isn't *really* thunder from the sky again, a sound like a tear in the sky. It's raining, but it isn't water that falls. Anne shuts her eyes tight, no ruby-slipper heels to click, so she repeats Morris' name, again and again and again, while the scalding filth drips down to blister her face and turn the pool red and steaming at her feet.

Morning now, and the storms have passed, blown away south to Bantry and Skibbereen, the Celtic Sea beyond, and the sky is perfect blue as Anne makes her way back to the cliffs alone. A rusty purple bicycle borrowed from the hotel's cook, and she follows the winding road north through the Glanleam woods, on past the lighthouse, and then takes a narrower road west, little more than a footpath for sheep, really, past the steep rise of Reenadrolaun and down to Culloo. The sea air chilly on her face, on her hands, and her legs are aching by the time she reaches the site.

She sees the girl standing by the cliffs long before she's close enough to recognize it's Máire, tousled black hair and one of her heavy wool cardigans, and she's staring out at the foam-white rollers, something dark held in her right hand. Anne stops, lowers the bike's kickstand and walks the last ten or twenty yards. But if Máire hears her approach, she makes no sign that she's heard. She stands very still, watching the uneasy, storm-scarred sea.

"Máire?" Anne calls out. "Hello? I didn't expect to find you out here."

The girl turns slowly, moving stiff and slow like someone half asleep, and Anne thinks that maybe she's been crying, the red around her eyes, wet green eyes and bruise-dark circles underneath like she hasn't slept in awhile.

"I want to ask you a question, about one of the photographs. I have it with…" But then Anne can see exactly what she's holding, the small black handgun, and Máire smiles for her.

"Good morning, Dr. Campbell."

A moment before she can reply, two heartbeats before she can even look away from the revolver, the sun glinting dully off its stubby chrome barrel. "Good morning, Máire," she finally says. Her mouth is dry, and the words come out small and flat.

"Did ye sleep well, then?" the girl asks, and Anne nods her head. Máire turns back towards the ledge, back towards the sea. "I was afraid you might have bad dreams," she says. "You know, after lookin' at them pictures."

"What is it, Máire, the disc in the photograph? You *know* what it is, don't you?" and Anne takes one step closer to the girl, one step closer to the point where the sod ends and the grey stone begins.

"I didn't kill him," the girl says. "I want ye to *know* that. I didn't do it, and neither did Billy." Her finger's tight and trembling around the trigger now, and Anne is only a few feet away, only two or three more steps left between them. "It's bad enough, what we've done," Máire says. "But it wasn't murder."

"You're going to have to tell me what you're talking about," Anne says, afraid to move, also afraid to stand still, and the girl turns towards her again.

"You weren't meant to see the pictures, Dr. Campbell. I was supposed to burn them. After we'd done with the tracks, we were supposed to burn everything."

There are fresh tears from the girl's bright eyes, and Anne can see where she's chewed her lower lip raw, fresh blood on her pale chin. Anne takes another step towards her.

"Why were you supposed to burn the pictures? Did Morris tell you to burn the pictures, Máire?"

A blank, puzzled expression passes across the girl's face then, her ragged smile gone for a moment before she shakes her head, rubs the barrel of the gun rough against her corduroy pants.

And then she says something that Anne doesn't understand, something that sounds like "Theena dow'an."

"I don't know Irish," Anne says, pleading now, wanting to understand, and she can see the hurt and anger in Máire's eyes, the bottomless guilt growing there like a cancer. The girl raises the revolver and sets the barrel against her right temple.

"Oh god, no Máire." The girl whispers those two words again, "Theena dow'an," and she then turns back towards the sea in the same instant that she squeezes the trigger. The sound the gun makes is the sound from Anne Campbell's nightmare, and it's the sound of the sky ripping itself apart, the sound of the waves breaking against the ragged, rocky shore.

In the west there is still a tradition of the Fomorii who dwelt in Ireland before the arrival of the Gael. They are perhaps the most feared of all the water fairies and are sometimes known as the Daoine Domhain, the Deep Ones, though they are rarely spoken of aloud.

–Lady Wilde, *Ancient Legends of Ireland* (1888)

So Runs the World Away

A falling star for your thoughts," she says, and Gable, the girl with foil-silver eyes and teeth like the last day of winter, points at the night sky draped high above Providence and the wide Seekonk River. Night-secret New England sky, and a few miles farther north you have to call it the Pawtucket River, but down here, where it laps fishy against Swan Point and the steep cemetery slopes, down here it's still the Seekonk, and way over there are the orange, industrial lights of Phillipsdale. Dead Girl blinks once or twice to get the taste out of her mouth, and then she follows Gable's grimy finger all the way up to Heaven, and there's the briefest streak of white light drawn quick across the eastern sky.

"That's very nice, but they aren't really, you know," she says, and Gable makes a face, pale face squinched up like a very old woman, dried-apple face to say she doesn't understand, and "Aren't really *what?*" she asks.

"Stars," says Dead Girl. "They're only meteorites. Just chunks of rock and metal flying around through space and burning up if they get too close. But they aren't stars. Not if they fall like that."

"Or angels," Bobby whispers and then goes right back to eating from the handful of blackberries he's picked from the brambles growing along the water's edge.

"I never said anything about angels," Gable growls at the boy, and he throws a blackberry at her. "There are *lots* of different words for angels."

"And for falling stars," Dead Girl says with a stony finality so they'll know that's all she wants to hear about it; meteorites that stop being mete-ors, Seekonk changing into Pawtucket, and in the end, it's nothing but the distance between this point and that. As arbitrary as any change, and so she presses her lips against the jogging lady's left wrist again. Not even the sheet-thin ghost of a pulse left in there, cooling meat against her teeth, flesh that might as well be clay except there are still a few red mouthfuls,

29

and the sound of her busy lips isn't all that different from the sound of the waves against the shore.

"I know seven words for grey," Bobby says, talking through a mouthful of seeds and pulp and the dark juice dribbling down his bloodstained chin. "I got them out of a dictionary."

"You're a little faggot," Gable snarls at the boy, those narrow mercury eyes and her lower lip stuck way out like maybe someone's been beating her again, and Dead Girl knows she shouldn't have argued with Gable about falling stars and angels. *Next time,* she thinks, *I'll remember that. Next time, I'll smile and say whatever she wants me to say.* And when she's finally finished with the jogging lady, Dead Girl's the first one to slip quiet as a mouse in silk bedroom slippers across the mud and pebbles, and the river is as cold as the unfalling stars speckling the August night.

An hour and four minutes past midnight in the big house on Benefit Street, and the ghouls are still picking at the corpses in the basement. Dead Girl sits with Bobby on the stairs that lead back up to the music and conversation overhead, the electric lights and acrid-sweet clouds of opium smoke; down here there are only candles, and the air smells like bare dirt walls and mildew, like the embalmed meat spread out on the ghouls' long carving table. When they work like this, the ghouls stand up on their crooked hind legs and press their canine faces close together. The very thin one named Barnaby (his nervous ears alert to every footfall overhead, every creaking door, as if anyone Up There even cares what they're doing Down Here) picks up a rusty boning knife and uses it to lift a strip of dry flesh the colour of old chewing gum.

"That's the gastrocnemius," he says, and the yellow-orange iris of his left eye drifts nervously towards the others, towards Madam Terpsichore, especially, who shakes her head and laughs the way that all ghouls laugh. *The way starving dogs would laugh,* Dead Girl thinks, *if they ever dared,* and she's starting to wish she and Bobby had gone down to Warwick with Gable and the Bailiff after all.

"No, that's the soleus, dear," Madam Terpsichore says and sneers at Barnaby, that practiced curl of black lips to flash her jaundiced teeth like sharpened piano keys, a pink-red flick of her long tongue along the edge of her muzzle. "*That's* the gastrocnemius, there," she says. "You haven't been paying attention."

Barnaby frowns and scratches at his head. "Well, if we ever got anything fresh, maybe I could keep them straight," he grumbles, making excuses again, and Dead Girl knows the dissection is beginning to bore Bobby. He's staring over his shoulder at the basement door and at the warm sliver of light getting in around the edges.

"Now, show me the lower terminus of the long peroneal," Madam Terpsichore says, her professorial litany and the impatient clatter of Barnaby digging about in his kit for a pair of poultry shears or an oyster fork, one or the other or something else entirely.

"You want to go back upstairs for a while?" Dead Girl asks the boy, and he shrugs, but doesn't take his eyes off the basement door, doesn't turn back around to watch the ghouls.

"Well, come on then," and she stands up, takes his hand, and that's when Madam Terpsichore finally notices them.

"Please don't go, dear," she says. "It's always better with an audience, and if Master Barnaby ever finds the proper instrument, there may be a flensing yet," and the other ghouls snicker and laugh.

"I don't think I like them very much," Bobby whispers very quietly, and Dead Girl only nods and leads him back up the stairs to the party.

Bobby says he wants something to drink, so they go to the kitchen first, to the noisy antique refrigerator, and he has a Coke, and Dead Girl takes out a Heineken for herself. One chilly apple-green bottle, and she twists the cap off and sips the bitter German beer; she never liked the taste of beer, before, but sometimes it seems like there were an awful lot of things she didn't like before. The beer is very, very cold and washes away the last rags of the basement air lingering stale in her mouth like a dusty patch of mushrooms, basement-dry earth and a billion microscopic spores looking for a place to grow.

"I don't think I like them at all," Bobby says, still whispering even though they're upstairs. Dead Girl starts to tell him that he doesn't have to whisper anymore, but then she remembers Barnaby, his inquisitive, dog-cocked ears, and she doesn't say anything at all.

Almost everyone else is sitting together in the front parlor, the spacious, book-lined room with its stained-glass lamp shades in all the sweet and sour colours of hard candy, sugar-filtered light that hurts her eyes. The first time she was allowed into the yellow house on Benefit Street, Gable showed her all the lamps, all the books, all the rooms, like they were hers. Like she belonged here, instead of the muddy bottom of the Seekonk River, another pretty, broken thing in a house filled up with things that are pretty or broken or both. Filled up with antiques, and some of them breathe and some of them don't. Some, like Miss Josephine, have forgotten how or why to breathe, except to talk.

They sit around her in their black funeral clothes and the chairs carved in 1754 or 1773, rough circle of men and women that always makes Dead Girl think of ravens gathered around carrion, crows about a raccoon's corpse, jostling each other for all the best bits; sharp beaks for her bright and sapphire eyes, for the porcelain tips of her fingers, or that silent, unbeating heart. *The empress as summer road kill,* Dead Girl thinks, and doesn't laugh out loud, even though she *wants* to, wants to laugh at these stiff and obsolescent beings, these tragic waxwork shades sipping absinthe and hanging on Miss Josephine's every word like gospel, like salvation. Better to slip in quiet, unnoticed, and find some place for her and Bobby to sit where they won't be in the way.

"Have you ever *seen* a firestorm, Signior Garzarek?" Miss Josephine asks, and she looks down at a book lying open in her lap, a green book like Dead Girl's green beer bottle.

"No, I never have," one of the waxworks says, tall man with slippery hair and ears that are too big for his head and almost come to points. "I dislike such things."

"But it was *beautiful,*" Miss Josephine assures him, and then she pauses, still looking at the green book in her lap, and Dead Girl can tell from the way her eyes move back and forth, back and forth, that she's reading what-ever's printed on the pages. "No, that's not the right word," she says, "That's not the right word at all."

"I was at Dresden," one of the women volunteers, and Miss Josephine looks up, blinks at the woman as if she can't quite remember what this particular waxwork is called.

"No, no, Addie, it wasn't like that. Oh, I'm sure Dresden was exquisite, too, yes. But this wasn't something man did. This was something that was *done* to men. And that's the thing that makes it truly transcendent, the thing that makes it…" and she trails off and glances back down at the book as if the word she's missing is in there somewhere.

"Well, then, read some of it to us," Signior Garzarek says and points a gloved hand at the green book, and Miss Josephine looks up at him with her blue-brilliant eyes, eyes that seem grateful and malicious at the same time.

"Are you sure?" she asks them all. "I wouldn't want to bore any of you."

"Please," says the man who hasn't taken off his bowler, and Dead Girl thinks maybe his name is Nathaniel. "We always like to hear you read."

"Well, only if you're sure," Miss Josephine says, and she sits up a little straighter on her divan, clears her throat, and fusses with the shiny folds of her black, satin skirt, the dress that only looks as old as the chairs, before she begins to read.

"'*That* was what came next – the fire,'" she says, and this is her reading voice now; Dead Girl closes her eyes and listens. "'It shot up everywhere. The fierce wave of destruction had carried a flaming torch with it – agony, death and a flaming torch. It was just as if some fire demon was rushing from place to place with such a torch. Flames streamed out of half-shattered buildings all along Market Street.

"'I sat down on the sidewalk and picked the broken glass out of the soles of my feet and put on my clothes.

"'All wires down, all wires down!'"

And that's the way it goes for the next twenty minutes or so, the kindly half dark behind Dead Girl's eyes and Miss Josephine reading from her green book while Bobby slurps at his Coke and the waxwork ravens make no sound at all. She loves the rhythm of Miss Josephine's reading voice, the cadence like rain on a hot day or ice cream, that sort of a voice. But it would be better if she were reading something else, 'The Rime of the Ancient Mariner,' maybe, or Keats or Tennyson. But this is better than nothing at all, so Dead Girl listens, content enough, and never mind that it's only earthquakes and conflagration, smoke and the screams of dying men and horses. It's the *sound* of the voice that matters, not the words or anything they mean, and if that's true for her, it's just as true for the silent waxworks in their stiff colonial chairs.

When she's finished, Miss Josephine closes the book and smiles, showing them all the stingiest glimpse of her sharp white teeth.

"Superb," says Nathaniel.

"Oh yes, superb," says Addie Goodwine.

"You are indeed a wicked creature, Josephine," says the Signior, and he lights a fat cigar and exhales a billowing phantom from his mouth. "Such delicious perversity wrapped up in such a comely package."

"I was writing as James Russell Williams, then," Miss Josephine says proudly. "They even paid me."

Dead Girl opens her eyes, and Bobby's finished his Coke, is rolling the empty bottle back and forth across the rug like a wooden rolling pin on cookie dough. "Did you like it?" she asks him, and he shrugs.

"Not at all?"

"Well, it wasn't as bad as the ghouls," he says, but he doesn't look at her, hardly ever looks directly at her or anyone else these days.

A few more minutes pass, and then Miss Josephine suddenly remembers something in another room that she wants the waxworks to see, something they *must* see, an urn or a brass sundial, the latest knick-knack hidden somewhere in the bowels of the great cluttered house. They follow her out of the parlor, into the hallway, chattering and trailing cigar and cigarette smoke, and if anyone even notices Bobby and Dead Girl sitting on the floor, they pretend that they haven't. Which is fine by Dead Girl; she dislikes them, the lifeless smell of them, the guarded desperation in their eyes.

Miss Josephine has left her book on the cranberry divan, and when the last of the vampires has gone, Dead Girl gets up and steps inside the circle of chairs, and she stands staring down at the cover of the green book.

"What does it say?" Bobby asks, and so she reads the title to him.

"San Francisco's Horror of Earthquake, Fire, and Famine," she reads, and then Dead Girl picks the book up and shows him the cover, the letters stamped into the green cloth in faded gold ink. And underneath, a woman in dark-coloured robes, her feet in fire and water, chaos wrapped about her ankles, and she seems to be bowing to a shattered row of marble columns and a cornerstone with the words "In Memoriam of California's Dead – April 18th, 1906."

"That was a long time ago, wasn't it?" Bobby asks, and Dead Girl sets the book down again. "Not if you're Miss Josephine, it isn't," she says. *If you're Miss Josephine, that was only yesterday, the day before yesterday. If you're her* – but that's the sort of thought it's best not to finish, better if she'd never thought it at all.

"We don't have to go back to the basement, do we?" Bobby asks, and Dead Girl shakes her head. "Not if you don't want to," she says. And then she goes to the window and stares out at Benefit Street, at the passing cars and the living people with their smaller, petty reasons for hating time. In a moment, Bobby comes and stands beside her, and he holds her hand.

Dead Girl keeps her secrets in an old Hav-A-Tampa cigar box, the few she can't just keep inside her head, and she keeps the old cigar box on a shelf inside a mausoleum at Swan Point. Beneath this manicured hillside that rises up so sharply from the river's edge, this steep and dead-adorned hill, in the cool darkness below green grass in the summer and the wind-rustling branches of the trees. Only Bobby knows about the box, and she thinks he'll keep it to himself. He rarely says anything to anyone, especially Gable; Dead Girl knows what Gable would do if she found out about the box, *thinks* she knows, and that's good enough, bad enough, that she keeps it hidden in the mausoleum.

The caretakers bricked up the front of the vault years and years ago, but they left a small cast-iron grate set into the masonry just below the marble keystone and the verdigris-streaked plaque with the name "Stanton" on it, though Dead Girl can't imagine why. Maybe it's there so the bugs can come in and out, or so all those dead Stantons can get a breath of fresh air now and then, though there's not even enough room for bats to squeeze through, or the swifts or rats. But still plenty of space between the bars of the grate for her and Bobby to slip inside whenever she wants to look at the things she keeps inside the old cigar box.

Nights like tonight, after the long parties, after Miss Josephine finally loses interest in her waxwork ravens and chases them all away (everyone except the ghouls, of course, who come and go as they please through the tunnels in the basement); there's still a coal-grey hour left until dawn and the hateful, but she knows that Gable is probably already waiting for them in the river, but she can wait a few minutes more.

"She might come looking for us," Bobby says when they're inside the mausoleum and he's standing on tip toes to see out, but the grate is still a foot above his head.

"No, she won't," Dead Girl tells him, tells herself that it's true, that Gable's too glad to be back down there in the dark to be bothered. "She's probably already asleep by now."

"Maybe so," Bobby says, not sounding even the least bit convinced, and then he sits down on the marble floor and watches Dead Girl with his quick-silver eyes, mirror eyes so full of light they'll still see when the last star in the whole goddamned universe has burned itself down to a spinning cinder.

"You let me worry about Gable," she says and opens the box to find that everything's still inside, just the way she left it. The newspaper clippings and a handful of coins, a pewter St. Christopher's medal and a doll's plastic right arm. Three keys and a ragged swatch of indigo velvet stained maroon around the edges. Things that mean nothing to anyone but Dead Girl; her puzzle, and no one else knows the way that all these pieces fit together.

Or even *if* they all fit together. Sometimes even she can't remember, but it makes her feel better to see them, anyway, to lay her white hands on these trinkets and scraps, to hold them.

Bobby is tapping his fingers impatiently against the floor, and when she looks at him he frowns and stares up at the ceiling. "Read me the one about Mercy," he says, and she looks back down at the Hav-A-Tampa box.

"It's getting late, Bobby. Someone might hear me."

And he doesn't ask her again, just keeps his eyes on the ceiling directly above her head and taps his fingers on the floor.

"It's not even a story," she says and fishes one of the newspaper clippings from the box. Nut-brown paper gone almost as brittle as she feels inside and the words printed there more than a century ago. "It's almost like a story, when you read it," Bobby replies.

For a moment, Dead Girl stands very still, listening to the last of the night sounds fading slowly away and the stranger sounds that come just before sunrise; birds and the blind, burrowing progress of earthworms, insects and a ship's bell somewhere down in Providence Harbour, Bobby's fingers drumming on the marble. She thinks about Miss Josephine and the comfort in her voice, her ice-cream voice against every vacant moment of eternity. And, in a moment, she begins to read.

Letter from the *Pawtuxet Valley Gleaner,* dated March 1892:

"Exeter Hill"

Mr. Editor,

As considerable notoriety has resulted from the exhuming of three bodies in Exeter cemetery on the 17th inst., I will give the main facts as I have received them for the benefit of such of your readers as "have not taken the papers" containing the same. To begin, we will say that our neighbor, a good and respectable citizen, George T. Brown, has been bereft of his wife and two grown-up daughters by consumption, the wife and mother about eight years ago, and the eldest daughter, Olive, two years or no later, while the other daughter, Mercy Lena, died about two months since, after nearly one year's illness from the same dread disease. About two years ago Mr. Brown's only son Edwin A., a young married man of good habits, began to give evidence of lung trouble, which increased, until in hopes of checking and curing the same, he was induced to visit the famous Colorado Springs, where his wife followed him later on and though for a time he seemed to improve, it soon became evident that there was no real benefit derived, and this coupled with a strong desire on the part of both husband and wife to see their Rhode Island friends, decided then to return east after an absence of about 18 months and are staying with Mrs. Brown's parents, Willet Himes. We are sorry to say that Eddie's health is not encouraging at this time. And now comes in the queer part, viz: The revival of a pagan or other superstition regarding the feeding of the dead upon a living relative where consumption was the cause of death and now bringing the living person soon into a similar condition, etc. and to avoid this result, according to the same high authority, the "vampire" in question which is said to inhabit the heart of a dead consumptive while any blood remains in that organ, must be cremated and the ashes carefully preserved and administered in some form to the living victim, when a speedy cure may (un) reasonably be expected. I will here say that the husband and father of the deceased ones, from the first, disclaimed any faith at all in the vampire theory but being urged, he allowed other, if not wiser, counsel to prevail, and on the 17th inst., as before stated the three bodies alluded to were exhumed and then examined by Doctor Metcalt of Wickford (under protest, as it were, being an unbeliever). The two bodies longest buried were found decayed and bloodless, while the last one who has been only about two months buried showed some blood in the heart as a matter of course, and as the doctor expected but to carry out what was a forgone conclusion, the heart and lungs of the last named (M. Lena) were then and there duly cremated, but deponent saith not how the ashes were disposed of. Not many persons were present, Mr. Brown being among the absent ones. While we do not blame any one for these proceedings as they were intended without doubt to relieve the anxiety of the living, still, it seems incredible that any one can attach the least importance to the subject, being so entirely incompatible with reason and conflicts also with scripture, which requires us "to give a reason for the hope that is in us," or the why and wherefore which certainly cannot be done as applied to the foregoing.

With the silt and fish shit settling gentle on her eyelids and her lungs filled up with cold river water, Dead Girl sleeps, the soot-black ooze for her blanket, her cocoon, and Bobby safe in her arms. Gable is there, too, lying somewhere nearby, coiled like an eel in the roots of a drowned willow.

And in her dreams, Dead Girl counts the boats passing overhead, their prows to split the day-drenched sky, their wakes the roil and swirl of thunderstorm clouds. Crabs and tiny snails nest in her hair, and her wet thoughts slip by as smooth and capricious as the Seekonk, one instant or memory flowing seamlessly into the next. And *this* moment, this one here, is the last night that she was still a living girl. Last frosty night before Halloween, and she's stoned and sneaking into Swan Point Cemetery with a boy named Adrian that she only met a few hours ago in the loud and smoky confusion of a Throwing Muses show, Adrian Mobley and his long yellow hair like strands of the sun or purest spun gold.

Adrian won't or can't stop giggling, a joke or just all the pot they've been smoking, and she leads him straight down Holly Avenue, the long paved drive to carry them across the Old Road and into the vast maze of the cemetery's slate and granite heart. Headstones and more ambitious monuments lined up neat or scattered wild among the trees, reflecting pools to catch and hold the high white moon, and she's only having a little trouble finding her way in the dark.

"*Shut up,*" she hisses, casts anxious serpent sounds from her chapped lips, across her chattering teeth. "Someone's going to fucking hear us," she says. She can see her breath, her soul escaping mouthful by steaming mouthful.

Then Adrian puts his arm around her, sweater wool and warm flesh around warm flesh, and he whispers something in her ear, something she should have always remembered but doesn't. Something forgotten, the way she's forgotten the smell of a late summer afternoon and sunlight on sand, and he kisses her.

And for a kiss she shows him the place where Lovecraft is buried, the quiet place she comes when she only wants to be alone, no company but her thoughts and the considerate, sleeping bodies underground. The Phillips family obelisk and then his own little headstone; she takes a plastic cigarette lighter from the front pocket of her jeans and holds the flame close to the ground so that Adrian can read the marker: August 20, 1890 – March 15, 1937, "I am Providence," and she shows him all the offerings that odd pilgrims leave behind. A handful of pencils and one rusty screw, two nickels, a small rubber octopus, and a handwritten letter folded neat and weighted with a rock so the wind won't blow it away. The letter begins "Dear Howard," but she doesn't read any farther, nothing there written for her, and then Adrian tries to kiss her again.

"No, wait. You haven't seen the tree," she says, wriggling free of Adrian Mobley's skinny arms, dragging him roughly away from the obelisk; two steps, three, and they're both swallowed by the shadow of an enormous, ancient birch, this tree that must have been old when her great grandfather was a boy. Its sprawling branches are still shaggy with autumn-painted leaves, its roots like the scabby knuckles of some sky-bound giant, clutching at the earth for fear that it will fall and tumble forever towards the stars.

"Yeah, so it's a tree," Adrian mumbles, not understanding, not even trying to understand, and now she knows that it was a mistake to bring him here.

"People have carved things," she says and strikes the lighter again, holds the flickering blue-orange flame so that Adrian can see all the pocket-knife graffiti worked into the smooth, pale bark of the tree. The unpronounceable names of dark, fictitious gods and entire passages from Lovecraft, razor steel for ink to tattoo these occult wounds and lonely messages to a dead man, and she runs an index finger across a scar in the shape of a tentacle-headed fish, a parody of the Christian ichthus.

"Isn't it beautiful?" she whispers, and that's when Dead Girl sees the eyes watching them from the lowest limbs of the tree, *their* shimmering, silver eyes like spiteful coins hanging in the night, like strange fruit, and "This shit isn't the way it happened at all," Gable says. "These aren't even *your* memories. Just memories stolen from some bitch we killed."

"Oh, I think she knows that," the Bailiff laughs, and it's worse than the ghouls snickering for Madam Terpsichore.

"I only wanted him to see the tree," Dead Girl says. "I wanted to show him something carved into the Lovecraft tree."

"Liar," Gable sneers, and that makes the Bailiff laugh again. He squats in the dust and fallen leaves and begins to pick something stringy from his teeth.

And she would run, but the river has almost washed the world away, nothing left now but the tree and the moon and the thing that clambers down its trunk on spider-long legs and arms the colour of chalk dust.

Is that a Death? and are there two?

"We know you would forget us," Gable says, "if we ever let you. You would pretend you were an innocent, a *victim*." Her dry tongue feels as rough as sandpaper against Dead Girl's wrist, a dead cat's tongue, and above them the northern constellations swirl in a mad kaleidoscope dance about the moon; the tree moans and raises its swaying branches to Heaven, praying for dawn, for light and mercy from everything it's seen and will ever see again.

Is Death that woman's mate?

And at the muddy bottom of the Seekonk River, in the shadow of the Henderson Bridge, Dead Girl's eyelids flutter as she stirs uneasily, frightening fish, fighting sleep and her dreams. But the night is still hours away, waiting on the far side of the scalding day, and so she holds Bobby tighter, and he sighs and makes a small, lost sound that the river snatches and drags away towards Narragansett Bay.

Dead Girl sits alone on the floor in the parlor of the house on Benefit Street, alone because Gable has Bobby with her tonight; Dead Girl drinks her Heineken and watches the yellow and aubergine circles that the wax-work voices trace in the stagnant, smoky air, and she tries to recall what it was like before she knew the colours of sound.

Miss Josephine raises the carafe and carefully pours tap water over the sugar cube on her slotted spoon; the water and dissolved sugar sink to the bottom of her glass, and at once the liqueur begins to louche, the clear and emerald-bright mix of alcohol and herbs clouding quickly to a milky, opaque green.

"Oh, of course," she says to the attentive circle of ravens. "I remember Mercy Brown, and Nellie Vaughn, too, and that man in Connecticut. What was his name?"

"William Rose," Signior Garzarek suggests, but Miss Josephine frowns and shakes her head. "No, no. Not Rose. He was that peculiar fellow in Peace Dale, remember? No, the man in Connecticut had a different name."

"They were maniacs, every one of them," Addie Goodwine says nervously and sips from her own glass of absinthe. "Cutting the hearts and livers out of corpses and burning them, eating the ashes. It's ridiculous. It's even worse than what *they* do," and she points confidentially at the floor, towards the basement and the ghouls below.

"Of course it is, dear," Miss Josephine says.

"But the little Vaughn girl, Nellie, I understand she's still something of a sensation among the local high school crowd," Signior Garzarek says and smiles, dabs at his wet red lips with a lace handkerchief. "They do love their ghost stories, don't you know. They must find the epitaph on her tombstone an endless source of delight."

"What does it say?" Addie asks, and when Miss Josephine turns and stares at her, Addie Goodwine flinches and almost drops her glass.

"You really should get out more often, dear," Miss Josephine says, and "Yes," Addie stammers. "Yes, I know. I should."

The waxwork named Nathaniel fumbles with the brim of his black bowler. "I remember," he says. "'I am watching and waiting for you.' That's what it says, isn't it?"

"Delightful, I tell you," Signior Garzarek chuckles, and then he drains his glass and reaches for the absinthe bottle on its silver serving tray.

"What do you see out there?"

The boy that Dead Girl calls Bobby is standing at the window in Miss Josephine's parlor, standing there with the sash up and snow blowing in, a small drift of snow at his bare feet, and he turns around when she says his name.

"There was a bear on the street," he says and puts the glass paperweight in her hands, the glass dome filled with water, and when she shakes it, all the tiny white flakes inside swirl around and around. A miniature blizzard trapped in her palm, plastic snow to settle slow across the frozen field, the barn, the dark and winter-bare line of trees in the distance.

"I saw a bear," he says again, more insistent than before, and points at the open window.

"You did *not* see a bear," Dead Girl says, but she doesn't look to see for herself, doesn't take her silver eyes off the paperweight; she'd almost forgotten about the barn, that day and the storm, January or February or March, more years ago than she'd have ever guessed, the wind howling like hungry wolves.

"I *did*," Bobby says indignantly. "I saw a big black bear dancing in the street. I know a bear when I see one."

Dead Girl closes her eyes and lets the globe fall from her fingers, lets it roll from her hand, and she knows that when it hits the floor it will shatter into a thousand pieces. World shatter, water-sky shatter to bleed Heaven away across the floor, and so there isn't much time if she's going to make it all the way to the barn.

"I think it knew our names," the boy says, and he sounds afraid, but when she looks back, she can't see him anymore. Nothing behind her now but the little stone wall to divide this field from the next, the slate and granite boulders already half buried by the storm, and the wind pricks her skin with icy needle teeth. The snow spirals down from the leaden clouds, and the wind sends it spinning and dancing in dervish crystal curtains.

"We forget for a reason, child," the Bailiff says, his rust-crimson voice woven tightly between the air and every snowflake. "Time is too heavy to carry so much of it strung about our necks."

"I don't hear you," she lies, and it doesn't matter anyway, whatever he says, because Dead Girl is already at the barn door; both the doors left standing open, and her father will be angry, will be furious if he finds out. The horses could catch cold, he will say to her. The cows, he will say, the cows are already giving sour milk, as it is.

Shut the doors and don't look inside. Shut the barn doors and run all the way home.

"It fell from the sky," he said, the night before. "It fell screaming from a clear blue sky. No one's gone looking for it. I don't reckon they will."

"It was only a bird," her mother said.

"No," her father said. "It wasn't a bird."

Shut the doors and run.

But she doesn't do either, because that isn't the way this happened, the way it *happens,* and the naked thing crouched there in the straw and the blood looks up at her with Gable's pretty face. It takes its mouth away from the mare's mangled throat, and blood spills out between clenched teeth and dribbles down its chin.

"The bear was singing our names," Bobby says.

And then the paperweight hits the floor and bursts in a sudden, merciful spray of glass and water that tears the winter day apart around her. "Wake up," Miss Josephine says, spitting out impatient words that smell like anise and dust, and she shakes Dead Girl again.

"I expect Madam Terpsichore is finishing up downstairs. And the Bailiff will be back soon. You can't sleep here."

Dead Girl blinks and squints past Miss Josephine and all the colorful, candy-shaded lamps. And the summer night outside the parlor window, the night that carries her rotten soul beneath its tongue, stares back with eyes as black and secret as the bottom of a river.

In the basement, Madam Terpsichore, lady of rib spreaders and carving knives, has already gone, has crept away down one of the damp and brick-throated tunnels with her snuffling entourage in tow. Their bellies full and all their entrail curiosities sated for another night, and only Barnaby is left behind to tidy up; part of his modest punishment for slicing too deeply through a sclera and ruining a violet eye meant for some graveyard potentate or another, the precious vitreous humour spilled by his hand, and there's a fresh notch in his left ear where Madam Terpsichore bit him for ruining such a delicacy. Dead Girl is sitting on an old produce crate, watching while he scrubs bile from the stainless steel tabletop.

"I'm not very good with dreams, I'm afraid," he says to her and wrinkles his wet black nose.

"Or eyes," Dead Girl says, and Barnaby nods his head.

"Or eyes," he agrees.

"I just thought you might listen, that's all. It's not the sort of thing I can tell Gable, and Bobby, well – "

"He's a sweet child, though," Barnaby says, and then he frowns and scrubs harder at a stubborn smear the colour of scorched chestnuts.

"But I can't tell anyone else," Dead Girl says; she sighs, and Barnaby dips his pig-bristle brush into a pail of soapy water and goes back to work on the stain.

"I don't suppose I can do *very* much damage, if all I do is listen," and the ghoul smiles a crooked smile for her and touches a claw to the bloody place where Madam Terpsichore nicked the base of his right ear with her sharp incisors.

"Thank you, Barnaby," she says and draws a thoughtless half circle on the dirt floor with the scuffed toe of one shoe. "It isn't a very long dream. It won't take but a minute," and what she tells him, then, isn't the dream of Adrian Mobley and the Lovecraft tree, and it isn't the barn and the blizzard, the white thing waiting for her inside the barn. This is another dream, a moonless night at Swan Point, and someone's built a great, roaring bonfire near the river's edge. Dead Girl's watching the flames reflected in the water, the air heavy with wood smoke and the hungry sound of fire. Bobby and Gable are lying on the rocky beach, laid out neat as an undertaker's work, their arms at their sides, copper on their eyes. And they're both slit open from collarbone to crotch, stem to stern, ragged Y-incisions, and their innards glint wetly in the light of the bonfire.

"No, I don't think it was me," Dead Girl says, even though it isn't true, and she draws another half circle on the floor to keep the first one company. Barnaby has stopped scrubbing at the table and is watching her uneasily with his distrustful scavenger eyes.

"Their hearts are lying there together on a boulder," and she's speaking very quietly now, almost whispering as if she's afraid someone upstairs might be listening, too, and Barnaby perks up his ears and leans towards her. Their hearts on a stone, and their livers, too, and she burns the organs in a brass bowl until there's nothing left but a handful of greasy ashes.

"I think I eat them," Dead Girl says. "But there are blackbirds then, a whole flock of blackbirds, and all I can hear are their wings. Their wings bruise the sky."

And Barnaby shakes his head, makes a rumbling, anxious sound deep in his throat, and he starts scrubbing at the table again. "I should learn to quit while I'm only a little ways behind," he snorts. "I should learn what's none of my goddamn business."

"Why, Barnaby? What does it mean?" and at first he doesn't answer her, only grumbles to himself and the pig-bristle brush flies back and forth across the surgical table even though there are no stains left to scrub, nothing but a few soap suds and the candlelight reflected in the scratched and dented silver surface.

"The Bailiff would have my balls in a bottle of brine if I told you that," he says. "Go away. Go back upstairs where you belong and leave me alone. I'm busy."

"But you do know, don't you? I heard a story, Barnaby, about another dead girl named Mercy Brown. They burned *her* heart – "

And the ghoul opens his jaws wide and roars like a caged lion, hurls his brush at Dead Girl, but it sails over her head and smashes into a shelf of Ball mason jars behind her. Broken glass and the sudden stink of vinegar and pickled kidneys, and she runs for the stairs.

"Go pester someone else, *corpse*," Barnaby snarls at her back. "Tell your blasphemous dreams to those effete cadavers upstairs. Ask one of *those* snotty fuckers to cross the Bailiff," and then he throws something else, something shiny and sharp that whizzes past her face and sticks in the wall. Dead Girl takes the stairs two at a time, slams the basement door behind her and turns the lock. And if anyone's heard, if Miss Josephine or Signior Garzarek or anyone else even notices her reckless dash out the front door and down the steps of the old yellow house on Benefit Street, they know better than Barnaby and keep it to themselves.

In the east, there's the thinnest blue-white sliver of dawn to mark the horizon, the light a pearl would make, and Bobby hands Dead Girl another stone. "That should be enough," she says, and so he sits down in the grass at the edge of the narrow beach to watch as she stuffs this last rock inside the hole where Gable's heart used to be. Twelve big rocks shoved inside her now, granite-cobble viscera to carry the vampire's body straight to the bottom of the Seekonk, and this time that's where it will stay. Dead Girl has a fat roll of grey duct tape to seal the wound.

"Will they come after us?" Bobby asks, and the question takes her by surprise, not the sort of thing she would ever have expected from him. She stops wrapping Gable's abdomen with the duct tape and stares silently at him for a moment, but he doesn't look back at her, keeping his eyes on that distant, jagged rind of daylight.

"They might," she tells him. "I don't know for sure. Are you afraid, Bobby?"

"I'll miss Miss Josephine," he says. "I'll miss the way she read us stories," and Dead Girl nods her head.

"Yes," she says. "Me too. But I'll always read you stories," and he smiles when she says that.

When Dead Girl is finally finished, they push Gable's body out into the water and follow it all the way down, wedge it firmly between the roots of the sunken willow tree below Henderson Bridge. And then Bobby nestles close to Dead Girl, and in a moment he's asleep, lost in his own dreams, and she closes her eyes and waits for the world to turn itself around again.

From Cabinet 34, Drawer 6

5:46 p.m.

The old theater on Asylum Street smells of stale popcorn and the spilled soft drinks that have soured on the sticky floors. The woman sitting in the very back row, the woman with the cardboard box open in her lap, shuts her eyes. A precious few seconds free of the ridiculous things on the screen, just the theater stink and the movie sounds – a scream and a splash, a gunshot – and then the man coughs again. Thin man in his navy-blue fedora and his threadbare gabardine jacket, the man with the name that sounds like an ice-cream flavor, and when she opens her eyes he's still sitting there in the row in front of her, looking at her expectantly over the back of his seat. The screen become a vast rectangular halo about his head, a hundred thousand shades of grey.

"Well," he says, "there you have it."

"I don't know what I'm seeing anymore," she says. He nods his head very slowly, up and down, up and down, like a small, pale thing on the sea, and she looks up at the screen again, at the man in the rubber monster suit revealed in the flickering light and the soft, insectile flutter from the projector in the booth above her head.

"Just an old movie," Dr. Solomon Monalisa says, not bothering to whisper because there's no one else in the theater but the two of them, him and her, the skinny, antique man and the bookish woman with her cardboard box. "A silly old movie to scare children at Saturday afternoon matinees, to scare teenage girls."

"Is that what it is? Is that the truth?"

"The truth," he says, smiles a tired sort of a smile and coughs again. A handkerchief from his breast pocket to wipe his thin lips clean, and then the man with the ice-cream name stares for a moment into his own spit and phlegm caught in folds of linen as though they were tea leaves and he could read the future there.

"Yes, I suppose that's what you would call it," he tells her, stuffing the soiled handkerchief back into his pocket. "You would call it that, until something better comes along."

On screen, a cavern beneath the black Amazonian lake, glycerin mist and rifle smoke, and the creature's gills rise and fall, struggling for breath; its bulging eyes are as blank and empty as the glass eyes of a taxidermied fish.

"It's almost over," Dr. Solomon Monalisa says. "Are you staying for the end?"

"I might talk," the woman whispers, even though they are alone, and the creature roars as its plated, scaly flesh is torn by bullets, by knives and spears. Rivulets of dark blood leak from its latex hide as the old man nods his head again. She hasn't answered his question.

"You might," he says. "You wouldn't be the first."

"Would someone try to stop me?"

"Someone already has, Miss Morrow."

And now it's her turn to nod, and she looks away from the movie screen, the man in the latex suit's big death scene up there, the creature drifting limp and lifeless to the bottom of its lonely, weedy lagoon. Lacey Morrow looks down at the box in her lap.

If I'd never found the goddamned thing, she thinks. *If someone else had found it instead of me.* All the things she would give away for that to be true, years of memories, her life if she could die without knowing the things she knows now.

"Well, there it is," Dr. Solomon Monalisa says again, as the last frames flicker past before the screen goes white and the red velvet curtain comes down and the house lights come up. "Not quite as silly as I remember. Not a bad way to pass an afternoon."

"Will they mind if I sit here a little longer?" she asks, and he shrugs his thin shoulders, stands and straightens the lapels of his jacket, fusses with the collar of his shirt.

"No," he says. "I shouldn't think they'd mind at all."

She doesn't watch him leave, keeps her eyes fixed on the box, and his shoes make small, uneven sounds against the sticky floor.

1:30 p.m.

Waking from an uneasy dream of childhood, a seashore and her sisters and something hanging in the wide, carnivorous sky, something terrible that she wouldn't look at no matter what they promised her. Lacey blinks and squints through the streaky train window at the Connecticut countryside rushing by, surely Connecticut by now, probably somewhere well past Springfield and headed for Hartford. A crazy quilt of fields and pastureland stitched together with October leaves, the fiery boughs of birch and beech and hickory to clothe red Jurassic sandstone. Then she catches sight of the winding, silver-grey ribbon of the river to the west, flashing bright beneath the morning sun. She rubs her eyes, blinks at all that sunlight and wishes that she hadn't dozed off. But trains almost always lull her to sleep, sooner or later, the steady heartbeat rhythm of the wheels against the rails, steel-on-steel lullaby, and the more random rattle and clatter of the couplings for punctuation.

She checks to see that the cardboard box is still resting on the empty aisle seat beside her, that her satchel is still stowed safely at her feet. They are. Reassured, Lacey glances quickly about the car, slightly embarrassed at having fallen asleep. That strangers have been watching her sleep, and she might have snored or drooled or mumbled foolish things in her dreams, but the car is mostly empty, anyway – a teenage girl reading a paperback, a priest reading a newspaper – and she looks back to the window, her nightmare already fading in the warmth of the day. The train is closer to the river now, and she can see a small boat – a fishing boat, perhaps – cutting a V-shaped wake on the water.

"Have yourself a nice little nap, then?" and Lacey turns, startled, clipping the corner of the box with her elbow, and it almost tumbles to the floor before she can catch it. There's a woman in the seat directly behind her, someone she hadn't noticed only a moment before, a painfully thin woman with tangled, oyster-white hair, neither very old nor very young, and she's staring at Lacey with watery blue eyes that seem to bulge slightly, intently, from their sockets. Her skin is dry and sallow, and there's a sickly, jaundiced tint to her cheeks. She's wearing a dingy black raincoat and a heavy sweater underneath, wool the color of instant oatmeal, and her nubby fingernails are painted an incongruous flamingo pink.

"I didn't mean to frighten you," the woman says in a deliberate, gravelly voice, but Lacey shakes her head.

"No, it's okay. I guess I'm not quite awake, that's all."

"I was starting to think I'd have to wake you up myself," the woman says impatiently, still staring. "I'm only going as far as Hartford. I don't have the time to go any farther than that."

As she talks, Lacey has begun to notice a very faint fishy smell, fish or low-tide mud flats, brine and silt and stranded, suffocating sea creatures, bladderwrack and rockweed. The odor seems to be coming from the white-haired woman, her breath or her clothes, and Lacey pretends not to notice.

"You're sitting there thinking, 'Who's this lunatic?' ain't you? 'Who's this deranged woman, and how can I get her to shut the hell up and leave me alone?'"

"No, I just don't – "

"Oh, yes you are," the woman says, and she jabs an index finger at Lacey, candy-pink polish and her knuckles like dirty old tree roots. "But that's okay. You don't know me from Adam. You aren't *supposed* to know me, Miss Morrow."

Lacey glances at the other passengers, the girl and the priest. Neither of them are looking her way, still busy with their reading, and if they've even noticed the white-haired woman they're pretending that they haven't. Not like she's their problem. Lacey says a silent, agnostic's prayer that it isn't much farther to the Hartford station; she smiles, and the woman makes a face like she's been insulted.

"It ain't *me* you got to be afraid of, Miss. Get that straight. I'm sticking my neck out, just talking to you."

"I'm very sorry," Lacey says, trying hard to sound sorry instead of nervous, instead of annoyed. "But I really don't have any idea what you're talking about."

"Me, I'm nothing but a messenger. A courier," the woman replies, lowering her voice almost to a whisper and glaring suspiciously towards the other two passengers. "Of course, that wouldn't make much difference, if you know what I mean."

"I don't have any idea what you mean."

"Well, you got the package right there," the woman says, and now she's pointing over the back of Lacey's seat at the cardboard box with the Innsmouth fossil packed inside. "That makes you a courier, too. Hell, to some that almost makes you a goddamn holy prophet on Judgment Day. But you probably haven't thought of it that way, have you?"

"Maybe it would be better if we talked later," Lacey whispers, playing along. The woman's probably perfectly harmless, but Lacey puts one hand protectively on the box, anyway.

"*They* might be listening," the woman says and nods her head towards the teenager and the priest. "They might hear something we don't want them to hear."

She makes an angry, hissing sound between her yellow teeth and runs the long fingers of her left hand quickly through her tangled white hair, slicking it back against her scalp, pulling a few strands loose, and they lie like pearly threads on the shoulder of her black raincoat.

"You think you got it all figured out, don't you?" she growls. "Put some fancy letters after your name, and you don't need to listen to anybody or anything, ain't that right? Can't nobody tell you no different, 'cause you've seen it *all,* from top to bottom, pole to pole."

"Calm down, *please,*" Lacey says, glancing towards the other passengers again, wishing one of them would look up so she could get their attention. "If you don't, I'm going to have to call the conductor. Don't make me do that."

"Goddamn stuck-up dyke," the woman snarls, and she spits on the floor, turns her head and stares furiously out the window with her bulging blue eyes. "You think I'm crazy. Jesus, you just wait till you come out the other side, and *then* let's see what the hell you think sane looks like."

"I didn't mean to upset you," Lacey says, standing, reaching for the satchel with her laptop. "Maybe I should just move to another seat."

"You *do* that, Miss Morrow. Won't be no skin off *my* nose. But you better take this with you," and the woman's left hand disappears inside her raincoat, reappears with a large, slightly crumpled manila envelope, and she holds it out to Lacey. "They told me you'd figure it out, so don't ask me no more questions. I've already said too goddamn much as it is."

Lacey sets her satchel down beside the cardboard box and stares at the envelope for a moment, yellow-brown paper, and there's what looks like a grease stain at one corner.

"Well, go on ahead. It ain't got teeth. It ain't gonna bite you," the white-haired woman sneers, not taking her eyes off the window, the farms and houses rushing past. "Maybe if you take it," she says, "the scary woman will leave you alone."

Lacey snatches the envelope, hastily gathers her things, the satchel and the box, and moves quickly up the aisle towards the front of the car. The priest and the girl don't even look up as she passes them. *Maybe they don't see me at all,* she thinks. *Maybe they haven't heard a thing.* She presses the black, rectangular panel to open the door to the next car, but the door doesn't budge; she presses it again, and again, with no greater success. Then the train lurches, sways suddenly to one side, and she almost drops the box, imagines the fossil inside shattering into a hundred pieces.

Stupid girl. Stupid, silly girl.

She forces herself to be still, then, presses her forehead against the cool aluminum door. She takes a deep breath of air that doesn't smell like dead fish, that only smells like diesel fumes and disinfectant, perfectly ordinary train smells, comforting familiarity, and the cadence of the rails is the most reassuring sound in the world.

Go on ahead. It ain't got teeth. It ain't gonna bite you, the white-haired woman said, nothing at all but a crazy lady that someone ought to be watching out for, not letting her ride about on trains harassing people. Lacey looks down at the grease-stained envelope in her hand, held tenuously between her right thumb and forefinger.

"Do you need me to help you with that?" and it's only the priest, scowling up at her from his newspaper; he sighs a loud, irritated sigh, then points at the exit. "Would you like me to get the *door* for you?"

"Yes," she says. "Thank you, Father. I'd really appreciate it. My hands are full."

Lacey glances anxiously past him towards the back of the car, and there's no sign of the white-haired woman now, but the door at the other end is standing wide open.

"There," the priest says; she smiles and thanks him again.

"No problem," he says, and as she steps into the short connecting corridor, he continues speaking in low, conspiratorial tones, "But don't wait too long to have a look at what's in that envelope she gave you. There may not be much time left." Then the door slides shut again, and Lacey turns and runs to the crowded refuge of the next car.

Her twenty-fifth birthday, the stormy day in early July when Lacey Morrow found the Innsmouth fossil, working late and alone in the basement of the Pratt Museum. Almost everyone else had gone home already, but there was nothing unusual about that. Lacey pouring over the contents of Cabinet 34, drawers of Devonian fishes collected from Blossburg,

Pennsylvania and Chaleur Bay, Quebec, slabs of shale and sandstone the dusky color of charcoal, the color of cinnamon; ancient lungfish and the last of the jawless ostracoderms, lobe-finned *Eusthenopteron* and the boxy armour plates of the antiarch *Bothriolepis*. Relics of an age come and gone hundreds of millions of years before the dinosaurs, a time when the earliest forests lined the shores of lakes and rivers teeming with strange and monstrous fish, and vertebrates had begun to take their first clumsy steps onto dry land. And that transition has been her sole, consuming obsession since Lacey was an undergraduate, that alchemy of flesh and bone – fins to feet, gills to lungs – the puzzles that filled her days and nights, that filled her dreams. Her last girlfriend walking out because she'd finally had enough of Lacey's all-night kitchen dissections, the meticulously mutilated sea bass and cod, eels and small sharks sliced up and left lying about until she found time to finish her notes and sketches. Dead things in plastic bags crammed into the freezer, and the ice cubes starting to taste like bad sushi, their Hitchcock Road apartment stinking of formalin and fish markets.

"If I grow fucking scales maybe I'll give you a call sometime," Julie said, hauling her boxes of clothes and CDs from their front porch to the back of her banged-up little car. "If I ever meet up with a goddamn mermaid, I'll be sure to give her your number."

Lacey watched her drive away, feeling less than she knew she *ought* to feel, wishing she would cry because any normal person would cry, would at least be angry with herself or with Julie. But the tears never came, nor the anger, and after that she figured it was better to leave romantic entanglements for some later stage in her life, some faraway day when she could spare a spark of passion for anything except her studies. She kept a picture of Julie in a pewter frame beside her bed, though, so she could still pretend, from time to time, when she felt alone, when she awoke in the middle of the night and there was nothing but the sound of rain on the roof and the wind blowing cold through the streets of Amherst.

But that August afternoon she wasn't lonely, not with the tall rows of battleship-grey steel Lane cabinets and their stony treasures stacked neatly around her, all the company she needed and no thoughts but the precise numbers from her digital calipers – the heights and widths of pelvic girdles and scapulocoracoids, relative lengths of pectoral fins and radials. She was finishing up with a perfectly preserved porolepiform that she suspected might be a new species, when Lacey noticed the box pushed all the way to the very back of the drawer, half-hidden under a cardboard tray of shale and bone fragments. Something overlooked, even though she'd thought she knew the contents of those cabinets like the back of her hand, and any further surprises would only be in the details.

"Well, hello there," she said to the box, carefully slipping it from its hiding place beneath the tray. "How'd I ever miss you?" It wasn't a small box – only a couple of inches deep, but easily a foot and a half square, sagging just a bit at the center from having supported the weight of the tray for who knows how many years. There was writing on one corner of the lid, spidery fountain-pen ink faded as brown as dead leaves: *from Naval dredgings,* USS Cormorant *(April, 1928), Lat. 42°40'N., Long. 70°43'W, NE. of old Innsmouth Harbor, Essex Co., Mass. ?Devonian.* But there was no more information provided, no catalog or field number, no identification either, and then Lacey opened the box and stared amazed at the thing inside.

"Jesus," she whispered, swallowing a metallic taste like foil or a freshly filled tooth, that adrenaline-silver aftertaste. Her first impression was that the thing in the box was a hand, the articulated skeleton of a human hand lying palm-side up, its fingers slightly curled and clutching at the ceiling or the bright fluorescent lights overhead. She set the box down on one of the larger Chaleur Bay slabs then, stared in turn at the tips of her own trembling fingers and the petrified bones resting in a bed of excelsior. The fossil was dark, the waxy black of baker's chocolate, and shiny from a thick coating of varnish or shellac.

No, not human, but certainly the forelimb of *something,* something big, at least a third again larger than her own hand. "Jesus," she whispered again. Lacey lifted the fossil from the excelsior, gently because there was no telling how stable it was, how many decades since anyone had even bothered to open the box. She counted, ticked off the elements of the manus – carpals and metacarpals, phalanges – and the lower part of the forearm, sturdy radius and ulna ending abruptly in a ragged break, the dull glint of gypsum or quartz flakes showing from the exposed interior of the fossil. There was bony webbing or spines preserved between the fingers, and the three that were complete ended in short, sharp ungual claws. There was a small patch of what appeared to be scales or dermal ossicles on the palm just below the fifth metacarpal, oval disks with deeply concave centers unlike anything she could remember ever having seen before. Here and there, small bits of greenish-grey limestone still clung to the bones, but most of the hard matrix had been scraped away.

Lacey sat down on a wooden stool near Cabinet 34, her dizzy head too full of questions and astonishment, heart racing with the giddy, breathless excitement of discovery, rediscovery, and she forced herself to shut her eyes for a moment. Gathering shreds of calm from the darkness behind her lids, she counted backwards from thirty until her pulse began to return to normal. She opened her eyes again and turned the fossil over to examine the other side. The bone surface on the back of the hand was not so well preserved, weathered as though that side had been exposed to the forces of erosion for some time before it was collected, the smooth, cortical layer cracked and worn completely away in places. There was a lot more of the greenish limestone matrix remaining on that side, too, and a small snail's shell embedded in the rock near the base of the middle finger.

"What *are* you?" she asked the fossil, as if it might tell her, as simple as that, and everything else forgotten now, all her fine coelacanths and rhipidistians, for this newest miracle. Lacey turned it over again, examining the palm-side more closely, the pebbly configuration of wrist bones, quickly identifying the ulnare, what she thought must be the intermedium, and when she finally glanced at her watch it was almost six-thirty. At least an hour had passed since she'd opened the box; she'd have to hurry to make her seven o'clock lecture. She returned the hand to the excelsior, paused a moment for one last, lingering glimpse of the thing before putting the lid back on. Overhead, high above the exhibits halls and the slate-tiled roof of the Pratt Museum, a thunderclap boomed and echoed across the valley, and Lacey tried to remember if she'd left her umbrella in her apartment.

1:49 p.m.

She's sitting next to a woman who smells like wintergreen candy and mothballs, listening to the steady *clackclackclack* of razor wheels against the rails. Lacey's been staring at the photograph from the manila envelope for almost five minutes now. A movie still, she thinks, the glossy black-and-white photograph creased and dog-eared at one corner, and it shows an old man with a white mustache standing with two Indians beside a rocky outcrop. Someplace warm, someplace tropical because there are palmetto fronds at one edge of the photograph. It isn't hot on the train, but Lacey's sweating, anyway, her palms gone slick and clammy, tiny beads like nectar standing out on her forehead and upper lip. The old man in the photograph is holding something cradled in both hands, clutching it like a holy relic, a grail, the prize at the end of a life-long search.

…'cause you've seen it all, from top to bottom and pole to pole…

The man in the photograph is holding the Innsmouth fossil. Or he's holding a replica so perfect that it must have been cast from the original, and it really doesn't make much difference, either way. She turns the picture over, and there's a label stuck to the back – Copyright © 1954 U$_n$iversal-I$_n$ter$_n$atio$_n$al – typed with a typewriter that drops its N's.

There was a letter in the envelope, as well. A faded photocopy of a letter, careless, sprawling handwriting that she can only just decipher:

Mr. Zacharias R. Gilman, Esq.
7 High Street
Ipswich, Mass.

15 January 1952
Mr. William Alland
Universal Studios
Los Angeles, Cal.

Dear Mr. Alland,

Sir, I have seen your fine horror picture "It Came From Outer Space" six times as of this writing and must say that I am in all ways impressed with your work. You have a true artist's eye for the uncanny and deserve to be proud of your endeavors. I am enclosing newspaper clippings which may be of some small interest to a mind such as yours, regarding certain peculiar things that have gone on hereabouts for years. Old people here talk about the "plagues" of 1846, but they will tell you it wasn't really no plague that set old Innsmouth on the road to ruin, if you've a mind to listen. They will tell you lots of things, Mr. Alland, and I lie awake at night thinking about what might still go on out there at the reef. But you read the newspaper clippings for yourself, sir, and make of it what you will. I believe you might fashion a frightful film from these incidents. I will be at this address through May, should you wish to reply.

Respectfully, your avid admirer,
Zacharias Gilman

"Do you like old monster movies?" the wintergreen and mothball woman asks her, and Lacey shakes her head no.

"Well, that photograph, that's a scene from – "

"I don't watch television," she says.

"Oh, no, I didn't mean made-for-TV movies. I meant real movies, the kind you see in theaters."

"I don't go to theaters, either."

"Oh," the woman says, sounding disappointed, and in a moment she turns away again and stares out the window at the autumn morning rushing by outside.

10:40 a.m.

"Well, I like it," Dr. Morgan says, finally. "It looks good on paper." He chews absently at the stem of his cheap pipe and puffs pungent grey smoke clouds that smell like roasting apples. "And a binomen should look good. It should sound good, rolling off the tongue. There should be a measure of poetry in it."

Lacey doesn't point out that the name Morgan chose the year before for a new mosasaur – *Selmasaurus kiernanae* – had been strictly utilitarian.

More than three months since she found the Innsmouth fossil tucked away in Cabinet 34, and Lacey sits with Dr. Jasper Morgan in his tiny third-floor office: all the familiar, musty comforts of that small room with its high ceilings and ornate, molded plaster walls hidden behind solid oak shelves stuffed with dust-washed books and fossils and all the careful clutter of an academic's life. A huge geologic map of Massachusetts is framed and hanging slightly askew. The rheumy hiss and clank from the radiator below the window, and if the glass wasn't steamed over, she could see across the rooftops of Amherst, south to the low, autumn-stained hills beyond the town, the weathered trap-rock slopes of the Holyoke Range rising blue grey in the hazy distance.

The past three months have seemed more like three weeks to her, days and nights, dreams and waking all become a blur of questions and hardly any answers, the fossil become her secret, shared only with Dr. Morgan, and also with Dr. Hanisak over in the zoology department. Hers and hers alone, until she could at least begin to get her bearings and a preliminary report on the specimen could be drafted. When she was ready and her paper had been peer-reviewed and accepted by *Nature,* Dr. Morgan arranged for the press conference at Yale, where she would sit in the shadow of Rudolph Zallinger's *The Age of Reptiles* and Othniel Marsh's dinosaurs and reveal the Innsmouth fossil to the whole wide world.

"I had to call it something," she replies. "Seemed a shame not to have some fun with it. I have a feeling that I'm never going to find anything like this again."

"Exactly," Jasper Morgan says and leans back in his creaky wooden chair, takes the pipe from his mouth and stares intently into the smoldering bowl. Like a gypsy with her polished crystal ball, this old man with his glowing cinders. "'Words,'" he says in the tone of voice he reserves for quoting anyone he holds in higher esteem than himself, "'are in themselves among the most interesting objects of study, and the names of animals and plants are worthy of more consideration than biologists are inclined to give them.' Unfortunately, no one seems to care very much about the aesthetics these days, no one but rusty old farts like me."

He slides the manuscript back across his desk to Lacey, seventeen double-spaced pages held together with a green plastic paper clip. She nods once, reading over the text again silently to herself. Her eyes drift across his wispy red pencil marks: a missing comma here, there a spelling or date she should double-check.

"That's not true," Lacey says.

"What's not true?"

"That no one but you cares anymore."

"No? Well, maybe not. But, please, allow me the conceit."

"Dr. Hanisak insists the name's too fanciful. She said I should have called it something more descriptive. She suggested *Eocarpus.*"

"Of course she did. Hanisak has all the imagination of a stripped wing nut," and the paleontologist slips his pipe back between his ivory-yellow teeth.

"*Grendelonyx innsmouthensis,*" Lacey whispers, the syllables across her tongue as smooth as good brandy.

"See? There you are. 'Grendel's claw from Innsmouth,'" Jasper Morgan mutters around his pipe. "What the hell could be more descriptive than that?"

Across campus, the steeple chimes begin to ring the hour – nine, ten, ten and three-quarters – later than Lacey had realized, and she frowns at her watch, not ready to leave the sanctuary of the office and his company.

"Shit. I'll miss my train if I don't hurry," she says.

"Wish I were going with you. Wish I could be there to see their faces."

"I know, but I'll be fine. I'll call as soon as I get to New Haven," and she puts the manuscript back inside its folder and returns it to the battered black leather satchel that also holds her iBook and the CD with all the slides for the presentation, the photographs and cladograms, her character matrix and painstaking line drawings. Then Dr. Morgan smiles and shakes her hand, like they've only just met this morning, like it hasn't been years, and he sees her to the door. She carries the satchel in one hand and the sturdy cardboard box in the other. Last night, she transferred the fossil from its original box to this one, replaced the excelsior with cotton and foam-rubber padding. Her future lies in this box, her box of wonders.

"Knock 'em dead, kiddo," he says and hugs her, wraps her tight in the reassuring scents of his tobacco and aftershave lotion, and Lacey hugs him back, twice as hard.

"Don't you go losing the damned thing. That one's going to make you famous," he says and points at the cardboard box.

"Don't worry. It's not going to leave my sight, not even for a minute."

A few more words, encouragement and hurried last thoughts, and then Lacey walks alone down the long hallway past classrooms and tall display cabinets, doors to other offices, and she doesn't look back.

"I couldn't find it on the map," she said, watching the man's callused, oil-stained hands as he counted out her change, the five dollars and two nickels that were left of the twenty after he'd filled the Jeep's tank and replaced a windshield-wiper blade.

"Ain't on no maps," the man told her. "Not no more. Ain't been on no maps since sometime way back in the thirties. Wasn't much left to put on a map after the Feds finished with the place."

"The Feds?" she asked. "What do they have to do with Innsmouth?" and the man stepped back from the car and eyed her more warily than before. He was tall, with stooped shoulders and gooseberry-grey eyes, a nose that looked like it'd been broken more than once. He shrugged and shook his head.

"Hell, I don't know. You hear things, that's all. You hear all sorts of things. Most of it don't mean shit."

Lacey glanced at the digital clock on her dashboard, then up at the low purple-black clouds sailing by, the threat of more rain and nightfall not far behind it. Most of the day wasted on the drive from Amherst, a late start in a downpour, then a flat tire on Route 2, a flat tire *and* a flat spare. By the time she made Cape Ann, it was almost four o'clock.

"What business you got up at Innsmouth, anyhow?" the man asked suspiciously.

"I'm a scientist," she said. "I'm looking for fossils."

"Is that a fact? Well, ma'am, I never heard of anyone finding any sort of fossils around here."

"That's because the rocks are wrong for fossils. All the rocks around the Cape are igneous and – "

"What's that mean, *igneous?*" he interrupted, pronouncing the last word like it's something that might bite if he wasn't careful.

"It means they formed when molten rock – magma or lava – cooled down and solidified. Around here, most of the igneous rocks are plutonic, which means they solidified deep underground."

"I never heard of no volcanoes around here."

"No," Lacey says. "There aren't any volcanoes around here, not now. But there were a very long time ago."

The man watched her silently for a moment, rubbed at his stubbly chin, as if trying to make up his mind whether or not to believe her.

"All these granite boulders around here, those are igneous rock. For fossils, you usually need sedimentary rocks, like sandstone or limestone."

"Well, if that's so, then what're *you* doing looking for them out here?"

"It's kind of a long story," she said impatiently, tired of this distrustful man and the acrid stink of gasoline, just wanting to get back on the road again if he can't, or won't, tell her anything useful. "I wanted to see Innsmouth Harbor, that's all."

"Ain't much left to see," he said. "When I was a kid, back in the fifties, there was still some of the refinery standing, a few buildings left along the waterfront. My old man, he used to tell me ghost stories to keep me away from them. But someone or another tore all that shit down years ago. You take the road up to Ipswich and Plum Island, then head east. If you really wanna see for yourself, that is."

"Thank you," Lacey said, and she turned the key in the switch and wrestled the stick out of park.

"Any time at all," the man replied. "You find anything interestin', let me know."

And, as she pulled away from the gas station, lightning flashed bright across the northern sky, somewhere off towards Plum Island and the cold Atlantic Ocean.

3:15 p.m.

The train slips through the shadow cast by the I-84 overpass, a brief ribbon of twilight from concrete and steel eclipse and then bright daylight again, and in a moment the *Vermonter* is pulling into the Hartford station. Lacey looks over her shoulder, trying not to *look* like she's looking, to see if they're still standing at the back of the car watching her – the priest and the oyster-haired crazy woman who gave her the envelope with the photograph and letter. They are, one on each side of the aisle like mismatched gargoyle bookends. It's been ten minutes or so since she first noticed them back there, the priest with his newspaper folded and tucked beneath one arm and the oyster-haired woman staring at the floor and mumbling quietly to herself. The priest makes eye contact with Lacey, and she turns away, glancing quickly towards the front of the train again. A few of the passengers are already on their feet, already retrieving bags and briefcases from overhead compartments, eager to be somewhere else, and the woman sitting next to Lacey asks if this is her stop.

"No," she says. "No, I'm going on to New Haven."

"Oh, do you have family there?" the woman asks. "Are you a student? My father went to Yale, but that was – "

"Will you watch my seat, please?" Lacey asks her, and the woman frowns at being interrupted, but nods her head yes.

"Thanks. I promise I won't be long. I just need to make a phone call."

Lacey gets up, and the oyster-haired woman stops mumbling to herself and takes a hesitant step forward. The priest lays one hand on her shoulder, and she halts, but glares at Lacey with her bulging eyes and holds up one palm like a crossing guard stopping traffic.

"I'll only be a moment," Lacey says.

"You can leave that here, too, if you like," the woman who smells like wintergreen and mothballs says, and Lacey realizes that she's still holding the box with the Innsmouth fossil.

"No. I'll be right back," Lacey tells her, gripping the box a little more tightly. Before the woman can say anything else, before the priest has a chance to change his mind and let the oyster-haired woman come after her, Lacey turns and pushes her way along the aisle towards the exit sign.

"Excuse me," she says, repeating the words like a prayer, a hasty mantra as she squeezes past impatient, unhelpful men and women. She accidentally steps on someone's foot, and he tells her to slow the fuck down, just wait her turn, what the fuck's *wrong* with her, anyway. Then she's past the last of them and moving quickly down the steps, out of the train and standing safe on the wide and crowded platform. Glancing back at the tinted windows, she doesn't see the priest or the crazy woman who gave her the envelope. Lacey asks a porter pulling an empty luggage rack where she can find a pay phone, and he points to the terminal.

"Right through there," he says, "on your left, by the rest rooms." She thanks him and walks quickly across the platform towards the doors, the wide electric doors sliding open and closed, spitting some people out and swallowing others whole.

"Miss Morrow!" the priest shouts, his voice small above the muttering crowd. "Please, wait! You don't understand!"

But Lacey doesn't wait, only a few more feet to the wide terminal doors and never mind the damned pay phones. She can always call Jasper Morgan *after* she finds a security guard or a cop.

"Please!" the priest shouts, and the wide doors slide open again.

It ain't me *you got to be afraid of, Miss. Get that straight.*

"You'll have to come with us now," a tall, pale man in a black suit and black sunglasses says as he steps through the doors onto the platform. The sun shines like broken diamonds off the barrel of the pistol in his left hand and the badge in his right. Lacey turns to run, but there's already someone there to stop her, a black woman almost as tall as the pale man with the gun.

"You'll only make it worse on yourself," she says in a thick Caribbean accent, and Lacey looks back towards the train, desperately searching the crowd for the priest, and there's no sign of him anywhere.

After the gas station, Lacey followed Highway 1 south to Kent Corner and from there she took Haverhill Street to the 1A, gradually working her way south and east, winding towards Ipswich and the sea. The sky has been beaten black and blue by the storms and the day was dissolving slowly into a premature North Shore night while lightning fingers flicked greedily across the land. At Ipswich, she asked directions again, this time from a girl working behind the counter of a convenience store. The girl had heard of Innsmouth, though she'd never seen the place for herself, had only picked up stories at school and from her parents – urban legends mostly, wild tales of witches and sea monsters and strange lights floating above the dunes. She sold Lacey a Diet Coke and a bag of Fritos and told her to take Argilla Road out of town and stay on it all the way down to the river.

"Be careful," the girl said worriedly, and Lacey smiled and assured her that she would.

"Don't worry about me," she said. "I just want to have a quick look around."

Twenty minutes later she reached the dead end of Argilla Road, a locked gate and chain-link fence crowned with loops of razor wire, stretching east and west as far as she could see. There were two rusty Army Corps of Engineers signs on the gate – NO TRESPASSING. VIOLATORS WILL BE PROSECUTED AND THIS AREA PATROLLED BY ARMED GUARDS – DO NOT ENTER. She parked the Jeep in a sandy spot near the fence and sat for a few minutes staring at the signs, wondering how many years they had been there, how many decades since they were hung on the gate and why. Then she cut the engine and got out.

The wind smelled like rain and the sea, ozone and the fainter silty stink of the salt marshes, commingled smells of life and sex and death. She sat on the cooling hood of the car with a folded topographic map and finished the bag of Fritos. Below her the land dropped quickly away to stunted trees, billowing swells of goldenrod and spike grass, and a few stingy outcroppings of granite poking up here and there through the sand. The Manuxet River snaked along the bottom of the valley, wandering through thickets of bullrush and silverweed, tumbling over a few low falls on its way down to the mouth of Ipswich Bay.

But there was no indication that there had ever been a town of any sort here, certainly no evidence that this deserted stretch of coastline had once been the prosperous seaport of Innsmouth, with its mills and factories, a gold refinery and bustling waterfront, its history stretching back to the mid-17th century. So maybe she was in the wrong place after all. Maybe the ruins of Innsmouth lay somewhere farther east, or back towards Plum Island. Lacey watched two seagulls struggling against the wind, raucous grey-white smudges drifting in the low indigo sky. She glanced at the topo map and then northwest towards a point marked "Castle Hill," but there was no castle there now, if indeed there ever had been, no buildings of any sort, only a place where the land rose up one last time before ending in a weathered string of steep granite cliffs.

She'd drawn a small red circle on the map just offshore, to indicate the coordinates written on the lid of the old box from Cabinet 34 – Latitude 42°40'N, Longitude 70° 43'W – and Lacey scanned the horizon, wishing she'd remembered her binoculars, left hanging useless in her bedroom closet at home. But there was *something* out there, a thin, dark line a mile or more beyond the breakwater, barely visible above the stormy sea. Perhaps it was only her imagination – something she *needed* to see – or a trick of the fading light, or both. She glanced back down at the map. Not far from her red circle were contour lines indicating a high, narrow shoal hiding beneath the water, and the spot was labeled simply "Allen's Reef." If the tide were out and the ocean calm, maybe there would be more to see, perhaps an aplitic or pegmatitic dike cutting through the native granite, an ancient river of magma frozen, crystallized, scrubbed smooth by the waves.

"What do you think you'll find out there?" Jasper Morgan had asked her the day before. He'd come by her office with the results of a microfossil analysis of the sediment sample she'd scraped from the Innsmouth fossil. "There sure as hell aren't any Devonian rocks on Cape Ann," he'd said. "It's all Ordovician, and igneous to boot."

"I just want to see it," she'd replied, skimming the letter typed on Harvard stationary, describing the results of the analysis.

"So, what does it say?" Dr. Morgan had asked, but Lacey read all the way to the bottom of the page before answering him.

"The rock's siltstone, but we already knew that. The ostracods say Early Devonian, probably Lochkovian. And that snail's definitely *Loxonema*. So, there you go. Devonian rocks somewhere off Cape Ann."

"Damn," he'd whispered, grinning and scratching his head, and they'd spent the next half hour talking about the thing from Cabinet 34, more than a hundred million years older than anything with a forearm like that had a right to be. No getting around the fact that it looked a lot more like a hand, something built for grasping, than a forefoot.

"Maybe we ought to just put it *back* in that drawer," Jasper Morgan had said, shaking his head. "Do you have any idea what kind of shitstorm this thing's gonna cause?"

"I think maybe I'm beginning to."

"You might as well have found a goddamn cell phone buried in an Egyptian pyramid."

Thunder rumbled somewhere nearby, off towards Rowley, and a few cold drops of rain spattered her skin. Lacey glanced down at the topo map and then out at the distant black line of Allen's Reef one last time. Such a long drive to find so little, the whole day wasted, the night and the time it would take her to drive back to Amherst. Money spent on gasoline that could have gone for rent and groceries. She slid off the hood of the Jeep and was already folding the map closed when something moved out on the reef. She caught the briefest glimpse from the corner of one eye, the impression of something big and dark, scuttling on long legs across the rocks before slipping back into the water. There was another thunderclap, then, and this time lightning like God was taking pictures, but she didn't move, stared at the reef and the angry sea crashing over it.

"Just my imagination," she whispered. Or maybe it had been a bird, or a particularly high wave falling across the rocks, something perfectly familiar made strange by distance and shadow.

The thunder rolled away, and there were no sounds left but the wind blowing through the tall grass and the falls gurgling near the mouth of the Manuxet River. In an instant, the rain became a torrent, and her clothes and the map were soaked straight through before she could get back inside the Jeep.

3:25 p.m.

Handcuffs and a blindfold tied too tightly around her face before the man and woman who clearly aren't FBI agents shoved her into the back of a rust-green Ford van. And now she lies shivering on wet carpeting as they speed along streets that she can't see. The air around her is as cold as a late December night and thick with the gassy, sour-sweet stench of something dead, something that should have been buried a long, long time ago.

"I already *told* you why," the man in the black suit and sunglasses growls angrily, and Lacey thinks maybe there's fear in his voice, too. "She didn't *have* it, okay? And we couldn't risk going onto the train after it. Monalisa's people got to her first. I already fucking *told* you that."

Whatever is in the back of the van with her answers him in its ragged, drowning voice like her grandmother dying of pneumonia when Lacey was seven years old. There are almost words in there, broken bits and pieces of words, vowel shards and consonant shrapnel, and the woman with the Caribbean accent curses and mumbles something to herself in French Creole.

"Please," Lacey begs them. "I don't know what you want. Tell me what the fuck you want, and I'll give it to you."

"You think so?" the woman asks. "You think it would be that easy now? After all this shit, and you just gonna hand it over, and we just gonna go away and leave you alone?"

"*Merde…*"

The van squeals around a corner without bothering to slow down, and Lacey is thrown sideways into something that feels like a pile of wet rags. She tries to roll away from it, but strong hands hold her fast, and icy fingers brush slowly across her throat, her chin, her lips. There's skin like sandpaper and Jell-O, fingertips that may as well be icicles, and she bites at them, but her teeth close on nothing at all, a mouthful of frigid air that tastes like raw fish and spoiled vegetables.

"We had strict fucking instructions to *avoid* a confrontation," the man says, and the car takes another corner, pitching Lacey free of the ragpile again.

"You just shut up and drive this damn car," the woman says. "You gonna get us all killed. You gonna have the cops on us."

"Then *you* better tell that slimy, half-breed motherfucker back there to shut the hell up and stop threatening me," the man snarls at the woman. "I'm just about ready to say *fuck* you and him both. Pop a fucking cap in his skull and take my chances with the Order."

The rag pile gurgles and then makes a hollow, gulping noise. Lacey thinks it's laughing, as close as it can ever come to laughing, and she wonders how long before it touches her again, wonders if they'll kill her first, and which would be worse. She presses her face against the soggy carpeting, both eyes open but nothing there to see, rough fabric against her cheek, and she tries to wipe its touch from her skin. Nothing she'll ever be able to scrub off, though, she knows that, something that's stained straight through to her soul.

"Is it the fossil?" she asks. "Is this about the fossil?"

"Now you startin' to use that big ol' brain of yours, missy," the woman says. "You tell us where it's hid, who you gave it to, and maybe you gonna get to live just a little bit longer."

"She ain't gonna tell you jack shit," the man sneers.

The rag pile makes a fluttering, anxious sound, and Lacey tries to sit up, but the van swerves and bounces over something, a pothole or a speed bump, a fucking old lady crossing the street for all she knows, and she tumbles over on her face again.

"It's in the box," she says, rolling onto her back, and she kicks out with her left foot and hits nothing but the metal side wall. The rag pile gurgles and sputters wildly, and so Lacey kicks the van again, harder than before. "Haven't you even *opened* the goddamn box?"

"Bitch, ain't *nothin'* we want in that box," the woman says. "You already handed it off to Monalisa, didn't you?"

"Of course she fucking gave it to him. What the fuck else do you *think* she did with it?"

"I *told* you to shut up and drive."

"*Fuck* you," and then a car horn blares and everything dissolves into the banshee wail of squealing brakes, tires burning themselves down to naked, steel-belt bones, the impact hardly half a heartbeat later, and Lacey is thrown backwards into the gurgling rag pile. *Something soft to cushion the blow, at least,* she thinks, wondering if she's dead already and just hasn't figured it all out yet, and the man in the sunglasses screams like a woman.

There's light, a flood of clean, warm sunlight across her face before the gunfire – three shots – *blam, blam, blam.* The rag pile abruptly stops gurgling, and someone takes her by the arm, someone pulling her out of the van, out of hell and back into the world again.

"I can't see," she says, and the blindfold falls away to leave her squinting and blinking at the rough brick walls of an alleyway, a sagging fire escape. There's the heady stink of a garbage dumpster, but even that smells good after the van.

"Wow," the old man says, the grinning scarecrow of an old man in a blue fedora and a shiny gabardine suit, blue bow tie to match his hat. "I saw someone do that in a movie once. I never imagined it would actually work."

There's a huge revolver clutched in his bony right hand, the blindfold dangling from the fingers of his left, and his violet-grey eyes sparkle like amethysts and spring water.

"Professor Solomon Monalisa, at your service," he says, letting the blindfold fall to the ground, and he holds one twig-thin hand out to Lacey. "You had us all worried, Miss Morrow. You shouldn't have run like that."

Lacey stares at his outstretched hand. There are sirens now.

"Oh, I'm sorry. I forgot about the handcuffs. I'm afraid we'll have to attend to those elsewhere, though. I don't think we should be here when the police show up and start asking questions, do you?"

"No," she says, and the old man takes her arm again and starts to lead her away from the wrecked van.

"Wait. The box," she says and tries to turn around, but he stops her and puts a hand across her eyes.

"What's back there, Miss Morrow, you don't want to see it."

"They have the box. The Innsmouth fossil – "

"I have the fossil," he says. "And it's quite safe, I assure you. Come now, Miss Morrow. We don't have much time."

He leads her away from the van, down the long, narrow alley. There's a door back there, a tall wooden door with peeling red paint, and he opens it with a silver key.

Excerpt from *New American Monsters: More Than Myth?*
by Gerald Durrell (Hill and Wang, New York, 1959):

…which is certainly enough to make us pause and wonder about the possibility of a connection between at least some of these sightings and the celluloid fantasies being churned out by Hollywood film-makers. If we insist upon objectivity and are willing to entertain the notion of unknown animals, we must also, it seems, be equally willing to entertain the possibility that a few of these beasts may exist as much in the realm of the psychologist as that of the biologist. I can think of no better example of what I mean than the strange and frightening reports from Massachusetts that followed the release of *The Creature from the Black Lagoon* five years ago.

As first reported in the *Ipswich Chronicle,* March 20th, 1954, there was a flurry of sightings, from Gloucester north to Newburyport, of one or more scaly man-like amphibians, monstrous things that menaced boaters and were blamed for the death of at least one swimmer. On the evening of March 19th, Mrs. Cordelia Eliot of Rowley was walking along the coast near the Annisquam Harbor Lighthouse when she saw what she later described as a "horrible fishman" paddling about just off shore. She claims to have watched it for half an hour, until the sun set and she lost sight of the creature. Four days later, there was another sighting by two fishermen near the mouth of the Annisquam River, of a "frogman with bulging red eyes and scaly greenish-black skin" wading through the shallows. When one of the men fired a shotgun at it (I haven't yet concluded if the men routinely carried firearms on fishing trips), it slipped quietly away into deeper water.

But the lion's share of the sightings that spring seem to have occurred in the vicinity of the "ghost town" of Innsmouth, at the mouth of the Castle Neck River (previously known by its Agawam Indian name, *Manuxet,* a name which still persists among local old-timers). Most of these encounters are merely brief glimpses of scaly man-like creatures, usually seen from a considerable distance, either swimming near the mouth of the river or walking along its muddy banks at low tide. But one remarkable, and disturbing, account, reported by numerous local papers, involves the death of a nine-year-old boy named Lester Sargent, who drowned while swimming with friends below a small waterfall on the lower Castle Neck River. His companions reported that the boy began screaming, and immediately a great amount of blood was visible in the water. There were attempts to reach the swimmer, but the would-be rescuers were driven back by "a monster with blood-red eyes and sharp teeth." The boy finally disappeared beneath the surface; his mutilated and badly decomposed body turned up a week later on Crane Beach, a considerable distance from the falls where he disappeared. The Essex County coroner listed the cause of death as shark attack.

"I've seen plenty of sharks," Harold Mowry, one of the swimmers, told reporters. "This wasn't a shark, I swear. It had hands, with great long claws, and it dragged Lester right down and drowned him."

Another notable sighting occurred along the old Argilla Road near Ipswich on April 2. The Rev. Henry Waite and his wife, Elizabeth, both avid bird watchers, claimed to have observed a "monster" strolling along the east bank of the Castle Neck River for more than an hour, before it dove into the river and vanished in a swirl of bubbles. Mrs. Waite described it as "tall and dark, and it walked a little hunched over. Through the binoculars, we could see its face quite plainly. It did *have* a face, you know, with protruding eyes like a fish, and gills. At one point it turned and seemed to be watching us. I admit I was afraid and asked Henry if we shouldn't go for the police. Have you ever seen that *Monster from the Black Lagoon* [sic] movie? Well, that's what it looked like."

The last of the sightings were made in early May and no further records of amphibious man-monsters near Cape Ann or Ipswich Bay are available. One report of April 27th claimed that a group of school children had, in fact, found the monster dead, but their discovery later proved to be nothing but the badly decomposed carcass of a basking shark. It is impossible, I think, not to draw connections with the release of the Universal-International horror flick on March 5th. The old bugaboo of "mass hysteria" raises its shaggy head once more.

10:23 a.m.

She's late for her meeting with Jasper before the drive to the train station, and Lacey rushes upstairs from the collections, is already halfway across the central rotunda of the Pratt Museum's exhibit hall when Dr. Mary Hanisak calls out her name. Lacey stops and stands in the skeletal shadows of the mammoth and mastodon, the stuffed Indian elephant, and Dr. Hanisak is walking quickly towards her, carrying the cardboard box with the Innsmouth fossil inside.

"Can you believe you almost forgot this thing?" she asks. "That would have been pretty embarrassing, don't you think?"

Lacey laughs a little too loudly, her voice echoing in the museum. "Yeah," she says. "It would have," and she takes the box from the woman, chubby little Dr. Hanisak like a storybook gnome, Dr. Hanisak whose specialty is the evolution of rodent teeth. The box is wrapped tight with packing tape, so there's no danger of its coming open on the train.

"Then you're all set now?"

"Ready as I'm ever going to be."

"And you're *certain* you want to do this? I mean, it's awfully high profile. I expect you'll be in newspapers all over the world when the reporters get a look at what's in that box. You might even be on CNN. Aren't you scared?"

Lacey stares for a moment at the dusty bones of a saber-tooth cat mounted near the mammoth's feet. "You bet," she says. "I'm terrified. But maybe it'll at least bring in some new funding for the museum. We could sure use it."

"Perhaps," Dr. Hanisak replies uncertainly, and she folds her hands and stares at the box. "You never can tell how these things will turn out, in the end."

"I suppose not," Lacey says, and then she looks at her watch and thanks Dr. Hanisak again. "I really have to get going," she says and leaves the woman standing alone with the skeletons.

Excerpt from *Famous Film Monsters and the Men
Who Made Them* by Ben Browning
(The Citadel Press, Secaucus, NJ, 1972):

Certainly there are several interesting stories floating about Hollywood regarding producer William Alland's inspiration for the story. The one most often repeated, it would seem, recounts how Alland heard a tale during a dinner party at Orson Welles' home regarding an ancient race of "fish-men" called the *dhaghon* inhabiting remote portions of the Amazon River. Local natives believed these creatures rose from the depths once a year, after floods, and abducted virgins. Naturally, the person telling the story is said to have sworn to its veracity. Another, less plausible, source of inspiration may have been a tradition in some parts of Massachusetts, in and around Gloucester, of humanoid sea monsters said to haunt a particularly treacherous stretch of coast near Ipswich Bay, known appropriately enough as "Devil Reef." Rumor has it Alland knew of these legends, but decided to change the story's setting from maritime New England to the Amazon because he preferred a more exotic and primeval locale. At any rate, one or another of these "fish stories" might have stuck with him and become the germ for the project he eventually pitched and sold to Universal.

3:47 p.m.

She goes through the peeling red door, and she follows the old man down long hallways dimly lit by bare incandescent bulbs, is led upstairs and downstairs, and finally, through a door he opens with another silver key. A steel fire door painted all the uncountable shades of dried gore and butcheries, and it swings slowly open on creaking hinges and pours the heavy scents of frigid air and formaldehyde at their feet. There's light in there, crimson light to match the door. Lacey looks at Dr. Solomon Monalisa, and he's smiling a doubtful, furtive smile.

"What am I going to see in there?"

"That's a matter of opinion," he says and holds one skinny arm out like a theater usher leading her to an empty seat.

"I asked you a simple question. All I wanted was a simple answer."

"Yes, but there are no *simple* answers, are there?"

"What's waiting for me in there?"

"All things are but mirrors, Miss Morrow. They reflect our deepest pre-conceptions, our most cherished prejudices."

"Never fucking mind," she says and steps quickly across the threshold into a room as cold as the back of the Ford van. The room is almost empty, high concrete walls and a concrete ceiling far overhead, banks of darkroom red lights dangling on chains, and a single huge tank, sitting alone in the center of it all.

"You're a very lucky woman," Dr. Monalisa says, and the steel door clicks shut behind her. "Have you any idea, my dear, how few scientists have had this privilege? Why, I could count them all on my left hand."

The tank is at least seven feet tall, sturdy aquarium glass held together with strips of rusted iron, filled with murky preservative gone bloody beneath the lights, and Lacey stares at the thing floating lifeless behind the glass.

"What do *you* see, Miss Morrow?"

"My god," she whispers and takes another step towards the tank.

"Now that's a curious answer."

Neither man nor fish, neither fish nor amphibian, long legs and longer arms, and its bald, misshapen skull is turned upwards, as if those bulging, blind white eyes are gazing longingly towards Heaven. Solomon Monalisa rattles his keys and slips the handcuffs from her aching wrists.

"*Grendelonyx innsmouthensis – that's* what I thought you'd see, Miss Morrow. Grendel's claw."

"But it's impossible," she whispers.

"Quite completely," Dr. Solomon Monalisa says. "It is entirely, unquestionably impossible."

"Is it real?"

"Yes, of course it's real. Why would I show it to you otherwise?"

Lacey nods her head and crosses the room to stand beside the tank, placing one hand flat against the glass. She's surprised that it isn't cold to the touch. The creature inside looks pale and soft, but she knows that's only the work of time and the caustic preserving chemicals.

"It got tangled in a fishing net, dragged kicking into the light of day," the old man says. His footsteps are very loud in the concrete room. "Way back in November '29, not too long after the Navy finished up with Innsmouth. I suspect it was wounded by the torpedoes," and he points to a deep gash near the thing's groin. "They kept it in a basement at the university in Arkham for a time, and then it went to Washington, the Smithsonian. They moved it here right after the war."

She almost asks him which war, and who "they" are, but she doubts he would tell her, not the truth, anyway. She can't take her eyes off the beautiful, terrible, impossible creature in the tank – its splayed hands, the bony webbing between its fingers, the recurved, piercing claws. "Why are you showing me this?" she finally asks, instead.

"It seemed a shame not to," he replies, his smile fading now, and he also touches the aquarium glass. "There are so few who can truly comprehend the…" and he pauses, furrowing his brow. "The *wonder* – yes, that's what I mean, the wonder of it all."

"You said you have the fossil."

"Oh, yes. We do. I do. Dr. Hanisak was kind enough to switch the boxes for us last night, while you were finishing up at the museum."

"Dr. Hanisak – "

"Shhhhhh," and Monalisa holds a wrinkled index finger to his lips. "Let's not ask *too* many questions, dear. I assure you, the fossil is safe and sound. I'll give it back to you very soon. Ah, and we have all your things from the train. You'll be wanting those back as well, I should imagine. But I wanted you to see our friend here first, before you see the film."

"What film?" she asks, then remembers the photograph from the manila envelope, the letter, the nosy woman asking her if she liked old monster movies.

"What odd sort of childhood did you have, Miss Morrow? Weren't you allowed to watch television? Have you truly never seen it?"

"My mother didn't like us watching television," Lacey says. "We didn't even own a TV set. She bought us books, instead. I've never cared much for movies. I don't know what you're talking about."

"Then that may be the most remarkable part of it all. You may be the only adult in America who's never seen *The Creature from the Black Lagoon*," and he chuckles softly to himself.

"I've heard of it."

"I should certainly hope so."

At last she turns away from the dead thing floating in the tank and looks into Dr. Solomon Monalisa's sparkling eyes. "You're not going to kill me?" she asks him.

"Why would I have gone to all the trouble to save you from those thugs back there if I only wanted you dead? They'd surely have seen to that for me, once they figured out you didn't have the fossil any longer."

"I don't understand any of this," Lacey says and realizes that she's started to cry.

"No," he says. "But you weren't meant to. No one was. It's a secret."

"What about my work?"

"Your article has been withdrawn from *Nature*. And Dr. Hanisak was good enough to cancel the press conference at the Peabody Museum."

"And now I'm just supposed to pretend I never saw any of this?"

"No, certainly not. You're just supposed to keep it to yourself."

"It doesn't make any sense. Why don't you just destroy the fossil? Why don't you destroy *this* thing?" and she slaps the glass hard with the palm of her hand. "If it's a goddamn secret, if no one's supposed to know, why don't you get rid of it all? Erase it?"

"Could *you* destroy these things?" the old man asks her. "No, I didn't think so. Haven't you taken an oath, of sorts, to search for answers, even when the answers are uncomfortable, even when they're *impossible?* Well, you see, dear, so have I."

"It was just lying in that drawer. Anyone could have found it. Anyone at all."

"Indeed. The fossil has been missing for decades. We have no idea how it ever found its way to Amherst. But you will care for it now, yes?"

She doesn't answer him, because she doesn't want to say the words out loud, stares instead through her tears at the creature in the tank.

"Yes, I thought you would. You have an uncommon strength. Come along, Miss Morrow. We should be going now," he says and takes her hand. "The picture will be starting soon."

For David J. Schow, Keeper of the Black Lagoon.

The Drowned Geologist
(1898)

10 May 1898

My Dear Dr. Watson,

At the urgent behest of a mutual acquaintance, Dr. Ogilvy, lately of the British Museum, I am writing you regarding a most singular occurrence which I experienced recently during an extended tour of the Scottish lowlands and the east English coast south on through North Yorkshire. The purpose of my tour was the acquisition of local geological specimens and stratigraphic data for the American Museum here in Manhattan, where I have held a post these last four years. As one man of science writing openly to another, I trust you will receive these words in the spirit which they are intended, indeed, the only spirit in which I presently know how to couch them: as the truthful and objective testimony of a trained observer and investigator who has borne witness to a most peculiar series of events, which, even now, many months hence, I am yet at a loss to explain. I fear that I must expect you to question the veracity of my story, and no doubt my sanity as well, if you are even half the man of medicine and of science that your reputation has led me to believe. As to why Ogilvy has suggested that I should entrust these facts to you, Sir, in particular, that will shortly become quite clear. Moreover, if my voice seems uncertain and strained at times, if my narration seems to falter, please understand that even though the better part of a year has passed since those strange days by the sea, only by the greatest force of will am I able to finally set this account down upon paper.

My travels in your country, which I have already mentioned, began last June with my arrival in Aberdeen after a rather uneventful and regrettably unproductive month spent studying in Germany. Moving overland by coach and locomotive, alone and availing myself always of the most convenient and inexpensive modes of transportation for my often unorthodox purposes, I wandered throughout the full length of June and July, on a course winding crookedly ever southwards, across rugged bands of Palaeozoic and Mesozoic strata, usually exposed best, as my luck would have it, along the most inaccessible coastal cliffs and beachheads. So it was that by mid August, on the morning of the 12th to be precise, I had worked my way down to Whitby and taken up residence in a small hotel overlooking the harbour.

After the long weeks spent on the road and often on foot, making my way across the rugged countryside, even these modest accommodations seemed positively luxuriant, I can assure you. To have a hot bath at the ready and cooked meals, a roof to keep the rain off one's head, such little things become an extravagance after only a little time without them. I settled into my single room on Drawbridge Road, excited at the prospect of exploring the ancient, saurian-bearing shales along the shoreline, but also relieved to be out of the dratted weather for a time. A fortnight earlier, I had cabled Sir Elijah Purdy, a fellow of the Geological Society of London and a man with great experience regarding the Liassic strata at Whitby and the fossil bones and mollusca found therein, and he was to meet me no later than the afternoon of the 14th, at which time we would begin our planned week-long survey of the rocks. Meanwhile, I was to examine specimens in the small Whitby Museum on the Quayside, perusing what type specimens of ammonites and Reptilia resided in that institution's collection.

I will endeavour not to bore you with a travelogue, for I know from Ogilvy that you are familiar with the village of Whitby, with its quaint red roofs and white-washed walls, the crumbling Abbey ruins at East Cliff, & etc. And I had, by the time, I must confess, taken in more than my share of maritime scenery, and had little interest or patience remaining for anything save the fossil shells and bones, and fossiliferous strata, which I had come so many thousands of miles to see.

After a good night's sleep, despite a terrible storm towards dawn, I dressed and went down to breakfast, where there was some considerable excitement and discussion among other guests and the proprietor regarding a Russian schooner, *Demeter,* which had run aground only a few days prior at Tate Hill Pier. As I have said, I was quite beyond caring about ships and scenery at this point, and paid little attention to the conversation, though I do recall that the circumstances of the ship's grounding were somewhat mysterious and seemed the source of no small degree of anxiety. Regardless, my mind was almost entirely on my work. I finished my eggs and sausages, a pot of strong black coffee, and set off for the Museum. The morning air was not especially warm nor cool, and it was an easy walk, during which I hardly noticed my surroundings, lost instead in my thoughts of all things palaeontological.

I reached the Quayside shortly before eleven o'clock and was met, as planned, by the Rev. Henry Swales, who has acted now for many years in a curatorial capacity, caring for the Museum's growing cabinet. Though established originally as a repository for fossils, in the last several decades the Museum's mission has been significantly expanded to encompass the general natural history of the region, including large assemblages of beetles, botanical materials, Lepidoptera, and preserved fishes. Rev. Swales, a tall, good-natured fellow with a thick grey mustache and the eyebrows to match, eagerly directed his Yankee guest to the unpretentious gallery where many wall-mounted saurians and other fossils are kept on display for the public. I listened attentively as he related the stories of each specimen, as a man might relate another man's biography, the circumstances of their individual discoveries and conservation. I was taken almost at once with a certain large plesiosaur which had preserved within its ribcage the complete skeleton of a smaller plesiosaur, and much of the afternoon was passed studying this remarkable artefact, making my sketches, and losing myself ever deeper in my fancies of a lost, prediluvian world of monstrous sea dragons.

Eventually, the Rev. Swales returned and reminded me that the Museum would be closing for the day at four, but I was welcome to stay later if I wished. I did, as I'd only just begun to scratch the surface of this marvelous collection, but didn't wish to abuse the Rev's. hospitality. After all, I had many more days to pour over these relics and my eyes were beginning to smart from so many hours scrutinizing the plesiosaurs and ichthyosauria.

"Thank you," said I. "But that really won't be necessary. I'll return early tomorrow morning." He reminded me that the Museum did not open until eight, which I assured him was entirely agreeable. I tidied my notes and left Rev. Swales to lock up for the night.

Leaving the Quayside behind, I decided to take a leisurely stroll towards the seaside, as it was still early, the weather was fine, and I'd little else to occupy my time except my books and notes. My route took me north along

Pier Road, with the dark brown waters of the narrow River Esk flowing swiftly along on my right-hand side. High above the river, of course, rose East Cliff and the venerable ruins of the old abbey.

Though earlier it had interested me not even in the least, I found myself gazing, fascinated, at the distant, disintegrating walls, the lancet archways, perhaps somewhat more disposed to appreciate "local colour" now that some small fraction of my desire to examine Whitby's famous saurians had been sated by the day's work. I knew little of the site's history, only that the original abbey had been erected on the cliff-side in 657 A.D., destroyed two centuries later by Viking raiders, and that the ruins of the present structure were the remains of a Norman abbey built on the same spot at some later date. I thought perhaps there had been some Saint or another associated with the abbey, that I had read this somewhere, but could not recollect the details. However, as I proceeded along the Pier Road, those towering ruins began to elicit from me strange feelings of dread, which I was, then and now, Sir, completely at a loss to explain, and I decided it was best to occupy myself with other, less foreboding sights. So it was that, in short order, I came to West Cliff, there above the beach, where the old cobbles of Pier Road turn sharply back to the south again towards the village, forming something like the crooked head of a shepherd's staff.

I must apologize if I have drifted into the sort of tedious travelogue I earlier promised to avoid, but it is important to impress upon you, at this point in my account, my state of mind, the odd and disquieting effect the abbey had elicited from me. I am not someone accustomed to such emotions and generally regard myself as a man not the least bit dogged by superstition. I told myself that whatever I felt was no more than the cumulative product of light and shadow, compounded by some exhaustion from my long day, and was only what most any other rational man might feel gazing upon those ruins.

At West Cliff, I was at once distracted from my intended goal, the Liassic shales themselves, by the extraordinary sight of a schooner run aground on the eastern side of the quay, across the Esk, and quickly realised that I was, in fact, seeing the very schooner, the *Demeter,* which I'd heard discussed with such excitement and foreboding over breakfast. I assure you, Dr. Watson, that the dead Russian ship cut a peculiar and lonely spectacle, cast up as she was on the jagged shingle of Tate Hill Pier, at the foot of East Cliff and the old graveyard. Her pathetic, shattered masts and bowsprit at once put me in mind of the tall spines of some pre-Adamite monster, not an odd association, of course, for someone in my profession. The tangled rigging and torn canvas hung loose, sagging like some lifeless mass of raw hide and sinew, flapping in the ocean's breeze.

And once again, that unaccustomed sense of dread assailed me, though even stronger than it had before, and I admit to you that I considered turning at once back towards the comfort of the inn. However, as I have said, I count my freedom from baser beliefs and superstitions as a particular point of pride, and, knowing there was nothing here to fear and determined to have a look at the Alum beds, not to be deterred by such childish thoughts nor emotions, I began searching for some easy access to the beach below me, where I might better examine the rocks.

Within only a very few minutes I'd located a spiral, wooden stairway affixed to the cliff near the wall of the quay. However, the years and ravages of the sea had done much damage to the structure and it swayed most alarmingly as I carefully descended the slick steps to the sands below. Having finally reached the bottom, I paused briefly and stared back up the rickety stairway, sincerely hoping that I might find an alternate means of reaching the top again. The tide was out, revealing a broad swath of clean sand and the usual bits of flotsam, and I rightly supposed that I still had a good hour or so to have a look about the foot of West Cliff, before setting out to discover such an alternative became a pressing concern.

Almost at once, then, I came across the perfectly-preserved test of a rather large example of spiny echinodermata, or sea urchin, weathered all but entirely free of the Alum shales which had imprisoned it for so many epochs, and deposited on the sand. I brushed it off and examined it more closely in the sunlight, unable to place either its genus or species, and suspecting that it might perhaps be of a form hitherto unrecognized by palaeontologists; I deposited my prize in my right coat pocket and continued to scan the steep rocks for any other such excellent fossils. But, as the evening wore on, I failed to spot anything else quite as interesting, all my additional finds consisting in the main only of broken pieces of ammonoid and mussel shells embedded in hard limestone nodules, a few fish bones, and what I hoped might prove to be a small fragment from one of the characteristic hourglass-shaped flipper bones of an ichthyosaur or plesiosaur. I glanced out to sea, and then back to the dark grey rocks, trying to envision, as I had so often done before, the unimaginable expanse of time which had transpired since the stones before me were only slime and ooze at the bottom of an earlier and infinitely more alien sea.

"You are a geologist?" someone asked at that point, a man's voice, giving me a start, and I turned to see a very tall, gaunt fellow with a narrow, aquiline nose watching me from only a few feet away. He was smiling very slightly, in a manner that I thought oddly knowing at the time. For all I guessed, he might well have been standing there for an hour, as I have a habit of becoming so intent upon my collecting that I may often neglect to glance about me for long stretches.

"Yes sir," I said. "A paleontologist, to be more precise."

"Ah," he said. "Of course you are. I would have seen that for myself, but I'm afraid the wreck has had me distracted," and the man motioned in the direction of the quay, the Esk, and the stranded *Demeter* beyond. "You are an American, too, and a New Yorker, unless I miss my guess."

"I am," I replied, though by this point I confess that the stranger was beginning to annoy me somewhat with his questions. "Dr. Tobias Logan, of the American Museum of Natural History," I introduced myself, holding out a hand which he only stared at curiously and smiled that knowing smile at me again.

"You're hunting the sea monsters of Whitby," he said, "and, I gather, having blasted little luck at it."

"Well," I said, taking the urchin from my pocket and passing it to the man, "I admit I've had better days in the field."

"Extraordinary," the tall man said, carefully inspecting the fossil, turning it over and over in his hand.

"Quite so," replied I, relaxing a bit, as I'm not unaccustomed to explaining myself to curious passerby. "But, still, not precisely the quarry I had in mind."

"Better the luck of Chapman, heh?" he asked and winked.

I realised at once that he was referring to the discovery by William Chapman in 1758 of a marine crocodile on the Yorkshire Coast, not far from where we were standing.

"You surprise me, sir," I said. "Are you a collector?"

"Oh no," he assured me, returning the urchin. "Nothing of the sort. But I read a great deal, you see, and I'm afraid few subjects have managed to escape my attention."

"Your accent isn't Yorkshire," I said, and he shook his head.

"No, Dr. Logan, it isn't," he replied, and then he winked at me once again. The man turned and peered out the sea, and it was at this point that I realised that the tide was beginning to rise, the beach being appreciably more constricted than the last time I'd noticed.

"I fear that we shall certainly be getting our feet wet if we don't start back," I said, but he only nodded his head and continued to stare at the restless grey expanse of the sea.

"We should talk at greater length sometime," he said. "There is a matter, concerning an object of great antiquity, and uncertain provenance, that I should very much appreciate hearing your trained opinion on."

"Indeed," I said, eyeing the rising tide. "A fossil?"

"No, a stone tablet. It appears to have been graven with hieroglyphics resembling those of the ancient Egyptians."

"I'm sorry, sir, but you'd surely be better off showing it to an archaeologist, instead. I wouldn't be able to tell you much."

"Wouldn't you?" he asked, cocking an eyebrow and looking thoughtfully back at me. "I pried it from those very strata which you've spent the last hour examining. It's really quite an amazing object, Dr. Logan."

I believe I must have stared at the man for some time then without speaking, for I am sure I was too stunned and incredulous to find the words. He shrugged, then picked up a pebble and tossed it at the advancing sea.

"Forgive me," I said, or something of the sort. "But either you're having me on or you yourself have been the victim of someone else's joke. You're obviously an educated man, so – "

"So," he said, interrupting me, "I know that these strata are too old by many millions of years to contain the artefact I've told you I found buried in them. Obviously."

"Then you are joking?"

"No, my good man," he said, selecting another pebble to fling at the tide. "Quite the contrary, I assure you. I was as skeptical as you when first I laid eyes upon the thing, but now I am fairly convinced of its authenticity."

"Poppycock," I said to him, though I had many far more vulgar expressions in mind by this point. "What you're proposing is so entirely absurd – "

"That it doesn't even warrant the most casual consideration of learned men," he said, interrupting me for the second time.

"Well, yes," I replied, somewhat impatiently I'm afraid, and then returned the urchin to its place in my coat pocket. "The whole idea is perfectly absurd, man, right there on the face of it. It runs contrary to everything we've discovered in the last one hundred years about the evolution and development of life and the rise of humanity."

"I suspected," he said, as though I'd not even spoken, "at first, that someone might have planted the artefact, you see, that perhaps I had stumbled upon a prank aimed at someone else. Someone who, unlike me, makes a habit of collecting shells and rocks and old bones on the seashore.

"But I was able to identify – Oh, what is it that you geologist fellows say? The positive and negative impressions – yes, that's it. The positive and negative impressions of the tablet were pressed quite clearly, unmistakably, into the layers of shale immediate above and below it. I have succeeded in recovering those as well."

"I'm sure you did," I said doubtfully.

"But, even more curiously, this isn't the first such inappropriate artefact, Dr. Logan. Two years ago, a very similar stone was found by a miner up the coast at Staithes, where, as you surely know, these same shales are mined for their alum. I have seen it myself, in a private cabinet in Glasgow. And there was a third, discovered in 1865, I think, or 1866, down at Frylingdales. But it seems to have vanished and, regrettably, only a drawing remains."

The man stopped talking then, for a moment, and gazed towards the walls of the quay. From where we were standing, one could just make out the splintered fore-mast of the ill-fated *Demeter* and he presently motioned towards it.

"There are dark entities afoot here in Whitby, Dr. Logan. Ay, darker things than even I'm accustomed to facing down, and I assure you I'm no coward, if I do say so myself."

"The tide, sir," I said, for now each wave carried the sea within mere feet of where we stood.

"Indeed, the tide," he said in a distracted, annoyed way and nodded his head again. "But perhaps we can talk of this another time, before you leave Whitby. I will be glad for the chance to show you the tablet. I will be here another week, myself. I would rather prefer, though, if you kept this matter between us."

"Gladly," I assured him. "I have no particular wish to be thought a madman."

"Even so," he said, and, with that enigmatic pronouncement, at once began the perilous ascent up the rickety stairs to the Pier Road. I stood there a bit longer, watching as he climbed, expecting those slippery and infirm planks to give way at any second, dashing him onto the rocks and sand at my feet. But they held and, seeing that the sea had already entirely engulfed the beach to the west of me, and having only the high and inaccessible quay wall to the east, I summoned my courage and followed him. By no small stroke of luck, I also survived the climb, though the structure swayed and creaked and I was quite certain that my every footfall would be my last.

By now, Dr. Watson, I have but little doubt that you must have begun to understand why Ogilvy has urged me to write you. I have read in the press several accounts of the extraordinary Mr. Holmes' death in Switzerland, and I hope that the remarkable possibility, which I will not explicitly suggest here, but rather let stand as an unstated question for your consideration, will bring you no further pain. I have been made well-aware of the great friendship that existed between you and Mr. Sherlock Holmes, and had not my reason been so vexed and controverted by the bizarre events at Whitby last August, I would have preferred to keep the encounter forever to myself. I would never have been led to reflect at such length upon the identity of the man on the beach, a man whose appearance and demeanor I think you might recognize.

But I should continue my story now, and must continue to hope that you see here anything more than the ravings of an overtaxed mind and an overindulged imagination.

By the time I had at last finished my climb and regained secure footing at the crumbling summit of West Cliff, storm clouds were moving swiftly in from the southwest, darkening the murmuring waters of the Esk and creating an ominous backdrop for the abbey ruins. Fearing that I might lose my way among the unfamiliar streets should I attempt to discover a shorter route back to the hotel, I hurried instead along Pier Road, retracing my steps back to the inn on Drawbridge Road. But I'd gone only a little way when the wind and thunder began and, in short order, a heavy, chilling downpour. I had neglected to bring an umbrella with me, thinking that the day would remain pleasant and clear, and not having planned on the walk down to the beach beforehand. As a result, I was now treated to a most thorough and proper soaking. I must have made for a dreary and pitiful sight, indeed, slogging my way down those narrow, rain-swept avenues.

When at last I reached the hotel, I was offered a hot cup of tea and a seat at the hearth. As tempting as the latter was, I told the innkeeper that I preferred instead to retire at once to my room and acquire some dry clothes and rest until dinner. As I started up the stairs, he called me back, having forgotten a message that had been left for me that afternoon. It was written on a small, plain sheet of stationary and read:

Toby, will call again first thing in the morning. Please await my arrival. Reached Whitby earlier than expected. I have much to relate re: unusual fossils found in Devon Lias and now in my care. Are you familiar with Phoenician (?) god Dagon or Irish Daoine Domhain? Until the morrow,

Yrs., E. P.

Though rightly intrigued and excited at the prospect of the new Devon fossils which Purdy had mentioned, I was quite completely baffled by his query regarding Phoenician gods and those two words of unpronounceable Gaelic. Deciding that any mysteries would readily resolve themselves in the morning, I retired to my room, where I at once changed clothes and then busied myself until dinner with some brief notes on the urchin and other specimens from West Cliff.

I slept fitfully that night, while the storm raged and banged at the shutters. I am not given to nightmares, but I recall odd scraps of dream where I stood on the shore at West Cliff, watching as the *Demeter* sailed majestically into the harbour. The tall man stood somewhere close behind me, though I don't think I ever saw his face, and spoke of my wife and child. I finally awoke for the last time shortly after dawn, to the smell of coffee brewing and breakfast cooking downstairs, and the comforting sound of rain dripping from the eaves. The storm had passed and, despite my rather poor sleep, I recall feeling very rested and ready for a long day prospecting the seaside outcrops with Purdy. I dressed quickly and, armed with my ashplant and knapsack, my hammer and cold chisels, I went down to await my colleague's arrival.

However, at eleven o'clock I was still waiting, sipping at my second pot of coffee and beginning to feel the first faint twinges of annoyance that so much of the day was being squandered when my time in Whitby was to be so short. I am almost Puritanical in my work habits and despise the wasting of perfectly good daylight, and could not imagine what was taking Purdy so long to show.

The terrible things that soon followed, I must tell you, occurred with not the slightest hint of the lurid or sensual air that is usually attached to the macabre and uncanny in the penny dreadfuls and Gothic romances. There was not even the previous day's vague sense of foreboding. They simply happened, Sir, and somehow that made them all the worse. It would be long weeks before I would begin to associate with the events a singular trepidation, indeed a genuine horror, which would gradually come to so consume my thoughts.

I was reading, for the second time, a long article in an Edinburgh paper (the paper's name escapes me now, as does the precise subject of the article), when a young boy, possibly eight years of age, came in and announced that he'd been sent to retrieve me. A man, he said, had paid him six-pence to bring me to West Cliff, where there had been a drowning in the night.

"I'm sorry, but I am not a medical doctor," I told him, thinking this must surely be a simple case of mistaken identity, but no, he assured me at once, he'd been instructed to bring the American Dr. Tobias Logan to the beach at West Cliff, with all possible haste. As I sat there scratching my head, the boy grew impatient and protested that we should hurry. Before I left the hotel on Drawbridge Road, however, I scribbled a quick note to Purdy and left it with the proprietor, in case he should arrive in my absence. Then I quickly gathered my belongings and followed the excited boy, who told me his name was Edward and that his father was a cobbler, through the narrow, winding streets of Whitby and once again down to West Cliff.

The body of the drowned man lay on the sand and clearly the gulls and crabs had been at him for some considerable time before he was discovered by a beachcomber. Yet, despite the damage done by the cruel beaks of the birds, I had no trouble in recognising the face of Elijah Purdy right off. Several men had crowded about, including the constable and harbour master, none of whom, I quickly gathered, had paid the boy six-pence to bring me to West Cliff.

"First that damned Russian ghost ship," the constable grumbled, lighting his pipe. "Now this."

"A foul week, to be sure," the harbour master muttered back.

I introduced myself at once and then kneeled down beside the tattered earthly remains of the man whom I had known and of whom I'd been so fond. The constable coughed and exhaled a great grey cloud of pipe smoke.

"Here," he said. "Did you know this poor fellow?"

"I did, and very well," I replied. "I was to meet him this very morning. I was waiting for him when the boy there fetched me from the inn on Drawbridge Road."

"Is that so now," the constable said. "What boy is that?"

I looked up and there was, to be sure, no sign of the boy who had led me to the grisly scene.

"The cobbler's son," I said, and looked back down at the ruined face of Purdy. "He said that he was paid to summon me here. I assumed you'd sent for me, sir, though I'm not at all sure how you could have known to do so."

At that, the harbour master and constable exchanged perplexed stares and the latter went back to puffing at his pipe.

"This man was an associate of yours, then?" the harbour master asked me.

"Indeed," said I. "He is Sir Elijah Purdy, a geologist from London. He arrived in Whitby only yesterday. I believe he may have taken a room at the Morrow House on Hudson Street."

The two men looked at me and then the constable whispered something to his companion and the two nodded their heads in unison.

"You're an American," the constable said, raising an eyebrow and chewing at the stem of his pipe.

"Yes," I said. "I'm an American."

"Well, Dr. Logan, you may be certain that we'll get straight to the bottom of this," he assured me.

"Thank you," I said, and it was at that moment that I noticed something odd, about the diameter of a silver dollar, clutched in the drowned man's hand.

"Murders here in Whitby do not go unsolved."

"What makes you think he was murdered?" I asked the constable, prying the curious, iridescent object from Elijah Purdy's grasp.

"Well, for one, the man's pockets were filled with stones to weight the body down. See there for yourself."

Indeed, the pockets of his wool overcoat were bulging with shale, but on quick inspection I saw that they all contained fossils and explained to the man that, in all likelihood, Elijah Purdy himself had placed the stones there. One of his vest pockets was likewise filled.

"Ah," the constable said thoughtfully and rubbed at his mustache. "Well, no matter. We'll find the chap what did this, I promise you."

In no mood to argue the point, I answered a few more questions, told the constable that I would be available at the inquest, and made my way back up the rickety stairway to Pier Road. I stood there for a short time, surveying the scene below, the men arranged in a ring around the drowned man's corpse, the dark sea lapping tirelessly at the shore, the wide North Sea sky above. After a bit I remembered the object I'd taken from Purdy's hand and held it up for a closer inspection. But there was no doubt of what it was, a small ammonite of the genus *Dactylioceras,* a form quite common in sections of the English Liassic. Nothing extraordinary, except that this specimen, though deceased, was not fossilized, and the squid-like head of the cephalopod stared back at me with silvery eyes, its ten tentacles drooping limply across my fingers.

I fear that there is little else to tell, Dr. Watson, and glancing back over these few pages I can see that there is not nearly so much sense in what I've written as I'd hoped for. I returned to the hotel, where I would spend the next three days, making one more visit to the Rev. Swales' museum, only to discover my enthusiasm for work had dissolved. After the inquest, during which it was determined that Sir Elijah Purdy's drowning was accidental, having occurred while he collected fossils along the beach, and that no foul play was involved – that he had simply misjudged the tides – I packed up my things and returned home to Manhattan. I delivered the very recently dead *Dactylioceras,* preserved in alcohol, to the curator of fossil invertebrates, who greeted the find with much fanfare and promised to name the surprising new species for the man from whose grip I had pried it. One final detail, which will be of interest to you, and which forms the primary reason of this writing, is a letter which I received some weeks after coming back to the States.

Posted from Whitby on the 12th of September, one month to the day after my arrival there, it carried no return address and had been composed upon a typewriter. I will duplicate the text below:

Dear Dr. Logan,

I trust that your trip home will have passed without incident. I have written to offer my sincerest apologies for not having attended to the matter of your friend's untimely death, and for not having found the time to continue our earlier conversation. But I must implore you to forget the odd matter of which I spoke, the three tablets from Whitby, Staithes, and Frylingdales. All are now lost, I fear, and I have come to see how that outcome is surely for the best. Dark and ancient powers, the whim of inhuman beings of inconceivable antiquity and malignancy, may be at work here and, I suspect, may have played a direct role in the death of Sir Elijah. Take my words to heart and forget these things. To worry at them further will profit you not. Perhaps we will meet again some-day, under more congenial circumstances.

S. H.

Whether or not the letter's author was, in fact, your own associate, Mr. Sherlock Holmes, and if that was the selfsame man with whom I spoke at West Cliff, I cannot say. Any more than I can explain the presence in the waters off Whitby of a mollusk believed vanished from the face of the Earth for so many millions of years or the death of Elijah Purdy, an excellent swimmer, or so I have been told. Having never seen the tablets first-hand, I can profess no reliable opinion regarding them, and feel I am better off not trying to do so. I have never been a nervous man, but I have taken to hearing strange sounds and voices in the night, and my sleep and, I am very much afraid, peace of mind are beginning to suffer. I dream of – no, I will not speak here of the dreams.

Before I close, I should say that on Friday last there was a burglary at the Museum here, which the police have yet to solve. The Whitby ammonite and all written records of it were the only things stolen, though some considerable vandalism was done to a number of the palaeontology and geology offices and to the locked cabinet where the specimen was being kept.

I thank you for your time, Dr. Watson, and, if you are ever in New York, hope to have the pleasure of meeting you.

Dr. Tobias H. Logan
Department of Vertebrate Palaeontology
American Museum of Natural History
New York City, New York

(unposted letter discovered among the effects of Dr. Tobias Logan, subsequent to his suicide by hanging, 11 May 1898)

The Dead and
the Moonstruck

Beneath Providence, below the ancient yellow house on Benefit Street where silver-eyed vampires sleep away the days and pass their dusty waxwork evenings with Spanish absinthe and stale memories; this house that once belonged to witches, long ago, this house with as many ghosts and secrets and curses as it has spiders and silverfish – beneath the yellow house, at half past midnight on a bitter February night, Mesdames Terpsichore and Mnemosyne are finishing a lecture with corporeal demonstrations. Lessons for ghoul pups and for the children of the Cuckoo – the changeling brats stolen as babies and raised in the warrens – and for an hour the two old hounds have droned on and on and on about the most efficacious methods for purging a corpse of embalming fluid and other funereal preservatives before it can be safely prepared in the kitchens. The skinny, mouse-haired girl named Starling Jane nodded off twice during the lecture, earning a snarl from Madam Mnemosyne and a mean glare from Madam Terpsichore's blazing yellow eyes.

"That's all for tonight," Madam Terpsichore growls, folding shut the leather satchel that holds her scalpels and syringes, her needles and knives. "But every one of you'd best know *all* the purgatives and detoxicants by the morrow. And you, young lady," and now the ghūl points a long and crooked finger at Starling Jane, one ebony claw aimed straight at her heart. "*You* need to learn that the day, not the classroom, is the proper place for sleeping."

"Yes, ma'am," Starling Jane whispers and keeps her eyes on the dirt floor of the basement, on her bare feet and an ivory scrap of bone protruding from the earth. "It won't happen again."

There's a hushed titter of laughter and guttural yapping from the rest of the class, and Jane pretends that she's only a beetle or a small red worm, something unimportant that can scurry or slither quickly away, something that can tuck itself out of sight in an unnoticed cranny or crevice, and she'll never have to sit through another dissection lecture or be scolded for dozing off again. Madam Mnemosyne silences the muttering class with a glance, but Jane can still feel their eyes on her, and "I'm sorry," she says.

"I should think that you are," Madam Terpsichore barks. "You're plenty old enough to know better, child," and then, to the other students sitting cross-legged on the basement floor, "Mistress Jane's Third Confirmation is scheduled for the full Hunger Moon, four nights hence. But perhaps she isn't ready, hmmmm? Perhaps she'll be found wanting, and the razor jaws will close tight about her hands. Then maybe we'll have *her* meat on the slab before much longer."

"And no nasty embalming fluid to contend with," Madam Mnemosyne adds.

"Ah, she would be sweet," Madam Terpsichore agrees.

"I'm sorry," Jane says again. "But I'll be ready on the moon."

Madam Terpsichore flares her wide black nostrils, sniffs at the musty cellar air, and her eyes glitter in the candlelight. "See that you are, child," she says. "It would be a shame to lose another sprout so very soon after young Master Lockheart's unfortunate rejection," and then she dismisses the class, and Jane follows all the others from the basement into the old tunnels winding like empty veins beneath the city.

Later, after Elementary Thaumaturgy and Intermediate Necromancy and a rambling, unscheduled address on the history of the upper night-lands by Master Tantalus, visiting Providence from the Boston warrens. After dinner and the predawn free hour, after all the time lying awake in her narrow bunk, wishing she were asleep but afraid to close her eyes, Starling Jane finally drifts out and down, slipping through the familiar dormitory smells of wet masonry and mildew and millipedes, past the snores and grunts and gentle breathing noises of those who aren't afraid of their dreams. A hundred feet beneath the day-washed pavement of Angell Street, and she spirals easily through velvet folds of consciousness and uncon-sciousness. Countless bits of senseless, inconsequential remembrance and fancy – simple dreams – leading and misleading her step by step, moment by moment, to the nightmare place she's visited almost every morning or afternoon for two months.

That place where there is a wide blue sky, and the sun hanging inconceivably bright directly overhead. Where there is grass and the scent of flowers, and she stands at the top of a hill looking down on a sparkling sea.

"You should have stayed with me," her mother says from somewhere close behind her, and Jane doesn't turn around, because she doesn't want to see. "If you'd have stayed with me, I'd have loved you, and you'd have grown up to be a beautiful woman."

The salt-warm wind off the sea makes waves in the tall grass and whistles past Starling Jane's ears.

"I would have stayed," she says, just like she always says. "If they'd have let me. I would have stayed, if I'd had a choice."

"I knew I'd lose you," her mother replies. "Before you were even born, I knew the monsters would come and steal you away from me. I knew they'd hide you from me and make you forget my face."

"How could you have known all that?" Jane asks. Down on the beach, there are children playing with a big yellow-brown dog. They throw pieces of driftwood, and the dog runs after them, and sometimes it brings them back again.

"Oh, I knew, all right," her mother says. "Trust me, I *knew* what was coming. I heard them in the night, outside my bedroom window, scratching at the glass, wanting in."

"I have to pass one more test, Mother. I just have to pass one more test, and they'll let me live."

"You would have been such a beautiful girl. Just look at what they've made of you instead."

On the beach, the children chase the yellow-brown dog through the surf, laughing and splashing so loudly that Starling Jane can hear them all the way up at the top of the hill.

"They'll make you a monster, too," her mother says.

"I wish they could," Jane mutters to herself, because she knows it doesn't matter whether or not her mother hears the things she's saying. "I wish to all the dark gods that they could make me like them. But that's not what happens. That's not what happens at all."

"You could come home. Every night, I sit up, waiting for you to come back, for them to bring you back to me."

"You shouldn't do that," Jane whispers, and the hill rumbles softly beneath her. Down on the beach, the children stop playing and turn towards her. She waves to them, but they don't seem to see her.

Or they're afraid of me, she thinks.

"If you fail the test, they might bring you back to me," her mother says hopefully.

"If I fail, they'll kill me," Jane replies. "They'll kill me and eat me. No one ever goes back, once they're chosen by the Cuckoo. No one."

"But you would have been such a beautiful girl," her mother says again. "I would have given you everything."

"It's the last test," Jane whispers.

Beneath her, the hill rumbles again, and the sea has turned to blood, and there are wriggling white things falling from the sky. On the beach, the children and the yellow-brown dog have vanished.

"I'll be waiting," her mother says.

And Jane opens her eyes, tumbling breathlessly back into flesh and bone, and she lies awake until sunset, listening to her heart and the sounds the sleepers make and the faraway din of traffic up on Angell Street.

"You're scared," the ghoul pup named Sorrow says, not asking her but telling her, and then he scratches determinedly at his left ear.

"I'm not scared," Starling Jane tells him, and shakes her head, but she knows it's a lie and, worse still, knows, too, that *he* knows it's a lie.

"Sure, and neither was Lockheart."

"Lockheart wasn't ready. Everyone knew he wasn't ready."

They're sitting on stools near one of the tall kitchen hearths, scrubbing tin plates clean with wire-bristle brushes, sudsy water up to their elbows and puddled on the cobbles at their feet. The washtub between them smells like soap and grease.

"Would *you* eat me?" she asks Sorrow. And he grunts and drops the plate he was scrubbing back into the washtub, then tugs thoughtfully at the coarse, straw-colored tuft of hair sprouting from the underside of his muzzle.

"That's not a fair question. You know underlings never get delicacies like that. Not a scrap. You'd be served to Master Danaüs and the – "

"I was speaking hypothetically," Jane says and adds another plate to the stack drying in front of the fire. "If they made an exception and you had the opportunity, would you eat me?"

Sorrow stares at her for a long moment, furrows his brow uncertainly and blinks his yellow eyes. "Wouldn't you *want* me to?" he asks her, finally.

"It wouldn't bother you, eating your best friend?"

Sorrow pulls another plate from the washtub and frowns, looking down at the dishwater now instead of Starling Jane. He scrubs halfheartedly at the bits of meat and gravy and potatoes clinging to the dented tin and then drops the plate back into the tub.

"That wasn't clean, and you know it."

"It's just not a fair question, Jane. Of *course,* I'd eat you. I mean, speaking hypothetically and all. I'm not saying I wouldn't *miss* you, but – "

"You'd eat me anyway."

"It'd be awful. I'd probably cry the whole time."

"I'm sure you would," Starling Jane says with a sigh, pulling the plate Sorrow didn't wash out of the tub again. There's a piece of burnt potato skin big as her thumb stuck to it. "I hope I'd give you indigestion. You'd have it coming."

"You really are scared," Sorrow scowls and spits into the washtub.

"You're a disgusting pig, you know that?"

"Oink," Sorrow oinks and wrinkles his nostrils.

"I'm *not* scared," Jane says again, because she needs to hear the words. "There's no reason for me to be scared. I've made it past the Harvest Moon and the full Frost Moon. I know my lessons – "

"Book lessons don't get you past the moons. You know that, Jane. Nobody's ever been confirmed because they got good marks."

"It doesn't hurt."

"It doesn't help, either."

"But it doesn't *hurt,*" Jane snarls at him and flings her wire-bristle brush at his head. Sorrow ducks, and it hits the wall behind him and clatters to the floor.

"You're crazy," Sorrow says, and then he hops off his stool, knocking it over in the process. "I might be a pig, but you're crazy."

"You *want* me to fail. You want me to fail so you can go through all my things and take whatever you want."

"You don't *have* anything I want," Sorrow barks defensively and takes a quick step backwards, putting more distance between himself and Starling Jane.

"Yes, I do. That owl skull the Bailiff brought me from Salem. You want that. You've *told* me more than once that you wish he'd given it to you instead of me."

"I just said I liked it, that's all."

"And that Narragansett Indian arrowhead I found in the tunnels last summer, you want that, too, don't you?"

"Jane, stop and listen to yourself," Sorrow pleads and takes another step or two away from the hearth. "I do not want you to fail your Confirmation and die, just so I can have your things. That's crazy. You're my *friend*. And I don't have a lot of friends."

"Friends don't eat each other!"

"Someone's gonna *hear* you," Sorrow hisses, and holds a long finger up to his thin black lips. "If old Melpomene finds out you're making such a racket, we'll both be scrubbing pots and plates from now till Judgment Day," and he glances nervously over a shoulder into the shadows waiting just beyond the firelight's reach.

"So maybe I don't care anymore!" Jane shouts at him, and then she reaches into the washtub and yanks out a particularly filthy plate. "I'd rather spend the rest of my life washing dishes for that old bat than wind up in her stew pot or roasting on her spit with a turnip stuffed in my mouth!"

"You're *not* going to fail," Sorrow says, glancing over his left shoulder again. "You're not going to fail, and no one's going to eat you."

"You don't know that."

"Sure I do."

"Go away. Leave me alone," Jane says, letting the filthy plate slip from her fingers. Soapy, lukewarm dishwater splashes out onto her patchwork apron. "That's all I want, Sorrow. I want to be alone. I think I'm going to cry, and I don't want anyone to see. I especially don't want you to see."

"You sure?" Sorrow asks. "Maybe I should stay," and he sits down on the floor as if she's just agreed with him when she hasn't. "I don't mind if you cry."

"Lockheart wasn't ready," she whispers. "That's the difference. He wasn't ready, and I am."

"You bet. I've never seen anyone so ready for anything in my whole life."

"Liar," Jane says and glares at him. In the hearth, one of the logs cracks and shifts and, for a moment, the fire flares so brightly that Sorrow has to squint until it settles down again.

"I wouldn't eat you," he tells her. "Not even if they stewed both your kidneys in crabapples and carrots and parsnips and served them to me with mint jelly, I wouldn't eat you. I swear."

"Thank you," Jane replies, and she tries to smile, but it comes out more of a grimace than a smile. "I wouldn't eat you, either."

"Are you going to throw anything else at me?"

"No," she says. "I'm not going to throw anything else at you. Not ever," and she gets up and retrieves her brush from the floor behind Sorrow's stool.

In a life filled past bursting with mysteries – a life where the mysterious and the arcane, the cryptic and the magical, are the rule, not the exception – if anyone were to ever ask Starling Jane what one thing she found the *most* mysterious, she would probably say the Bailiff. If he has a name, she's never heard it, this very large, good-natured man with his shiny, bald head and full grey beard, his pudgy link-sausage fingers and rusty iron loop of keys always jangling on his wide belt. Not a vampire nor a ghoul nor any of the other night races, just a man, and Jane's heard rumors that he's a child of the Cuckoo, too, a changeling, but also something more than a changeling. And there are other rumors – that he's an exiled demon, or a wizard who's forgotten most of his sorcery, or an ancient, immortal thing no one's ever made up a word for – but to Starling Jane he's just the Bailiff. A link between the yellow house on Benefit Street and other dark houses in other cities, courier for the most precious packages and urgent messages that can be trusted to no one else.

On the last night before her final rite of Confirmation, the ceremony on the night of the full Hunger Moon, the Bailiff returns from a trip to New Orleans, and after his business with the dead people upstairs and his business with the hounds downstairs, he takes his dinner in the long candlelit dining room where the changeling children and the ghoul pups are fed.

"You'll do fine," he assures Starling Jane, nibbling the last bit of meat from a finger bone. "Everyone gets the shakes before their third moon. It's natural as mold and molars, and don't let no one tell you any different."

Sorrow stops picking his teeth with a thumb claw. "You heard about Lockheart?" he asks the Bailiff.

"Everyone's heard about Lockheart," a she-pup named Melancholy says and rolls her yellow eyes. "Of course he's heard about Lockheart, you slubberdegullion."

Sorrow snorts and bares his eyeteeth at Melancholy. "What the heck's a slubberdegullion?" he demands.

"If you weren't one, you'd know," she replies brusquely, and Sorrow growls and tackles her. A moment later and they're rolling about on the floor between the dinner tables, a blur of fur and insults and dust and someone starts shouting, "Fight! Fight!" so everyone comes scrambling to see.

Jane keeps her seat and picks indifferently at the green-white mound of boiled cabbage on her plate. "You have heard about Lockheart?" she asks the Bailiff.

"As it so happens, and with all due respect paid to the sesquipedalian Miss Melancholy down there," and he glances at the commotion on the dining-room floor, "no, my dear, I haven't."

"Oh," Starling says and jabs her cabbage with the bent tines of her fork. "He failed his second."

"Ah, I see. Well, now, I'd have to say that's certainly a bloody shame, of one sort or another."

"He was scared. He froze up right at the start, didn't even make it past the sword bridge. They had to bring him down in a burlap sack."

The Bailiff belches, politely says pardon me, please, then asks her "Was the boy a friend of yours?" he asks her.

"No," Jane says. "I always thought he was a disgusting little toad."

"But now you're thinking him failing has something to do with you, is that it? Perhaps an ill omen."

"Maybe," Jane replies. "Or maybe I was scared to start with, and that only made it worse."

On the floor, Melancholy pokes Sorrow in his left eye, and he yelps and punches her in the belly.

"Don't seem fair, sometimes, does it?" the Bailiff asks, and then he takes a bite of her cabbage.

"What doesn't seem fair?"

"All these trials for them that never asked to be taken away from their rightful mommas and brought down here to the dark, all these tribulations, while *others* – not naming names, mind you," but Starling Jane knows from the way he raised his voice when he said "others" that he means Sorrow and Melancholy and all the ghūl pups in general. "All they have to do is be born, then watch their p's and q's, keep their snouts clean, and not a deadly deed in sight."

"Madam Terpsichore says nothing's fair, and it's only asking for misery, expecting things to turn out that way."

"Does she now?"

"All the time."

"Well, you listen to your teachers, child, but, on the other hand, Madam Terpsichore never had to face what's waiting down in that pit during the full Hunger Moon, now did she?"

"No," Jane says, pushing her plate over to the Bailiff's side of the table. "Of course not."

"See, that's what really draws the line between you and her, Miss Starling Jane. Not a lot of words written in some old book by gods no one even remembers but the hounds, not the color of your eyes or how sharp your teeth might be. What matters…" and he pauses to finish her cabbage and start on her slice of rhubarb-and-liver pie. Jane pushes Sorrow's plate across the table to the Bailiff, as well.

"Thank you," he says with his mouth full. "I do hate to see good food go to waste. Now, as I was saying, what matters, Miss Jane, what you need to understand come tomorrow night…" and then he trails off again to swallow.

"You really shouldn't talk with your mouth full," Jane says. "You'll choke."

The Bailiff takes a drink from his cup and nods his bald head. Now there are a few beads of red wine clinging to his whiskers. "My manners ain't what they used to be," he says.

"You were saying, what I need to understand – " she prompts.

The Bailiff stops eating, puts his fork down and looks at her, his moss-green eyes like polished gems from the bottom of a deep stream. "You're a brave girl," he says, and smiles, "and one day soon you'll be a fine, brave woman. *That's* the difference, and that's what you need to understand. Madam Terpsichore won't ever have to prove herself the way you already have. What makes us brave isn't lacking the good sense to be afraid, it's looking back at what we've lived through and seeing if we faced it well. The ghouls are your masters, and don't you ever forget that, but they'll never have your courage, because no one's ever gonna make them walk the plank, so to speak."

And then he reaches into a pocket of his baggy coat and pulls out a small gold coin with a square hole punched in the center. The metal glimmers faintly in the candlelight as he holds it up for Jane to see.

"I want you to have this," he says. "But not to keep, mind you. No, when you offer your hands up to old Nidhogg's mouth tomorrow night, I want you to leave this on his tongue. I can't say why, but it's important. Now, do you think you can do that for me?"

Starling nods her head and takes the coin from his hand. "It's very pretty," she says.

"Now, don't you get scared and forget. I want you to put that right there on that old serpent's tongue."

"I won't forget. I promise. Put it on his tongue."

The Bailiff smiles again and goes back to eating, and Jane holds the coin tightly and watches Sorrow and Melancholy tumbling about on the floor, nipping at each other's ears, until Madam Melpomene comes to break up the fight.

In the dream, she watches the children on the beach with their dog, and the crimson thunderheads piling up higher and higher above the darkening sea. Her mother has stopped talking, and, because this has never been part of the dream before, Starling Jane turns to see why. But there's no one standing behind her now, only the tall grass and the wind whispering furtively through it and the world running on that way forever.

And then there are no more nights left between Starling Jane and the full Hunger Moon, no more anxious days or hours or minutes, because all moons are inevitable and no amount of fear or desire can forestall their coming. This is the year of her Third Confirmation, her time for the Trial of the Serpent, because she's survived the first two rites, the Trial of Fire and the Trial of Blades. There are no lessons or chores on the day of a trial, for Jane or any other changeling child, and by the appointed hour the warrens have emptied into the amphitheater carved from solid stone one hundred and fifty feet beneath Federal Hill.

Jane wears the long silver robes of passage and waits alone with blind, decrepit Master Solace in a tiny curtained alcove on the northern rim of the pit. The air stinks of wet stone and rot and the myrrh smoldering in a small brass pot on the floor. Her face is a mask of soot and drying blood, the red and black runes drawn on her skin by Madam Hippodamia, that she might make the descent with all the most generous blessings of the Old Ones. From the alcove she can hear the murmuring crowd and knows that Sorrow's out there somewhere, crouched nervously on one of the stone benches, and she wishes she were sitting beside him, and it were someone else's turn to stand before the dragon.

"It's almost time, child," Master Solace barks and blinks at her, his pale, cataract-shrouded eyes the color of butter. "If you are ready, there's nothing to fear."

If I'm ready, she thinks and shuts her eyes tight.

And then the horn, and the ship's bell, and the steady *thump-thump-thump* of the drums begins.

"Walk true," Master Solace says and blinks at her again.

Jane opens her eyes, and the tattered curtain has been pulled back so she can see the torchlight and shadows filling the amphitheater and the pit.

"Walk this path with no doubt in your heart," Master Solace says, and then he ushers Starling Jane out of the alcove to stand on a narrow wooden platform jutting out over the abyss. Above and all around her, the murmuring rises to an excited, expectant crescendo, and ghūl drum-wraiths hammer at their skins so loudly she wonders that the cavern doesn't collapse from the noise and bury them all alive. *That would be preferable,* she thinks. *That would be easier than dying alone.*

The drumming stops as abruptly as it began, and gradually the murmuring follows suit, and for a moment or two there's no sound from the great chamber but Jane's heartbeat and Master Solace sucking the dull stubs of his teeth. And then one note rings out from the ship's bell, and "All stand," Madam Terpsichore says, shouting to the assembled through her bullhorn.

"Tonight we have come down to this sacred place of truth and choice to witness the deserved confirmation or the just rejection of Mistress Starling Jane of the Providence warrens. It has been eight years since she was delivered to us by the grace of the Cuckoo, and on this night of the full Hunger Moon we shall all know, once and for all, whether she will serve us until the end of her days."

"Watch your step, girl," Master Solace whispers. "It's a long way down," and then Jane hears the curtain drawn shut again, and she knows that he's left her alone on the wooden platform.

"Go down, Starling Jane," Madam Terpsichore growls. "Go down into the dark and find the hungry jaws of Nidhogg, the dragon that gnaws the very roots of the World Tree, drawing ever closer the final days. Find him, changeling, and ask him if you are worthy."

And then the ghoul bows once before she pulls the mahogany lever on her right, and far overhead secret machineries begin to grind, the hesitant turning of iron wheels, the interlocking teeth of ancient, rusted gears, and somewhere on the surface a trapdoor opens and moonlight pours into this hollow place inside the earth.

"Walk true, Starling Jane," Madam Terpsichore says, and then passes the bullhorn to an underling before she sits down again.

The moonlight forms a single, brilliant shaft reaching from the vaulted ceiling of the amphitheater to the very bottom of the black pit, argent lunar rays held together by some clever trick of photomancy Jane knows she'll probably never learn, even if the dragon doesn't take her hands. The crowd makes no sound whatsoever as she turns right and begins her descent along the steep and rickety catwalk set into the walls of the pit. And the drum-wraiths begin drumming again, marking her every footstep with their mallets of bone and ivory.

Starling Jane keeps to the right side of the catwalk, because she's afraid of falling, because she's afraid she might look over the edge and lose her balance. She places one foot after the next, and the next, and the next after that, walking as slowly as she dares, spiraling around the pit, down and down, and each circuit is smaller than the last so that the distance to the moonbeam shrinks until she could reach out and brush it with her finger-tips. The old planks creak and pop beneath her bare feet, and she tries not to imagine how many decades, how many centuries, it's been since they were anchored to the rock face.

And then, at last, she's standing at the bottom, only one final moment remaining to carry her from the darkness into the blazing white shaft; Jane hesitates a second, half a second, takes a deep breath and lets it out again, and then she steps into the light of the full Hunger Moon.

It's stolen my eyes, she thinks. *It's stolen away my eyes and left me as blind as Master Solace.* This pure and perfect light distilled and concentrated, focused on the dingy reflecting mirror of her soul. It spills over her, dripping from the silver robe, burning away anything less immaculate than itself. She realizes that she's crying, crying at the simple beauty of it. When she wipes her cheeks, the light dances in furious motes across the back of her hand, and she sees that she hasn't gone blind after all. So she kneels on the stone, and the dragon rumbles beneath her like an empty belly waiting to be filled.

Above her, the drum-wraiths fall silent.

"It's okay," she whispers. "It's all okay," and death's not such a terrible thing now that she's seen that light, felt it burrowing its way into her, washing her clean. On the ground in front of her there are two holes, each no more than a few inches across and ringed with seals of hammered gold and platinum.

Right hand gold, left hand platinum.

She remembers the Bailiff's coin, gold for gold, and reaches into the deep pocket in the robe where she tucked it safely away before Madam

Hippodamia led her down to wait in the tiny myrrh-scented alcove with Master Solace. Gold for gold, and the hole at the center of the coin is not so very different from the twin mouths of the dragon.

"Just get it over with," she says and leans forward, plunging both arms into the holes, the Bailiff's coin clutched tightly in her right hand.

Inside, the holes are warm, and the stone has become flesh, flesh and slime and dagger teeth that eagerly caress her fingers and prick her wrists. Nidhogg's poisonous breath rises from the twin holes – sulfur and brimstone, ash and acid steam – and Jane opens her hand and presses the coin against the thorny tongue of the dragon. The earth rumbles violently again, and Starling Jane waits for the jaws to snap shut.

But then the pit sighs, making a sound like the world rolling over in its sleep, and there's only cold, hard stone encircling her arms. She gasps, pulls her hands quickly from the holes and stares at her fingers in disbelief, all ten still right there in front of her, and only a few scratches, a few drops of dark blood, to prove that there was ever any danger at all.

High above, the amphitheater erupts in a thunderous clamor, a joyful, relieved pandemonium of barks and shouts and clapping hands, howls and laughter and someone ringing the ship's bell again and again.

Jane sits back on her heels and stares up into the moonlight, letting it pour down into her, drinking its impossible radiance through her strangling pinpoint pupils and every pore of her body, letting it fill her against all the endless nights to come, all the uncountable darknesses that lie ahead. And when she cannot hold another drop, Starling Jane stands up again, bows once, and only once, to Nidhogg Rootnibbler, exactly the way that Madam Terpsichore said she should, and then the changeling starts the long walk back up the catwalk to the alcove. With the applause raining down around her and the moonlight in her eyes, it doesn't seem to take any time at all.

Houses Under the Sea

1.

When I close my eyes, I see Jacova Angevine.

I close my eyes, and there she is, standing alone at the end of the breakwater, standing with the foghorn as the choppy sea shatters itself to foam against a jumble of grey boulders. The October wind is making something wild of her hair, and her back's turned to me. The boats are coming in.

I close my eyes, and she's standing in the surf at Moss Landing, gazing out into the bay, staring towards the place where the continental shelf narrows down to a sliver and drops away to the black abyss of Monterey Canyon. There are gulls, and her hair is tied back in a ponytail.

I close my eyes, and we're walking together down Cannery Row, heading south towards the aquarium. She's wearing a gingham dress and a battered pair of Doc Martens that she must have had for fifteen years. I say something inconsequential, but she doesn't hear me, too busy scowling at the tourists, at the sterile, cheery absurdities of the Bubba Gump Shrimp Company and Mackerel Jack's Trading Post.

"That used to be a whorehouse," she says, nodding in the direction of Mackerel Jack's. "The Lone Star Cafe, but Steinbeck called it the Bear Flag. Everything burned. Nothing here's the way it used to be."

She says that like she remembers, and I close my eyes.

And she's on television again, out on the old pier at Moss Point, the day they launched the ROV *Tiburón II*.

And she's at the Pierce Street warehouse in Monterey; men and women in white robes are listening to every word she says. They hang on every syllable, her every breath, their many eyes like the bulging eyes of deep-sea fish encountering sunlight for the first time. Dazed, terrified, enraptured, lost.

All of them lost.

I close my eyes, and she's leading them into the bay.

Those creatures jumped the barricades
And have headed for the sea.

All these divided moments, disconnected, or connected so many different ways, that I'll never be able to pull them apart and find a coherent narrative. That's my folly, my conceit, that I can make a mere *story* of what has happened. Even if I could, it's nothing anyone would ever want to read, nothing I could sell. CNN and *Newsweek* and *The New York Times, Rolling Stone* and *Harper's,* everyone already knows what they think about Jacova Angevine. Everybody already knows as much as they want to know. Or as little. In those minds, she's already earned her spot in the death-cult hall of fame, sandwiched firmly in between Jim Jones and Heaven's Gate.

I close my eyes, and "Fire from the sky, fire on the water," she says and smiles; I know that this time she's talking about the fire of September 14, 1924, the day lightning struck one of the 55,000-gallon storage tanks belonging to the Associated Oil Company and a burning river flowed into the sea. Billowing black clouds hide the sun, and the fire has the voice of a hurricane as it bears down on the canneries, a voice of demons, and she stops to tie her shoes.

I sit here in this dark motel room, staring at the screen of my laptop, the clean liquid-crystal light, typing irrelevant words to build meandering sentences, waiting, waiting, waiting, and I don't know what it is that I'm waiting for. Or I'm only afraid to admit that I know exactly what I'm waiting for. She has become my ghost, my private haunting, and haunted things are forever waiting.

"In the mansions of Poseidon, she will prepare halls from coral and glass and the bones of whales," she says, and the crowd in the warehouse breathes in and out as a single, astonished organism, their assembled bodies lesser than the momentary whole they have made. "Down there, you will know nothing but peace, in her mansions, in the endless night of her coils."

"*Tiburón* is Spanish for shark," she says, and I tell her I didn't know that, that I had two years of Spanish in high school, but that was a thousand years ago, and all I remember is *si* and *por favor.*

What is that noise now? What is the wind doing?

I close my eyes again.

The sea has many voices.

Many gods and many voices.

"November 5, 1936," she says, and *this* is the first night we had sex, the long night we spent together in a seedy Moss Point hotel, the sort of place the fishermen take their hookers, the same place she was still staying when she died. "The Del Mar Canning Company burned to the ground. No one ever tried to blame lightning for that one."

There's moonlight through the drapes, and I imagine for a moment that her skin has become iridescent, mother-of-pearl, the shimmering motley of an oil slick. I reach out and touch her naked thigh, and she lights a cigarette. The smoke hangs thick in the air, like fog or forgetfulness.

My fingertips against her flesh, and she stands and walks to the window.

"Do you see something out there?" I ask, and she shakes her head very slowly.

I close my eyes.

In the moonlight, I can make out the puckered, circular scars on both her shoulder blades and running halfway down her spine. Two dozen or more of them, but I never bothered to count exactly. Some are no larger than a dime, but several are at least two inches across.

"When I'm gone," she says, "when I'm done here, they'll ask you questions about me. What will you tell them?"

"That depends what they ask," I reply and laugh, still thinking it was all one of her strange jokes, the talk of leaving, and I lie down and stare at the shadows on the ceiling.

"They'll ask you everything," she whispers. "Sooner or later, I expect they'll ask you everything."

Which they did.

I close my eyes, and I see her, Jacova Angevine, the lunatic prophet from Salinas, pearls that were her eyes, cockles and mussels, alive, alive-o, and she's kneeling in the sand. The sun is rising behind her, and I hear people coming through the dunes.

"I'll tell them you were a good fuck," I say, and she takes another drag off her cigarette and continues staring at the night outside the motel windows.

"Yes," she says. "I expect you will."

2.

The first time that I saw Jacova Angevine – I mean, the first time I saw her in *person*. I'd just come back from Pakistan and had flown up to Monterey to try and clear my head. A photographer friend had an apartment there, and he was on assignment in Tokyo, so I figured I could lay low for a couple of weeks, a whole month maybe, stay drunk and decompress. My clothes, my luggage, my skin, everything about me still smelled like Islamabad. I'd spent more than six months overseas, ferreting about for real and imagined connections between Muslim extremists, European middlemen, and Pakistan's leaky nuclear arms program, trying to gauge the damage done by the enterprising Abdul Qadeer Khan, rogue father of the Pakistani bomb, trying to determine exactly what he'd sold and to whom. Everyone already knew – or at least thought they knew – about North Korea, Libya, and Iran, and American officials suspected that al-Qaeda and other terrorist groups belonged somewhere on his list of customers, as well, despite assurances to the contrary from Major-General Shaukat Sultan. I'd come back with a head full of apocalypse and Urdu, anti-India propaganda and Mushaikh poetry, and I was determined to empty my mind of everything except scotch and the smell of the sea.

It was a bright Wednesday afternoon, a warm day for November in Monterey County, and I decided to come up for air. I showered for the first time in a week and had a late lunch at the Sardine Factory on Wave Street – Dungeness crab remoulade, fresh oysters with horseradish, and grilled sanddabs in a lemon sauce that was a little heavy on the thyme – then decided to visit the aquarium and walk it all off. When I was a kid in Brooklyn, I spent a lot of my time at the aquarium on Coney Island, and, three decades later, there were few things a man could do sober that relaxed me as quickly and completely. I put the check on my MasterCard and followed Wave Street south and east to Prescott, then turned back down Cannery Row, the glittering bay on my right, the pale blue autumn sky stretched out overhead like oil on canvas.

I close my eyes, and that afternoon isn't something that happened three years ago, something I'm making sound like a goddamn travelogue. I close my eyes, and it's happening now, for the first time, and there she is, sitting alone on a long bench in front of the kelp forest exhibit, her thin face turned up to the high, swaying canopy behind the glass, the dapple of fish and seaweed shadows drifting back and forth across her features.

I recognize her, and that surprises me, because I've only seen her face on television and in magazine photos and on the dust jacket of the book she wrote before she lost the job at Berkeley. She turns her head and smiles at me, the familiar way you smile at a friend, the way you smile at someone you've known all your life.

"You're in luck," she says. "It's almost time for them to feed the fish." And Jacova Angevine pats the bench next to her, indicating that I should sit down.

"I read your book," I say, taking a seat because I'm still too surprised to do anything else.

"Did you? Did you really?" and now she looks like she doesn't believe me, like I'm only saying that I've read her book to be polite, and from her expression I can tell that she thinks it's a little odd, that anyone would ever bother to try and flatter her.

"Yes," I tell her, trying too hard to sound sincere. "I did really. In fact, I read some of it twice."

"And why would you do a thing like that?"

"Truthfully?"

"Yes, truthfully."

Her eyes are the same color as the water trapped behind the thick panes of aquarium glass, the color of the November sunlight filtered through salt-water and kelp blades. There are fine lines at the corners of her mouth and beneath her eyes that make her look several years older than she is.

"Last summer, I was flying from New York to London, and there was a three-hour layover in Shannon. Your book was all I'd brought to read."

"That's terrible," she says, still smiling, and turns to face the big tank again. "Do you want your money back?"

"It was a gift," I reply, which isn't true, and I have no idea why I'm lying to her. "An ex-girlfriend gave it to me for my birthday."

"Is that why you left her?"

"No, I left her because she thought I drank too much, and I thought she drank too little."

"Are you an alcoholic?" Jacova Angevine asks, as casually as if she were asking me whether I liked milk in my coffee or if I took it black.

"Well, some people say I'm headed in that direction," I tell her. "But I did enjoy the book, honest. It's hard to believe they fired you for writing it. I mean, that people get fired for writing books." But I know that's a lie, too; I'm not half that naïve, and it's not at all difficult to understand how or why *Waking Leviathan* ended Jacova Angevine's career as an academic. A reviewer for *Nature* called it "the most confused and preposterous example of bad history wedding bad science since the Velikovsky affair."

"They didn't fire me for writing it," she says. "They politely asked me to resign because I'd seen fit to publish it."

"Why didn't you fight them?"

Her smile fades a little, and the lines around her mouth seem to grow the slightest bit more pronounced. "I don't come here to talk about the book, or my unfortunate employment history," she says.

I apologize, and she tells me not to worry about it.

A diver enters the tank, matte-black neoprene trailing a rush of silver bubbles, and most of the fish rise expectantly to meet him or her, a riot of kelp bass and sleek leopard sharks, sheephead and rockfish and species I don't recognize. She doesn't say anything else, too busy watching the feeding, and I sit there beside her, at the bottom of a pretend ocean.

I open my eyes. There are only the words on the screen in front of me.

I didn't see her again for the better part of a year. During that time, as my work sent me back to Pakistan, and then to Germany and Israel, I reread her book. I also read some of the articles and reviews, and a brief online interview that she'd given Whitley Strieber's *Unknown Country* website. Then I tracked down an article on Inuit archaeology that she'd written for *Fate* and wondered at what point Jacova Angevine had decided that there was no going back, nothing left to lose and so no reason not to allow herself to become part of the murky, strident world of fringe believers and UFO buffs, conspiracy theorists and paranormal investigators that seemed so eager to embrace her as one of its own.

And I wondered, too, if perhaps she might have been one of them from the start.

3.

I woke up this morning from a long dream of storms and drowning and lay in bed, very still, sizing up my hangover and staring at the sagging, water-stained ceiling of my motel room. And I finally admitted to myself that this isn't going to be what the paper has hired me to write. I don't think I'm even trying to write it for them anymore. They want the dirt, of course, and I've never been shy about digging holes. I've spent the last twenty years as a shovel-for-hire. I don't think it matters that I may have loved her, or that a lot of this dirt is mine. I can't pretend that I'm acting out of nobility of soul or loyalty or even some selfish, belated concern for my own dingy reputation. I would write exactly what they want me to write if I could. If I knew how. I need the money. I haven't worked for the last five months, and my savings are almost gone.

But if I'm not writing it for them, if I've abandoned all hope of a paycheck at the other end of this thing, why the hell then am I still sitting here typing? Am I making a confession? Bless me, Father, I can't forget? Do I believe it's something I can puke up like a sour belly full of whiskey, that writing it all down will make the nightmares stop or make it any easier for me to get through the days? I sincerely hope I'm not as big a fool as that. Whatever else I may be, I like to think that I'm not an idiot.

I don't know why I'm writing this, whatever this turns out to be. Maybe it's only a very long-winded suicide note.

Last night, I watched the tape again.

I have all three versions with me – the cut that's still being hawked over the internet, the one that ends right after the ROV was hit, before the lights came back on; the cut that MBARI released to the press and the scientific community in response to the version circulating online; and I have the raw footage, the copy I bought from a robotics technician who claimed to have been aboard the *R/V Western Flyer* the day that the incident occurred. I paid him two thousand dollars for it, and the kid swore to both its completeness and authenticity. I knew that I wasn't the first person to whom he'd sold the tape. I'd heard about it from a contact in the chemistry department at UC Irvine. I was never sure exactly how she'd caught wind of it, but I gathered that the tech was turning a handsome little profit peddling his contraband to anyone willing to pony up the cash.

We met at a Motel 6 in El Cajon, and I played it all the way through before I handed him the money. He sat with his back to the television while I watched the tape, rewound and started it over again.

"What the hell are you doing?" he asked, literally wringing his hands and gazing anxiously at the heavy drapes. I'd pulled them shut after hooking up the rented VCR that I'd brought with me, but a bright sliver of afternoon sunlight slipped in between them and divided his face down the middle. "Jesus, man. You think it's not gonna be the exact same thing every time? You think if you keep playing it over and over it's gonna come out any different?"

I've watched the tape more times than I can count, a couple hundred, at least, and I still think that's a good goddamned question.

"So why didn't MBARI release this?" I asked the kid, and he laughed and shook his head.

"Why the fuck do you think?" he replied.

He took my money, reminded me again that we'd never met and that he'd deny everything if I attempted to finger him as my source. Then he got back into his ancient, wheezy VW Microbus and drove off, leaving me sitting there with an hour and a half of unedited color video recorded somewhere along the bottom of the Monterey Canyon. Everything the ROV *Tiburón II*'s starboard camera had seen (the port pan-and-tilt unit was malfunctioning that day), twenty miles out and three kilometers down, and from the start I understood it was the closest I was ever likely to come to an answer, and that it was also only a different and far more terrible sort of question.

Last night I got drunk, more so than usual, a *lot* more so than usual, and watched it for the first time in almost a month. But I turned the sound on the television down all the way and left the lights burning.

Even drunk, I'm still a coward.

The ocean floor starkly illuminated by the ROV's six 480-watt HMI lights, revealing a velvet carpet of grey-brown sediment washed out from Elkhorn Slough and all the other sloughs and rivers emptying into the bay. And even at this depth, there are signs of life: brittle stars and crabs cling to the shit-colored rocks, sponges and sea cucumbers, the sinuous, smooth bodies of big-eyed rattails. Here and there, dark outcroppings jut from the ooze like bone from the decaying flesh of a leper.

My asshole editor would laugh out loud at that last simile, would probably take one look at it and laugh and then say something like, "If I'd wanted fucking purple I'd have bought a goddamn pot of violets." But my asshole editor hasn't seen the tape I bought from the tech.

My asshole editor never met Jacova Angevine, never listened to her talk, never fucked her, never saw the scars on her back or the fear in her eyes.

The ROV comes to a rocky place where the seafloor drops away suddenly, and it hesitates, responding to commands from the control room of the *R/V Western Flyer*. A moment or two later, the steady fall of marine snow becomes so heavy that it's difficult to see much of anything through the light reflecting off the whitish particles of sinking detritus. And sitting there on the floor between the foot of the bed and the television, I almost reached out and touched the screen.

Almost.

"It's a little bit of everything," I heard Jacova say, though she never actually said anything of the sort to me. "Silt, phytoplankton and zooplankton, soot, mucus, diatoms, fecal pellets, dust, grains of sand and clay, radioactive fallout, pollen, sewage. Some of it's even interplanetary dust particles. Some of it fell from the stars."

And *Tiburón II* lurches and glides forward a few feet, then slips cautiously over the precipice, beginning the slow descent into this new and unexpected abyss.

"We'd been over that stretch more than a dozen times, at least," Natalie Billington, chief ROV pilot for *Tiburón II,* told a CNN correspondent after the internet version of the tape first made the news. "But that drop-off wasn't on any of the charts. We'd always missed it somehow. I know that isn't a very satisfying answer, but it's a big place down there. The canyon is over two hundred miles long. You miss things."

For a while – exactly 15.34 seconds – there's only the darkness and marine snow and a few curious or startled fish. According to MBARI, the ROV's vertical speed during this part of the dive is about 35 meters per minute, so by the time it finds the bottom again, depth has increased by some five hundred and twenty-five feet. The seafloor comes into view again, and there's not so much loose sediment here, just a jumble of broken boulders, and it's startling how clean they are, almost completely free of the usual encrustations and muck. There are no sponges or sea cucumbers to be seen, no starfish, and even the omnipresent marine snow has tapered off to only a few stray, drifting flecks. And then the wide, flat rock that is usually referred to as "the Delta stone" comes into view. And this isn't like the face on Mars or Von Daniken seeing ancient astronauts on Mayan artifacts. The ∂ carved into the slab is unmistakable. The edges are so sharp, so clean that it might have been done yesterday.

The *Tiburón II* hovers above the Delta stone, spilling light into this lightless place, and I know what's coming next, so I sit very still and count off the seconds in my head. When I've counted to thirty-eight, the view from the ROV's camera pans violently to the right, signaling the portside impact, and an instant later there's only static, white noise, the twelve-second gap in the tape during which the camera was still running, but no longer recording.

I counted to eleven before I switched off the television, and then sat listening to the wind, and the waves breaking against the beach, waiting for my heart to stop racing and the sweat on my face and palms to dry. When I was sure that I wasn't going to be sick, I pressed EJECT and the VCR spat out the tape. I returned it to its navy-blue plastic case and sat smoking and drinking, helpless to think of anything but Jacova.

4.

Jacova Angevine was born and grew up in her father's big Victorian house in Salinas, only a couple of blocks from the birthplace of John Steinbeck. Her mother died when she was eight. Jacova had no siblings, and her closest kin, paternal and maternal, were all back east in New Jersey and Pennsylvania and Maryland. In 1960, her parents relocated to California, just a few months after they were married, and her father took a job teaching high-school English in Castroville. After six months, he quit that job and took another, with only slightly better pay, in the town of Soledad. Though he'd earned a doctorate in comparative literature from Columbia, Theo Angevine seemed to have no particular academic ambitions. He'd written several novels while in college, though none of them had managed to find a publisher. In 1969, his wife five months pregnant with their daughter, he resigned from his position at Soledad High and moved the family north to Salinas, where he bought the old house on Howard Street with a bank loan and the advance from his first book sale, a mystery novel titled *The Man Who Laughed at Funerals* (Random House; New York).

To date, none of the three books that have been published about Jacova, the Open Door of Night, and the mass drownings off Moss Landing State Beach, have made more than a passing mention of Theo Angevine's novels. Elenore Ellis-Lincoln, in *Closing the Door: Anatomy of Hysteria* (Simon and Schuster; New York), for example, devotes only a single paragraph to them, though she gives Jacova's childhood an entire chapter. "Mr. Angevine's works received little critical attention, one way or the other, and his income from them was meager," Ellis-Lincoln writes. "Of the seventeen novels he published between 1969 and 1985, only two – *The Man Who Laughed for Funerals* [sic] and *Seven at Sunset* – are still in print. It is notable that the overall tone of the novels becomes significantly darker following his wife's death, but the books themselves never seem to have been more to the author than a sort of hobby. Upon his death, his daughter became the executor of his literary estate, such as it was."

Likewise, in *Lemming Cult* (The Overlook Press; New York), William L. West writes, "Her father's steady output of mystery and suspense potboilers must surely have been a curiosity of Jacova's childhood, but were never once mentioned in her own writings, including the five private journals found in a cardboard box in her bedroom closet. The books themselves were entirely unremarkable, so far as I've been able to ascertain. Almost all are out of print and very difficult to find today. Even the catalog of the Salinas Public Library includes only a single copy each of *The Man Who Laughed at Funerals, Pretoria,* and *Seven at Sunset.*"

During the two years I knew her, Jacova only mentioned her father's writing once that I can recall, and then only in passing, but she had copies of all his novels, a fact that I've never seen mentioned anywhere in print. I suppose it doesn't seem very significant, if you haven't bothered to read Theo Angevine's books. Since Jacova's death, I've read every one of them. It took me less than a month to track down copies of all seventeen, thanks largely to online booksellers, and even less time to read them. While William West was certainly justified in calling the novels "entirely unremarkable" when considered only as works of fiction, even a casual examination reveals some distinctly remarkable parallels between the fiction of the father and the reality of the daughter.

I've spent the whole afternoon, the better part of the past five hours, on the preceding four paragraphs, trying to fool myself into believing that I can actually write *about* her as a journalist would write about her. That I can bring any degree of detachment or objectivity to bear. Of course, I'm wasting my time. After seeing the tape again, after almost allowing myself to watch *all* of it again, I think I'm desperate to put distance between myself and the memory of her. I should call New York and tell them that I can't do this, that they should find someone else, but after the mess I made of the Musharraf story, the agency would probably never offer me another assignment. For the moment, that still matters. It might not in another day or two, but it does for now.

Her father wrote books, books that were never very popular, and though they're neither particularly accomplished nor enjoyable, they might hold clues to Jacova's motivation and to her fate. And they might not. It's as simple and contradictory as that. Like everything surrounding the "Lemming

Cult" – as the Open Door of Night has come to be known, as it has been labeled by people who find it easier to deal with tragedy and horror if there is an attendant note of the absurd – like everything else about *her,* what seems meaningful one moment will seem irrelevant the next. Or maybe that's only the way it appears to me. Maybe I'm asking too much of the clues.

Excerpt from *Pretoria,* pp. 164–165;
Ballantine Books, 1979:

Edward Horton smiled and tapped the ash from his cigar into the large glass ashtray on the table. "I don't like the sea," he said and nodded at the window. "Frankly, I can't even stand the sound of it. Gives me nightmares."

I listened to the breakers, not taking my eyes off the fat man and the thick grey curlicues of smoke arranging and rearranging themselves around his face. I'd always found the sound of waves to have a welcomed, tranquilizing effect upon my nerves and wondered which one of Horton's innumerable secrets was responsible for his loathing of the sea. I knew he'd done a stint in the Navy during Korea, but I was also pretty sure he'd never seen combat.

"How'd you sleep last night?" I asked, and he shook his head.

"For shit," he replied and sucked on his cigar.

"Then maybe you should think about getting a room farther inland."

Horton coughed and jabbed a pudgy finger at the window of the bungalow. "Don't think I wouldn't, if the choice were mine to make. But she wants me *here.* She wants me sitting right here, waiting on her, night and day. She knows I hate the ocean."

"What the hell," I said, reaching for my hat, tired of his company and the stink of his smoldering Macanudo. "You know where to reach me, if you change your mind. Don't let the bad dreams get you down. They ain't nothing but that, bad dreams."

"That's not enough?" he asked, and I could tell from his expression that Horton wished I'd stay a little longer, but I knew he'd never admit it. "Last night, goddamn people marching into the sea, marching over the sand in rows like the goddamn infantry.

Must of been a million of them. What you think a dream like that means, anyway?"

"Horton, a dream like that don't mean jack shit," I replied. "Except maybe you need to lay off the spicy food before bedtime."

"You're always gonna be an asshole," he said, and I was forced to agree. He puffed his cigar, and I left the bungalow and stepped out into the salty Santa Barbara night.

Excerpt from *What the Cat Dragged In*, p. 231;
Ballantine Books, 1980:

Vicky had never told anyone about the dreams, just like she'd never told anyone about Mr. Barker or the yellow Corvette. The dreams were her secret, whether she wanted them or not. Sometimes they seemed almost wicked, shameful, sinful, like something she'd done that was against God, or at least against the law. She'd almost told Mr. Barker once, a year or so before she left Los Angeles. She'd gone so far as to broach the subject of mermaids, and then he'd snorted and laughed, so she'd thought better of it.

"You got some strange notions in that head of yours," he'd said. "Someday, you're gonna have to grow out of crap like that, if you want people 'round here to start taking you seriously."

So she kept it all to herself. Whatever the dreams meant or didn't mean, it wasn't anything she would ever be able to explain or confess. Sometimes, nights when she couldn't sleep, she lay in bed staring at the ceiling, thinking about the ruined castles beneath the waves and beautiful, drowned girls with seaweed tangled in their hair."

Excerpt from *The Last Loan Shark of Bodega Bay*,
pp. 57–59; Bantam Books, 1982:

"This was way the hell back in the fifties," Foster said and lit another cigarette. His hands were shaking, and he kept looking over his shoulder. "Fifty-eight, right, or maybe early fifty-nine. I know Eisenhower was still president, though I ain't precisely sure of the year. But I was still stuck in Honolulu, right, still hauling lousy tourists around the islands in the *Saint Chris* so they could fish and snap pictures of goddamn Kilauea and what have you. The boat was on its last leg, but she'd still get you where you were goin', if you knew how to slap her around."

"What's this got to do with Winkie Anderson and the girl?" I asked, making no effort to hide my impatience.

"Jesus, Frank, I'm getting to it. You want to hear this thing or not? I swear, you come around here asking the big questions, expecting the what's-what, you can at least keep your trap shut and listen."

"I don't have all night, that's all."

"Yeah, well, who the hell does, why don't you tell me that? Anyway, like I was saying, back about fifty-nine, and we was out somewhere off the north shore of Molokai. Old Coop was fishing the thousand fathom line, and Jerry – you remember Jerry O'Neil, right?"

"No," I said, eyeing the clock above the bar.

"Well, whatever. Jerry O'Neil was mouthing off about a twelve-hundred pounder, this big-ass marlin some Mexican businessman from Tijuana had up and hooked just a few weeks before. Fish even made the damn papers, right. Anyway, Jerry said the Mexican was bad news, and we should keep a sharp eye out for him. Said he was a regular Jonah."

"But you just said he caught a twelve-hundred pound marlin."

"Yeah, sure. He could haul in the fish, this chunt son of a bitch, but he was into some sort of Spanish voodoo shit and had these gold coins he'd toss over the side of the boat every five or ten minutes. Like goddamn clockwork, he'd check his watch and toss out a coin. Gold doubloons or some shit, I don't know what they were. It was driving Coop crazy, 'cause it wasn't enough the Mexican had to do this thing with the coins, he was mumbling some sort of shit non-stop. Coop kept telling him to shut the hell up, people was trying to fish, but this guy, he just keeps mumbling and tossing coins and pulling in the fish. I finally got a look at one of those doubloons, and it had something stamped on one side looked like a damn octopus, and on the other side was this star like a pentagram. You know, those things witches and warlocks use."

"Foster, this is crazy bullshit. I have to be in San Francisco at seven-thirty in the morning." I waved to the bartender and put two crumpled fives and a one on the bar in front of me.

"You ever heard of the Momma Hydra, Frank? That's who this chunt said he was praying to."

"Call me when you run out of bullshit," I said. "And I don't have to tell you, Detective Burke won't be half so understanding as I am."

"Jesus, Frank. Hold up a goddamn second. It's just the way I tell stories, right. You know that. I start at the beginning. I don't leave stuff out."

These are only a few examples of what anyone will find, if he or she should take the time to look. There are many more, I assure you. The pages of my copies of Theo Angevine's novels are scarred throughout with yellow highlighter.

And everything leaves more questions than answers.

You make of it what you will. Or you don't. I suppose that a Freudian might have a proper field day with this stuff. Whatever I knew about Freud I forgot before I was even out of college. It would be comforting, I suppose, if I could dismiss Jacova's fate as the end result of some overwhelming Oedipal hysteria, the ocean cast here as that Great Ur-Mother savior-being who finally opens up to offer release and forgiveness in death and dissolution.

5.

I begin to walk down some particular, perhaps promising, avenue and then, inevitably, I turn and run, tail tucked firmly between my legs. My memories. The MBARI video. Jacova and her father's whodunits. I scratch the surface and then pull my hand back to be sure that I haven't lost a fucking finger. I mix metaphors the way I've been mixing tequila and scotch.

If, as William Burroughs wrote, "Language is a virus from outer space," then what the holy hell were you supposed to be, Jacova?

An epidemic of the collective unconscious. The black plague of belief. A vaccine for cultural amnesia, she might have said. And so we're right back to Velikovsky, who wrote, "Human beings, rising from some catastrophe, bereft of memory of what had happened, regarded themselves as created from the dust of the earth. All knowledge about the ancestors, who they were and in what interstellar space they lived, was wiped away from the memory of the few survivors."

I'm drunk, and I'm not making any sense at all. Or merely much too little sense to matter. Anyway, you'll want to pay attention to this part. It's sort of like the ghost story within the ghost story within the ghost story, the hard nugget at the unreachable heart of my heart's infinitely regressing babooshka, matryoshka, matrioska, matreshka, babushka. It might even be the final straw that breaks the camel of my mind.

Remember, I am wasted, and so that last inexcusable paragraph may be forgiven. Or it may not.

"When I become death, death is the seed from which I grow." Burroughs said that, too. Jacova, you will be an orchard. You will be a swaying kelp forest. There's a log in the hole in the bottom of the sea with your name on it.

Yesterday afternoon, puking sick of looking at these four dingy fucking walls, I drove down to Monterey, to the warehouse on Pierce Street. The last time I was there, the cops still hadn't taken down all the yellow CRIME SCENE – DO NOT CROSS tape. Now there's only a great big for-sale sign and an even bigger no-trespassing sign. I wrote the name and number of the realty company on the back of a book of matches. I want to ask them what they'll be telling prospective buyers about the building's history. Word is the whole block is due to be rezoned next year, and soon those empty buildings will be converted to lofts and condos. Gentrification abhors a void.

I parked in an empty lot down the street from the warehouse, hoping that no one happening by would notice me, hoping, in particular, that any passing police would not notice me. I walked quickly, without running, because running is suspicious and inevitably draws the attention of those who *watch* for suspicious things. I was not so drunk as I might have been, not even so drunk as I *should* have been, and I tried to keep my mind occupied by noting the less significant details of the street, the sky, the weather. The litter caught in the weeds and gravel – cigarette butts, plastic soft-drink bottles (I recall Pepsi, Coke, and Mountain Dew), paper bags and cups from fast-food restaurants (McDonalds, Del Taco, KFC), broken glass, unrecognizable bits of metal, a rusted Oregon license plate. The sky was painfully blue, the blue of nausea, with only very high cirrus clouds to spoil that suffocating pastel heaven. There were no other cars parked along the street and no living things that I noticed. There were a couple of garbage dumpsters, a stop sign, and a great pile of cardboard boxes that had been soaked by rain enough times it was difficult to tell exactly where one ended and another began. There was a hubcap.

When I finally reached the warehouse – the warehouse become a temple to half-remembered gods become a crime scene, now on its way to becoming something else – I ducked down the narrow alley that separates it from the abandoned Monterey Peninsula Shipping and Storage Building (established 1924). There'd been a door around that way with an unreliable lock. If I was lucky, I thought, no one would have noticed, or if they had noticed, wouldn't have bothered fixing it. My heart was racing, and I was dizzy (I tried hard to blame that on the sickening color of the sky) and there was a metallic taste in the back of my mouth, like a freshly filled tooth.

It was colder in the alley than it had been out on Pierce, the sun having already dropped low enough in the west that the alley must have been in shadow for some time. Perhaps it is always in shadow and never truly warm there. I found the side door exactly as I'd hoped to find it, and three or four minutes of jiggling about with the wobbly brass knob was enough to coax it open. Inside, the warehouse was dark and even colder than the alley, and the air stank of mold and dust, bad memories and vacancy. I stood in the doorway a moment or two, thinking of hungry rats and drunken bums, delirious crack addicts wielding lead pipes, the webs of poisonous spiders. Then I took a deep breath and stepped across the threshold, out of the shadows and into a more decided blackness, a more definitive chill, and all those mundane threats dissolved. Everything slipped from my mind except Jacova Angevine, and her followers (if that's what you'd call them), dressed all in white, and the thing I'd seen on the altar the one time I'd come here when this had been a temple of the Open Door of Night.

I asked her about that thing once, a few weeks before the end, the last night that we spent together. I asked where it had come from, who had made it, and she lay very still for a while, listening to the surf or only trying to decide which answer would satisfy me. In the moonlight through the hotel window, I thought she might have been smiling, but I wasn't sure.

"It's very old," she said, eventually. By then I'd almost drifted off to sleep and had to shake myself awake again. "No one alive remembers who made it," Jacova continued. "But I don't think that matters, only that it was made."

"It's fucking hideous," I mumbled sleepily. "You know that, don't you?"

"Yeah, but so is the Crucifixion. So are bleeding statues of the Virgin Mary and images of Kali. So are the animal-headed gods of the Egyptians."

"Yeah, well, I don't bow down to any of them, either," I replied, or something to that effect.

"The divine is always abominable," she whispered and rolled over, turning her back to me.

Just a moment ago I was in the warehouse on Pierce Street, wasn't I? And now I'm in bed with the Prophet from Salinas. But I will not despair, for there is no need here to stay focused, to adhere to some restrictive illusion of the linear narrative. It's coming. It's been coming all along. As Job Foster said in Chapter Four of *The Last Loan Shark of Bodega Bay*, "It's just the way I tell stories, right. You know that. I start at the beginning. I don't leave stuff out."

That's horseshit, of course. I suspect luckless Job Foster knew it was horseshit, and I suspect that I know it's horseshit, too. It is not the task of the writer to "tell all," or even to decide what to leave in, but to decide what to leave *out*. Whatever remains, that meager sum of this profane division, that's the bastard chimera we call a "story." I am not building, but cutting away. And all stories, whether advertised as truth or admitted falsehoods, are fictions, cleft from any objective facts by the aforementioned action of cutting away. A pound of flesh. A pile of sawdust. Discarded chips of Carrara marble. And what's left over.

A damned man in an empty warehouse.

I left the door standing open, because I hadn't the nerve to shut myself up in that place. And I'd already taken a few steps inside, my shoes crunching loudly on shards of glass from a broken window, grinding glass to dust, when I remembered the Maglite hidden inside my jacket. But the glare of the flashlight did nothing much to make the darkness any less stifling, nothing much at all but remind me of the blinding white beam of *Tiburón II*'s big HMI rig, shining out across the silt at the bottom of the canyon. *Now,* I thought, *at least I can see anything, if there's anything to see,* and immediately some other, less familiar thought-voice demanded to know why the hell I'd want to. The door had opened into a narrow corridor, mint-green concrete walls and a low concrete ceiling, and I followed it a short distance to its end – no more than thirty feet, thirty feet at the most – past empty rooms that might once have been offices, to an unlocked steel door marked in faded orange letters, EMPLOYEES ONLY.

"It's an empty warehouse," I whispered, breathing the words aloud. "That's all, an empty warehouse." I knew it wasn't the truth, not anymore, not by a long sight, but I thought that maybe a lie could be more comforting than the comfortless illumination of the Maglite in my hand. Joseph Campbell wrote, "Draw a circle around a stone and the stone will become an incarnation of mystery." Something like that. Or it was someone else said it and I'm misremembering. The point is, I knew that Jacova had drawn a circle around that place, just as she'd drawn a circle about herself, just as her father had somehow drawn a circle about her –

Just as she'd drawn a circle around me.

The door wasn't locked, and beyond it lay the vast, deserted belly of the building, a flat plain of cement marked off with steel support beams. There was a little sunlight coming in through the many small windows along the east and west walls, though not as much as I'd expected, and it seemed weakened, diluted by the musty air. I played the Maglite back and forth across the floor at my feet and saw that someone had painted over all the elaborate, colorful designs put there by the Open Door of Night. A thick grey latex wash to cover the intricate interweave of lines, the lines that she believed would form a bridge, a *conduit* – that was the word that she'd used. Everyone's seen photographs of that floor, although I've yet to see any that do it justice. A *yantra*. A labyrinth. A writhing, tangled mass of sea creatures straining for a distant black sun. Hindi and Mayan and Chinook symbols. The precise contour lines of a topographic map of Monterey Canyon. Each of these things and *all* of these things, simultaneously. I've heard that there's an anthropologist at Berkeley who's writing a book about that floor. Perhaps she will publish photographs that manage to communicate its awful magnificence. Perhaps it would be better if she doesn't.

Perhaps someone should put a bullet through her head.

People said the same thing about Jacova Angevine. But assassination is almost always unthinkable to moral, thinking men until *after* a holocaust has come and gone.

I left that door open, as well, and walked slowly towards the center of the empty warehouse, towards the place where the altar had been, the spot where that divine abomination of Jacova's had rested on folds of velvet the color of a massacre. I held the Maglite gripped so tightly that the fingers of my right hand had begun to go numb.

Behind me, there was a scuffling, gritty sort of noise that might have been footsteps, and I spun about, tangling my feet and almost falling on my ass, almost dropping the flashlight. The child was standing maybe ten or fifteen feet away from me, and I could see that the door leading back to the alley had been closed. She couldn't have been more than nine or ten years old, dressed in ragged jeans and a T-shirt smeared with mud, or what looked like mud in the half light of the warehouse. Her short hair might have been blonde, or light brown, it was hard to tell. Most of her face was lost in the shadows.

"You're too late," she said. She sounded tired. Or lost. Or both.

"Jesus *Christ,* kid, you almost scared the holy shit out of me."

"You're too late," she said again.

"Too late for what? Did you follow me in here?"

"The gates are shut now. They won't open again, for you or anyone else."

I looked past her at the door I'd left open, and she looked back that way, too.

"Did you close that door?" I asked her. "Did it ever occur to you that I might have left it open for a reason?"

"I waited as long I dared," she replied, as though that answered my question, and turned to face me again.

I took one step towards her, then, or maybe two, and stopped. And at that moment, I experienced the sensation or sensations that mystery and horror writers, from Poe on down to Theo Angevine, have labored to convey – the almost painful prickling as the hairs on the back of my neck and along my arms and legs stood erect, the cold knot in the pit of my stomach, the goose across my grave, a loosening in my bowels and bladder, the tightening of my scrotum. My blood ran cold. Drag out all the fucking clichés, but there's still nothing that comes within a mile of what I felt standing there, looking down at that girl, her looking up at me, the feeble light from the windows glinting off her eyes.

Looking into her face, I felt *dread* as I'd never felt it before. Not in war zones with air-raid sirens blaring, not during interviews conducted with the muzzle of a pistol pressed to my temple or the small of my back. Not waiting for the results of a biopsy after the discovery of a peculiar mole. Not even the day she led them into the sea, and I sat watching it all on fucking CNN from a bar in Brooklyn.

And suddenly I knew that the girl hadn't followed me in from the alley, or closed the door, that she'd been here all along. I also knew that a hundred coats of paint wouldn't be enough to undo Jacova's labyrinth.

"Was you ever bit by a dead bee?"

"You shouldn't be here," the girl said, her minotaur's voice lost and faraway and regretful.

"Then where *should* I be?" I asked, and my breath fogged in air gone as frigid as the dead of winter or the bottom of the sea.

"All the answers were here," she replied. "Everything that you're asking yourself, the things that keep you awake, that are driving you insane. All the questions you're putting into that computer of yours. I offered all of it to you."

And now there was a sound like water breaking against stone, and something heavy and soft and wet, dragging itself across the concrete floor, and I thought of the thing from the altar, Jacova's Mother Hydra, that corrupt and bloated Madonna of the abyss, its tentacles and anemone tendrils and black, bulging squid eyes, the tubeworm proboscis snaking from one of the holes where its face should have been.

Mighty, undying daughter of Typhaôn and serpentine Echidna – Udra Lernaia, Hydra Lernaia, gluttonous whore of all the lightless worlds, bitch-bride and concubine of Father Dagon, Father Kraken.

I smelled rot and mud, saltwater and dying fish.

"You have to go now," the child said urgently, and she held out a hand as though she meant to show me the way. Even in the gloom, I could see the barnacles and sea lice nestled in the raw flesh of her palm. "You are a splinter in my soul, always. And she would drag you down to finish my own darkness."

And then the girl was gone. She did not vanish, she was simply not *there* anymore. And those other sounds and odors had gone with her. There was nothing left behind but the silence and stink of any abandoned building, the wind brushing against the windows and around the corners of the warehouse, the traffic along roads in the world waiting somewhere beyond those walls.

6.

I know *exactly* how all this shit sounds. Don't think that I don't. It's just that I've finally ceased to care.

7.

Yesterday, two days after my trip to the warehouse, I watched the MBARI tape again. This time when it reached the twelve-second gap, when I'd counted down to eleven, I continued on to twelve, and I didn't switch the television off, and I didn't look away. Surely, I've come too far to allow myself that luxury. I've seen so goddamn much – I've seen so much that there's no reasonable excuse for looking away, because there can't be anything left that's more terrible than what has come before.

And, besides, it was nothing that I hadn't seen already.

Orpheus' mistake wasn't that he turned and looked back towards Eurydice and Hell, but that he ever thought he could *escape.* Same with Lot's wife. Averting our eyes does not change the fact that we are marked.

After the static, the picture comes back, and at first it's just those boulders, same as before, those boulders that ought to be covered with silt and living things – the remains of living things, at least – but aren't. Those strange, clean boulders. And the lines and angles carved deeply into them that cannot be the result of any natural geological or biological process, the lines and angles that can be nothing but what Jacova said they were. I think of fragments of the Parthenon, or some other shattered Greek or Roman temple, the chiseled ornament of an entablature or pediment. I'm seeing something that was *done,* something that was consciously fashioned, not something that simply happened. The *Tiburón II* moves forward very slowly, because the blow before the gap has taken out a couple of the port thrusters. It creeps forward tentatively, floating a few feet above the seafloor, and now the ROV's lights have begun to dim and flicker.

After the gap, I know that there's only 52.2 seconds of video remaining before the starboard camera shuts down for good. Less than a minute, and I sit there on the floor of my hotel room, counting – one-one thousand, two-two thousand – and I don't take my eyes off the screen.

The MBARI robotics tech is dead, the nervous man who sold me – and whoever else was buying – his black-market dub of the videotape. The story made the Channel 46 evening news last night and was second page in the *Monterey Herald* this morning. The coroner's office is calling it a suicide. I don't know what else they would call it. He was found hanging from the lowest limb of a sycamore tree, not far from the Moss Landing docks, both his wrists slashed nearly to the bone. He was wearing a necklace of *Loligo* squid strung on baling wire. A family member has told the press that he had a history of depression.

Twenty-three seconds to go.

Almost two miles down, *Tiburón II* is listing badly to starboard, and then the ROV bumps against one of the boulders, and the lights stop flickering and seem to grow a little brighter. The vehicle appears to pause, as though considering its next move. The day he sold me the tape, the MBARI tech said that a part of the toolsled had wedged itself into the rubble. He told me it took the crew of the *R/V Western Flyer* more than two hours to maneuver the sub free. Two hours of total darkness at the bottom of the canyon, after the lights and the cameras died.

Eighteen seconds.

Sixteen.

This time it'll be different, I think, like a child trying to wish away a beating. *This time, I'll see the trick of it, the secret interplay of light and shadow, the hows and whys of a simple optical illusion –*

Twelve.

Ten.

The first time, I thought that I was only seeing something carved into the stone or part of a broken sculpture. The gentle curve of a hip, the tapering line of a leg, the twin swellings of small breasts. A nipple the color of granite.

Eight.

But there's her face – and there's no denying that it's *her* face – Jacova Angevine, her face at the bottom the sea, turned up towards the surface, towards the sky and Heaven beyond the weight of all that black, black water.

Four.

I bite my lip so hard that I taste blood. It doesn't taste so different from the ocean.

Two.

She opens her eyes, and they are *not* her eyes, but the eyes of some marine creature adapted to that perpetual night. The soulless eyes of an anglerfish or gulper eel, eyes like matching pools of ink, and something darts from her parted lips –

And then there's only static, and I sit staring into the salt-and-pepper roar.

All the answers were here. Everything that you're asking yourself... I offered all of it to you.

Later – an hour or only five minutes – I pressed EJECT, and the cassette slid obediently from the VCR. I read the label, aloud, in case I'd read it wrong every single time before, in case the timestamp on the video might have been mistaken. But it was the same as always, the day before Jacova waited on the beach at Moss Landing for the supplicants of the Open Door of Night. The day before she led them into the sea. The day before she drowned.

8.

I close my eyes.

And she's here again, as though she never left.

She whispers something dirty in my ear, something profane, and her breath smells like sage and toothpaste.

The protestors are demanding that the Monterey Bay Aquarium Research Institute (MBARI) end its ongoing exploration of the submarine canyon immediately. The twenty-five mile long canyon, they claim, is a sacred site that is being desecrated by scientists. Jacova Angevine, former Berkeley professor and leader of the controversial Open Door of Night cult, compares the launching of the new submersible Tiburón II to the ransacking of the Egyptian pyramids by grave robbers. (San Francisco Chronicle)

I tell her that I have to go to New York, that I have to take this assignment, and she replies that maybe it's for the best. I don't ask her what she means; I can't imagine that it's important.

And she kisses me.

Later, when we're done, and I'm too exhausted to sleep, I lie awake, listening to the sea and the small, anxious sounds she makes in her dreams.

The bodies of fifty-three men and women, all of whom may have been part of a religious group known as the Open Door of Night, have been recovered following Wednesday's drownings near Moss Landing, CA. Deputies have described the deaths as a mass suicide. The victims were all reported to be between 22 and 36 years old. Authorities fear that at least two dozen more may have died in the bizarre episode and recovery efforts continue along the coast of Monterey County. (CNN.com)

I close my eyes, and I'm in the old warehouse on Pierce Street again; Jacova's voice thunders from the PA speakers mounted high on the walls around the cavernous room. I'm standing in the shadows all the way at the back, apart from the true believers, apart from the other reporters and photographers and camera men who have been invited here. Jacova leans into the microphone, angry and ecstatic and beautiful – *terrible,* I think

126

– and that hideous carving is squatting there on its altar beside her. There are candles and smoldering incense and bouquets of dried seaweed, conch shells and dead fish, carefully arranged about the base of the statue.

"We can't remember where it began," she says, "where *we* began," and they all seem to lean into her words like small boats pushing against a violent wind. "We can't remember, of course we can't remember, and they don't want us to even *try*. They're afraid, and in their fear they cling desperately to the darkness of their ignorance. They would have us do the same, and then we would never recall the garden nor the gate, would never look upon the faces of the great fathers and mothers who have returned to the deep."

None of it seems the least bit real, not the ridiculous things that she's saying, or all the people dressed in white, or the television crews. This scene is not even as substantial as a nightmare. It's very hot in the warehouse, and I feel dizzy and sick and wonder if I can reach an exit before I vomit.

I close my eyes, and I'm sitting in a bar in Brooklyn, watching them wade into the sea, and I'm thinking, *Some son of a bitch is standing right there taping this and no one's trying to stop them, no one's lifting a goddamn finger.*

I blink, and I'm sitting in an office in Manhattan, and the people who write my checks are asking me questions I can't answer.

"Good god, you were fucking the woman, for Christ's sake, and you're telling me you had no *idea* whatsoever that she was planning this?"

"Come on. You had to have known *something.*"

"They all worshipped some sort of prehistoric fish god, that's what I heard. No one's going to buy that you didn't see this coming – "

"People have a right to know. You still believe that, don't you?"

Answers are scarce in the mass suicide of a California cult, but investigators are finding clues to the deaths by logging onto the Internet and Web sites run by the cult's members. What they're finding is a dark and confusing side of the Internet, a place where bizarre ideas and beliefs are exchanged and gain currency. Police said they have gathered a considerable amount of information on the background of the group, known as the Open Door of Night, but that it may be many weeks before the true nature of the group is finally understood. (CNN.com)

And my clumsy hands move uncertainly across her bare shoulders, my fingertips brushing the puckered chaos of scar tissue there, and she smiles for me.

On my knees in an alley, my head spinning, and the night air stinks of puke and saltwater.

"Okay, so I first heard about this from a woman I interviewed who knew the family," the man in the Radiohead T-shirt says. We're sitting on the patio of a bar in Pacific Grove, and the sun is hot and glimmers white off the bay. His name isn't important, and neither is the name of the bar. He's a student from LA, writing a book about the Open Door of Night, and he got my e-mail address from someone in New York. He has bad teeth and smiles too much.

"This happened back in '76, the year before Jacova's mother died. Her father, he'd take them down to the beach at Moss Landing two or three times every summer. He got a lot of his writing done out there. Anyway, apparently the kid was a great swimmer, like a duck to water, but her mother never let her go very far out at that beach because there are these bad rip currents. Lots of people drown out there, surfers and shit."

He pauses and takes a couple of swallows of beer, then wipes the sweat from his forehead.

"One day, her mother's not watching, and Jacova swims too far out and gets pulled down. By the time the lifeguards get her back to shore, she's stopped breathing. The kid's turning blue, but they keep up the mouth-to-mouth and CPR, and she finally comes around. They get Jacova to the hospital up in Watsonville, and the doctors say she's fine, but they keep her for a few days anyhow, just for observation."

"She drowned," I say, staring at my own beer. I haven't taken a single sip. Beads of condensation cling to the bottle and sparkle like diamonds.

"Technically, yeah. She wasn't breathing. Her heart had stopped. But *that's* not the fucked-up part. While she's in Watsonville, she keeps telling her mother some crazy story about mermaids and sea monsters and demons, about these things trying to drag her down to the bottom of the sea and drown her, and how it wasn't an undertow at all. She's terrified, convinced that they're still after her, these monsters. Her mother wants to call in a shrink, but her father says no, fuck that, the kid's just had a bad shock, she'll be fine. Then, the second night she's in the hospital, these two nurses turn up dead. A janitor found them in a closet just down the hall from Jacova's room. And here's the thing you're not gonna believe, but I've seen the death certificates and the autopsy reports, and I swear to you this is the God's honest truth."

Whatever's coming next, I don't want to hear it. I know that I don't *need* to hear it. I turn my head and watch a sailboat out on the bay, bobbing about like a toy.

"They'd drowned, both of them. Their lungs were full of saltwater. Five miles from the goddamn ocean, but these two women drowned right there in a *broom closet.*"

"And you're going to put this in your book?" I ask him, not taking my eyes off the bay and the little boat.

"Yeah," he replies. "I am. It fucking happened, man, just like I said, and I can prove it."

I close my eyes, shutting out the dazzling, bright day, and wish I'd never agreed to meet with him.

I close my eyes.

"Down there," Jacova whispers, "you will know nothing but peace, in her mansions, in the endless night of her coils."

We would be warm below the storm
In our little hideaway beneath the waves.

I close my eyes. Oh god, I've closed my eyes. She wraps her strong, sun-tanned arms tightly around me and takes me down, down, down, like the lifeless body of a child caught in an undertow. And I'd go with her, like a flash I'd go, if this were anything more than a dream, anything more than an infidel's sour regret, anything more than eleven thousand words cast like a handful of sand across the face of the ocean. I would go with her, because, like a stone that has become an incarnation of mystery, she has drawn a circle around me.

Pickman's Other Model (1929)

1.

I have never been much for the movies, preferring, instead, to take my enter-tainment in the theater, always favoring living actors over those flickering, garish ghosts magnified and splashed across the walls of dark and smoky rooms at twenty-four frames per second. I've never seemed able to get beyond the knowledge that the apparent motion is merely an optical illusion, a clever procession of still images streaming past my eye at such a rate of speed that I only perceive motion where none actually exists. But in the months before I finally met Vera Endecott, I found myself drawn with increasing regularity to the Boston movie houses, despite this longstanding reservation.

I had been shocked to my core by Thurber's suicide, though, with the unavailing curse of hindsight, it's something I should certainly have had the presence of mind to have seen coming. Thurber was an infantryman during the war – *La Guerre pour la Civilisation,* as he so often called it. He was at the Battle of Saint-Mihiel when Pershing failed in his campaign to seize Metz from the Germans, and he survived only to see the atrocities at the Battle of the Argonne Forest less than two weeks later. When he returned home from France early in 1919, Thurber was hardly more than a fading, nervous echo of the man I'd first met during our college years at the Rhode Island School of Design, and, on those increasingly rare occasions when we met and spoke, more often than not our conversations turned from painting and sculpture and matters of aesthetics to the things he'd seen in the muddy trenches and ruined cities of Europe.

And then there was his dogged fascination with that sick bastard Richard Upton Pickman, an obsession that would lead quickly to what I took to be no less than a sort of psychoneurotic fixation on the man and the blasphemies he committed to canvas. When, two years ago, Pickman vanished from the squalor of his North End "studio," never to be seen again, this fixation only worsened, until Thurber finally came to me with an incredible, nightmarish tale which, at the time, I could only dismiss as the ravings of a mind left unhinged by the bloodshed, madness, and countless wartime horrors he'd witnessed along the banks of the Meuse River and then in the wilds of the Argonne Forest.

But I am not the man I was then, that evening we sat together in a dingy tavern near Faneuil Hall (I don't recall the name of the place, as it wasn't one of my usual haunts). Even as William Thurber was changed by the war and by whatever it is he may have experienced in the company of Pickman, so too have I been changed, and changed *utterly,* first by Thurber's sudden death at his own hands and then by a film actress named Vera Endecott. I do not believe that I have yet lost possession of my mental faculties, and if asked, I would attest before a judge of law that my mind remains sound, if quite shaken. But I cannot now see the world around me the way I once did, for having beheld certain things there can be no return to the unprofaned state of innocence or grace that prevailed before those sights. There can be no return to the sacred cradle of Eden, for the gates are guarded by the flaming swords of cherubim, and the mind may not – excepting in merciful cases of shock and hysterical amnesia – simply forget the weird and dismaying revelations visited upon men and women who choose to ask forbidden questions. And I would be lying if I were to claim that I failed to comprehend, to suspect, that the path I was setting myself upon when I began my investigations following Thurber's inquest and funeral would lead me where they have. I knew, or I knew well enough. I am not yet so degraded that I am beyond taking responsibility for my own actions and the consequences of those actions.

Thurber and I used to argue about the validity of first-person narration as an effective literary device, he defending it and me calling into question the believability of such stories, doubting both the motivation of their fictional authors and the ability of those character narrators to accurately recall with such perfect clarity and detail specific conversations and the order of events during times of great stress and even personal danger. This is probably not so very different from my difficulty appreciating a moving picture because I am aware it is *not,* in fact, a moving picture. I suspect it points to some conscious unwillingness or unconscious inability, on my part, to effect what Coleridge dubbed the "suspension of disbelief." And now I sit down to write my own account, though I attest there is not a word of *intentional* fiction to it, and I certainly have no plans of ever seeking its publication. Nonetheless, it will undoubtedly be filled with inaccuracies following from the objections to first-person recitals that I have already belabored above. What I am putting down here is my best attempt to recall the events preceding and surrounding the murder of Vera Endecott, and it should be read as such.

It is my story, presented with such meager corroborative documentation as I am here able to provide. It is some small part of her story, as well, and over it hang the phantoms of Pickman and Thurber. In all honesty, already I begin to doubt that setting any of it down will achieve the remedy which I so desperately desire – the dampening of damnable memory, the lessening of the hold that those memories have upon me, and, if I am most lucky, the ability to sleep in dark rooms once again and an end to any number of phobias which have come to plague me. Too late do I understand poor Thurber's morbid fear of cellars and subway tunnels, and to that I can add my own fears, whether they might ever be proven rational or not. "I guess you won't wonder now why I have to steer clear of subways and cellars," he said to me that day in the tavern. I *did* wonder, of course, at that and at the sanity of a dear and trusted friend. But, in this matter, at least, I have long since ceased to wonder.

The first time I saw Vera Endecott on the "big screen" it was only a supporting part in Josef von Sternberg's *A Woman of the Sea,* at the Exeter Street Theater. But that was not the first time I saw Vera Endecott.

2.

I first encountered the name and face of the actress while sorting through William's papers, which I'd been asked to do by the only surviving member of his immediate family, Ellen Thurber, an older sister. I found myself faced with no small or simple task, as the close, rather shabby room he'd taken on Hope Street in Providence after leaving Boston was littered with a veritable bedlam of correspondence, typescripts, journals, and unfinished compositions, including the monograph on weird art that had played such a considerable role in his taking up with Richard Pickman three years prior. I was only mildly surprised to discover, in the midst of this disarray, a number of Pickman's sketches, all of them either charcoal or pen and ink. Their presence among Thurber's effects seemed rather incongruous, given how completely terrified of the man he'd professed to having become. And even more so given his claim to have destroyed the one piece of evidence that could support the incredible tale of what he purported to have heard and seen and taken away from Pickman's cellar studio.

It was a hot day, so late into July that it was very nearly August. When I came across the sketches, seven of them tucked inside a cardboard portfolio case, I carried them across the room and spread the lot out upon the narrow, swaybacked bed occupying one corner. I had a decent enough familiarity with the man's work, and I must confess that what I'd seen of it had never struck me quiet so profoundly as it had Thurber. Yes, to be sure, Pickman was possessed of a great and singular talent, and I suppose someone unaccustomed to images of the diabolic, the alien, and the monstrous would find them disturbing and unpleasant to look upon. I always credited his success at capturing the weird largely to his intentional juxtaposition of phantasmagoric subject matter with a starkly, painstakingly realistic style. Thurber also noted this, and, indeed, had devoted almost a full chapter of his unfinished monograph to an examination of Pickman's technique.

I sat down on the bed to study the sketches, and the mattress springs complained loudly beneath my weight, leading me to wonder yet again why my friend had taken such mean accommodations when he certainly could have afforded better. At any rate, glancing over the drawings, they struck me, for the most part, as nothing particularly remarkable, and I assumed that they must have been gifts from Pickman, or that Thurber might even have paid him some small sum for them. Two I recognized as studies for one of the paintings mentioned that day in the Chatham Street tavern, the one titled *The Lesson*, in which the artist had sought to depict a number of his subhuman, doglike ghouls instructing a young child (a *changeling*, Thurber had supposed) in their practice of necrophagy. Another was a rather hasty sketch of what I took to be some of the statelier monuments in Copp's Hill Burying Ground, and there were also a couple of rather slapdash renderings of hunched gargoyle-like creatures.

But it was the last two pieces from the folio that caught and held my attention. Both were very accomplished nudes, more finished than any of the other sketches, and given the subject matter, I might have doubted they had come from Pickman's hand had it not been for his signature at the bottom of each. There was nothing that could have been deemed pornographic about either, and considering their provenance, this surprised me, as well. Of the portion of Richard Pickman's *oeuvre* that I'd seen for myself, I'd not once found any testament to an interest in the female form, and there had even been whispers in the Art Club that he was a homosexual. But there were so many rumors traded about the man in the days leading up to his disappearance, many of them plainly spurious, that I'd never given the subject much thought. Regardless of his own sexual inclinations, these two studies were imbued with an appreciation and familiarity with a woman's body that seemed unlikely to have been gleaned entirely from academic exercises or mooched from the work of other, less-eccentric artists.

As I inspected the nudes, thinking that these two pieces, at least, might bring a few dollars to help Thurber's sister cover the unexpected expenses incurred by her brother's death, as well as his outstanding debts, my eyes were drawn to a bundle of magazine and newspaper clippings that had also been stored inside the portfolio. There were a goodly number of them, and I guessed then, and still suppose, that Thurber had employed a clipping bureau. About half were write-ups of gallery showings that had included Pickman's work, mostly spanning the years from 1921 to 1925, before he'd been so ostracized that opportunities for public showings had dried up. But the remainder appeared to have been culled largely from tabloids, sheetlets, and magazines such as *Photoplay* and *The New York Evening Graphic,* and every one of the articles was either devoted to or made mention of a Massachusetts-born actress named Vera Marie Endecott. There were, among these clippings, a number of photographs of the woman, and her likeness to the woman who'd modeled for the two Pickman nudes was unmistakable.

There was something quite distinct about her high cheekbones, the angle of her nose, an undeniable hardness to her countenance despite her starlet's beauty and sex appeal. Later, I would come to recognize some commonality between her face and those of such movie "vamps" and *femmes fatales* as Theda Bara, Eva Galli, Musidora, and, in particular, Pola Negri. But, as best as I can now recollect, my first impression of Vera Endecott, untainted by film personae (though undoubtedly colored by the association of the clippings with the work of Richard Pickman, there among the belongings of a suicide) was of a woman whose loveliness might merely be a glamour concealing some truer, feral face. It was an admittedly odd impression, and I sat in the sweltering boarding-house room, as the sun slid slowly towards dusk, reading each of the articles, and then reading some over again. I suspected they must surely contain, somewhere, evidence that the woman in the sketches was, indeed, the same woman who'd gotten her start in the movie studios of Long Island and New Jersey, before the indus-try moved west to California.

For the most part, the clippings were no more than the usual sort of picture-show gossip, innuendo, and sensationalism. But, here and there, someone, presumably Thurber himself, had underlined various passages with a red pencil, and when those lines were considered together, removed from the context of their accompanying articles, a curious pattern could be dis-cerned. At least, such a pattern might be imagined by a reader who was either *searching* for it, and so predisposed to discovering it whether it truly existed or not, or by someone, like myself, coming to these collected scraps of yel-low journalism under such circumstances and such an atmosphere of dread as may urge the reader to draw parallels where, objectively, there are none to be found. I believed, that summer afternoon, that Thurber's *idée fixe* with Richard Pickman had led him to piece together an absurdly macabre set of notions regarding this woman, and that I, still grieving the loss of a close friend and surrounded as I was by the disorder of that friend's unfulfilled life's work, had done nothing but uncover another of Thurber's delusions.

The woman known to moviegoers as Vera Endecott had been sired into an admittedly peculiar family from the North Shore region of Massachusetts, and she'd undoubtedly taken steps to hide her heritage, adopting a stage name shortly after her arrival in Fort Lee in February of 1922. She'd also invented a new history for herself, claiming to hail not from rural Essex County, but from Boston's Beacon Hill. However, as early as '24, shortly after landing her first substantial role – an appearance in Biograph Studios' *Sky Below the Lake* – a number of popular columnists had begun printing their suspicions about her professed background. The banker she'd claimed as her father could not be found, and it proved a straightforward enough matter to demonstrate that she'd never attended the Winsor School for girls. By '25, after her starring role in Robert G. Vignola's *The Horse Winter*, a reporter for *The New York Evening Graphic* claimed Endecott's actual father was a man named Iscariot Howard Snow, the owner of several Cape Anne granite quarries. His wife, Make-peace, had come either from Salem or Marblehead, and had died in 1902 while giving birth to their only daughter, whose name was not Vera, but Lillian Margaret. There was no evidence in any of the clippings that the actress had ever denied or even responded to these allegations, despite the fact that the Snows, and Iscariot Snow in particular, had a distinctly unsavory reputation in and around Ipswich. Regardless of the family's wealth and prominence in local business, it was notoriously secretive, and there was no want for back-fence talk concerning sorcery and witchcraft, incest and even cannibalism. In 1899, Make-peace Snow had also borne twin sons, Aldous and Edward, though Edward had been a stillbirth.

But it was a clipping from *Kidder's Weekly Art News* (March 27th, 1925), a publication I was well enough acquainted with, that first tied the actress to Richard Pickman. A "Miss Vera Endecott of Manhattan" was listed among those in attendance at the premiere of an exhibition that had included a couple of Pickman's less provocative paintings, though no mention was made of her celebrity. Thurber had circled her name with red pencil and drawn two exclamation points beside it. By the time I came across the article, twilight had descended upon Hope Street, and I was having trouble reading. I briefly considered the old gas lamp near the bed, but then, staring into the shadows gathering amongst the clutter and threadbare furniture of the seedy little room, I was gripped by a sudden, vague apprehension – by what, even now, I am reluctant to name *fear*. I returned the clippings and the seven sketches to the folio, tucked it under my arm and quickly retrieved my hat from a table buried beneath a typewriter, an assortment of paper and library books, unwashed dishes and empty soda bottles. A few minutes later, I was outside again and clear of the building, standing beneath a streetlight, staring up at the two darkened windows opening into the room where, a week before, William Thurber had put the barrel of a revolver in his mouth and pulled the trigger.

3.

I have just awakened from another of my nightmares, which become ever more vivid and frequent, ever more appalling, often permitting me no more than one or two hours' sleep each night. I'm sitting at my writing desk, watching as the sky begins to go the grey violet of false dawn, listening to the clock ticking like some giant wind-up insect perched upon the mantel. But my mind is still lodged firmly in a dream of the musty private screening room near Harvard Square, operated by a small circle of aficionados of grotesque cinema, the room where first I saw "moving" images of the daughter of Iscariot Snow.

I'd learned of the group from an acquaintance in acquisitions at the Museum of Fine Arts, who'd told me it met irregularly, rarely more than once every three months, to view and discuss such fanciful and morbid fare as Benjamin Christensen's *Häxan,* Rupert Julian's *The Phantom of the Opera,* Murnau's *Nosferatu, eine Symphonie des Grauens,* and Todd Browning's *London After Midnight.* These titles and the names of their directors meant very little to me, since, as I have already noted, I've never been much for the movies. This was in August, only a couple of weeks after I'd returned to Boston from Providence, having set Thurber's affairs in order as best I could. I still prefer not to consider what unfortunate caprice of fate aligned my discovery of Pickman's sketches of Vera Endecott and Thurber's interest in her with the group's screening of what, in my opinion, was a profane and a deservedly unheard-of film. Made sometime in 1923 or '24, I was informed that it had achieved infamy following the director's death (another suicide). All the film's financiers remained unknown, and it seemed that production had never proceeded beyond the incomplete rough cut I saw that night.

However, I did not sit down here to write out a dry account of my discovery of this untitled, unfinished film, but rather to try and capture something of the dream that is already breaking into hazy scraps and shreds. Like Perseus, who dared to view the face of the Gorgon Medusa only indirectly, as a reflection in his bronze shield, so I seem bound and determined to reflect upon these events, and even my own nightmares, as obliquely as I may. I have always despised cowardice, and yet, looking back over these pages, there seems in this account something undeniably cowardly. It does not matter that I intend that no one else shall ever read this. Unless I write honestly, there is hardly any reason in writing it at all. If this is a ghost story (and, increasingly, it feels that way to me), then let it *be* a ghost story and not this rambling reminiscence.

In the dream, I am sitting in a wooden folding chair in that dark room, lit only by the single shaft of light spilling forth from the projectionist's booth. And the wall in front of me has become a window, looking out upon or into another world, one devoid of sound and almost all color, its palette limited to a spectrum of somber blacks, dazzling whites, and innumerable shades of grey. Around me, the others who have come to see smoke their cigars and cigarettes, and they mutter among themselves. I cannot make out anything they say, but, then, I'm not trying particularly hard. I cannot look away from that silent, grisaille scene, and little else truly occupies my mind.

"Now, do you understand?" Thurber asks from his seat next to mine, and maybe I nod, and maybe I even whisper some hushed affirmation or another. But I do *not* take my eyes from the screen long enough to glimpse his face. There is too much there I might miss, were I to dare look away, even for an instant, and, moreover, I have no desire to gaze upon the face of a dead man. Thurber says nothing else for a time, apparently content that I have found my way to this place, to witness for myself some fraction of what drove him, at last, to the very end of madness.

She is there on the screen – Vera Endecott, Lillian Margaret Snow – standing at the edge of a rocky pool. She is as naked as in Pickman's sketches of her, and is positioned, at first, with her back to the camera. The gnarled roots and branches of what might be ancient willow trees bend low over the pool, their whip-like branches brushing the surface and moving gracefully to and fro, disturbed by the same breeze that ruffles the actress' short, bob-cut hair. And though there appears to be nothing the least bit sinister about this scene, it at once inspires in me the same sort of awe and uneasiness as Doré's engravings for *Orlando Furioso* and the *Divine Comedy*. There is about the tableau a sense of intense foreboding and anticipation, and I wonder what subtle, clever cues have been placed just so that this seemingly idyllic view would be interpreted with such grim expectancy.

And then I realize that the actress is holding in her right hand some manner of phial, and she tilts it just enough that the contents, a thick and pitchy liquid, drip into the pool. Concentric ripples spread slowly across the water, much *too* slowly, I'm convinced, to have followed from any earthly physics, and so I dismiss it as merely trick photography. When the phial is empty, or has, at least, ceased to taint the pool (and I am quite sure that it *has* been tainted), the woman kneels in the mud and weeds at the water's edge. From somewhere overhead, there in the room with me, comes a sound like the wings of startled pigeons taking flight, and the actress half turns towards the audience, as if she has also somehow heard the commotion. The fluttering racket quickly subsides, and once more there is only the mechanical noise from the projector and the whispering of the men and women crowded into the musty room. Onscreen, the actress turns back to the pool, but not before I am certain that her face is the same one from the clippings I found in Thurber's room, the same one sketched by the hand of Richard Upton Pickman. The phial slips from her fingers, falling into the water, and this time there are no ripples whatsoever. No splash. Nothing.

Here, the image flickers before the screen goes blindingly white, and I think, for a moment, that the filmstrip has, mercifully, jumped one sprocket or another, so maybe I'll not have to see the rest. But then the glitch corrects itself, and it all comes flooding back again, the woman and the pool and the willows, playing out frame by frame by frame. She kneels at the edge of the pool, and I think of Narcissus pining for Echo or his lost twin, of jealous Circe poisoning the spring where Scylla bathed, and of Tennyson's cursed Shalott, and, too, again I think of Perseus and Medusa. I am not seeing the thing itself, but only some dim, misguiding counterpart, and my mind grasps for analogies, signification, and points of reference.

On the screen, Vera Endecott, or Lillian Margaret Snow – one or the other, the two who were always only one – leans forward and dips her hand into the pool. And again, there are no ripples to mar its smooth obsidian surface. The woman in the film is speaking now, her lips moving deliberately, making no sound whatsoever, and I can hear nothing but the mumbling, smoky room and the sputtering projector. And this is when I realize that the willows are not precisely willows at all, but that those twisted trunks and limbs and roots are actually the entwined human bodies of both sexes, their skin perfectly mimicking the scaly bark of a willow. I understand that these are no wood nymphs, no daughters of Hamadryas and Oxylus. These are prisoners, or condemned souls bound eternally for their sins, and for a time I can only stare in wonder at the confusion of arms and legs, hips and breasts and faces marked by untold ages of the ceaseless agony of this contortion and transformation. This is William Blake's Wood of Self-Murderers, Dante's Forest of Suicides. I want to turn and ask the others if they see what I see, and how the deception has been accomplished, for surely these people know more of the prosaic magic of filmmaking than do I. Worst of all, the bodies have not been rendered entirely inert, but writhe ever so slightly, helping the wind to stir the long, leafy branches first this way, then that.

Then my eye is drawn back to the pool, which has begun to steam, a grey-white mist rising languidly from off the water (if it still is water). The actress leans yet farther out over the strangely quiescent mere, and I find myself eager to look away. Whatever being the cameraman has caught her in the act of summoning or appeasing, I do not want to *see,* do not want to *know* its daemonic physiognomy. Her lips continue to move, and her hands stir the waters that remain smooth as glass, betraying no evidence that they have been disturbed in any way.

> At Rhegium she arrives; the ocean braves,
> And treads with unwet feet the boiling waves.

But desire is not enough, nor trepidation, and I do not look away, either because I have been bewitched along with all those others who have come to see her, or because some deeper, more disquisitive facet of my being has taken command and is willing to risk damnation in the seeking into this mystery.

"It is only a moving picture," dead Thurber reminds me from his seat beside mine. "Whatever else she would say, you must never forget it is only a dream."

And I want to reply, "Is that what happened to you, dear William? Did you forget it was never anything more than a dream and find yourself unable to waken to lucidity and life?" But I do not say a word, and Thurber does not say anything more.

> *But yet she knows not, who it is she fears;*
> *In vain she offers from herself to run,*
> *And drags about her what she strives to shun.*

"Brilliant," whispers a woman in the darkness at my back. "Sublime," mumbles what sounds to be a very old man. My eyes do not stray from the screen. The actress has stopped stirring the pool, has withdrawn her hand from the water, but still she kneels there, staring at the sooty stain it has left on her fingers and palm and wrist. *Maybe,* I think, *that is what she came for, that mark, that she will be known,* though my dreaming mind does not presume to guess what or whom she would have recognize her by such a bruise or blotch. She reaches into the reeds and moss and produces a black-handled dagger, which she then holds high above her head, as though making an offering to unseen gods, before she uses the glinting blade to slice open the hand she previously offered to the waters. And I think perhaps I understand, finally, and the phial and the stirring of the pool were only some preparatory wizardry before presenting this far more precious alms or expiation. As her blood drips to spatter and *roll* across the surface of the pool like drops of mercury striking a solid tabletop, something has begun to take shape, assembling itself from those concealed depths, and, even without sound, it is plain enough that the willows have begun to scream and to sway as though in the grip of a hurricane wind. I think, perhaps, it is a mouth, of sorts, coalescing before the prostrate form of Vera Endecott or Lillian Margaret Snow, a mouth or a vagina or a blind and lidless eye, or some organ that may serve as all three. I debate each of these possibilities, in turn.

Five minutes ago, almost, I lay my pen aside, and I have just finished reading back over, aloud, what I have written, as false dawn gave way to sunrise and the uncomforting light of a new October day. But before I return these pages to the folio containing Pickman's sketches and Thurber's clippings and go on about the business that the morning demands of me, I would first confess that what I have dreamed and what I have recorded here are not what I saw that afternoon in the screening room near Harvard Square. Neither is it entirely the nightmare that woke me and sent me stumbling to my desk. Too much of the dream deserted me, even as I rushed to get it all down, and the dreams are never exactly, and sometimes not even remotely, what I saw projected on that wall, that deceiving stream of still images conspiring to suggest animation. This is another point I always tried to make with Thurber, and which he never would accept, the fact of the inevitability of unreliable narrators. I have not lied; I would not say that. But none of this is any nearer to the truth than any other fairy tale.

4.

After the days I spent in the boarding house in Providence, trying to bring some semblance of order to the chaos of Thurber's interrupted life, I began accumulating my own files on Vera Endecott, spending several days in August drawing upon the holdings of the Boston Athenaeum, the Public Library, and the Widener Library at Harvard. It was not difficult to piece together the story of the actress' rise to stardom and the scandal that led to her descent into obscurity and alcoholism late in 1927, not so very long before Thurber came to me with his wild tale of Pickman and subterranean ghouls. What was much more difficult to trace was her movement through certain theosophical and occult societies, from Manhattan to Los Angeles, circles to which Richard Upton Pickman was, himself, no stranger.

In January '27, after being placed under contract to Paramount Pictures the previous spring, and during production of a film adaptation of Margaret Kennedy's novel, *The Constant Nymph,* rumors began surfacing in the tabloids that Vera Endecott was drinking heavily and, possibly, using heroin. However, these allegations appear at first to have caused her no more alarm or damage to her film career than the earlier discovery that she was, in fact, Lillian Snow, or the public airing of her disreputable North Shore roots. Then, on May 3rd, she was arrested in what was, at first, reported as merely a raid on a speakeasy somewhere along Durand Drive, at an address in the steep, scrubby canyons above Los Angeles, not far from the Lake Hollywood Reservoir and Mulholland Highway. A few days later, after Endecott's release on bail, queerer accounts of the events of that night began to surface, and by the seventh articles in the *Van Nuys Call, Los Angeles Times,* and the *Herald-Express* were describing the gathering on Durand Drive not as a speakeasy, but as everything from a "witches' Sabbat" to "a decadent, sacrilegious, orgiastic rite of witchcraft and homosexuality."

But the final, damning development came when reporters discovered that one of the many women found that night in the company of Vera Endecott, a Mexican prostitute named Ariadna Delgado, had been taken immediately to Queen of Angels-Hollywood Presbyterian, comatose and suffering from multiple stab wounds to her torso, breasts, and face. Delgado died on the morning of May 4th, without ever having regained consciousness. A second "victim" or "participant" (depending on the newspaper), a young and unsuccessful screenwriter listed as Joseph E. Chapman, was placed in the psychopathic ward of LA County General Hospital following the arrests.

Though there appear to have been attempts to keep the incident quiet by both studio lawyers and also, perhaps, members of the Los Angeles Police Department, Endecott was arrested a second time on May 10th, and charged with multiple counts of rape, sodomy, second-degree murder, kidnapping, and solicitation. Accounts of the specific charges brought vary from one source to another, but regardless, Endecott was granted and made bail a second time on May 11th, and four days later, the office of Los Angeles District Attorney Asa Keyes abruptly and rather inexplicably asked for a dismissal of all charges against the actress, a motion granted in an equally inexplicable move by the Superior Court of California, Los Angeles County (it bears mentioning, of course, that District Attorney Keyes was, himself, soon thereafter indicted for conspiracy to receive bribes, and is presently awaiting trial). So, eight days after her initial arrest at the residence on Durand Drive, Vera Endecott was a free woman, and, by late May, she had returned to Manhattan, after her contract with Paramount was terminated.

Scattered throughout the newspaper and tabloid coverage of the affair are numerous details which take on a greater significance in light of her connection with Richard Pickman. For one, some reporters made mention of "an obscene idol" and "a repellent statuette carved from something like greenish soapstone" recovered from the crime scene, a statue which one of the arresting officers is purported to have described as a "crouching, dog-like beast." One article listed the item as having been examined by a local (unnamed) archaeologist, who was supposedly baffled at its origins and cultural affinities. The house on Durand Drive was, and may still be, owned by a man named Beauchamp who'd spent time in the company of Aleister Crowley during his four-year visit to America (1914–1918), and who had connections with a number of hermetic and theurgical organizations. And finally, the screenwriter Joseph Chapman drowned himself in the Pacific somewhere near Malibu only a few months ago, shortly after being discharged from the hospital. The one short article I could locate regarding his death made mention of his part in the "notorious Durand Drive incident" and printed a short passage reputed to have come from the suicide note. It reads, in part, as follows:

> *Oh God, how does a man forget, deliberately and wholly and forever, once he has glimpsed such sights as I have had the misfortune to have seen? The awful things we did and permitted to be done that night, the events we set in motion, how do I lay my culpability aside? Truthfully, I cannot and am no longer able to fight through day after day of trying. The Endecotte* [sic] *woman is back East somewhere, I hear, and I hope to hell she gets what's coming to her. I burned the abominable painting she gave me, but I feel no cleaner, no less foul, for having done so. There is nothing left of me but the putrescence we invited. I cannot do this anymore.*

Am I correct in surmising, then, that Vera Endecott made a gift of one of Pickman's paintings to the unfortunate Joseph Chapman, and that it played some role in his madness and death? If so, how many others received such gifts from her, and how many of those canvases yet survive so many thousands of miles from the dank cellar studio near Battery Street where Pickman created them? It's not something I like to dwell upon.

After Endecott's reported return to Manhattan, I failed to find any printed record of her whereabouts or doings until October of that year, shortly after Pickman's disappearance and my meeting with Thurber in the tavern near Faneuil Hall. It's only a passing mention from a society column in the *New York Herald Tribune,* that "the actress Vera Endecott" was among those in attendance at the unveiling of a new display of Sumerian, Hittite, and Babylonian antiquities at the Metropolitan Museum of Art.

What is it I am trying to accomplish with this catalog of dates and death and misfortune, calamity and crime? Among Thurber's books, I found a copy of Charles Hoy Fort's *The Book of the Damned* (Boni and Liveright; New York, December 1, 1919). I'm not even sure why I took it away with me, and having read it, I find the man's writings almost hysterically belligerent and constantly prone to intentional obfuscation and misdirection. Oh, and wouldn't that contentious bastard love to have a go at this tryst with "the damned"? My point here is that I'm forced to admit that these last few pages bear a marked and annoying similarity to much of Fort's first book (I have not read his second, *New Lands,* nor do I propose ever to do so). Fort wrote of his intention to present a collection of data which had been excluded by science (*id est,* "damned"):

Battalions of the accursed, captained by pallid data that I have exhumed, will march. You'll read them – or they'll march. Some of them livid and some of them fiery and some of them rotten.

Some of them are corpses, skeletons, mummies, twitching, tottering, animated by companions that have been damned alive. There are giants that will walk by, though sound asleep. There are things that are theorems and things that are rags: they'll go by like Euclid arm in arm with the spirit of anarchy. Here and there will flit little harlots. Many are clowns. But many are of the highest respectability. Some are assassins. There are pale stenches and gaunt superstitions and mere shadows and lively malices: whims and amiabilities. The naïve and the pedantic and the bizarre and the grotesque and the sincere and the insincere, the profound and the puerile.

And I think I have accomplished nothing more *than* this, in my recounting of Endecott's rise and fall, drawing attention to some of the more melodramatic and vulgar parts of a story that is, in the main, hardly more remarkable than numerous other Hollywood scandals. But also, Fort would laugh at my own "pallid data," I am sure, my pathetic grasping at straws, as though I might make this all seem perfectly reasonable by selectively quoting newspapers and police reports, straining to preserve the fraying infrastructure of my rational mind. It's time to lay these dubious, slipshod attempts at scholarship aside. There are enough Forts in the world already, enough crackpots and provocateurs and intellectual heretics without my joining their ranks. The files I have assembled will be attached to this document, all my "battalions of the accursed," and if anyone should ever have cause to read this, they may make of those appendices what they will. It's time to tell the truth, as best I am able, and be done with this.

5.

It is true that I attended a screening of a film, featuring Vera Endecott, in a musty little room near Harvard Square. And that it still haunts my dreams. But as noted above, the dreams rarely are anything like an accurate replaying of what I saw that night. There was no black pool, no willow trees stitched together from human bodies, no venomous phial emptied upon the waters. Those are the embellishments of my dreaming, subconscious mind. I could fill several journals with such nightmares.

What I *did* see, only two months ago now, and one month before I finally met the woman for myself, was little more than a grisly, but strangely mundane, scene. It might have only been a test reel, or perhaps 17,000 or so frames, some twelve minutes, give or take, excised from a far longer film. All in all, it was little more than a blatantly pornographic pastiche of the widely circulated 1918 publicity stills of Theda Bara lying in various risqué poses with a human skeleton (for J. Edward Gordon's *Salomé*).

The print was in very poor condition, and the projectionist had to stop twice to splice the film back together after it broke. The daughter of Iscariot Snow, known to most of the world as Vera Endecott, lay naked upon a stone floor with a skeleton. However, the human skull had been replaced with what I assumed then (and still believe) to have been a plaster or papier-mâché prop that more closely resembled the cranium of a mandrill, baboon, or some malformed, macrocephalic dog. The wall or backdrop behind her was a stark matte grey, and the scene seemed to me purposefully underlit in an attempt to bring more atmosphere to a shoddy production. The skeleton (and its ersatz skull) were wired together, and Endecott caressed all the osseous angles of its arms and legs and lavished kisses upon its lipless mouth, before masturbating, first with the bones of its right hand and then by rubbing herself against the crest of an ilium.

The reactions from the others who'd come to see the film that night ranged from bored silence to rapt attention to laughter. My own reaction was, for the most part, merely disgust and embarrassment to be counted among that audience. I overheard, when the lights came back up, that the can containing the reel bore two titles, *The Necrophile* and *The Hound's Daughter,* and also bore two dates: 1923 and 1924. Later, from someone who had a passing acquaintance with Richard Pickman, I would hear a rumor that he'd worked on scenarios for a filmmaker, possibly Bernard Natan, the prominent Franco-Romanian director of blue movies, who recently acquired Pathé and merged it with his own studio, Rapid Film. I cannot confirm or deny this, but certainly, I imagine what I saw that evening would have delighted Pickman to no end.

However, what has lodged that night so firmly in my mind, and what I believe is the genuine author of those among my nightmares featuring Endecott in an endless parade of nonexistent horrific films transpired only in the final few seconds of the film. Indeed, it came and went so quickly that the projectionist was asked by a number of those present to rewind and play the ending over four times, in an effort to ascertain whether we'd seen what we *thought* we had seen.

Her lust apparently satiated, the actress lay down with her skeletal lover, one arm about its empty ribcage, and closed her kohl-smudged eyes. And in that last instant, before the film ended, a shadow appeared, something passing slowly between the set and the camera's light source. Even after five viewings, I can only describe that shade as having put me in mind of some hulking figure, something considerably farther down the evolutionary ladder than Piltdown or Java man. And it was generally agreed among those seated in that close and musty room that the shadow was possessed of an odd sort of snout or muzzle, suggestive of the prognathous jaw and face of the fake skull wired to the skeleton.

There, then. *That* is what I actually saw that evening, as best I now can remember it. Which leaves me with only a single piece of this story left to tell, the night I finally met the woman who called herself Vera Endecott.

6.

"Disappointed? Not quite what you were expecting?" she asked, smiling a distasteful, wry sort of smile, and I think I might have nodded in reply. She appeared at least a decade older than her twenty-seven years, looking like a woman who had survived one rather tumultuous life already and had, perhaps, started in upon a second. There were fine lines at the corners of her eyes and mouth, the bruised circles below her eyes that spoke of chronic insomnia and drug abuse, and, if I'm not mistaken, a premature hint of silver in her bobbed black hair. What had I anticipated? It's hard to say now, after the fact, but I was surprised by her height, and by her irises, which were a striking shade of grey. At once, they reminded me of the sea, of fog and breakers and granite cobbles polished perfectly smooth by ages in the surf. The Greeks said that the goddess Athena had "sea-grey" eyes; I wonder what they would have thought of the eyes of Lillian Snow.

"I have not been well," she confided, making the divulgence sound almost like a *mea culpa,* and those stony eyes glanced towards a chair in the foyer of my flat. I apologized for not having already asked her in, for having kept her standing in the hallway. I led her to the davenport sofa in the tiny parlor off my studio, and she thanked me. She asked for whiskey or gin, and then laughed at me when I told her I was a teetotaler. When I offered her tea, she declined.

"A painter who doesn't drink?" she asked. "No wonder I've never heard of you."

I believe that I mumbled something then about the Eighteenth Amendment and the Volstead Act, which earned from her an expression of commingled disbelief and contempt. She told me that was strike two, and if it turned out that I didn't smoke, either, she was leaving, as my claim to be an artist would have been proven a bald-faced lie, and she'd know I'd lured her to my apartment under false pretenses. But I offered her a cigarette, one of the *brun* Gitanes I first developed a taste for in college, and at that she seemed to relax somewhat. I lit her cigarette, and she leaned back on the sofa, still smiling that wry smile, watching me with her sea-grey eyes, her thin face wreathed in gauzy veils of smoke. She wore a yellow felt cloche that didn't exactly match her burgundy silk chemise, and I noticed there was a run in her left stocking.

"You knew Richard Upton Pickman," I said, blundering much too quickly to the point, and, immediately, her expression turned somewhat suspicious. She said nothing for almost a full minute, just sat there smoking and staring back at me, and I silently cursed my impatience and lack of tact. But then the smile returned, and she laughed softly and nodded.

"Wow," she said. "There's a name I haven't heard in a while. But, yeah, sure, I knew the son of a bitch. So, what are you? Another of his protégés, or maybe just one of the three-letter-men he liked to keep handy?"

"Then it's true Pickman was light on his feet?" I asked.

She laughed again, and this time there was an unmistakable edge of derision there. She took another long drag on her cigarette, exhaled, and squinted at me through the smoke.

"Mister, I have yet to meet the beast – male, female, or anything in between – that degenerate fuck wouldn't have screwed, given half a chance." She paused, here, tapping ash onto the floorboards. "So, if you're not a fag, just what are you? A kike, maybe? You sort of look like a kike."

"No," I replied. "I'm not Jewish. My parents were Roman Catholic, but me, I'm not much of anything, I'm afraid, but a painter you've never heard of."

"Are you?"

"Am I what, Miss Endecott?"

"Afraid," she said, smoke leaking from her nostrils. "And do *not* dare start in calling me 'Miss Endecott.' It makes me sound like a goddamned schoolteacher or something equally wretched."

"So, these days, do you prefer Vera?" I asked, pushing my luck. "Or Lillian?"

"How about Lily?" she smiled, completely nonplussed, so far as I could tell, as though these were all only lines from a script she'd spent the last week rehearsing.

"Very well, Lily," I said, moving the glass ashtray on the table closer to her. She scowled at it, as though I were offering her a platter of some perfectly odious foodstuff and expecting her to eat, but she stopped tapping her ash on my floor.

"Why am I here?" she demanded, commanding an answer without raising her voice. "Why have you gone to so much trouble to see me?"

"It wasn't as difficult as all that," I replied, not yet ready to answer her question, wanting to stretch this meeting out a little longer and under-standing, expecting, that she would likely leave as soon as she had what she'd come for. In truth, it had been quite a lot of trouble, beginning with a telephone call to her former agent, and then proceeding through half a dozen increasingly disreputable and uncooperative contacts. Two I'd had to bribe, and one I'd had to coerce with a number of hollow threats involving nonexistent contacts in the Boston Police Department. But, when all was said and done, my diligence had paid off, because here she sat before me, the two of us, alone, just me and the woman who'd been a movie star and who had played some role in Thurber's breakdown, who'd posed for Pickman and almost certainly done murder on a spring night in Hollywood. Here was the woman who could answer questions I did not have the nerve to ask, who knew what had cast the shadow I'd seen in that dingy pornographic film. Or, at least, here was all that remained of her.

"There aren't many left who would have bothered," she said, gazing down at the smoldering tip-end of her Gitane.

"Well, I have always been a somewhat persistent sort of fellow," I told her, and she smiled again. It was an oddly bestial smile that reminded me of one of my earliest impressions of her – that oppressive summer's day, now more than two months past, studying a handful of old clippings in the Hope Street boarding house. That her human face was nothing more than a mask or fairy glamour conjured to hide the truth of her from the world.

"How did you meet him?" I asked, and she stubbed out her cigarette in the ashtray.

"Who? How did I meet who?" She furrowed her brow and glanced nervously towards the parlor window, which faces east, towards the harbor.

"I'm sorry," I replied. "Pickman. How is it that you came to know Richard Pickman?"

"Some people would say that you have very unhealthy interests, Mr. Blackman," she said, her peculiarly carnivorous smile quickly fading, taking with it any implied menace. In its stead, there was only this destitute, used-up husk of a woman.

"And surely they've said the same of you, many, many times, Lily. I've read all about Durand Drive and the Delgado woman."

"Of course, you have," she sighed, not taking her eyes from the window. "I'd have expected nothing less from a persistent fellow such as yourself."

"How did you meet Richard Pickman?" I asked for the third time.

"Does it make a difference? That was so very long ago. Years and years ago. He's quite dead and buried."

"No body was ever found."

And, here, she looked from the window to me, and all those unexpected lines on her face seemed to have abruptly deepened; she might well have been twenty-seven, by birth, but no one would have argued if she laid claim to forty.

"The man is dead," she said flatly, then added, cryptically. "And if by chance he's *not*, well, we should all be fortunate enough to find our heart's desire, whatever it might be." Then she went back to staring at the window, and for a minute or two neither of us said anything more.

"You told me that you have the sketches," she said, finally. "Was that a lie, just to get me up here?"

"No, I have them. Two of them, anyway," and I reached for the folio beside my chair and untied the string holding it closed. "I don't know, of course, how many you might have posed for. There were more?"

"More than two," she replied, almost whispering now.

"Lily, you still haven't told me how the two of you met."

"And you are a persistent fellow."

"Yes," I assured her, taking the two nudes from the stack and holding them up for her to see, but not yet touch. She studied them a moment, her face remaining slack and dispassionate, as if the sight of them elicited no memories at all.

"He needed a model," she said, turning back to the window and the blue October sky. "I was up from New York, staying with a friend who'd met him at a gallery or lecture or something of the sort. My friend knew that he was looking for models, and I needed the money."

I glanced at the two charcoal sketches again, at the curve of those full hips, the round, firm buttocks, and the tail – a crooked, malformed thing sprouting from the base of the spine and reaching halfway to the bend of the subject's knees. As I have said, Pickman had a flair for realism, and his eye for human anatomy was almost as uncanny as the ghouls and demons he painted. I pointed to one of the sketches, to the tail.

"That isn't artistic license, is it?"

She did not look back to the two drawings, but simply, slowly, shook her head. "I had the surgery done in Jersey, back in '21," she said.

"Why did you wait so long, Lily? It's my understanding that such a defect is usually corrected at birth, or shortly thereafter."

And she almost smiled that smile again, that hungry, savage smile, but it died, incomplete, on her lips.

"My father, he has his own ideas about such things," she said quietly. "He was always so proud, you see, that his daughter's body was blessed with evidence of her heritage. It made him very happy."

"Your heritage – " I began, but Lily Snow held up her left hand, silencing me.

"I believe, sir, I've answered enough questions for one afternoon. Especially given that you have only the pair, and that you did not tell me that was the case when we spoke."

Reluctantly, I nodded and passed both the sketches to her. She took them, thanked me, and stood up, brushing at a bit of lint or dust on her burgundy chemise. I told her that I regretted that the others were not in my possession, that it had not even occurred to me she would have posed for more than these two. The last part was a lie, of course, as I knew Pickman would surely have made as many studies as possible when presented with so unusual a body.

"I can show myself out," she informed me when I started to rise from my chair. "And you will not disturb me again, not ever."

"No," I agreed. "Not ever. You have my word."

"You're lying sons of bitches, the whole lot of you," she said, and with that, the living ghost of Vera Endecott turned and left the parlor. A few seconds later, I heard the door open and slam shut again, and I sat there in the wan light of a fading day, looking at what grim traces remained in Thurber's folio.

7. (October 24th, 1929)

This is the last of it. Just a few more words, and I will be done. I know now that having attempted to trap these terrible events I have not managed to trap them at all, but merely given them some new, clearer focus.

Four days ago, on the morning of October 20th, a body was discovered dangling from the trunk of an oak growing near the center of King's Chapel Burial Ground. According to newspaper accounts, the corpse was suspended a full seventeen feet off the ground, bound round about the waist and chest with interwoven lengths of jute rope and baling wire. The woman was identified as a former screen actress, Vera Endecott, née Lillian Margaret Snow, and much was made of her notoriety and her unsuccessful attempt to conceal connections to the wealthy but secretive and ill-rumored Snows of Ipswich, Massachusetts. Her body had been stripped of all clothing, disemboweled, her throat cut, and her tongue removed. Her lips had been sewn shut with cat-gut stitches. About her neck hung a wooden placard, on which one word had been written in what is believed to be the dead woman's own blood: *apostate.*

I almost burned Thurber's folio this morning, along with all my files. I went so far as to carry them to the hearth, but then my resolve faltered, and I just sat on the floor, staring at the clippings and Pickman's sketches. I'm not sure what stayed my hand, beyond the suspicion that destroying these papers would not save my life. If they want me dead, then dead I'll be. I've gone too far down this road to spare myself by trying to annihilate the physical evidence of my investigation.

I will place this manuscript, and all the related documents I have gathered, in my safe deposit box, and then I will try to return to the life I was living before Thurber's death. But I cannot forget a line from the suicide note of the screenwriter Joseph Chapman – *how does a man forget, deliberately and wholly and forever, once he has glimpsed such sights.* How, indeed. And, too, I cannot forget that woman's eyes, that stony, sea-tumbled shade of grey. Or a rough shadow glimpsed in the final moments of a film that might have been made either in 1923 or 1924, that may have been titled either *The Hound's Daughter* or *The Necrophile.*

I know the dreams will not desert me, not now nor at some future time, but I pray for such fortune as to have seen the last of the waking horrors that my foolish, prying mind has called forth.

The Thousand-and-Third Tale
of Scheherazade

I never much cared for those stories," the changeling woman says, staring out at all the fresh snow blanketing the rooftops and streets and the stingy front yards of Federal Hill. The January storm that began just after sunset is finally starting to taper off, and the woman sits at the little table by the window, cleaning her guns and watching the large, wet flakes spiraling down through the orange-white glow of the streetlights. The lean young man whom she has taken as her odalisque is lying naked on the narrow bed, not far away from her. In the room there are only three pieces of furniture: the little table where the woman cleans her guns, the narrow bed where the man lies wrapped in a dingy patchwork quilt, and the creaky wooden chair in which the woman is seated. The only light comes from the window and a small desk lamp sitting on the floor near the foot of the bed. The lamp has a stained-glass shade, but the shade is cracked and so dusty that it's hard to make out any sort of pattern or the particular tints of the glass. The oyster-colored walls are bare, save for a single framed tintype photograph hung above the headboard. Neither the man nor the changeling woman know the provenance of the photograph, and it might have been hanging here since long before either of them were born. It shows a nude woman standing in some sort of washtub or basin, a very large python cradled in her arms, and someone has written the names Biancabella and Samaritana across the bottom of the tintype in sepia ink.

"They're marvelous tales," the young man says very quietly, not precisely contradicting her. All things considered, the changeling woman is not unkind, at least not to him. Tonight, for instance, she brought him a pint bottle of Jacquin's ginger-flavored brandy. She opened it after they fucked, and now he's pleasantly drunk and grateful for the gift, which has helped to push back the cold air and the raw sound of the wind blowing hard around the eaves of the terrible old house on Federal Hill.

"After all the trouble they've caused you," she mutters and shakes her head. The woman wets a bit of fabric with forty-weight Remington bore cleaner, then uses a metal rod to work the cloth back and forth through the barrel of the revolver. She does this several times, then stops and stares at him.

He smiles and stares back, and she wonders, not for the first time, if the things he knows and the months he's spent in the stables might have unhinged his mind. Not many last as long as he's lasted, the men and women kept downstairs, inside the filthy cages built into the sub-basement of the old house.

For more than two centuries now, this place has served as a refuge for the Children of the Cuckoo, those stolen as infants and raised up in the warrens below College Hill to labor and officiate for the Hounds of Cain, to walk abroad in the day-lit world where the ghouls dare not venture. Those trained to see to the Hounds' more prosaic concerns, and to make certain that their secrets *remain* secret. To kill, or only maim, or perhaps merely intimidate, as necessary. In all the city, it is only within the walls of *this* house that the changelings are safe from the watchful eyes of their task-masters. There is no other sanctuary afforded them, no other place where they may do as they please without fear of recrimination.

"It's not such an awful price to pay," he says, "not for the privilege of knowing, beyond any shadow of a doubt, that there are still such wonders among us."

"I'm never going to figure you out," she sighs, and glances at the window again, the window and the subsiding storm, the snow and the heavy winter night crouched above Providence.

"No," he agrees. "I don't think you ever will. Now, do you want to hear the story or not?"

"You didn't grow up on that crap," she says. "It's not the same for you as it is for me."

"You haven't answered my question," he tells her, and considers having another sip from the bottle of brandy. It's still more than half full and sitting on a corner of the little table just beyond the edge of the bed.

"I think, maybe, that's because it's disguising another question altogether, and I'd *prefer* to answer the one that you're *really* asking me." And then she goes back to working on the revolver.

"Fine," the young man says and reaches for the bottle. "Would you please *allow* me to tell you the story?" He sits up and unscrews the plastic cap, then tilts the pint to his lips. She laughs again and nods her head.

"And the truth shall set you free," the changeling woman says, selecting the brass bore brush from her tools.

"You probably meant that to be ironic," he says, twisting the cap back onto the bottle of brandy and returning the bottle to its place on the table. "But I don't take it that way. Finding those books, reading what I read, having seen what I've seen, it truly *has* set me free."

She puts down the bore brush and goes back to watching the snow. "It very nearly got you killed," she says. "But the Hounds took pity, or what they consider pity. So, instead, you live in filth, in a pen, like an animal. Instead, you're a slave and a whore."

"Yes," he replies. "I do. I am. But that doesn't change what I know, nor in any way lessen the sublimity of the knowledge. What has become of me, it's only the *price* of the knowledge."

"I still don't know why they didn't just kill you outright."

"I have no idea," he says. "Perhaps we don't give them enough credit."

The changeling woman laughs, shaking her head again, and she reaches for the ginger brandy. "Yeah, sure. They're sweet as you please, given half the chance. Sweet as strawberry-rhubarb pie. Regular fucking teddy bears, and here *we* are, the two of us, living proof."

"Here we *are*, regardless, and that's more than I expected. May I please tell you the story now. It really is one of the very best, in my opinion."

"They're just stories," she says, "though it's beyond me how you remember them all. You couldn't have had the *Red Book* all that long before they caught on."

"It's one of my favorites, this story."

"I already told you I'd listen, but it better not be 'The Fisherman and the Djinn' again, or 'Gulnare of the Sea,' or any of that silly shit about Ali Baba or Sinbad the Sailor."

"It isn't any of those," he assures her, lying down on his back and staring up at the water stains and cracks in the ceiling.

"And nothing about Esmeribetheda and the damn grey witches."

"It's not," he says.

"I've already told you, I have to be out of here and on my way down to Warwick by three, so you best keep that in mind." She takes a long, hot swallow from the bottle, then wipes her mouth and rubs at her eyes, trying, and failing, to remember the last time that she got a full night's – or day's – sleep.

"I will," he says.

"Then get on with it," she tells him and twists the cap tightly back onto the bottle.

"It's one of the stories that Scheherazade relates to Shahryar and Dinazade, but one that didn't make it into Burton's *The Book of the Thousand Nights and a Night,* or into any of the earlier European translations. I suspect it was originally imported into the *Red Book of Riyadh* from another source, possibly the Persian *Isíhtsöornot* or from the writing of Abd-al-Hazred, though I was never able to confirm this, mind you. It's possible – "

"Just the story, please," she cuts in, trying not to sound annoyed, but sounding annoyed, regardless.

He apologizes and keeps his eyes trained on the ceiling, on the ruined plaster and paint above the bed. He was a scholar, once, and to him the origins of the tales are almost as fascinating as the tales themselves; he has trouble remembering that not everyone shares his enthusiasm.

"I'm listening," she says, prompting him. "The clock's ticking," (even though there is no clock in the room, and she doesn't wear a wristwatch).

And so, his head and belly warm from the brandy, and the howling wind seeming not so close and not so cold, the young man begins his story with the usual preamble. Scheherazade whispering the opening lines of a story to her sister; the King awakening, and at once captivated by what he hears; the Queen consort informing Shahryar, regretfully, that the sun is rising, and so her beheading would mean that she'd be unable to conclude the tale; and, finally, the King granting yet another stay of execution, so that he might hear the remainder of her cliffhanger.

"You *think* the silly bastard would see through her maneuvers, sooner or later," the changeling woman says. She's gone back to cleaning her revolver. "No one ever bothers to point out what an idiot this Sassanid 'king of kings' must have been."

"Most don't even remember that he *is* Sassanid, and therefore Zoroastrian, instead of Muslim."

"That's because most don't give two shits," she replies, then turns her attention to the revolver's extractor assembly.

He agrees this is true and then resumes his story.

"This was, of course, long, long before the war between the Ghūl and the other races of the Djinn – the *Ifrit,* the *Sila,* and the *Marid.* In those days, the men of the desert still looked upon all the Djinn as gods, though they'd already learned to fear the night shades and guarded their children and the graves of their dead against them. Among all the fates that might befall the soul of a man or woman, to have one's corpse stolen and then devoured by the Ghūl was counted as one of the most gruesome and tragic conceivable. It was thought by many that to be so consumed would mean that the deceased would be taken from the cold sleep of *barzakh,* never to meet with the angels Nakir and Munkar, and so never be interrogated and prepared for Paradise.

"It was thought that the Ghūl, the night shades, were also shape shifters. It was said that they were especially fond of appearing in the form of hyenas, but that they could also come as scorpions, vipers, and even vultures."

"Are you entirely certain that you're not making this up?" the changeling woman asks, without pausing in her work or even glancing at the young man.

"I'm not," he replies. "Not making this up, I mean. Why?"

"Because I know the tales of the *Red Book,* backwards and forwards, as well as any warren rat, and this is the first I've heard about hyenas and vultures and shape shifting, that's why."

"Have you ever read from the book yourself? Have you ever even held a copy in your hands?" There's no challenge in these questions, as the young man has long since learned not to impugn his captors; rather, there's only curiosity, and curiosity is the only thing the changeling woman hears.

"Of course I haven't," she replies. "It's forbidden. We learn the book, what we are told we need to know of it, from the ghouls."

He's silent a moment, listening to the rumble of a snow plow passing by somewhere not far away, and the young man considers the glamours that keep the terrible old house on Federal Hill, and its inhabitants and prisoners, hidden in plain view.

"I'm telling you what I read," he says, and when she doesn't argue, he goes back to the story.

"In those days, there lived a woman to whom Allah had gifted seven sons. Naturally, she was very grateful for them, and yet, regardless, she still desired with all her heart to bear a daughter. So she asked this of Allah, that she might give birth to a baby girl.

"And soon afterwards, she was walking alone through a marketplace, this woman with seven sons. When she saw a mound of white goat cheese, she was moved by the sight so that she exclaimed, 'My Lord Allah! Give me,

I entreat thee, a daughter every bit as white and fair and beautiful as this goat's cheese, and I will call her Ijbeyneh.'

"Allah heard her prayer, and very soon she was sent an exceedingly beautiful girl, with skin as fair as goat-milk cheese, a daughter with the delicate throat of a gazelle, with blue eyes like blazing sapphires, and hair as black as pitch. The woman kept her word, and the girl was named Ijbeyneh. Everyone in the village who chanced to look upon her loved her at once and without reservation, with the exception of the daughters of her mother's sisters, her cousins, and *they* were very jealous."

"She was named after goat cheese?" the changeling woman asks, and she glares at the man on the bed, naked and wrapped in the threadbare patchwork quilt.

"That's what the *Red Book* says," he replies. "That's what I read there."

She laughs, and shakes her head skeptically, then tells him to continue.

"So, when she was seven, Ijbeyneh begged her jealous cousins to please take her with them on one of their walks in the forest. The girl was innocent and had no inkling of her cousins' true feelings for her. They often went deep into the forest, to pick the fruit and berries there, and came back with tales of the marvels they saw. Anyway, the cousins agreed, much to the girl's delight, and Ijbeyneh went with them. The day passed quickly, and when she'd filled her *tarbi'ah* with ripe berries – "

"Wait, what?" the changeling woman interrupts, and she sets aside the revolver's extractor assembly and the worn-out toothbrush she's been using to clean it. "She filled her what with berries?"

"Her *tarbi'ah,*" the man answers patiently. "It's a traditional linen veil, still worn, for example, by Palestinian women."

The changeling nods and stares out the single window in the room, and she frowns when she sees that it's snowing hard again. "You can bet the roads are going to be a bitch," she says.

Then, when a minute or two has passed, and she hasn't said anything more, the lean young man asks her if he can please go on with the story.

"Sure," she replies, wondering if she should call the Bailiff and suggest that maybe the drive to Warwick, and what she has to do there, could be postponed until the roads are clear.

"As I was saying," the man on the bed continues, "Ijbeyneh left her berries at the base of a tree and, on her own, wandered off to pick the wildflowers growing between the enormous sycamore figs. But, later, when she returned, she found that her *tarbi'ah* was filled with ugly, poisonous

160

berries, instead of the delicious, sweet ones she'd worked so hard to gather. Also, her jealous cousins were gone, and she was left alone in the forest. She wandered through the hills, calling out to them, but no one and nothing answered her calls, except for the birds and a few buzzing insects. Finally, when Ijbeyneh tried to find her way home again, she discovered that she'd strayed from the trail, and she quickly became disoriented and lost in the forest.

"When the sun had set, a fearsome Ghūl woman crept up from a cave and came upon her. Surely, the ghoul would have devoured Ijbeyneh, but, as the child was Allah's gift to her mother, she was protected, after a fashion. Instead of eating the girl, the ghoul found her heart was filled with pity for her. And, seeing the ghoul, Ijbeyneh cried out, 'Oh, my Aunt! Please tell me which way my cousins have gone! And which way is home!' The ghoul answered her, 'I don't know, Beloved, but come back and live with me, at least until your cousins return for you.'

"Ijbeyneh agreed, and the *ghoūlah* took her to a cave near the very summit of the mountain. There, the child became a shepherdess, and, as the years passed – for her cousins never did come back – the Ghūl grew extremely fond of her. Every night, when the ghoul woman hunted in the forest, and in the rocky desert beyond the forest, she brought only her choicest kills back to the girl. The *ghoūlah* would not ever eat until after the girl had eaten. And in a hundred other ways, the Djinn tried to make Ijbeyneh happy and her life a comfortable one. For her, fine silks and ointments were stolen from caravans bound for the city, and for her, too, the ghoul woman found precious stones deep in the cave and polished them for Ijbeyneh to wear. In many ways, as the months came and went, the fair child grew in habit very much like her mistress, learning, for example, to eat the flesh of men and women taken from the village graves that the ghoul sometimes robbed.

"But, despite the *ghoūlah*'s best and most determined efforts, despite her love and constant attentions, the girl was not ever happy there on the mountain. Often, she wept for her home and her parents, and she cursed her jealous, traitorous cousins. Meanwhile, in the village, all the many white doves belonging to her father, which Ijbeyneh had fed and tended before she was lost, longed endlessly for the missing daughter's return. They did not coo, as they once had. And whenever they flew, their eyes searched all the wide land for any sign of her. In time, a day came when the doves espied the girl, there on the mountainside, minding the *ghoūlah*'s flock.

Even though she was now a young woman, they recognized her immediately, and they went straight away to Ijbeyneh, lighting on the ground all about her, and showed their joy at having found her alive and well."

"This is starting to sound more like something you looted from Charles Perrault or the Brothers Grimm," the changeling woman says. She presses a thumb gently to the pistol's extractor rod and begins to clean the underside of the assembly.

"I assure you that I didn't," the young man tells her. "But, if you wish for me to stop – "

"I didn't fucking *say* that, now did I?"

"No, you didn't."

"Whatever and whoever you were before," the woman says, "you are *now* a whore, a whore who doesn't even get paid for his services, a whore whom I could kill and no one would even bother to ask why. So don't second-guess me, or presume what I do and don't want. Just finish the damned story."

The man nods. This is nothing he hasn't heard before, from her lips and from the lips of others. These are words that have become casual, that have long since lost their sting and become no more to him than any other truism: crows are black, water's wet, fire burns, and he's a slave in the service of the changelings, completely at their mercy, and will be until the day he's outlived his usefulness.

"Should I remind you I don't have all night," the woman mutters, trying to scrub away an especially stubborn and all-but inaccessible bit of grime. "The doves found the girl named after goat cheese, and then what?"

The young man rolls over on his right side, rolling towards the changeling woman, and he reaches for the bottle of brandy. The bed springs squeak loudly. "When she saw them," he says, "Ijbeyneh wept with delight, and she commanded them, 'O ye doves of my mother and of my father, go to them and tell them that their daughter, the dear one, keeps sheep in the high meadows of the mountain. Let them know I have not perished.' And, at once, they flew back to the village.

"Now, years before, the jealous cousins had claimed that the girl had been lost in the forest, though sometimes they told the story so that she'd been set upon by jackals, or a lion, and eaten alive. Her father and her brothers, her uncles and many other men from the village, had searched the hills for her. Her mother took the blame upon herself, weeping endlessly and declaring that this was Allah's curse upon her for not having been content with seven sons."

The lean young man pauses to sip from the rim of the bottle of brandy, and for a moment he watches the changeling clean her gun. The wind is blowing so hard now that even the liquor cannot keep a shiver at bay, and he wraps himself tighter in the frayed quilt.

"As I said, the doves had stopped cooing, when they were no longer cared for by Ijbeyneh. However, after they found her on the mountain, their disposition suddenly changed. The birds ceased to mourn and became lively again. What's more, it seemed as though they were endeavoring to communicate something to their keepers. A neighbor, struck by the very odd behavior of the doves, convinced Ijbeyneh's father he should learn which way the birds flew every day. He did this, and when he was sure, he gathered together the brothers and the uncles and all those in the village who still adored the fair girl, and, together, this band followed the doves deep into the mountains and up to the high grazing meadows.

"But it had never been Ijbeyneh's intention to be rescued. She'd only wished to have her parents know that she'd not died. In the year's since the Djinn had taken her in, the girl had grown to love the *ghoŭlah,* and had even consented to become the night shade's concubine. Her home was no longer her father's house, or the safety of the village, but the wild mountainside and the grotto where the *ghoŭlah,* whom she still called Aunt, pampered her and taught her dark secrets unknown to the sons and daughters of Allah."

"Stop," the changeling woman says, and she puts down the gun and the oily scrap of linen she'd been scrubbing at it with. She turns in her chair and glowers at the young man, who does as he's been told, and is now having another sip of the ginger brandy.

"You said that the *ghoŭlah* had *failed* to make her happy. But now you're saying that they're lovers, and that goat-cheese girl doesn't want to be rescued and go home to mamma and papa?"

The young man nods his head and again screws the cap back onto the pint bottle. "Yes," he says. "You're right. But the contradiction is present in the *Red Book of Riyadh.* I'm only repeating it. It's possible that Ijbeyneh had a change of heart somewhere along the way that the original author failed to note, or that whoever transcribed the story from an older text simply got it wrong. At any rate, I *am* telling the tale just as the book records it. But, if you'd prefer, I'll gladly backtrack and tell it so that the narrative is more consistent."

The changeling woman scowls and sighs and tells him no, just get on with it, and so he does.

"When Ijbeyneh saw the men coming up the mountain, she knew, of course, that she'd made a dire mistake speaking with the doves as she had. She understood that the *ghoūlah* would either destroy her father and brothers and uncles – whom she did still care for – or else *they* would succeed in killing her beloved Djinn. Wishing to forestall any such bloodshed, Ijbeyneh abandoned her sheep and raced back to the cave where her Aunt was sleeping. She woke the ghoul in time to warn her that men from the village had learned, somehow, that the fair daughter of the woman with seven sons still lived, and now these men were quickly approaching."

"Had learned *somehow*," the changeling woman mutters. "Lying little cunt."

"A lie of omission, at most," the young man says. "But, regardless, her Aunt told her that, rather than confront the men, there was another way out of the grotto. Or, more precisely, there was a boulder that when rolled back would reveal stairs cut into the limestone, leading down into a great cavern, where an underground lake lapped at subterranean shores. The *ghoūlah* said there was a boat there that would ferry them to safety, to the hidden realm of the Ghūl, which no man would ever find.

"You can well imagine Ijbeyneh's profound relief upon hearing this, for she'd already resigned herself to either a violent death fighting at the side of her mistress or to watching as the men from her family were slaughtered and then having little choice but to do what was expected of her and dine upon their remains."

"Poor baby," the changeling woman laughs. Satisfied that the revolver's extractor assembly is clean, she goes to work brushing out the cylinder.

"Her Aunt told her to get what few belongings she wished to carry with them, though Ijbeyneh protested that there wasn't time. The *ghoūlah* woman kissed her and told her not to worry, that men were, by nature, slow to find the things they sought, and, since there were so many caves in the mountainside, it was unlikely these men would hit upon the one they were looking for right off. Reluctantly, still convinced they should not be wasting time, the girl gathered up some of the gems that her Aunt had given her, and some of her favorite silks, a crocodile's tooth, the dagger she'd carved from a vizier's shin bone, and a few other things. She bundled them together inside a piece of camel hide while the *ghoūlah* crouched in the mouth of the cave and kept watch for the men.

"When she was done, the *ghoŭlah* led her deeper into the grotto than Ijbeyneh had ever gone before. And just as she heard the triumphant shouts of her own father and her seven brothers, who had discovered the entry to the *ghoŭlah*'s cave, the girl and the Djinn reached the immense boulder concealing the path down to the secret sea below the hills. The *ghoŭlah*, fearing now that they *had* indeed tarried too long, shoved against the stone with all her might, only to discover that it wouldn't budge."

The changeling woman's cell phone rings, then, and she sets the revolver down and makes an annoyed, dismissive motion with her left hand, silencing the young man on the bed. He rolls back over on his back and resumes his examination of the plaster ceiling while she talks to whoever's on the other end. The call lasts less than a minute, and when it's done, the woman sits staring out the window, cursing the snow.

"You have to go now," the young man says.

"Yeah, I have to go now. That was fucking Pentecost. I'll have someone take you back down to the stables. You can have whatever's left of the brandy. I'll tell them not to take it from you."

"Thank you," he says, keeping his eyes on the ceiling, wishing he could have spent the whole night Above, wishing she'd have stayed in bed after they made love, instead of insisting that she needed to clean the revolver.

He lies still, listening to the January wind, and doesn't talk while she hastily reassembles the gun. There's one crack in the plaster that leads all the way from the top of the doorframe, across the ceiling, to the wall above the headboard, and it reminds him of a river glimpsed from orbit, wending its way along a wide desert plain.

"So," the changeling woman says, "what happened? Did they get away? Or did goat-cheese girl's father catch up with them?"

"It's complicated," he replies.

"Is it now?"

"Very much so," he says. "A shame I don't have time to finish the story. Maybe…"

"…next time?" she asks and spares the young man a sidewise glance. "You are really *not* going to tell me how it all ends, are you?"

"I fear that rushing it would spoil the tale," the young man says, "and all I have left to me are these stories. Surely you understand."

"Fine. If that's the way you want to play, Scheherazade, and if we're *both* lucky enough to live through another goddamn day."

"Just keep your head down," he whispers, trying not to think about the stables below the terrible old house, or whatever it is the changeling woman will do before dawn. "And I'll do the same, to the best of my abilities."

And five minutes later, when she's gone out into the snowy, windy night, he lies alone on the bed with his bottle of ginger-flavored brandy and tries to get a few minutes sleep, there in the relative warmth and comfort of the shabby room, before they come to take him downstairs again.

The Bone's Prayer

The sea pronounces something, over and over, in a hoarse whisper;
I cannot quite make it out.

Annie Dillard

1.

She has been walking the beach all afternoon, which isn't unusual for days when she cannot write. And there have been several dry days now in a row, one following wordlessly after the next. A mute procession of empty hours, or, worse still, a procession of hours spent carefully composing sentences and paragraphs that briefly deceive her into thinking that the drought has finally passed. But then she reads back over the pages, and the prose thuds and clangs artlessly against itself, or it leads off somewhere she has not the time nor the skill nor the inclination to follow. She has deadlines, and bills, and the expectations of readers, and all these things must be factored into the question of whether a productive hour is, indeed, productive.

It becomes intolerable, the mute procession and the false starts, the cigarettes and coffee and all those books silently watching her from their places on the shelves that line her office. And, so, she eventually, inevitably, goes to the beach, which is not so very far away, hardly an hour's drive south from the city. She goes to the beach, and she tries very hard not to think of what isn't getting written. She tries only to hear the waves, the gulls and cormorants, the wind, tries to take in so much of the sand and the sky and the blue-green sea that there is no room remaining for her anxieties.

And sometimes it even works.

Today is a Thursday near the end of winter, and there are violent gusts off the sound that bite straight through her gloves and her long wool coat.

Gusts that have twice now almost managed to dislodge the fleece-lined cap with flaps to keep her ears warm. Thick clouds the color of Wedgwood china hide the sun and threaten snow. But, thanks to the inclement weather, she has the beach all to herself, and that more than makes up for the discomfort. This solitude, like the breathy rhythm of the surf and the smell of the incoming tide, is a balm. She begins at Moonstone Beach and walks the mile or so south and west to the scatter of abandoned summer cottages at Greenhill Point. Then she walks back, following the narrow strip of beach stretching between Block Island Sound and the low dunes dividing the beach from Card Pond.

The estuary is frozen solid, and when she climbs the dunes and stares out across the ice, there are flocks of mallards there, and Canadian geese, and a few swans wandering disconsolately about, looking lost. In the summer, the land around the salt pond is a verdant tangle of dog roses, poison ivy, greenbriers, and goldenrod. But now it is ringed by a homogenous brown snarl, and the only sign of green anywhere in this landscape are a few spruce trees and red cedars, dotting the southern edge of the forest to the north.

She turns back towards the sea and the cobble-strewn sand. It doesn't seem to her that the sea changes its hues with the season. Today, it wears the same restless shade of celadon that it wears in June, quickly darkening to a Persian blue where the water begins to grow deep, only a little ways out from shore. Ever shifting, never still, it is her only constant, nonetheless. It is her comfort, the sight of the sea, even in a month as bleak and dead as this.

She begins gathering a handful of pebbles, meaning to carry them back towards the dunes and find a dry place to sit, hopefully somewhere out of the worst of the wind. This beach is somewhat famous for the pebbles that fetch up here from submerged outcroppings of igneous stone, earth that was the molten-hot core of a mountain range millions of years before the coming of the dinosaurs. Here and there among the polished lumps of granite are the milky white moonstones that give the beach its name. She used to collect them, until she had a hundred or so, and they lost their novelty. There are also strands of kelp and bladderwrack, the claws, carapaces, and jointed legs of dismembered crabs and lobsters, an occasional mermaid's purse – all the usual detritus. In the summer months, there would be added to this an assortment of human jetsam – water bottles, beer cans, stray flip-flops, styrofoam cups, and all manner of plastic refuse – the thoughtless filth that people leave behind. And this is another reason that she prefers the beach in winter.

She has selected six pebbles, and is looking for a seventh (having decided she would choose seven and only seven), when she spots a small, peculiar stone. It's shaped like a teardrop and is the color of pea soup. The stone glistens wetly in the dim afternoon light, and she can clearly see that there are markings etched deeply into its smooth surface. One of them looks a bit like a left-facing swastika, and another reminds her of a Greek *ichthus*. For a moment, the stone strikes her as something repulsive, like coming upon a rotting fish or a discarded prophylactic, and she draws her hand back. But that first impression quickly passes, and soon she's at a loss even to account for it. It is some manner of remarkable artifact, whether very old or newly crafted, and she adds it to the six pebbles in her hand before turning once more towards the frozen expanse of Card Pond.

2.

It's Friday evening, two days after her trip from Providence to the beach. Usually, she looks forward to Fridays, because on Friday nights Sammie almost always stops by after work. Sammie is the closest thing she has to a close friend, and, from time to time, they've been lovers, as well. The writer, whose name is Edith (though that isn't the name that appears on the covers of her novels), is not an outgoing person. Crowds make her nervous, and she avoids bars and nightclubs, and even dreads trips to the market. She orders everything she can off the internet – clothing, books, CDs, DVDs, electronics – because she hates malls and shopping centers. She hates the thought of being seen. To her knowledge, psychiatrists have yet to coin a term for people who have a morbid fear of being looked at, but she figures *antisocial* is accurate enough. However, most times, she enjoys having Sammie around, and Sammie never gets angry when Edith needs to be left alone for a week or two.

They've been mistaken for sisters, despite the fact that they really don't look very much alike. Sammie is two or three inches taller and has striking jet-black hair just beginning to show strands of grey. Edith's hair in an unremarkable dishwater blonde. Sammie's eyes are a bright hazel green, and Edith's are a dull brown. Sammie has delicate hands and the long, tapered fingers of a pianist, and Edith's hands are thick, her fingers stubby. She keeps her nails chewed down to the quick, and there are nicotine stains on her skin. Sammie quit smoking years ago, before they met.

"Well, it was just lying there on the sand," Edith says. "And it really doesn't look all that old."

"It's a rock," Sammie replies, still peering at the peculiar greenish stone, holding it up to the lamp on the table next to Edith's bed. "What do you mean, it doesn't look old? All rocks look old to me."

"The carving, I mean," Edith replies, trying to decide if she really wants another of the stale petite madeleines that Sammie brought with her; they taste faintly of lemon extract and are shaped like scallop shells. "I mean the *carving* in the rock looks fresh. If it had been rolling around in the ocean for any time at all the edges would be worn smooth by now."

"I think it's soapstone," Sammie says and turns the pebble over and over, examining the marks on it. "But I don't think you find soapstone around here."

"Like I was saying, I figure someone bought it in a shop somewhere and lost it. Maybe it was their lucky charm. Or maybe it didn't mean anything much to them."

"It feels funny," Sammie says, and before Edith can ask her to explain what she means, Sammie adds. "Slippery. Oily. Slick. You know?"

"I haven't noticed that," Edith says, although she has. The lie surprises her, and she can't imagine why she didn't just admit that she's also noticed the slithery sensation she gets whenever she holds the stone for more than a minute or two.

"You should show it to someone. A geologist or an archaeologist or someone who knows about this stuff."

"I honestly don't think it's very old," Edith replies, deciding against a fourth madeleine. Instead, she lights a cigarette and thinks about going to the kitchen for a beer. "If I took it to an archaeologist, they'd probably tell me the thing was bought for five bucks in a souvenir shop in Misquamicut."

"I really don't like the way it feels," Sammie says.

"Then put it down."

"Is that supposed to be a Jesus fish?" Sammie asks, pointing to the symbol that reminded Edith of an *ichthus*.

"Sort of looks like one," Edith replies.

"And *this* one, this one right here," Sammie says and taps the nail of her index finger against the stone. "That looks like astrology, the symbol for Neptune."

"I thought it was a trident, or a pitchfork," Edith sighs, wishing Sammie would put the stone away so they could talk about something else, almost anything else at all. The stone makes her uneasy, and three times in two days she's almost thrown it into the trash so she wouldn't have to think about it or look at it anymore. "Can we please talk about something else for a while? You've been gawking at that awful thing for half an hour now."

Sammie turns her head, looking away from the stone, looking over her left shoulder at Edith. She's frowning slightly, and her neatly waxed eyebrows are furrowed.

"You *asked* me what I thought of it," she says, sounding more defensive than annoyed, more confused than angry. *"You're* the one who started this."

"It's not like I meant to find it, you know."

"It's not like you had to bring it home, either."

Sammie watches her a moment or two longer, then turns back to the tear-shaped stone.

"This one is a sun cross," she says, indicating another of the symbols. "Here, the cross held inside a circle. It's something else you see in astrology, the sign for the earth."

"I never knew you were into horoscopes," Edith says, and she takes a long drag on her cigarette and holds the smoke in her lungs until she begins to feel dizzy. Then she exhales through her nostrils.

"Why does it bother you?" Sammie asks.

"I never said it did."

"You just called it 'that awful thing,' didn't you?"

"I'm going to get a beer," Edith tells her. "Do you want one, as long as I'm up."

"Sure," Sammie says and nods, not looking away from the stone. "I'd love a beer, as long as you're up."

Edith stands and pulls her bathrobe closed, tugging roughly at the terrycloth belt. The robe is a buttery yellow and has small blue ducks printed on it. "You can have it if you want it," she tells Sammie, who frowns softly, then sets the stone down on the bedside table.

"No," she replies. "It's yours. You found it, so you should keep it. Besides, it's a hell of a lot more interesting than most of the junk you haul back from the shore. At least this time the house doesn't smell like dead fish and seaweed. But I still say you should find an archaeologist to take a look at it. Might turn out to be something rare."

"Perhaps," Edith says. "But I was just thinking, maybe it wasn't lost. Maybe someone got rid of it on purpose."

"Anything's possible."

"I'm afraid all I have is Heineken," Edith says, nodding towards the kitchen.

"Heineken's fine by me. Moochers can't be choosers."

"I meant to get something else, because I know you don't like Heineken. But I haven't been to the store in a few days."

"The Heineken's fine, really. I promise."

Edith manages the ghost of a smile, then goes to the kitchen, leaving Sammie (whose birth name is Samantha, but everyone knows better than to call her that) alone in the bedroom with the peculiar greenish stone. Neither of them mentions it again that night, and later, for the first time in almost three weeks, they make love.

3.

"Well, for one thing, continents don't just *sink,*" Edith says, and she's beginning to suspect that she might only be dreaming. She's sitting on the closed toilet lid in her tiny bathroom, and Sammie is standing up in the claw-foot tub. Sammie was the one who started talking about Atlantis, and then Mu and Madame Blavatsky's Lemuria.

"And I read about another one," she says. "When I was a kid, I found a book in the library, *Mysteries of the Sea,* or something like that. Maybe one of those *Time-Life* series. Anyhow, one of the stories was about a ship finding an uncharted island somewhere in the South Pacific, back in the twenties, I think. They found an island, complete with the ruins of a gigantic city, but then the whole thing sank in an earthquake. Islands can sink, right?" she asks.

"Not overnight," Edith says, more interested in watching Sammie bathe than all this nonsense about lost worlds.

"What about Krakatoa? Or Santorini?"

"Those were both volcanic eruptions. And the islands didn't sink, they exploded. *Boom,*" and Edith makes a violent motion in the air with her right hand. "For that matter, neither was completely submerged."

"Sometimes you talk like a scientist," Sammie says, and she stares down at the water in the cast-iron tub.

"Are you saying I'm pedantic?"

"No, I'm not saying that. It's kind of sexy, actually. Big brains get me wet."

172

There's a sudden fluttering noise in the hallway, and Edith looks in that direction. The bathroom door is standing half open, but the hallway's too dark to see whatever might have made the sound.

"Okay," Sammie continues, "so maybe, instead, there have been cities that never sank, because the things that built them never lived on land. Or maybe they lived on land a long time ago, but then returned to the water. You know, like whales and dolphins."

Edith frowns and turns back to the tub. "You're sort of just making this up as you go along, aren't you?"

"Does that matter?" Sammie asks her.

"Whales don't build cities," Edith says, and there's a finality in her voice that *should* have been sufficient to steer the conversation in another direction. But when Sammie's been drinking and gets something in her head, she can go on about it for hours.

"Whales sing songs," she says. "And maybe if we were able to understand those songs, we'd know about whoever built the cities."

Edith frowns at her, trying not to think about the fluttering noise from the hall. "If we could understand those songs," she says, "I suspect we'd mostly hear about horny whales and which sort of krill tastes the best."

"Maybe," Sammie replies, and then she shrugs her narrow shoulders. "But the whales *would* know about the cities. Especially sperm whales, because they dive so deep and all."

"You're still working from an *a priori* assumption that the cities have ever existed. You're trying to find evidence to solve an imaginary problem."

Sammie holds up the greenish stone from the beach, then, as if it offers some refutation, or maybe she thinks Edith has forgotten about it. In the light from the fluorescent bulb above the sink, the stone looks greasy. Sammie's fingers look greasy, too, as if something has seeped out of the rock and stained her hands.

I really don't like the way it feels.

"It's just something one of the summer people dropped," Edith says, wondering why Sammie didn't leave the stone lying on the table beside the bed, why she's in the tub with it. "The thing was probably made on an Indian reservation in Arizona. It's just a piece of junk."

"Can't you hear it?" Sammie asks her. "If you listen very closely, it's singing. Not the same song that whales sing, but it's singing, all the same."

"Stones don't sing," Edith says, "no matter what someone's carved on them. I don't hear anything at all."

Sammie looks mildly disappointed, and she shrugs again. "Well, I hear it. I've been hearing it all night. It's almost a lamentation. A dirge. And I don't just hear it, Edith, I can *feel* it. In my bones, I can feel it."

"Really, I don't know what you mean," Edith says, and before she can add, *and I don't care, either,* Sammie is already talking again.

"My body hears the song. Every cell in my body hears the song, and it's like they want to answer. It's a song the ocean sings, that the ocean has always *been* singing. But, suddenly, my body remembers it, from a very, very long time ago, I think. Back when there were still only fish, maybe, and nothing had crawled out to live on the land."

"You were making more sense with Atlantis and the theosophists," Edith sighs. She sits there on the toilet, staring at the greasy-looking stone in Sammie's greasy-looking hands. The rock's surface is iridescent, and it shimmers with a riot of colors, a rainbow film on an oil-slick mud puddle, or the nacreous lining of an abalone shell. Sammie's hands have become iridescent, as well, and she's saying something about inherited memories, the collective unconscious, somatic and genetic recollection. Edith wants to ask her, *Now who sounds like a scientist?* But she doesn't.

"We don't know what's down there," Sammie says. "Not really. I read somewhere that we know more about the surface of the moon than about the deep sea. Did you even know that? Do you know about the Marianas Trench? It's so deep, Edith, that if you were to set Mount Everest at the bottom, there would still be more than a mile of water covering the mountaintop."

"Yes, I know a little about the Marianas Trench," Edith replies, trying to be patient without trying to *sound* like she's having to try to be patient. And that's when Sammie stops rolling the tear-shaped stone between her fingers and quickly slips it down to the clean-shaven space between her legs and into her vagina. There's no time for Edith to try to stop her.

"Do you think that was such a good idea?" she asks.

Sammie only smiles back, a furtive sort of smile, and doesn't answer the question. But she finally sits down in the tub, and Edith sees that where only a few moments before the water was clear and clean, now it has become murky, and dark strands of kelp float on the surface. There's a sharp crust of tiny barnacles clinging to the white enamel, and she opens her mouth to tell Sammie to be careful, that they're sharp, and she could cut herself. But then the fluttering noise comes from the hallway again, louder than before, and, hearing it, she's afraid to say anything at all.

"It's a message in a bottle," Sammie whispers. "Or those golden phonograph records they sent off on the *Voyager* probes. Messages like that, no one ever expects to get an answer, but we keep sending them off, anyway."

"I don't hear anything," Edith lies.

"Then I suggest you should try listening more closely. It's the most beautiful song I've ever heard. And it's taken so terribly long to get here."

Edith shuts her eyes and smells the ocean, and she smells an evaporating tide pool trapped between rime-scarred boulders, and a salt-marsh mudflat, and all the soft, pale creatures that live in the briny ooze, and, last of all, the sweet hint of pink dog roses in the air. She keeps her eyes shut tightly, straining not to hear the strange, unpleasant commotion in the hallway, which sounds nothing at all like any music she's ever heard. And for a hopeful moment, Edith begins to believe she's waking up, before the dream abruptly drops away beneath her feet, the dream and the tile floor of the bathroom, and she understands that the water's only getting deeper.

4.

There are dreams that stack in tiers, like a gaily frosted birthday cake, and, too, there are dreams that sit nested snuggly one within the other, the way that Russian matryoshka dolls may be opened to reveal a regression of inner dolls. Edith cannot say if *this* dream is falling into itself, or merely progressing from tier to tier, whether up or down. She is sitting on the sand among the cobbles at Moonstone Beach, listening to the surf. Above her, the sky is low and looks like curdled milk. In her right hand, she's holding a stick that the retreating tide left stranded, and all about her, she's traced the designs from the peculiar greenish stone. They form a sort of mandala, and she sits at its center. If asked, she could not say whether the circle is meant to contain her or to protect her. Possibly, it's meant to do both. Possibly, it is insufficient to either task.

The wind is the half-heard voice of the beach, or it's the voice of the sea. Behind her, it rattles the dry reeds at the edge of Card Pond, and before her, it whips the crests of the breakers into a fine spray.

There is something else there with her, tucked in amongst the sand and the cobbles and the symbols she's traced on the shore. Something that desperately needs to be seen, and that would have her gaze upon nothing else. But she doesn't look at it, not yet. She will *not* look at it until she can no longer bear the pain that comes from averting her eyes.

Only a few moments ago, Sammie was standing somewhere behind her, standing very near, and talking about the January thirteen winters before, when a tank barge and a tug ran aground here. The barge spilled more than eight hundred thousand gallons of toxic heating oil into the sea and onto the beach. The name of the barge was *North Cape,* and the tug was named *Scandia,* and during a storm they'd run afoul of the rocks in the shallows just offshore. Both Card and Trustom ponds were contaminated by the spill, and the beach was littered with the corpses of tens of millions of poisoned sea birds, lobsters, surf clams, and starfish.

"It was a massacre," Sammie said, before she stopped talking. There was an unmistakable trace of bitterness in her voice, Edith thought. "She doesn't forget these things. Maybe people do. Maybe the birds come back, and the lobsters come back, and no one tells tourists what happened here, but the *sea* remembers."

Edith asked her if that was why the song from the stone is a dirge, if it laments all the creatures killed in the oil spill. But Sammie said no, that the stone was made to keep the memory of a far more appalling day, one that predated the coming of man and was now otherwise lost to the mind of the world.

"Why are we here?" Edith asked.

"Because you would not hear the song," Sammie replied. She said nothing else after that, and Edith assumes she's alone now, sitting here alone on Moonstone Beach, buffeted by the icy wind and doing her best not to see the thing half buried in the sand only a foot or so away. She understands perfectly well that she's fighting a losing battle.

I will close my eyes, she thinks. *I can't see anything with my eyes shut. I'll close my eyes and keep them closed until I wake up.*

But shutting her eyes only releases the next doll in the stack, so to speak, and Edith finds herself adrift in an all but impenetrable blackness, a blackness that is almost absolute. She recalls, clearly, standing and walking out into Block Island Sound, recalls the freezing saltwater lapping at her ankles, and then her knees, recalls it rushing up her nostrils and down her throat, searing her lungs as she sank. But she was *not* drowned, and maybe that was the magic of the carved stone at work, and maybe it was some other magic, entirely. The currents carried her away from land and into the Atlantic, ferrying her north and east past Cape Cod, and at last she'd left the sheer bluffs of the continental shelf behind. Far below her, hidden in veils of perpetual night, lie flat abyssal plains of clay and silt and diatomaceous slime. She is suspended above them, unable to fall any farther, and yet incapable of ever again rising to the surface.

All around her – over and below and on every side – indistinct shapes come and go. Some are very small, a parade of eyeless fish and curious squid, jellies and other bathypelagic creatures that she knows no names for. Others, though, move by like enormous, half-glimpsed phantoms, and she can only guess at their identity. Some are surely whales, and probably also enormous deep-water sharks and cephalopods. But others are indescribable and plainly much too vast to be any manner of cetacean or squid. Occasionally, she reaches out a hand, and her fingers glide over that alien flesh as it rushes by in the gloom. Sometimes it seems smooth as any silk and other times rough as sandpaper. The haunted, endless night is filled with phantoms, and *I am just one more,* she thinks. *They must wonder at me, too, at what I am, at where so strange a beast could have come from.*

And the next leviathan glares back at her with a bulging ebony eye the size of a dinner plate. There's no pupil in that eye, nor evidence of an iris, nothing to mar such an unfathomable countenance. And then the eye is gone, replaced by a flank adorned with huge photophores, each one glowing with a gentle pale-blue light. The sight delights her, and she extends a hand to stroke the thing as it moves past. And Edith clearly sees the thin, translucent webbing that's grown between her own fingers and the hooked claws that have replaced the nails she chews to nubs. In the muted blue light cast by the bioluminescent creature, she sees that there are fine scales dappling the backs of both her hands, and they shimmer dully, reminding her of the oily, prismatic stone.

Edith opens her eyes, and she is once more merely sitting within the mandala that she's drawn on Moonstone Beach, thirteen years after the wreck of the *North Cape.* She's still clutching the piece of driftwood and shivering in the wind. She looks over her shoulder, hoping to find Sammie there, but sees at once that she's still alone.

"Sam, I don't *know* what I'm *meant* to be listening for," she says, almost shouting to hear herself over the wind. "I don't *know* what it is, but I *am* listening."

When there's no reply, she isn't disappointed or surprised, because she understood well enough that she *wouldn't* be answered. Any answer she needs is right here before her, held within a crab-gnawed and gull-pecked anatomy, that misshapen mound of rotting flesh coughed up by whatever indifferent gods or goddesses or genderless deities call the globe's ocean their domain.

In the sand before her is a slit, and at first she thinks it is no more than some depression fashioned with her own busy fingers. She leans towards it, and now the wind is speaking, though she cannot say that the words are meant for her ears. She cannot say they are meant for any ears at all:

There are stories that have no proper beginning. Stories for which no convenient, familiar "Once upon a time…" praeambulum exists. They may, for instance, be contained within larger stories, interwoven with the finest of gradations, and so setting them apart is a necessarily arbitrary undertaking. Let us say, then, that this story is of that species. Where it truly began is not where we will start its telling, for to attempt such a thing would require a patience and the requisite time for infinite regression. I may say that the sea had a daughter, though she has spent every day of her life on dry land. At once, the tumult of a hundred questions about how such a thing ever came to be will spring to mind. What is the nature of the sea's womb? With what or whom did she or he have congress to find himself or herself with child? What of the midwife? What is the gestation time of all the oceans of the world, or its sperm count, when considered as a single being? And, while we're at it, being, and from which pantheon, do I mean when I say "the sea"? Am I speaking of the incestuous union of Oceanus and his sister Tethys? Do I mean to say Poseidon, or Neptune, Ægir and Rán, or Susanoo of the Shinto, or Arnapkapfaaluk of the Inuit?

I mean only to say the sea.

The sea had a daughter, but she was orphaned. She grew up in a city of men, a city at the mouths of two rivers that flowed down into a wide bay, fed by other rivers and dotted by more than thirty rocky, weathered islands. Here she was a child, and then a young woman. Here, she thought, she would grow to be an old woman. She'd never desired to travel and had never ventured very far inland. She had seen photographs of mountain ranges and read descriptions of the world's great deserts, and that was sufficient.

Edith places the tip of one index finger into the nearer end of the slit in the sand. Except it is not merely sand, though there is something of quartz granules and mica flakes and dark specks of feldspar in its composition. *It is flesh crafted from sand,* she thinks, *or sand painstakingly crafted from flesh.* The gross physiology is self-evident now, the labia majora and labia minora, the glans clitoris and clitoral hood. It weeps, or simply secretes, something not so different from sea foam. And lying within it is the teardrop-shaped stone that Sammie slipped inside herself while standing in the tub.

Do you think that was such a good idea?

It's a message in a bottle. Messages like that, no one ever expects to get an answer, but we keep sending them off, anyway.

And Edith removes the stone from the slit in the sand, which then immediately closes, leaving behind no trace that it was ever actually there. She stares at the spot for a moment, comprehending, and then she flings the stone into the sea. There's no splash; the waves take it back without any sound and without so much as a ripple.

The circuit has been closed, she thinks, though the metaphor strikes her as not entirely appropriate.

She looks to the sky, and sees birds wheeling against the curdled clouds. The dream pushes her back into wakefulness, then, and, for a while, Edith lies still, squinting at the half-light of dawn and listening to a woman sobbing softly somewhere in the room.

5.

When Edith was seven years old, she saw a mermaid. One summer's day, she'd gone on a picnic with the aunt and uncle who raised her (after the death of her parents), to the rocky shore below Beavertail Lighthouse on Conanicut Island. There are tidal pools there, deep and gaping clefts opened between tilted beds of slate and phyllite, and in one of them she saw the mermaid. It rose, suddenly, towards the surface, as if lunging towards her. What most surprised her child's mind was how little it resembled any of the mermaids she'd seen in movies and storybooks, in that it was not a pretty girl with the tail of a fish. Still, she recognized it at once for what it was, if only because there was nothing else it could have been. Also, she was surprised that it seemed so hungry. The mermaid never broke the surface of the pool, but floated just beneath that turbulent, glistening membrane dividing one world from the other.

I may say that the sea had a daughter, though she has spent every day of her life on dry land.

The mermaid watched her for a while, and Edith watched the mermaid. It had black eyes, eyes like holes poked into the night sky, and did not seem to have eyelids of any sort. At least, Edith never saw it blink. And then, as abruptly as it had risen, the mermaid sank back into the deep cleft in the rock, leaving behind nothing for a seven-year-old girl to stare at but the sloshing surface of the pool. Later, she told her aunt and uncle what she'd seen, and they both smiled and laughed (though not unkindly) and explained that it had only been a harbor seal, *not* a mermaid.

When they got back home that evening, her uncle even showed her a color picture of a harbor seal in one of his encyclopedias. It made Edith think of a fat dog that had learned to live in the ocean, and looked nothing whatsoever like the mermaid that had watched her. But she didn't say this to her uncle, because she'd begun to suspect that it was somehow *wrong* to see mermaids, and that any time you saw one, you were expected to agree that what you'd really seen was a harbor seal, instead. Which is what she did. Her aunt and uncle surely had enough trouble without her seeing mermaids that she shouldn't see.

A week later, they had her baptized again.

Her uncle nailed her bedroom window shut.

Her aunt made her say the Lord's Prayer every night before bed and sewed sprigs of dried wormwood into her clothes.

And they never went back down to the rocky place below the lighthouse at Beavertail and always thereafter had their picnics far from the sea.

6.

Edith does not doubt that she's now awake, any more than a moment before she opened her eyes she doubted that she was still dreaming. This is not the next tier, nor merely the next painted wooden doll in the matryoshka's stack. This is the world of her waking, conscious mind, and this time she will not deny that for the sake of sanity or convenience. There has always been too much of lies about her, too much pretend. When her eyes have grown accustomed to the early morning light, she sits up in bed. Sammie is still crying, somewhere in the room, somewhere very close by, and as soon as Edith sits up, she sees her crouching naked on the hardwood floor near the foot of the bed. All around her, the floor is wet. She has her back turned to Edith, and her head is bowed so that her black hair hangs down to the pine floorboards. Edith glances immediately to the little table beside the bed, but the peculiar tear-shaped pebble from Moonstone Beach is gone. She knew that it would be, but she looked anyway. The air in the room smells like a fish market.

Sammie, or the thing that now occupies the place in this universe where Sammie used to be, has stopped sobbing and has begun a ragged sort of trilling chant in no language that Edith knows or thinks she's ever heard. It sounds much more like the winter wind, and like waves rolling against sand, and the screech of herring gulls, than it sounds like human speech. Edith opens her mouth and almost calls out to Sammie, but then she stops herself. The thing on the floor probably wouldn't answer to that name, anyway. And she'd rather not use any of the names to which it might respond.

Its skin is the same murky pea green as the vanished stone and bears all the same marks that were carved into the stone. All the same wounds, each pregnant with significance and connotations that Edith has only just begun to grasp. There is a pentacle – or something almost like a pentacle – cut deeply into each of Sammie's shoulders, and a vertical line of left-facing swastikas decorates the length of her spine. Wherever this new flesh has been sliced open, it leaks a greasy black substance that must be blood. Below the swastikas, there is the symbol that reminded them both of a Greek *ichthus,* centered just above Sammie's ass. Edith cannot help but wonder if Sammie was reborn with these wounds already in place, like birth marks, or if they came later, not so differently than the stigmata of Catholic saints. Or if maybe they're self inflicted, and Edith remembers her own hands in the dream, the sharp claws where her nails had been. In the end, it hardly matters how the marks came to be; the meaning is the same, either way.

Do you think that was such a good idea?

It's a message in a bottle. No one ever expects to get an answer, but we keep sending them off.

"When you're ready," Edith says, almost whispering, "I'll be right here. There's no hurry. I know how long you've been waiting." Then she lies back down and turns to face the wall.

The Peril of Liberated Objects, or The Voyeur's Seduction

Arabella Hopestill can no longer recall, precisely, where or when she acquired the ancient red book. She remembers only that the day was very, very hot, so she assumes it was during the summer, or possibly early autumn. It was a hot day, and the air stank of dust and mothballs and her own sour sweat, and oftentimes she thinks that there were many *other* books involved. It seems, sometimes, there was a sort of necessary trial to gain this treasure, the task of choosing this *one* book from among hundreds or thousands of others. But the truth, which she has not yet even begun to suspect, is that the book acquired *her,* as has always been, and ever shall be, its way. In the millennium since it escaped the dreamlands, it has only once, briefly, been bound by the will of a human being, and, in the end, that man paid dearly for the privilege and the insult.

But Arabella Hopestill knows nothing of the red book's captivity at the hands of that forgotten Italian astrologer and alchemist – now five-hundred years dead and buried in the catacombs beneath Palermo – any more than she knows of the book's origins in the onyx seaport of Inquanok, below the towering, polished walls of the Temple of the Elder Ones. She does not know of the inhuman priests who there guarded it in lightless subterranean chambers. Or of the accident or miscalculation that allowed it to slip, at last, from their watchful gaze and be carried across the sea to Celephaïs in Ooth-Nargai, and from there, in time, to the basalt towers of Dylath-Leen, and on to Nir and Ulthar, and across the green plains bordering the River Skai. Arabella will never guess at the dire pact that allowed the nameless red book to find its way past the priests Nasht and Kaman-Thah in the cavern of flame, then up the seventy steps to the waking world. These things are secrets the book has hidden from all prying eyes and minds, that it might never be delivered back into the hands of its keepers in the Temple of the Elder Ones.

Arabella knows only that she can no longer bear to live without the book. Just the thought of someday losing it brings cold sweats and sleepless nights. She has spent too many years in its company, and is terrified at the prospect of her life devoid of the unspeakable, perverse revelations it readily surrenders whenever she takes it down from its place on a particularly high shelf and opens the red leather covers. The paper is brittle and the yellowish brown of fossil ivory. There is no title page, for the book was never named. There is no author, for it needed none. Indeed, there's not a single written word to be found anywhere inside the volume. It is not a book of letters, but a book of images. One does not simply read the red book. Rather, *it* reads the fondest nightmares and most repressed appetites of those who gaze into it and subsequently shows them what they have always longed to see (even though they may never have been conscious of these longings). In this way, it might fairly be said to be as much a mirror as a book, and Arabella Hopestill, lost and alone and content for the first time in her life, has become a devotee to its endless reflections.

She has little use of any other looking glass, having been convinced when still a young woman that she was too plain to be of interest to any lover, far too humdrum and dim-witted to attract a suitor of any stripe, and hopelessly beyond even the most remote chance for marriage. "Hardly fit for whoring, this one," a comely man said to her, the same year she turned twenty. He told her that, spoke those six words, then laughed, and whatever atrophied stub of dignity and self-worth had managed to survive the first two decades of her life was entirely consumed in that instant.

The book has become her lover, or so she sometimes pretends. The book has become all she will ever need.

This evening in August, Arabella lays the book on a table near an open window, so that she can feel and smell the cool salt breeze blowing in off the harbor. There's no light in the room but the feeble glow of the moon (two nights past the first quarter), getting in through that window. She's learned that the book is at its most forthcoming when kept away from the harsh glare of electric bulbs, and that even candlelight can mute the visions it offers up. She opens it at random, seeking no particular page, and there's a faint whistling sort of noise, as though she has unsealed a vacuum, but it only lasts a moment. Then the room is quiet, save the sound of the traffic on the street below and muffled voices from the apartment next door, the songs of night birds, and the eager pounding of her own caged heart.

"Show me," she whispers. "Show me something I haven't seen before. Show me something new, and something awful."

And, immediately, the book obliges, as it always does. The blank page on Arabella's right goes suddenly sooty and strangely translucent. She has the distinct impression that some inner, half-concealed luminosity is struggling to tear itself free of the paper, something caught for unknown eons between the covers like a wasp sealed in a lump of amber. If it *is* a struggle, and not merely an overture before the curtain rises, it never lasts long, and seconds later she's gazing into and *through* the red book, at a small meadow surrounded on all sides by spruces and oaks grown so lofty their uppermost boughs seem to rasp at the exposed belly of the sky. Across the green meadow, violet blooms of columbine compete with anemones and starry yellow flowers that Arabella doesn't recognize. There's a wide brook winding through the meadow and its banks are muddy and crowded with reeds, starwort, and water-crowfoot. Here and there, the brook ripples and furls as it glides smoothly over a barely submerged outcropping of stone.

"Something *awful*," she says again, as though it were possible the book misunderstood the first time.

And then she sees the unicorn and the maiden, not far from the brook. They must surely have been there all along, but, somehow, she didn't see them before. The woman is very young, and her dress, which hangs from her in shreds, seems to have been woven of golden thread, the way the tatters shine beneath the bright sun falling across the meadow. Even the muddy spatters do not seem to diminish the gleam of that golden dress. The woman is down on her hands and knees, and her long auburn hair hides her face from view. She seems to grip the earth as if she's afraid of falling. Not down, for surely she cannot fall any farther down, but up, into the wide sky sprawling blue and vacant and hungry above the meadow. Her fingers are sunk deeply into the mud.

"Yes," Arabella whispers. "Thank you. Yes." She once dreamed this scene, many years ago, though she has no recollection of the dream. The book knows all the dreams of humanity, and of many other beings, besides, and vomits them forth whenever it sees fit.

This unicorn is a *true* unicorn, not merely a white mare with a horn sprouting from its skull. In equal measure it resembles a billy-goat or a doe, or some fabulous species of white antelope, as much as it resembles any horse. Its restless tail is very like that of a lion, and the spiraling horn that is its namesake could have been plucked from the upper left maxilla of a bull narwhal. It stands over the woman, snorting and stamping at the muddy ground with its cloven hooves. Its prodigious cock is almost the same exact shade of red as the leather in which the book was bound. The unicorn bares its teeth, and when it snorts steam seems to billow from its flaring nostrils.

So, this is the scene being played out upon the page for Arabella, the fallen woman trampled beneath the feet of an angry, rutting unicorn. And Arabella looks as closely as she can, squinting to note each and every detail, no matter how terrible or minute or seemingly inconsequential, drinking it all in, for she's learned that the book never gives up the same vision twice. And this is one she knows she'll want to savor again and again and again.

The unicorn bows its shaggy head, and with that gleaming horn, tears away what's left of the golden dress. With another swipe of the horn, it leaves a deep gash in the pale flesh of the woman's lower back. She screams, in pain and fear, and then the unicorn mounts her. She tries to struggle free, to shake the beast off and crawl towards the brook. But thick roots burst from the mire and twine themselves tightly about her wrists and ankles and throat, as though Nature herself has conspired against the maiden, or, Arabella thinks, as though the unicorn commands all green and growing things. The woman screams again when the creature enters her.

Arabella licks at her thin, dry lips and grips the edges of the table by the open window.

And in the dreamlands, past the seventy steps and through the wild, enchanted fungal woods that lie just beyond the Gate of Deeper Slumber, past the River Skai and the narrow, cobbled streets of Ulthar and across the shimmering sea in the onyx city of Celephaïs, the priests within the sixteen-sided Temple of the Elder Ones pause in their prayers. Even after so many centuries, they have not lost all connection to the nameless red book, and in those hours when it works its deceits in the waking world, they bleed a foul, caustic ichor from their palms and the bottoms of their feet. Far below the Temple, in the catacombs that once imprisoned the tome, one among their number has been chained in its place, as a constant reminder of their inexcusable failure. This unfortunate, become a sort of willing proxy, bears the greater part of their conjunction with the escaped book. The martyr's tongue was cut out, that he might never utter the fell apparitions the book reveals to those waking men and women who, like Arabella Hopestill, have become catalysts for its depredations. What the chained priest bleeds is not to be described.

Arabella stares *into* the page, while the red book stares into her, and by way of its immemorial sorceries she feels every bit of the maiden's hurt and terror and humiliation, her outrage and despair. But Arabella Hopestill *also* is given access to all the sensations and sentiments of the unicorn. She tastes the violated woman's blood upon its tongue, and grows drunk with waves of triumph and the boundless cruelty that infects all immortal beings. She perceives the unicorn's every violent thrust, but is no less the victim than the rapist, no more the ravager than she is the ravaged, broken maiden. And she would have it no other way. The experiences the book bequeaths to her would be incomplete and entirely unsatisfying were she given only one half of any of its tableaus (or, in other, more elaborate cases, were she given only a third, or a fifth, or one fiftieth).

Arabella shudders and comes, even as the unicorn comes. She finds the strength to glance away from the page for a moment, trembling and listening to a mockingbird running through its repertoire of borrowed songs. Its impossible to be sure if the bird is in that meadow within the book or somewhere just outside the open window. The breeze through the window reeks of the exhaust of passing automobiles, and Arabella realizes that she's bitten her tongue hard enough that it's bleeding. With an unsteady hand, she wipes blood and spittle from her lips and chin, and she laughs nervously. Already, the ecstasy is fading quickly from her mind and body, as are the torments visited upon the maiden, those vales of anguish and degradation she has known now as though they were her own. Arabella looks back to the book, and already the page is growing murky around the edges.

"As long as I live," she whispers, "I will guard you. As long as I live, I will keep you safe."

At the edge of the brook, the maiden lies shattered, a wreck of meat and golden cloth. Her hazel-green eyes are not lifeless, but they seem as empty as the glass eyes of a porcelain doll. The roots that held her have retreated back into the muck.

"As long as I live," Arabella whispers.

The unicorn uses one cloven forefoot to roll the woman over onto her back, and then it stands perfectly still for a moment, motionless and white as a figurine carved from alabaster or bone. And then it turns and walks, unhurried, towards the shelter of those towering oaks and spruces. Arabella knows everything the beast knows, and the unicorn is quite entirely certain that the woman lying in the mud will bear it a daughter, and that the child will come shortly after the first winter snowfalls smother the meadow and the brook has frozen over.

And then the page is only a blank and brittle page again, and, with trembling hands, Arabella Hopestill closes the red book and sits watching the cars coming and going on the street below her apartment.

Far down in the dreamlands, the hands and feet of the priests who kneel inside the Temple of the Elder Ones cease to display that vile stigmata, and the sacrifice chained far below them finally stops fighting against his unbreakable bonds. As the sun rises over the ebony towers of Inquanok, pushing the night away, that madman slips away into the nightmares that visit the inhabitants of this land, and he dreams his bitter, splintered dreams within dreams.

At the Gate of Deeper Slumber

05.

It would be easier if I were only watching her die. But I know that I'm witnessing something far worse, a transition that will not conclude with the finality and peaceful oblivion of death. She's alone inside the wide circle we prepared with a paste of white chalk and pig's blood, and I've sworn to Suzanne that I'll never dare cross its terrible circumference, no matter what I might see or hear, and no matter what she may say. She is alone in there with the metal box and what it contains, and I am alone out here, with all the world about me. It only *seems* as though the world has gone away. It only seems that the entire universe has somehow contracted down to a space no farther across than the diameter of her circle. It would be easier, perhaps, if this dwindling of the cosmos *were* more than an illusion.

Two women, alone together, at the end of all that ever was and will ever be.

That would be easier.

Suzanne lies shivering on her left side, her eyes following me as I use the stub of a charcoal pencil to retrace the ring of protective runes and symbols about the periphery of the circle. I've lost track now of how many times I've drawn them on the hardwood floor. I draw them, and the wood absorbs them. Or they evaporate, or they simply cease to be. I can't say which; it hardly matters. I can only keep watch and restore them each time the thing inside the box, the shining thing trapped inside the circle with Suzanne, takes them away.

I am trying to think of it as nothing more insidious than an infection – a virus or bacterium – this force slowly devouring and transfiguring her. But that's a lie, a bald-faced lie, and I've never been a very good liar.

"Is it morning?" she asks, her voice hardly more than a raw whisper. I look up at the tall windows, at the summer sun streaming in, but the daylight seems far away and completely inconsequential. I know the thing inside the box is preventing the light from entering our circle, and that there's only darkness for Suzanne. I saw it very briefly, before she pushed me away. I saw it, and, what's more, I *felt* it, that black that would put even the perpetual night at the bottom of the deepest ocean trench to shame.

"Yes, it is," I reply. "It's a beautiful day. The sky is blue. There are no clouds, and the sky is blue."

"Nothing's getting past me," she says, and then I nod and go back to drawing on the floorboards. I want to say more, want to tell her anything reassuring, anything that's comforting, but, like I said, I'm a shitty liar. And Suzanne has moved forever beyond reassurances and comfort. She makes a hurtful sound that's almost like crying, and I try hard not to look. I've seen too much already, and every new glimpse only weakens my resolve. I can't possibly help her. No one and nothing can. And I can't run away and leave the circle untended, any more than I could leave Suzanne more alone than she is already. So, I grit my teeth and scribble at the varnished wood with my bit of charcoal pencil. The room is hot, and a stinging rivulet of sweat runs down my forehead, into my left eye; I try to blink it away.

"I know the names of the messenger," she mutters hoarsely, and I think it's a miracle she can still talk after what the thing in the box has done with her lips and teeth and tongue. I wouldn't exactly call that seeping hole in her face a mouth, not anymore. "The Black Pharaoh, I know all the names he's ever worn."

"Well, do me just one goddamn favor," I tell her, and I know I'm being selfish. "Do us *both* a favor, and keep them to yourself."

"But he so loves to hear his name spoken aloud by living beings," Suzanne whispers. There's a wet, shuddering sound from inside the circle, and she's silent again. There is, however, no mercy in her silence. I think there's no mercy remaining, or, more likely, mercy was only ever a fairy tale we told ourselves to get from one minute to the next. At the edge of this circle, in the presence of the thing not quite held inside that box, all our cherished illusions ravel and diminish. This, I suspect, is why the charcoal symbols on the floor dissolve almost as quickly as I can draw them. They were never *more* than symbols, never anything more vital than wishful thinking. Benevolent gods have not bequeathed us any safeguard against the void, and all our desperate sorceries have conjured only impotent figments.

I *know* this, as surely as I know that the glistening trapezohedral engine inside the box is corrupting and reshaping her to suit the needs of whatever made it, however many innumerable eons ago. It is an open window, and some abomination on the other side is gazing through it into her, even as she is gazing across those unfathomable gulfs of time and space into the watcher on the other side.

From the open box Suzanne fished out of a rocky tidal pool, I can hear the pipes playing again, and also the frantic, careless footfalls of the dancers who swoop and careen and howl before the throne of Chaos. Bleeding from all the symmetrically staggered kite-faces of the shining trapezohedron, I clearly hear that toneless, monotonous music. It would be so easy, I think, to join Suzanne. Easy *and* just. This is the most wicked deed in all my life, allowing her to face the abyss alone.

And finally I raise my head and look directly at her for the first time in hours, and, in this moment, I understand that I am exactly the same sort of coward as Perseus, only braving the countenance of Medusa secondhand, and that Suzanne has become a warrior's polished shield.

03.

We're lying together in bed. I kiss her, and she tastes like the sea. Or maybe it's only the smell from the shop below her tiny, cluttered apartment on Wickenden Street, the place that sells tropical fish and aquariums, that I'm mistaking for the taste of her. But that's never happened before. Too many things are happening that have never happened before. For example, I look into her eyes, and for a moment I'm unable to find *her* in her eyes. For that moment, I see nothing that could ever be confused with humanity. And then she blinks, and smiles, and Suzanne's eyes are only Suzanne again.

"It's under the bed," she says, though I haven't asked where she's keeping the box from the tide pool.

"Couldn't you think of some other place to keep it? Someplace that *isn't* under the bed?"

"It doesn't bother you, does it?" she asks, still smiling, and I believe she's only pretending to sound surprised. Of course, it bothers me, just the thought of the metal box and its contents stashed in the shadows and dust beneath us. It bothers me that it was there while I made love to her, and that I didn't know. It bothers me that we didn't leave it where she found it almost a week ago, washed up among the rocks, stranded with the kelp and crabs below the lighthouse.

"Yeah, as a matter of fact, it makes me a little nervous," I admit, reluctantly, and Suzanne laughs and nuzzles my naked breasts. Her lips brush across my left nipple, and I flinch. I can't say *why*, not exactly. Only that there is some unexpected and almost painful sensation from that brief contact, something that causes me to flinch. I cannot describe it, except by contradictory analogies. It feels like a static shock. It feels like an ice cube pressed against my skin. It feels sharp and hot, like the needle of a tattoo gun.

She looks up at me and frowns.

"It's just a strange old box," she says.

"Well, there must be some other place in the apartment where you can keep it, besides under the bed." I'm trying not to appear unreasonable. After all, it's not my apartment, or my bed. But if her expression is any indication, I'm not doing a very good job.

"Sure," Suzanne says, raising herself on one elbow and staring at me. "If it upsets you that much, I'll move it. I can stash it on top of the bookcase, or in the bottom of the closet. You want to pick which?"

"The closet seems like a pretty good idea," I reply, and she sighs and nods her head.

"Don't think I've ever seen you spooked like this," she says, getting out of bed and pulling on her bathrobe. It's the one I gave her last Christmas, dark red sateen with white roses. She doesn't cinch the belt or tie it, but lets the robe hang open.

"So, are you disappointed?" I ask her, watching Suzanne as she stoops to retrieve the box from beneath the bed. "Maybe having second thoughts?"

"No, I'm most definitely *not* having second thoughts. It's just, you always try to come on so butch and all, and now you're creeped out by an old box."

"Yeah, well, it's a fucking creepy old box," I say, "and you *know* it's fucking creepy." Then she stands again, holding it in both her hands. It isn't at all heavy. I know that because I'm the one who carried it from the tide pool back to her car. The whitish-yellow metal gleams dully in the glow from the lamp on the bedside table. The hinged lid and all six sides of the box have been stamped or engraved with bas-relief images, worn and dented now, but still plainly discernable. I think the designs are meant to depict living creatures, but they put me in mind of nothing so much as the biomechanoid monstrosities of H. R. Giger's paintings and sculptures. I don't like looking at the box's grotesqueries, and yet I find it very hard to look away. Giger's work has always had this same morbid affect on me.

Suzanne carries the box across the small bedroom and opens the closet door, then stands staring for a moment at the disarray of clothing jammed inside.

"You're saying it doesn't make you uncomfortable?" I ask. "Not even a little biddy bit?" She shrugs, and sets the box down on the floor. Then Suzanne begins excavating a hole in her dirty laundry, making a space large enough that the metal box can sit on the closet floor. She tosses a pair of jeans over her shoulder, and they land not far from the foot of the bed, the legs splayed in two different directions.

"I want to know what it is," she tells me. "I want to know what it is, and where it came from, and who made it, and why."

"You don't want very much, do you?"

"Only the moon," she laughs again. "And don't you go telling me how curiosity killed the cat. I never met a cat yet who would have been better off without curiosity."

"I wasn't going to say that."

"Good," she says, and out comes a great wad of panties and T-shirts and more jeans. "But, if you swear you won't freak out, there is something weird I want to tell you. I made some rubbings of the box this afternoon. One from each side."

I roll over on my back and stare at the ceiling, wishing that I had a cigarette, that Suzanne hadn't convinced me to quit. "Something weird," I say, like a wary echo.

"Well, the box has six sides, right, like most boxes. I mean, it's basically a hollow cube. And I used one sheet of paper for each side. But, and here's where it gets weird, when I was finished, I had eight rubbings on eight sheets of paper. I didn't even realize that I was *making* eight rubbings, not until it was over."

"You lost track and did two of the sides twice," I suggest, but my mouth has gone dry, and there's gooseflesh on my arms. I doubt I sound anything like convincing.

"Sure, I thought of that, right off. But when I compared the rubbings, they were all different. And when I tried to match them all up with the images on the box, I could only find six. On the box, I mean."

I sit up and stare at her. Suzanne has her back to me. She's just placed the box inside the closet and is busy piling dirty clothes in on top of it.

"And *then,* after that, you put it beneath the bed?" I ask.

"It's only a box," she says again and shuts the closet door. "I'm sure I'll figure it all out later. Weird shit like that happens, you know? But you can't let it go and freak you out. When I was a little girl, I was sure I'd seen a sea monster, but, turned out, it was only a seal."

I lie there, staring up at the ceiling, trying not to think about the box or the shining thing inside, and unable to think of anything else. In a minute or two, she comes back to bed.

04.

It's almost dark, and I'm watching something on television when Suzanne gets back from Salem. I reach for the remote, press a button, and the screen instantly goes black. She's complaining about the traffic between Boston and Providence, and about Boston drivers, in general. I sip at the glass of cheap Scotch I've been nursing for the last half hour. All the ice has melted, and the sides of the tumbler are slick with beads of condensation. I try not to notice the oddly intimate way she's holding the box, and I'm grateful when she sets it down on the kitchen counter. I'm grateful when she's no longer *touching* it.

"Well, that wasn't altogether unprofitable," Suzanne says, and then sits down on one of the barstools at the counter. There are three of them, the cushions upholstered in some sort of shiny red vinyl fabric embedded with flakes of gold glitter. I want to call it Naugahyde, but I'm not sure that's right. Suzanne found the stools cheap at the Salvation Army over on Pitman Street. Here and there, the upholstery is marred by cigarette burns.

"I thought you'd be back sooner."

"Like I said, all the fucking traffic," she reminds me, then produces a manila folder from her pea-green laptop bag. She lays the folder on the countertop and taps it twice with her right index finger.

"So, what'd you find out?" I ask, and Suzanne taps the folder a third time, and answers me with a question of her own.

"Ever heard of the Church of Starry Wisdom?"

"Wasn't that one of Aleister Crowley's little clubs?" I ask, and watch the blank television screen.

"No, it isn't. Or wasn't. Whichever." I hear her open the folder, but I don't turn around. "This was way before Crowley's time. Near as anyone can tell, the order was founded by an Egyptologist and occultist named Enoch Bowen, sometime around 1844. At least, in May of that year he came back from a dig on the east bank of the Nile, at a site near Thebes. The following July, he bought an abandoned Free-Will Baptist sanctuary on Federal Hill and started the Church of Starry Wisdom."

"Never heard of it," I tell her.

"Neither had I. But that's not too surprising. Whatever Bowen and his followers were up to, seems it didn't sit too well with the locals. By December 1844, ministers in Providence were denouncing the Starry Wisdom. Four years later, there were rumors of blood sacrifices, devil worship, that kind of thing. Various sordid scandals and hostilities ensued. Though by 1863 there appear to have been at least two hundred people in Bowen's congregation. And sometime in 1876 Thomas Doyle, who was the mayor of Providence at the time, stepped in and the church was summarily shut down. After that, it seems that Professor Bowen and most of his followers left Providence. There are rumors of the Starry Wisdom cult reemerging in other places. First in Chicago, then, near the end of the Nineteenth Century, somewhere in Yorkshire."

Suzanne reminds me of someone reading a book report to her high-school classmates.

"Colorful story," I say and take another sip of the watery, lukewarm Scotch. "But what's any of this got to do with your box and its bauble?"

"Just about everything," Suzanne replies, her tone growing exasperated, and I glance at her over my shoulder. She looks tired, tired but excited. Jittery. On edge. She forces a smile for me and continues.

"Look, now you're being dense on purpose," she says. "When Bowen returned from Egypt in 1844, he brought back an artifact he discovered during an excavation there. A carving or stone or cartouche. This artifact, which is only ever referred to as 'the Shining Trapezohedron,' was supposed to be some sort of magical gateway. Bowen and his cohorts thought they could use it to talk to ancient Egyptian gods, or maybe gods older than the Egyptians. That part's not clear, exactly who or what they were worshipping. But the artifact was used to summon them. In return for blood offerings and profane sexual rites – the usual suspects – the Starry Wisdom cult believed these gods would offer up all the hidden secrets of the universe."

I turn back towards the television and consider switching it on again.

"You're not believing a word of this, are you?"

"Not especially," I reply.

"It isn't like I'm making it up. I have photocopies of contemporary newspaper accounts – "

"I didn't *say* I think you're making it up. That's not what I meant. That's not what I said."

"That's sure what it *sounded* like," Suzanne sighs, and God, I hate it when she sulks. I finish the Scotch and set the empty glass on the floor beside the futon.

"So, you're saying the thing in your peculiar yellow box, that it's Bowen's Shining Trapezohedron?"

"Yeah, that's what I'm saying."

"But wouldn't the cultists have hauled their holy of holies away with them when they fled Providence?"

"If you're not going to take this seriously, I'm going to stop right now, okay?"

I close my eyes. I'm beginning to get a headache, that dull, faint throb winding itself up tight and jagged somewhere directly behind my eyes.

"I have to be at work in half an hour," I say. "I traded shifts with that new guy. The restaurant will be packed wall to wall tonight, and I'm not looking forward to it, that's all. I'm not trying to be a bitch. It just seems strange, that these Starry Wisdom fruitcakes wouldn't have taken their sacred relic with them when they left."

"It seems strange to me, too," Suzanne says, and the tone of her voice has become hard and defensive, all the enthusiasm drained away. "But the church building was still standing in the thirties, and even that long after the Starry Wisdom left Providence, people on Federal Hill were scared of the place. In 1935, a painter named Robert Blake broke in – "

"Robert Blake?" I ask, opening my eyes again. "Like the guy who played Baretta?"

"Yeah, like the guy who played Baretta. He apparently broke into the abandoned church and found the trapezohedron on an altar in the steeple." I hear her turn a page. "He was from Milwaukee, but was staying near Brown, someplace on College Street close to the John Hay Library. And he died there, not long after he broke into the church. Struck by lightning, if you can believe that."

"This is what you drove all the way to Salem to find out?" I ask. "This is what Tirzah told you?"

"Yeah, but it's not exactly a secret. These articles, they're mostly from the *Providence Journal.* I just never heard of any of it. I guess it's not the sort of stuff you learn in history class. Anyway, showing the box to Tirzah was *your* idea."

And yeah, that part's true. We met Tirzah a few years back, during a lesbian-only retreat out on the Cape. She runs a witchcraft shop in Salem, reads Tarot cards for tourists, etc. & etc. "She's undoubtedly the weirdest person we know," I say. "It made sense, letting her see it. So…Baretta steals this thing and gets struck by lightning."

"I wish you wouldn't drink before work," Suzanne says.

"And I wish you'd left that damned box where you found it. If wishes were horses…" There's a drawn out few moments of quiet then, as if neither of us knows our next line and we're waiting on a helpful prompt from backstage.

"At any rate," she says, finally breaking the silence. "One of the men who investigated Blake's death, a doctor named Ambrose Dexter, found the stone among the dead man's effects. He chartered a fishing boat in Newport, and dropped the metal box into Narragansett Bay, somewhere off Castle Hill. That's the deepest part of the bay, you know. There in the Eastern Passage, between Newport and Beavertail."

"No," I say. "No, I didn't know that. But I *do* know I'm gonna be late if I don't get dressed and get out of here. We'll talk about this later." I stand, feeling dizzy, unsure if it's from the Scotch or the nascent headache, or maybe from a bit of both. I look at Suzanne, who's still staring at the contents of the manila folder, and I point at the dented metal box on the counter. "You should just get rid of it," I tell her. "Hell, sell the thing on eBay. I'm sure some freak would pay a pretty penny for it."

She looks up and glares at me. "Jesus. You don't *sell* something like this on eBay. Whether or not Enoch Bowen was a lunatic, it has historical significance."

"Fine," I tell her. "Whatever. Then give it to a museum." Suzanne shakes her head and goes back to reading the sheaf of photocopied pages.

"I found it," she whispers. "It's mine to do with as I please." And I don't disagree. I'm not in the mood for arguments, especially not one I know I'll lose.

01.

"Hey! I think I've found something," Suzanne shouts. The waves slamming against the rocks and the wind off the bay obscure her voice so that I can only just make out the words. I'm lying on the blanket we've spread out over a relatively flat place among the tilted, contorted beds of slate and phyllite. I'm lying there with my eyes shut, the sun too warm on my face, shining straight through my eyelids and making me sleepy. I don't want to get up. If I get up to see whatever it is she's found, I'll have to bring the blanket along, or it'll blow away.

"Come see!" she shouts.

"Bring it *to* me!" I shout back without bothering to open my eyes. Often, it seems that Suzanne and I love the rugged coast around the old Beavertail Lighthouse for entirely different reasons. I come here to get away from the city, for the smells and sounds of the sea. And she comes for the flotsam and jetsam, for whatever she can find dead or dying in the tide pools. Her apartment is littered with the garbage she's brought back from the edge of the sea. Shells and bones, weathered shards of Wedgwood china, unusually shaped pieces of driftwood, rounded pebbles and cobbles, fishing lures, rusted and unrecognizable pieces of machinery, a ruined lobster pot. You could decorate a good-sized chowder house with all the junk Suzanne's scavenged from beaches up and down Rhode Island and Massachusetts, Maine and Nova Scotia. She has more jars of beach glass than I've ever bothered to count.

"It's *big!*" she calls out. "Get off your lazy ass and come look!"

I open my eyes, squinting at the afternoon light, and I see now that there's a herring gull standing only a few feet away, watching me. It cocks its head to one side, and its pale irises seem simultaneously startled and filled with questions. I make a shooing motion with my hands, and the bird squawks, then spreads its grey wings, and the wind seems to snatch it away.

"Hold your horses," I say, not shouting, though, not really caring whether Suzanne's heard me or not. I stand and wad the blanket into a tight bundle, tucking it under my right arm. I'd thought that her voice was coming from somewhere to the south, but I soon spot her ten or fifteen yards north of me, kneeling on the smooth, dark shale next to one of the deeper pools of seawater left behind by the retreating tide. Her head is bowed slightly, her hands clasped in front of her, and I think she looks like someone praying to the bay. Then she turns towards me and points at something in the water. By the time I reach the edge of the pool, she's already pulled it out onto the rocks, along with a rubbery, fat tangle of kelp and bladderwrack. The box gleams dully in the sun.

"What is it?" she asks me, and I tell her I have no idea. I stand there, gazing down at the yellow-white metal and the slippery knot of seaweed tangled around it. There are intricate, spiraling images worked into the gleaming surface of the box, and seeing them, the first word that comes to mind is *unwholesome.* Whatever the artist was trying to depict in these bas-reliefs, from life or only his or her imagination, it was unwholesome.

"I can't figure out how it opens," Suzanne says, sounding puzzled and chewing thoughtfully at her lower lip. She pulls away the strands of seaweed. "There are hinges, *here* and *here,* but no sign of a latch. I'm not even sure I can tell where the top and bottom parts fit together. I can't find the seam. Is that gold?"

And I want to say, *Put it back, Suzanne. For god's sake, put it back. Don't touch it.* I want to ask why she can't see the obvious *unwholesomeness* of it. But I don't, and then she presses her right thumb into a very subtle depression or indentation on the front of the box and it opens with an audible pop, easy as you please. She laughs, like a child delighted at having gotten all the sides of a Rubik's Cube to match up.

Suzanne lifts the lid, and at first, all I can see in there is darkness, such an entirely complete darkness that my eyes are useless against it, and I have the distinct and disquieting impression that sunlight is unable to penetrate that umbral space.

"Shut it," I say, but she doesn't seem to have heard me. She doesn't close the box or tell me that I'm being silly. Instead, Suzanne reaches *into* that inviolable blackness, and I'm absolutely *certain* that she's going to scream, and when she pulls her arm back all that will be left is the bloody, spurting stump of her wrist. I'll scream, too, as if in reply.

She lifts something out of the box, and it also gleams beneath the sun.

"A crystal," she says. "Some kind of crystal." I feel sick, just looking at it. The same way I get nauseous on the deck of a listing boat, I feel sick when I look at the thing from the metal box. But, nonetheless, I *do* look at it. I *don't* turn away. Its glassy, kite-shaped facets are vaguely iridescent, and I'm having a lot of trouble figuring out what color it is, if, indeed, it's any *one* color. At first, it appears to be greenish black, like an overripe avocado skin. But I catch hints of crimson, too, then hints of violet, and *then* the whole thing glimmers a very deep cobalt blue. Suzanne holds it up, turning it this way and that so that I can get a better view. There's an ugly, greasy quality to the light flashing off its perfectly delineated, four-sided faces.

"Put it back, please," I say, speaking very softly. "Put it back inside." Suzanne stares at me a second or two, then nods and does as I've asked. She closes the metal box, and there's another pop when it shuts. I sit with her, at the edge of the tide pool, with the box between us. The pool is full of tiny mussels and the whorled shells of periwinkle snails, with seaweed and small scuttling crabs. The rock beneath the water is scabbed with sharp barnacles.

There's never any discussion about whether we're keeping the box or leaving it there. Never any question. When she's ready to go, I carry it for her, and it weighs a lot less than I expected.

02.

And now I sit down to write about the dream, the dream I have the night after we find Enoch Bowen's trapezohedron. It's the same dream I have when I can no longer stay awake to draw vigilant runes around the binding circle where Suzanne lies, the circle and the star, the flaming, all-seeing eye and the shattered wreck of her. I can no longer take solace in a clock face or the track of the sun or moon across the sky. I am not contained in any single moment, and the assumed order of the world is lost on me. I've heard the piping flutes, and the drums, and the lumbering footfalls of titan gods who've danced away the eons of their exile. I've felt the precious safety net of time falling away. There's only now. This moment, which I may call past or present or future. Suzanne sleeps peacefully beside me, and she's whole, but she also lies broken and transformed within the Elder Sign carefully chalked upon the floor of her apartment. I've torn the story apart, no longer able to perceive the illusion of chronology, and I've haphazardly strewn the scenes, just as Suzanne has been torn and as she's been strewn. I rearrange and lie. I present the gorgon's face reflected in a polished shield, and I will never be even half so strong as I'd need to be to tell the full, vicious truth of it. I'm amazed to have made it this far. I come to confess, but can at best drop hints and innuendo. Suzanne was the sacrifice, not me. It was Suzanne who swallowed the pomegranate seeds. Ask her.

Surely some revelation is at hand…

I used to think so.

All our roughest beasts have come and gone, slouching past, and now wait together impatiently at the threshold of what we, in our cherished ignorance, have named a *universe*. We see inconvenient shards of truth in dream, perhaps, or in the contents of a metal box coughed up by the sea.

I shouldn't tarry, or digress. There is too little coherence remaining within me to squander even an ounce. *This* is the dream. The rest is hardly better than window dressing. Quit stalling and spit it out; the ocean has obliged, and now it's my turn:

Suzanne and I are walking along a sandy beach, not the rocks at Beavertail, and the summer sun beats mercilessly down on the bloated corpses of innumerable thousands of crabs and huge lobsters and dead fish that have been tossed ashore by the waves. Haddock and cod, flounder and striped bass, tautog and weakfish and pollock. I ask her if it was a red tide did this, and she asks me if there's ever been any other sort. The air is far too foul and heavy and hot to breathe, and I'm relieved when she turns away from the Atlantic and towards the low dunes. There's a narrow, winding trail, almost overgrown by dog roses and poison ivy, and it leads to the old church on Federal Hill. I remember that the church was demolished decades ago, all its derelict secrets become anonymous landfill. But in the dream, the shrine of the Starry Wisdom has been restored, or it has never precisely fallen, or we are removed to a time before its destruction. It hardly matters which. No, that's not true. It matters not at all.

Suzanne leads me from the sun-blighted day into night and into that crumbling antique sanctuary, past the fearful, praying throng that has gathered on its steps, those shriveled old Italian women clutching their onyx and coral rosaries. They spare a hateful peek at me, each and every one in her turn, and the curses that spill from their lips are more befitting witches than good New England Catholics.

"Oh, don't mind them," Suzanne says. "They're bitter, that's all. They can't hear the music. Not a one of them has ever danced, and now they're old and won't ever have the opportunity."

She leads me through silent vales of dust and shadows, and our path is as indirect as this cockeyed, wandering narrative. Together, we wind our way between apparently endless rows of warped and buckled pews, between chiseled marble columns rising around us to shoulder the awful, sagging burden of the church's vaulted roof. Then we move away from the nave, revisiting the vestibule, and she shows me the concealed stairway spiraling up and up and up into the sky. We climb the wooden steps until the moon is only a silver coin far below us.

"Wipe your feet," Suzanne tells me, and I see we've finally reached the top of the stairs and gained the steeple. If this place has ever held a peal of bells to chime the hour and call the faithful to worship, they've been removed. There are four tall lancet windows, painted over so that the daylight might never enter the circular room.

"You should have waited for me below," Suzanne says, and her eyes flash yellow-white in the gloom. "You should have waited on the beach. I can see that now."

I don't reply, and I don't glance back the way we've come. I know it's much too late to retrace that route, and I don't try. There's a ring of seven high-backed chairs arranged about a low stone pillar. And in each chair sits a robed figure, their faces veiled with folds of golden silk. They don't look up when we enter the steeple, but keep their attentions focused on the peculiar metal box sitting on the stone pillar. The box is open. There can be no doubt whatsoever that it's the same box she found in the tide pool, the box Enoch Bowen brought home from Thebes, so I don't have to peer inside to know its contents.

The seven seated figures have begun to chant, and I watch while Suzanne undresses, then takes her place before the altar. I watch as a tangible, freezing blackness is disgorged by the box, by the thing *inside* the box. I watch as those hungry tendrils wrap themselves tightly about her, and draw her down, and enter her.

"Yes," she whispers. "I will be the bride. I will be the doorway. I will be the conduit." And there is so much more. I don't doubt that I could write page after page setting down the blasphemous things that I dreamt I saw in the steeple of the rotting church. I could never spend a moment doing anything else, and what remains of my life would be utterly insufficient to record more than a fraction of those depredations. There is no bottom to this dream. Wherever I choose to stop, the point is chosen arbitrarily.

I stand among the dunes, looking out across a dying sea, and watch while clouds gather on the bruised horizon.

The wind is scalding, and I cannot find the sun.

There is another shore, you know, upon the other side.

00.

The afternoon is fading quickly towards dusk, and I sit outside the chalk and blood circle drawn on the floorboards. From time to time, I glance at the sky outside, or at the door leading to the hallway. Or I scrounge the courage to look inside the circle again. But she's gone forever, even the ruin it made of her. She's gone, and the box is gone, and the trapezohedron is gone. There's very little remaining to prove she was ever here. I cannot conceive that one woman's body and soul were possibly enough to appease that hunger. It is all beyond my comprehension.

There is a bloody spot where she lay, blood and bile, and a few lumps of something colorless and translucent that remind me of beached jellyfish. There are scorch marks where the box sat. There's the faint odor of ammonia and charred wood.

"It was a beautiful day," I say, and at first the sound of my own voice startles me. "The sky was blue, Suzanne. There were no clouds, and the sky was blue. I think it will be a beautiful night."

And then, with the heel of my bare palm, I begin to erase the protective circle, and the five-pointed star, and the burning eye.

> *We cannot think of a time that is oceanless*
> *Or of an ocean not littered with wastage*
> *Or of a future that is not liable*
> *Like the past, to have no destination.*
> T. S. Eliot, *The Dry Salvages*

Fish Bride
(1970)

We lie here together, naked on her sheets which are always damp, no matter the weather, and she's still sleeping. I've lain next to her, watching the long cold sunrise, the walls of this dingy room in this dingy house turning so slowly from charcoal to a hundred successively lighter shades of grey. The weak November morning has a hard time at the window, because the glass was knocked out years ago, and she chose as a substitute a sheet of tattered and not-quite-clear plastic she found washed up on the shore now, held in place with mismatched nails and a few thumbtacks. But it deters the worst of the wind and rain and snow, and she says there's nothing out there she wants to see, anyway. I've offered to replace the broken glass, a couple of times I've said that, but it's just another of the hundred or so things that I've promised I would do for her and haven't yet gotten around to doing; she doesn't seem to mind. That's not why she keeps letting me come here. Whatever she wants from me, it isn't handouts and pity and someone to fix her broken windows and leaky ceiling. Which is fortunate, as I've never fixed anything in my whole life. I can't even change a flat tire. I've only ever been the sort of man who does the harm and leaves it for someone else to put right again, or simply sweep beneath a rug where no one will have to notice the damage I've done. So, why should she be any different? And yet, to my knowledge, I've done her no harm so far.

I come down the hill from the village on those interminable nights and afternoons when I can't write and don't feel like getting drunk alone. I leave that other world, that safe and smothering kingdom of clean sheets and typescript, electric lights and indoor plumbing and radio and window frames with windowpanes, and follow the sandy path through gale-stunted trees and stolen, burned-out automobiles, smoldering trash-barrel fires and suspicious, under-lit glances.

They all know I don't belong here with them, all the other men and women who share her squalid existence at the edge of the sea, the ones who have come down and never gone back up the hill again. When I call them her apostles, she gets sullen and angry.

"No," she says, "it's not like that. They're nothing of the sort."

But I understand well enough that's exactly what they are, even if she doesn't want to admit it, either to herself or to me. And so they hold me in contempt, because she's taken me into her bed – me, an interloper who comes and goes, who has some choice in the matter, who has that option because the world beyond these dunes and shanty walls still imagines it has some use for me. One of these nights, I think, her apostles will do murder against me. One of them alone, or all of them together. It may be stones or sticks or an old filleting knife. It may even be a gun. I wouldn't put it past them. They are resourceful, and there's a lot on the line. They'll bury me in the dog roses or sink me in some deep place among the tide-worn rocks, or carve me up like a fat sow and have themselves a feast. She'll likely join them, if they are bold enough and offer a few scraps of my charred, anonymous flesh to complete the sacrifice. And later, much, much later, she'll remember and miss me, in her sloppy, indifferent way, and wonder whatever became of the man who brought her beer and whiskey, candles and chocolate bars, the man who said he'd fix the window, but never did. She might recall my name, but I wouldn't hold it against her if she doesn't.

"This used to *be* someplace," she's told me time and time again. "Oh, sure, you'd never know it now. But when my mother was a girl, this used to be a town. When I was little, it was still a town. There were dress shops, and a diner, and a jail. There was a public park with a bandshell and a hundred-year-old oak tree. In the summer, there was music in the park, and picnics. There were even churches, *two* of them, one Catholic and one Presbyterian. But then the storm came and took it all away."

And it's true, most of what she says. There was a town here once. A decade's neglect hasn't quite erased all signs of it. She's shown me some of what there's left to see – the stump of a brick chimney, a few broken pilings where the waterfront once stood – and I've asked questions around the village. But people up there don't like to speak openly about this place, or even allow their thoughts to linger on it very long. Every now and then, usually after a burglary or before an election, there's talk of cleaning it up, pulling down these listing, clapboard shacks and chasing away the vagrants and squatters and winos. So far, the talk has come to nothing.

A sudden gust of wind blows in from off the beach, and the sheet of plastic stretched across the window flaps and rustles, and she opens her eyes.

"You're still here," she says, not sounding surprised, merely telling me what I already know. "I was dreaming that you'd gone away and would never come back to me again. I dreamed there was a boat called the *Silver Star,* and it took you away."

"I get seasick," I tell her. "I don't do boats. I haven't been on a boat since I was fifteen."

"Well, you got on this one," she insists, and the dim light filling up the room catches in the facets of her sleepy grey eyes. "You said that you were going to seek your fortune on the Ivory Coast. You had your typewriter and a suitcase, and you were wearing a brand new suit of worsted wool. I was standing on the dock, watching as the *Silver Star* got smaller and smaller."

"I'm not even sure I know where the Ivory Coast is supposed to be," I say.

"Africa," she replies.

"Well, I know that much, sure. But I don't know *where* in Africa. And it's an awfully big place."

"In the dream, you knew," she assures me, and I don't press the point further. It's her dream, not mine, even if it's not a dream she's actually ever had, even if it's only something she's making up as she goes along. "In the dream," she continues, undaunted, "you had a travel brochure that the ticket agent had given you. It was printed all in color. There was a sort of tree called a bombax tree, with bright red flowers. There were elephants and a parrot. There were pretty women with skin the color of roasted coffee beans."

"That's quite a brochure," I say, and for a moment I watch the plastic tacked over the window as it rustles in the wind off the bay. "I wish I could have a look at it right now."

"I thought what a warm place it must be, the Ivory Coast," and I glance down at her, at those drowsy eyes watching me. She lifts her right hand from the damp sheets, and patches of iridescent skin shimmer ever so faintly in the morning light. The sun shows through the thin, translucent webbing stretched between her long fingers. Her sharp nails brush gently across my unshaven cheek, and she smiles. Even I don't like to look at those teeth for very long, and I let my eyes wander back to the flapping plastic. The wind is picking up, and I think maybe this might be the day when I finally have to find a hammer, a few ten-penny nails, and enough discarded pine slats to board up the hole in the wall.

"Not much longer before the snow comes," she says, as if she doesn't need to hear me speak to know my thoughts.

"Probably not for a couple of weeks yet," I counter, and she blinks and turns her head towards the window.

In the village, I have a tiny room in a boardinghouse on Darling Street, and I keep a spiral-bound notebook hidden between my mattress and box springs. I've written a lot of things in that book that I shouldn't like any other human being to ever read – secret desires, things I've heard and read, things she's told me and things I've come to suspect all on my own. Sometimes, I think it would be wise to keep the notebook better hidden. But it's true that the old woman who owns the place, and who does all the housekeeping herself, is afraid of me, and she never goes into my room. She leaves the clean linen and towels in a stack outside my door. Months ago, I stopped taking my meals with the other lodgers, because the strained silence and fleeting, leery glimpses that attended those breakfasts and dinners only served to give me indigestion. I expect the widow O'Dwyer would ask me to find a room elsewhere, if she weren't so intimidated by me. Or, rather, if she weren't so intimidated by the company I keep.

Outside the shanty, the wind howls like the son of Poseidon, and, for the moment, there's no more talk of the Ivory Coast or dreams or sailing gaily away into the sunset aboard the *Silver Star*.

Much of what I've secretly scribbled there in my notebook concerns that terrible storm you claim rose up from the sea to steal away the little park and the bandshell, the diner and the jail and the dress shops, the two churches, one Presbyterian and the other Catholic. From what you've said, it must have happened sometime in September of '57 or '58, but I've spent long afternoons in the small public library, carefully pouring over old newspapers and magazines. I can find no evidence of such a tempest making landfall in the autumn of either of those years. What I can verify is that the village once extended down the hill, past the marshes and dunes to the bay, and there was a lively, prosperous waterfront. There was trade with Gloucester and Boston, Nantucket and Newport, and the bay was renowned for its lobsters, fat black sea bass, and teeming shoals of haddock. Then, abruptly, the waterfront was all but abandoned sometime before 1960. In print, I've found hardly more than scant and unsubstantiated speculations to account for it, that exodus, that strange desertion. Talk of overfishing, for instance, and passing comparisons with Cannery Row in faraway California and the collapse of the Monterey Bay sardine canning industry back in the 1950s. I write down everything I find, no matter how unconvincing, but I permit myself to believe only a very little of it.

"A penny for your thoughts," she says, then shuts her eyes again.

"You haven't got a penny," I reply, trying to ignore the raw, hungry sound of the wind and the constant noise at the window.

"I most certainly do," she tells me and pretends to scowl and look offended. "I have a few dollars, tucked away. I'm not an indigent."

"Fine, then. I was thinking of Africa," I lie. "I was thinking of palm trees and parrots."

"I don't remember any palm trees in the travel brochure," she says. "But I expect there must be quite a lot of them, regardless."

"Undoubtedly," I agree. I don't say anything else, though, because I think I hear voices, coming from somewhere outside her shack – urgent, muttering voices that reach me despite the wind and the flapping plastic. I can't make out the words, no matter how hard I try. It ought to scare me more than it does. Like I said, one of these nights, they'll do murder against me. One of them alone, or all of them together. Maybe they won't even wait for the conspiring cover of nightfall. Maybe they'll come for me in broad daylight. I begin to suspect my murder would not even be deemed a crime by the people who live in those brightly painted houses up the hill, back beyond the dunes. On the contrary, they might consider it a necessary sacrifice, something to placate the flotsam and jetsam huddling in the ruins along the shore, an oblation of blood and flesh to buy them time.

Seems more likely than not.

"They shouldn't come so near," she says, acknowledging that she too hears the whispering voices. "I'll have a word with them later. They ought to know better."

"They've more business being here than I do," I reply, and she silently watches me for a moment or two. Her grey eyes have gone almost entirely black, and I can no longer distinguish the irises from the pupils.

"They ought to know better," she says again, and this time her tone leaves me no room for argument.

There are tales that I've heard, and bits of dreams I sometimes think I've borrowed – from her or one of her apostles – that I find somewhat more convincing than either newspaper accounts of depleted fish stocks or rumors of a cataclysmic hurricane. There are the spook stories I've over-heard, passed between children. There are yarns traded by the half dozen or so grizzled old men who sit outside the filling station near the widow's boarding house, who seem possessed of no greater ambition than checkers and hand-rolled cigarettes, cheap gin and gossip. I have begun to believe the truth is not something that was entrusted to the press, but, instead, an ignominy the town has struggled, purposefully, to forget, and which is now recalled dimly or not at all. There is remaining no consensus to be had, but there *are* common threads from which I have woven rough speculation.

Late one night, very near the end of summer or towards the beginning of fall, there was an unusually high tide. It quickly swallowed the granite jetty and the shingle, then broke across the seawall and flooded the streets of the harbor. There was a full moon that night, hanging low and ripe on the eastern horizon, and by its wicked reddish glow men and women saw the things that came slithering and creeping and lurching out of those angry waves. The invaders cast no shadow, or the moonlight shone straight through them, but was somehow oddly distorted. Or, perhaps, what came out of the sea that night glimmered faintly with an eerie phosphorescence of its own.

I know that I'm choosing lurid, loaded words here – *wicked, lurching, hungry, eerie* – hoping, I suppose, to discredit all the cock and bull I've heard, trying to neuter those schoolyard demons. But, in my defence, the children and the old men whom I've overheard were quite a bit less discreet. They have little use, and even less concern, for the sensibilities of people who aren't going to believe them, anyway. In some respects, they're almost as removed as she, as distant and disconnected as the other shanty dwellers here in the rubble at the edge of the bay.

"I would be sorry," she says, "if you were to sail away to Africa."

"I'm not going anywhere. There isn't anywhere I want to go. There isn't anywhere I'd rather be."

She smiles again, and this time I don't allow myself to look away. She has teeth like those of a very small shark, and they glint wet and dark in healthy pink gums. I have often wondered how she manages not to cut her lips or tongue on those teeth, why there are not always trickles of drying blood at the corners of her thin lips. She's bitten into me enough times now. I have ugly crescent scars across my shoulders and chest and upper arms to prove that we are lovers, stigmata to make her apostles hate me that much more.

"It's silly of you to waste good money on a room," she says, changing the course of our conversation. "You could stay here with me. I hate the nights when you're in the village and I'm alone."

"Or you could go back with me," I reply. It's a familiar sort of futility, this exchange, and we both know our lines by heart, just as we both know the outcome.

"No," she says, her shark's smile fading. "You know that I can't. You know they'd never have me up there," and she nods in the general direction of the town.

And yes, I do know that, but I've never yet told her that I do.

The tide rose up beneath a low red moon and washed across the waterfront. The sturdy wharf was shattered like matchsticks, and boats of various shapes and sizes – dories and jiggers, trollers and Bermuda-rigged schooners – were torn free of their moorings and tossed onto the shivered docks. But there was no storm, no wind, no lashing rain. No thunder and lightning and white spray off the breakers. The air was hot and still that night, and the cloudless sky blazed with the countless pin-prick stars that shine brazenly through the punctured dome of Heaven.

"They say the witch what brought the trouble came from some place up Amesbury way," I heard one of the old men tell the others, months and months ago. None of his companions replied, neither nodding their heads in agreement, nor voicing dissent. "I heard she made offerings every month, on the night of the new moon, and I heard she had herself a daughter, though I never learned the girl's name. Don't guess it matters, though. And the name of her father, well, ain't nothing I'll ever say aloud."

That night, the cobbled streets and alleyways were fully submerged for long hours. Buildings and houses were lifted clear of their foundations and dashed one against the other. What with no warning of the freakish tide, only a handful of the waterfront's inhabitants managed to escape the deluge and gain the safety of higher ground. More than two hundred souls perished, and for weeks afterwards the corpses of the drowned continued to wash ashore. Many of the bodies were so badly mangled that they could never be placed with a name or a face and went unclaimed, to be buried in unmarked graves in the village beyond the dunes.

I can no longer hear the whisperers through the thin walls of her shack, so I'll assume that they've either gone or have simply had their say and subsequently fallen silent. Possibly, they're leaning now with their ears pressed close to the corrugated aluminum and rotting clapboard, listening in, hanging on her every syllable, even as my own voice fills them with loathing and jealous spite.

"I'll have a word with them," she tells me for the third time. "You should feel as welcome here as any of us."

The sea swept across the land, and, by the light of that swollen, sanguine moon, grim approximations of humanity moved freely, unimpeded, through the flooded thoroughfares. Sometimes they swam, and sometimes they went about deftly on all fours, and sometimes they shambled clumsily along, as though walking were new to them and not entirely comfortable.

"They weren't men," I overheard a boy explaining to his friends. The boy had ginger-colored hair, and he was nine, maybe ten years old at the most. The children were sitting together at the edge of the weedy vacant lot where a traveling carnival sets up three or four times a year.

"Then were they women?" one of the others asked him.

The boy frowned and gravely shook his head. "No. You're not listening. They weren't women, neither. They weren't *anything* human. But, what I heard said, if you were to take all the stuff gets pulled up in trawler nets – all the hauls of cod and flounder and eel, the dogfish and the skates, the squids and jellyfish and crabs, *all* of it and whatever else you can conjure – if you took those things, still alive and wriggling, and could mush them up together into the *shapes* of men and women, *that's* exactly what walked out of the bay that night."

"That's not true," a girl said indignantly, and the others stared at her. "That's not true at all. God wouldn't let things like that run loose."

The ginger-haired boy shook his head again. "They got different gods than us, gods no one even knows the names for, and that's who the Amesbury witch was worshipping. Those gods from the bottom of the ocean."

"Well, I think you're a liar," the girl told him. "I think you're a blasphemer *and* a liar, and, also, I think you're just making this up to scare us." And then she stood and stalked away across the weedy lot, leaving the others behind. They all watched her go, and then the ginger-haired boy resumed his tale.

"It gets worse," he said.

A cold rain has started to fall, and the drops hitting the tin roof sound almost exactly like bacon frying in a skillet. She's moved away from me and is sitting naked at the edge of the bed, her long legs dangling over the side, her right shoulder braced against the rusted iron headboard. I'm still lying on the damp sheets, staring up at the leaky ceiling, waiting for the water tumbling from the sky to find its way inside. She'll set jars and cooking pots beneath the worst of the leaks, but there are far too many to bother with them all.

"I can't stay here forever," she says. It's not the first time, but, I admit, those words always take me by surprise. "It's getting harder being here. Every day, it gets harder on me. I'm so awfully tired, all the time."

I look away from the ceiling, at her throat and the peculiar welts just below the line of her chin. The swellings first appeared a few weeks back, and the skin there has turned dry and scaly, and has taken on a sickly greyish-yellow hue. Sometimes, there are boils or seeping blisters. When she goes out among the others, she wears the silk scarf I gave her, tied about her neck so that they won't have to see. So they won't ask questions she doesn't want to answer.

"I don't have to go alone," she says, but doesn't turn her head to look at me. "I don't want to leave you here."

"I can't," I say.

"I know," she replies.

And this is how it almost always is. I come down from the village, and we make love, and she tells me her dreams, here in this ramshackle cabin out past the dunes and dog roses and the gale-stunted trees. In her dreams, I am always leaving her behind, buying tickets on tramp steamers or signing on with freighters, sailing away to the Ivory Coast or Portugal or Singapore. I can't begin to recall all the faraway places she's dreamt me leaving her for. Her nightmares have sent me round and round the globe. But the truth is, *she's* the one who's leaving, and soon, before the first snows come.

I know it (though I play her games of transference), and all her apostles know it, too. The ones who have come down from the village and never gone back up the hill again. The vagrants and squatters and winos, the lunatics and true believers, who have turned their backs on the world, but only after it turned its back on them. Destitute and cast away, they found the daughter of the sea, each of them, and the shanty town is dotted with their tawdry, makeshift altars and shrines. She knows precisely what she is to them, even if she won't admit it. She knows that these lost souls have been blinded by the trials and tribulations of their various, sordid lives, and *she* is the soothing darkness they've found. She is the only genuine balm they've ever known against the cruel glare of the sun and the moon, which are the unblinking eyes of the gods of all mankind.

She sits there, at the edge of the bed. She is always alone, no matter how near we are, no matter how many apostles crowd around and eavesdrop and plot my demise. She stares at the flapping sheet of plastic tacked up where the windowpane used to be, and I go back to watching the ceiling. A single drop of rainwater gets through the layers of tin and tarpaper shingles and lands on my exposed belly.

She laughs softly. She doesn't laugh very often anymore, and I shut my eyes and listen to the rain.

"You can really have no notion how delightful it will be, when they take us up and throw us, with the lobsters, out to sea," she whispers, and then laughs again.

I take the bait, because I almost always take the bait.

"But the snail replied 'Too far, too far!' and gave a look askance," I say, quoting Lewis Carroll, and she doesn't laugh. She starts to scratch at the welts below her chin, then stops herself.

"In the halls of my mother," she says, "there is such silence, such absolute and immemorial peace. In that hallowed place, the mind can be still. There is serenity, finally, and an end to all sickness and fear." She pauses and looks at the floor, at the careless scatter of empty tin cans and empty bottles and bones picked clean. "But," she continues, "it will be lonely down there, without you. It will be something even worse than lonely."

I don't reply, and in a moment, she gets to her feet and goes to stand by the door.

The Alchemist's Daughter
(A Fragment)

Her father died in the hot, dry season before the coming of the mid-summer rains, when all the cobbled streets of Ulthar sizzle and the sky assumes a hue almost indistinguishable from the many-tiered expanse of roofs tiled with terra-cotta slate. He was very old and very sick, and his passing was in no way eased by the heat, nor by the reddish dust that sifted in through the shutters and settled over every surface in the house. The alchemist's daughter, whose name is Sála, sat vigil at his bedside and did everything within her meager abilities to comfort him. But the man had led a strange and ruthless life, and he feared dying, and feared still more the nameless beings who waited for him on the other side of death. Often they'd been summoned, by black sorceries and the most obscure hermetic sciences, and bound, and forced to do his bidding, these demons and more ancient, formless things. Always, the alchemist had been keenly aware that the day would arrive, and soon, when the brittle veil of his life would be parted, and all those beyond, whom he'd pressed into this or that distaste-ful labor, would be eagerly waiting to greet him.

"Eternity will be too short a span to settle that debt," he whispered fearfully through parched lips, as Sála wiped the sweat from his brow with a damp cloth.

"Well then, father, if that's the case," she said, "they will never collect their due. You'll emerge the victor, for even ages of their vengeance shall prove futile to the task." And though she meant the words as solace, he took them some other way, moaning louder, grimacing, gnashing his toothless gums, and rolling his rheumy blue eyes.

Afterwards, Sála kept any such thoughts to herself. It wasn't hard; he died only a few hours later, just as the bloated sun was finally setting behind the spires and gables of the city.

She covered the body with a yellowed linen sheet, and sat listening to the peal of bells ringing from the Temple of the Elder Ones, chiming the twilight in. To her ears, the bells sounded much farther away than they ever had before. She left the old man's corpse and went alone out onto the railed terrace, the balcony where they'd spent so many evenings together, where he'd charted the stars and spoken to her of other worlds bordering the dreamlands. The balcony where she'd listened. Now, Sála gazed down upon the narrow thoroughfares of the lower town and up at the high towers of the temple. It was plain that no distance had changed, whether absolute or relative, no matter how far off the bells might seem, unless it had changed somehow *within* herself.

As she watched, matches were struck, and whale-oil lamps and beeswax tapers were lit behind a hundred windowpanes, evidencing no gratitude whatsoever for the coolness and relief that night might bring. And there was movement now in the shadows, all along the balustrades and the tops of walls, in alleyways and the stalls of the deserted marketplace. Innumerable cats crept or scampered or simply sat watching, gathering for whatever secret feline affairs needed tending between dusk and dawn. Long before her birth, the burgesses of Ulthar had made the killing of any cat a crime punishable by death. On occasion, her father had sought their wise counsel in his studies and experiments, but never once had a cat been made to assist him in defiance of their own freewill.

After a time, Sála tired of watching the comings and goings of the busy cats and went back inside to tend what little remained of her father and to make ready for the arrival of the undertaker.

Long had the alchemist served the venerable patriarch Atal and the priests of the Temple of the Elder Ones, and so her father would be accorded a place of honor deep within the catacombs. And his house, his library and laboratory and all the peculiar contents thereof, including the journals containing his painstaking notes and calculations, the fruits of his researches, were willed to his daughter.

Following the elaborate funereal rites and the proper duration of her mourning, Sála left the city, for she had always longed to travel. She'd dreamed of Nir and Parg and the basalt turrets of Dylath-Leen, of sailing on black galley ships to the islands and port towns that lay across the wide Southern Sea, of wandering, perhaps, so far as gleaming Celephaïs in Ooth-Nargai beyond the Tanarian Hills and even the bhole-haunted vale of Pnath. And so she did, and many long years passed before she at last returned home to her father's house in the city of her birth. The tales of those voyages must await some other telling, or many other tellings, but it *should* be here noted that the woman who came back was not precisely the one who'd left, for the journey had worked its own magicks upon her, as journeys almost inevitably do. Very little remained of the girl she'd once been, for no species of innocence or naïveté can very long endure the rigors and revelations of the places where Sála had dared to tarry.

And before long she took up the alchemist's researches exactly where death had forced him to leave off. The old man had been a constant and demanding pedagogue, and Sála had proven a most attentive and gifted pupil. His lessons, combined with the knowledge she'd accumulated in her far-flung travels, had prepared her well. Within a month she mastered the fundaments of elemental and metallic transmutation and moved along to greater and more daunting problems.

Though she was a striking woman, fair skinned and tall, ebony haired, and with her father's gray-blue eyes, she did not take a husband. Though her beauty survived the passing of her youth, she had no suitors, and no one shared her bed. Sála lived alone, with only the company of her books and a few transient cats and the changing seasons. As it was, she had hardly time enough for the work, without squandering it on such trivialities as love and family. Besides, in her years away, Sála had frequented almost every brothel and bordello she happened upon, and she had taken a ghoul lover in a necropolis beneath the slopes of Mount Ngarnek. In Dylath-Leen, she'd been courted by, and, in a moment of weakness, had almost married the son of a wealthy wool merchant. In Celephaïs, she'd been willingly inducted into a certain notorious marquise's imbroglio. So, it was difficult for Sála to imagine there could be anything more remaining of sex that was worth the learning. She turned, instead, to more advanced transmutations and to questions of immortality, seeking the elixir that had eluded her father, though he'd sought after it as desperately as any before him.

The work become Sála's life, and very few interruptions or intrusions were permitted. Her days and nights were passed with flasks and beakers bubbling above the hot blue flames of spirit lamps. She puzzled over vexing, seemingly insoluble matters of filtration, sublimation, distillation, with acidic and alkali compounds, bismuth and antimony and salts of mercury. She devised her own improved numerology and also an elaborate new cryptography for setting down her inquiries and their results. Her notebooks were filled with alphanumeric snares, deadly incantations that would be triggered by the uninitiated and uninvited. She delved more deeply into both hyperbolic and elliptic geometry than her father had ever dared, constructing nine-dimensional lattices of crystal, light, and sound. She conjured and commanded djinn and the souls of the dead and even dared invoke servants of the blind and lunatic daemon sultan Azathoth, to whom all the Outer Gods are but marionettes in an endless shadowplay.

Day by day her power was compounded, and within only a single decade her mastery of the alchemical and thaumaturgical arts outstripped everything her father had required a lifetime to accomplish. In all the lands surrounding the prefecture of Ulthar, she was respected and feared in equal measure. Both her opinion and skill were always in great demand, from those in her own city as well as from foreign scholars, merchants, priests, and royalty.

And, then, on an autumn evening, one night past the new moon, as she attempted the *putrefactio* of a bothersome baetylic idol, and despite having taken especial precautions, there was an accident at the forge. The particulars were not set down, for she could be a prideful woman, and had on more than one occasion hidden any evidence of a logistical error on her part. What is known is that she might well have died from her injuries that night, or soon thereafter, if not for the timely intervention of a fat old tabby, a tom who'd been watching from the shadows of her workshop. He slipped silently, soundlessly, up the stairs and out a window, quickly spreading news of the mishap to many other cats and also to a physician named Zath, who'd attended Sála on more than one occasion.

"That cat surely saved your life," the physician told Sála a few days later, after the fever had broken, after she'd regained consciousness and her wounds had begun to heal. "I'd keep him close, were I you."

And Zath also insisted that she enlist the services of a nurse, at least until she was again able to walk and to see to her own needs. Reluctantly, Sála consented, and allowed the physician to retain a dependable young woman from the lower town. Her name was Anissa, and, unknown to Sála, she was the granddaughter of the midwife who had seen to Sála's own delivery, the labor that had claimed her mother's life and left her father, the alchemist, to raise their daughter alone and by his own wits.

"If she becomes a nuisance, I'll not hesitate to send her away," Sála warned Zath as he changed the dressing on a burn that covered most of her left leg below the knee.

"Of course," the physician replied. "But she won't become a nuisance. You'll see."

"I've no time for these distractions, and no need of a companion," she said, wincing as Zath began reapplying a thick blue salve to the burn.

"If these wounds become infected, Sála, and sepsis sets in, you'll find yourself with no time at all and in need of no one but the embalmer." He scowled at her a moment, and then began wrapping her calf with a fresh length of bandage.

Anissa arrived early the next morning and was installed in a disused, and particularly musty, portion of the attic. She was permitted access to Sála's bedchamber, of course, and the kitchen, and to all other areas of the house that a nurse, cook, and maid might fairly need to gain during the pursuit of her duties. But she was strictly forbidden entry to the library and conservatory and to the lower levels of the house, the basement and subbasement, where her mistress' laboratories were located. Also, she was to speak to no other living being of *anything* she saw or heard within those walls, and Zath made it clear to her that even the most minor breach of these directives would result, at the *very* least, in her immediate dismissal and the forfeiture of a reference and any wages owed.

And so the comfortable and long-held rhythms of Sála's existence were suddenly supplanted by new routines and by the almost constant presence of this low-born girl. At first, Sála rarely missed an opportunity to complain about the inconveniences visited upon her by the accident and the over-cautious physician's insistence that she employ a nurse, and, endlessly, she lamented the work that wasn't getting done while she lay there in bed. Sála groused and grumbled and carped. But, in truth, she found Anissa comely and not without charm, possessing of an unexpectedly sharp mind for one with so little formal education.

As the weeks passed and Sála's condition slowly improved, she worried less and less over her neglected researches, and began, instead, to look forward to her conversations with Anissa. She found herself anticipating the girl's every lightest touch, the very sight and smell of her, and soon discovered that she'd actually come to cherish her nurse's ministrations. Indeed, Sála began to wonder how and why she'd suffered so many years of self-imposed isolation, and though she would not have admitted these things to anyone, and not for any price, they were, nonetheless, true.

Often, she and Anissa would talk well into the small hours of the night, and it was not uncommon for their tête-à-têtes to last until the cocks had begun to crow and the stars to dim in a sky gone grayish-purple with dawn. Anissa discovered no great effort was needed to coax from Sála the bizarre and rambling stories of her travels. Since her return to Ulthar, she'd had scant occasions to talk with others in anything but a professional capacity, and, even then, she'd always tended to be curt and furtive. In some indefinable way, the girl put her at ease and loosened her tongue, set her mind wandering back upon those days of caravans and sailing ships and distant lands.

"You have so very many wonderful tales," Anissa told her one evening, as the nurse busied herself with the dressing on Sála's left wrist. "And not merely tales you've heard, no, but tales that you have *lived* to tell. Myself, I've never gone any farther than the bridge across the river, and I've only done that once."

It must be acknowledged that Sála had inherited from her father various imperfections of character, and one of those weaknesses was surely vanity, and another was just as surely a susceptibility to fawning palaver and all sorts of flattery. But, it would be wrong to say here that Anissa exploited these weaknesses in her mistress, for the girl had no designs to that end. If she burbled or displayed an excess of enthusiasm, it was done honestly, and arose from a genuine adoration and a desire to hear of Sála's adventures and misadventures. Since childhood, Anissa had been curious of the world beyond the walls of Ulthar, and she'd heard little enough of it before coming to the alchemist's house.

"I would not trade those days cheaply," Sála replied, glancing quickly at the ugly scars on her wrist and palm, wondering if she'd ever again have full use of that hand. "They often seem as though they happened to some other, more daring woman, and I've only managed to steal her memories for my own."

"A most fortunate theft," Anissa said and smiled for Sála, before hiding her mistress' injured hand in swaths of clean gauze. "Would that I might someday prove so skilled a cutpurse. And then find so fine a mark."

The talk helped somewhat to distract from the pain of her difficult recovery, but Sála also turned, in time, to tinctures of opium, including laudanum and paregoric, as well as a strong solution of morphia, ethyl alcohol, citrus juice, and anise oil. These potions were not prescribed by the physician Zath, but purchased by Anissa from a local chemist or concocted from the contents of Sála's own cabinets. And while they did act to ease much of Sála's discomfort, they also took their inevitable toll on her mental faculties; under their influence she dreamt queer and disquieting dreams, both waking and while asleep. Sometimes, she spoke aloud to no one and nothing that Anissa could see, and, other times, she might lay perfectly still, her unblinking eyes open wide and gazing into such dreadful and marvelous gulfs as the nurse could only dare imagine. In the throes of her deliriums, Sála railed against unseen adversaries, or wept inconsolably, or she would cringe pitifully in obvious terror, as though some monstrous entity loomed nearby. While these paroxysms greatly disconcerted Anissa, who more than once seemed herself the object of her mistress' hysteria, the nurse did what she was able to do in order to calm Sála and make certain she didn't harm herself.

Late one evening, for example, as Anissa was pulling the bedroom shutters closed for the night and in advance of a storm, a horrified sort of gasp or wheeze was loudly uttered by the alchemist (and by now, Sála had certainly inherited this appellation, so from hereon, and unless otherwise stated, when "the alchemist" is spoken of, it is her, and not her father, whom is meant). Anissa turned quickly about and found her charge sitting bolt upright in the bed, one bandaged arm raised towards the low ceiling beams.

"Do you not *see* it?" the alchemist asked, barely speaking above a whisper. "Right *there,* floating, floating in the sea, *watching* me with those abominable lifeless eyes. Can *no one* see it watching me?"

"Yes, I can see it," Anissa answered, and what matter if she lied, so long as her words allayed Sála's panic. "But that was long ago, and you are only remembering. You're home, in your own bed, and you are *safe.* Safe with *me.* It cannot find you here."

"But it's still watching," Sála insisted, turning her head only slightly towards Anissa, who felt a chill at the conviction in the alchemist's voice.

"Of course," she assured Sála. "But *you are safe,* and no matter *how* diligently it keeps this awful lookout, it will *not* find you, not *ever.*"

And at that, Sála began to relax somewhat, though she continued to stare intently up at the ceiling for the better part of an hour. Only when the thunder commenced and a cold rain started to pepper the windows did she at last look away. Yet, later, even after sleep found and claimed her, the alchemist tightly gripped Anissa's hand in hers, much the same way a frightened child clutches its mother's hand when startled or threatened.

As with all tales possessed of so many twists and turns and complications, decisions must perforce be made as to what shall be related and what set aside. In this unfortunate imperative lies the difference between the truth of things and those extracts or distillates which we call *history* and *biography,* which can only ever be a rough approximation of *actual* events and lives, a necessary fiction conveying what any given author may perceive as the most significant points along a timeline comprised of vastly more moments than any reasonable narrative may contain. To wit, there are always omissions. The lion's share of the moments comprising all the days and hours bounded by "Once upon a time" and "The End" are simply omitted, while others may be given only the most cursory treatment.

In the instance of *this* tale, there is only space here to mention, in passing, that Sála's nurse was able, with great patience and the aid of the physician Zath, to wean the alchemist off her addiction to these varied potions of opium and morphia. And, also, as Sála recovered from both her injuries and dependencies, that she discovered her fondness for Anissa had become love. Not the love between dear friends or even sisters, but, rather, that genus of love the Grecian poets and philosophers ascribed to the realm of the god Eros. To the reader, it may seem a great negligence on the part of the narrator not to elaborate on exactly *how* it happened, or to detail the first awkward intimacies between the two women, or treat at length Anissa's sexual education at the hands, literally, of one who'd known all the disparate and exotic carnal pleasures the alchemist had experienced during her journeys. It must suffice to know this *was* the case, and that Anissa was, in all ways, receptive and returned her mistress' affections.

Bit by bit, the alchemist's body healed, and, as the latter part of autumn gave way to bare branches and the first snows of winter, she found that she could walk again, with a cane and with Anissa's aid. For short durations, she could even return to her studies. Though, by necessity, Sála broke with her earlier dictates, allowing the nurse to accompany her, and even at times assist, in the laboratories that Anissa, heretofore, had been barred from entering.

The alchemist began by inspecting a number of timeworn, moldering books and parchments that had been delivered during her convalescence. One, a papyrus or *wadj* protected inside a baked-clay cylinder, was reputed by the dealer who had sold it to her to have been removed from an unmarked tomb, somewhere near the fabled ruins of Sarkomand, where it is said that titanic winged lions of stone guard a well leading all the way down to the Great Abyss and which lies not so very far from the cold wastes of cursed Leng. Although she was unable to translate the papyrus in full, it was plainly concerned with that unspeakable Elder Hierophant, the High Priest Not to Be Described, who dwells always in his monastery on the Plateau of Leng, his face perpetually concealed behind a yellow mask of silk.

And yet, among these several new acquisitions, there was still one item which excited the alchemist much more than the undoubtedly priceless

Sarkomand papyrus. To Anissa's eyes, it was only a letter, postmarked from one of the farming villages beyond the River Skai, and bearing no return address. It had arrived almost a full month previous, sealed with a dribble of crimson sealing wax. But as Sála silently read what was scrawled on the single page her eyes widened and her hands began to tremble, this time not from any infirmity or ague, but from excitement. A few moments later, she read it aloud to Anissa:

My Dear Madame Professor,

As for introductions, I should say only that I am a bo'sun aboard the dogger *Mock Turtle,* in the employ of a fine skipper who fishes the river and transports wool and other dry goods. Not long ago, a most unusual object fetched up in our nets, which appears very like a gigantic egg as dark and smooth as a shard of obsidian glass. Never have I seen the like of it. I have measured the egg – for I am certain it is an egg – and can say to you that it is a full nine palms in length, though without much heft (and so, I fear, empty). At night, or whenever out of direct sunlight, it has been seen to emit a faint and bluish glow. I was told such an oddity might be of interest to you, and would ask only a modest finder's fee to have it transported from the docks, where it is now safely put aside. There are those who, upon glimpsing it, have whispered prayers and named it a Drake's egg, and who swear it has been washed all the way down from the eyries and rookeries of those mighty worms. As you may know, many men hold that these beasts still dwell in high and inaccessible mountain passes. I do not know of such things myself, but can attest to this object's singular deviance from anything I have heretofore witnessed in all my long years on the river or at sea. I await your kind reply, and such remittance as you generously deem fit.

The letter had been written, in a coarse hand, with what appeared to be a charcoal pencil upon a scrap of butcher's paper. When the alchemist unexpectedly passed the page to Anissa, she saw that it was signed only with the initials R. O. and was stained at one corner with some unpleasant, greasy substance.

"I *must* have this thing," Sála said, reaching for a quill and a bottle of ink. "You'll carry my reply and make payment and arrange for the egg's portage. If, of course, we are not already too late and our bo'sun, having despaired of a reply, has sold it to another."

There were questions that Anissa wanted to ask, but she kept them all to herself, hopeful that they would eventually be addressed. She also worried about leaving Sála alone and unattended, and suggested Zath might be bidden to come and sit with the alchemist until the errand was finished, but Sála shook her head and glowered, dismissing the idea out of hand.

"I'm done with playing an invalid," she said, "and we've lost much too much time as it is." And, with that, she found a sheet of stationary and wrote a quick response to the boatswain's query. This she gave to Anissa, along with what the alchemist deemed sufficient gold to secure the egg and pay to see it brought safely to her doorstep.

"As you wish," Anissa sighed, and she slipped both the letter and coins into a sturdy leather pouch that served as her purse and pulled its drawstrings tight. Then she helped the alchemist from her desk in the laboratory, back upstairs to what was now *their* bed.

"Please, Sála," she said, "stay put until I return. I'll try not to be long, no longer than I must be. And I'll surely have enough to worry over, what with this mysterious Mr. R. O. and his black egg, without *also* having to worry whether you've stumbled and taken a bad fall."

"*Don't* dote on me," Sála replied, rather more sternly than was necessary. "And do not rush this task on my account. I have to have it, Anissa."

And then, because she could not help herself, Anissa said, "My mother taught me they were only fairy tales. Dragons, I mean. Drakes, and fire worms, and what have you. You believe this man?"

"I will believe what my eyes reveal," the alchemist replied, clearly growing anxious that Anissa stop fussing and posing questions and be on her way. "But, yes, there once were dragons in the world, unequivocally, from the isle of Oriab west to Mnar and north across the Cerenarian Sea to the shores of Kaar. They were not entirely uncommon beings, long ago. Now, *please* – "

And so Anissa left the house in the shadow of the Temple of the Elder Ones, and she hurried through the snowy streets of Ulthar, weaving her way between pedestrians and the omnipresent, mewling carpet of cats, dodging zebra-drawn carriages and carts of vegetables pulled by oxen. She passed through the lower city, down to the quayside and the docks that line the eastern shore of the Skai. The wide river was slate colored beneath the clouds, and there was a thin fringe of new ice near the shore. Anissa thought it a great good fortune to find the *Mock Turtle* moored in one of the first berths she explored. However, after speaking to a pair of deckhands and the first mate, she learned that the man who'd sent the letter to Sála had drowned only a week earlier.

The dogger had been returning from the port at Dylath-Leen, just entering into an especially worrisome stretch of water where boats were often lost to the sharp, stony reefs that lay hidden, here and there, below the rippling surface. The elderly navigator, who was growing near-sighted, had made a small error at his charts, and, as a result, the *Mock Turtle*'s bow had struck one of the reefs – only a glancing blow, and no real harm was done to the hull. But the boatswain (and none among the sailors could tell what the initials R. O. stood for, though they'd known and worked alongside the man for many years) was jolted from the rigging, where he'd been overseeing the untangling of a snarled cable. An alarm was raised and a lifeline immediately lowered, but not before he'd vanished beneath the swirling water, never to be seen again.

"But we know well enough where he stowed the black egg," the first mate volunteered, as soon as Anissa explained why she'd come seeking after the lost man. "And we'll not be sorry to see it go, I'll tell you *that* for nothing. A small enough wonder no one's cast it back into the river. I'd have done it myself, only I can't be sure it wouldn't do more harm there than locked away ashore."

And when she asked what, specifically, he meant when he spoke of "harm," the first mate grew suddenly taciturn, unwilling to discuss the matter any further. Instead, he barked an order at one of the deckhands to take her to a nearby net shed, where R. O. had placed his treasure inside a locker. No one had the key, but the steel hasp was prised open easily enough with one end of a broken gaff hook. The egg was still right there, beneath a tattered section of canvas that had once been part of a ship's sail. Inside the shed, the air was close and stunk of mildew, rotting wood, and fish, but at least the walls provided a brief respite from the cold wind blowing off the Skai.

"Now, you take it and be off," the man told her gruffly, and when Anissa offered him two of the gold coins Sála had given her, he refused. "Take it and be off," he said again, then left her alone in the net shed.

Anissa stood staring a moment at the egg. It was just as the letter had described, smooth and dark as volcanic glass, vaguely translucent, and in the half light of the shed it emitted a faint, but unmistakable and uncanny blue glow. When she touched the egg, she was surprised to find it warm, not at all cold, as she'd expected. Anissa lifted it warily, half anticipating some reaction or resistance. But if the thing truly *was* an egg and ever had held the embryo of a living creature, along with whatever albumen and yolk might have been present, it seemed empty now and weighed no more than a brass kettle. She wrapped it carefully in the canvas, and, as twilight fell over the avenues of Ulthar, made her way from the waterfront back to the house where her mistress waited.

Anissa did not find Sála in the bedchamber, nor anywhere else upstairs, but once more downstairs, in the laboratory, pouring over a particularly thick sheaf of notes that had been made decades before by her dead father.

"It's a miracle you didn't take a tumble on the stairs and break your neck," Anissa said, exasperated and frowning as she gently sat the canvas bundle down on the table in front of the alchemist.

"This is it?" Sála asked, ignoring the reprimand. Her voice wavered slightly with expectation and the state of dismay that often visits women or men who are about to lay eyes on some trinket of their heart's desire that they've never actually dared hope to see.

"Yes, love. This is it. But the bo'sun was dead, drowned as it turns out, and – "

"No matter," Sála said. "No matter at all," and with the thumbs and forefingers of both hands, she gingerly pulled back the sailcloth and unwrapped the black egg. In the dim light of the laboratory, which was illumined only with candles and oil lamps, the bluish glow was almost as evident as it had been to Anissa when first she'd glimpsed it in the net shed. Amazed, the alchemist squinted through her spectacles and muttered the names of several among the Great Old Ones which are rarely ever spoken aloud (and with very good reason).

"Is it? From a dragon, I mean?" Anissa asked, and Sála nodded. "But it's so light," Anissa said, and through force of habit, she bent down and placed a palm on Sála's forehead; she was relieved to detect no hint of fever. "I'm afraid it no longer holds anything. There's no telling how long it lay at the bottom of the river. Ages, I'd think."

"All the better," the alchemist replied. She was smiling now, and it was an expression Anissa saw cross her mistress' face all too infrequently. "After all, what conceivable use have I of a dragon hatchling? It would be a nuisance, and a hazard, and no end of trouble. But the *egg* of a dragon," and she almost touched the glossy black shell, then, but stopped herself, and returned, instead, to the notes she'd been examining when Anissa had found her.

"While studying in Ilarnek," she said, tapping at the sheaf of papers, "at the library there, my father saw a fossilized shard from a dragon's egg, which was said to have prolonged the life of the sorcerer who'd uncovered it by almost two centuries, until he was betrayed and poisoned by a professional rival."

Anissa considered this, then asked, "The egg didn't protect him from the poison?"

"Oh, it would have, most assuredly. But the rival succeeded in pilfering the shard *before* the poison was administered to his victim. At any rate, the murderer was found dead some days later, having hung himself." Sála paused and glanced back at Anissa. "Mind you, my father only half believed this tale, though he noted the purported eggshell displayed many peculiar properties when subjected to various reagents. And he said not one word about it being luminous."

Anissa reached out and brushed the fingertips of her right hand across the slick ebony surface, curious whether it sill retained the warmth she'd felt in the net shed. She found that it did and was about to ask Sála what might possibly be the source of this heat, when she discovered a tiny breach – hardly any wider than the breadth of a hair – running lengthwise along one side of the egg.

"Sála," she said. "Could it be this crack that allowed the contents to spill out?"

The alchemist looked up from her father's notes, turning back to the egg, which she herself had not yet touched. But before she could reply to Anissa's question, or examine the crack for herself, she noticed a bright drop of blood welling from the pad of Anissa's middle finger.

"You've cut yourself," she said. "Go and find a sticking plaster. And be sure to clean the wound thoroughly."

"You're beginning to sound like me," the nurse replied and stared at the end of her finger, at the minute laceration she hadn't even felt, but must have received while examining the edges of the breach. It wasn't much more than a paper cut.

"The shell not only reminds the eye of obsidian," Sála said, and for the first time she touched the black egg, "but like obsidian, when broken the shards are razor sharp. They must be handled with caution." She glanced at Anissa again, still smiling. "It's warm. Why didn't you tell me it was warm?"

"Well, I was just about to do that very thing," Anissa told her, then sucked at the cut, tasting the rusty tang of her own blood.

"That *is* remarkable," the alchemist said, turning back to the egg, and wondering to herself if the source of the heat radiating from it might share a common cause with the indisputable luminescence. Could it be this egg, unlike the shard in Ilarnek, was not ancient, but had passed into the river quite recently and still retained some unknown vitae or other essential essence that would disperse and be lost with time? And if so, would it not stand to reason that dragonkind still persisted somewhere in the dreamlands? Sála's mind reeled from the sight of her prize and the weight of these and a hundred other questions. What novel and invaluable compounds might be extracted from a dragon's egg that had so lately contained the living foetus? What fabulous cures and solvents might it yield, and if a petrified shard had prolonged a man's life for twice a hundred years, then could it be that a relatively whole and fresh egg might be the key to that elixir of immortality her father had sought so fervently.

"There are tests I must perform straight away," she told Anissa. "Please, leave me to the work. I'll call should I need anything."

"You're certain you're strong enough?"

The alchemist laughed softly and rolled the egg over so she might examine the opposite hemisphere. "Are you worried I'll catch my death down here, and then you'll have to answer to old Zath for the loss of a patient?"

"No," Anissa replied, and she lightly kissed the top of Sála's head, though the alchemist hardly seemed to take notice. "That's not it at all. If you need me – "

"I won't hesitate to let you know," and Sála pointed to the brass bell resting on the table nearby. Its stout mahogany handle had been carved to resemble the head and coils of some manner of ferocious serpent. Its jaws were open, baring wooden fangs.

And so Anissa went back upstairs, and began preparing the evening meal – a roast hare and cabbage with onions – all the while listening for the clang of the brass bell with the mahogany handle. She did remember to wash out the very slight cut on her finger, though it had long since ceased to bleed. There was no discomfort, and she didn't bother to bandage it. After all, she'd learned it was sometimes preferable to allow an injury, especially one so minor, to remain exposed to the air, to "breathe," as the physician Zath had said.

A day passed, and another, and then another, while the snow piled up on the roof and eaves and in the streets of Ulthar. Anissa did her best to see that Sála rested as she should, that she ate and slept and did not forget to take the medications that had been prescribed to hasten her renaissance.

But the black egg had become an obsession, and it was almost impossible to divert Sála's attention from her questing after whatever could be learned of the artifact's structure and properties and origins. That first night, it had ceased to glow, almost as soon as Anissa had left her alone in the laboratory, and this phenomenon, in and of itself, had beget no small amount of consternation from the alchemist. Sála discovered that the egg was far more resilient than she'd first believed and found that the application of a diamond stylus was necessary to cut away even the few stingy fragments required for her analyses. She had difficulty conceiving a force sufficient to have produced the longitudinal crack in the egg without also having shattered it.

And on the morning of the fourth day after Anissa had retrieved the egg from the shed where the drowned boatswain had placed it for safe keeping, she awoke sweating and breathless from a nightmare she would not later be able to recall in any detail. Only that there had been a roaring, billowing inferno moving steadily across the land, a wall of fire that extended north and south as far as the eye could see. It swept hungrily over the land, turning the snow and ice to floodwater as it bore down upon the old city on the banks of the Skai. In the dream, Anissa had known that the fire was seeking her, and she woke with a fever and chills that lasted well into the late afternoon, but which she managed to keep secret from Sála. That night, she felt well enough again not to spurn her lover's advances, though they caught her completely off her guard. For days, Sála had exhibited an interest in nothing except the black egg. But, then, when the two women went down to sleep, and the candles were extinguished so that there was only the soothing orange light from the hearth, Anissa felt the alchemist's hands on her breasts.

"I have neglected you," Sála whispered in her ear.

"You have been occupied," Anissa replied, "and rightly so. Such a find – "

"It's no excuse," Sála replied, whispering as though someone might overhear. "I have no desire to return to being the woman I once was, consumed only by my work."

Beneath her gown, Anissa's nipples had begun to stiffen. She shivered, and rolled over onto her side to face Sála, though the shadows hid her features from view.

"All the same, I have not *felt* neglected," Anissa whispered. "And I would not wish you to think I have."

They kissed, then, and Sála thought that perhaps there was the faintest taste of brimstone and soot on Anissa's breath. But it was an impression that passed almost immediately, as soon as Anissa slipped a finger inside her.

Houndwife

1.

Memory fails, moments bleeding one against and into the next or the one before, merging and diverging and commingling again farther along. Rain streaking glass, muddy rivers flowing to the sea or blood on a slaughterhouse floor, wending its way towards a drain. There was a time, I am still reasonably certain, when all this might have been set forth as a mere *tale,* starting at some more or less arbitrary, but seemingly consequential, moment: the day I first met Isobel Endecott, the evening I boarded a train from Savannah to Boston, or the turning of frail yellowed pages in a black magician's grimoire and coming upon the graven image of a jade idol. But I am passed now so far out beyond the conveniences and conventions of chronology and narrative and gone down to some place so few (and so very many) women before me have ever gone. It cannot be a tale, any more than a crystal goblet dropped on a marble floor may ever again hold half an ounce of wine. I have been dropped, like that, from a great height, and I have shattered on a marble floor. Or I may not have been dropped. I may have only fallen, but that hardly seems to matter now. I may have been pushed, also. And, too, it might well be I was dropped, fell, *and* was pushed, none of these actions necessarily being mutually exclusive of the others. I am no different from the broken goblet, whose shards do not worry overly about how they came to be divided from some former whole.

Memory fails. I fall. Not one or the other, but both. I tumble through the vulgar, musty shadows of sepulchers. I lie in my own grave, dug by my own hands, and listen to hungry black beetles and maggots busy at my corporeal undoing. I am led to the altar on the dais in the sanctuary of the Church of Starry Wisdom, to be bedded and worshipped and bled dry. I look up from a hole in the earth and see the bloated moon. There

is no ordering these events, no matter how I might try, if I even *cared* to
try. They occurred, or I am yet rushing towards them. They are past and
present and future, realized and unrealized and imagined and inconceivable; I would be a damned fool to worry over such trivialities. Better I be
only damned.

"It was lost," Isobel tells me. "For a very long time it was lost. There
were rumors it had gone to Holland, early in the Fifteenth Century, that
it was buried there with one who'd worn it in life. Other stories say it was
stolen from the grave of that man sometime in the 1920's and carried off
to England."

I sip coffee while she talks.

"It's all bound up in irony and coincidence, and, really, I don't give
that sort of prattle much credence," she continues. "The Dutchman who's
said to have been buried with the idol, some claim he was a grave robber,
that he fancied himself a proper ghoul. Charming fellow, sure, and then,
five hundred years later, along come these two British degenerates – from
somewhere in Yorkshire, I think. Supposedly, they dug him up and stole
the idol, which they found hung around his neck."

"But before that...I mean, before the Dutchman, where might it have
been?" I ask, and Isobel smiles. Her smile could melt ice, or freeze the
blood, depending on one's perspective and penchant for hyperbole and
metaphor. She shrugs and sets her coffee cup down on the kitchen table.
We're sitting together in her loft on Atlantic Avenue. The building was
constructed in the 1890's, as cold storage for the wares of fur merchants.
The walls are thick and solid and keep our secrets. She lights a cigarette and
watches me a moment.

My train is pulling into South Station. I've never visited Boston before,
and I shall never leave. It's a rainy day, and I've been promised that Isobel
will be waiting for me on the platform.

"Well, before Holland – assuming, of course, it was ever *in* Holland – I've
spoken with a man who thinks it might have spent time in Greece, hidden
at the Monastery of Holy Trinity at Metéora. But the monastery wasn't built
until 1475, so this really doesn't jibe with the story of the Dutch grave robber. Of course, the hound is mentioned in *Al Azif*. But you know that." And
then the conversation shifts from the jade idol to archaeology in Damascus,
and then Yemen, and, finally, the ruins of Babylon. In particular, I listen to
Isobel describe the blue-glazed tiles of the Ishtar Gate, with their golden bas-
reliefs of lions and auroch bulls and the strange, dragon-like *sirrush*. She saw

a reconstructed portion of the gate at the Pergamon Museum when she was in Berlin, many years ago.

"In Germany, I was still a young woman," she says, and glances at a window and the city lights, the Massachusetts night and the yellow-orange skyglow that's there so no one ever has to look too closely at the stars.

This is the night of the new moon, and Isobel kneels before me and bathes my feet. I'm naked save the jade idol on its silver chain, hung about my neck. The temple of the Starry Wisdom smells of frankincense, galbanum, sage, clove, myrrh, and saffron smoldering in iron braziers suspended from the high ceiling beams. Her ash-blonde hair is pulled back from her face, pinned into a neat chignon. Her robes are the color of raw meat. I don't want her to look me in the eyes, and yet I cannot imagine going up the granite stairs to the dais without first having done so, without that easy, familiar reassurance. Dark figures in robes of half a dozen other shades of red and black and grey press in close from all sides. The colors of their robes denote their rank. I close my eyes, though I have been forbidden to do so.

"This is our daughter," barks the High Priestess, the old one crouched near the base of the altar. Her voice is phlegm and stripped gears, discord and tumult. "Of her own will does she come, and of her own will and the will of the Nameless Gods will she make the passage."

And even in this instant – here at the end of my life *and* the beginning of my existence – I cannot help but smile at the High Priestess' choice of words, at force of habit, her calling them *the Nameless Gods,* when we have given them so very many names over the millennia.

"She will see what we cannot," the High Priestess barks. "She will walk unhindered where our feet will never tread. She will know their faces and their embrace. She will suffer fire and flood and the frozen wastes, and she will dine with the Mother and the Father. She will take a place at their table. She will know their blood, as they will know hers. She will fall and sleep, be raised and walk."

I am pulling into South Station.

I am drinking coffee with Isobel.

I am nineteen years old, dreaming of a Dutch churchyard and violated graves. My dream is filled with the rustle of leathery wings and the mournful baying of some great, unseen beast. I smell freshly broken earth. The sky glares down at all the world with a single cratered eye which humanity, in its merciful ignorance, would mistake for a full autumnal moon. There are two men with shovels and pick axes. Fascinated, I watch their grim,

233

determined work, an unspeakable thievery done sixty-three years before my own birth. I hear the shovel scrape stone and wood.

In the temple, Isobel rises and kisses me. It's no more than the palest ghost of all the many kisses we've shared during our long nights of lovemaking, those afternoons and mornings spent exploring one another's bodies and desires and most taboo fancies.

The Hermit passes a jade cup to the Hierophant, who in turn passes it to Isobel. Though, in this place and in this hour, Isobel is *not* Isobel Endecott. She is the Empress, as I am here named the Wheel of Fortune. I have never seen this cup until now, but I know well enough that it was carved untold thousands of years before this night and from the same vein of leek-green *piedra de ijada* as the pendant I wear about my throat. The mad Arabian author of the *Al Azif* believed the jade to have come from the Plateau of Y'Pawfrm e'din Leng, and it may be he was correct. The Empress places the rim of the cup to my lips, and I drink. The bitter ecru tincture burns going down, and it kindles a fire in my chest and belly. I know this is the fire that will make ashes of me, and from those ashes will I rise as surely as any phoenix.

"She stands at the threshold," the High Priestess growls, "and soon will enter the Hall of the Mother and the Father." The crowd murmurs blessings and blasphemies. Isobel's delicate fingers caress my face, and I see the longing in her blue eyes, but the High Priestess may not kiss me again, not in this life.

"I will be waiting," she whispers.

My train leaves Savannah.

"Do you miss Georgia?" Isobel asks me, a week after I arrive in Boston, and I tell her yes, sometimes I do miss Georgia. "But it always passes," I say, and she smiles.

I am almost twenty years old, standing alone on a wide white beach where the tannin-stained Tybee River empties into the Atlantic Ocean, watching as a hurricane barrels towards shore. The outermost rain bands lash the sea, but haven't yet reached the beach. The sand around me is littered with dead fish and sharks, crabs and squid. On February 5th, 1958, a B-47 collided in midair with an F-86 Sabre fighter 7,200 feet above this very spot, and the crew of the B-47 was forced to jettison the Mark 15 hydrogen bomb it was carrying; the "Tybee bomb" was never recovered, and lies buried somewhere in silt and mud below the brackish waters of Wassaw Sound, six or seven miles southwest of where I'm standing. I draw a line in the sand, connecting one moment to another, and the hurricane wails.

I am sixteen, and a high-school English teacher is telling me that if a gun appears at the beginning of a story, it should be fired by the end. If it's a bomb, the conscientious author should take care to be certain it explodes, so that the reader's expectations are not neglected. It all sounds very silly, and I cite several examples to the contrary. The English teacher scowls and changes the subject.

In the temple of the Church of Starry Wisdom, I walk through the flames consuming my soul and take my place on the altar.

2.

It's a sweltering day in late August 20__, and I walk from the green shade of Telfair Square, moving north along Barnard Street. I would try to describe here the violence of the alabaster sun on this afternoon, hanging so far above Savannah, but I know I'd never come close to capturing in words the sheer *spite* and *vehemence* of it. The sky is bleached as pallid as the cement sidewalk and the whitewashed bricks on either side of the street. I pass what was once a cotton and grain warehouse, when the New South was still the Old South, more than a century ago. The building has been "repurposed" for lofts and boutiques and a trendy soul-food restaurant. I walk, and the stillness of the summer afternoon makes my footsteps seem almost loud as thunderclaps. I can feel the dull beginnings of a headache, and wish I had a Pepsi or an orange drink, something icy cold in a perspiring bottle. I glance through windows at the air-conditioned sanctuaries on the other side of the glass, but I don't stop and go inside.

The night before this day, there were dreams I will never tell anyone until I meet Isobel Endecott, two years farther along. I had dreams of a Dutch graveyard, and of a baying hound, and awoke to find an address on West Broughton scribbled on the cover of a paperback book I'd been reading when I fell asleep. The handwriting was indisputably mine, though I have no memory of having picked up the ballpoint pen on my nightstand and writing the address. I did not get back to sleep until sometime after sunrise, and then there were only more dreams of that cemetery and the spire of a cathedral and the two men, busy with their picks and shovels.

I glance directly at the sun, daring it to blind me.

"You knew where to go," Isobel says, my first evening in Boston, my first evening with her, and already I felt as though I'd known her all my life. "The time was right, and you were chosen. I can't even imagine such an honor."

It is late August, and I sweat and walk north until I come to the intersection with West Broughton Street. I am clutching the paperback copy of *Absalom, Absalom!* in my left hand, and I pause to read the address again. Then I turn left, which also means I turn west.

"The stars were right," she says and pours me another brandy. "Which is really only another way of saying these events cannot occur until it is *time* for them to occur. That there is a proper sequence. A protocol."

I walk west down West Broughton until I come to the address that my sleeping self wrote on the Faulkner book. It's a dingy shop (calling itself an "emporium") specializing in antique jewelry, porcelain figurines, and Oriental curios. Inside, after the scorching gaze of the sun, the dusty gloom seems almost frigid. I find what I did not even know I was looking for in a display case near the register. It is one of the most hideous things I've ever seen, but it's one of the most beautiful, too. I guess the stone is jade, but it's only a guess. I know next to nothing about gemstones and the lapidary arts. That day, I do not even know the word *lapidary*. I won't learn it until later, when I begin asking questions about the pendant.

There's a middle-aged man sitting on a stool behind the counter. He watches me through the lenses of his spectacles. He has about him a certain mincing fastidiousness. I notice the mole above his left eyebrow and that his clean nails are trimmed almost to the quick. I notice there's a hair growing from the mole. My mother always said I had an eye for detail.

"Anything I can show you today?" he wants to know, and I only *almost* hesitate before nodding and pointing to the jade pendant.

"Now, that is a very peculiar piece," he says, leaning forward and sliding the back of the case open. He reaches inside and lifts the pendant and its chain from a felt-lined tray. The felt is a faded shade of burgundy. He sits up again and passes the pendant across the counter to me. I'd not expected it to be so heavy or to feel so slick in my fingers, almost as though it were coated with oil or wax.

"Picked it up at an estate sale, a few years back," says the fastidious seller of antiques. "Never liked the thing myself, but different strokes, as they say. If I only stocked what I liked, wouldn't make much of a living, now would I?"

"No," I reply. "I don't suppose you would."

I stand alone on a beach at the south end of Tybee Island, watching the arrival of a hurricane. I've come to the beach to drown. However, I already know that's not what's going to happen, and the realization brings with it a faint pang of disappointment.

"Came from an old house down in Stephen's Ward," the man behind the counter says. "On East Hall Street, if memory serves. Strange bunch of women lived there, years ago, but then, one June, all of a sudden, the whole lot up and moved away. There were nine of them living in that house, and, well, you know how people talk."

"Yes," I say. "People talk."

"Might be better if we all tended to our own business and let others be," the man says and watches me as I examine the jade pendant. It looks a bit like a crouching dog, except for the wings, and it also puts me in mind of a sphinx. Its teeth are bared. Here, in my palm, carved from stone, is the countenance of every starving, tortured animal that has ever lived and also the face of every madman, pure malevolence given form. I shiver, and the sensation is not entirely unpleasant. I realize that I am becoming aroused, that I am wet. There are letters from an alphabet I don't recognize inscribed about the base of the figurine, and a stylized skull has been etched into the bottom. The pendant is wholly repellent, and I know I cannot possibly leave the shop without it. It occurs to me that I might kill to own this thing.

"I think it would be," I tell him. "Be better if we all tended to our own business, I mean."

"Still, you can't change human nature," he says.

"No, you can't do that," I agree.

The train is pulling into South Station.

The hurricane bears down on Tybee Island.

And I'm only eleven and standing at a wrought-iron gate set into a brick wall, a wall that surrounds a decrepit mansion on East Hall Street. The wall is yellow, not because it has been painted yellow, but because all the bricks used in its construction have been glazed the color of goldenrods. They shimmer in the heat of a late May afternoon. On the other side of the gate is a woman named Maddy (which she says is short for Madeleine). Sometimes, like today, I walk past and find Maddy waiting, as though I'm expected. She never opens the gate; we only ever talk through the bars, there in the cool below the live oak branches and Spanish moss. Sometimes, she reads my fortune with a pack of Tarot cards. Other times, we talk about books. On this day, though, she's telling me about the woman who owns the house, whom she calls Aramat, a name I'm sure I've never heard before.

"Isn't that the mountain where the Bible says Noah's Ark landed after the flood?" I ask her.

"No, dear. That's Mount Ararat."

"Well, they *sound* very much alike, Ararat and Aramat," I say, and Maddy stares at me. I can tell she's thinking all sorts of things she's not going to say aloud, things I'm not meant to ever hear.

And then Maddy says, almost whispering, "Write her name backwards sometime. Very often, what seems unusual becomes perfectly ordinary, if we take care to look at it from another angle." She peers over her shoulder and tells me that she has to go and that I should be on my way.

I'm twenty-three, and this is the day I found the pendant in an antique shop on West Broughton Street. I ask the man behind the counter how much he wants for it, and after he tells me, I ask him whether it's jade or whether it only *looks* like jade.

"Seems like real jade to me," he replies, and I know from his expression that the question has offended him. "It's not glass or plastic, if that's what you mean. I don't sell costume jewelry, Miss. The chain, that's sterling silver. You want it, I'll take ten bucks off the price on the tag. Frankly, it gives me the creeps, and I'll be happy to be shed of it."

I pay him twenty-five dollars, in cash, and he puts the pendant into a small brown paper bag, and I go back out into the blazing sun.

I dream of a graveyard in Holland, and the October sky is filled with flittering bats. There is another sound, also of wings beating at the cold night air, but *that* sound is not being made by anything like a bat.

"This card," says Maddy, "is the High Priestess. She has many meanings, depending."

"Depending on what?" I want to know.

"Depending on many things," Maddy says and smiles. Her Tarot cards are spread out on the mossy paving stones on her side of the black iron gate. She taps at the High Priestess with an index finger. "In this instance, I'd suspect a future that has yet to be revealed, and duality, too, and also hidden influences at work in your life."

"I'm not sure what you *mean* by duality," I tell her, so she explains.

"The Empress, she sits there on her throne, with a pillar on either side. Some say, these are two pillars from the Temple of Solomon, king of the Israelites and a powerful mystic. And some say that the woman on the throne is Pope Joan."

"I never knew there was a woman pope," I say.

"There probably wasn't. It's just a legend from the Middle Ages." And then Maddy brushes a stray wisp of hair from her eyes before she goes back to explaining duality and the card's symbolism. "On the Empress' right hand is a dark pillar, which is called Boaz. It represents the negative life principle. On her left is a white pillar, Jakin, which represents the positive life principle. Positive and negative, that's duality, and because she sits here between them, we know that the Empress represents balance."

Maddy turns over another card, the Wheel of Fortune, but it's upside down, reversed.

I am twenty-five years old, and Isobel Endecott is asleep in the bed we share in her loft on Atlantic Avenue. I lie awake, listening to her breathing and the myriad of noises from the street three stories below. It's four minutes after three a.m., and I briefly consider taking an Ambien. But I don't *want* to sleep. That's the truth of it. There's so little time left to me, and I'd rather not spend it in dreams. The night is fast approaching when the Starry Wisdom will meet on my behalf, because of what I've brought with me on that train from Savannah, and on that night I will slip this mortal coil (or be pushed, one or the other or both), and there'll be time enough for dreaming when I'm dead and in my grave, or during whatever's to come after my resurrection.

I find a pencil and a notepad. The latter has the name of the law firm that Isobel works for printed across the top of each page: Jackson, Monk, & Rowe, with an ampersand instead of "and" being written out. I don't bother to put on my robe. I go to the bathroom wearing only my panties and stand before the wide mirror above the sink and stare back at my reflection a few minutes. I've never thought of myself as pretty, and I still don't. Tonight, I look like someone who hasn't slept much in a while. My hazel eyes seem more green than brown, when it's usually the other way around. The tattoo between my breasts is beginning to heal, the ink worked into my skin by the thin, nervous man designated the Ace of Pentacles by the High Priestess of the Church of Starry Wisdom.

I write *Aramat* on the notepad, then hold it up to the mirror. I read it aloud, as it appears in the looking glass, and then I do the same with *Isobel Endecott,* speaking utter nonsense, my voice low so I won't wake Isobel. In the mirror, my jade amulet does its impossible trick, which I first noticed a few nights after I bought it from a fastidious man in a shop on West Broughton Street. The reflection of the letters carved around the base, beneath the claws of the winged dog-like beast, are precisely the same as when I look directly at them. The mirror does not reverse the image of the pendant. I have never yet found a mirror that will. I turn away from the sink, gazing into the darkness framed by the bathroom door.

I stand on a beach.

I sit on a sidewalk, eleven years old, and a woman named Maddy passes me the Wheel of Fortune between the bars of an iron gate.

3.

Memory fails, and my thoughts become an apparently disordered torrent. I'm a dead woman recalling the events of a life I have relinquished, a life I have repudiated. I sit in this chair at this desk and hold this pen in my hand because Isobel has asked it of me, not because I have any motivation of my own to speak of all the moments that have led me here. I'm helpless to deny her, so I didn't bother asking *why* she would have me write this. I did very nearly ask why she didn't request it *before,* when I was living and still bound by the beeline perception of time that marshals human recollection into more conventional recitals. But then I experience an epiphany, or something like an epiphany, and I understood, without having asked. No linear account would ever satisfy the congregation of the Church of Starry Wisdom, for they seek more occult patterns, less intuitive paths, some alternate perception of the relationships between past and present, between one moment and the next (or, for that matter, one moment and the last). Cause and effect have not exactly been rejected, but have been found severely wanting.

"That *is* you," says Madeleine, passing me the Tarot card. "You *are* the Wheel of Fortune, an avatar of Tyche, the goddess of fate."

"I don't understand," I tell her, reluctantly accepting the card, taking it from her because I enjoy her company and don't wish to be rude.

"In time," she says, "it may make sense," then gathers her deck and hurries back inside that dilapidated house on East Hall Street, kept safe from the world behind its moldering yellow brick walls.

Burning, I lie down upon the cold granite altar. Soon, my lover, the Empress, climbs on top of me – straddling my hips – while the ragged High Priestess snarls her incantations, while the Major Arcana and the Minor Arcana and all the members of the Four Suits (Pentacles, Cups, Swords, and Staves) chant mantras borrowed from the *Al Azif.*

The train rattles and sways and dips as it hurries me through Connecticut, and then Rhode Island, on my way to South Station. *Because I could not stop for Death, He kindly stopped for me...* The woman sitting next to me is reading a book by an author I've never heard of, and the man across the aisle is busy with his laptop.

I come awake to the dank embrace of the clayey soil that fills in my grave. It presses down on me, that astounding, unexpected weight, wishing to pin me forever to this spot. I am, after all, an abomination and an outlaw in the eyes of biology. I've cheated. The ferryman waits for a passenger who will never cross his river, or whose crossing has been delayed indefinitely. I lie here, not yet moving, marveling at every discomfort and at my collapsed lungs and the dirt filling my mouth and throat. I was not even permitted the luxury of a coffin.

"Caskets offend the Mother and the Father," said the High Priestess. "What use have they of an offering they cannot touch?"

I drift in a fog of pain and impenetrable night. I cannot open my sunken eyes. And even now, through this agony and confusion, I'm aware of the jade pendant's presence, icy against the tattoo on my chest.

I awaken in my bed, in my mother's house, a few nights after her funeral. I lie still, listening to my heartbeat and the settling noises that old houses make when they think no one will hear. I lie there, listening for the sound that reached into my dream of a Dutch churchyard and dragged me back to consciousness – the mournful baying of a monstrous hound.

On the altar, beneath those smoking braziers, the Empress has begun to clean the mud and filth and maggots from my body. The Priestess mutters caustic sorceries, invoking those nameless gods burdened with innumerable names. The congregation chants. I am delirious, lost in some fever that afflicts the risen, and I wonder if Lazarus knew it, or Osiris, or if it is suffered by Persephone every spring. I'm not certain if this is the night of my rebirth or the night of my death. Possibly, they are not even two distinct events, but only a single one, a serpent looping forever back upon itself, tail clasped tightly between venomous jaws. I struggle to speak, but my vocal cords haven't healed enough to permit more than the most incoherent, guttural croaking.

> *...I am Lazarus, come from the dead,*
> *Come back to tell you all, I shall tell you all...*

"Hush, hush," says the Empress, wiping earth and hungry larvae from my face. "The words *will* come, my darling. Be patient, and the words will come back to you. You didn't crawl into Hell and all the way up again to be struck mute. Hush." I know that Isobel Endecott is trying to console me, but I can also hear the fear and doubt and misgiving in her voice. "Hush," she says.

All around me, on the sand, are dead fish and crabs and the carcasses of gulls and pelicans.

It's summer in Savannah, and from the wide verandah of the house on East Hall Street, an older woman calls to Maddy, ordering her back inside. She leaves me holding that single card, *my* card, and I sit there on the sidewalk for another half hour, staring at it intently, trying to make sense of the card *and* what Maddy has told me. A blue sphinx squats atop the Wheel of Fortune, and below it there is the nude figure of a man with red skin and the head of a dog.

"You are *taking too long,*" snaps the High Priestess, and Isobel answers her in an angry burst of French. I cannot speak French, but I'm not so ignorant that I don't know it when I hear it spoken. I wonder dimly what Isobel has said, and I adore her for the outburst, for her brashness, for talking back. I begin to suspect something has gone wrong with the ritual, but the thought doesn't frighten me. Though I'm still more than half blind, my eyes still raw and rheumy, I strain desperately for a better view of Isobel. In all the wide world, at this instant, there is nothing I want but her and nothing else I can imagine needing.

This is a Saturday morning, and I'm a few weeks from my tenth birthday. I'm sitting in the swing on the back porch. My mother is just inside the screen door, in the kitchen, talking to someone on the telephone. I can hear her voice quite plainly. It's a warm day late in February, and the sky above our house is an immaculate and seemingly inviolable shade of blue. I've been daydreaming, woolgathering, staring up at that sky, past the sagging eaves of the porch, when I hear something and notice that there's a very large black dog only a few yards away from me. It's standing in the gravel alleyway that separates our tiny backyard from that of the next house over. I have no way of knowing how long the dog has been standing there. I watch it, and it watches me. The dog has bright amber eyes and isn't wearing a collar or tags. I've never before seen a dog smile, but *this* dog is smiling. After five minutes or so, it growls softly, then turns and trots away down the alley. I decide not to tell my mother about the smiling dog. She probably wouldn't believe me anyway.

"What was that you said to her?" I ask Isobel, several nights after my resurrection. We're sitting together on the floor of her loft on Atlantic, and there's a Beatles album playing on the turntable.

"What did I say to whom?" she wants to know.

"The High Priestess. You said something to her in French, while I was still on the altar. I'd forgotten about it until this morning. You sounded angry. I don't understand French, so I don't know what you said."

"It doesn't really matter what I said," she replies, glancing over the liner notes for *Hey Jude*. "It only matters that I said it. The old woman is a coward."

Somewhere in North Carolina, the rhythm of the train's wheels against the rails lulls me to sleep. I dream of a neglected Dutch graveyard and the amulet, of hurricanes and smiling black dogs. Maddy is also in my dreams, reading fortunes at a carnival. I can smell sawdust and cotton candy, horseshit and sweating bodies. Maddy sits on a milking stool inside a tent beneath a canvas banner emblazoned with the words *Lo! Behold! The Strikefire & Z. B. Harbinger Wonder Show!* in bold crimson letters fully five feet high.

She turns another card, the Wheel of Fortune.

I lie in my grave, fully cognizant but immobile, unable to summon the will or the physical strength to begin worming my way towards the surface, six feet overhead. I lie there, thinking of Maddy and the jade pendant. I lie there considering, in the mocking solitude of my burial place, what it does and does not mean that I've returned with absolutely no conscious knowledge of anything I may have experienced in death. Whatever secrets the Starry Wisdom sent me off to discover remain secrets. After all that has been risked and forfeited, I have no revelations to offer my fellow seekers. They'll ask their questions, and I'll have no answers. This should upset me, but it doesn't.

Now I can hear footsteps on the roof of my narrow house. Something is pacing heavily, back and forth, snuffling at the recently disturbed earth where I've been planted like a tulip bulb, like an acorn, like a seed that *will* unfold, but surely never sprout.

It goes about on four feet, I think, *not two.*

The hound bays.

I wonder, will it kindly dig me up, this restless visitor? And I wonder, too, about the rumors of the others who've worn the jade pendant before me, and the stories of their fates. Those two ghoulish Englishmen in 1922, for instance; they cross my reanimated mind. As does a passage from Francois-Honore Balfour's notorious grimoire, *Cultes des Goules,* and a few stray lines from the *Al Azif.* My bestial caller suddenly stops pacing and begins scratching at the soft dirt, urging me to move.

In the temple, as my lover takes my hand and I'm led towards the altar stone, through the fire devouring me from the inside out, the High Priestess of the Starry Wisdom reminds us all that only once in every thousand years does the hound choose a wife. Only once each millennium is any living woman accorded that privilege.

My train pulls into a depot somewhere in southern Rhode Island, grumbling to a slow stop, and my dreams are interrupted by other passengers bustling about around me, retrieving their bags and briefcases, talking too loudly. Or I'm jarred awake by the simple fact that the train is no longer moving.

After sex, I lie in bed with Isobel, and the only light comes from the television set mounted on the wall across the room. The sound is turned down, so the black-and-white world trapped inside that box exists in perfect grainy silence. I'm trying to tell her about the pacing thing from the night I awoke. I'm trying to describe the snuffling noises and the way it worried at the ground with its sharp claws. But she only scowls and shakes her head dismissively.

"No," she insists. "The hound is nothing but a metaphor. We weren't meant to take it literally. Whatever you heard that night, you imagined it, that's all. You heard what some part of you expected, and maybe even needed, to hear. But the hound, it's a superstition, and we're not superstitious people."

"Isobel, I fucking *died*," I say, trying not to laugh, gazing across her belly towards the television. "And I came *back* from the dead. I tunneled out of my grave with my bare hands and then, blind, found my way to the temple alone. My flesh was already rotting, and now it's good as new. Those things actually happened, to *me*, and you don't *doubt* that they happened. You practice necromancy, but you want me to think I'm being superstitious if I believe that the hound is real?"

She's quiet for a long moment. Finally, she says, "I worry about you, that's all. You're so very precious to me, to all of us, and you've been through so much already." And she closes her hand tightly around the amulet still draped about my neck.

On a sweltering August day in Savannah, a fastidious man who sells antique jewelry and Chinese porcelain makes no attempt whatsoever to hide his relief when I tell him I've decided to buy the jade pendant. As he rings up the sale, he asks me if I'm a good Christian girl. He talks about Calvary and the Pentecost, then admits he'll be glad to have the pendant out of his shop.

I stand on a beach.

I board a train.

Maddy turns another card.

And on the altar of the Church of Starry Wisdom, I draw a deep, hitching breath. I smell incense burning and hear the lilting voices of all those assembled for my homecoming. My heart is a sledgehammer battering at my chest, and I would scream, but I can't even speak. Isobel Endecott is straddling me, and her right hand goes to my vagina. With her fingers, she scoops out the slimy plug of soil and minute branches of fungal hyphae that have filled my sex during the week and a half I've spent below. When the pad of her thumb brushes my clit, every shadow and shape half glimpsed by my wounded eyes seems to glow, as if my lust is contagious, as though light and darkness have become sympathetic. I lunge for her, my jaws snapping like the jaws of any starving creature; there are tears in her eyes as I'm restrained by the Sun and the Moon. The Hanged Man dutifully places a leather strap between my teeth.

Madness rides on the star-wind…

"Hush," Isobel whispers. "Hush, hush," whispers the Empress. "It'll pass."

It's the day I leave Savannah for the last time. In the bedroom of the house where I grew up, I pack the few things that still hold meaning for me. These include a photo album, and tucked inside the album is the Tarot card that the woman named Madeleine gave me.

4.

Isobel is watching me from the other side of the dining room. She's been watching, while I write, for the better part of an hour. She asks, "How does it end? Do you even know?"

"Maybe it doesn't end," I reply. "I half think it's hardly even started."

"Then how will you know when to stop?" she asks. There's dread wedged in between every word she speaks, between every syllable.

"I don't think I will," I say, this thought occurring to me for the first time. She nods, then stands and leaves the room, and when she's gone, I'm glad. I can't deny that there is a certain solace in her absence. I've been trying not to look too closely at Isobel's eyes. I don't like what I see there anymore.

Tidal Forces

Charlotte says, "That's just it, Em. There wasn't any pain. I didn't feel anything much at all." She sips her coffee and stares out the kitchen window, squinting at the bright Monday morning sunlight. The sun melts like butter across her face. It catches in the strands of her brown hair, like a late summer afternoon tangling itself in dead cornstalks. It deepens the lines around her eyes and at the corners of her mouth. She takes another sip of coffee, then sets her cup down on the table. I've never once seen her use a saucer.

And the next minute seems to last longer than it ought to last, longer than the mere sum of the sixty seconds that compose it, the way time stretches out to fill in awkward pauses. She smiles for me, and so I smile back. I don't want to smile, but isn't that what you do? The person you love is frightened, but she smiles anyway. So you have to smile back, despite your own fear. I tell myself it isn't so much an act of reciprocation as an acknowledgement. I could be more honest with myself and say I only smiled back out of guilt.

"I *wish* it had hurt," she says, finally, on the other side of all that long, long moment. I don't have to ask what she means, though *I* wish that *I* did. I wish I didn't already know. She says the same words over again, but more quietly than before, and there's a subtle shift in emphasis. "I wish it *had* hurt."

I apologize and say I shouldn't have brought it up again, and she shrugs.

"No, don't be sorry, Em. Don't let's be sorry for anything."

I'm stacking days, building a house of cards made from nothing but days. Monday is the Ace of Hearts. Saturday is the Four of Spades. Wednesday is the Seven of Clubs. Thursday night is, I suspect, the Seven of Diamonds, and it might be heavy enough to bring the whole precarious thing tumbling down around my ears. I would spend an entire hour watching cards fall, because time would stretch, the same way it stretches out to fill in awkward pauses, the way time is stretched thin in that thundering moment of a car crash. Or at the edges of a wound.

If it's Monday morning, I can lean across the breakfast table and kiss her, as if nothing has happened. And if we're lucky, that might be the moment that endures almost indefinitely. I can kiss her, taste her, savor her, drawing the moment out like a card drawn from a deck. But no, now it's Thursday night, instead of Monday morning. There's something playing on the television in the bedroom, but the sound is turned all the way down, so that whatever the something may be proceeds like a silent movie filmed in color and without intertitles. A movie for lip readers. There's no other light but the light from the television. She's lying next to me, almost undressed, asking me questions about the book I don't think I'm ever going to be able to finish. I understand she's not asking them because she needs to know the answers, which is the only reason I haven't tried to change the subject.

"The Age of Exploration was already long over with," I say. "For all intents and purposes, it ended early in the Seventeenth Century. Everything after that – reaching the north and south poles, for instance – is only a series of footnotes. There were no great blank spaces left for men to fill in. No more 'Here be monsters.'"

She's lying on top of the sheets. It's the middle of July and too hot for anything more than sheets. Clean white sheets and underwear. In the glow from the television, Charlotte looks less pale and less fragile than she would if the bedside lamp were on, and I'm grateful for the illusion. I want to stop talking, because it all sounds absurd, pedantic, all these unfinished, half-formed ideas that add up to nothing much at all. I want to stop talking and just lie here beside her.

"So writers made up stories about lost worlds," she says, having heard all this before and pretty much knowing it by heart. "But those made-up worlds weren't really *lost*. They just weren't *found* yet. They'd not yet been imagined."

"That's the point," I reply. "The value of those stories rests in their insistence that blank spaces still do exist on the map. They *have* to exist, even if it's necessary to twist and distort the map to make room for them. All those overlooked islands, inaccessible plateaus in South American jungles, the sunken continents and the entrances to a hollow earth, they were important psychological buffers against progress and certainty. It's no coincidence that they're usually places where time has stood still, to one degree or another."

"But not really so much time," she says, "as the processes of evolution, which require time."

"See? You understand this stuff better than I do," and I tell her she should write the book. I'm only half joking. That's something else Charlotte knows. I lay my hand on her exposed belly, just below the navel, and she flinches and pulls away.

"Don't do that," she says.

"All right. I won't. I wasn't thinking." I was thinking, but it's easier if I tell her that I wasn't.

Monday morning. Thursday night. This day or that. My own private house of cards, held together by nothing more substantial than balance and friction. And the loops I'd rather make than admit to the present. Connecting dot to dot, from here to there, from there to here. Here being half an hour before dawn on a Saturday, the sky growing lighter by slow degrees. Here, where I'm on my knees, and Charlotte is standing naked in front of me. Here, now, when the perfectly round hole above her left hip and below her ribcage has grown from a pinprick to the size of the saucers she never uses for her coffee cups.

"I don't think it will hurt," she tells me. And I can't see any point in asking whether she means, *I don't think it will hurt me* or *I don't think it will hurt you.*

"Now?" I ask her, and she says, "No. Not yet. Wait."

So, handed that reprieve, I withdraw again to the relative safety of the Ace of Hearts – or Monday morning, call it what you will. In my mind's eye, I run back to the kitchen washed in warm yellow sunlight. Charlotte is telling me about the time, when she was ten years old, that she was shot with a BB gun, her brother's Red Ryder BB gun.

"It wasn't an accident," she's telling me. "He meant to do it. I still have the scar from where my mother had to dig the BB out of my ankle with tweezers and a sewing needle. It's very small, but it's a scar all the same."

"Is that what it felt like, like being hit with a BB?"

"No," she says, shaking her head and gazing down into her coffee cup. "It didn't. But when I think about the two things, it seems as if there's a link between them, all these years apart. Like, somehow, this thing was an echo of the day he shot me with the BB gun."

"A meaningful coincidence," I suggest. "A sort of synchronicity."

"Maybe," Charlotte says. "But maybe not." She looks out the window again. From the kitchen, you can see the three oaks and her flower bed and the land running down to the rocks and the churning sea. "It's been an awfully long time since I read Jung. My memory's rusty. And, anyway, maybe it's not a coincidence. It could be something else. Just an echo."

"I don't understand, Charlotte. I really don't think I know what you mean."

"Never mind," she says, not taking her eyes off the window. "Whatever I do or don't mean, it isn't important."

The warm yellow light from the sun, the colorless light from a color television. A purplish sky fading towards the light of false dawn. The complete absence of light from the hole punched into her body by something that wasn't a BB. Something that also wasn't a shadow.

"What scares me most," she says (and I could draw *this* particular card from anywhere in the deck), "is that it didn't come back out the other side. So, it must still be lodged in there, *in* me."

I was watching when she was hit. I saw when she fell. I'm coming to that.

"Writers made up stories about *lost* worlds" she says again, after she's flinched, after I've pulled my hand back from the brink. "They did it because we were afraid of having found all there *was* to find. Accurate maps became more disturbing, at least unconsciously, than the idea of sailing off the edge of a flat world."

"I don't want to talk about the book."

"Maybe that's why you can't finish it."

"Maybe you don't know what you're talking about."

"Probably," she says, without the least bit of anger or impatience in her voice.

I roll over, turning my back on Charlotte and the silent television. Turning my back on what cannot be heard and doesn't want to be acknowledged. The sheets are damp with sweat, and there's the stink of ozone that's not *quite* the stink of ozone. The acrid smell that always follows her now, wherever she goes. No. That isn't true. The smell doesn't follow her. It comes *from* her. She radiates the stink that is almost, but not quite, the stink of ozone.

"Does *Alice's Adventures in Wonderland* count?" she asks me, even though I've said I don't want to talk about the goddamned book. I'm sure that she heard me, and I don't answer her.

Better not to linger too long on Thursday night.

Better if I return, instead, to Monday morning. Only Monday morning. Which I have carelessly, randomly, designated here as the Ace of

Hearts, and hearts are cups, so Monday morning is the Ace of Cups. In four days more, Charlotte will ask me about Alice, and though I won't respond to the question (at least not aloud), I *will* recall that Lewis Carroll considered the *Queen* of Hearts – who rules over the Ace and is also the Queen of Cups – I will recollect that Lewis Carroll considered her the embodiment of a certain type of passion. That passion, he said, which is ungovernable, but which exists as an aimless, unseeing, furious thing. And he said, also, that the Queen of Cups, the Queen of Hearts, is not to be confused with the *Red* Queen, whom he named another brand of passion altogether.

Monday morning in the kitchen.

"My brother always claimed he was shooting at a blue jay and missed. He said he was aiming for the bird and hit me. He said the sun was in his eyes."

"Did he make a habit of shooting songbirds?"

"Birds and squirrels," she says. "Once he shot a neighbor's cat, right between the eyes." And Charlotte presses the tip of an index finger to the spot between her brows. "The cat had to be taken to a vet to get the BB out, and my mom had to pay the bill. Of course, he said he wasn't shooting at the cat. He was shooting at a sparrow and missed."

"What a little bastard," I say.

"He was just a kid, only a year older than I was. Kids don't mean to be cruel, Em, they just are sometimes. From our perspectives, they appear cruel. They exist outside the boundaries of adult conceits of morality. Anyway, my dad took the BB gun away from him. So, after that, he always kind of hated cats."

But here I am neglecting Wednesday, overlooking Wednesday, even though I went to the trouble of drawing a card for it. And it occurs to me now I didn't even draw one for Tuesday. Or Friday, for that matter. It occurs to me that I'm becoming lost in this ungainly metaphor, that the tail is wagging the dog. But Wednesday was of consequence. More so than was Thursday night, with its mute TV and the Seven of Diamonds and Charlotte shying away from my touch.

The Seven of Clubs. Wednesday, or the Seven of Pentacles, seen another way round. Charlotte, wrapped in her bathrobe, comes downstairs after taking a hot shower, and she finds me reading Kip Thorne's *Black Holes and Time Warps,* the book lying lewdly open in my lap. I quickly close it, feeling like I'm a teenager again, and my mother's just barged into my room to find me masturbating to the *Hustler* centerfold. Yes, your daughter is a lesbian, and yes, your girlfriend is reading quantum theory behind your back.

Charlotte stares at me awhile, staring silently, and then she stares at the thick volume lying on the coffee table, *Principles of Physical Cosmology.* She sits down on the floor, not far from the sofa. Her hair is dripping, spattering the hardwood.

"I don't believe you're going to find anything in there," she says, meaning the books.

"I just thought…" I begin, but let the sentence die unfinished, because I'm not at all sure *what* I was thinking. Only that I've always turned to books for solace.

And here, on the afternoon of the Seven of Pentacles, this Wednesday weighted with those seven visionary chalices, she tells me what happened in the shower. How she stood in the steaming spray watching the water rolling down her breasts and *across* her stomach and *up* her buttocks before falling into the hole in her side. Not in defiance of gravity, but in perfect accord with gravity. She hardly speaks above a whisper. I sit quietly listening, wishing that I could suppose she'd only lost her mind. Recourse to wishful thinking, the seven visionary chalices of the Seven of Pentacles, of the Seven of Clubs, or Wednesday. Running away to hide in the comfort of insanity, or the authority of books, or the delusion of lost worlds.

"I'm sorry, but what the fuck do I say to that?" I ask her, and she laughs. It's a terrible sound, that laugh, a harrowing, forsaken sound. And then she stops laughing, and I feel relief spill over me, because now she's crying, instead. There's shame at the relief, of course, but even the shame is welcome. I couldn't have stood that terrible laughter much longer. I go to her and put my arms around her and hold her, as if holding her will make it all better. The sun's almost down by the time she finally stops crying.

I have a quote from Albert Einstein, from sometime in 1912, which I found in the book by Kip Thorne, the book Charlotte caught me reading on Wednesday: "Henceforth, space by itself, and time by itself, are doomed to fade away into mere shadows, and only a kind of union of the two will preserve an independent reality."

Space, time, shadows.

As I've said, I was watching when she was hit. I saw when she fell. That was Saturday last, two days before the yellow morning in the kitchen, and not to be confused with the *next* Saturday which is the Four of Spades. I was sitting on the porch and had been watching two noisy grey-white gulls wheeling far up against the blue summer sky. Charlotte had been working in her garden, pulling weeds. She called out to me, and I looked away from the birds. She was pointing towards the ocean, and at first I wasn't sure what it was she wanted me to see. I stared at the breakers shattering themselves against the granite boulders, and past that, to the horizon where the water was busy with its all but eternal task of shouldering the burden of the heavens. I was about to tell her that I didn't see anything. This wasn't true, of course. I just didn't see anything out of the ordinary, nothing special, nothing that ought not occupy that time and that space.

I saw nothing to give me pause.

But then I did.

Space, time, spacetime, shadows.

I'll call it a shadow, because I'm at a loss for any more appropriate word. It was spread out like a shadow rushing across the waves, though, at first, I thought I was seeing something dark moving *beneath* the waves. A very big fish, perhaps. Possibly a large shark or a small whale. We've seen whales in the bay before. Or it might have been caused by a cloud passing in front of the sun, though there were no clouds that day. The truth is I knew it was none of these things. I can sit here all night long, composing a list of what it *wasn't,* and I'll never come any nearer to what it might have been.

"Emily," she shouted. "Do you *see* it?" And I called back that I did. Having noticed the shadow, it was impossible *not* to see that grimy, indefinite smear sliding swiftly towards the shore. In a few seconds more, I realized, it would reach the boulders, and if it wasn't something beneath the water, the rocks wouldn't stop it. Part of my mind still insisted it was only a shadow, a freakish trick of the light, a mirage. Nothing substantial, certainly nothing malign, nothing that could do us any mischief or injury. No need to be alarmed, and yet I don't ever remember being as afraid as I was then. I couldn't move, but I yelled for Charlotte to run. I don't think she heard me. Or if she heard me, she was also too mesmerized by the sight of the thing to move.

I was safe, there on the porch. It came no nearer to me than ten or twenty yards. But Charlotte, standing alone at the garden gate, was well within its circumference. It swept over her, and she screamed, and fell to the ground. It swept over her, and then was gone, vanishing into the tangle of green briars and poison ivy and wind-stunted evergreens behind our house. I stood there, smelling something that smelled almost like ozone. And maybe it's an awful cliché to put to paper, but my mind *reeled*. My heart raced, and my mind reeled. For a fraction of an instant I was seized by something that was neither déjà vu nor vertigo, and I thought I might vomit.

But the sensation passed, like the shadow had, or the shadow of a shadow, and I dashed down the steps and across the grass to the place where Charlotte sat stunned among the clover and the dandelions. Her clothes and skin looked as though they'd been misted with the thinnest sheen of…what? Oil? No, no, no, not oil at all. But it's the closest I can come to describing that sticky brownish iridescence clinging to her dress and her face, her arms and the pickets of the garden fence and to every single blade of grass.

"It knocked me down," she said, sounding more amazed than hurt or frightened. Her eyes were filled with startled disbelief. "It wasn't *anything*, Em. It wasn't anything at all, but it knocked me right off my feet."

"Are you hurt?" I asked, and she shook her head.

I didn't ask her anything else, and she didn't say anything more. I helped her up and inside the house. I got her clothes off and led her into the downstairs shower. But the oily residue that the shadow left behind had already begun to *evaporate* – and again, that's not the right word, but it's the best I can manage – before we began trying to scrub it away with soap and scalding clean water. By the next morning, there would be no sign of the stuff anywhere, inside the house or out of doors. Not so much as a stain.

"It knocked me down. It was just a shadow, but it knocked me down." I can't recall how many times she must have said that. She repeated it over and over again, as though repetition would render it less implausible, less inherently ludicrous. "A shadow knocked me down, Em. A shadow knocked me down."

But it wasn't until we were in the bedroom, and she was dressing, that I noticed the red welt above her left hip, just below her ribs. It almost looked like an insect bite, except the center was…well, when I bent down and examined it closely, I saw there *was* no center. There was only a hole. As I've said, a pinprick, but a hole all the same. There wasn't so much as a drop of blood, and she swore to me that it didn't hurt, that she was fine, and it was nothing to get excited about. She went to the medicine cabinet and found a Band-Aid to cover the welt. And I didn't see it again until the next day, which as yet has no playing card, the Sunday before the warm yellow Monday morning in the kitchen.

I'll call that Sunday the Two of Spades.

It rains on the Two of Spades. It rains cats and dogs all the damn day long. I spend the afternoon sitting in my study, parked there in front of my computer, trying to find the end to Chapter Nine of the book I can't seem to finish. The rain beats at the windows, all rhythm and no melody. I write a line, then delete it. One step forward, two steps back. Zeno's "Achilles and the Tortoise" paradox played out at my keyboard – "That which is in locomotion must arrive at the halfway stage before it arrives at the goal," and each halfway stage has it's own halfway stage, *ad infinitum*. These are the sorts of rationalizations that comfort me as I only pretend to be working. This is the *true* reward of my twelve years of college, these erudite excuses for not getting the job done. In the days to come, I will set the same apologetics and exculpations to work on the problem of how a shadow can possibly knock a woman down and how a hole can be explained away as no more than a wound.

Sometime after seven o'clock, Charlotte raps on the door to ask me how it's going and what I'd like for dinner. I haven't got a ready answer for either question, and she comes in and sits down on the futon near my desk. She has to move a stack of books to make a place to sit. We talk about the weather, which she tells me is supposed to improve after sunset, that the meteorologists are saying Monday will be sunny and hot. We talk about the book – my exploration of the phenomenon of the literary *Terrae Anachronismorum,* from 1714 and Simon Tyssot de Patot's *Voyages et Aventures de Jacques Massé* to 1918 and Edgar Rice Burroughs's *Out of Time's Abyss* (and beyond; see Aristotle on Zeno, above). I close Microsoft Word, accepting that nothing more will be written until at least tomorrow.

"I took off the Band-Aid," she says, reminding me of what I've spent the day trying to forget.

"When you fell, you probably jabbed yourself on a stick or something," I tell her, which doesn't explain *why* she fell, but seeks to dismiss the result of the fall.

"I don't think it was a stick."

"Well, whatever it was, you hardly got more than a scratch."

And that's when she asks me to look. I would have said no, if saying no were an option.

She stands and pulls up her T-shirt, just on the left side, and points at the hole, though there's no way I could ever miss it. On the rainy Two of Spades, hardly twenty-four hours after Charlotte was knocked off her feet by a shadow, it's already grown to the diameter of a dime. I've never seen anything so black in all my life, a black so complete I'm almost certain I would go blind if I stared into it too long. I don't say these things aloud. I don't remember what I say, so maybe I say nothing at all. At first, I think the skin at the edges of the hole is puckered, drawn tight like the skin at the edges of a scab. Then I see that's not the case at all. The skin around the periphery of the hole in her flesh is *moving,* rotating, swirling about that preposterous and undeniable blackness.

"I'm scared," she whispers. "I mean, I'm *really* fucking scared, Emily."

I start to touch the wound, and she stops me. She grabs hold of my hand and stops me.

"Don't," she says, and so I don't.

"You *know* that it can't be what it looks like," I tell her, and I think maybe I even laugh.

"Em, I don't know anything at all."

"You damn well know *that* much, Charlotte. It's some sort of infection, that's all, and – "

She releases my hand, only to cover my mouth before I can finish. Three fingers to still my lips, and she asks me if we can go upstairs, if I'll please make love to her.

"Right now, that's all I want," she says. "In all the world, there's nothing I want more."

I almost make her promise that she'll see our doctor the next day, but already some part of me has admitted to myself this is nothing a physician can diagnose or treat. We have moved out beyond medicine. We have been pushed down into these nether regions by the shadow of a shadow. I have stared directly into that hole, and already I understand it's not merely a hole in Charlotte's skin, but a hole in the cosmos. I could parade her before any number of physicians and physicists, psychologists and priests, and not a one would have the means to seal that breach. In fact, I suspect they would deny the evidence, even if it meant denying all their science and technology and faith. There are things worse than blank spaces on maps. There are moments when certitude becomes the greatest enemy of sanity. Denial becomes an antidote.

Unlike those other days and those other cards, I haven't chosen the Two of Spades at random. I've chosen it because on Thursday she asks me if Alice counts. And I have begun to assume that everything counts, just as everything is claimed by that infinitely small, infinitely dense point beyond the event horizon.

"Would you tell me, please," said Alice, a little timidly, *"why you are paint-ing those roses?"*

Five and Seven said nothing, but looked at Two. Two began, in a low voice, "Why, the fact is, you see, Miss, this here ought to have been a red rose-tree, and we put a white one in by mistake..."

On that rainy Sunday, that Two of Spades with an incriminating red brush concealed behind its back, I do as she asks. I cannot do otherwise. I bed her. I fuck her. I am tender and violent by turns, as is she. On that stormy evening, that Two of Pentacles, that Two of *Coins* (a dime, in this case), we both futilely turn to sex looking for surcease from dread. We try to go *back* to our lives before she fell, and this is not so very different from all those "lost worlds" I've belabored in my unfinished manuscript: Maple White Land, Caprona, Skull Island, Symzonia, Pellucidar, the Mines of King Solomon. In our bed, we struggle to fashion a refuge from the present, populated by the reassuring, dependable past. And I am talking in circles within circles within circles, spiraling inward or out, it doesn't matter which.

I am arriving, very soon now, at the end of it, at the Saturday night – or more precisely, just before dawn on the Saturday morning – when the story I am writing here ends. And begins. I've taken too long to get to the point, if I assume the validity of a linear narrative. If I assume any one moment can take precedence over any other or assume the generally assumed (but unproven) inequity of relevance.

A large rose-tree stood near the entrance of the garden; the roses growing on it were white, but there were three gardeners at it, busily painting them red.

We are as intimate in those moments as two women can be, when one is forbidden to touch a dime-sized hole in the other's body. At some point, after dark, the rain stops falling, and we lie naked and still, listening to owls and whippoorwills beyond the bedroom walls.

On Wednesday, she comes downstairs and catches me reading the dry pornography of mathematics and relativity. Wednesday is the Seven of Clubs. She tells me there's nothing to be found in those books, nothing that will change what has happened, what may happen.

She says, "I don't know what will be left of me when it's done. I don't even know if I'll be enough to satisfy it, or if it will just keep getting bigger and bigger and bigger. I think it might be insatiable."

On Monday morning, she sips her coffee. We talk about eleven-year-old boys and BB guns.

But here, at last, it is shortly before sunup on a Saturday. Saturday, the Four of Spades. It's been an hour since Charlotte woke screaming, and I've sat and listened while she tried to make sense of the nightmare. The hole in her side is as wide as a softball (and were this more obviously a comedy I would list the objects that, by accident, have fallen into it the last few days). Besides the not-quite-ozone smell, there's now a faint but constant whistling sound, which is air being pulled into the hole. In the dream, she tells me, she knew exactly what was on the other side of the hole, but then she forgot most of it as soon as she awoke. In the dream, she says, she wasn't afraid, and that we were sitting out on the porch watching the sea while she explained it all to me. We were drinking Cokes, she said, and it was hot, and the air smelled like dog roses.

"You know I don't like Coke," I say.

"In the dream you did."

She says we were sitting on the porch, and that awful shadow came across the sea again, only this time it didn't frighten her. This time I saw it first and pointed it out to her, and we watched together as it moved rapidly towards the shore. This time, when it swept over the garden, she wasn't standing there to be knocked down.

"But you said you saw what was on the other side."

"That was later on. And I would tell you what I saw, if I could remember. But there was the sound of pipes, or a flute," she says. "I can recall that much of it, and I knew, in the dream, that the hole runs all the way to the middle, to the very center."

"The very center of what?" I ask, and she looks at me like she thinks I'm intentionally being slow-witted.

"The center of everything that ever was and is and ever will be, Em. The *center*. Only, somehow the center is both empty and filled with…" She trails off and stares at the floor.

"Filled with what?"

"I can't *say*. I don't *know*. But whatever it is, it's been there since before there was time. It's been there alone since before the universe was born."

I look up, catching our reflections in the mirror on the dressing table across the room. We're sitting on the edge of the bed, both of us naked, and I look a decade older than I am. Charlotte, though, she looks *so* young, younger than when we met. Never mind that yawning black mouth in her abdomen. In the half light before dawn, she seems to shine, a preface to the coming day, and I'm reminded of what I read about Hawking radiation and the quasar jet streams that escape some singularities. But this isn't the place or time for theories and equations. Here, there are only the two of us, and morning coming on, and what Charlotte can and cannot remember about her dream.

"Eons ago," she says, "it lost its mind. Though I don't think it ever really *had* a mind, not like a human mind. But still, it went insane, from the knowledge of what it is and what it can't ever stop being."

"You said you'd forgotten what was on the other side."

"I have. Almost all of it. This is *nothing*. If I went on a trip to Antarctica and came back and all I could tell you about my trip was that Antarctica had been very white, that would be like what I'm telling you now about the dream."

The Four of Spades. The Four of Swords, which cartomancers read as stillness, peace, withdrawal, the act of turning sight back upon itself. They say nothing of the attendant perils of introspection or the damnation that would be visited upon an intelligence that could never look *away*.

"It's blind," she says. "It's blind, and insane, and the music from the pipes never ends. Though, they aren't really pipes."

This is when I ask her to stand up, and she only stares at me a moment or two before doing as I've asked. This is when I kneel in front of her, and I'm dimly aware that I'm kneeling before the inadvertent avatar of a god, or God, or a pantheon, or something so immeasurably ancient and pervasive that it may as well be divine. Divine or infernal; there's really no difference between the two, I think.

"What are you doing?" she wants to know.

"I'm losing you," I reply, "that's what I'm doing. Somewhere, some-*when,* I've *already* lost you. And that means I have nothing *left* to lose."

Charlotte takes a quick step back from me, retreating towards the bedroom door, and I'm wondering if she runs, will I chase her? Having made this decision, to what lengths will I go to see it through? Would I force her? Would it be rape?

"I know what you're going to do," she says. "Only you're *not* going to do it, because I won't let you."

"You're being devoured."

"It was a dream, Em. It was only a stupid, crazy dream, and I'm not even sure what I actually remember and what I'm just making up."

"Please," I say, "please let me try." And I watch as whatever resolve she might have had breaks apart. She wants as badly as I do to hope, even though we both know there's no hope left. I watch that hideous black gyre above her hip, below her left breast. She takes two steps back towards me.

"I don't think it will hurt," she tells me. And I can't see any point in asking whether she means, *I don't think it will hurt me* or *I don't think it will hurt you.* "I don't think there will be any pain."

"I can't see how it possibly matters anymore," I tell her. I don't say anything else. With my right hand, I reach into the hole, and my arm vanishes almost up to my shoulder. There's cold beyond any comprehension of cold. I glance up, and she's watching me. I think she's going to scream, but she doesn't. Her lips part, but she doesn't scream. I feel my arm being tugged so violently I'm sure that it's about to be torn from its socket, the humerus ripped from the glenoid fossa of the scapula, cartilage and ligaments snapped, the subclavian artery severed before I tumble back to the floor and bleed to death. I'm almost certain that's what will happen, and I grit my teeth against that impending amputation.

"I can't feel you," Charlotte whispers. "You're inside me now, but I can't feel you anywhere."

Then.

The hole is closing. We both watch as that clockwise spiral stops spinning, then begins to turn widdershins. My freezing hand clutches at the void, my fingers straining for any purchase. Something's changed; I understand that perfectly well. Out of desperation, I've chanced upon some remedy, entirely by instinct or luck, the solution to an insoluble puzzle. I also understand that I need to pull my arm back out again, before the edges of the hole reach my bicep. I imagine the collapsing rim of curved spacetime slicing cleanly through sinew and bone, and then I imagine myself fused at the shoulder to that point just above Charlotte's hip. Horror vies with cartoon absurdities in an instant that seems so swollen it could accommodate an age.

Charlotte's hands are on my shoulders, gripping me tightly, pushing me away, shoving me as hard as she's able. She's saying something, too, words I can't quite hear over the roar at the edges of that cataract created by the implosion of quantum foam.

Oh, Kitty, how nice it would be if we could only get through into Looking-glass House! I'm sure it's got oh! such beautiful things in it! Let's pretend there's a way of getting through into it, somehow, Kitty. Let's pretend the glass has got all soft as gauze, so that we can get through…

I'm watching a shadow race across the sea.

Warm sun fills the kitchen.

I draw another card.

Charlotte is only ten years old, and a BB fired by her brother strikes her ankle. Twenty-three years later, she falls at the edge of our flower garden.

Time. Space. Shadows. Gravity and velocity. Past, present, and future. All smeared, every distinction lost, and nothing remaining that can possibly be quantified.

I shut my eyes and feel her hands on my shoulders.

And across the space within her, as my arm bridges countless light years, something brushes against my hand. Something wet, and soft, something indescribably abhorrent. Charlotte pushed me, and I was falling backwards, and now I'm not. It has seized my hand in its own – or wrapped some celestial tendril about my wrist – and for a single heartbeat it holds on before letting go.

...whatever it is, it's been there since before there was time. It's been there alone since before the universe was born.

There's pain when my head hits the bedroom floor. There's pain and stars and twittering birds. I taste blood and realize that I've bitten my lip. I open my eyes, and Charlotte's bending over me. I think there are galaxies trapped within her eyes. I glance down at that spot above her left hip, and the skin is smooth and whole. She's starting to cry, and that makes it harder to see the constellations in her irises. I move my fingers, surprised that my arm and hand are both still there.

"I'm sorry," I say, even if I'm not sure what I'm apologizing for.

"No," she says, "don't be sorry, Em. Don't let's be sorry for anything. Not now. Not ever again."

John Four

The Temple is called the Temple because it is a place of prayer, even though no one prays anymore because it's better that the gods don't notice you. It's better to be an anonymous mote in the eye than a mote in the eye that has called attention to itself. It may be this is what happened to the world, in that final age of humanity, before the beginning of this interminable eschatology. It may be that the gods finally sat up and took notice. After two million years of prayer and blood sacrifice and magical thinking, it may only be that they took notice and crawled down from heaven and up from hell to see what was making such an awful racket. This may only be a plea by the gods for peace and quiet.

But those who remember Before tell a different story, those from before who can still speak. Those from Before who can still speak and remember how. Those from Before who can still speak and remember how and are stupid enough to do so. That ever-diminishing subset recalls that Something came from Somewhere Else, and that astronomers saw it coming twenty, twenty-five, thirty years before its arrival. There's no consensus on what the Something might have been, only that it has always traveled between galaxies, and finally, inevitably, it came much too near, and swallowed all the Milky Way and shat out this new world where the Temple in which no one prays rises from a horizonless charcoal plain. It was not built here, the temple, but is a secretion, an architectural excrescence. Those from Before call it crooked, because they remember that other geometry, the one in which words like *crooked* still had meaning.

So, a crooked Temple rises from a crooked charcoal plain, and all about the Temple is the last crooked city of mankind, spread out below the crooked black sky. It becomes tedious, the cataloging of all this crookedness, and entirely absurd, as there remains nothing *straight* to provide a point of reference. If there were still clouds, the spires of the Temple would brush against their bellies. If there were still stars, it would seem as if the Temple were an accusatory finger pointing towards them.

The plain. The city. The Temple. The starless sky.

That's quite enough for now.

A woman who was never given a name – and who mercifully doesn't recall Before – sits inside the vast narthex of the Temple. She tends to one of the pools of greater darkness that spring, here and there, from the greasy, resinous walls and floors, because sipping or bathing or drowning in one of these pools temporarily blots out the incessant piping of flutes and the constant drumming that pours always down from the inaccessible upper regions of the spire. A balm from waters that are not water, but can dim those monotonous hymns devised for the pleasure of Chaos, in that era before the coming of time. She tends the pool whose blood can muffle the laughter, and the screams, and even the crying sounds. So, the pools are precious, and those who have the strength, the gift, the requisite madness to keep them, to milk them, these people are the only solace remaining in all the shattered mind of the shattered race that once was humanity.

She might be called Mercy, had that word not been forgotten. She might be called Release, but the concept of release has dwindled until it's hardly more than the unreachable itch of a phantom limb. Release was amputated along with Death and Hope, Blindness and Sleep.

Oh yes, she *can* see. All who dwell in the city on the plain can see perfectly well, though no light remains anywhere, only a complex continuum of darkness. So, the nameless woman who isn't blind sits at the edge of this pool, which is one of half a hundred such springs in the city. She has a thimble, a spoon, a mug, and a bowl. The thimble can hardly hold enough to ease one's suffering. The spoon is rusted, and its edges are sharp as a razor. The mug is cracked and missing its handle. The bowl has several small holes in the bottom. And these are the only vessels by which she is permitted to dispense what passes for surcease to the ruined and misshapen pilgrims who come to her.

She has been kneeling so long at the edge of the pool that she has no memory of ever standing, walking, or running. This is just as well, because, at some point, the living floor of the narthex decided that her legs and feet must surely be a part of its excreted self, and so she was incorporated, partly absorbed, and became a fixture of the Temple; an appendage, at most. She sprouts from the greasy, sweating stone, and all the lurching masses come to her.

There is in the city a sort of lottery, determining when any given person may visit the Temple, so she will not ever be overwhelmed. Even so, there's never a moment when the needful, impatient bodies do not press in all about her. But they do not dare to press *too* impatiently, for *she* decides the dosage one receives from the pool – whether a spoonful, or a cup, or a bowl – and no one argues with her, because she may also withhold the pool's blessings. She may refuse, and then the pool shuts itself tightly, and no one can even have so much as the thimble. In this way, there are still manners in a world devoid of Order. Fear and desperation have preserved their barest semblance. And also promote acts of generosity, for on very rare occasions a pilgrim may come to her bearing some stingy shard of Before. The offering is presented and set down on the floor, on that indefinite place where she becomes the floor of the narthex and the floor of the narthex becomes her.

"Kind," she might whisper, or "Thoughtful." She is infrequently heard to utter more than a single word at once, as her jaws and tongue, palate and teeth, are ill suited to conversation. But always there is at least *one* word before she takes the offering into herself, which is also the jealous Temple's way of claiming these alms for *it*self. A pilgrim may present her with a melted lump of windowpane, or a gnawed bone, or a penny, or the effigy of a disremembered saint fashioned from injection-molded plastic. Cherished treasures from the rubble. Quaint keepsakes from Before. She finds them amusing.

Though this is an age without seconds or minutes or hours, it's not precisely an age without time. Or perhaps it is more accurate to say it is an age during which the *illusion* of time stubbornly persists, hardwired as it is into the primate brain. Moments still *seem* to follow one after the next, even though there exists no means of keeping track of them. There are not days, as there is no sun. It might be claimed that when the globe capsized, tumbling pole over pole into this abyss, an era of unending night began. Only, there are remaining no stars nor moon nor any other luminous body that once helped define the night as night. Nor is this darkness merely the absence of daylight. This darkness is a positive state, something of tangible substance that writhes overhead and underfoot.

The woman who keeps the well in the narthex of the Temple usually has no need of the illusion of time. She has a sense of purpose, something denied almost everyone still living. Without her, there would be no conduit to deliver the waters of the pool to the people who seek its faintest of anodynes. If she keeps track of anything, it's the thirsty parade, and when it strikes her, she counts them, until counting them becomes more tedious than not counting them, and it's once again enough merely to have a purpose. It occurs to her, occasionally, to catalog the pilgrims, to sort them into types. She knows this ordering is an act of heresy, a blasphemy against the Dæmon Sultan and his messenger, the Black Pharaoh, who dwell in the Temple's spire. But she tends the pool, and so is favored, and the gods rarely pause to peer inside her thoughts.

She's busy devising a new scheme – one by which the pilgrims are classed according to the noises their flesh makes as they move – when she looks up to see that a woman from Before is next in line. Not only a woman from Before, no, but something so rarely glimpsed as to have vanished almost into the realm of myth. The pilgrim's naked body bears few marks from the passage. She's very nearly a vision of humanity as it existed prior to the coming of the gods and the sundering of the gates of Creation. Startled, the woman who keeps the well almost lets the spoon slip from her fingers and be lost forever in the depths.

"Oh," she whispers, and those crowded in about her bow their heads (or what pass for heads), privileged as they are to have heard her speak without having first *paid* for that privilege with an offering. But the woman from Before doesn't bow her head. She stands on the far side of the pool, watching, waiting, unseemly in her apparent calm. None who come to the pool hide their need of it. Few would even be capable of doing so, and yet this woman shows no evidence of any want. Her eyes (she has two and only two) have remained clear and blue, like the ghost of every lost autumn sky. Her gaze is disarming, and the woman who keeps the pool does something she cannot ever remember having previously done. She looks away.

"I've tried not to need the waters," the pilgrim says. And her voice, like her eyes, is impossibly clear. "You're so burdened already, I've tried not to come here."

"How?" demands the woman rooted at the edge of the pool, wishing she were able to turn the trick of stringing words together into sentences. There are at least a dozen questions in her skull that she would have answered, if she could manage to ask them. With some considerable effort, she forces herself to raise her head again. She forces herself to behold the *wholeness* of this unlikely pilgrim.

"I have alms," the pilgrim tells her, and the woman by the pool sees, then, that there's a stained and raggedy bundle of linen held in those perfectly formed hands, five fingers to each, no more, no less. Her ebony eyes dart up and down the pilgrim's body, searching for deformities that aren't there to find. The woman by the pool feels cheated and inadequate, and she cannot recall ever having felt either of these emotions before. After all, was she not *chosen?* Was she not singled out by the Temple acolytes, those whose faces are always hidden behind masks of yellow silk? Was she not led here and *forged* to this spot because she is special? Yes, all these things are certain and true. So, how can she possibly envy any among the beggars, those wretches whom she is free to placate or to ignore, as her moods and whims dictate?

In the days preceding apocalypse (when there still *were* days), the pilgrim would have been called *beautiful,* and the woman knows that much, no matter how little lore she may possess of Before. Pale hair hangs down to cover the pilgrim's shoulders and half conceal her perfectly formed breasts. She carries but a single scar, that her skin has taken on the appearance of a dark green stone – marble or schist or serpentinite – carved and polished so that it glimmers smoothly in the gloom. Her hips and belly, legs and face and arms are crosscut by what appear to be narrow, branching veins of milky white quartz or calcite. She might be a caryatid come down from her Athenian pillar, no longer willing to bear the weight of the stone entablature upon her head. Or a viridian Galatea, kissed by Venus but unable to complete her divine metamorphosis. And while this flesh may *appear* as stone, it's incongruent suppleness is plainly visible to the woman by the pool.

She knows spite for the first time, and the gods' faithful emissary growing from the resinous floor of the Temple tries hard to imagine the pilgrim cast out of the city and slowly weathering to rock dust and crystalline granules in the winds that scour the charcoal plains. Wishing this, there's a pang of guilt, which only serves to double and treble her envy. All her life, she's served the Temple in the last city of men without question or expectation of reward, and now this abomination has the gall to come asking her for comfort.

"No," the woman by the pool says flatly, shaking her head and staring into the darkness to catch sight of the next in line, an armless man with too many eyes, appropriately deformed and therefore worthy of her ministrations.

"But...I have a gift," the pilgrim insists. "I have a gift, something I swore I'd never be parted from. I've brought it to you."

"No," the woman by the pool says a second time, delivering the word as firmly and with as much finality as she can muster. She gestures with

her hands, signaling the armless man to step forward, motioning the green pilgrim to step aside.

The former tries, eagerly, to do as he's been bidden, but the latter refuses to budge.

"I don't understand," the green pilgrim says, wrinkling her green brow, frowning and glaring over her shoulder at the armless man. "How have I offended you?"

The woman at the edge of the pool flares her nostrils and tilts her head a bit to one side, her expression become one part curiosity and one part indignation. No one argues with her. No one *ever* argues with her. The consequences of incurring her wrath are too dire to consider, and so no seeker after the pool's meager blessings – even those who have, for whatever reason, been turned away – has seen fit to question her.

"Leave," she snarls, her lips curling back to expose obsidian teeth. *"Go."*

And now the crowd has grown anxious, but also curious how this will play out, how the green pilgrim will be punished for her transgression. The circle of gnarled bodies withdraws a scant few yards in all directions, dilating as a pupil dilates, and only two figures are left beside the pool of greater darkness. From somewhere in the spire high above the narthex, there's a sudden wet flutter, almost loud as tolling bells, and all assembled in the Temple know that the confrontation has attracted the attention of the acolytes and also of the Black Pharaoh, Nyarlathotep. Few eyes look upwards, and a dozen or so of the pilgrims creep fearfully from the narthex back out into the atrium and onto the uppermost of the five thousand steps that descend to the city below.

"At least let me show you what I've brought," the green pilgrim implores. If she's heard the fluttering sounds, she shows no evidence of having heard. If she grasps their provenance and significance, it's not obvious that she does. "Please, look at the offering before you send me away. I promise, there's nothing else like it remaining in all the wide world. I'm sure it's the last. The very last."

The woman by the pool flares her nostrils again and grits her bared teeth. Something oily and putrid leaks from the wound that was her sex before the Temple claimed her and, in so doing, changed her forever. The oily substance, her dingy stigmata, sizzles and seethes on the floor.

"Just look. Please. I've come so far, do that much before I go."

Above the narthex, the fluttering cacophony grows more urgent, the Black Pharaoh's curiosity piqued and piqued again. The woman by the pool wonders, briefly, why he can't simply look through those tatters of linen and see the offering for himself, without forcing her to acquiesce to the petition of this lovely, unseemly creature.

Because I exist only at his discretion, at his pleasure. Because I exist only to serve his caprice.

The woman by the pool snorts derisively, the way horses and cows snorted when there still were horses and cows, and she hides her sharp teeth and points at the raggedy bundle in the green pilgrim's hands.

"Yes," she reluctantly hisses.

"Thank you," the green pilgrim says, and then she bows her head once before lifting the folds of her bundle to reveal the corroded metal tube cradled within. It's bigger around at one end than the other, and the larger end is fitted with a glass lens. The glass is cracked. It probably cracked long ago, in the cataclysm, or maybe even before. Maybe it was cracked by some perfectly mundane, unremarkable event.

Overhead, the fluttering stops as abruptly as it began, and the woman at the edge of the pool stares at the artifact, which seems like nothing much at all. She can't be sure if the fluttering has stopped because the Black Pharaoh's curiosity is sated and he's lost interest or because the metal tube truly *is* as rare a sight as the green pilgrim claims. She reminds herself it's always better to err on the side of caution and holds out her hands to receive the oblation. The wet fluttering resumes. The gods exhale, having quickly tired of holding their breath. The green pilgrim looks down at the metal tube, which hardly glints at all in the murk. She actually seems to hesitate, but only for an instant before stepping around the border of the pool and relinquishing her gift.

"Why?" the woman at the edge of the pool asks, and it takes the green pilgrim the space of several heartbeats to realize that the keeper of the well is inquiring as to the function of the thing.

"On the side, there's a switch. You only have to move it forward with your thumb. The batteries still work. I've cared for them and kept them dry." The pilgrim's about to add that she's devoted herself to protecting the silver tube and its four batteries since before the city and before the black, when the fluttering stops a second time. In its place, an expanding series of concentric ripples begins at the center of the pool and spreads rapidly across its surface to lap thickly at the low, steep banks.

And too late it occurs to the keeper that this might be a warning of some sort, a dispatch from the spire that she should proceed with great caution. Her thumb has already pushed against the switch, and the flash-light flickers once, twice, then pours forth a brilliant flood of light. Actual *light* – not merely some lesser shade of dim – which is a thing the woman by the pool has never seen or even imagined. It is as alien to her as once this world was alien to those who have claimed it for their own. And having become part of the Temple, it isn't only alien to her, but wholly antithetical. Just as the incandescent beam parts and banishes the gloom, so too does it part and banish the woman, for she's nothing but the gloom made solid and given shape. And when her hands are no longer there to support it, the silver tube clatters to the floor and rolls into the pool. The water that is not water swallows it and takes away that hateful glow forever.

All the rotten, unfathomable corners of this dimension seem to wince, and a terrible, keening cry rises up from the remaining pilgrims as they shrink back against the walls and vaulted columns and finally flee the nar-thex. The cry is horror, and loss, and dazzled confusion.

The green pilgrim has dropped to her knees, is about to plunge her right arm deep into the pool in an attempt to rescue the lost flashlight, when she feels a sudden, violent tug at her ankles. She gasps and struggles as freezing tendrils curl tightly about her feet and slither up her calves, pull-ing her back from the well. What the floor has lost, it will now reclaim as the Temple metes out justice in the manner that seems to it most fitting. If there were still time, the transition would require hardly any time at all. Where there was before some pretense at skin and muscle and bone and blood there now remains only the nameless greasy matter of the floor. It reaches as high as the green pilgrim's hips, her thighs, the lower part of her belly, fixing her to the place the lost keeper so long occupied. The essence of it flows hungrily into its new helpmate, through her veins and marrow, invading every cell, and soon those vivid blue irises bruise, turning drab and inky as the tenebrous sky. Her pale hair is made dark, that it will never prove an affront to the watchful denizens of the spire.

If the Temple in the city on the horizonless charcoal plain wobbled for a second, it's been set right again. The high spire has gone back to seeping its endless atonal whine of fluting and the pounding of drums, and noth-ing more. Azathoth and its minions are otherwise occupied. The house is in proper disorder.

And what remains of the green pilgrim, this variegated shade she has become, stares into the pool of greater darkness and wonders at the utility of the thimble, the spoon, the mug, and the bowl. Whatever she'd come to the Temple to find is forgotten, inadvertently traded for something far, far more valuable. She is possessed of a purpose, infused with whyfor and wherefore and consumed with the exigency of her newfound station. When the thirsty, needful press of pilgrims returns, she realizes that she's always been waiting for them.

On the Reef

Man is least himself when he talks in his own person.
Give him a mask, and he will tell you the truth.

Oscar Wilde (1891)

There are rites that do not die. There are ceremonies and sacraments that thrive even after the most vicious oppressions. Indeed, some may grow stronger under such duress, stronger and more determined, so that even though devotees are scattered and holy ground defiled the rituals will find a way. The people will find a way back, down long decades and even centuries, to stand where strange beings were summoned – call them gods or demons or numina; call them what you will, as all words only signify and may not ever define or constrain the nature of these entities. Temples are burned and rebuilt. Sacred groves are felled, but new trees take root and flourish.

And so it is with this ragged granite skerry a mile and a half out from the ruins of a Massachusetts harbor town that drew its final, hitching breaths in the winter of 1928. Cartographers rarely take note of it, and when they do, it's only to mark the location for this or that volume of local hauntings or guides for legend trippers. Even the teenagers from Rowley and Ipswich have largely left it alone, and the crumbling concrete walls are almost entirely free of the spray-painted graffiti that nowadays marks their comings and goings.

Beyond the lower falls of the Castle Neck (which the Wampanoag tribes named Manuxet), where the river takes an abrupt southeastern turn before emptying into the Essex Bay, lies the shattered waste that once was Innsmouth. More than half buried now by the tall advancing dunes sprawls this tumbledown wreck of planks weathered grey as oysters, a disarray of cobblestone streets and brick sidewalks, the stubs of chimneys, and rows of warehouses and docks rusted away to almost nothing. But the North Shore wasteland doesn't end at the shore, for the bay is filled with sunken trawlers and purse seiners, a graveyard of lobster pots and steel hulls, rotting jute rope and oaken staves, where sea robins and flounder and spiny blue crabs have had the final word.

However, the subject at hand is not the fall of Innsmouth town, nor what little remains of its avenues and storefronts. The subject at hand is the dogged persistence of ritual, and its tendency to triumph over adversity and prejudice. The difficulty of forever erasing belief from the mind of man. We may glimpse the ruins, as a point of reference, but are soon enough drawn back around to the black granite reef, its rough spine exposed only at low tide. We are drawn back to now, and now it's one hour after sundown on a Halloween night, and a fat Harvest Moon as fiery orange as molten iron has just cleared the horizon. You'd think the sea would steam from the light of such a moon, but the water's too cold and far too deep.

On this night, there's a peculiar procession of headlights along the lonely Argilla Road, a solemn motorcade passing all but unnoticed between forests and fallow fields, nameless streams and wide swaths of salt marsh and estuary mudflat. *This* night, because this night is one of two every year when the faithful are drawn back to worship at their desecrated cathedral. The black reef may have no arcade, gallery, or clerestory, no flying buttresses or papal altar, but it *is* a cathedral, nonetheless. Function, not form, makes of it a cathedral. The cars file down to the ghost town, the town which is filled only with ghosts. They park where the ground is firm, and the drivers and passengers make their way by moonlight, over abandoned railroad tracks and fallen telegraph poles, skirting the pitfalls of old wells and barbed-wire tangles. They walk silently down to this long stretch of beach, south of Plum Island and west of the mouth of the Annisquam River and Cape Ann.

Some have come from as far away as San Francisco and Seattle, while others are locals, hailing from Boston and Providence and Manhattan. Few are dwellers in landlocked cities.

Each man and each woman wears identical sturdy cloaks sewn from cotton velveteen and lined with silk, cloth black as raven feathers. Most have pulled the hoods up over their heads, hiding their eyes and half hiding their faces from view. On the left breast of each cape is an embroidered symbol, which bears some faint resemblance to the *ikhthus,* secret sign of early Christian sects, and before that, denoting worshipers at the shrines of Aphrodite, Isis, Atargatis, Ephesus, Pelagia, and Delphine.

There are thirteen boats waiting for them, a tiny flotilla of slab-sided Gloucester dories that, hours earlier, were rowed from Halibut Point, six miles to the east. The launching of the boats is a ceremony in its own right, presided over by a priest and priestess who are never permitted to venture to the reef out beyond the ruins of Innsmouth.

As the boats are filled, there's more conversation than during the walk down to the beach; greetings are exchanged between friends and more casual acquaintances who've not spoken to one another since the last gathering, on the thirtieth of April. News of deaths and births is passed from one pilgrim to another. Affections are traded like childhood Valentines. These pleasantries are permitted, but only briefly, only until the dories are less than a mile out from the reef, and then all fall silent in unison and all eyes watch the low red moon or the dark waves lapping at the boats. Their ears are filled now with the wind, wild and cold off the Atlantic, and with the rhythmic slap of the oars.

There is a single oil lantern hung upon a hook mounted on the prow of each dory, but no other light is tolerated during the crossing from the beach to the reef. It would be an insult to the moon and to the darkness the moon pushes aside. In the boats, the pilgrims remove their shoes.

By the time the boats have gained the rickety pier – water-logged and slicked with algae, its pilings and boards riddled by the boring of shipworms and scabbed with barnacles – there is an almost tangible air of anticipation among these men and women. It hangs about them like a thick and obscuring cowl, heavy as the smell of salt in the air. There's an attendant waiting on the pier to help each pilgrim up the slippery ladder. He was blinded years ago, his eyes put out, that he would never glimpse the faces of those he serves; it was a mutilation he suffered gladly. It was a small enough price to pay, he told the surgeon.

Those who have come from so far, and from not so far, are led from the boats and the rotting pier out onto the reef. Each must be mindful of his or her footing. The rocks are slippery, and those who fall into the sea will be counted as offerings. No one is ever pulled out, if they should fall. Over many thousands of years, since the glaciers retreated and the seas rose to flood the land, this raw spit of granite has been shaped by the waves. In the latter years of the Eighteenth Century and the early decades of the Nineteenth – before the epidemic of 1846 decimated the port – the reef was known as Cachalot Ledge, and also Jonah's Folly, and even now it bears a strong resemblance to the vertebrae and vaulted ribs of an enormous sperm whale, flayed of skin and muscle and blubber. But after the plague and the riots that followed, as outsiders began to steer clear of Innsmouth and its harbor, and as the heyday of New England whaling drew to a close, the rocks were rechristened Devil Reef. There were odd tales whispered by the crews of passing ships, of nightmarish figures they claimed to have seen clambering out of the sea and onto those rocks, and this new name stuck and stuck fast.

Late in the winter of 1928, the submarine USS *O-10* was deployed to these waters, from the Boston Navy Yard. The one hundred and seventy-three foot vessel's tubes were armed with a complement of twenty-nine torpedoes, all of which were discharged into an unexpectedly deep trench discovered just east of Devil Reef. The torpedoes detonated almost a mile down, devastating a target that has never been publicly disclosed. But the pilgrims know what it was, and that attack is to them no less a blasphemy than the destruction of synagogues and cathedrals during the firestorms of the two World Wars, no less a crime than the razing of Taoist temples by Chinese communists, or the devastation of the Aztec Templo Mayor by Spaniard conquistadores after the fall of Tenochtitlan in 1521. And they remember the benthic mansions of Y'ha-nthlei and the grand altars and the beings murdered and survivors left dispossessed by those torpedoes. They remember the gods of that race, and the promises, and the rites, and so they come this night. They come to honor the Mother and the Father and all those who died and who have survived and all those who have yet to make the passage, but yet may. The old blood is not gone from the world.

Two are chosen from among the others. A box carved from jet is presented, and two lots are drawn. On each lot is graven the true name of one of the supplicants, the names bestowed in dream quests by Father Dagon and Mother Hydra. One male and one female, or two female, or two male. But always the number is two. Always only a single pair to enact the most holy rite of the Order. There is no greater honor than to be chosen, and all here desire it. But, too, there is trepidation, for one may not become an avatar of gods without the annihilation of self, to one degree or another. And becoming the avatars of the Mother and the Father means utter and complete annihilation. Not physical death. Something far more destructive to both body and mind than mere death. The jet box is held high and shaken once, and then the lots are drawn, and the names are called out loudly to the pilgrims and the night and the waters and the glaring, lidless eye of the moon.

"The dyad has been determined," declares the old man who drew the lots, and then he steps aside, making way for the two women who have been named. One of them hesitates a moment, but only a moment and only for the most fleeting of moments. They have names, in the lives they have left behind, lives and families and careers and histories, but tonight all this will be stripped away, sloughed off, just as they now remove their heavy black cloaks to reveal naked, vulnerable bodies. They stand facing one another, and a priestess steps forward. She anoints their forehead, shoulders, bellies, and vaginas with a stinking paste made of ground angelica and mandrake root, the eyes and bowels of various fish, the aragonite cuttlebones of Sepiidae, from foxglove, amber, frankincense, dried kelp and bladderwrack, the blood of a calf, and powdered molybdena. Then the women join hands, and each receives a wafer of dried human flesh, which the priestess carefully places beneath their tongues. Neither speaks. Even the priestess does not speak.

Words will come soon enough.

And now it is the turn of the Keeper of the Masks, and he steps forward. The relics he has been charged with protecting are swaddled each in yellow silk. He unwraps them, and now all the pilgrims may look upon the artifacts, shaped from an alloy of gold and far more precious metals, some still imperfectly known (or entirely unknown) to geologists and chemists, and some which have fallen to this world from the gulfs of space. To an infidel, the masks might seem hideous, monstrous things. They would miss the divinity of these divine objects, too distracted by forms they have been taught are grotesque and to be loathed, too unnerved by the almost inexplicable angles into which the alloy was shaped long, long ago, geometries that might seem "wrong" to intellects bound by conventional mathematics. Sometime in the early 1800s, these hallowed relics were brought to Innsmouth by the hand of Captain Obed Marsh himself, delivered from the Windward Islands of French Polynesia and ferried home aboard the barque *Sumatra Queen*.

The Keeper of Masks makes the final choice, selecting the face of Father Dagon for one of the two women and the face of Mother Hydra for the other. The women are permitted to look upon the other's mortal countenance one last time. And then the Keeper hides their faces, fitting the golden masks and tying them tightly in place with cords woven from the tendons of blood sacrifices, hemp, and sisal. When it is certain that the masks are secure, only then does the Keeper step back into his place among the others. And the two women kneel bare-kneed on stone worn sharp enough to slice leather.

"Iä!" cries the priestess, and then the Keeper of the Masks, and, finally, the man who drew the lots. Immediately, the pilgrims all reply, "Iä! Iä! Rh'típd! Cthulhu fhtagn!" And then the man who drew the lots, in a somber voice that barely is more than an awed whisper, adds "Ph'nglui mglw'nafh Cthulhu R'lyeh wgah'nagl fhtagn. Rh'típd qho'tlhai mal." His words are lost on the wind, which greedily snatches away each syllable and strews them to the stars and sinks them to that immemorial city far below the waves, its spires broken and crystalline roofs splintered by naval munitions more than eighty years before this night.

"You are become the Mother and the Father," he says. "You are become the living incarnation of the eternal servants of R'lyeh. You are no more what you were. Those former lives and forms are undone. You are become the face of the deep and the eyes of the heavens. You are on this night forever more wed."

The two kneeling women say nothing at all. But the wind has all at once ceased to blow, and around the reef the water has grown still and smooth as glass. The moon remains the same, though, and leers down upon the scene like a jackal waiting for its turn at someone else's kill or Herod Antipas lusting after dancing Salomé. But no one among the pilgrims looks away from the kneeling women. No one ever looks away, for to avert their eyes from the sacrament would be unspeakable offense. They watch, as the moon watches, with great anticipation, and some with envy, that their names were not chosen from the bag of lots.

To the west – over the wooded hills beyond Essex Bay and the vast estuarine flats at the mouth of the Manuxet River – there are brilliant flashes of lightning, despite the cloudless sky. And, at this moment, as far away as Manchester-By-The-Sea, Wenham and Topsfield, Georgetown and Byfield, hounds have begun to bay. Cats only watch the sky in wonder and contemplation. The waking minds of men and women are suddenly, briefly, obscured by thoughts too wicked to ever share. If any are asleep and dreaming, their dreams turn to hurricane squalls and drownings and impossible beasts stranded on sands the color of a ripe cranberry bog. In this instant, the land and the ocean stand in perfect and immemorial opposition, and the kneeling women who wear the golden masks are counted as evolutionary apostates, deserting the continent, defecting to brine and abyssal silt. The women are tilting the scales, however minutely, and on this night the sea will claim a victory, and the shore may do no more to protest their desertion than sulk and drive the tides much farther out than usual.

No one on the reef turns away. And they don't make a sound. There's nothing left for the pilgrims but to bear silent witness to the transition of the anointed. And that change is not quick, nor is it in any way merciful; neither woman is spared the least bit of agony. But they don't give voice to their pain, if only because their mouths have been so altered that they will nevermore be capable of speech or any other utterance audible to human ears. The masks have begun to glow with an almost imperceptible phosphorescence and will shortly drop away, shed skins to be retrieved later by the Keeper.

Wearing now the mercurial forms of Mother Hydra and Father Dagon, the lovers embrace. Their bodies coil tightly together until there's almost no telling the one from the other, and the writhing knot of sinew and organs and rasping teeth glistens wetly in the bright moonlight. The two are all but fused into a single organism, reaffirming a marriage first made among the cyanobacterial mats of warm paleoarchaen lagoons, three and a half billion years before the coming of man. There is such violence that this coupling looks hardly any different from a battle, and terrible gaping wounds are torn open, only to immediately seal themselves shut again. The chosen strain and bend themselves towards inevitable climax, and the strata of the reef shudders repeatedly beneath the feet of the pilgrims. Several have to squat or kneel to avoid sliding from the rocks to be devoured by the insincere calm of the sea. In the days to come, none of them will mutter a word about what they've seen and heard and smelled in the hour of this holy copulation. This is a secret they guard with their lives and with their sanity.

No longer sane, the lovers twist, unwind, and part. The Father has already bestowed his gift, and now it is the Mother's turn. A bulging membrane bursts, a protuberance no larger than the fist of a child, and the resulting lacuna weeps blood and ichor and a single black pearl. It is *not* a pearl, but by way of the roughest sort of analogy or approximation. One may as well call it a pearl as not. The true name for the Mother's gift is forbidden. It drops from her and lies quivering in a sticky puddle, to be claimed as the masks will be claimed. And then they drag themselves off the steep eastern lip of the reef, slithering from view and sinking into the ocean as the waves and wind return. They will spend the long night spiraling down and down, descending into that same trench the *O-10* torpedoed eighty-two Januaries ago. And by the time the sun rises, and Devil Reef is once more submerged, they will have found the many-columned vestiges of the city of Y'ha-nthlei, where they will be watched over by beings that are neither fish nor men nor any amphibious species cataloged by science.

By then, the cars parked above the ghost town will have gone away, carrying the pilgrims back to the drab, unremarkable lives they will live until the end of April and the next gathering. And they will all dream their dreams and await the night they may be chosen to wear the golden masks.

The Transition of Elizabeth Haskings

Elizabeth Haskings inherited the old house on Water Street from her grandfather. It would have passed to her mother, but she'd gone away to Oregon when Elizabeth was six years old, leaving her daughter with the old man. She'd said she would return, but she never did, and after a while the letters stopped coming, and then the postcards stopped coming, too. And now Elizabeth Haskings is twenty-nine, and she has no idea whether her mother is alive or dead. It's not something she thinks about very often. But she does understand *why* her mother left, that it was fear of the broad, tea-colored water of the Ipswich River, flowing lazily down to the salt marshes and the Atlantic. Flowing down to Little Neck and the deep channel between the mainland and Plum Island, finally emptying into the ocean hardly a quarter of a mile north of Essex Bay. Elizabeth understands it was the ruins surrounding the bay, there at the mouth of the Manuxet River – labeled the Castle Neck River on more recent maps, maps drawn up after the late 1920s.

She's never blamed her mother for running like that. But here, in Ipswich, she has the house and her job at the library, and in Oregon – or *wherever* she might run – she'd have nothing at all. Here she has roots, even if they're roots she does her best not to dwell on. But this is only history, the brief annals of a young woman's life. Relevant, certainly, but only as prologue. What happened in the town that once ringed Essex Bay, the strange seaport town that abruptly died one winter eighty-four years ago, where her grandfather lived as a boy.

It's a Saturday night in June, and on most Saturday nights Elizabeth Haskings entertains what she quaintly thinks of as her "gentleman caller." She enjoys saying, "Tonight, I will be visited by my gentleman caller." Even though Michael's gay. They work together at archives at the Ipswich Public Library, though, sometimes, he switches over to circulation. Anyway, he knows about Elizabeth's game, and usually he brings her a small bouquet of flowers of one sort or another – calla lilies, Peruvian lilies, yellow roses fringed with red, black-eyed susans – and she carefully arranges them in one of her several vases while he cooks her dinner. She feels bad that Michael is always the one who cooks, but, truthfully, Elizabeth isn't a very good cook and tends to eat from the microwave most nights.

They might watch a DVD afterwards, or play Scrabble, or just sit talking at the wide dinner table she also inherited from her grandfather. About work or books or classical music, something Michael knows much more about than does she. Truth is, he often makes her feel inadequate, but she's never said so. She loves him, and it's not a simple, Platonic love, so she's always kept it a secret, allowed their "dates" to seem like nothing more than a ritual between friends who seem to have more in common with one another than with most anyone else they know in the little New England town (whether that's true or not). Sometimes, she lies in bed, thinking about him lying beside her, instead of thinking about all the things she works so hard *not* thinking about: the river, the sea, her lost mother, the grey, weathered boards and stone foundations where there was once a dingy town, etcetera & etcetera. It's her secret, and she'll never tell him.

Though, Michael knows the most terrible secret that she'll ever have, and she's fairly sure that his knowing it has kept her sane for the five years they've known one another. In an odd way, it doesn't seem fair, the same way his always cooking doesn't seem fair. No, it's obviously something worse than unfair, his knowing this awful thing about her, and her keeping secret how she feels for him. Still, Elizabeth assures herself, telling him that would only ruin their friendship. A bird in the hand being worth two in the bush, and in this instance it really is better not to have one's cake and eat it, too.

They don't always play board games after dinner, or watch movies, or talk. Because there are nights that his just *knowing* her secret isn't enough. There are nights it weighs so much Elizabeth imagines it might crush her flat, like the pressure at the bottom of the deep sea. Those nights, after dinner, they go upstairs to her bedroom, and he runs a porcelain bowl of water from the bathtub faucet. He adds salt to it while she undresses before the tall mirror affixed to one wall, taller than her by a foot, and framed with ornately carved walnut. She pretends that it's only carved with acanthus leaves and cherubs. It's easier that way. It doesn't embarrass her for Michael to see her nude, not even with the disfigurements of her secret uncovered and plainly visible to him. After all, that's why he's returned from the bathroom with the bowl of salty water and a yellow sponge (he leaves the tap running). That's why they've come upstairs, because she can't always be the only one to look at herself.

"It's bad tonight?" he asks.

She doesn't answer straightaway. She's never been one to complain if she can avoid complaining, and it's bad enough that he knows. She doesn't also want to seem weak. After a minute or half a minute she answers, "It's been worse." That's the truth, even if it's also a way of evading his question.

"Betsy, just tell me when you're ready." He always calls her Betsy, never Elizabeth. She's never called him Mike, though.

"I'm ready," she says, leaning her neck to the left or to the right, exposing the pale skin below the ridge of her chin. *But I'm not ready at all. I'm never ready, am I?*

"Okay, then. I'll be as gentle as I can."

He's always as gentle as anyone could be.

"You've never hurt me, Michael. Not even once."

But she has no doubt he can see the discomfort in her eyes when the washcloth touches her skin. She tries hard not to flinch, but, usually, she flinches regardless.

"Was that too hard?"

"No. I'm fine. I'm okay," she tells him, so he continues administering the saltwater to her throat, dabbing carefully, and Elizabeth Haskings tries to concentrate on his fingertips, whenever they happen to brush against her. It never takes very long for the three red slits on each side of her throat to appear, and not much longer for them to open. They never open very far, not until later on. Just enough that she can see the barn-red gills behind the stiff, crescent-shaped flaps of skin that weren't there only moments before. That never are there until the saltwater. Here, she always loses her breath for a few seconds, and the flaps spasm, opening and closing, and she has to gasp several times to find a balance between the air being drawn in through her nostrils and mouth, and the air flowing across the feathery red gill filaments. Sometimes her legs go weak, but Michael has never let her fall.

"Breathe," he whispers. "Don't panic. Take it slow and easy, Betsy. Just breathe."

The dizziness passes, the dark blotches that swim before her eyes, and she doesn't need him to support her any longer. She stares at herself in the mirror, and by now her eyes have gone black. No irises, no pupils, no sclerae. Just inky black where her hazel-green eyes used to be.

"I'm right here," he says.

He doesn't have to tell her that again. He's always there, behind her or at her side.

Unconsciously, she tries to blink her eyes, but all trace of her lids have vanished, and she can only stare at those black, blank eyes. Later, when they begin to smart, Michael will have the eye drops at the ready.

"It's getting harder," she says. He doesn't reply, because she says this almost every time. *All his replies have been used up*, Elizabeth thinks. *No matter how much he might want to calm me or offer comfort, he's already said it all a dozen times over.*

Instead, he asks, "Keep going?"

She nods.

"We don't have to, you know."

"Yes we do. It's bad if we do. It's worse if we don't. It hurts more if we don't." Of course, Michael knows this perfectly well, and there's the briefest impatience that she has to remind him. Not anger, no, but an unmistakable flash of impatience, there and gone in the stingy space of a single heartbeat.

He dips the sponge into the saltwater again, not bothering to squeeze it out, because the more the better. The more, the easier. Water runs down his arm and drips to the hardwood floor. Before they're finished, there will be a puddle about her bare feet and his shoes, too. Michael gingerly swabs both her hands with the sponge, and at once the vestigial webbing between her fingers, common to all men and women, begins to expand, pushing the digits farther away from one another.

Elizabeth watches, biting her lip against the discomfort and watches. It doesn't horrify her the same way that the appearance of the gills and the change to her eyes does, but it's much more painful. Not nearly so much as the greater portion of her metamorphosis to come, but enough she *does* bite her lip (careful not to draw blood). Within five minutes, the webbing has grown enough that it's attached at the uppermost joint between each finger, and is at least twice as thick as usual. And the texture of the skin on the backs of her hands and her palms is becoming smoother and faintly iridescent, more transparent, gradually taking on the faintest tinge of turquoise. She used to think of the color as *celeste opaco,* because the Italian sounded prettier. But now she settles for *turquoise.* Not as lyrical, no, but it's not opaque, and turquoise is somehow more honest. Monsters should be honest. Before half an hour has passed, most of her skin will have taken on variations of the same hue.

"Yesterday," she says, "during my lunch break, when I said I needed to go to the bank, I didn't."

There are a few seconds of quiet before he asks, "Where did you go, Elizabeth?"

"Choate Bridge," she answers. "I just stood there a while, watching the river." It's the oldest stone-arch bridge anywhere in Massachusetts, built in 1764. There are two granite archways through which the river flows on its easterly course.

"Did it make you feel any better?"

"It made me want to swim. The river always makes me want to swim, Michael. You know that."

"Yeah, Betsy. I know."

She wants to add, *Please don't ask me questions you already know the answers to,* but she doesn't. It would be rude. He means well, and she's never rude if she can help it. Especially not to Michael.

All evidence of her fingernails has completely vanished.

"It terrified me. It always terrifies me."

"Maybe one day it won't. Maybe one day you'll be able to look at the water without being frightened."

"Maybe," she whispers, hoping it isn't true. Pretty sure what'll happen if she ever stops being afraid of the river and the sea. *I can't drown. I can't ever drown. How does a woman who can't drown fear the water?*

There are things in the water. Things that can *hurt me. And places I never want to see awake.*

Now he's running the sponge down her back, beginning at the nape of her neck and ending at the cleft between her buttocks. This time, the pain is bad enough she wants to double over, wants to go down on her knees and vomit. But that would be weak, and she won't be weak. Michael used to bring her pills to dull the pain, but she stopped taking them almost a year ago because she didn't like the fogginess they brought, the way they caused her to feel detached from herself, as though these transformations were happening to someone else.

Monsters should be honest.

At once, the neural processes of her vertebrae begin to broaden and elongate. She's made herself learn a lot about anatomy: human, anuran, chondrichthyan, osteichthyan, *et alia.* Anything and everything that seems relevant to what happens to her on these nights. *The devil you know,* as her grandfather used to say. So, Elizabeth Haskings knows that the processes will grow the longest between her third and seventh thoracic vertebrae, and between her last lumbar, sacrals, and coccygeals (though less so than in the thoracic region), greatly accenting both the natural lumbar curve of her back. Musculature responds accordingly. She knows the Latin names of all those muscles, and if there were less pain, she could recite them for Michael. She imagines herself laughing like a madwoman and reciting the names of the shifting, straining tendons. In the end, there won't quite be fins, *sensu stricto*. Almost, but not quite.

Aren't I a madwoman? How can I possibly still be sane?

"Betsy, you don't have to be so strong," he tells her, and she hates the pity in his voice. "I know you think you do, but you don't. Certainly not in front of me."

She takes the yellow sponge from him, her hands shaking so badly she spills most of the saltwater remaining in the bowl, but still manages to get the sponge sopping wet. Her gums have begun to ache, and she smiles at herself before wringing out the sponge with both her webbed hands so that the water runs down her belly and between her legs. In the mirror, she sees Michael turn away.

She drops the sponge to the floor at her feet (she doesn't have to look to know her toes have begun to fuse one to the next), and gazes into her pitchy eyes until she's sure the adjustments to her genitals are finished. When she does look down at herself, there's a taut, flat surface in place of the low mound of the mons pubis, and the labia majora, labia minora, and clitoris – all the intricacies of her sex – have been reduced to the vertical slit of an oviduct where her vagina was moments before. On either side of the slit are tiny, triangular pelvic fins, no more than an inch high and three inches long.

"We should hurry now, Betsy," Michael says. He's right, of course. She has to reach the bathtub full of warm salty water while she can still walk. Once or twice before she's waited too long, and he's had to carry her; that humiliation was worse than all the rest combined. In the tub, she curls almost fetal, and the flaps in front of Elizabeth's gills open and close, pumping in and out again, extracting all the oxygen she'll need until sunrise. Michael will stay with her, guarding her, as he always does.

She can sleep without lids to shield her black eyes, and, *when* she sleeps, she dreams of the river flowing down to the ruined seaport, to Essex Bay, and then out into the Atlantic due south of Plum Island. She dreams of the craggy spine of Devil Reef rising a few feet above the waves and of those who crawl out onto the reef most nights to bask beneath the moon. Those like her. And, worst of all, she dreams of the abyss beyond the reef, and towers and halls of the city there, a city that has stood for eighty thousand years and will stand for eighty thousand more. On these nights, changed and slumbering, Elizabeth Haskings can't lie to herself and pretend that her mother fled to Oregon, or even that her grandfather lies in his grave in Highland Cemetery. On these nights, she isn't afraid of anything.

A Mountain Walked

Excerpts from the Field Journal of Arthur Lakes During His
Explorations for Saurians and Fossil Remains in the Wyoming
Territory (June 1879):

MAY 25TH: I spent the morning in sketching bones in [Quarry] No. 3
and the locality of the *Ichthyosaurus* quarry. Being alone in the tent I had
the usual company of the spermophiles. In the evening I walked along
RR track to meet men returning in the handcar. Stationmaster Carlin
[William Edward] had shot an elk and they were bringing back the hams.
Following supper, the tale of the hunt was recounted which set [William
Hallow] Reed to the cheerful spinning of many yarns of their hunting
misadventures.

MAY 27TH: Reed discovered portion of saurian jaw poßeßed of herbivo-
rous teeth in it at Quarry No. 3. So we went up on the handcar to see it.
Was about six inches of jaw, but rather weathered and portions of skull in
exceedingly friable condition attached. Saw couple of deer and fawn near
the quarry. Most of the day spent shovelling out dirt.

Had elk meat for our supper which was tender and nice. We fashioned a
cabinet for geological specimens from dry goods box. Caught axolotl [tiger
salamander, *Ambystoma mexicanum*] in water tank. Reed related story of
how he once found a broken fiddle in the old deserted camp of some party
in North Park. Broken, the fiddle, but of expert craftsmanship. Also found
blankets. Campers supposed, then, to have been wealthy people, likely of a
sudden run down by Indians and forced either to beat a hasty retreat, else

were maßacred and never heard of thereafter. He also told of finding skeleton of a man and also his gun in a fißure. He believed the man must have frozen to death.

MAY 28TH: Paßed morning sketching bluffs fr. North shore of the lake [Como]. Great clouds of cliff swallows whirling darting about on ledges or rock forming the bank of the lake or resting basking on sand near to the water. Strata to north belong to same geological horizons and groups as those forming bluffs at the station, viz Juraßic & Cretaceous.

Reed returned from Quarry No. 3 with report of find of a very large humerus bone. Men discovered enormous claw of carnivorous Dinosaur much curved, sharp and long. Walked out by shore of lake near to sunset, and saw muskrat cavorting in the rushes. Couple of ducks flew close in under the bank unconscious of my presence the female quacking lustily. Could have dropped a stone on them! A wild scene with flaming glare of the sunset so distant and solitary on the desolate Wyoming prairie. As we turned to head back to camp, a most peculiar booming was heard sounding acroß the lake followed by complete silence. Gave us a right start. Reed speculates may be meteorological phenomenon as yet unknown though it sounded to me nothing like thunder. We did not speak of it to the others.

MAY 29TH: Went to Quarry No. 3 in company of Reed. Uncovered respectable portions of two fused vertebrae [allosaurus sacral] lying beneath humerus. While digging, Reed had misfortune to tap into a small spring which at once flooded part of the diggings. Water foul and oily, owing poßibly to mineral composition of enclosing strata. A most noisome odour as if from decaying vegetation and it is hoped we shall not be forced to abandon quarry on its account. Reed also found three small and somewhat constricted vertebrae roughly one yard from humerus. In the evening arranged Reed's cabinet of foßils.

MAY 30TH: Spent in shovelling earth at No. 3. All signs of flood have drained away, leaving only hole from which it sprung and which I filled in post haste lest we have a repeat of that deluge. Odd sunset.

MAY 31ST: Spotted antelope herd as we made our way back to camp. Reed the hunter started in pursuit whilst I continued on to the quarry. Soon I heard the report of his rifle, and looking up saw him lying on the prairie firing shot after shot. But not at the herd which had vanished. Puff after puff of white smoke came from his rifle's barrel and I could see nothing of his target. I saw dust rise where the bullets struck ground. After twenty shots he remained for a bit lying there in the graß.

On the way home on the handcar asked Reed what had become of the antelope and what he might have been shooting at in their stead. But he was uncharacteristically taciturn and refused to speak on the subject. Minutes later though he did point out to me a distinct trail several feet wide and a half mile long which he said was made by jack rabbits. I saw no sign of their feet but the graß grew up in a defined line as distinct from the prairie turf.

JUNE 1ST: In tent read to Reed from *Vestiges of Creation*. He has spoken little since yesterday and starts at the smallest of sounds. Have not asked again about the antelopes.

JUNE 2ND: Hired another man. Watched coyote creeping along through sage until Reed shot it. Later found small saurian bones 500 yds. west of No. 3. They were small vertebrae hollow but filled with carbonate of lime. Also curved sabre tooth about one inch in length from a carnivorous Dinosaur. In the afternoon I sketched our camp. The last discovery Reed calls Quarry No. 6. He is not so anxious as on yesterday – to my relief.

JUNE 4TH: Profeßor [Othniel Charles] Marsh whom we had been expecting arrived and breakfasted with hands at sectionhouse. Quickly made himself to home with all the men. After breakfast we set forth on the handcar, a large party of us, the "rubbed car" being attached to it for Marsh and my benefit. A lovely morning & Profeßor Marsh much amused by innumerable spermophiles, hares and rabbits leaping from RR track as we did speed along. Stopped first at Quarry No. 3 only to find worse flooding from Reed's spring, as if I had not filled in the source! A great disappoint all round, and the odour was many times worse it seemed than previously. Profeßor Marsh dismayed and visibly angered that ilium and caudals of carnivorous dinosaur lost, even after I explained all were too rotten for excavation. In addition to iridescent oily sheen on water's surface witneßed a yellow foam about the periphery of the submerged quarry.

Thence we proceeded to our latest discovery No. 6, in hopes of lifting Profeßor Marsh's spirits somewhat. After close and careful examination of bones Profeßor M. devolved many of them to destruction as much too imperfect or rotten for preservation and lest Cope's men come upon them and conclude otherwise. But bones we had taken to be those of a crocodile with scutes of armour deeply pitted proved just so. Profeßor M. thinks one bone to be that of a pterodactyl, and a small half inch jaw to belong to early mammal. The loose teeth were also those of a crocodile of a species long vanished from the globe.

From there again by handcar to Quarry No. 4, which is situated on the slope of a deep ravine washed out by Rock Creek, some four or five miles east of Como. Quarry has been well worked by Reed previous to my arrival at Como. Many large bones plainly were visible. Near this quarry Profeßor Marsh found exceedingly unusual Indian stone fetish or lithic artefact which could be, at a casual glance, taken for the effigy of some winged demon as from the illustrations of Gustave Doré. Reed straightaway grew troubled again and advised the Proffßor to leave it be, as its removal could anger Sioux or Cheyenne with whom we have had no trouble heretofore. But Profeßor Marsh insisted the piece would be a valuable addition to the Peabody collection back in New Haven and all Reed's effort could not dißuade him. Profeßor M. carried the artefact away in his coat pocket. Also found a foßil snail or helix in concretion between quarry and overlying Dakota sandstone (Cretaceous).

From a nearby ravine a doe elk suddenly sprang from the bushes and dashed up to the top of the ravine. Reed who happened to be on ahead did not see it at first till the Profeßor shouted at him. Hearing us he wheeled round and fired directly. Beast struck him near the hip but wound insufficient to stop him, and Reed got off another shot but without succeß. The elk was lost to sight over the ridge. Reed followed and tracked him [sic] for an hour by drips of blood which later he insisted were "not right," being of a darker hue than proper for any elk and stinking of sulfur. Profeßor Marsh suggests doe may have drunk from befouled pool at No. 6 [sic], resulting in contamination of its fluids but this rational explanation did little if anything to soothe Reed's nerves. Again, he implored Profeßor M. to leave behind the artefact and again without result, except to set him in an ill humour. He wondered aloud at having employed a superstitious collector given to fear of Indian relics, and this did nothing to settle Reed.

Turning his attention back to the quarry, Profeßor Marsh determined the bones there – a sacrum – to belong to a great sauropod. We returned to the handcar for lunch. Railroad hands and our party made quite a fine picnic arranged around the viands which were spread out upon the rubber car. Afterwards, went to Quarry 1 and prospecting on our stomachs or on hands and knees all hunted for small bones in a microscopic manner and were well rewarded finding what Marsh thought might be toe bone of either pterodactyl or bird. Still this did not improve Reed's disposition I am sad to say.

After supper, Profeßor M. regaled us with stories of his exploits searching for Tertiary bones near to Fort Bridger. Reed, however, did remain in the tent.

JUNE 5TH: Profeßor M. has resolved to stay on another day with us. Immediately upon finishing breakfast we started for the lake and when we had arrived he brought to our attention the small crustaceans [amphipods] to be found amongst the waterweed which grows in such profusion on the lakebed. We stopped at the old quarry situated on the lake's north shore, and Marsh was much interested in the medium-sized sacrum we have exposed there. He believes it belongs to the Allosauridae, and he wishes to see this quarry expanded further in hopes of additional discoveries of a similar merit. From the lake we walked the RR tracks west to the bridge acroß Rock Creek where desperadoes had last August purposed wrecking the train by the removal of a rail (along with its spikes).

Our party croßed excellent outcroppings of tawny and yellow strata of the Cretaceous and Juraßic group as we climbed down into the selfsame hollow where those desperadoes encamped, and I remarked it was certainly a spot well adapted to their ends. In the shade of the identical cottonwoods that sheltered the thwarted bandits, we sat – Marsh, Reed, Ashley [Edward G.], and I. As mourning doves, which had nested above, flew about to and fro, I managed a quick sketch of the pastoral scene. We lunched below the trees, and discußion soon turned from the brigand gang's plot to wreck the Union Pacific Westbound Expreß No. 3 to the jaw of a little mammal (*Dryolestes*) Reed had found at the base of a nearby cliff, about which Profeßor M. is very excited. Soon though Reed steered the conversation back to the matter of the Indian artefact found the previous day at Quarry No. 4. He remains most unaccountably agitated on the subject, and insists we are inviting calamity of one sort or another by not returning it.

Unexpectedly he spoke also, but briefly, of that queer episode with the antelope on the last day of May yet refused to provide any details, saying only that there are many perils of the prairie we do not understand and would be wise not to be so reckleß. Profeßor M. listened and asked him what he believed he was shooting at that day but Reed grew tight-lipped and wouldn't say. Now here is a respected man, a seasoned hunter and guide and RR employee, former infantryman in the Union Army, and always have I held him in high esteem, certainly not regarding him as the sort given to the wild and frankly credulous attitude he seems to have adopted in the past few days. It was he and the stationmaster who first alerted Marsh to the presence of giant saurian bones at Como. It was impoßible not to detect an apprehensive look in the Profeßor's eyes. In any case it is clear he will do no such thing as part with the curious relic, which I will admit is not a pleasant object to look upon as is the case with many of the redskins' fetishes, but hardly is it either cause for such behaviour as Reed's.

After visiting a couple of other promising outcrops, one of which turned up a jaw with diminutive crenated teeth reminiscent of the *Iguanodon*.

After our supper Ashley drew our attention to an unusual halo about the moon (three nights past full) which shone almost red as blood and which greatly piqued Profeßor M.'s curiosity who suggested it might portend a coming dust storm. Reed would not look upon or speak of it.

JUNE 6TH: I am pleased to report Marsh has decided to remain with us a few days more before returning to the Eastern states. We returned to the new discovery which is probably of a *Laosaurus*. Three fir trees grow in an isolated clump near to the site and so we have christened the spot "Three Trees Quarry." The wind was blowing hard – seeming to confirm the Profeßor's suspicions – and with every blow of the pick the gusts blinded up with dust and grit. But we managed to unearth a fine femur and some other bones before returning to camp. Reed's demeanour is beginning to gnaw at my nerves and I daresay those of all of us.

JUNE 7TH: Weather windy as yesterday. It blew so hard and the dust was so intolerable we were forced to make a short day of it, much to Profeßor M.'s disappointment. Men washed their clothes back at camp. News has come to us of a great strike and attendant excitement at the North Park Mines and Reed has spoken of travelling there rather than staying on with us, talk which rightfully has angered Marsh.

JUNE 9TH: Reed's thirty-first birthday. I did a small coloured sketch of the lake and its surrounding painted bluffs to place above his cabinet of foßils back in Nebraska honouring his finds, the hardships he has faced, and his diligence. I will be the first to say Bill Reed is as fine an instance of the fact that education is hardly confined to those who have attended university but much is learnt by sharp wits put to the service of keen observation.

Which makes all the odder his continuing insistence that Marsh's artefact from Quarry No. 4 poses some unspoken threat to our party. He has actually gone as far as offering to purchase it that it might be returned by his hand to the spot where it was discovered. He talks increasingly in riddles that I find unsettling and Profeßor M. is adopting a decidedly belligerent attitude toward him for which I cannot fault our employer.

We returned to the diggings containing the curious little *Laosaurus* dinosaur. Its bones are hollow, and its appearance in life must have been akin to a kangaroo though with a disproportionately small and lizard-like skull. Its claws measure a good inch, and Marsh thinks it to have been ten feet in length.

Our labours were once more very unpleasant, as the gale of wind was blowing, blowing dust in blinding clouds as quickly as we exposed the bones. It lifted airbourne also particles of dry clay besides our papers, books, and packing materials, all being constantly spirited away so that we wasted much time in chasing them about the sandstone bluffs. Notwithstanding we stubbornly persisted tooth and nail and were rewarded by exposing a lot of bones. I sketched the bones *in situ,* but only with great difficulty the wind nearly ripping my [sketch]book from my hands and constantly blinding me with dust. Left early for camp, finally having had enough. Reed worked hard but muttered inceßantly about North Park and the artefact and the storm's being a portent of some sort. I fear for his sanity, and perhaps it would be best if he moved on.

JUNE 10TH: Despite continuing dust storm, returned to Three Trees and found more bones. Reed returned to camp in advance of the rest of us. When I suggested he might attempt to steal the Profeßor's artefact, Marsh took it from his pocket, aßuring me that was quite unlikely.

We all returned to camp about noon as heavy clouds loomed up over the south. The clouds loosed hailstones the size of bantam eggs, and yet through it all the dust blew. The heavy clouds rang with thunder and there were constant flashes of lightning in the sky, but no rain. The thunder and rushy noise of the hail brought with them an even greater sense of deep solitude than we have become accustomed to. I found Reed in the tent quite near tears, and he received a smart upbraiding from Profeßor M. They argued after I removed myself to the shelter of one of the wagons.

At sunset the storm at last abated taking with it the dust (finally!). Before supper I killed a large jack rabbit with a stone but it was stunted and somehow disquieting to look upon. I wisely did not allow Reed to see it, as its eyes had the same oily sheen as the water flooding the now abandoned No. 3. I did not dreß it for we immediately judged it unfit for eating. Even with this grim event, I was greatly relieved at the storm's departure and a peaceful night free of the howling wind.

JUNE 11TH: An extraordinary and uncanny occurrence was last evening visited upon the camp – seeming to bear out in the worst poßible ways Reed's anxieties – and has left the party in a state of disarray. Profeßor M. has departed for Como station, and vowed never to speak on this matter. Also asked the same of us and I am certain he would not be pleased were he to learn I am setting the event down though I do so only for the purposes of my own memory. What was witneßed, for all its horror, I cannot wish to forget as it hints at a world even more distant and ultimately impervious to our understanding than the bygone ages and their fauna hinted at by our diggings.

As the weather grew leß inclement, we departed in the early morning at half past five o'clock for the *Laosaurus* site. Reed did not accompany us, complaining of a headache and begging off. But Marsh and Ashley and I paßed the morning excavating and were rewarded with an ilium and most of the beast's tail. The sun was bright and the sky clear without any clouds in view. After our lunch however there came a clamour from the direction of the lake almost identical to that cacophony heard at Como by Reed and I on the afternoon of the 27th. We had only just returned to work removing a layer of hard clay we hoped would reveal additional bones of the Dinosaur, when the booming cry split the air and I would say almost seeming to rend it apart. We all stopped our work and sat stock still, listening should the sound recur. I will confeß there were goose bumps on my arms and the small hairs upon the nape of my neck had stood up at the booming. Marsh stared easterly, the direction from which the sound had seemed to emanate and Ashley sat staring at his boots. After some minutes Marsh turned towards me and he was clearly unsettled. He asked if I knew the source of the booming and at once I told him I did not but reported we had heard it on the one other occasion. He sat rubbing his beard muttering to himself for several minutes before we got back to work – though we no longer were poßeßed of our former enthusiasm and returned to camp quite early, having exposed no more bones of the *Iguanodon*-like creature.

In camp we found Reed engaged in an argument with Carlin and the cook. The latter we learned had been plucking several sage hens [*Centrocercus urophasianus*] for our supper, fine cock birds. I have mentioned already that some in the camp are not fond of the fowl partly from prejudice and partly on account of its strong sage-like flavour. However Carlin was all in a rage not over those early objections but was raving all the while swinging one of the partially plucked birds about by its broken neck. It was a sight. All the while – though Carlin tried his best to calm him – Reed shouted that all the game hereabouts has become poisonous and how we must confine our meals only to dry goods and canned foodstuffs. As we joined Carlin in attempting to urge Reed to simmer down the head of the sage hen parted company with its body and the corpse went sailing away into one of the tents. I saw then that indeed the bird's blood was afflicted with the same unwholesome sheen I'd noticed in the eyes of the jack rabbit. Straightaway we agreed with Reed and this at last eased his distreß to a degree, though not entirely. Profeßor M. instructed the cook to dispose of the sage hens and to bury them well away from camp. Reed disappeared and spent the next hour or so alone in his tent while Carlin, Ashley, Marsh, and I mulled over the poßible source of the contamination, at last agreeing it must originate from some mineral impregnating the local water table, first witneßed when Reed struck the spring that flooded Quarry No. 3 more than two weeks ago now. It was resolved that we must unfortunately – as Reed had advised – cease relying on the plentiful elk, black-tailed deer, grouse, & etc. and send a man post haste to Medicine Bow for extra supplies. Here it was that Marsh announced his plans to leave us the next day and I can hardly say I was surprised.

I spoke of the events which followed sunset as extraordinary and uncanny, but it would be more truthful to refer to them as *inexplicable* as I cannot imagine science shall ever discover an explanation for them.

After sunset and our supper we were sitting about the fire having a second cup of coffee. We did not resign ourselves to the disagreeable prospect of a dry meal, in spite of our misgivings about the water though perhaps we should have. No one detected any unusual flavour. Reed had joined us, but sat a little ways apart with his rifle acroß his knee as the rest of us talked (he had refused the coffee). Our conversation was largely of the Profeßor's imminent return to the East, but also on the *Laosaurus* as well as the prospects of finding more remains of primitive mammals. Also talk of cavalry movements and Indian troubles. It should be said Profeßor M. has a great sympathy for the natives regardleß of the dangers they have posed to his collectors.

Our second pot of coffee finished, Ashley retired to bed. Carlin produced his Jew's harp which has so often provided us with a small measure of entertainment and he played a number of tunes as the silence of night stole over the camp. Reed was first to note the absence of the usual nocturnal noise from coyotes & owls & such other nocturnal birds as we have become accustomed to. Carlin stopped playing and it was plain that Reed was in fact correct. There was not even a breath of wind to stir the graß or the canvas of our tents and wagons. It was an eerie silence and disconcerting after the strangeneß of the day.

I think none were in the least surprised when Reed again pleaded with Marsh to divest himself of the artefact and they argued over the thing. The Profeßor remained adamant in his determination to see the admittedly hideous object safe in the Yale collections. I could not fault him over his insistence that so peculiar a find ought be studied and conserved. But Reed cursed and spat into the fire which I think we all understood as good as his spitting on Marsh himself and then Reed went to stand muttering at the farthermost reach of the firelight.

At this point Carlin pointed to the sky but before he could tell us why and before we could ask him, Reed raised his gun and fired two shots into the darkneß, hollering loudly at something he had apparently seen but which still remained hidden to the rest of us. In an instant we were all on our feet and I had drawn my Colt revolver in anticipation of what I aßumed was an imminent attack on the camp either by an animal or by redskins or bandits.

This is when the woman stepped out of the darkneß, or it seemed more that the night parted like a theatre curtain to reveal her. Reed lowered his rifle and stepped back, putting distance between her and him. I call her a woman but in truth I readily acknowledge this to be only the best word, an approximation, I know to describe what stood before us. Certainly no other description would come any closer to the truth of it. So I will say "her" and "she" and "the woman" and be satisfied with that as I may be. She stepped out of the darkneß, taking only one step towards us. Her movement was as slow and smooth and graceful as a lion bracing itself to pounce upon its prey, which is not to say she struck me as poised to attack, because this was certainly not the impreßion I had. There were in that moment and surrounding her many *contradictory* impreßions and I am at a loß to explain much of the feelings she inspired in me. Afterwards – though we did not talk very much about her or the events that were about to unfold – I got the notion my companions felt very much the same.

There she stood before us, and her skin and hair were as white as a fresh snowfall. No blemish sullied that whiteneß and I swear it almost burned my eyes to gaze upon. Her own eyes were a bright blue and shone as if imbued with an inner light, as though perhaps an inferno had been stoked within her skull. She was obviously no Indian, not even an albino individual of that race. Her arms and legs were disproportionately long, relative to her body, so that she must have stood a good seven and a half or even eight feet tall, much taller than any of us. Indeed the lankineß of her arms and legs gave her a faintly insectile semblance. She was both grotesque and unspeakably beautiful, wraithlike as anything ever dreamt up by Mr. Poe and still glorious as an Olympian goddeß, as are so many aspects of Nature. Yet nothing I'd ever seen in all my explorations and studies had prepared me for the sight of her. She wore not a stitch of clothing, and was hairleß save that on her scalp. Still I will say that I felt not the least bit of carnal excitement, for the sight of her was far to [sic] strange to permit such arousal.

Profeßor Marsh called out to her, his voice quavering somewhat. I had never before heard him shaken, but it was clearly the case that he was now shaken. The woman canted her face to one side as if regarding him with an intense curiosity. He called out to her again, but she made no reply and I suspected either she did not speak English or might be a mute, even deaf and dumb.

And then I happened to glance upwards, recalling how Carlin had pointed heavenward immediately prior to her arrival (though I wondered if poßibly she'd been standing just out of reach of the firelight for sometime). I saw what he had seen, and by God I do wish I had not. Towering above her, even as a cottonwood tree will tower above a pebble – such was the scale – was some indistinct *shadow* that blotted out any evidence of the stars. She had approached from the south, and in that direction it was as if – I dare put this down only because I mean these pages never to be read by any man – as if a titanic form stood, blotting out both the stars and moon. It was not clouds, as only seconds before I am sure the stars had shone brightly in a clear summer sky. Later, in our hasty discußion, we did all reluctantly agree on this fact. It was one of the very few we did agree upon. The enormity of that eclipsing shape was almost beyond comprehension and as I stared at it, I could discern the faintest of silhouettes, and also saw that it shifted the slightest bit to and fro, not unlike a man shifting from one foot to the other. Before my eyes were drawn back to the woman, I wondered how such an abomination could move without drawing from the very earth beneath our feet temblor waves to shame even the most terrible ocean tempest.

Reed was next to speak, and he told Profeßor M. that we all knew what she had come for, and that we would all be damned were it not returned without hesitation. Marsh replied by admonishing Reed with the harshest words ever I have heard him speak, but Reed would not waver from his conviction. He had raised his voice and it had taken on a tone of genuine hysteria. He once more lifted his rifle and this time it was aimed squarely at Profeßor M.

The woman stretched out her left hand as if to confirm the rightneß of Reed's demands. She blinked several times, and I was reminded of the flashing of a lighthouse beacon.

Reed cocked his Winchester, and this is when I raised my revolver and took aim at the woman. I had no hope of killing her, understanding on some level that such a singular entity as this visitor was beyond destruction by a mere bullet, just as the shadow behind her, that vast and mountainous thing, existed untold leagues beyond the ken of man. I cannot say now why I aimed my Colt at her except it is ever the way of humanity to run from or endeavour to drive back that which means us harm. And it was clear any attempt to flee would be futile.

Carlin did not move. Ashley emerged from his tent, and several of the men had also joined us. None of them uttered a sound. Wrapped about us was a silence so profound it might dwarf that which must have existed in the ages before Creation. The woman lowered her head, keeping her startling blue eyes on us, and I realised on Profeßor M. in particular. Reed said that he would not ask again but that it would be his gun that spoke next. He ordered Marsh to produce the artefact and return it forthwith to her.

Marsh cursed Reed and he cursed the impoßibly pale woman. I think he had not noticed the shadow looming above her, which surely was for the best. He cursed them both to Perdition and swore he would see Reed in prison, but he also reached into his coat pocket and produced the figurine. In the firelight it struck me as much more hideous than it had previously. I lowered my pistol and realised I must not have drawn a breath for almost a full minute.

Marsh cursed her again, spitting words with spiteful vehemence, the earlier tremble gone now from his voice. He held out the artefact and the woman smiled. I will not here make any effort to describe that smile. Better it be forgotten though I know it will haunt my dreams for the rest of my life.

Profeßor M. told the woman to go on ahead and take it, and if ever I meant to speak to another soul of that night I would swear before a court of law, hand on Holy Bible, to the veracity of what next occurred. That carved image that had so reminded me of one of Doré's fallen angels vanished from Marsh's hand and reappeared in hers. Not the smallest fraction of a second could have paßed in between. Marsh cried out and gripped the hand that had held the heathen idol (for now this is how I thought of it, as something the woman who could not be a woman surely worshipped). In the morning, I learned that a circular portion of Marsh's palm no larger than a gold Indian-head dollar was badly frostbitten.

The woman folded her fingers about the object of her desire, and she seemed almost to flow back into the darkneß at her back. I looked up at the southern sky again, and that damnable silhouette remained. It lingered for I cannot say how long, long enough that all would bear witneß to it (save Marsh, who was too busy with his frostbit hand). And then it withdrew, making no sound at all. How its footfalls failed to shake the earth, as the Profeßor has proposed the stride of the mighty sauropod Dinosaurs must surely have, I do not know. The unnatural eclipse almost seemed to blow away, leaving no vestige behind. The stars and the waning moon were restored, and soon the night was once more alive with all the usual nighttime noises – a coyote, the hooting of owls, wind blowing through the prairie graß, the chirruping of crickets. I understood then that it truly had *only* been a shadow, as of the shadow cast by a mountain when the sun sets behind it, and I dared not contemplate what being could cast so prodigious a shadow.

Reed sat down on the ground, the Winchester slipping from his fingers and he cried. Carlin went off to check on the horses, which had remained oddly quiet throughout the duration of the woman's appearance. It was long after midnight before any of us went to our bedrolls, and I did not sleep. I cannot speak for the others. Never have I been so grateful for a dawn.

JUNE 15TH: Following Profeßor M.'s departure, Reed went away to North Park to seek what fortune or misfortune there as might await him. He says his days as a bone sharp are over. But all the rest have decided, to my surprise, to stay on, and we resumed work at Three Trees, exposing more of the *Laosaurus*. Not a one of us has spoken of the events of the evening of the 12th. I imagine none of us ever shall. Yet I catch myself every night now fighting back an undeniable dread and glancing repeatedly towards the stars, ever expecting to find they have been obscured, by what I will not ever be able to say.

Love Is Forbidden, We Croak & Howl

Here's the scene: One hour past twilight on the night of a full Hay Moon – so an evening in June – an hour and spare change, and the last bend of the Castle Neck River vomits out the estuaries and salt marshes and sand bars that is, by turns, known as Essex Bay and Innsmouth Harbor. Lovecraft called the river the Manuxet, but that was never its true name. That was only some portmanteau spun from Algonquian – *man,* island fused with *uxet,* "at the river's widest part." Not inaccurate, as the Castle Neck here abandons any pretense at *being* a river, and is, instead, only the sluggish maze of shallow streams, sloughs, impassable tracts of swamps, dunes, and thickly wooded islands prefacing Essex Bay (id est, Innsmouth Harbor). On this night in June of 1920 the Hay Moon has only just cleared the horizon and shines low and red across the Atlantic beyond *Ipswich* Bay. To men and women alien to the decaying seaport of Innsmouth, that moon might bring a shiver. It might cause one to look away, because it could be the single eye of any god gazing out across a world to which it means to do mischief. The peculiar inhabitants of the seaport, however, revel on these nights. They strip and swim through the cold water out to the low granite spine of Devil Reef, and, by the moonlight, there they do cavort with the sorts of beings their slow metamorphoses will one day make of them. This has been the way of things since Captain Obed Marsh returned from the South Seas just prior to the year of someone else's lord, 1846 (possibly as far ago as the early 1820s), sailing back on the *Sumatra Queen* with new prosperity for an ailing town and the gift of transcendence and ever-lasting life for all. Returning to preach the gospel of Father Dagon and Mother Hydra…

But, this is neither a geography nor a history lesson. This is something else.

Some would say this is a love story. Alright, let's settle for that, if only for the sake of convenience. Some would go so far to make an analogy with Shakespeare's *Romeo and Juliet,* though that may be interjecting an unnecessary and, too, inappropriate degree of sentimentality into what is to come.

Once upon a time, there was a ghoul who fell in love with a daughter of the port of Innsmouth. To say the least, her parents would hardly have looked upon this as an acceptable state of affairs. She destined one day to descend through abyssal depths to the splendor of many spired Y'ha-nthlei in the depths well beyond the shallows of Jeffreys Ledge. She might have the fortune to marry well, perhaps, even, taking for herself a husband from among the amphibious Deep Ones who inhabit the city, or, at the very least, a fine and only once-human devotee of the Esoteric Order. She would be adorned in nothing less (and nothing more) than the fantastic, partly golden alloy diadems and bracelets and anklets, the lavallières of uncut rubies, emeralds, sapphires, and diamonds. What caring parent would *not* be alarmed that their only daughter might foolishly forsake so precious an inheritance, and all for an infatuation with so lowborn and vile a creature as a ghoul?

The girl's name is (or was, if you dislike tense shifts) Elberith Gilman, and on the night in question she is a few months past her sixteenth birthday. Likely, she has long since been betrothed and is only awaiting the completion of her transition.

The ghoul has no name that could ever be spoken in any tongue of man. With a small tribe of his kind, he passes the days in the moldering tunnels beneath the Old Hill Burying Ground, those passages roofed with long-emptied, shattered caskets and the roots of elderly oaks and hemlocks. Unlike Elberith, the ghoul has not much more to look forward to but a few fresh corpses here and there, the gnawing of dry bones devoid of the least scrap of marrow, and the grumbling company of his own vicious kin. Possibly, if great luck should someday shine down upon him, the ghoul may one day descend into the underworld of the Dreamlands and dwell among the peaks of Thok, above the Vales of Pnath (carpeted with a billion skeletons), where the most celebrated ghouls never lack for the fleshiest of rotted corpses.

On a night almost a full year before *this* night, the ghoul first emerged from the tunnels – something his race rarely does – and crept almost seven miles across field and wood and fen down to Innsmouth town. For he is an uncommon sort of ghoul, given to curiosities, fascinations, and obsessions not entirely healthy for subterranean creatures who wisely shun the cruel light of the sun. And he'd heard rumors of the seaport, and of its peculiar citizens, and of the pact they'd made with those immortal beings who are neither frogs nor fish, but bear a striking (some would say discomfiting, even nauseating) resemblance to both at once. He much desired to look upon such things for himself. It seemed unlikely he would be missed, so occupied are most with their own grisly and individual affairs. Surely, he could escape the eyes of man and be back before dawn. So it was he climbed the forty-seven steps up and up and up to the mausoleum whose bronze door led out into the forbidden World Above.

On that night, when the moon was still several nights from full, Elberith went with her mother and father and three sisters (it was the greatest tragedy in her father's life that he had no sons) to the nightly services in the Hall of Dagon at New Church Green, the same building that had once held the port's Masonic temple. With her family and her fellow inhabitants of Obed Marsh's fair community, she raised her coarse voice in the rattling, gurgling hymns to the Father and the Mother and to Great Cthulhu. She much enjoyed singing the hymns, and, as it happens, was said to possess one of the finest voices in all Innsmouth. Following the services, she walked along the wharves with her family and that of Mister Zebidiah Waite, savoring the muddy reek of an especially and unexpectedly low tide. It was almost midnight by the time the Gilmans at last returned to their listing and somewhat dilapidated home on Lafayette Street.

Never before had the ghoul imagined such wonders – almost beyond comprehension to one who has lived his life in the darkness below a bone yard – as the cobbled streets, the gas- and candlelight through windows, the fieldstone and redbrick chimneys, steeples, the widow's walks and cupolas of Georgian architecture, the handful of rusting automobiles parked here and there. The ghoul could not see, of course, all the signs of disuse and neglect that shrouded the avenues and alleys of Innsmouth, having no point of reference. Even the boarded windows and doorways seemed the product of amazing skill. The parallel lines of abandoned railways and telegraph poles that had long since lost their wiring to one or another nor'easter or hurricane were evidence of a carefully calculated brilliance he had never suspected could exist. The ghouls knew the World Below, and they knew very little else. Indeed, he had been taught it was anathema to *seek* anything more, as such an act would surely be an offense to the gods who guarded and watched over carrion feeders.

It was only happenstance that he chose to squat beneath the bedroom window of Elberith Gilman. Most of Lafayette Street was dark and deserted (which, so far as the ghoul knew, was a normal condition for any town), so it was, naturally, the yellow-orange glow of the windows of her house that drew his attention. Perhaps, then, it was *not* happenstance, but quite the opposite. It may have been the inevitability that so often attends curiosity. Darkness and shadows were familiar to the ghoul; lighted windows, however, these were a novelty. In a patch of weeds and beneath the limbs of an elderberry tree, he squatted and listened intently to the noises – all quite routine, though he had no way of knowing this – of Elberith readying herself for bed. He pressed his ear to the weathered grey clapboard, savoring every sound. But it wasn't until he heard the creak of mattress springs, not until the light from the room was extinguished, that the ghoul summoned the courage to rise on its hooved and shaggy fetlocked hindlimbs and gaze in through the windowpane.

It so happened that Elberith had not yet even closed her eyes, much less drifted away and down to her usual and sweet, welcomed dreams of the bioluminescent terraces and silt courtyards of Y'ha-nthlei, or of that name-less sunken city in the Middle Sea of the Dreamlands which lies in the strait between Dyath-Leen and the city of Oriab. When the ghoul began softly tapping and scraping on the glass, at first she took it for nothing more than a breeze causing the branches of the elderberry tree to brush against the house. But then the tap-tap-tapping grew more insistent, and she sensed in it both a purpose and a pattern that never could be attributed to wind and tree limbs. So she rose and went to the window. She was met by the scarlet eyes of the ghoul peering in at her and its wet nose pressed to the pane, and at first she was taken aback by such a monstrous sight and very nearly called for her father, whom she still trusted to keep her safe from all the malevolent bogeys and goblins that go bump in the night.

Seeing the beauty of her, another thing completely alien to the ghoul, he quite unintentionally – or, at least, without forethought – coughed out a short bark and a few words of wonder. Of course, Elberith didn't speak the language of ghouls, so, to her, this was only the guttural din that might be heard from any animal. But she didn't recoil, and she didn't scream. She stared back, and the ghoul tapped several more times on the glass.

"If you meant to do me harm," she asked aloud, "would you not simply shatter the glass and crawl in across the sill?"

As the ghoul didn't know the language of humans, not even that of humans evolving into that which may no longer rightly be considered human, the question meant no more to him than his utterances had meant to her.

Linguists would call this unfortunate situation a "language barrier."

"You would do that, wouldn't you, if you meant me harm?" asked Elberith Gilman. "You would, and by now I would have been slaughtered and near to half devoured."

Catching the absence of fear in the girl's voice, the ghoul raised its eyebrows and twisted its short muzzle into the grimace that passes as a smile among ghouls. Elberith did wince the tiniest bit at the sight of his rows of crooked yellowed teeth, the canines robust as those of any wolf or black bear. She bravely pressed her open palm and outstretched fingers against the windowpane, and certainly the ghoul took this as a sign of welcome. In response he did the same, though his hand was not a hundredth as fair as hers and his talons clicked loudly upon the glass even when he hadn't intended them to do so.

"You mean me no harm," she said, "and if I raise the sash you won't eat me," she said, having silently arrived at this unlikely conclusion. "You want to be friends, I do believe. It may be that, whatever manner of a beast you are, you want nothing more than to dispel a loneliness that has long troubled your heart."

Elberith had always been a bold girl, and one given to questionable deductions.

She unlocked the window, lifted it, and then stared face to face with the ghoul who'd walked all the way from Ipswich. Uncertain of what he ought do next, he took a step back, lest he make some move that would startle the girl. All the men and women and children he'd ever glimpsed had been dead and consigned to their narrow houses (though others he knew had peered out at gravediggers, mourners, and ministers), but none had been anywhere near as beautiful as *this* human girl. Her forehead sloped slightly backwards, and she had hardly any chin at all. Her lips were uncommonly thick (if the corpses upon which he'd stolen and fed were any indication), her skin vaguely iridescent in the moonlight, and there were the faintest delicate folds on the sides of her throat. Her green eyes bulged more than he would have expected. Her long yellow hair was pulled back in a braid, and when she'd opened the window the ghoul had noted a sort of webbing between her long fingers.

"Well, there," she said, "I've gone and done it. So, if you mean to eat me, do be quick about it, please."

The ghoul did his best to decipher her words, but it was hopeless. Instead, he decided upon another action that he did hope would be taken as friendly. He held out one hand to her, that which he'd used to tap and scratch at the girl's window. His long arm reached into the room, and for almost a full minute, she regarded the proffered hand with what Elberith considered the necessary dose of caution and suspicion. The skin was calloused, with tufts of coarse hair sprouting here and there in no discernable pattern. The claws could easily have gutted a shark, should the opportunity arise, and several plainly unwholesome species of fungus grew upon the ghouls flesh. But then, arriving at one of her questionable verdicts, she took the ghoul's hand. It was altogether warmer than she'd expected it would be.

The ghoul, unaccountably pleased by the gesture, folded up her hand in his.

And that's how it went on the first night. For a time, they stood there, holding hands and staring at one another with ever increasing fondness. Until, somewhere in the seaport, a clock chimed the hour, so startling the ghoul that he released her and scampered away from the window and the elderberry trees, back down empty lanes and once more into the marshes. He made it back to the bronze door of the mausoleum well before dawn. As for Elberith, she stood staring at her hand and the smudgy, moldy stain the ghoul had left on her jaundiced skin until at last she grew sleepy, closed the window, locked it against less amiable visitors, and crawled back into bed. This night, she did not dream of submarine palaces nor of her grandparents and aunts and uncles and cousins who'd long since gone down to the sea without ships, rising to the surface only on appointed nights to cavort upon the jagged strata of Devil Reef. No, this night she dreamt of the ghoul, of his face and the touch of his hand upon her own.

Pushing the Sky Away
(Death of a Blasphemer)

The water is gone. The morphine is gone. My knapsack is now all but empty, containing nothing but the memory of useful things, of things that kept me alive. Of course, these winding, endless hallways were not ever intended for anything alive. These granite and limestone blocks were not lain here two and a half millennia ago that any breathing woman or man would ever find hospitality within the corridors and chambers and antechambers that their union forms. To be sure, I am an intrusion, an interloper in a city of the dead. Though, it's a passing violation that will soon enough be rectified.

Miles and miles and miles of shimmering green glass.

A tiny sun in my hand.

Fusion, fission in my palm.

I lie here shivering, delirious and feverish within my skin burned first by the summoned fires and then burned again by the Saharan days. I lie here and stare through shadows and guttering torchlight at limestone blocks and gypsum mortar. Occasionally, I permit my eyes to leave the precision of right angles and linger on the jumbled chaos of bones that litters the corridor. So far as I can see, not even the meanest scrap of flesh remains on any of them. Long, long ago they were picked clean, and the ghouls are impressively thorough. A matter of necessity, I would imagine; it can't be very often that they happen upon even a stingy morsel of flesh; nothing is wasted. Most of the bones have been cracked open for their precious store of marrow, broken by teeth as suited to the task as the teeth of hyenas.

I lie here and stare into the shadows.

The irony is not lost on me, that I'll die in darkness, fatally wounded by the light. The gods have a sense of humor, no matter how cruel.

She has come to speak to me of the gods and of many other matters. She has come either down from the world Above or up from the world Below. I can't say which. I haven't asked, as it doesn't seem especially relevant. I lie with my head in her lap, my duster folded beneath my head for a pillow. She has olive oil for my cracked lips and my eyelids. For tending to me is more a casual diversion, I know, than any sort of sympathy or compassion. One such as her knows neither.

"You've come so far to go no farther," she says, her whisper loud in the silence of the pyramid. "It was unfortunate, your ever having arrived in the desert."

"I had no choice," I reply. I'm not sure if, strictly speaking, this is true.

"I know," she says, whether it's true or not.

She delicately touches my blistered forehead with her fingertips. Her touch is soothing, even if relieving my suffering isn't her intent. I'll never know her *intentions;* no one ever has, I suspect. I won't lie, not here at the end. I wish I knew them. Just as I wish I had a few mouthfuls of cool water or another syringe filled with morphine.

"You're a brash woman," she says. "Bold and skillful, clever, but brash. To rob the Ghūl of a thing so precious to them as *la clé pour les manilles.*"

She is unaccountably fond of French, which I hardly speak at all. Perhaps it's something she picked up from French colonists a hundred years ago. Perhaps she has walked the streets of Paris and Versailles.

"*Et la griffe de Khoshilat Maqandeli,* as if burgling a single treasure were not enough to earn their rancor."

I will note that it is not the ghouls' thirst for vengeance that has brought me here. They've merely gotten lucky. This isn't even, I think, some karmic retribution visited upon me for that specific crime, but only the end result of my general hubris.

"The Ghūl stole both," I whisper. "And I've returned the Claw to the Djinn."

My voice sounds like antique papyrus being torn into strips.

"But only in exchange for a favor," she says. "Don't pretend there was anything noble in your motives. Not that your motives are of any consequence to ghouls."

When the australopithecine progenitors of *Homo sapiens* still struggled to master the most rudimentary tools, the Djinn and the Ghūl waged a terrible war in the wastes of what geographers would one day name Arabia. The latter were defeated and were cast down into the Underworld at the very threshold of Dream. But not before they'd sacked temples and reliquaries, and so they departed this world with many objects holy to their foes. In exile, at least they could gloat over these small victories. In the vaults below the plateau of Thok, the ghouls hid their plunder, and in time even they forgot what they'd stolen, until a sleeper came among them to thieve from thieves. But in this *waking* world, the hounds of Pnath may only reach so far and no farther. Here, they are bound to the necropoleis we have provided them, never meaning to do so. They fear the sun and are loathe even to walk beneath the moon.

"Why did you come to me?" I ask again.

"I was curious," she replies, predictably, same as each time before that I've put the question to her. I have no reason whatsoever to doubt that she's telling me the truth. Demons have no need to hide the truth from dying women.

"You must have seen the deaths of millions," I whisper.

"But never the death of a woman who was so audacious as to enter the domain of the Ghūl and rob them, then to insert herself into the center of an ancient feud by bargaining with the Djinn. And *then* to try and wield the Key of Shackles." This is the first time she's named the Key in English. I'd begun to wonder if there were some prohibition against doing so or if the language were simply insufficient to the task.

A tiny sun blazing in my palm.

Molten sand to cool and solidify into miles of green glass.

"I may not have the opportunity to witness the death of such a fool again before Skarl at last stops beating his drum and the silence startles MĀNA-YOOD-SUSHĀĪ from his slumber to unmake the cosmos."

The names of gods roll off her tongue like drops of honey casually spilled from a beehive, free of reverence, disdain, or fear. I hear subtle wickedness in such nonchalance.

"And you've been sent round to collect the errant child," I say. "When I'm dead, you'll take the Key."

"Of course," she replies. "You can't possibly imagine it would be forgotten and left to molder here among your bones. My Lady and Lord have patiently waited half an aeon and more for the Key to pass near enough that they might finally see it restored to its rightful place and its rightful keepers."

It's true the ghouls stole the Key of Shackles from the Djinn, but it was the Djinn who, ages before, lifted it from off its hook in the halls of Abriymoch and carried it away from Phlegethos. So, a theft, a theft, and a theft, the procession ending here in the perpetual night beneath the pyramid. It might well have ended anywhere, but all those innumerable might-have-beens now deftly swept aside by a single actuality.

"I smell death all about you," she says, pushing white hair back from my forehead and eyes. "It won't be much longer now."

"Are you to take me, as well?" I've needed hours to gather up the courage to ask this question.

"No," she says, and I think that there's a hint – at least a hint – of regret in her voice. "There is a price for your part in this crime. None of the Nine Hells will have you, nor, of course, will Heaven."

So, my spirit will be set adrift forever to haunt that liminal twilight for all the time remaining to this universe. I'll be a ghost, denied perdition or salvation.

Her soothing fingertips wander down my chin to my throat, over tissue that would become an ugly mass of keloid scars if I would only live so long that it might have time to heal. She gently touches the glistening shrapnel embedded there, the milky emerald-green flecks of the glass formed by the furnaces of my recklessness. I didn't even feel the blast that shredded my clothing and peppered my entire body with a thousand scalding bits of trinitite, Alamogordo glass, atomite, forged at ~137° Celsius and laced with a mild dose of radiation. Not enough of the cesium isotopes to be fatal, not in and of itself, at least not in the short run, which is all I had left.

She says that she is dying. She says that she is dying. She says that she is dying, and it has become so tiresome a cadence.

"How much longer?" I ask. There is only so much suffering any mind can endure, and it is becoming difficult for me to comprehend even another heartbeat of this agony.

"Soon," she says. "Soon. Rest."

After that Mosaical last pillar of fire rose high about the dunes, when the near perfect stillness of the wilderness had again descended over me, I was much too shattered to complete the work I'd begun. No mortal had ever mastered that Key, nor any other from the Sulfur Plane. I wouldn't be the first. I barely managed to shut the portal again, my body made the lock, the lover required by *la clé pour les manilles* if it was to complete its appointed task. A fire bloomed, sunrise in the wee, cold hours; metaphorical bow and shank turned and the single rectangular tooth turned the tumblers of the warded lock that had been made, metaphorically, of my soul. Phallic and vulvic analogies. Hell loves a good metaphor.

One of the ghouls peers into the corridor, a big son of a bitch, all tattered ears and red-brown fur and short muzzle marked by the battles of its long life. They're impatient for the feast to come. I don't know why they didn't just kill me on sight and have done with it when they found me dragging my breathing corpse through the basalt and obsidian canyons northeast of the pyramid. There are so many goddamn things I do not and will not be allowed to understand. I have not arrived in a place of understanding, but of concluding mystery. She looks back at the ghoul, and it frowns and vanishes into the gloom once more.

"Talk to me," I say. "Tell me a story."

"You believe you've earned that much solace? The comfort of the story from a succubus' lips?"

"I didn't say that," I reply.

"No, that's true. You didn't."

She combs my matted hair with her long, delicate fingers while she tells me *two* stories, both lays of the five small gods. First, how Kib and Sish and Roon, Mung and Slid, raised their hands and fashioned from the void the eye of the Moon for a Watcher and a silver Comet as a Wanderer and Earth to stand in awe and ponder all creation. And this she follows with the tale of Mosahn – the Bird of Doom – and the Last Day of All. I suppose it's not inappropriate to the occasion:

"For, when the sleep of MĀNA-YOOD-SUSHĀĪ is done, shall the thunder, fleeing to escape the doom of the gods, roar most dreadfully between and above and round the worlds and the space between the stars; and Time, the undoer, the scythe, the *hound* of the gods, hungrily bay to his masters, for he has grown lean with age."

I gasp in the fetid air stale twice a thousand years. I listen. My stinging eyes make a game of counting the skeletons in the corridor and identifying those I recognize: horse, camel, goat, sheet, jackal, and, of course, man.

She finishes and leans close, kissing my left cheek. I feel an electric spark arc between us. I feel it stab the innermost recesses of my fading consciousness.

"You are ready, Elisheba?" she wants to know, her honey voice tracing the further irony of my name.

"Would you be?"

"No, but that wasn't the question, was it?"

It wasn't, but I don't agree. I'm no longer in the mood to be agreeable. The precipice is too steep, and the vale below is smothered in a blackness so absolute that I do not have to be told nothing that enters, during the breadth of all eternity, will ever be permitted exit. I am afraid, and for once I don't feel ashamed of my fear.

I turned the Key, and the Key turned me.

And I held a tiny sun in my hand.

And the light ate me alive.

And that blackness is the price I'll pay for my audacity.

The Ghūl, who will very soon now take their sloppy, unholy communion of my flesh and bones and congealing blood, mingle just beyond the flicker of the torchlight. Above me, in richly appointed chambers, sleep pharaohs and the wives of pharaohs, and beyond the pyramid the desert wind howls across the vast plateau. Here is what I have earned, an ignominious death in a tomb constructed for kings and queens. A third irony.

"The Key of Shackles will never forget your name," she says.

Cold comfort.

And then her robes fall away, and she enters me, and nothing now remains of me but shards that before were miles and miles and miles of shimmering green glass.

For Cybin Orion Nelsen, aka Nis Talio, aka Lucy Crown.

Black Ships Seen South of Heaven

The clouds will part and the sky cracks open,
And God himself will reach his fucking arm through...

Nine Inch Nails

Before, in the time that was before, this was a city of the living and the whole. It was not a city of blank-eyed warriors and broken women and pregnancies mercifully terminated before fresh teratisms can be born. It was not wasted and besieged. There were no watchful ramparts, and Midway and O'Hare International ferried civilian traffic, because there was civilian traffic. Before. There were unguarded highways into the city, before the fall of Manhattan and Boston and D.C. and Atlanta and pretty much everything else bordering the Atlantic, from Greenland to Tierra del Fuego. Before the city became a pounding ring of field, medium, and heavy batteries, 105 mm howitzers, 155 mm, 203 mm, anti-aircraft and rocket artillery. Before the sea turned black and engulfed the East, and before the waters of Lake Michigan froze over with jaundiced ice that's immune to the heat of burning skies and molten shores.

Before the probe came home from the Kuiper belt, when it was never supposed to come home at all.

Before the beginning of the war.

The beginning of The End, which some will say is simply the Beginning. Even within the ragged fortress of Chicago, there are zealous priests and necromancers who pray day and night to the Old Things for the fall of all mankind. They have the books. They know the names. They spill blood on secret altars. Agents of the Guard hunt them, but it's a hunt as futile as stalking the swarms of rats and the dogs and cats gone feral and vicious.

The once-were names for the days have been discarded.

This is Thunderday.

And on this Thunderday, Susannah takes her weekly turn on the eastern wall, with all the others who come on at dawn. She hardly ever sleeps anymore. She can, in fact, only just recall the last time she slept more than one or two hours at once. It's better that way; the dreams that are no longer merely dreams are kept at bay by wakefulness. But because insomnia weakens, the infirmaries handed out amphetamines and methamphetamine as long as the supplies lasted. Which wasn't long. Besides, the hallucinations that visited her after several drugged days without any sleep at all were almost as bad as the nightmares.

"Stay sharp," the Captain of the Guard says as she settles into one of the plastic patio chairs tucked inside the concrete pillbox. As if it's necessary to remind her, but she supposes he has to say *something,* so she's never complained. Futility is the rule After, not the exception.

She smokes stale tobacco and listens to the skinny kid from what used to be Elmwood Park, back when, back before the crimson drifters and the rain that sets fires. Back before. Before that island rose up from the South Pacific, from very near that oceanic pole of inaccessibility – the point on the planet farthest from any landmass. Near to Point Nemo. 47°9'S 126°43'W. And maybe you didn't know jack shit about geography before, but now those coordinates are etched into the mind of the survivors, as indelible as their own names. The zealots and the enemies of man call it R'lyeh. Susannah just calls it Hell.

"Sue, you see that?" asks the Elmwood kid. She wishes he wouldn't call her Sue, because that's what her mother called her. But she always lets it go. The kid's pointing across No Man's Land towards Indiana. "You *see* that?"

She picks up the one pair of binoculars allotted to the pillbox and tries to spot whatever it is the kid thinks he saw. But there's only the glistening polychromatic canopy of the forest that presses in at the walls and stretches away, seemingly, forever.

"I don't see anything," she replies, and he curses.

"I know what I saw."

"Then why don't you tell me, and then we'll both know?"

But he doesn't. He sulks, instead. He sits in his patio chair reading an old paperback, neglecting the job that insures him room and rations.

Susannah knows better, but she lets the binoculars linger on the forest. The stalks of fungus that once were men and women, back before the plague. Before. Not that it's well and truly over. But most people in the city talk about the plague like it was something that's come and gone, and they do their best to ignore the infected who cower in the alleyways and otherwise deserted husks of buildings. They stay indoors or in the bunkers on days when the prevailing winds bring clouds of spores north. They stay inside until the decon teams have done their best to scrub away the microscopic contagion. If they find a growth on their own bodies, they keep it a secret as long as they can. They cloak themselves in denial. Which is how Susannah has made it through the last month, since she found the shiny wet spot on her left hip.

Only a matter of time now, but so is everything else.

It's all winding down.

The world has known the war is lost for years, since the nukes that failed to scratch the pillars of that vast island that shrugged off the sea. Since the fireballs and fallout failed to do anything but piss off the titans who stride across the world, bringing havoc at their leisure.

Susannah wishes that the ceaseless movement of the forest were only an illusion created by distance and the heat haze. But she knows it's no mirage. She knows all those men, women, and children who've been assimilated, absorbed, transformed, what the fuck ever, are still alive and still conscious and still in agony. As she will be soon enough.

She knows too much of what the CDC and WHO and etcetera learned before the airwaves and satellites went silent.

The Survivors' Prayer: Lord, let me be ignorant.

But she's an atheist. Susannah has no prayer.

"They're not gods," she said on the Worstday she met the boy, when he wouldn't shut up about the monsters. "They're just shit from other places. That's all they are."

Maybe it's easier to accept The End if it's being brought by a malevolent pantheon than by indifferent aliens. She wouldn't know.

"I don't see anything," she says again, right as the sirens go off. She still jumps at the sirens, as if they meant something more than the opening of the southern gates to send the latest batch of fungal terminals out to join those who have gone before them. She always jumps as if it were ebony wings bearing down on the city.

"Jesus, Sue. Get a grip," the boy tells her, not even looking up from his paperback.

She tells him to go fuck himself, flicks the butt of her cigarette away, then trains the binoculars on the asphalt scab of I-394, Forest Road. There are only a couple dozen today. Susannah watches as they stagger away towards writhing stalks and the shadows below the enormous iridescent caps. She watches for five, ten, maybe fifteen minutes. It's easy to lose track of time on the wall.

She knows that forest all too well. Susannah arrived with one of the last groups of refugees, and the convoy came much, much too near to the fruiting bodies. She was sixteen then. Her mother had died back in Ohio. Her father had not even made it out of Boston. That was five years ago. Five years and spare change. Back when stupid motherfuckers and military strategists still talked about offensives, pushing back, *winning*.

They called the invaders gods, and they talked about winning.

It's one of the sickest jokes Susannah knows.

The moon rises like a boil, bloated, livid. No one bothers asking anymore how the moon can rise when the sun never seems to set.

"Did you hear that?" the Elmwood kid asks, dropping his paperback, his eyes all at once wild, but looking at her instead of looking out over the wastes.

"I didn't hear anything," she says, which is true.

He's silent a moment, then says, "They've left us alone for almost a week. You know this can't go on, Sue. You know they must be planning something big."

"Go back to your book," she replies.

"I heard wings," he all but whispers.

"Go back to your book."

"I swear to god, Sue, I'm putting in a request for a new partner. I'm not joking with you."

"You do that. But right now, you shut up and go back to your book."

"I swear I'm going to."

"Fine with me."

She wants to tell him not to bother. She wants to confess her infection. Her hip itches constantly, and she knows that in another week or two she'll be one of the alley lurkers, and by next month she'll be staggering out the gate, unable to resist the siren song, dragging what's left of her body towards the forest. Maybe the kid will watch her go. Maybe he'll even recognize her.

Probably he won't.

She's never recognized any of those who've left to take their places as part of that vast colonial organism.

Susannah still remembers the TV broadcasts in those first few weeks after the island rose, after the earthquakes and tsunamis that devastated coastlines and erased cities on both sides of the Pacific. Quakes measuring 9.9+, possibly one or two as strong as 12.0, exceeding the parameters of Mercalli-Cancani-Sieberg scale. Quakes so strong they broke apart the atomic structure of stone. She remembers watching on CNN and MSNBC, the floods, the fire, the few blurred, grainy bits of footage that were ever filmed of the coast of R'lyeh before there were no longer any ships left to sail the bruised-black seas. Susannah even recalls an interview with two physicists who attributed the inability of video to capture clear footage of the island's titanic monoliths to the bending of light rays by the angles of poorly understood geometries and "physics beyond the standard model." Her dad had said it was all a load of crap, that no one had any idea what was happening, and she's inclined to agree with her dead father.

New Horizons returned, ignoring its programming and using Pluto for a gravitational slingshot back towards the inner Solar System, hurtling across near vacuum and cold and all those millions of miles back to earth. The probe crashed somewhere in the Sahara, or the Caspian Sea, or Scandinavia. No one was ever certain, as tracking stations seemed to show it coming down in multiple locations.

But it returned with secrets, and the scientists could grasp at straws forever and never have one iota what those secrets were. *New Horizons* returned, and R'lyeh rose, and the one sleeping there awoke.

And The End began.

Or the Beginning.

Susannah remembers those grainy clips, played over and over until all the channels all went off the air, and her family joined the steady stream of refugees heading inland. She even recalls the final broadcast and what emerged from those strange angles into the light of day. Just a distorted hint of its impossible bulk glimpsed between crackling bursts of static. She remembers the screams.

She asked questions that her parents would never answer, but she had the TV and Twitter and Facebook, while they lasted. All the contradictory reports, the events that were only explicable if one were willing to believe the inexplicable. News of the friends and family who died or simply vanished. So many people vanished so quickly there was no way to keep track. Here one day, gone the next. Here one hour, one minute, then…poof.

The conspiracy nuts, fringe theorists, and pseudoscientists had a field day, their fifteen minutes in the sun. It was their moment to shine, because, obviously, this was all the result of top-fucking-secret black-ops NSA DOD ESA CIA NASA acronym, acronym, acronym ancient astronaut Roswell Area 51 chemtrails secret electromagnetic directed-energy weaponry cold god-damn fusion and strangelets spawned by the Large Hadron Collider and, and, and HAARP program disruptions in the ionosphere and the ghosts of John F. Kennedy, Nikola Tesla, and Madame Blavatsky. They all ran together just exactly like that in Susannah's mind, like melted steel. Naturally, the religious end-timers got a word in edgewise. This had to be the Rapture, the Second Coming, the opening of the Seven Seals, what the hell else could that thing that crawled forth from the New Land be *but* the Anti-Christ?

There were a few who went so far as to propose that *all* conceivable claims were true.

Five years farther on, in the ruins of Babylon, she and the Elmwood kid sit in the pillbox. She watches, and he reads. At precisely 13:00 hours a "squadron" of the blood-red driftgliders appears to the south, swooping low above No Man's. They shimmer wetly, those wings a hundred feet from tip to tip, those insectile heads, the tails that trail out behind them throwing blue-white sparks of electricity. Minutes later, there's the dull whup-whup-whup of a modified National Guard UH-60 Blackhawk helicopter. It goes as near to the driftgliders as it dares, but never engages, never opens fire.

She watches it all through the binoculars. The Elmwood kid only looks up for a few seconds.

At 15:07 something on towering stilt legs strides through the mush-room forest. She reports it, but HQ O'Hare says it isn't a clear and present danger. Just neofauna. But she notes the walker in the logbook, anyway. Susannah even sketches a decent likeness of the creature. It calls out across the wastes with a cry like all the foghorns ever built. Maybe it's lonely and looking for a mate. Maybe it's praying. She isn't curious enough to ponder the problem for very long.

"That's it for me," the kid says at 16:55, even though they won't be relieved for another twenty minutes. "There's meatloaf tonight," he says and grins, tucking his book into a pocket of his coat.

"How can you eat that shit?" she asks. It comes heavy on the loaf and light on anything that can be called meat, just enough Spam or Vienna sausage to create the illusion, and all the rest grain and Crisco filler from the rapidly dwindling stores.

"Gotta eat something," he replies. "There's worse. Then again, maybe you ain't never been down that low, Sue. Maybe you never were a scrounger before your paperwork went through and you got the wall."

And sure, that's true, though she doesn't like the tone in the Elmwood kid's voice when he reminds her. She waited out quarantine in the camps, then pulled various shit civil service and Army duties before finally rising up the ranks. All she had to keep her sane was ambition. That and her own secrets, which she will never share with the Elmwood kid. Even without the infection, even if she had all the time in the world, she'd never share those secrets. *New Horizons* had its mysteries, and Susannah has hers, which are even more secret than the probes because no one suspects that she *has* secrets.

She doesn't let the kid leave early.

Technically, Susannah bunks with the other members of the Guard in the barracks at the converted State Street Subway tunnel. That's what her ID badge says, and that's where she takes most of her meals. But she isn't the only person who seeks other lodgings from time to time. Her rank gives her a freedom of movement not afforded by civilians. The curfews don't apply, and she has very little trouble at checkpoints.

The stingy luxuries that keep people at their posts, gazing out across the horrors of No Man's Land.

Fringe benefits.

Susannah has claimed a basement room below what once was the Biograph Theater. Dillinger was shot dead just outside the theater, way, way back before. But some people still remember that. A lot of people squat in the derelict movie palace, and sometimes there are gatherings and meetings of one sort or another that use the stage. The squatters don't ever seem to mind. It's something to break up the grinding tedium here at the end of the world. But none of the Biograph's other inhabitants or occasional interlopers ever fuck with Susannah. She's painted the Mark of the Guard on her rusty steel door, and that keeps them away in droves.

There is a second mark, down low. Bottom left hand corner, near the hinges that creak and strain every time the door is opened and closed.

A mark no larger than a dime.

It's another secret in the dregs of a world that has all descended into secrets. If military intelligence could ever learn this secret, then the city might stop rotting from the inside out. A drop in the bucket of the tide might be turned. Maybe. It's the sign of the Eyes and Mouths and Hands of the Black Pharaoh. He has many names, many titles, but that's the one Susannah prefers, even if she can't say why. Perhaps because so many of the others are all but unpronounceable. She used a Swiss army knife to carve the symbol there herself, almost two years back now, after she first glimpsed the tall, dark man lingering in the doorway of a burned-out house in Sheridan Park. He saw her, as she saw him. He looked into her, and she was afforded the thinnest rind of the truth of it all. Just the oily scum floating on the surface, but that was more than enough to seduce.

Now she is among the hundreds in the city who have answered his call, and that seems a far, far greater purpose than numbering among the paper tigers who go through the motions of watching over the ignorant, the unseeing, the souls just counting off the days until deaths or fates much worse than death. Unlike them, her existence has *true* meaning, even if only a shred.

There isn't much to her room below the stage. A few pieces of furniture she dragged in down the stairs: an old office chair, a loveseat upholstered in tatters of mildewed linen, a dead television set that was already there when she claimed the place, a hotplate, an Army cot, a wobbly table (one leg's too short) heaped with books and unbound pages and a ceramic coffee cup filled with pens and pencils. One side of the cup has the glowering face of a red bull printed on it and THE CHICAGO BULLS. The horns of the bull form the U in BULLS. The only light comes from the stubs of candles that she hoards, and that she only lights when she needs illumination. Most of her time here is passed in complete darkness.

As, Susannah knows, is appropriate.

The ceiling is low enough that she can reach it by standing on the Coleman cooler she scavenged from the ruins of a sporting-goods store. And there on the cement ceiling is the place that she's creating her celestial map, which is, of course, more than a mere map. When it's finally finished, at that undisclosed but nonetheless appointed hour, it will also be a hole.

That word, *hole,* is entirely inadequate to describe what she's slowly, slowly, slowly fashioning. Just as all the names and epithets worn by the Black Pharaoh are entirely inadequate. In her mind, she can see what she's making, piecemeal, on the ceiling, because He showed her.

Hole.

Breach.

Tear.

Whatever.

When she left the wall, she and Elmwood boy going their separate ways until next week, she went to her hiding place below the Biograph. She sits on the loveseat, trying to ignore her itching, infected hip, and listens to the ticking of the alarm clock, which she also keeps on the wobbly table, perched atop a crooked stack of books capped off with *Quantum Mechanics and Experience*. She's always careful to wind the clock whenever she leaves the room below the stage, checking it against the wristwatch supplied by the Guard. She listens and waits impatiently. In the darkness, it's easy to lose track of time. The tick, tick, ticking of the clock seems to do more to blur moments than to delineate, and so she sometimes wonders why it's so important to her to keep it wound. But eventually she hears heavy, shuffling footsteps coming down the corridor. They stop just outside the room, and then there's a protracted moment of silence before the faint, dry sound of an envelope being slipped beneath the door. Sweating, her heart pounding, almost too anxious to breathe, she waits until the footsteps have retreated back the way they came before she lights the candle.

It's an envelope sealed with a few drops of yellow wax stamped with the same mark scratched at the bottom left hand corner of her door. Susannah crouches over the envelope, almost reluctant to touch it, even now, when she can no longer recall how many times this ritual has been repeated. It isn't necessary to hold a thing in one's hands in order to recognize the significance with which it has been imbued. She reaches down, her fingers no more than an inch or two above the paper, but she hesitates. Susannah suspects that they all hesitate, the ones who have seen the Black Pharaoh and been chosen to receive these significant messages sealed with yellow wax.

"Do you mean to wait all night?" a voice whispers from a corner of the room, an inky spot where the unsteady flame of the candle isn't reaching. But Susannah knows that the candlelight wouldn't brighten that corner even if she walked over and stood there. Something in the corner is immune to light. She isn't sure if that something was there when she found the room, or if it followed her. She isn't sure if all the disciples have black corners and voices that speak to them from black corners.

Still crouching, Susannah looks over her shoulder, peering at the corner even though she knows there's absolutely no chance of seeing who or what is there.

"When I was seven," she says, "we took a vacation to Yosemite, a camping trip. It was summer, and I lay on the hood of the car. Just me and my father, staring up at the stars. He would point to one and tell me its name. What astronomers called it."

"Astronomers were always arrogant fools," the voice tells her, "thinking they could name a star."

"I'd never seen anything like it. The whole sky seemed bathed in white fire. The Milky Way stretched from one horizon to the other."

And, she thinks, *the sight of them absolutely fucking terrified you, though you never told Dad that. You wanted to crawl beneath the car and hide there until sunrise when there would only be that one familiar star, close and warm.*

She says, "He pointed out the specks that were Mars and Venus and Jupiter."

Susannah can hear whatever speaks to her from the corner smile. It smiles in a way that can *be* heard. "Be grateful to his memory, then. He paved your way to glory. He set the stage that night."

"He taught me about the speed of light," she replies, even if it isn't a proper reply. "He told me a lot of those stars had died billions of years before we looked up and saw them."

That was the first night she understood how small she was, how her only perfection would ever lie in her perfect insignificance in the face of all that universe stretched out above her.

"You should open the envelope," the voice says.

I wanted to crawl beneath the car and lie with my face pressed to the ground. That sky was hungry, and I expected that any moment I would fall up, up, up – forever falling into its jaws.

"You'd not even be a crumb," says the corner. It knows the way into her head, so when it hears her thoughts and answers them she isn't ever surprised. "Doesn't mean the sky would spare you, but you wouldn't make a decent morsel. Heaven eats entire galaxies and is still ravenous."

Which reminds her of one of the last newscasts before there were no more newscasts and never would be. One of those foolish astronomers described the discovery of an apparent black hole between Saturn and Neptune. He talked about X-ray emissions, the event horizon and accretion disk. He talked about the death of planets.

"There are no paths that lead away from the black hole."

The scientist might have said that, or it may only be a false memory.

The sky is eating us alive.

"The clock is ticking," says the voice, not meaning, specifically, the clock on the table. Meaning, of course, a clock so vast as to be inconceivable.

Her hip itches like hell, but she doesn't scratch it. She picks up the envelope and carries it to the table. She uses a thumbnail to peel back the sticky yellow wax, which smells very faintly of honey. There is an expensive looking piece of stationary inside, folded over once. As always, the message has been composed in sepia, writing that looks old fashioned, and Susannah always has imagined that the messages are each written out with an antique fountain pen.

Each man and woman who receives these envelopes has also received a key to a cryptographic code. No two of these ciphers are identical. She spent a week memorizing hers, then destroyed the ruled index card on which it had been written. Just for her. The Black Pharaoh speaks joyfully in an endless parade of languages learned from his father, and so he has one to spare for each of his chosen.

"You are a special snowflake," sneers the voice, and she tries to ignore it, but that works about as well as trying to ignore the prickling irritation where the fungus has taken root in her flesh. "You are a unique butterfly," laughs the voice.

Susannah reads the message over several times, and then several times more to be certain that she's worked it out precisely right. She isn't permitted to copy it down as she decodes the encrypted equations and stellar coordinates; she has to hold it all in her mind. Copies are much too dangerous when there are so many out there trying their damnedest to ferret out the servants of the tall, thin man who waits in doorways for lost sheep. And as soon as she's certain she's got it right, before she climbs atop the ice chest with blue Sharpie in hand, she has to burn it. Not after, which is why she has to be more sure than sure can be that she's made not even the most minute mistake. She touches one corner of the stationary to the candle's flame, and the paper catches and burns. She drops it onto the floor and waits until nothing remains but ashes. The whole floor of the room is carpeted in a fine grey layer of ash, smeared beneath her bare feet. She'll leave wearing ash. She always does.

"Your own moveable feast," the voice in the corner whispers. "Remember that thou art dust, and to dust thou shalt return."

Star dust.

"In the end," the voice reminds her, "not even that much will remain."

Susannah needs only fifteen minutes to copy the message onto the concrete ceiling. The Guard can hide inside their pillboxes and lob mortars at the demons who/that come too near the city. The jets and helicopters can fire their air-to-air missiles at the driftgliders and the polyp clouds. The infantry can spray all the napalm it wishes. Let them. Because *this* is where the real offensive strikes of the war are being executed and carried out, in this dark, musty room and countless others like it all around the globe.

The tip of the marker squeaks as she draws lines to connect the dots between stars that only foolish men would try to name. She is laying a minefield. She is building a siege engine.

Susannah only *hardly* ever sleeps. If her insomnia were complete, that would be a mercy. Because even a woman touched by the hand of that tall, dark man to hasten The End, even such a woman as that, as Susannah, is not immune to fear. To terror. To dread. To be a whirlwind's concubine is not to be immune from the wind. And, long after midnight, when she has finished with the instructions delivered to her cramped room below the Biograph Theater, she extinguishes the candle and sits down to rest in the loveseat. She only means to get her breath, to clear her head, for the translation, transcription, then the act of laying down those new pieces of his stratagem has left her as drained as it always does.

But, there in the comforting arms of the darkness, thinking of the wall and No Man's Land, of the forest and the Elmwood kid, she slips.

She sleeps.

She dreams.

No one is spared in dreams.

There is no protective ward against the revelations riding on the double helix of REM and NREM, spat up and out by the amygdala and limbic system to come crawling up from the recesses buried deep in the convolutions of grey matter. In her dreams, Susannah has never been *aware* that she's dreaming, never in all her life; that would be another sort of mercy. The worlds of her dreams – before and after the return of *New Horizons* and the sundering of reality – have always, always, always been as authentic as her waking world.

She walks along a boulevard that seems to have no beginning and no end. The shells of dead buildings rise up tall on either side of the street, and every empty window frame is another eye. Above Susannah, the sky seethes red with unopposed squadrons of driftgliders. The asphalt beneath her bare feet is sticky, as if it has either never cooled or is melting again. She's going somewhere, even if she could never say where that might be. She can hear distant artillery, the impotent booming of howitzers. But there is no one here to make a stand. This place, she knows, has fallen to chaos.

The itch from her infection is maddening, and has spread from her hip all the way down to her leg and across her belly. But she doesn't scratch, because that only spreads it faster, and she still has so much work to do before she joins the others in the forest.

"Is this the very last day?" she asks, uncertain whom she intends the question for and not expecting an answer.

"No," says a voice very close behind her. It sounds like her mother's voice, but she doesn't turn or even look over her shoulder to see. "No, Susannah. It's not quite as far along as that. On that day, the stars will wink out, one by one. Isn't that what you're doing when you draw on the ceiling? Erasing the stars?"

"Then there are still stars up there, behind the monsters?"

"Watch where you put your feet," says the woman who may or may not be her dead mother. "Watch your step. There are no maps here."

"No one repairs the roads anymore," Susannah replies.

And then she's come to a crucifix welded together from rusted steel girders, and hung there with coils of baling wire and with railroad spikes is the Elmwood kid. He isn't dead yet. Like Christ at Calvary, he stares Heavenward, as though he might yet be delivered.

"No one's coming for us," she tells him.

There's a happy ring of ebony beetles dancing about the base of the cross, singing ebony beetle songs of sacrifice. She thinks about crushing them beneath her heel, all of them, so at least the boy could suffer in peace.

"We'll see," the Elmwood kid whispers through blood and a mouthful of broken teeth. "Nothing is certain. Ain't that the New Rule?"

"Nothing is new about uncertainty," she tells him.

His blood is the same color as the bellies, throats, and the undersides of the wings of the driftgliders.

The Elmwood kid says, "I'll go for all of them, because there must be someone who will go for all of them."

"Who said that?" she asks the Hanged Man.

"I did. Just now."

"No. Someone said it before you."

And this is when she sees that there are dozens and dozens of other crucifixes – hundreds, possibly – stretching away along the boulevard before her. *This is,* she thinks, *the Road of Needles. The Road of Infidels.*

"Go away, witch," he says. "I'm dying. I don't want you to be here when I die."

Susannah does as he asks.

She walks along the shore of the risen island on the very afternoon that it emerged, when it still dripped with the silt and slime of the seafloor. Heaps of hagfish, ratfish, brittle stars, and sea cucumbers squirm around her ankles, but she feels no revulsion whatsoever. Her back is to R'lyeh, with its warped spacetime and tortured geometry, that utterly alien architecture where the sleeper was imprisoned three hundred million years before the rise of mankind, as the continents slammed one against another in the birth throes of Pangaea and the first tiny reptiles scurried beneath the boughs of steaming Carboniferous jungles.

Ph'nglui mglw'nafh Cthulhu R'lyeh wgah'nagl fhtagn.

No, sing that song no more. He is awakened.

A sanguine sea laps at the basalt shore.

The second angel poured out his bowl into the sea, and it became like the blood of a corpse, and every living thing died that was in the sea.

There are fleets of destroyers and aircraft carriers out there, the ships of war, bobbing like toys in a bathtub. Soon enough, the sleeper, no longer sleeping, will wipe them all away, send them straight down to the bottom of the ocean. The bombs begin to fall, shat out of submarines and silos in China, Nebraska, Russia, India. The clock on a crooked stack of books in a concrete room below Chicago ticks, and then all the world is made of light and fire.

The fire is a path into cool shade.

Holocaust to blessed, perpetual gloom.

This is the day when gates open for Susannah, when the plague fungus has eaten enough that there's more of it than her. Now she only ever dreams of the gulfs out beyond Pluto and Charon. What's left of her brain is soothed by narcotic effects of the spores coursing through the sludgy remnants of her bloodstream. So there's no more pain. There will never again be pain. She goes to the forest with a dozen staggering others. She walks the shadowed lanes between stalks that would put redwoods to shame (if any redwoods still grew). And she finds her place among those who have come before her, a gaping, wet vulvic nook in one of the stalks, and she allows that honeyed cleft to receive her. If this is Dante's Wood of the Suicides, William Blake's Forest of Self-Murderers, at least there are no harpies to tear at the bodies of the damned.

And there is peace in unity.

All wars end, even this last war. Even this wholesale massacre, as it can never truly be said to have been a war. As Mr. Wells wrote, "bows and arrows against the lightning." And many weeks later, many wax-sealed envelopes later, many nightmares later, many turns at the wall later, on a Sighday the end of this war does finally arrive.

Susannah watches from the ramparts as the wave rolls across the land, crushing, obliterating, consuming everything in its path. The wave is as high and wide as the sky. It isn't a wave of water. It moves so slowly that there was time for news of it to reach the city days before it became visible, rolling in from the southwest. From, she supposes, the direction of R'lyeh. Of Hell. Some have fled the city, bound for the deserts that once were Wisconsin. But those refugees are few, a scattered parade of the last enclaves of Hope and Determination. They are the doomed unwilling to accept an impending fate, and so Susannah can only think of them as cowards. Better to stand here and bear witness at the conclusion of human history. The wave is a theater curtain drawing shut after the actors have all taken their final bows and retreated to the wings. If asked, she would have to admit that the sight of it is not unwelcomed. After more than five years, almost a quarter of her life, Susannah is ready, and she has done her part to usher in this moment.

"It can't be real," the Elmwood kid whispers in a whisper that is more awe than terror. "Sue, it can't be real."

"It's real," she assures him. "Few things have ever been more real than that."

He raises his left arm and points towards the place where the horizon used to be.

"Nothing can be that..." But then he trails off.

"In its way," she says, "it's beautiful." She stands, moving in an effort not to scratch at the welts and boils and spongy tissue that has spread from her hip across her belly, between her legs, up her entire back. In the old days, no one with such an advanced stage of the plague would ever have been permitted to remain on the wall.

But beggars can't be choosers.

The wave oozes forward, rolling inch by inch by inch.

Her final envelope simply called it Shuggoth.

Despair, for by your hand comes the annihilator even of time, and those once rebels who were legion have been made whole and imbued with inconceivable intent, and the name placed upon it is Shuggoth.

The Black Pharaoh has allowed her to play a role in this extinction. The lines, angles, and remaining interstices marked off on so many secret walls within the city, they are all, in their way, midwives and heralds of the wave. As a reward, those who crafted them will pass from the cosmos, or, more accurately, into the post-cosmic void, with some small part of their dignity intact. Of course, this gift is a subjective perception and nothing more; the star-born harbingers of oblivion – conceived outside the quantum-foam cradle of this universe – offer no gifts, no favors to the faithful.

No one mans the howitzers. No jets are scrambled for a closing show of defiance. There is not even panic in the streets. The people who have remained in the city have accepted what is coming, and now there is only the waiting. They have a few more hours at the most.

The Elmwood kid points at the sky now. When Susannah looks up, she can see that the stars are winking out, one by one.

Pickman's Madonna

In the perpetual twilight of the Lower Dream Lands, the twins stand at the precipice, with the desolate plateau and peaks of Thok stretching behind them. Far below the precipice, lost in shadows, stretches the bone-littered vales of Pnath. They have imagined, these two from Above, that if they shut their eyes and listen very carefully, they can hear the rattle and rumble of gigantic bholes plowing through those jackstraw heaps. No one has ever set eyes on those creatures and lived to tell the tale. But, from time to time, the noise of their busy habits rises up the high cliffs of slate to the ears of any who are listening.

The twins, though partway human, are neither guests nor tourists in the abyss. They belong here as much as any ghoul. They may travel awake down the seven hundred steps to the Gates of Deeper Sleep. They may pass freely; none dare bar their way.

His name is Isaac, and her name is Isobel. They were born, not by chance, in the final minutes of an All Hallows Eve twenty-two years ago. One look at either and anyone at all would appreciate the aptness of their surname: Snow. Their skin is milk, and their corn-silk hair is white as white can be. But their eyes are the deep crimson of rubies, eyes that see as well in this gloom almost as any eyes may see. Their birth was not an easy passage, and it took the life of their mother, Hera. She saw them briefly, and then death came and delivered her from the blood-spattered crypt where the two were dragged out of the amniotic peace of Womb into the clamorous purgatory of the World. Had Hera Snow survived, herself only one third a true Daughter of Eve, she'd have loved them and been proud, for the twins grew to be all that would have been expected of them by the three families and their Ghūl father.

Hera Salem Snow, a Boston Brahmin Yankee born to the fortune and power her family bargained for centuries before. Deals with the ghouls and with dark gods, obligating each of the four families – Snow, Cabot,

Tillinghast, and Endicott – to offer once in every generation a daughter for the Ghūl to do with as they see fit. And as they see fit is almost always the birthing of half-breed children. Hera was herself the child of such a pairing, and was also such an offering, when the moon decided it was her time to bleed. She was neither fair of skin nor hair, but she shared the twins red eyes, and she shared their hungers. However, she could only ever have aspired to the ferocity of *their* terrible appetites and desires, for the son and daughter have excelled in the expectations of their father.

Long before they were finally shown the way down through secret tunnels beneath Mount Auburn Cemetery they'd stalked and killed. They'd taught themselves the arts and sciences of torture, how to prolong the suffering of their victims as long as possible before the mercy of a killing stroke. It began – with kittens, puppies, songbirds, a hutch of rabbits – before their fifth birthday. As teenagers, they moved along to adult dogs and cats, a horse from the Snow stables, before, finally, they graduated to the cook. When they were done with her, they, appropriately, butchered the corpse and stewed the finest bits. They shared that meal, and then, for the first time, fucked beneath a full moon, upon an altar they'd fashioned to honor Shub-Niggurath, the All Mother and consort of the Not-to-Be-Named. That night they first tasted one another's blood, and that night they became truly intertwined. They were wedded beneath and by the darkness between the stars, the void that watched on as they consecrated unholy, unspoken vows.

Now.

Here they stand, hand in hand, above the black gulf of Pnath. They have brought with them, in a burlap sack, the dry skeleton of their mother; they drop the bones, one by one, over the cliff, saving her skull for last. Isaac kisses its forehead. Isobel does the same. And then she releases Hera to her final resting place among the bholes. The twins drew lots to see which of them would be afforded that honor and responsibility. Isaac did a poor job of hiding his bitterness at losing the roll of a single soapstone die. Isobel has always found his sour moods especially endearing, particularly exciting.

Their sacred duty done, the two walk together along the narrow, cobbled road leading back to the great necropolis of Zin, a city once held by the race of gugs until two years ago when the twins led an army of ghouls to shatter the ramparts and breach the walls and rain fire. For the twins have become what was never suspected any half-*modab* beings ever *could* become. Together, by bold and secret sorceries, they unseated the King of Bones, the Queen of Rags – *Qqi d'Tashiva* and *Qqi Ashz'sara,* respectively

– and took for themselves the thrones of Thok. They put to death any who dared oppose them or question their right to rule, all traitors and rabble-rousers. These public executions were accomplished by such cruel and unsightly means that very few were necessary to quiet the dissidents. And they made the kingdom anew. No longer did the ghouls cower in mold and offal, gnawing gristle and marrow from withered, pilfered corpses. Isaac and Isobel raised them up and made a proper army. The gugs were enslaved, and the night gaunts, as well. Here every foul thing that slithers, flies, hops, or goes about on two legs fell under their domain.

The forever twilight became a *new* twilight.

Rarely do the twins bother climbing the seven hundred steps back to the Gate of Deeper Slumber and the cavern of flame beyond leading up and up and up to those catacombs beneath Mount Auburn. Never except when returning cannot be avoided. Those times come, as Isobel and Isaac are still the rightful matriarch and patriarch of the Snow clan. Too, there are other occasions when their duties force their return, as was the case with the exhumation of their mother. As was the case when the location of the Basalt Madonna – *Qqi d'Evai Mubadieb* – was discovered in a cave in the Sultanate of Oman, a hole in the Selma Plateau long known locally as Khoshilat Maqandeli and to the Arabs as Majlis al Jinn. Since the "death" of an artist named Richard Upton Pickman, the idol had been lost, as Pickman neglected to bring it with him when he made his own descent into the Underworld of the Lower Dream Lands. It disappeared in 1926, taken from the painter's effects by some unknown woman or man or something that was neither. How it came to be hidden below the sun-blasted canyons near the southeastern coasts of the Arabian Peninsula no one knows. But the answer to that mystery is hardly important. All that matters is that it is no longer lost. The twins know well enough not to question the winds of Fortune, but only accept her boons when all too rarely they are handed down.

The cobblestones twist and turn, coming at last to the towering gardens of fungi and more unspeakable vegetation. They've spent many wonderful private hours here alone in one another's company. Beyond the gardens rise the fantastic archway framing the entrance to Zin, fashioned of obsidian, chrome tourmaline, and green fluorite. Isaac and Isobel cross the bridge above the moat, and she pauses a moment to observe a ring of bubbles rising from the inky waters. The trumpets of the Guards of the Wall announce the arrival of King and Queen, and the mighty doors to the city swing open on copper hinges. Isobel points into the moat, and her brother is quick to look for himself. It wouldn't be the first time the moat has whispered a portent. This time, though, the disturbance seems to be no more than gas escaping from the bottom. He looks a little disappointed, and she whispers promises of consolation. Then they pass into the royal city, and the door draws shut again.

"What if the preparations are not complete?" Isaac asks his sister. They've left the gatehouse fortifications behind and come to the first gloomy avenues. Per their standing orders, none have come to meet them, and at the sound of their approach every ghoul falls to his or her knees, head bowed.

"Then there will be a feast in the dungeon," she says and smiles. Her smile, like his, is an unpleasant thing: uneven yellow teeth that she had no need to file to cannibal points because she and Isaac were both born with the teeth of carnivores. "Don't worry. The preparations will be complete."

For a reply, he only nods. Isobel is more often correct than she is wrong.

When they reach the palace, there are more trumpets, ordering all within earshot to drop to their knees. They stroll hand in hand through the lightless corridors, acknowledging none of the supplicants.

"Are we hungry, brother?"

Isaac doesn't answer her straightaway, so she asks again.

"Well, *are* we?"

He laughs and kisses her right cheek. "When are we ever not?"

"There is time before the hour," she tells him.

"There is," he agrees.

So she calls for a meal to be prepared, and servants get to their splayed feet and rush off to the larder and busy themselves at the dining table in the Great Hall.

So far as is recorded, the Basalt Madonna first appeared sometime in the Fifth Century *Anno Domini Nostri Iesu Christi*. Well, not the lord of any of the inhabitants of the city of Zin or, for that matter, in all the Lower Dream Lands. Nor even the *Upper* Dream Lands. In Constantinople, a monk happened across one of the Ghūl who, in those days, slunk through the alleys and abandoned buildings of so many cities. The few ghouls still inhabiting the World Above were bolder than they are today, and they didn't confine themselves to graveyards and to sewers. So, the pious monk encountered what he mistook for a wretched leprous man gnawing on something in a gutter (he wisely did not look too closely at what it was the ghoul gnawed), and he led the wretch back to his abbot. The abbot, being sharper of wit than the monk, was quick to realize that the man from the gutter wasn't any sort of man at all, and thus did the "Hounds of Cain" – as they were *christ*ened – come to the attention of citizens of *Christ*endom. As assimilation is inherent to that system, the abbot (his name and that of the monk are lost to history, and just as well) sent his monastic agents out to evangelize to and convert these misbegotten creatures, regardless of their foul habits and appearance and dubious origins.

The effort was met with less success than the abbot would have wished.

For, of course, ghouls have their own gods. When humanity had yet to move beyond their australopithecine progenitors, already did the ghouls worship their pantheon of Fifty, the *Qqi*. Ages before their fateful war with the Djinn, they had come to know the Hands of the Five, the Ten Hands, the *fifty* fingers. They weren't about to cast aside their veneration of Great Amylostereum or Mother Paecilomyces, Camponotus the Tireless Maw or eyeless, all-seeing Claviceps, in exchange for one god who'd not even seen fit to send his martyr down to the Lower Dream Lands. Still, there's always a gullible element in any assemblage, and a tiny but strident number, while not abandoning the *Qqi,* did engage in a notable act of syncretism. They wove their own rough patchwork of holy entities from the teachings of the monks. They brought into being the Maghor Rostrum (patron of the starving and toothless), Mortifien the Crypt Mason, Mistress Praxedes the Many-Limbed (midwife to the transformed who once were only women and men), bat-winged Pteropidion, the maimed bride Saint Lilit (invoked for the endurance of exile and pain). These names and many others besides were set down in 1702 for the prying eyes of brave and foolish seekers after mystery by Francois-Honore Balfour in his infamous *Cultes des Goules,* a volume almost immediately consigned to the Church's *Index Librorum Prohibitorum.*

It is not known precisely how Francois-Honore Balfour learned the names, though his association with a handful of Jesuits would be sagely blamed.

And those ghouls who so cleverly fashioned these new "gods" also fashioned for themselves a new idol, their own Pietà, a *Beáta Maria Virgo Perdolens* to fit their needs, and among men it became known as the Basalt Madonna, *id est Basaltes Maria Virgo.*

When Isaac and Isobel Snow have finished their raw meal of the tongue, kidneys, ovaries, and heart of librarian, a woman lately of Providence, Rhode Island, they lick clean one another's faces and hands before proceeding to the chamber where the priests have erected – to their exacting specifications – an altar of stacked skulls and blocks of volcanic rock mined from the quarries of Thok. The altar rests on a wide dais, and before the dais the priests have lain a bed of mammoth furs and tanned skins peeled from off half a hundred embalmed corpses. The smoky candles that illuminate the room have been made from the fat of both humans and ghouls.

"Are we ready?" asks Isobel. Before Isaac answers her, he examines the brass contraption near the altar. A single shaft of pale moonlight is shining down through a hole in the high domed roof of the chamber, and it falls across the contraption. It looks a bit like a sextant, a bit like a sundial, yet also suggests an elaborate clockwork.

"We are," he says, and she smiles. It's been a long and arduous path to this hour.

What they are about to do cannot ever be undone, which, obviously, is what makes what they are about to do sublime. The twins stand at the hairline threshold of the realization of a prophecy first uttered more than four million years ago, in the days after the end of the war with the Djinn, well in advance of the ghouls' exposure to the tenets of Christianity and what they made of it. The teachings of the Abbot were only – to those who understood – a means to an end. A means to fulfillment of a prophecy that might never have had a *chance* of fulfillment had not a monk found a ghoul in a gutter and led it back to a monastery. There can be hope, and dreams, and the illusion of design, but it's the accidents of history that *propel* history, for history is no more than innumerable tangled strands of happenstance.

Isobel spares a glance at the well that opens just a couple of feet behind the bed that has been prepared for her and her brother. Even a mind as gleefully, unapologetically wicked as her own feels a slight shiver at the sight of the well, hewn from the native rock and eight feet across, the candlelight making no dint whatsoever in its implacable darkness. A mouth like that needs no teeth to be taken seriously. It was here long before this chamber was built, long before the city of Zin.

"Better, Sister, that we don't look at it." He is thinking of basilisks and the gorgon Medusa, but he doesn't tell her that.

"Yes," she says, turning her face away from the well. "But – "

"It's better," he says again.

She undresses, and he follows her example. Their robes of yellow silk and wool damask form pretty puddles at their feet.

It is a shame, she thinks, this could not have been our wedding bed.

"It's a shame," says Isaac, "that *this* couldn't have been our wedding bed," and she smiles and nods. Isobel smiles far more than Isaac; she sometimes thinks him far too serious for their own good. In all matters, it seems to her, a little levity is advisable.

The Basalt Madonna has been placed on the altar.

Half hidden in the ten arms of Mother Hydra rests the slain body of the messiah. Not the one that the monks of Constantinople hoped the Ghūl would come, in time, to venerate. This is a messiah fit for the Lower Dream Lands. It might be the graven image of almost any ghoul, from its vaguely canine face to its hooves. Which is the point. It *might* be any ghoul, were any ghoul made perfect. There is no describing perfection; it is seen, and it is understood. Or it isn't. Over the centuries, many forgeries of the Basalt Madonna have surfaced. Some arose from within the blasphemous sect sometimes referred to (as in Balfour's book) as the "Byzantine Ghūl." Others were created by charlatans and also by occultists hoping a copy might prove as powerful as the lost (or only hidden) original. They were wrong, for without the blessings bestowed upon the first, the true *Basaltes Maria Virgo,* these counterfeits were no more than unnerving chunks of igneous stone. Here, in this place, at this appointed time, Isobel Snow lies in her twin's embrace, watching as the candlelight plays over the angles and curves of the idol. The pyritized nautiloid crowning Mother Hydra, her golden gloriole, only the geometry of its spiral are wholly an expression of any known mathematics. That organic manifestation of the golden curve, circular arcs connecting the opposite corners of squares in the Fibonacci tiling – 1, 1, 2, 3, 5, 8, 13, 21, and 34. That lone Paleozoic shell, pried from Turkish shale, is a comfort to any eye that lingers on the idol. Only it is not somehow alien to the sight of one born in the World Above or in the Dream Lands. For the hands of those who exist Outside had too great a hand in the conception and sculpting of the Madonna.

In their defeat and humiliation, a hierophant of the Ghūl foretold of the coming of a mighty warrior priest who would lead them in a second war against their ancient foes and fully restore them to the waking world. The father and mother of this savior would be twins born of a mongrel bitch. And now the tribulations are ending, passing with the sacrifice of Hera Snow, grandmother of God. With the birth of Isobel and Isaac Snow.

In the shadow of the altar, he enters her, and she wraps her legs tightly about him. A distant piping music rises from the well, and the candles burn the sickly blue of the phosphorescent fungi in the garden beyond the city walls. There are no other words between them. There never will be. Once he's come and is asleep beneath her, she gazes at the obsidian dagger waiting on the altar. It will cut her hands when she wields it, that her own blood will mingle with her brother's when she slices his throat from ear to ear. She'll be alone when their child is born, but Isaac always understood that he'd never live to see the exodus from Zin and the deliverance of his people and the Age of the Second Kingdom.

"I love you," she whispers, knowing that she will never love another. Not even the daughter who will grow within her to be born before another year is out. Soon, she will cast his bones upon the vales of Pnath, to join their mother's.

"You'll not ever be forgotten, Isaac," she whispers.

Somewhere in the twilight that hangs always above the city, there's the rumble of thunder and the sound of vast wings bruising the air. She kisses him, then rises to take up the knife.

With thanks to Vic Ruiz, my partner in Ghūl lore.

The Peddler's Tale,
or Isobel's Revenge

I f you are very sure that's the story you wish to hear," said the peddler, the seller of notions and oddments, to the tow-headed girl child who called her Aunty. They were not related, neither by blood nor marriage, but very many people in Ulthar called the peddler Aunt or Aunty or the like. Few people living knew her right name or her history. Most felt it impolite to ask, and she never volunteered the information.

"You should be certain, and then be *certain* you're certain, before I begin. I've come a long, long way. And tomorrow I leave the city and will not soon return. So, be *sure* this is the tale you wish to hear."

"Aunty, I *am* very certain," said the girl impatiently, and the other two children – both boys – agreed. "I have no doubt whatsoever."

"Well, then," said the old woman who wasn't her aunt. She sat back in her chair and lit her pipe, then squinted through grey smoke at the youngsters who'd arranged themselves on the floor between her and the crackling hearth fire. Also, there were five cats, none of whom seemed the least bit interested in peddlers' yarns.

She took a deep pull on her pipe, then began.

"You've all heard the name of the King of Bones, and you've heard the tales of how he came to power. And of his Queen, his twin sister, Isobel."

The children nodded eagerly. And the peddler paused, because she knew that the making of beginnings is, as many have noted, a matter not to be undertaken lightly. And, too, the girl had requested of her a very grim tale, which made the beginning that much more delicate an undertaking. The old woman watched her audience, and they watched her right back. She was well versed at hiding exhaustion, disguising an aching back and sore feet behind a pleasant demeanor, not letting on how her weary sinews wished for the rare luxury of a soft mattress. Duty before rest. This tale was the price of her night's lodging and board, and she was a woman who paid her debts.

Shortly after dawn, the peddler had led the strong draught pony that pulled her wagon over the ancient stone bridge spanning the River Skai, that wild path of meltwater gurgling down from the glaciers girdling Mount Lerion and flowing northwards towards the Cerenarian Sea. She'd lingered a while on the bridge, admiring the early autumn sunrise, the clean smell of the river, and the view to the east. This was always a welcome sight, the cottages and farms speckling the hills beyond the bridge. Behind her lay Nir and Hatheg, neither of which had proven as profitable as she'd hoped. With so many merchants and craftsmen – and it seemed there were more every year – few in the villages and cities had use for a traveling tinker and a seller of oddments and notions, a peddler of medicinals and salves, a woman up to almost any menial job for a few coins. She'd become an anachronism, but at so advanced an age it was hardly practical to seek some other more lucrative trade.

Out beyond the farmland, just visible in a gauzy mist starting to burn away beneath the new day, she had been able to discern the suburbs of Ulthar. She was born in that city and hoped to spend her last years there, fate willing. She did not ever think *gods willing,* as she had long since learned the folly and dangers of placing one's hope in the hands of gods and things that fancy themselves gods.

"Isobel and Isaac, the earthborn ghouls," said the girl, prompting the peddler to continue.

"Yes, well," said the peddler. "But they were not true and proper ghouls, only mongrels, birthed of a mostly human mother. They were fair, some even say beautiful to behold, their skin white as milk, their eyes clear and blue as sapphires. Their Ghūl heritage barely showed, excepting in their appetites and ruthlessness. Still, they wished to *rule* as ghouls. By the procurement of a powerful, terrible artifact, they raised an army and threw down the rightful King and Queen of Bones and Rags, and – "

"The *Qqi d'Tashiva* and *Qqi Ashz'sara,*" the tow-headed girl interrupted. "And the artifact is the Basalt Madonna – *Qqi d'Evai Mubadieb* – and, Aunty, I've heard – "

The old woman raised an eyebrow and scowled, silencing the girl.

"Now, which of us is telling this tale?" she asked. "And, besides, I'd not guess your ma and pa would think so highly of your palavering in the corpse tongue."

One of the cats, a fat tabby tom, leapt into the peddler's lap, stretched, then curled up for a nap. She stroked its head. In her wanderings far and wide from the cobblestone streets of radiant Ulthar, the cats were, perhaps, what she missed above all else. For an age, the citizens of the city had been forbidden to harm any cat for any reason, upon pain of death or banishment. There were not many laws of man she counted wise and unquestionably just, but that surely was one of the few.

"Yes. Those were the titles that the Snow twins took for themselves when all the forces of Thok had fallen before them and the fire they wielded, after even the city of the gugs and the vaults of Zin lay at their feet, after even the great flocks of night gaunts had surrendered. In the days that followed the war, when I was only a very small girl myself, there was fear even here that Isaac Snow might not be content to rule the shadows of the Lower Dream Lands, that he might have greater ambitions and rise up against the world of men.

"You know, of course, no such thing happened. We'd not be sitting here, me telling you this story, if matters had gone that way. We were, all of us, fortunate, for many are the generals who'd believed the might of the twins was so awful that none could ever stand against it. It is written that the Snows were content to remain below, and that they still – to this day – rule over and enslave the creatures of the Lower Dream Lands."

"But – " began the tow-headed girl, and this time the peddler interrupts *her*.

"But, child, though this is what most count as the truth, there are those who whisper a secret history of the Ghûl Wars. And if this *other* account is to be believed – and I warrant there are a few priests and scholars who will swear that it is so – the twins were never of one mind. Indeed, it is said that Isaac greatly feared his sister, for the same prophecy that had foretold their victory also spoke of the birth of a daughter to them."

"He feared his own child?" asked the boy seated to the tow-headed girl's right.

"He did."

"But why?" the boy asked.

"If you'll kindly stop asking questions, I was, as it happens, coming to that."

The peddler chewed the stem of her pipe a moment and stroked the tabby tom's head. It purred, and she briefly considered changing horses in the middle of this stream and *insisting* they hear some other tale, one not populated with ghouls, half ghouls, and moldering necropoleis, and not a tale of war and the horrors of war. Likely, if she continued, it would end in nightmares for her and the children both. The plains of Pnath and the peaks of Thok might lie far away, and the battles in question long ago, but neither space nor time, she knew, could be depended upon to hold phantoms at bay.

Still, this was the tale they'd asked for, and this was the tale she'd promised, and the peddler was not a woman to go back on her word.

"The prophecy," she continued, "had been passed down since the ghouls were defeated by the Djinn and cast out of the wastes of the Arabian deserts into the Lower Dream Lands, so thrice a million years before the first city of humankind was built. It foretold that someday a daughter would be born to half-ghoul twins, half-*modab* albino twins, and this daughter would grow to be a savior, a messiah, who'd be more powerful by far than even her terrible parents. She would, so said the prophecy, lead the Ghūl through the Enchanted Wood and up the seven hundred steps to the Gates of Deeper Slumber and through the gates into the Waking World. Once above, the mighty Djinn would find their doom by the same hellish weapon her mother and father had wielded in Thok. But…"

And here the peddler paused for effect and puffed at her pipe a moment. The air in the room had gone as taut as a harp string, and the three children leaned very slightly forward.

"But?" whispered the tow-headed girl.

"But," continued the peddler, smoke leaking from her nostrils, "the rise of the ghouls would also be the downfall of the father of their champion. Because first, or so went the prophecy, the daughter would have to murder the father and claim both thrones for herself. She would spare her mother, but never again would there be a king and a queen in Thok. Those immemorial titles would vanish into memory and then pass from all recollection.

"The King of Bones and Rags, he did believe the prophecy, for, after all, had it not foretold of his and his sister's birth and their coming to the Underworld and of their ascension? Sure it had, and if that portion of it was not false then how could he *not* fear those passages that had yet to be realized? Sure he was terrified, because even so great a monster as he may fear his own undoing at the hands of such unfathomable mysteries as soothsaying. And, what's more, he soon learned that Isobel Siany Snow – for that was her earthborn name in full, given by their mother Hera – that Queen Isobel was already pregnant. That she had become so shortly before the war began, when she and he were hardly more than storm clouds gathering on the horizon."

And here the peddler departed briefly from her simple narrative, for the bare bones of a tale are a dull affair and should be dressed appropriately in the attire of atmosphere and the garb of mood. Too easily might this story become a dry recitation of *perhaps it was, and so they say,* and *might have been.* So, with words she deftly painted images of the perpetual twilight that lay over the dreaded Vale of Pnath, where gigantic bholes burrowed through unplumbed strata of gnawed bones heaped into the wide valley. She told of towering forests of phosphorescent fungi that pressed in all about the borders of that land in the shadow of the ragged peaks of Thok, mountains so lofty they reached almost to the rocky, stalactite-festooned ceiling of the Lower Dream Lands. It was the ghouls, she explained, who'd made Pnath a plain of dry ribs and broken skulls, for they'd spent untold ages tossing the leavings of their unspeakable feasts over the cliffs into the abyss below. In those lands, the peddler assured them, every breath of air was redolent of death and rot. For it was the *realm* of the grave. It was the abode of nightmares beyond reckoning.

"Oh, and the ghasts," she nodded. "I shouldn't neglect to mention them. Terrible, vile, creeping beasts with a bite so venomous none can survive it. The gugs, the architects of Zin, hunted them, and probably hunt them still. But the gugs fear them as well."

Now the eyes of the children were wide, and occasionally they glanced over their shoulders towards the fire or upwards at the autumn night pressing against the windows of the room.

"Oh, but I *have* strayed terribly, haven't I," said the peddler, and she frowned and knitted her brows, feigning mild exasperation with herself. "Must be the wind brushing around the eaves of the house making my mind wander so."

"Aunty, we don't mind," the tow-headed girl whispered, and the other children nodded in unison.

"That's all well and good, but, we'll be here until cock's crow if I keep nattering on that way. Where was I?"

"Isobel was already pregnant," said the boy who'd spoken before.

"Yes. Yes, that was it. Isobel, the Queen of Bones and Rags, was pregnant by her brother, and when Isaac Glyndwr Snow learned this he feared it would be the death of him. Everything was unfolding precisely as the prophecy had promised. For the first time ever he grew distant from his sister and withdrew from her, becoming ever more secretive, spending long hours alone or in the company of his concubines. He took to drink and to chasing the Dragon, trying to smother his worries in the embrace of opium. As Isobel's belly swelled, *his* scheming, anxious mind swelled with plots and designs by which he might prevent the fulfillment of the prophecy and cheat his own undoing.

"He would kill his sister. Yes. That's exactly what he *had* to do. Even though he truly did love Isobel, and even though he knew full well he'd never, ever, *ever* love another woman, he had to do murder against her. Because, you see, he loved himself far more. Still, the King of Bones also understood that he must take care to proceed with the utmost caution. For though it was true there was no end of ghouls so fanatically loyal to him they'd gladly turn assassin even against their queen, it was also true he had enemies. The inhabitants of Thok were, by large, a conquered, broken lot, and many were the ghouls who despised the twins and named them usurpers and conspired in secret, drawing plots against the Crown. Isaac Snow's advisors warned him that even the fires of the Basalt Madonna might not save him should there be open revolt. For before, he and Isobel had possessed the element of surprise. They'd never have that advantage again.

"Worse, there were rumors that some among the dissidents had begun making sacrifices to – well, I'll not say *that* name here, but I mean the dæmon sultan who serves the blind, insane chaos at the center of the universe. No one ought *ever* speak that name."

The children looked disappointed, and the tow-headed girl muttered to herself.

"Anyway, the King of Bones had made up his mind," continued the peddler, "and nothing could dissuade him from the cold and heartless resolve of his decision. He would see Isobel dead, and he chose the method, and he chose the hour. It was with an especial shame that he cowardly set another to the task. At first he'd intended to do the deed himself, which only seemed right and good to his twisted ideas of right and good. But his advisors convinced him it was much more prudent to *order* her death by another's hand. Then, afterwards, he could have the killer tried and publicly executed, and there would be fewer questions about the queen's sad fate. If it were discovered that the *Qqi d'Tashiva* had murdered the mother of the child who would deliver all Ghūl-kind and lead them to victory against the Djinn – "

"There'd have been a terrible count of angry ghouls," the tow-headed girl said.

The peddler nodded, not bothering to complain about yet another interruption.

"Indeed. It's no small thing to destroy the hope of an entire people, even if the people are so foul a bunch as the ghouls."

One of the children yawned, and the peddler asked, "Should I stop here? It's getting late, after all, and you three by rights should be in your beds."

"No, Aunty, please," said the tow-headed girl, and she thumped the boy who'd yawned smartly on the back of his head. "We're not tired, not at all. Please, do go on."

"Please," murmured the boy who'd yawned, who was now busy rubbing his head.

"Very well then," said the peddler, and she set her pipe aside, for it had gone out partway through her description of the Lower Dream Lands. "So, the king commanded that his sister die, and he chose the ghoul who would cut her throat while she slept. He told none but those closest to him, a handful whom he trusted and believed were beyond any act of treachery. But he was mistaken. The *Qqi Ashz'sara* was every bit as wicked and distrustful and perfidious as her brother, and she'd taken precautions. She'd placed a spy, a ghoul named Sorrow, within her brother's inner circle. Sorrow was as noble a ghoul as a ghoul may be, which is to say not particularly, but he was in love with his queen, and Isobel did not doubt that he would gladly perish to protect her, should it come to that."

"That's a very strange name," said the tow-headed girl.

"He was a ghoul," replied the peddler. "Would you expect he'd be named George or Juan Carlos or maybe Aziz? His name was Sorrow, a name he'd found on a gravestone stolen from a cemetery in the World Above and brought into the World Below."

"But you said," cut in the boy who'd yawned, "you told us that the Djinn had banished the Ghūl to – "

" – as a whole, yes. I said that, and they did. However, always have there been those few who braved the wrath of the Djinn, hiding among women and men of the Waking World, infesting catacombs and cemeteries."

"Oh," said the boy, clearly confused.

"As I was saying," the peddler began again, "Isobel Snow trusted this one ghoul to bring her word of her brother's doings, and as soon as Sorrow learned of the plot to murder the queen, he scampered back to her with the news."

"Scampered?" asked the tow-headed girl.

"Yes. Scampered. Ghouls do that. They lope and they creep and they scamper. And as the latter is the more expedient means of getting about,

Sorrow *scampered* back to Isobel to warn her she and her unborn child were in very terrible danger. Isobel listened, not desiring to believe it was true, but also never supposing that it wasn't. The twins were, as is generally the case with twins, two peas from the same ripe pod, and she admitted to Sorrow that in her brother's place she likely would have made the same decision. Sorrow advised her that she had two options. She could try and make a stand, possibly rallying the very ghouls who would see the King and Queen both deposed, currying their favor with promises that she would abdicate and by pointing out that she was, after all, the mother of the prophesied messiah. Or she could run."

"I'd have run," said the boy who'd yawned.

"But you're a poltroon," replied the boy on the tow-headed girl's right. "You always run from a fight."

"Yes, well," said the peddler, "have you never heard that discretion is the better part of valor? The greater wisdom lies in knowing when the odds are not in your favor, and Isobel Snow knew the odds were not in hers. So she dispatched Sorrow to enlist the aid of another earthborn ghoul, one who had once been a man of the Waking World, a man named Richard Pickman. In the century since Pickman had arrived in Thok, he'd risen to a station of some prominence among the ghouls, and during the Ghūl War he'd fought against the Snows. Afterwards, he'd gone into hiding, but Sorrow knew his whereabouts, and he knew also that Pickman possessed the influence to arrange the queen's hasty escape, and that for the right price he would help."

"But wasn't he afraid?" asked the tow-headed girl.

"Undoubtedly, but Pickman didn't believe the prophecy and was convinced that the coming of the albino twins was no more than a coincidence. He was of the opinion that the two were grifters and humbugs who'd seen a chance to exploit ignorance and superstition, and they'd seized it. He certainly did not believe that the infant who'd be born of their union would be the ghouls' deliverance. In fact, Richard Pickman doubted that there ever had *been* a war with the Djinn. He was a heretic of the first order, an unbeliever through and through. It wasn't that he was sympathetic to Isobel's plight. No. More that he was convinced that as long as her child lived, Isaac Snow would be weakened by his fear of their offspring. And, too, Pickman conjured that the brother's confidence would be weakened if he failed to murder his sister. Neither of the Snows were accustomed to failure."

"They were extremely arrogant," said the boy who'd yawned. He rubbed at his eyes and petted a ginger kitten that was curled on the floor near him.

"Sure he was," nodded the peddler, "and more than words ever can convey. It did not cross his mind that his plot would be foiled, once he set it in motion. They say that the first thing he felt upon receiving the news that one of his confidants, a ghoul named Sorrow – and *not* George or Juan Carlos or maybe Aziz – had lain in wait for the King's butcher and gotten the upper hand, the very first expression Isaac Snow's face showed that night was not rage, but amazement that he could possibly have failed."

"Serves him right," says the tow-headed girl.

The peddler shrugged. "Perhaps, if one excuses Isobel her own crimes and makes of her a hero merely because she'd fallen out of favor with her brother. Regardless, after the assassin was slain, Pickman, Sorrow, and several other ghouls led her from the palace and out of Thok, down narrow mountain trails and across the bhole-haunted Vale of Pnath. At last they gained the vaults of ruined Zin, that haunted city of the gugs, and went straightaway to a mighty central tower, the tallest among twice a hundred towers so tall no one could, from the ground, ever hope to glimpse the tops of those spires. They pushed open its enormous doors, which bore the sigil of Koth – a dreadful, awful bas-relief neither Isobel Snow nor Sorrow dared gaze upon – and I should tell you, children, that the history of that tower is a shuddersome tale in its own right, one all but lost to antiquity."

"Maybe you'll tell it next time," said the boy on the tow-headed girl's left.

"Maybe," replied the peddler. "We shall see. Anyhow, beyond that forbidding entryway was a stair that wound up and up and up…and *up*… to a massive trapdoor carved of slick black stone. It is said two hard days' climbing were necessary to at last reach the top of those stairs and that the strength of all the ghouls present was only *barely* enough to lift open that trapdoor. But open it they did, and so it was that Isobel Snow, Queen of Bones and Rags, *Qqi Ashz'sara,* slipped through her brother's icy fingers and fled to the Upper Dream Lands. Of the ghouls, only Sorrow went with her, the others turning back with Richard Pickman, who, as I've said, hoped her escape would be the beginning of the end for Isaac Snow's reign. Pickman had instructed Sorrow to lead the Queen in Exile through the Enchanted Wood to the River Xari, where a barge would be waiting to bear them down to the port city of Jaren, from whence they could book safe passage across the shimmering sea to Serannian. Sure, even Isaac Snow would never be half so bold as to venture so many leagues from the Underworld, much less attempt to breach the high walls of the island kingdom of Serannian."

"The people of Serannian let them enter?" the tow-headed girl asked skeptically. "A ghoul and an albino half ghoul?"

"You'd not think so, would you? But, see, the lords of Serannian were kindly," answered the peddler. "And as I have told you, there were generals and leaders of men who'd learned of the Snow's discovery of the long lost *Qqi d'Evai Mubadieb* and of the strife that followed, and how they feared the twins might not be content to rule the Lower Dream Lands. So, they saw the arrival of Isobel Snow and news of the division between king and queen as a good omen, indeed. Moreover, there is a thing I have not yet revealed, probably the most important part of the tale, the pivot on which turns its plot."

Each of the four children sat up a little straighter at that, for how could anything be more important than the ghoul queen's flight?

"When Isobel Snow departed the peaks of Thok and the palaces of the royal necropolis, she took with her the Basalt Madonna."

There was a collective gasp from the peddler's audience, and she felt the smallest rind of satisfaction at that. If she had to tell this story, at least the gravity of it was not being lost on the listeners, and at least she knew she was not slipping in her skill as a spinner of yarns. She wanted to rekindle her pipe, but this was no place to interrupt herself. She was getting very near the end.

"But if she had the weapon, why did she not turn it against her brother?" asked the boy on the tow-headed girl's right.

"I don't know," said the peddler. "No one knows, no one now living. Perhaps she didn't fully comprehend how, or possibly she was unable to use the Madonna without him. It may have required the two of them together. Or perhaps she simply loved Isaac too much to destroy him."

"Or she was afraid," whispered the boy who'd yawned.

"Or that," said the peddler. "Whatever the reason, she didn't use it against him. She carried it away with her, and by the time Isaac Snow discovered this she was far beyond his reach. When she arrived at Serannian she and Sorrow were arrested and taken to the Council of Lords to whom she told her story and to whom she revealed the *Qqi d'Evai Mubadieb*. She asked for sanctuary, and it was granted. And this even though she refused to surrender the Basalt Madonna to the men and women of that city on the sea. So, it was there her daughter was born, whom she named Elspeth

Isa Snow. There in the shining bustle and safety of Serannian it was that Elspeth grew to be a woman, a strong and fiercely intelligent woman, I should add. Indeed, in the spring of her nineteenth year she was offered a seat on the Council, which she accepted. That same year her mother succumbed to a disease of the blood that had plagued her and her brother since birth, and – "

"Aunty, you didn't mention that before," interrupted the tow-headed girl.

"It wasn't important before. Now it is. Anyway, when Elspeth Snow's mother died the Basalt Madonna passed into her keeping."

"And what happened to Sorrow?" the girl asked.

"Oh, he was still there. He was, in fact, ever Elspeth's dearest friend and confidant. She being one-quarter ghoul herself found his company comforting. But…this is not the end of the tale. There's more."

"It *sounds* like the end," said the boy who'd yawned.

"Very *much* like the end," said the tow-headed girl.

"Well, if you wish," said the peddler, "I can stop here. I am tired, and I – "

"No, no, please," said the boy on the girl's right. "Tell the rest. If there is more, then you cannot stop here."

"And why is that?" the peddler asked him.

"My da says that an unfinished tale is an indecent thing."

Somewhere in the house a door creaked open and was pulled shut just a little too roughly, and all three of the children started at the noise. The cat in the old woman's lap opened one eye and looked well and profoundly annoyed at having been awakened.

"So," said the peddler, who had not jumped at the slamming door, "your da believes that stories have endings, which means he must also believe they have beginnings. Do you believe that, child?"

The boy looked somewhat baffled at her question.

"Well…do they not?" he asked her.

"I don't think so," she told him. "Then again, I am only a poor peddler who sells oddments and notions and fixes broken wagon wheels and heals warts but…no, *I* do not believe so. Priests and learned scholars may disagree – though I daresay some of them may not. But I would ask you, did our story truly begin when the Snow twins waged their war and conquered Thok and Pnath and all the Lower Dream Lands, or was the beginning when they found the *Qqi d'Evai Mubadieb* in the Waking World, the World Above, where it had been hidden in a cavern known as Khoshilat Maqandeli, deep in the Arabian wastes? But no, more likely we'd have to say the beginning was earlier, the night the twins consummated their incestuous love on an altar they'd fashioned to honor Shub-Niggurath, the All Mother and consort of the Not-to-Be-Named."

The peddler paused a moment, quietly admonishing herself for having been careless and spoken the name of one of the Great Old Ones, and worse, for having spoken it to three children. She picked up her cold pipe and set the stem between her yellow teeth, chewing at it a moment before continuing.

"Might be," she said, "or might be, instead, the story began when they were born to Alma Shaharrazad Snow, who went by Hera. Or the night she was led by *her* mother into a ghoul warren in an earthly city known as Boston to be bedded by a ghoul. Or perhaps it all started much farther back, when the Snows and the Tillinghasts and the Cabots – all the members of that clan – entered into a pact with the ghouls whereby they'd be given riches and power in exchange for bearing half-caste children. Or much farther back still, when the Ghūl foolishly went to war against their ancient enemies, the Djinn. Or – "

"I think we get the idea," said the tow-headed girl.

"Good," said the peddler, and she managed a ghost of smile. "Good, for I think that is a very important lesson."

"So…what happened next?" the boy who'd yawned asked. He was now very much awake.

"Well, Elspeth Snow didn't only grow to be a brilliant woman and a leader of Serannian. She also studied military strategy and became proficient with a sword and a bow and with rifles, too. And she studied the mysteries of the Basalt Madonna, as well. She'd learned much of the history of the race of ghouls from Sorrow, who never did come to feel at home in the world of men and longed always to return to Thok. Too much sun, you see. The daughter of Isaac and Isobel Snow loved the old ghoul, and she wished always that he *could* return, and, for that matter, that she might have a chance to see for herself the lands her mother had once ruled, however briefly. She even desired, they say, to look upon the face of her father. She hated him for the strife he'd caused her mother and Sorrow, but some bit of her wanted also to love him as her mother had. In the end, I cannot say what single thing it was led Elspeth to become a soldier, but become a soldier she did. More than a soldier, she became a captain of the Serannian guard, and, by her thirtieth birthday, she'd risen to the highest rank.

"And it was then that she gathered an army from the people of Serannian to march against the despotic *Qqi d'Tashiva* and end his tyranny. Also women and men from Cydathria did she rally to her cause, and from Thran Kled, and the tribes of the Stony Desert and Oonai and even the fearsome shi'earya of the faraway hills of Implan. She took up the weapon her mother and father had used to crush the Old Kingdom of the Ghūl, and on a midsummer's night she led her army down into Zin and across the Vale of Pnath. There she was joined by another army, rebel ghoul soldiers who followed Richard Pickman, the earthborn ghoul and once-man. Pickman had become an outspoken foe of the King of Bones and Rags and had long since fled Thok to avoid the gallows. The night gaunts and what remained of the race of gugs also followed her when she rode out to meet her father's army in the abyss below the mountains. The battle was brief, for Elspeth Snow chose to unleash the fires roiling inside the Madonna. When she was done, her field of victory was a scorched plain where stone had been melted to slag, and of the bones of her enemies not even ash remained."

The tow-headed girl stopped chewing her lower lip long enough to ask, "And what of the King? Did she slay her father?"

"Ah, what of the King. This is where our tale begins to fray, for none seem certain precisely what became of him. Sure, some *do* say that Elspeth slew her father outright. Others claim that he survived and was taken prisoner and locked in the catacombs deep below the throne room where he'd once ruled. Some would have us believe that he was banished simply and unceremoniously to the World Above to live always among human men and women, stripped of all his power. There is, however, another account of his fate and, I believe, one that more likely is nearer the truth of the matter."

"And what *is* that?" asked the boy who'd yawned, but who was now wide awake and who, the peddler suspected, might not sleep at all that night.

"There is a story I heard the one time I ventured as far as Sinara – I dislike traveling through the Garden Lands, but that one time I did, and, by the way, it is said that soldiers of Sinara were also among those who joined with Elspeth – there is a story I heard there from a very old woman who once had been a priestess in a temple of the Elder Ones. Before that, she'd been a pirate and a smuggler, and before that – well, as I said, she was very old. She'd lived a long and strange life and knew many peculiar tales.

"We sat together in the back of a tavern on the banks of the River Xari, a tavern that served the wharves and all the shady, disreputable sorts one finds dockside, and she told me another version of the fate of Isaac Glyndwr Snow. She said, between fits of coughing and long drinks of whiskey – for she was ill and did, I learned, soon after we spoke succumb to her tubercular sickness – that Elspeth took pity on him, for, at the last she saw before her a father. Sure now, children, I grant this is the oddest of all the twists and turns of my story, but often the course of history is many times odder than any fable or fairy tale."

The peddler closed her eyes, taking care here to say only that part fit for the ears of youngsters and, too, only that part she would not in days to come find herself ruing having said. When she opened her eyes, the hearth fire seemed much brighter than it had before, and it ringed the three children like a halo.

"C'mon then," said the boy on the tow-headed girl's right side. "Aunty, what was it the woman in the tavern told you?"

The girl glared at him. "Don't be rude, or she might decide not to say."

"I ought not," said the peddler. Her voice was rubbed thin by the telling of so long a tale, and it sounded to her ears weak and worn thin. "Sure, I should keep it between me, myself, and I. And the cats, of course, for cats know all, or so proclaim the wizened priests and priestesses of Ulthar."

"Please," said the girl. "We'll tell no one else. I swear. It will be our secret."

"It has been my experience," replied the peddler, "that children are not especially good at keeping secrets." She laughed quietly and chewed at the stem of her pipe. "But I will tell you all I know, which is, I have no doubt, not as much by half as you three would wish to hear." The peddler shifted in the chair, and her back popped loudly.

"The sickly woman in Sinara claimed that her own father had stood with Elspeth Snow in the Battle of the Vale of Pnath, and that he had ridden with her after the defeat of the King of Bones and Rags, down winding, perilous canyon roads to witness the sundering of the onyx gates of the royal city of Amaakin'šarr. There he watched as the Twilight's Wrath – this is the sobriquet Elspeth had been given by her troops – confronted her father on the torch-lined steps of the palace. His guards bowed before her, praying she would spare their lives. But the *Qqi d'Tashiva* drew his sword against her and stood his ground. In the decades since his sister's escape he'd known only loneliness and regret, not one single hour of joy, and what was the loss of his life when he'd already lost the kingdom he'd hoarded at the cost of his only love?"

"'Father,' said Elspeth Snow to him, 'will you not now cast aside your folly and old misdeeds? Will you not put down your blade that I will not have to cause you further harm than already I have?'

"The King of Bones and Rags, he sneered hatefully and advanced towards her, blue eyes blazing, his sword glinting in the light of the flickering torches. There was naught remaining in him but bitterness and rage. 'Do not call *me* father, whore, for you are your mother's bitch and none of mine. Now, come down off your horse and face me.'

"Elspeth Snow, Twilight's Wrath, the Maiden of Serannian – for she was called that, as well – did not dismount, as she desperately did not wish to slay the man who'd sired her, no matter his crimes against her mother and against the ghouls and all of the denizens of the Underworld. In her heart, she knew mercy, which Isobel had taught her, having learned it herself from the actions of Pickman and Sorrow. Did they not have fair cause to slay her, rather than aid in her escape? Sure. She had been half the author of their pain and the subjugation of their race. But even the black hearts of ghouls may feel pity.

"'No, Father,' said Elspeth. 'I have brought too much death this day, and your blood will not also stain my hands. I shall not be the despoiler you have become. That will not be your legacy to me.'

'Thief,' he growled. 'Coward and thief, usurper and witch. You come to take my lands from me, but have not the courage to test your mettle against the rightful *Qqi d'Tashiva*. No whelp of mine would flinch from her final duty, cur.'

"At that, one of Elspeth's lieutenants drew an arrow from his quiver and nocked it, taking aim at Isaac Snow. But she was quick, and she stayed the man's hand. Again, her father cursed her as a coward."

"She should have killed him," said the boy who'd yawned.

"Of a certain," agreed the tow-headed girl.

"That may be. In the years to come, said the woman in the tavern in Sinara, Elspeth would sometimes doubt her choice that day, and sometimes she would wish him dead. But the fact, as this woman would have it, is that she did not kill him, nor did she permit any other to bring him harm. She declared that any who dared touch him would suffer a judgment far worse than death."

"Then what did she do?" asked the boy on the tow-headed girl's right.

"What she did do, child, was bestow upon him a gift."

All three children stared back at her now in stark disbelief.

"No," said the girl.

"Yes," replied the peddler, "if the woman who had been a priestess in a temple of the Elder Ones, and before that a pirate and a smuggler, if she is to be trusted. Though, of course, it may be she was a liar or mistaken or mad, and sure, you may choose to believe or not."

"Then…what did she do?" asked the boy who'd yawned. "I mean, what manner of gift did she give such a wicked man?"

At that the peddler smiled and slowly shook her head. "The woman in the tavern did not say, because she did not know. Her father had never told her, not specifically, but said only that it was a gift that lifted from the shoulders of Isaac Snow all his bitterness and insanity, all of his fury and grief. Elspeth's gift, said the woman in the tavern, restored to him that which he'd held so dear, though *how* this was accomplished we do not know. But he was changed – and changed utterly. Afterwards, Elspeth ordered him escorted to the seven hundred steps and up, up, up…and *up*… to the Gates of Deeper Slumber, where he was sent back to the Waking World to live out the remainder of his days and where he may yet dwell, for none in the Dream Lands have knowledge of what became of him. We can say only, by *this* version of the truth, that he passed beyond the ken of the world."

"That isn't a very good ending," frowned the tow-headed girl.

"It most assuredly isn't," said the boy who'd yawned.

"Not at all," added the boy on the girl's right side.

The peddler tilted her head, and she said sternly, "Do you imagine this is the way of tales, the way of the world, that it is somehow beholden to come with satisfying conclusions? If, indeed, it comes with any conclusions at all?"

The children didn't answer the question. The boy who'd yawned peered over his shoulder at the fire, which was beginning to burn down. The tow-headed girl stared down at her bare feet. And the boy on her right picked at a loose thread in his trousers. Only the girl spoke. She asked the old woman, "Aunty, did Elspeth Snow become the new Queen of Bones and Rags?"

"No, child, she did not. She had no taste for power, though the temptation must have weighed heavily on her soul. Elspeth entrusted Richard Pickman and his compatriots with the future of Thok and with the task of rebuilding Amaakin'šarr. She forsook what remained of the prophecy, vowing never again to be a soldier, and she rode away from Thok and back to the Upper Dream Lands. She took with her the Basalt Madonna, which, I have heard, she carried far across the Middle Ocean and even beyond the Eastern Desert and Irem, City of Pillars. It could not be destroyed, and she dared not entrust it to the hands of any being so mighty *they* could have undone the *Qqi d'Evai Mubadieb*. But she did hide it, and she hid it well. Some say she cast it over the edge of the world, though, personally, I think that is likely an exaggeration."

"And what became of her after that?" asked the girl, not looking up from her feet.

"Some say that she returned at last to Serannian, where she fell in love and bore a daughter, Idonnea, then finally died many years ago. And others say she went to Celephaïs, and still others say that by wielding the Madonna she'd become undying and was permitted a place among the Old Ones in the shining city of Kadath. But these are all rumors, and no more to be trusted than ever rumors should be," and with that, the peddler drew a deep breath and said that she'd told all she could tell in a night.

There were questions from the children, but she did not answer them. She sent the three away to their beds, and then went to the garret room she'd been provided for the night – in exchange for a story. Several of the cats followed her, including the tabby tom, and they stood sentry at the top of the stairs. However, despite her great exhaustion, the peddler did not immediately seek sleep. Rather, she opened the shutters of the garret's single small window, and there in Ulthar, she undressed before the brilliant eye of the moon and before all the icy, innumerable stars that speckle an early autumn evening sky. The night regarded her with perfect indifference, and she regarded it with awe. And the peddler, the seller of notions and oddments, the nameless old woman who wandered the cities on the plains below Mount Lerion, she recalled her mother, and a kindly ghoul named Sorrow, and the last face her father had worn. And she told herself a truer tale than she'd told the children.

The Cats of River Street
(1925)

1.

Essie Babson lies awake, listening to the soft, soft murmur of the Manuxet flowing by, on its way down to the harbor and the sea beyond. Unable to find sleep, or unable to be found *by* sleep, she listens to the voice of the river and thinks about the long trip the waters have made, all the way from the confluence of the Pemigewasset and the Winnipesaukee, and before that, the headwaters at Franconia Notch and faraway Profile Lake in the White Mountains of New Hampshire. The waters have traveled hundreds of miles just to keep her company in the stillness of this too-warm last night of July. Or so she briefly chooses to pretend. Of course, the waters of the river, like all the rest of the wide world, neither know nor care about this sleepless spinster woman, but it's a pretty thought, all the same, and she holds tightly to it.

Some insomniacs count sheep; Essie traces the courses of rivers.

"You're still awake?" asks her sister, Emiline.

"I thought you were asleep," Essie sighs and turns over onto her right side, rolling over to face Emiline.

"No, no, it's too hot to sleep," Emiline replies. "I'm so tired, but it's really much too hot. I'm sweating on my sheets. They're soaked right through with sweat."

"Me, too," says Essie. "Mine, too."

There's only a single window in the second-story bedroom, and both storm shutters are open and the sash is raised. But the night is so still there's no breeze to bring relief, to stir the stagnant air trapped inside the room with the two women.

"Think about the river," Essie tells her sister. "Shut your eyes and think about the river and how cool it must be, out there in the night. Think about the harbor and the bay."

"No, I won't do that," Emiline says. "You know I won't do that. Why would you even suggest such a thing, when you know I won't."

Essie shuts her eyes. The room smells of perspiration and dust, talcum powder, tea rose perfume, and the potpourri they order from a shop in Boston. The latter sits in a bowl on the chifforobe: a salmagundi of all-spice, marjoram leaves, rose hips, lavender, juniper and cinnamon bark, with a little mugwort thrown in to help keep the moths at bay. Emiline insists on having a bowl of the potpourri in every room in the high old house on River Street. She dislikes the smell of the Manuxet and the fishy, low-tide smells of the bay, whenever the wind blows from the east, and also the muddy odor of the salt-marshes, whenever the wind blows from the west or south or north. Essie has never minded these smells, and sometimes they even comfort her, the way the sound of the river sometimes comforts her. But she also rarely minds the scent of the potpourri. Tonight, though, the potpourri is cloying and unwelcome, and it almost seems as if it could smother her, as if it means to seep up her nostrils and drown her.

Emiline is deathly afraid of drowning, which, of course, is why it was foolishness to suggest that thinking of the river might help her to sleep.

Essie rolls onto her back once more, and the box springs squeak like a bucket of angry mice.

"I'm going to buy a new mattress," she says.

And, again, Emiline says, "It's much too hot to sleep." Then she adds, "It's very silly, lying here, not sleeping, when there's work to be done."

"Yes, in the autumn, I think I will definitely buy a new mattress."

"There's really nothing wrong with the mattress you have," says Emiline.

"You don't know," Essie replies. "You don't have to sleep on it. Sometimes I think there are stones sewn up inside it."

"I should get up," whispers Emiline, and Essie isn't sure if her sister is speaking to her or speaking to herself. "I could get some baking done. A pie, some biscuits. It'll be too hot to bake after sunrise."

"Em, it's too hot to bake now. Try to sleep."

Then the door creaks open, just enough to admit their striped ginger tom Horace to the bedroom, and Essie listens to the not-quite inaudible padding of velvet paws against the white-pine floorboards. Horace reaches the space between the women's beds, and he pauses there a moment, deciding which sister he's in the mood to curl up with. The moonlight coming in through the open window is bright, and Essie can plainly see the cat, sitting back on its haunches, watching her.

"Well, where have you been?" she asks the ginger tom. "Making certain we're safe from marauding rodents?"

The cat glances her way, then turns its head towards Emiline.

Emiline calls Horace their "tough old gentleman." His ears are tattered, and there are ugly scars crisscrossing his broad nose and marring his flanks and shoulders, souvenirs of the battles he's won and lost. The sisters have had him for almost seventeen years now, since he was a tiny kitten, since they were both still young women. They found him one afternoon in the alley out back of the Gilman House, hiding behind an empty produce crate, and Emiline named him Horace, after Horace Greeley. It seemed an odd choice to Essie, but she's never asked her sister to explain herself. It isn't a bad name for a cat, and the kitten seemed to grow into it.

"Well, make up your mind," Essie says. "Don't take all night."

"Don't rush him," Emiline tells her. "What's the hurry. It's not as if we're going anywhere."

Downstairs, the grandfather clock in the front parlor chimes midnight.

And then Horace chooses Emiline. He jumps – a little stiffly – up onto her bed and, after sniffing about the quilt and sheets for a bit, lies down near her knees. Essie feels slightly disappointed, but then the cat has always preferred her sister. She sighs and stares up at the fine cracks in the ceiling plaster, concentrating once again on the soft, wet sound of the Manuxet flowing between River and Paine streets. Across from her, Horace purrs himself and Emiline to sleep. After another hour or so, Essie also drifts off to sleep, and she dreams of tall ships and the sea.

2.

The brass bell hung over the shop door jingles, and Bertrand Cowlishaw – proprietor of River Street Grocery and Dry Goods – looks up from his newspaper just long enough to note that it's the elder Miss Babson who's come in. He nods to the woman as she eases the door shut behind her. Though the shades are drawn against the noonday heat, and despite the slowly spinning electric ceiling fan, it's stifling inside the dusty, dimly-lit shop.

"And how are you today, Miss Babson," he says, then turns his attention back to the front page of a two-week old edition of the *Gloucester Daily Times*. Bertrand remembers when it wasn't so hard to get newspapers from Gloucester and Newburyport, and even as far away as Boston, in a timely fashion. He's old enough to remember when the offices of the *Innsmouth Courier* were still in business, and also he remembers when it quietly folded amid rumors of threats from elders of the Esoteric Order, of which it had frequently been openly critical.

"A bit out of sorts, Bert," she replies. "Emiline and me, we're having trouble sleeping again. It's the heat, I suppose. You'd think it would rain, wouldn't you? I can't recall such a dry summer." And then she picks up a can of peaches in heavy syrup and stares at the label a moment before setting it back on the shelf.

"Hot as Hades," Bertrand agrees, "and dry as a bone, to boot. You got a list there, Miss Babson?"

She tells him yes, she certainly does, and takes her neatly-penned grocery list from a pocket of her gingham dress. It's written on the back of a letter from a cousin who moved away to Gary, Indiana several years ago. Essie goes to the counter, stepping around a barrel of apples piled so high it's a marvel they haven't spilled out across the floor, and she gives the envelope to Bertrand.

"I confess, we haven't had much of an appetite," she tells the grocer. "And neither of us wants to cook, the house being as terribly hot as it is."

While Bertrand examines the list, Essie steals a glance at his newspaper, reading it upside down. The headline declares SCOPES FOUND GUILTY OF TEACHING EVOLUTION, and there's a photograph of William Jennings Bryan, smug and smiling for the press. Farther down the page, there's an article on a coal strike in West Virginia and another on the great-grandnephew of Napoleon Bonaparte. Essie Babson tends to avoid news of the world outside of Innsmouth, as it never seems to be anything but unpleasant. In all her forty years, she's not traveled farther from home than Ipswich and Hamilton, neither more than six miles away, as the crow flies.

"Let's see," says Bertrand, as he gathers the items from her shopping list and places them in a cardboard box. "Condensed milk, icing sugar, one can of lime juice, baking powder, raspberry jam, a dozen eggs, a can of lima beans. We do have some nice fresh blueberries, as it happens, if you and – "

"No, no," she tells him. "Just what's on the list, please."

"Very well, Miss Babson. Just thought I'd mention the blueberries. They're quite nice, for baking and canning."

"It's really much too hot for either."

"Can't argue with you there."

"You'd think," she says, glancing again at the July 22nd *Gloucester Daily Times,* "people would want to be properly educated, in this day and age. Even in Tennessee, you'd think people wouldn't put up such a ridiculous fuss over a man just trying to teach his students science."

"Folks can be peculiar," he says, reaching for a box of elbow macaroni. "And when it comes down to religion, people get pigheaded and don't seem to mind how ignorant they might look to the rest of the world. Five cans of sardines, yes?"

"Yes, five cans. Emiline and I enjoy them for our luncheon. And soda crackers, please. Mother and Father, they were Presbyterians, you know. But they prided themselves on being enlightened people."

"Folks can be very peculiar," he says again, adding an orange tin of Y & S licorice wafers to the cardboard box. "And we are talking about Tennessee, after all."

"Still," says Essie Babson.

Just then, Bertrand Cowlishaw's fat calico cat – whose name is Terrapin – leaps from the shadows onto the counter, landing silently next to the cash register. Terrapin isn't as old as Horace, but she isn't a youngster, either. Bertrand has been known to boast that she's the best mouser in all of Essex County. Whether or not that's strictly true, there's no denying she's a fine cat.

"And what about you, Turtle," says Essie Babson. "Has the weather got you out of sorts, as well?" She always calls the cat Turtle, because she can never remember it's name is actually Terrapin.

The cat crosses the counter to Essie, walking over Bertrand's paper and the smug newsprint portrait of William Jennings Bryan. Terrapin purrs loudly and gently butts Essie in the arm with its head.

"Well, then I'm glad to see you, too."

"Molasses? I don't see it on the list, but – "

"Oh, yes please. I must have forgotten to write it down."

Essie scratches behind Terrapin's ears, and the cat purrs even louder. Then, apparently tired of the woman's affection, she retreats to the register and begins washing her front paws.

"Horace," says Essie, "has been acting a little odd."

"Maybe it's the full moon coming on," replies Bertrand. "The Hay Moon's tonight. The tide'll be high."

"Maybe."

"Animals, you know, they're more sensitive to the moon and the tides and whatnot than we are."

"Maybe," Essie says again, watching the cat as it fastidiously grooms itself.

"Well, I'm pretty sure I have everything you needed. If you're absolutely certain I can't interest you in a pint or two of these blueberries."

"No, that's all, thank you."

Bertrand Cowlishaw brings the box to the counter, and Essie checks it over, checking it against her list to be certain nothing's been overlooked. The cat meows at Bertrand, and he strokes its back and waits patiently until Essie is satisfied.

"I'll have Matthew bring these around to you just as soon as he gets back," the grocer tells her. "He had a delivery over on Lafayette, but he shouldn't be long."

Matthew Cowlishaw is Bertrand's only son. Next year, he goes away to college in Arkham to study mathematics, astronomy, and physics, which has always been the boy's dream, and Bertrand has reluctantly given up his own dream that Matthew would one day take over the store when his father retired. His son is much too bright, Bertrand knows, to spend his life selling groceries in a withering North Shore seaport.

"When it's cooler," Essie Babson says, "I'll bake some sugar cookies and bring some around to you. I will, or I'll have Emiline do it. She needs to get out more often. But it's much too hot to bake in this heat. It surely won't last much longer."

"One can only hope not," replies Bertrand. He licks the tip of his pencil, tallies up her bill, and writes it down in his ledger book. He rarely ever uses the fancy new nickel-plated machine he bought last year from the National Cash Register Company in Dayton, Ohio. It's noisy, and the keys make his fingers ache.

Essie gives Terrapin a parting scratch beneath the chin, and the cat shuts its eyes and looks as content as any cat ever has.

"You take care," says Bertrand Cowlishaw.

"Just hope we get a break in this weather," she says, then leaves the shop, and the brass bell jingles as the door opens and swings shut behind her. Bertrand goes back to his newspaper, and Terrapin, having gotten her fill of humans for the time being, leaps off the counter to prowl among the aisles and barrels and bushel baskets.

3.

Frank Buckles sits in his rocking chair on the front porch of his narrow yellow house on River Street, sweating and smoking hand-rolled cigarettes and drinking the bootlegged Canadian whiskey he buys down on the docks near the jetty. He stares at the green-black river flowing between the grey granite-and-mortar quay walls built half a century ago to contain it and keep the water flowing straight down to the harbor, a bulwark against spring floods. The river glistens brightly beneath the summer sun. He dislikes the river and often thinks of selling the house his grandfather built and getting a place set farther back from the Manuxet. Or, better yet, moving away from Innsmouth altogether, maybe all the way up to Portland or Bangor. Sometimes, he thinks he wouldn't stop until he was safely in the Maritimes, where no one had ever heard of Innsmouth or Obed Marsh or the Esoteric fucking Order of Dagon. But he isn't going anywhere, because he lacks the resolve, and what few tenuous roots he has, they're here, in this rotting town the outside world has done an admirable job of forgetting.

Lucky them, thinks Frank Buckles, as he shakes out a fresh line of Prince Albert, then licks the paper and twists it closed. He lights the cigarette with a kitchen match struck on the side of his chair, and for a few merciful seconds the smell of sulfur masks the musky stink of the river. It isn't so bad up above the falls, back in the marshes towards Choate and Corn and Dilly islands, where the waters are broad and still. When he was young, he and his brother Joe would often spend their days in those marshes, digging for quahogs and fishing for white perch, steelhead, and shad. Back there, away from the sewers that spill into the Manuxet below the falls, it was easy to pretend Innsmouth was only a bad dream.

In April of '18, both he and his brother were drafted, and they were sent off to the French trenches to fight the Huns. Joe died less than five months later in the Meuse-Argonne Offensive, blown limb from limb by a mortar round. The very next week, at the Battle of Blanc Mont Ridge, Frank lost his left foot and his right eye, and they shipped what was left of him back home to Massachusetts. Joe's remains were buried in Lorraine, in the American cemetery at Romagne-sous-Montfaucon, in a grave that

Frank has never seen and never expects to see. That his brother was killed and he was mangled only weeks before the end of the war to end all wars is a horrible irony that isn't lost on Frank. And now, seven years have gone by, and both his mother and father have passed, and Frank spends his days sitting on the porch, drinking himself numb, watching the filthy river roll by. He spends his nights tossing and turning, lying awake or dreaming of murdered men tangled in barbed wire and of skies burning red as blood and roses. Sometimes, he sits with a shotgun pressed to his forehead or his mouth around the muzzle, pretending that he'll pull the trigger. But he hasn't got that much courage left anywhere in him. He wonders if there would be time to smell the cordite before his soul winked out, if he would taste it, how much pain there would be in the split second before his brains were sprayed across the wall. He has a stingy inheritance that might or might not be enough to see him through however many years he's left to suffer, and he has the narrow yellow house on River Street. Sometimes, he sobers up enough to do odd jobs about town.

Frank exhales a steel-grey cloud of smoke, and the breeze off the river immediately picks it apart. The breeze smells oily, of dead fish and human waste; it smells of rot.

This is Hell, he thinks. *I'm alive, and this is Hell.* It's an old thought, worn smooth as the cobbles along the breakwater.

> *"Is it better to be a living coward,*
> *Or thrice a hero dead?"*
> *"It's better to go to sleep, my lad,"*
> *The Colour Sergeant said.*

One of the three tortoiseshell kittens – two female, one male – that have recently taken up residence beneath his porch scrambles clumsily up the steps and mews at him. It can't be more than a couple or three months old. He has no idea where the kittens came from, whether they were abandoned by their mother, or if the mother were killed. She might have gotten a belly full of poison left out for the rats. She might have perished under the wheels of an automobile. It could have been a hungry dog, or she might have run afoul of the tribes of half-feral boys who roam the streets and alleys and the wharves, happy for any opportunity to do mischief or cruelty that comes their way. It might simply have been her time. But it hardly matters. Now, the kittens live beneath the porch of his narrow yellow house.

The first is followed by a second, and then the third, the brother, comes scrambling up. The trio is thin and crawling with fleas. The little tom has already lost an eye to some infection or parasite. To Frank, that makes him a sort of comrade in the great shitstorm of the world. Frank has been told that a male tortoiseshell is a rare thing.

"What's it you three want, eh?" he asks them, and they loudly mewl in tandem. "That so?" he replies. "Well, people in Hell want ice water, or so I've heard."

One of the tortoiseshell girls parks herself between his boots, and she begins playing with the tattered laces. When the kittens first showed up, he seriously considered herding them all into an empty burlap potato sack from the pantry, putting a few stones in there to keep them company and weight it down, then dropping the sack into the river. It's what his father would have done with the strays. But the thought passed almost as soon as it had come. Frank Buckles knows he's a sorry son of a bitch, but he's not so heartless that he'd send anything to its death in those foul waters.

He scratches at the stubble on the chin he hasn't bothered to shave in days and stares down at the kitten. Ash falls from his cigarette, but it misses the cat.

"Yeah, okay," he says. "How about you moochers just give me a goddamn minute." Then he gets up and goes inside the dark house. The kittens all line up at the screen door, waiting and watching for Frank's return. After only five minutes or so he comes back with a third of a tin of Holly-brand canned salmon and a chipped china saucer. He empties what's left into the dish and gives it to the hungry kittens. They fall upon it with as much ferocity as any cat has ever shown a fish, living or dead. In only a few moments the saucer is licked clean.

"Greedy little shits," Frank mutters, tossing the empty tin at the Manuxet before sitting back down in the rocker. The chair was built by his paternal grandfather, as a gift to his grandmother, before he signed up with the 8th Massachusetts Volunteer Militia, left his pregnant wife behind, and marched off to die at the hands of a pro-secession mob in Baltimore, on the 19th day of April, 1861. His great grandfather made many chairs and cabinets and tables, and sometimes Frank Buckle wonders where they've all gone, how many have survived the sixty-four years since the man's untimely death.

The kittens, their hunger sated for the time being, have all disappeared back beneath the porch, to the cool shadows below.

"Yeah," Frank mutters, "beat it. The lot of you. Stuff your faces and leave me here holding an empty can. Lotta gratitude that is, you bums."

Lithe and supple lads they were
Marching merrily away –
Was it only yesterday?

Frank Buckle, he sips his illegal whiskey, and he rocks in his grandmother's chair, and he watches the demon sun shining bright as diamonds off the greasy river. He reminds himself that there's always the shotgun he keeps beside his bed, and he tries not to think about where that burning river leads.

4.

She was only fourteen years of age when Annie Phelps took a keen interest in the things that wash up along the sands and shingle beaches of Innsmouth Harbor, the breakwater, and the marshy shorelines to the north and south of the port. The strandings and junk, the flotsam and jetsam of commerce and mishap, the remains of dead and dying creatures, fronds and branches of the kelp and algae forests that grow below the waves. As a child, her parents didn't exactly encourage her boyish fascinations, but neither did they *discourage* them. When she was eighteen, she would have gone away to study natural history and anatomy and chemistry at a university in Arkham, maybe, or Boston, or even Providence. But there wasn't the money for her tuition. So, she stayed at home, instead, and cared for her ailing mother and father.

Annie didn't marry, preferring always the company of women to that of men. There is talk that she enjoys much more than their *platonic* company. However, in a shadowed and ill-starred place like Innsmouth, there are always far darker rumors than whispers of Sapphic passion to provide the grist for clothesline gossips. She was twenty-eight years when the influenza of '18 claimed Charles and Beulah Phelps, and afterwards she sold their listing Georgian house on Hancock Street and took up residence in three adjoining rooms in Hephzibah Peabody's boarding house on River Street. Her study and bedroom both have excellent views of the gurgling Manuxet.

Annie Phelps makes a modest living as a seamstress and a typist, keeping back most of the income from the sales of the house on Hancock for that proverbial rainy day. But her passion has remained for those treasures she finds on the shore, and hardly three days pass that she doesn't find time to make her way down to the fish markets or past the waterfront, where few women dare to venture alone, to see what the boats or the tides or a fortuitous storm have hauled in to arouse her curiosity. Most of the fishermen and fishmongers, the sailors, boatwrights, deckhands, and dockworkers, know her by sight and leave her be.

This day, this sweltering late Monday afternoon in July, she sits at her father's old roll-top desk, in her study, a small room lined with shelves loaded down with books and jars of biological specimens she's pickled in solutions of formaldehyde. There are squid and sea cucumbers, eels and baby dogfish. Among the books and jars, there are also the bones of whales and dolphins, the jaws of a Great White shark, the skull and shell of a loggerhead sea turtle. There are also fossils and minerals sent to her by correspondents – of which she has many – from as far away as Montana, California, and Mexico. The pride of her collection is an enormous petrified whale vertebra from the Eocene of Alabama, fully two feet long. She pays Mrs. Peabody a little extra to allow her to keep this cabinet of oddities, but that doesn't prevent the old woman from regularly grousing about Annie's peculiar collection or the unpleasant odors that sometimes leak from beneath her door.

Annie Phelps has four cats: a black-and-white tom she's named Huxley; a fat grey tom with one yellow eye and one blue eye, whom she's named Darwin; a perpetually thin calico lady, Mary Anning; and, finally, the skittish young girl she christened Rowena after a Saxon woman in *Ivanhoe*. When she's not entertaining a friend or a lover, the cats are all the companionship she needs, even if the apartment is rather too small for all five of them, and even though they claw her mother's already threadbare heirlooms and leave the rooms smelling of piss. The cats are another thing she pays Mrs. Peabody extra to overlook. Were it not for the fact that it's getting harder and harder to find lodgers, the landlady likely would not be willing to make these concessions to Annie's eccentricities.

On this afternoon, she sits drinking a lukewarm glass of lemonade, spiked with a dash of Jamaican ginger, the jake she gets from a pharmacist over on Federal. Annie is very careful how often she imbibes, because she's well aware of the cases of paralysis, and even death, that have resulted from excessive use of the extract.

Darwin and Huxley are both perched on the back of the roll-top. Darwin has scaled a stack of monographs on malacology and the hydromedusae of coastal New England. Meanwhile, Huxley has wedged himself between one of her compound microscopes and a copy of Lyell's *Geological Evidences of the Antiquity of Man*. Both cats are purring loudly and watching as she composes a letter to Dr. Osborn at the American Museum. Occasionally, she'll send him a few of her more intriguing specimens and is proud that some have become permanent additions to the museum's collections in Manhattan.

"What will he think of this piece, Mr. Darwin?" she asks the cat. "Frankly, I think it may be the most fascinating and curious object I've sent him yet."

Darwin shuts his yellow-green eyes.

"Yes, well, what do you know, you chubby old fool?"

Annie stops writing and stares at the jawbone in its cardboard box, cradled in wads of excelsior. It's a bit worn from having been rolled about in the surf, but is unbroken and still has all its teeth. At first glance, she took it for the jaw of a man or woman, some unfortunate soul drowned in the harbor or the cold sea beyond the Water Street jetty. But that impression was fleeting, lasting hardly longer than the time it took her to pick the bone up off the sand. It's much too elongate and slender to be the jaw of any normal human being, and both the condyle and the coronoid process are all but absent. The mental protuberance of the mandibular symphysis is almost blade-like. But the teeth are the strangest of all the strange jawbone's features. Instead of the normal adult human compliment of four incisors, two canines, and eight molars, the teeth are homodont – completely undifferentiated – and more closely resemble the fangs of a garpike than those of any mammal.

Standing at the edge of the murky harbor, low waves sloshing insistently against the shore, Annie Phelps was briefly gripped by an almost irresistible urge to toss the strange bone away from her, to give it back to the sea from whence it had come. To be rid of it. She squinted through the mist, out past the lines of ruined and decaying wharves, at the low dark line of rock that the people of Innsmouth call Devil Reef. Growing up, she heard all the tales about the reef, yarns of pirate gold, sirens, and sea demons, and she knows, too, of the locals who compete in swimming races out to the granite ridge on moonlit nights, a sport sponsored by the Esoteric Order, a religious sect who long ago took over the Masonic Hall at New Church Green.

But she didn't throw the bone away. She carefully wrapped it in newspaper and added it to her basket with the other day's finds.

Annie Phelps is a rational woman of the twentieth century, a woman of science and reason, even if her circumstances mean that she will never be more than an amateur naturalist. She is not bound by the fearful, superstitious ways of so many of the people of the town, all those citizens of Innsmouth who mistake the effects of inbreeding, disease, and poor nutrition among the Marshes, Eliots, Gilmans, Waites, and other old families of the town for some metaphysical transformation brought about by the secretive rites and rituals of the Order of Dagon – as certainly a witch-cult as any described in the scholarly works of Margaret Murray. Growing up, she heard all that bushwa, and she sometimes feels anger and embarrassment at the way so many of her neighbors live in terror of whatever goes on inside the dilapidated, pillared hall.

"It certainly isn't a fossil," she says to Huxley, ignoring the less-than-useful Mr. Darwin. "There's no sign whatsoever of permineralization. It's no sort of reptile, and I don't believe it's a fish, neither cartilaginous or osteichthyan. But I can't believe it's a mammal, either."

If the cat has an opinion, he keeps it to himself.

Annie writes a few more lines of her letter –

I am very grateful for the copy of your description of Hesperopithicus, *though I must confess it still looks to me very like a pig's tooth.*

– and then she glances at the jawbone again.

"The water gets deep out past the reef," she says to Huxley and Darwin, "and who knows what might be swimming around out there."

The cats purr, and Huxley begins vigorously cleaning his ears.

The enclosed specimen has entirely confounded all my best attempts at classification. Beyond the self-evident fact that it resides somewhere within the Vertebrata, *I'm entirely at a loss.*

Sometimes, Annie dares to imagine she will one day find something entirely new to science, and Dr. Osborn – or someone else – will name the new animal or plant after her. She stares at the jaw and considers a number of appropriate Latin binomina, if it should prove to be something novel, finally settling on *Deinognathus phelpsae,* Phelp's terrible jaw. She likes that. She likes that very much.

But then she feels the prickling at the back of her neck and along her forearms, and the sinking, anxious feeling she first experienced the day she found the bone, and she quickly looks away and tries to focus on finishing the day's correspondence:

…and at any rate, I hope this letter finds you well.

Outside, there's a sudden commotion, a loud splashing from the river, and Annie sets her pen aside and goes to the window to see what it might have been. But there's nothing, just the waters of the Manuxet swirling past the boarding house, dark and secret as the coming night.

"Someday," she says to the cats, "I'm gonna pack up and leave this place. You just watch me. Someday, we're gonna get out of here."

5.

Ephraim Asher Peaslee closes his wrinkled eyelids, sixty-one years old and thin as vellum paper, sinking into the sweet rush and warm folds of the heroin coursing through his veins. All the world bleeds to white, and he could well be staring into the noonday sun, patiently waiting to go mercifully blind, so bright does the darkness around him blaze. But it doesn't blind him. It doesn't ever blind him, and neither does it burn him. He lies cradled in the worn cranberry velvet of the chaise lounge in the parlor of his house at the corner of River and Fish streets, directly across from the shattered arch of the Fish Street Bridge. The heavy drapes are drawn, like his eyelids, against the last dregs of twilight, against the rising Hay Moon, Corn Moon, Red Moon, goddamn Grain Moon, whichever folk name suits your fancy. None suit his. The moon is a cruel cyclopean eye, lidless, watchful, prying, and this night it will drag the sea far inland, swelling the harbor and tidal river all the way back to the lower falls. It won't be the kindly, obscuring white of his opiate high, but will lie orange and bloated, low on the horizon. It will scrape its cratered belly against the sea, hemorrhaging for all the bloodthirsty mouths that lie in wait, always, just below the waves. Oh, Ephraim Asher Peaslee has seen so *many* of those slithering, spiny things, has drowned again and again in their serpent coils. He's been kissed by every undertow and riptide, dragged down screaming to bear witness to abyssal lands no human man ever was meant to see. Right now, this evening, he pushes back against those thoughts, awakened by the rising moon. He tries to cling to nothing but the heroin, the forever white expanse laid out before him after the needle kiss. The radio's on, "I'll Build a Stairway to Paradise," and the music makes love to his waking alabaster dream. *It's madness to be always sitting around in sadness, when you could be learning the steps of gladness.* He folds his bony hands in supplication, in prayer to St. Gershwin and the ghost of Guglielmo Marconi and the Crosley Model 51, that they have graced him with this balm, a sacred ward against the memories and the nightmares and the long hours to come before dawn. God bless, and take your choice of gods, but surely, please, bless the pharmaceutical manufacturers in faraway eastern Europe, in Turkey and Bulgaria, god bless the Chinese farmers and poppy fields, where moralizing tyrants have not yet obliterated his ragged soul's deliverance from the abominations of Innsmouth. Pray a rosary for the white powder that ferries him away to Arctic wastes, Antarctic plains, where water is stone and nothing can swim through those crystalline rivers. *I won't open my eyes,* thinks Ephraim Asher Peaslee. *I won't open my eyes until morning, and maybe not even then. Maybe I will never again open my eyes, but fall eternally, perpetually, into the saving grace of the heroin light.* Then he hears the rising moon, a sound like the sky being torn open, like steam engines and furnaces, and he turns his face into a brocade pillow, wishing he were able to smother himself, but knowing better. He's a failed suicide, several times over; a coward with straight razor and noose. And trying not to hear the moon or the sluice of the rising tide, trying only to drown in white and ancient snow and the fissured glaciers that course down the basalt flanks of Erebus, there is another sound, past the radio – *Dance with Maud the countess, or just plain Lizzy. Dance until you're blue in the face and dizzy. When you've learn'd to dance in your sleep, you're sure to win out* – past crooning and tinny strings, there is the thunder, earthquake, sundering purr of Bill Bailey, his gigantic Maine Coon, twenty-five pounds if he's an ounce. Bill Bailey, raised up from a kitten, and now he comes heroic, thinks the heroin addict hopefully, to pull my sledge up the crags of a dead and frozen volcano in the South Polar climes, Mr. Poe's Mount Yaanek, where the filthy, unhallowed Manuxet never, never will do them mischief on this hot August night. Risking so many things – his shredded sanity not the least of all – Ephraim Asher Peaslee opens his eyes, letting the world back in, releasing his desperate hold on the white. He rolls over, and Bill Bailey stands not far from the cranberry chaise, watching him, waiting cat-patient, those amber eyes secret filled. "You hear it, too, don't you? We ought to have run. We ought to have packed our bags and taken that rattletrap bus away to Newburyport. They'd have let us go. They have no use for the likes of us. They be *glad* to be rid of us." The cat merely blinks, then sets about licking its shaggy chocolate coat, grooming paws and chest. "You *do* hear it, I *know* you do." And then, close to tears and disappointed by the cat's apparent lack of concern, by Bill Bailey's usual pacific demeanor, the old man once more turns away and presses his face into the cushion. Sure, what has a cat to fear from the evils of an encroaching, salty sea? A holy temple child of Ubaste, privy to immemorial knowledge forever set beyond the ken of loping apes fallen from African trees and the grace of Jehovah. Bill Bailey purrs and bathes and does not move from his appointed station by the chaise. And Ephraim Asher Peaslee tries to give himself back to the white place, but finds that, in the scant handful of seconds it took him to converse with the cat, the luminous White Lands have deserted him. Left him to his own meager devices, none of which are a match for the monsters the mad and unholy men and women of the Esoteric Order see fit to call forth on nights when the moon sprawls so obscenely large in the Massachusetts heavens. Their oblations and devotions that rot and gradually discard their human forms, sending those lost souls tumbling backwards, descending the rungs of the evolutionary ladder towards steamy Devonian and Carboniferous yesteryears, muddy swamp pools, silty lagoons, dim memories held in bone and blood and cells of morphologies devised and then abandoned two-hundred and fifty, three hundred million ago. Ephraim Asher Peaslee of No. 7 River Street shuts his eyes more tightly than, he would say, he ever has shut his eyes before, skating his hypodermic fix down, down, *down,* but not down to the sanctuary of his alabaster realms. Some door slammed and bolted shut against him, and, instead, he has only clamoring, fish-stinking recollections of the waterfront, the docks where beings no longer human cast suspicious, swollen eyes towards interlopers. Grotesque faces half glimpsed in doorways and peering out windows. Shadows and murmurs. The squirming green-black mass he once caught a fleeting sight of before it slipped over the edge of a pier and, with a plop, was swallowed up by the bay. The chanting and hullabaloo that pours from the old Masonic Hall. All of this and a hundred other images, sounds, and smells burned indelibly into his mind's eye. Shuffling hulks. Naked dancers on New Church Green, seen on stormy, starless nights, whirling devil dervishes. *All you preachers who delight in panning the dancing teachers, let me tell you there are a lot of features of the dance that carry you through the gates of Heaven!* So many other citizens might turn their heads and convince themselves they've seen nothing, and anyway, what business is it of theirs, the pagan rites of the debased followers of Father Dagon and Mother Hydra? Oh, old Ephraim Asher Peaslee, *he* knows those names, because he can't seem to shut out the voices that ride between the crests and troughs. Out there, as night comes on and the last scrap of sunset fades, he prays to his own heathen deities, the narcotic molecules in his veins, the radio, to keep him insensible for all the hours between now and dawn. And Bill Bailey stands guard, and listens, and waits.

6.

When even the solar system was young, a fledgling, Pre-Archean Earth was kissed by errant Theia, daughter of Selene, and four and a half billion years ago all the cooling crust of the world became once more a molten hell. In that mighty collision, Theia was obliterated for her reckless show of affection and reborn as a cold, dead sphere damned always to orbit her intended paramour; she a planet no more, but only a satellite never again permitted to touch the Earth. And so it is that the moon, spurned, scarred, diminished, has always haunted the sky, gazing spitefully across more than a million miles of vacuum, hating silently – but not *entirely* powerless.

She has the tides.

A dance for three – sun, moon, and earth.

She can pull the seas, twice daily, and twice monthly her pull is vicious.

And so she has formed an alliance with those things within the briny waters of the world that would gain a greater foothold upon the land or would merely reach out and take what the ocean desires as her own.

For the ocean, like the moon, is a wicked, jealous thing.

Hold that thought.

Cats, too, have secrets rooted in antiquity and spanning worlds, secret histories known to very few living men and women, most of whom have only read books or heard tales in dreams and nightmares; far fewer have for themselves beheld the truth of the lives of cats, whether in the present day or in times so long past there are only crumbling monuments to mark the passage of those ages. The Pharaoh Hedjkheperre Setepenre Shoshenq's city of Bubastis, dedicated to the Cult of Bast and Sekhmet, where holy cats swarmed the temples and were mummified, as attested by the writings of Herodotus. And the reverence for the *Tamra Maew* shown by Buddhist monks, the breeds sacred to the Courts of Siam, the *Wichien-maat, Sisawat, Suphalak, Khaomanee,* and *Ninlarat.* In the Dream Lands, the celebrated cats of Ulthar, whom no man may kill on pain of death, and, too, the great battle the cats fought against the loathsome, rodent-like zoogs on the dark side of the moon.

Cats upon the moon.

Star-eyed guardians whose power and glory has been forgotten, by and large, by humanity, which has come to look upon them as nothing more than pets.

The stage has been set.

Here's the scene:

All the cats of Innsmouth have assembled on this muggy night, coming together at a designated place within the shadowed, dying seaport at the mouth of Essex Bay, south of Plum Island Sound, and west of the winking lighthouses of Cape Ann. The sun is finally down, and that swollen moon has cleared the Atlantic horizon to shine so bright and violent over the harbor and the wharves, over fishing boats, the meeting hall of the Esoteric Order of Dagon, and over all the gabels, balustrades, hipped Georgian and slate-shingled gambrel rooftops, the cupolas and chimneys and widow's walks, the high steeples of shuttered churches. The cats take their positions along the low stone arch of Banker's Bridge, connecting River Street with Paine Street, just below the lower falls of the Manuxet. They've slipped out through windows left open, through attic crannies and basement crevices, all the egresses known to cats whose "owners" believe they control the comings and goings of their feline charges.

The cats of Innsmouth town have come together to hold the line. They've come, as they've done twice monthly since the sailing ships of Captain Obed Marsh returned a hundred years ago with his strange cargoes from the islands of New Guinea, Sumatra, and Malaysia. Strange cargoes and stranger rituals that set the seaport on a new and terrible path, as the converts to Marsh's transplanted South Sea's cult of Cthulhu called out to the inhabitants of the drowned cities beyond Devil Reef and far out beyond the wide plateau of Essex Bay. They sang for the deep ones and all the other abominations of that unplumbed submarine canyon and the halls of Y'ha-nthlei and Yoharneth-Lahai. And their songs were answered. Their blasphemies and blood sacrifices were rewarded.

Evolution spun backwards for those who chose that road.

And even as the faithful went down, so did the deep ones rise.

On these nights, when the spiteful moon hefts the sea to cover the cobble beaches and slop against the edges of the tallest piers, threatening to overtop the Water Street jetty, on *these* nights do the beings called forth by the rites of the Esoteric Order seek the slip past the falls and gain the wet-lands and the rivers beyond Innsmouth, to spread inland like a contagion. On *these* nights, the Manuxet swells and, usually, is contained by the quays erected when the city was still young. But during *especially* strong spring tides, such as this one of the first night of August 1925, the commingled sea and river may flood the streets flanking the Manuxet. And things may crawl out.

But the cats have come to hold the line.

None among them – not even the very young or the infirm or the very old – shirk this duty.

Essie and Emiline Babson's tom Horace is here, as is shopkeeper Bertrand Cowlishaw's plump calico Terrapin. The three tortoiseshell kittens have scrambled out from beneath Frank Buckle's front porch to join the ranks. All four of Annie Phelps' cats – Darwin and Huxley, Mary Anning and Rowena – are here, and a place of honor has been accorded Mister Bill Bailey, the heroin addict Ephraim Asher Peaslee's enormous Maine Coon. Bill Bailey has led the cats of Innsmouth since his seventh year and will lead them until his death, when the burden will pass to another. *All* these have come to the bridge, and five score more, besides. The pampered and the stray, the beloved and the neglected and forgotten.

By the whim of gravity, the three celestial bodies have aligned, sun, moon, and earth all caught now in the invisible tension of syzygy, and within an hour the Manuxet writhes with scaled and slimy shapes eager and hopeful that this is the eventide that will see them spill out into the wider world of men. The waters froth and splash as the deep ones, hideous frog-fish parodies of human beings, clamber over the squirming mass of great eels long as Swampscott dories and the arms of giant squid and cuttlefish that might easily crush a man in their grip. There are sharks and toothsome fish no ichthyologist has ever seen, and there are armored placoderms with razor jaws and lobe-finned sarcopterygians, believed by science to have vanished from the world aeons ago. Other Paleozoic anachronisms, neither quite fish nor quite amphibians, beat at the quay with stubby, half-formed limbs.

The conspiring moon is lost briefly behind a sliver of cloud, but then that obstructing cataract passes from her eye and pale, borrowed light spills down and across the Belgian-block paving running the length of River and Paine, across all those rooftops and trickling down into alleyways. And there are those few, in this hour, who dare to peek between curtains pulled shut against the dark, and among them is Annie Phelps, distracted from her reading by some noise or another. She sees nothing more than the water growing perilously high between the quays, and she's grateful she has nothing of value stored in the basement, not after the flood of '18, when she lost her entire collection of snails and mermaids' purses, which she'd unwisely stored below street level. But she sees nothing more than the possibility of a flood, and she reminds herself again how she should move to some village where there would be crews with sandbags out on nights like this. She closes the curtain and goes back to her books.

Two doors down, Mr. Buckles sits near the bottom of the stairs, his 12-gauge, pump-action Browning across his lap. He carried the gun in France, and if it was good enough to kill Huns in the muddy trenches it ought to do just damn fine against anything slithering out of the muck to come calling at his door. The shotgun is cocked, both barrels loaded; he drinks from his bottle of whiskey and keeps his eye open. Even in the house he can smell the stench from the river, worse times ten than it ever is during even the hottest, stillest days.

On Banker's Bridge, Bill Bailey glares with amber eyes at the interlopers, as they surge forward, borne by the tide.

Farther up the street, Essie Babson looks down at the river, and she sees nothing at all out of the ordinary, despite what she plainly *hears*.

"Come back to bed," says Emiline.

"You didn't hear that?" she asks her sister.

"I didn't hear anything at all. Come back to bed. You're keeping me awake."

"The heat's keeping you awake," mutters Essie.

"Have you seen Horace?" Emiline wants to know. "I couldn't find him. He didn't come for his dinner."

"No, Emiline. I haven't seen Horace," says Essie, and she squints into the night. "I'm sure he'll be along later."

Bill Bailey's ears are flat against the side of his head. The eyes of all the other cats of Innsmouth are, in this moment, upon him.

Above his store, Bertrand Cowlishaw lies in his bed, exhausted from a long, hot afternoon in the shop, by all the orders filled and the shelves he restocked himself because Matthew was in and out all day, making deliveries. Bertrand drifts uneasily in that liminal space between waking and sleep. And he half dreams about a city beneath the sea, and he half hears the clamor below the arch of Banker's Bridge.

Bill Bailey tenses, and all the other cats follow his lead.

Something hulking and only resembling a woman in the vaguest of ways lurches free of the roiling, slippery horde, rising to her full height, coming eye to eye with the chocolate Maine Coon.

It's eyes are black as holes punched in a midnight sky.

Ephraim Asher Peaslee floats, coddled in the gentle, protective arms of Madame héroïne; after a long hour of pleading, he's been permitted to reenter the White Lands, where neither the sea nor the moon nor their demons may ever come. He isn't aware that Bill Bailey no longer sits near the cranberry velvet chaise lounge. And the radio is like wind through the branches of distant trees, wind through a forest in a place he but half recalls. He is blissfully ignorant of the rising river and the tide and the coming of the deep ones and all their retinue.

The scaled thing with bottomless pits for eyes opens its mouth, revealing teeth that Annie Phelps would no doubt recognize from the jaw she found on the shingle. Dripping with ooze and kelp fronds, its hide scabbed with barnacles and sea lice, the monster howls and rushes the bridge.

And the cats of Innsmouth town do what they have always done.

They hold the line.

They cheat the bitter moon, with claws and teeth, with the indomitable will of all cats, with iridescent eyeshine and with a perfect hatred for the invaders. Some of them are slain, dragged down and swallowed whole, or crushed between fangs and gnashing beaks, or borne down the riverbed and drowned. But most of them will live to fight at the next battle during New Moon spring tide.

Bill Bailey opens the throat of the black-eyed beast that once was a woman who lived in the town and cared for cats of her own.

Mary Anning is devoured, and Annie Phelps will spend a week searching for her.

One of the kittens from beneath Frank Buckles' front porch is crushed, its small body broken by flailing tentacles.

But there have been worse fights, and there will be worse fights again.

And when it is done and the soldiers of Y'ha-nthlei and Dagon and Mother Hydra have all been routed, retreating to the depths beyond the harbor, beyond the bay, when the cats have won, the survivors carry away the fallen and lay them in the reeds along the shore of Choate Island.

When the sun rises, there is left hardly any sign of the invasion, or of the bravery and sacrifice of the cats. Some will note dying crabs and drying strands of seaweed washed up along River and Paine streets, but most will not even see that much.

The day is hot again, but by evening rain clouds sweep in from the west, and from the windows of the Old Masonic lodge on New Church Green the watchers watch and curse. They say their prayers to forgotten gods, and they bide their time, patient as any cat.

M Is for Mars

1. The Proposition

This is likely not the most appropriate place or time to recount the numerous mistakes and misfortunes that had led me from the relative comfort and civilization of Herschel City to the squalor and disrepair of the Kayne agradome, some fifteen hundred kilometers east of Herschel, where the highlands drop away to the ragged edges of the Elysium Planitia. Geologists tell us it was once the shore of the great Martian ocean, billions of years ago, and they can show you the rocks and the fossils to support their claims. They can point to the winding course and exposed strata of the great Ma'adim Vallis, where it opens out onto the dry lake bed that is Gusev Crater, just east of Kayne. But no amount of geology or rumors of lost waterways can serve to make the frontier seem anything less than desolate, or conjure the sense that there were ever truly flowing rivers or waves breaking against those parched stones. But I am Marsborn, and so everything I know of the sea is secondhand knowledge.

It does not matter how I came to find myself living in Kayne, teaching math and reading and geography to the children of dew farmers and mechanics, living above a junkyard in a two-room housing module that was already an antique before my mothers were born. It only matters that I did, and that I was there on that windy night when they brought the waste runners in, three days past the summer solstice. They'd been found by a prospecting gang, somewhere in the hills out beyond the marker buoys. By the time the pair reached Kayne they were both unconscious and as near to death as any woman goes without slipping across. Their suits had failed or been breached (I never learned which), and both were suffering advanced decompression. The prospectors claimed the pair were still somewhat cognizant when they were discovered, huddled together inside a wrecked crawler, bogged down at the lip of a dust sink. The vehicle's tracks led off to the north, consistent with what the prospectors said the women had told them before finally losing consciousness. The runners both died before dawn. It is a wonder they lived as long as that, and it is a goddamned mercy they did not live any longer.

There would be an official inquest the next day, before the bodies were incinerated, and I had been asked by the dome constable to be present, so I'd headed back to my module above the junkyard to try and get a few hours sleep. I was already in bed and only half-awake when someone began pounding on my door. I rolled over and stared up through the dark for a few moments at the low ceiling, listening to the insistent knocking, wishing whoever it was would give up and go away. But they did not, and after five minutes or so I shouted for them to please stop banging at the door, that I was getting dressed. I pulled on my robe, stubbed my left big toe on a loose floor panel, and finally found the light switch, which immediately flooded the mod with the loathsome greenish-white radiance from the overheads. In that stark light, everyone looks like a corpse. By this time, the impatient knocking had resumed, even louder than before, and when I finally reached the entryway and slid back the bolt, opening the door only partway, I was greeted by the dark, deep-set eyes and hollow cheeks of my landlord, Narmeen Jericho. There were others with her, but I could not at first guess who they might be – only faint, uneasy silhouettes in the night, four or five bodies crowded onto the narrow catwalk outside the mod.

"Professor," Narmeen said, slurring the way she did when she'd been drinking, "we would like a word with you."

"We?" I asked, squinting at the faces I could not quite make out. "*Who* is *we,* and why the hell are you waking me at this hour? I have classes tomorrow, and the inquest."

"Oh, we already know about the inquest," Narmeen replied quickly. "We have heard you spoke with the prospectors, and that is why we would please now speak to you."

I glanced at the clock on the wall above the bed. The sun would be up in less than two hours.

"And there's a very good reason this can't wait until tomorrow?" I asked, and Narmeen Jericho frowned and tugged nervously at the frayed collar of her green coveralls. She was a heavyset woman, and as near I could tell had never in her life had dealings with a bar of soap.

"You spoke with the prospectors," she said again.

"Yes, I did," and one of the women crowded in behind her sneezed very loudly.

"Then we will speak to you *now*, Professor," she said, and at that Narmeen pushed the door the rest of the way open, shoving me back a step or two. I had long since grown accustomed to her manners, or rather the complete lack thereof. She'd grown up in Kayne, and her birth mother had owned the scrapyard before her. Narmeen's swap mother died in a federal prison down in Molesworth, a few years after she gutted a woman in a barroom brawl. Narmeen was rough, even for the frontier, and I'd long since learned not to expect much in the way of tact or consideration from her. It was usually best just to wait her out, like an autumn dust storm or a bad case of intestinal flu. Sooner or later, she would be done with me and move along.

Five or six minutes later, we were all sitting around what passed for both my desk and dinner table – an empty cargo crate that had once ferried several dozen rolls of polyform insulation all the way from Earth and then halfway around Mars before finally winding up in Kayne and Narmeen's dump heap. By the buzzing fluorescent light of my quarters, the five women I'd been unable to recognize in the dark resolved into familiar, and generally unwelcome, faces. There were only two chairs, and I took one and Narmeen Jericho took the other, leaving the rest to stand or sit on the floor or lean against the dingy plastic walls of the module.

"You spoke with the prospectors," Narmeen said for the third time. "We heard *they* talked to you, that they told you what it was the runners said out there on the flat. We thought maybe you wouldn't mind sharing."

I rubbed at my eyes, wishing for a strong cup of tea, thinking about putting on a kettle because the possibility of getting more sleep before work was starting to seem unlikely. Narmeen had a pebble in her shoe, as people say in Kayne, and she'd probably be another hour or two getting it all the way out again. I squinted at her across the crate.

"Well," I replied, "I think you'll find I'm a more generous person when I have not just been dragged out of bed."

"You can sleep when they plant you in the cold, cold ground, Professor," snorted Narmeen. One of the others laughed, a pie-faced dew farmer named Mary Sullivan whom I knew as one of Narmeen's regular drinking partners.

"That's so very fucking considerate of you," I sighed, getting up to fill the kettle from my water jug. I didn't offer a cup to any of the interlopers, and, to their credit, none of them asked for one.

"Them prospectors are both holed up in the transit hostel and won't talk," Narmeen said, "else we'd have gone straight to them. But what we heard, well, I didn't want to let it sit till morning."

I glanced over my shoulder at Narmeen Jericho, not bothering to ask her what it was she'd heard, because I figured we would come to that soon enough. As it happened, we came to it sooner than I'd expected.

"A ship from Earth," blurted out a black-skinned, blue-eyed woman I knew only as Cracker. "That's what we heard, that there was a ship from Earth."

Narmeen made an annoyed, grunting noise, clearly unhappy that her role as the group's spokesperson had been usurped by Cracker. I lit the stove with a match and waited for whatever was coming next.

"Yeah," said Narmeen Jericho, "that's what we heard. That those runners found a ship from offworld, somewhere up near the Patera. We heard there were *men* – "

"Men?" I laughed as I filled the tea ball with a stingy quarter scoop of Darjeeling. "You heard there were *men* at Apollinaris Patera, and you think *that's* what the prospectors told me?"

"I think that's *part* of it."

"Just part? Isn't that quite enough?"

There were a few seconds of silence then, and I didn't have to turn and look at Narmeen to know the expression on her face, the anger beginning to stir in those deep-set eyes.

"Got a mouth on her," grumbled Cracker.

"Maybe, Professor, you need to be reminded who it is *rents* you this place," said Narmeen.

"Why?" I asked her, pushing my luck, hanging the tea ball over the side of a mug and waiting for the water to get hot. "You got a line of people out there clamoring to take my place? Some other poor fuck gowed enough to pay you fifty creds a month for this box?"

Mary Sullivan laughed again, and Narmeen Jericho told her to shut the hell up.

"I don't recall anything in my lease," I continued, "requiring me to entertain half the dome at four a.m., or, for that matter, a clause stipulating that I have to be part of your little gossip circle here." A tentative wisp of steam rose from the aluminum spout, and I could feel Narmeen's drunken, embarrassed gaze boring into my back. I wondered which would boil first, the kettle or Narmeen. I didn't make a habit of picking fights with women almost twice my size, and I had no reason not to tell her what I'd heard that afternoon from the prospectors. But I have always had a contrary streak. Otherwise, I might never have left the university and Herschel and ended up teaching agradome brats at the cunt-end of the highlands.

"My sufferance has got limits," said Narmeen, in the breathless half-whisper she usually reserved for difficult customers or particularly bad hangovers. "All I'm asking is to know what you heard, and last I checked, that wasn't no kind of crime or goddamned profanation."

"Maybe we ought to come back tomorrow," muttered Cracker.

"You just shut the hell up and let *me* handle this," Narmeen growled at her. "I thought we had an agreement about *who* was gonna do the talking?"

Before the kettle began to whistle, I lifted it off the flame and filled my mug. "I'm sorry," I said, though I certainly wasn't. But I also wasn't in the mood to be looking for another place to sleep or to end up in the infirmary because I'd picked a fight with Squire Jericho. "It's not like me to be such a poor host," I added, turning to face the women gathered around the polyform crate. Narmeen was glaring down at her pudgy hands, which lay crossed in her lap.

"All I'm asking is what you heard," she said, and the way she sounded, I realized just how close I'd come to a beating. "Unless the constable or the coroner told you to keep it to yourself, and that don't seem likely, Professor, as it's gonna be a public inquest."

I nodded, then shut off the stove. "What I heard from the prospectors, it's not what I'd ever call reliable information. You didn't see those two they brought in, Narmeen. It's a wonder they could have talked at all. Frankly, I don't think any of it's true."

"All the more reason there's no harm in you passing it along to us," said Cracker, and Narmeen raised her head and furrowed her grey eyebrows. If looks alone could do the deed, Cracker would have been a dead woman right then and there, I have no doubt.

"Do you *know* what decompression does to the brain?" I asked Narmeen, ignoring Cracker and the others. "Never mind the delirium brought on by all the pain, or the massive hematomas, or the severe hypoxia caused by oxygen depravation, just stop a moment and consider that both their brains had swollen so badly that the internal pressure had fractured their skulls. Whatever they *said* they saw, I assure you, there's no reason to think that it's anything more than an hallucination."

Narmeen licked her thin lips and looked back down at her hands. "You ain't miserly with all those big damn words, are you, Professor? But then I guess that's what people pay you for."

"They were *raving,*" I told her, "which is nothing shy of a miracle, when you figure the mess their lungs were in, or that their tongues were so badly swollen they were both choking on them. Frankly, maybe the question you *ought* to be asking me right now is whether or not it was the prospectors made the whole thing up."

"Is that what *you* think?" Narmeen wanted to know, then laughed a dry sort of laugh and licked at her lips again. "What the hell would be the percentage in doing that?"

Probably half a dozen or more wise-ass, obvious replies occurred to me, but, instead, I only shrugged and checked on my tea. The hot water was turning the color of a bad bruise, and I considered dipping into my precious supply of sugar cubes.

"People don't do a thing like that unless they got a damn good reason," Narmeen said. "And I can't figure no way they stand to profit from a tale like that."

"It's getting pretty late," another of the women sighed. "Hell, at this point, it's started getting early." She was a habitat tech and the only off-worlder in all of Kayne City, a Pan-Asian immigrant named Sang Hee Trinh who spent her days, and often enough her nights, too, tending the dome's aging atmospherics and biofilters and patching thin spots in its venerable foil skin before they could become actual holes. I had no idea what she was doing tagging along with Narmeen's bunch, but then I have never once claimed to be a particularly keen judge of human behavior. At the time, I just supposed she had her reasons.

"We all got better places to be," Mary Sullivan said, and Cracker nodded.

I took the tea ball from my cup and set it on the edge of the sink, deciding against the sugar. There would be days when I needed it more than I needed it now.

"Do whatever suits you," muttered Narmeen, taking her pipe and a pigskin pouch of britch weed from a pocket of her vest. "But me, I ain't leaving until I hear what I came to hear."

"You're a stubborn lady," I said, taking my cup and returning to my place at the table.

"Professor, you don't even know the half of it," said Cracker, and she rubbed at her bright blue eyes.

I sipped my tea and watched while Narmeen Jericho packed the bowl of her pipe.

"We got as much right to that salvage as anyone else out here," she said, "and if we don't move soon, we'll wind up losing the whole damn thing to one of the big scrappers or the goddamn feds. I don't aim to let that happen. Something like this don't fall into a woman's lap but once in her life, and then only if she's lucky." She lit her pipe, and the air smelled like sulfur and the acrid britch smoke.

"So that's what this is about?" I asked. "Salvage rights?"

"That's exactly what this is about," Narmeen mumbled around the stem of her pipe. I've always hated the smell of britch weed, and the stuff available in Kayne is just about as skunky as it gets. I inhaled the steam coming off my tea, but nothing short of a chemical fire was going to mask the stink of Narmeen's pipe.

"I don't have the grid coordinates for the crawler," I said, "if that's what your asking. That's something they didn't tell me. I got the impression they came across the wreck somewhere between the eastern rim of High Wash and the north edge of Herbert, but you know as well as me, that's a whole lot of ground to cover, a whole lot of nothing."

Narmeen shook her head. "I ain't after the goddamned crawler. It ain't worth risking life and limb for a busted-up buggy that probably isn't worth the fuel it would take to haul it back here, or the oxygen I'd use up looking for the thing. What I'm after, Professor, is what those wasters said they saw on the Patera."

"An earth ship," I said, and my breath sent tiny ripples across the surface of my tea.

Narmeen plucked the pipe dramatically from her lips and sneered at me, then beamed up at the other women. "Jesus, Mary, and Buddha," she grinned, showing off her crooked yellow-brown teeth. "Ain't she a smart one, our dear Miss Fancy-Pants Professor Flanagan, come all the way out here from the shiny lights and amenities of Hershel to bring learning to us poor dumb dustfuckers."

Nobody but Mary Sullivan laughed, but I've always had the impression she's the sort who laughs at her own farts.

"Listen," I said to Narmeen, trying not to cough as the pipe smoke quickly began to fill up the mod. "Here's what I heard. And like I've been saying, if you want my opinion, it's all bullshit. But fuck that. I'm half asleep and tired of looking at you, Narmeen."

"You ain't no damned beauty your own self."

"So I have been told on more than one occasion," I replied, setting my cup down a little too quickly, and Darjeeling sloshed out onto the tabletop. And then I told them what I knew, all of it I could remember, what the two prospectors had told me. They'd come upon the dust crawler, missing a tread and half buried, nose down in a sink, and then they'd found the dying runners locked inside the cockpit. The pair hadn't been in any shape to talk, but, supposedly, they'd talked anyway, rambling on about having been somewhere out on the south slopes of the Apollinaris caldera, where they said they'd seen men and a wrecked transport with Earth registration. They claimed the ship had been sitting at the bottom of some sort of a cavern, and that they'd climbed down to get a better look. After all, they were wasters, the most desperate sort of scavengers, and they weren't about to let an opportunity like this get away from them. The cave was deep, they said. And there were bodies, mostly of men, in and around the transport. But that's as much as the prospectors had been able to make out before the two women had begun to slip away. I told Narmeen again that I didn't believe it, even if I couldn't say who'd made up such a story or why. There were just too many ways it didn't add up. All of them had listened while I talked, not interrupting, and when I was done, Narmeen relit her pipe and then sat staring at the mod's one small window and rubbing her chin.

"Fuck me sideways," she whispered. "You know what that thing would be worth? Hell, just tot up the fuel cells and wiring alone, and – "

"Plenty," I said, "*if* there's anything to it. But that's a long damned way to go to find nothing at all. And consider this, Narmeen. None of the geological surveys of the Patera have ever turned up anything like a cavern big enough to hold a transplanetary. Out on the Tharsis, sure, lots of them. But not out here, and not on that mountain."

"How the hell do you know?" Narmeen frowned and sucked at her pipe.

"I *know* because there's been almost a hundred and fifty years of field surveys, all around the rim, and if there were caverns anywhere on the Patera, they would have long since been logged and mapped, and, for that matter, probably domed over by the feds, *that's* how the hell I know. A cavern that size, that deep, I promise you, it wouldn't have been overlooked."

"Something else to think about," said a woman whose name I didn't know, and who had said nothing at all up to that point. She wore a threadbare green flight suit with the Shimizu-Mochizuki logo stenciled on one sleeve; I figured she'd found it in a rag bin somewhere. "If what they say is true – it being an Earth ship – I mean, whoever sent it's gonna come looking, sooner or later. There will be a retrieval team. There would be a navsat beacon."

"You don't fucking know that for a fact," Narmeen murmured, half to herself.

"No, not for a fact, I don't," the woman in the green flight suit said. "I'm just saying how it's likely the case."

"She's right," I told Narmeen. "And you know salvage law better than I do, so you know if a distress signal's been intercepted, it's hands off. You also need to consider, there aren't many people Earthside with the money laying around to make the trip this far out, so we're likely talking a government ship, or one of the bigger metanationals. And their fleets are off limits to salvors, *de facto,* signal or no signal."

"You weren't *born* here," Narmeen said to me, making it sound like an accusation. "You haven't spent your whole life stuck in this shithole, Professor, and I'd wager, sooner or later, no matter who or what you're hiding from, you'll find a way back to someplace more civilized than Kayne. Rest of us" – and she motioned to the others – "ain't so goddamn fortunate in our prospects. Not unless we happen to get lucky and something like this here falls into our laps, and even then we gotta have the balls not to let it get away from us, law or no law."

And then she stared at me, and I stared into my cup, and I could feel the anticipation coming off Cracker and Mary Sullivan and the rest, even if I had no idea what they were anticipating.

"I've told you what I know," I said, finally, because somehow that minute or so of silence had been the worst of it so far. "Now, unless there's something else – "

Narmeen coughed up smoke, then loudly cleared her throat before wiping her mouth on the back of her left hand. She glanced at Cracker, who sighed and frowned and nodded her head.

"Back in Herschel," said Narmeen, "at that university, you were studying geology, weren't you, Professor? I mean, before you called it quits and all."

I felt something heavy and cold roll over in my belly, and I knew then that they'd come for more than news of whatever I'd heard from the prospectors.

"I studied lots of things," I replied.

"Yeah, but you'd conjured how that would be your trade, ain't that the truth?"

"More or less," I admitted, beginning to guess where Narmeen Jericho was headed with this and wishing I were smart enough to talk my way out of it.

"Right, and that's why you know so much about the Patera and caves and surveys and the like. What we got planned, Professor, someone with your head for rocks, she'd be an asset."

"And just what *have* you got planned, Narmeen?"

She sucked at her pipe a moment, and when I looked at her, she was smiling.

"To try and change our fortunes," she said. "Maybe buy ourselves a little something more than hardscrabble and rust. Maybe. And with you along, well, that has to tip the scales in our favor just a smidgen."

"I'm a schoolteacher," I told her, but only rarely have words seemed more hollow or pointless, or the weight of inevitability pressed down upon me with such determined force. "I'm not a geologist, not by a long shot, and even if I were, I'd not risk trouble with the feds or worse over an illegal salvage."

"It wouldn't be the first time you've run afoul of the law," said Narmeen Jericho, still smiling, and the woman in the shopworn green flight suit laid a wrinkled sheaf of papers on the table in front of me. The topmost page was marked with the bright red stamp of the Council and a magistrate's blue seal.

"How long have you had those?" I asked, as though the question had any relevance.

"Since the first week you showed up here looking for work. We might be a bunch of dumb dustfuckers, Professor, but we do believe in checking up on the folks we let into the dome, the folks we trust with the schooling of our young and such. There's an outstanding warrant on the bottom of that stack, you know that? A warrant from Hershel City for a student named Babette Flanagan, accused of some pretty heinous misdeeds. First time I saw it, truth be told, I like to fainted dead away from shock. Never heard of such goings on."

I looked from Narmeen to the rest, one after the other, and only one or two of them turned away. "But you let me teach your children," I said.

"Well, now, we don't want them growing up to be ignorant, illiterate dustfuckers like their mammas – not when we got a perfectly good professor at hand – just on account of squeamishness and all."

"No call to be a prick about this, Jericho," said Sang Hee Trinh. "You just tell her what we want, what we came here for, and be done with it."

Narmeen stared up at Trinh for a few seconds, and Trinh stared back, and then Narmeen puffed hard at her pipe and rapped the knuckles of her right hand against the table.

"One day, Professor, perhaps I'll even tell you why this mouthy gook cunt here" – and she jabbed a thumb at Sang Hee – "was willing to cross quarantine and throw away any chance she had of ever seeing Earth again. Women will do the damnedest fool things when faced with prison."

"What do you want?" I asked, staring now at the papers lying on my table, not even bothering to wonder how my record had fallen into Narmeen Jericho's hands.

"You make this trip up to the Patera with us, help us find that cave the runners were on about, give a hand with the hard work if it should come to pass, and then keep your gob shut. That's all, Professor. What's more, we'll even cut you in for a full percentage of the take, whatever that might turn out to be."

"And I get these?" I asked, pointing to the papers.

Narmeen furrowed her brow and nodded. "Sure, if you got some need of them. We already made copies. But if what you're asking me is, you do this thing and we'll keep quiet about you being here next time the feddys or some Council bitch comes nosing about, yeah, that's the proposition. Plain and simple, take it or fucking leave it be."

Other things were said, including certain suggestions regarding my testimony at the inquest the next day, and it was dawn before Narmeen and her pack had finally shuffled off to their various dens and burrows. They took the court documents with them, along with the last wild hope that I might have actually managed to escape what had happened back in Herschel. I sat for a while on the catwalk outside the door to my mod, watching the dust drifting through dim shafts of morning, listening as the town woke up and the dome's drive-bots and servos whirred and clanked high above me, opening and closing skylights and recalibrating the solar array according to Sang Hee Trinh's instructions. I am not ashamed to say that I contemplated some of the less painless forms of suicide at my disposal, nor that I had contemplated them many times before. Indeed, looking back on all that has happened since – the horror to come, and the lingering consequences of that horror – my chief regret is that, unlike Narmeen Jericho, I lacked the requisite grit to do what needed to be done.

2. The Inquest

After Narmeen and her company had gone, I did not try to sleep. It likely would have been fruitless, and I feared that if I did manage to doze off again, I would almost certainly oversleep. Classes were set to begin at nine, but I posted a notice on the schoolhouse door advising my students that they could have the day off. I was too exhausted to teach, and as the coroner's inquest was scheduled for one p.m., at best I could have only managed half a day's lessons. I drank black strong coffee and took a couple of the pink and green pills I still use when the nightmares are so bad that I prefer not to sleep. I was first introduced to them by a pharmacist in Molesworth, where I hid myself briefly after my abrupt departure from Hershel City, and ever since they have been a boon or a crutch, depending how one chooses to look upon such things. They remind me that sometimes the low-tech solutions are still the best, as these pills differ very little in composition from the pain-killer ziconitide, which was first manufactured in the early 21st Century from conotoxin, the poisonous secretion of a now long-extinct group of terran marine snails, the Conidae. With a little refinement, ziconitide made from synthesized conotoxin was found to have a curious and beneficial side effect, that of lessening the severity of chronic nightmares and the psychological effects of trauma.

As for exactly what occurred during the inquest, I won't go into much detail here. The transcript is public record and may be accessed by anyone interested in precisely what was said and by whom. I was one of five witnesses called by the District Coroner, an elderly physician named Livia Morton who'd served in the infantry during the war and lost an arm for her trouble. Only a few odd ticks betrayed the mechanical prosthesis she wore. Besides myself, the two prospectors were questioned, as was one of the dome's two doctors, and the local constable, who was also present when the dying dust runners were brought in through the north gate. The prospectors repeated the story of how they'd come across the crawler, bogged down in a sink, and the things they claimed the runners had told them before losing consciousness. The doctor and I testified to the physical condition of the bodies upon their arrival at Kayne. When asked if we had any cause to suspect foul play, we both responded in the negative.

Narmeen and Cracker and Mary Sullivan watched the proceedings from their galley seats, though I can honestly say that nothing I said was in any way altered by their presence or Narmeen's suggestions the night before that I might omit any details that could lead the Coroner or other officials to inter-fere with her salvage plans. I told what I had seen, and I tried my best not to notice the way she scowled and glowered during and after my testimony.

By late afternoon, the jury had returned its verdict, which was simple, perhaps a little too simple given the evidence that had been presented. But these were all women with lives that had been interrupted by the hear-ing, women with crops to tend and machines to repair, women with wives and children and secrets all their own. The deaths of the runners were determined to have resulted from sudden, violent decompression and CO_2 toxicity, following the wreck of their vehicle and the failure of their suits and the crawler's air locks. Coroner Morgan seemed not the least bit inter-ested in the more puzzling aspects of the case; how, for example, the two had managed to survive for so long, when their deaths should have been almost instantaneous, or, for that matter, whether there was any truth to the story of an Earth transport and the corpses of men having been found in an immense cavern at the Patera. All parties were summarily discharged, much to the relief of the prospectors who were expected at a mineral-rights deliberation at Baldet City two days later.

For my part, by the time we were discharged I had little thought for anything but bed. I figured that I could deal with Narmeen later on, and somehow the formalities of the inquest had made the previous night's visi-tation seem hardly more substantial than a particularly lucid bad dream. In the light of afternoon, the thought of my being forced to tag along on some excuse for a salvor expedition was more than simply absurd – it was unthinkable. Other than a few field trips while at university, I'd hardly ven-tured outside a dome in my life. I'd always traveled by zeppelin, even when I made my hurried and illegal exit from Hershel.

Later on, I would tell Narmeen Jericho to go fuck herself, that I knew even she wasn't stupid enough to hand me over to the feds when it might well be years before another suitable and willing teacher showed up this far out on the rim. Not that she was the sort to care much one way or the other about the education of Kayne's children, but once word got out that *she* was the reason I'd been arrested, she'd be blessed and holding aces if her fellow citizens didn't chase her any farther than the Ma'adim foundries. I would go back to my shabby module, back to the corrosion and clutter of the scrapyard, back to my classroom, and by next week the dead waste runners and their crackbrained tales would be old news and half-forgotten. And it is a sad fucking testament to my ability to bullshit myself and underestimate the world's knack for flinging grief my way that by the time I'd left the courthouse, crossed the hub and headed down a side street that led to Narmeen's place I was actually pretty much convinced that this was how the whole mess would spin. Worst case, I thought, I'd soon be looking for new lodgings, which could only be a good thing, once I got past the immediate inconvenience.

I turned down a narrow, unpaved alley, only a few blocks west of the scrapyard, and found myself face-to-face with the offworlder habtech, Sang Hee Trinh. She hadn't been at the hearing, which had not really surprised me; as I've said already, she'd hardly seemed the sort to run with Narmeen's coterie of roughnecks and malcontents. I recognized her at once, and I also noticed that she hadn't changed clothes since leaving my module twelve or thirteen hours earlier. Then I saw she was holding a gun, and all those happy delusions of my life returning soon to its miserable, grinding routine evaporated in the space between one heartbeat and the next.

"Don't scream," she whispered, and I knew just enough about firearms to know the flashing green light on her pistol meant the safety had been toggled off. "Don't you dare go and scream, Professor. Too few thinking women in this cesspit as it is. I'd hate to find myself the cause of there suddenly being one less."

I stared at the barrel of the gun and tried not to wonder how long it would take me to die of a belly wound, or how much it would hurt before I did. "Seems to me," I said, "the blackmail was more than sufficient incentive to take up pirating with Squire Jericho. The firearm might be overstating your case just a grain."

"This isn't about the salvage," she replied. "There's something you need to see, and the way you came across last night, it seemed unlikely you're the sort who'd come running if I only asked nicely."

"And you didn't strike me as the sort who lurks about in alleyways waiting on a chance to do murder."

"Let's try our best not to see it come down to that," she said, then stepped to one side and nodded towards the far end of the alleyway. "Just start walking. Don't look back. I'll be right here behind you."

All these long years later, it still amuses me that what I recall most vividly about being ambushed at gunpoint by the Pan-Asian habtech was that, for the first time since fleeing Hershel, I found myself genuinely aroused by another woman. It wasn't only the fact that she was pretty and clean and appeared to have all her teeth, though these things certainly set her apart from the majority of Kayne City's populace. I'd seen Sang Hee around town since the day I first arrived, and I had gotten a good close look back in my module, so if the unexpected, half-forgotten tingle was purely physical, it was one hell of a delayed reaction. And I'm pretty sure it wasn't her gun, either, or the prospect of imminent bodily harm, as I have not found myself sexually responsive to such scenarios, either before or since. What does seem possible, though, is that my reaction had something to do with the cold determination in her eyes, eyes so brown that they were almost black. Genuine purpose was an uncommon property in Kayne, and I've always been a stooge for passion.

I walked down the alley until she told me to stop. There was an open doorway on my left, an irregular rectangle of deeper shadow framed by crumbling mortar and adobe bricks, and Sang Hee pointed at it with the muzzle of her pistol.

"There's a switch just a little ways inside," she told me. "Flip it, get the lights up, then I'll follow you. And don't try to run, because this hall's a dead end. You should take my word for that, Professor."

"The thought never even entered my mind," I lied, then stepped across the threshold into the building. The air in there was dank and stank of mildew and rats. I did exactly as Sang Hee had instructed, though it took a bit of fumbling about to locate the light switch. There was a loud, insectile buzz, and the bulbs set into the ceiling flickered reluctantly to life. I blinked and shaded my eyes against the sudden glare, and Sang Hee glanced back the way we'd come before stepping through the entryway.

"There's a door a little farther along," she said, and when I turned about, I saw it, a low iris of overlapping steel plates set into the right wall, just a few meters shy of the dead end she had assured me was there. A keypad was mounted next to the door, but the characters were all Chinese.

"I'll give you the code," she said. "You tap it in."

"Sorry. I don't read pinyin," I replied.

"You're kidding me?" she asked. "What the fuck kind of schools they got over in Hershel?"

"Hànyǔ Pīnyīn was a prestige, and my mothers were poor women. I only got the core."

"Then move out of my way, *gweipor,*" she said and prodded me roughly in the ribs with her pistol. I watched while Sang Hee punched seven of the keys, and then there was a stuttering series of clicks and thuds from the wall before the rusty diaphragm spiraled slowly open to reveal a somewhat less starkly lit corridor beyond. Past that, there was a rickety catwalk, worse even than the one rigged up outside my mod, and a ladder leading down to what I assumed was the basement. The iris closed automatically behind us, and the grating of metal against metal made my teeth ache. She surprised me by going down the ladder first, but then again, where the hell was I going to run?

From my vantage point on the catwalk, I looked over the railing into the deep basement and saw a jumbled maze of crates and shelving, exposed sewer pipes and electrical wiring, an assortment of machinery in various stages of decrepitude and disassembly. And near the center of it all, what I recognized at once as a sort of make-shift infirmary, dominated by a shiny grey isolation capsule that, unlike most everything else in the place, seemed a relatively new addition to the basement. One woman was busy at the capsule's control screen, and another sat not far away, perched atop a large aluminum crate with a sonic rifle resting across her lap. I'd never seen either of them before.

"Any minute now," I said, "I know someone's going to decide it's time to show me the courtesy of explaining what's going on and what exactly it has to do with me."

The woman sitting on the crate laughed, then grunted something rude in Portuguese, something that I only half understood, and pointed her rifle at me. Sang Hee Trinh had already reached the bottom of the ladder; she holstered her gun and told me to hurry. The ladder was even more rickety than the catwalk, and I thought with any luck at all the whole damned thing would give way and I'd be killed in the fall.

"The prospectors weren't lying," Sang Hee said, "even if it happens they weren't telling all there was to tell. The waste runners weren't lying, either."

"Fine," I told her, somewhat disappointed to have reached the last rung of the ladder alive and feel solid, hard-packed ground beneath my feet. "But haven't I already agreed to go along on this excursion with Narmeen – "

"This isn't about Jericho," the woman standing by the capsule said without looking away from the patchwork of readouts scrolling across the screen. "But in a moment you'll see that for yourself."

"Trinh, do your friends here have names, or should I feel free to make something up?"

"Why you think our names matter, schoolteacher?" growled the woman with the rifle. "What the fuck difference do our names make to you?"

"George, put down the goddamn gun," Sang Hee snapped back at her, then took my hand and led me between a heap of busted Laskar coils and a stack of warped harvester blades to the clearing where the isotank hovered above the basement floor, seemingly weightless. "Just look inside, Professor, and then we'll talk, *after* you've seen what's at stake."

And so I looked into the tank, because it seemed the only way out of this mess was straight ahead and because, to be perfectly honest, I wanted to know what they were going to so much trouble to hide from the rest of the dome. I don't know what I might have expected I would see, or if I'd had time to even think that far ahead. It hardly mattered, either way. It certainly doesn't matter now. Lying there inside the tube, cradled by a sterile white somaform mattress and jacked into a bewildering assortment of IV lines and data leads and EEG wires, was the battered, but very much living body of a man. A living man on Mars.

3. The Survivor

The last man on Mars died more than twenty years before I was born, only weeks after the trade wars drew to a rather anticlimactic close with the release of the newly developed Klein-Yamada virus. A handful of sprayer hybrots were launched from Phobos Station, and within a few days the contagion had been successfully dispersed across the entire surface of the planet. Metacorporate lawyers and defense ministers on Earth would later claim the virus had merely been intended to cause sterility and impotence in human males, as a means of demoralizing the majority of enemy soldiers. There are still lawsuits pending, half a century later. And, of course, no one of the XY persuasion here on Mars. As the atmosphere has yet to test negative for Klein-Yamada, and no effective vaccine or cure has been found, all male infants carried to term die within the first few months of birth. Most mothers simply choose to abort male fetuses.

I don't know how long I must have stood staring into the tank, slack-jawed and dumbfounded as any local would have been in my place. The city of my birth and my unfinished education might well have bestowed upon me a more or less useless degree of sophistication and civility, but it certainly had not prepared me for the sight of him. I'd seen men, of course, but only in photos and film. Never did I imagine that I would look upon the living, breathing item, so close that I could have reached out and laid a hand on his bare chest were it not for the protective layer of plastic dividing us.

He wasn't young, but neither was he old. He had a light growth of beard, though it was my impression that this was more the result of having been rendered unable to shave than a conscious decision to grow one. His eyes were shut and twitched in his sleep. His hair was clipped very close to his scalp, though I could see that it was, like his beard, a brownish blond. There was a slight hook to his nose and a scar across his forehead. His lips were full and were very slightly parted, somehow increasing the impression that he was only sleeping, only waiting to wake from whatever dreams men have.

"Jesus fucking Christ," I whispered. "Someone please tell me what's going on here."

"The prospectors weren't lying," Sang Hee Trinh said again. "He was found aboard the crawler with the two wasters, already sealed inside this containment tube."

"But I was *there,* when they came through the lock – " I began, and the woman at the screen interrupted me (I never did learn her name).

"Yes," she said, "but the prospectors contacted us the day before they arrived, and we met them a few klicks from the dome. The isotank was transferred then, and they were instructed to continue on to Kayne City with the two dying women. It seemed like an effective enough diversion."

"This *fellow* here," added Sang Hee, "he was brought in through the west locks."

"I don't understand," I said, closing my eyes and turning my head away from the tank, forcing myself to stop staring at its remarkable contents. "I mean, I can see the need for discretion. Certainly," and I opened my eyes again. All three women were watching me now, and it was easy to see that each of them was waiting for whatever reaction would follow on the heels of my initial shock. The woman with the sonic rifle still had her finger on the trigger, and Sang Hee's eyes were still filled with the determination I'd seen in the alleyway. But now it was tempered, I think, by an anxious sort of hope, that she had not made a mistake by bringing me to see their prize.

"There can be no word of what you've witnessed here," the woman at the screen said, and I realized then that I'd seen her before, that she worked as a chemist in the infirmary and apothecary. She was tall, and her black hair had only recently begun to grey. "No word at all, Professor. The Council and the feds have a strict euthanasia policy in place for this particular contingency."

"Jesus," I sighed and looked around for someplace to sit. My legs were beginning to feel weak. "I thought perhaps you *were* Council, or maybe Federal."

"Hardly fucking likely," said the woman with the gun, and Sang Hee glared at her.

"Don't worry," I replied, giving voice to that brash, contrary streak I mentioned earlier. "I never for a moment took *you* for anything more than a thug with a fancy gun." The woman Sang Hee had called George, who couldn't have been more than twenty or twenty-one, narrowed her hard green eyes and spat into the dirt at my feet.

"It's true, Professor," said Sang Hee, stepping in between me and the rifle. "If we gave him over, this man would be as good as dead."

"This *man...*" I began and trailed off. "I think I need a chair, please," I said, and she pointed to a nearby crate and apologized for that being the best she could offer me. I nodded and sat down, suddenly painfully thirsty and wishing for a shot of good whiskey or maybe a strong bowl of tea with brandy.

"Can we count on you?" Sang Hee asked. "Can we trust you not to speak of this to anyone?"

I kept my eyes on the hard-packed dirt floor of the basement, and I believe I may have laughed. "That seems the sort of question you might have bothered asking me *before* I was abducted and shown what I've been shown. Especially considering your trigger-happy friend over there."

"Keep in mind, there's just the one right answer," said the woman with the sonic rifle.

"Well," I replied, "then that rather simplifies the situation, doesn't it?"

Sang Hee sat down on the floor in front of me, and I glanced up at those determined eyes of hers, wondering just what *had* led her to cross quarantine and immigrate, when she'd known full well she'd never again be able to return to Earth.

"This is not the way I would have done things," she assured me, "if we were not so pressed for time. We are *not* thugs, Babette Flanagan, and we are not in this for salvage rights. We are not profiteers." I am certain this is the first time Sang Hee used my given name, which I'd grown unaccustomed to hearing. My students called me Miss Flanagan, and anyone else in the dome, on those rare instances when they had cause to speak with the peculiar woman from the west, the outlander, just called me *Professor*.

I said, "I have never heard of the Council having a euthanasia program – "

"It doesn't matter to us what *you* might or might *not* have heard," George grunted, and then she spat again. "It only matters to us that you can keep your mouth shut and do as you're fucking told."

"Miss Trinh," I said, trying hard to smile, but only managing a pleasant grimace. "I'm sure your gunsel is only doing her job, a job she has either been *paid* to do or has taken upon herself out of the conviction that your cause is just. But, with all due respect, you need to tell her to shut the fuck up, as I have a history of doing very stupid things, when so impelled, with no thought to my own safety. And I assume you need me alive."

"Don't you fucking talk about me like I'm not right here," George growled, but Sang Hee told her to shut up and go check topside, to be sure that no one had followed us in. The woman went reluctantly, but she went all the same, and she took the rifle with her.

When the steel iris had once again spiraled shut, I looked first at Sang Hee and then at the medic. "It's time one or the other of you got around to spelling out what it is you want from me," I said. "And yes, you can trust me not to speak of what I've seen. But I'm weary of trying to figure how the hell you think I fit into this thing."

"There is only so much I'm allowed to tell you," she replied. "And I'm afraid you'll have to accept that, Professor. But what we need is for you to accompany Narmeen Jericho, just as you have agreed to do. I'll be going, as well. I've read your transcripts. I know you have some expertise in geomorphology and seismic tomography, and I know that you once visited the caverns at Arsia Mons."

"That was a very long goddamned time ago, and I was a student. It was just a field exercise. We had guides and never left the marked trails."

"Beggars can't be choosers," she said. "You're the best we have."

"There are geologists at Kayne," I said. "*Certified* geologists."

"There's one hydrologist, one pedologist, and an engineering geologist, and none of them have the sort of training we may need. More importantly, we can't trust them."

"And you think you *can* trust me?"

Sang Hee exchanged uncertain glances with the woman at the isotank's screen. "*I* do," she said. "And there are people who trust my judgment. You are the best we have."

"Is he infected?" I asked and pointed at the burnished capsule hovering only a few feet away.

"No. Not if these readouts are correct," the chemist answered. "Which probably means that he was never exposed. He must not have left the ship."

"The ship from Earth," I added.

"It's the least unlikely way to explain his presence here, don't you think?" asked Sang Hee.

Once, before my indiscretions in Hershel and the indignities and hardships that followed after, I might have felt myself fortunate to have been drawn into whatever misadventures lay ahead. That earlier, vanished me certainly would have felt herself blessed to glimpse a thing so remarkable as a living man on the surface of Mars. But the years since university had taken a weighty toll on the enthusiasm and curiosity of my youth, and at that point I probably had no greater ambition than to stay holed up in my module above the scrapyard, unseen and anonymous to all the world outside. So, having seen the man for myself, it wasn't so much that I still doubted there actually was a derelict transport from Earth somewhere out on the Patera. It's just that I wanted no part in it.

"While we're on the subject of what I do and do not think," I said to Sang Hee Trinh, "I think the fact that those two wasters managed to survive decompression as long as they did is at least as stupefying as Mister Who-the-Hell-Ever-He-Is there. At the inquest, our good Dr. Livia Morton did everything but ignore the question."

"That's one I wish I *could* answer," said the chemist, finally stepping away from the tank's control screen. "I've examined some of the tissue samples myself, with the permission of the coroner."

"So she's in on this, too?"

"Not exactly," Sang Hee replied, and then the chemist continued.

"My best guess, Professor, is that they were dosed with something from the ship, possibly a new drug. Their bloodstreams were loaded down with what appears to be, at least, an unfamiliar isomer of dextrose monohydrate, which seems to have kept their muscles in an almost constant state of contraction. Possibly, it acted as a sort of full-body pressure bandage, minimizing the effects of decompression and so delaying their deaths. They also both had grossly elevated adrenaline levels and – "

" – truthfully," I cut in, "you have no idea *what* kept those poor wretches alive that long."

"Truthfully," she said, "it's utterly fucking baffling. They should have been dead within moments of their suits having failed. We both know that."

I looked back to Sang Hee, and she was watching me, waiting for my reaction, maybe searching for some sign that I thought I was being lied to. I didn't. Having already been told that I would be told only so much, I tended to believe what I was hearing, even if it didn't make a great deal of sense. I nodded and scuffed at the floor with the toe of one boot, leaving a shallow, uneven scrape in the hard clay.

"Are you with us?" Sang Hee asked.

"And I should keep in mind, there's only *one* correct answer to that question."

"There's a great deal at stake here," she said. "You have to believe me when I say that. At the very least, this man's life. And there may be other survivors out there."

Probably, I laughed again. Probably, they could both read the skepticism on my face. "I hope you don't seriously expect me to believe this is some sort of rescue mission, that the two of you and that bitch with the rifle are angels of mercy with nothing but honorable intent. I'd prefer to be credited with just a skid more intelligence, if you don't mind."

"We're both a terrible long way from home, you and I," Sang Hee said to me. "That's the truth, Professor, whether you're measuring the distance in kilometers or AU, in years or experience. Here we both are, an offworlder and an outlander serving out our time in this godforsaken wasteland, scraping by, hoping no one bothers to look at us too hard."

"You shouldn't presume to know *what* I spend my days hoping, Miss Trinh."

"But I *should* sit here and listen to your presumptions? Why is that, Babette?"

There was a long moment when neither of us spoke. The isotank's hover panels began to whine softly, and the chemist immediately went back to her screen.

"See, here's what I think," Sang Hee said, scooting a little nearer to my crate. "I think you *want* to believe there's nothing left for you now, that the most you can hope for is to spend the remainder of your days in this *pena do porco, perdido nisto em nenhuma parte.*"

"It's ironic," I said, drawing another scrape with my boot, "you being the one who keeps Kayne patched together, having such a low opinion of the place."

"No more ironic than a schoolteacher who figures there's nothing left worth learning, nothing left worth trying to understand. You wanted to be a scientist – "

"Yes, I *wanted* to be a scientist, but that was a whole goddamned lifetime ago."

"Not so long ago some part of you doesn't still think to ask how and why when no one else can be bothered. Not so long ago there's not some stingy sliver of you aching to know what the fuck's going on up there at Apollinaris."

Suddenly, the hover panels popped loudly, sparked once, and then stopped whining. The isotank listed alarmingly to one side, and the chemist cursed and frantically tapped at the screen. The basement air began to smell of ozone, but a few seconds later the panels had begun cycling normally again, and the tank righted itself.

"I *know* what this looks like," Sang Hee said, ignoring the noise and the stink and the thin wisps of smoke hanging in the air. She leaned close, speaking slowly now, as though she were afraid I might not comprehend her meaning. "It looks like maybe you've run afoul of seditionists or maybe a cell of anti-Council guerrillas. Am I right?"

"More or less," I admitted, still eyeing the malfunctioning isotank.

"Then bear with me. Because I promise you that's not the case, and you know as well as I do that things are often not what they appear to be at first fucking sight."

"Then you tell me, Sang Hee, what *is* it I'm seeing? What exactly am I missing here? Or do I need to learn the secret handshake before you are allowed to enlighten me?"

She glanced at the woman named George, and then at the chemist busy with the isotank's controls. I imagined I saw silent words passing between them, some heated last-moment debate as to whether or not the outlander was to be trusted. The chemist shrugged and shook her head, and George finally put down her gun. I felt only the smallest shred of relief.

"He's not the only thing the prospectors found on that crawler," Sang Hee said, and she turned away from me and walked across the basement to a low worktable cluttered with tools and grease cans and the disassembled innards of any number of machines. From all that junk she selected a bright green and red Christmas-colored tin that had once held pemmican biscuits. She opened it and removed an oily bundle of rags.

"I'm not going to ask you to believe me," she said. "All I'm asking is that you try and keep an open mind and hear me out." And then she motioned for me to join her at the table. I'd have run, if I'd been given a choice, all the way back to Narmeen's scrapyard and the sanctuary of my hovel. Instead, I walked over and watched while Sang Hee unwound those rags to reveal a roughly triangular chunk of blue-grey stone, small enough to fit snugly into the palm of her hand. One corner had been chipped off, and in the harsh overhead illumination, the stone seemed faintly iridescent. She held it out to me, and, all at once, I was unaccountably reluctant to touch it.

"Go on," she said. "I want your opinion, the opinion of someone with trained eyes."

"I'm not a geologist," I protested (again), but I took the stone from her, anyway. It was surprisingly light, and for a moment I thought maybe it was actually something that had been cast from plastic, not carved from rock. But the broken corner revealed a fine-grained, highly foliated crystalline structure, like slate or only slightly metamorphosed shale. Both sides were very subtly concave. One was polished smooth, but the other had been etched so that it was decorated with an assortment of symbols and characters that, at first glance, put me in mind of Egyptian or Mesoamerican hieroglyphic text. Indeed, the thing looked a lot like a stela or cartouche. The largest of the symbols resembled nothing so much as a winged serpent, its diamond-shaped head nestled in one of the vertices of the triangle, its sinuous body and tail trailing out behind. Another put me in mind of a frog, but an oddly anthropomorphic frog, that seemed to be bowing to the snake. There were three dots arranged above the frog's head, rather like a diadem.

"I'm not an archaeologist, either," I said, squinting at the designs. I asked Sang Hee if she had a hand lens, and she took a jeweler's loupe from a pocket of her jacket.

"Will this do?" she asked, and I said sure, that would do just fine. Then she asked me how old I thought the stone was. I didn't answer right away. I peered through the loupe at the broken corner. Examining the exposed cleavage planes, I thought I could make out quartz, muscovite, pyrite, maybe hematite. But mineralogy had never been my best subject. I also saw bits of fossilized shells and what I thought might have been part of a tiny trilobite.

"Are you asking me how old the rock is or how long ago this carving was done?"

"The carving," replied Sang Hee. "Not the rock."

"Then I'm afraid I can't help you," I told her and set both the stone and the loupe down on the table, near the pemmican tin. "The rock's from Earth, though. Maybe Cambrian or Ordovician. Maybe Silurian. You got this from the prospectors?"

She nodded and glanced at the others. "You really can't tell when it was carved?"

"No, I really can't," I said. "A month ago or a thousand years ago, I don't know. The etching doesn't look fresh, but there are lots of ways to age a fake artifact. Anyway, if that thing's supposed to somehow clear all this up for me or change how I feel about running off into the bled with Narmeen Jericho, I'm afraid we still have a problem."

"Show her," muttered George. "Go ahead. You've gone this far."

"Yeah," I said, "sure, whatever, you've gone this far. By all means, let's not get cold feet now."

And then Sang Hee took off her jacket, rolled up a shirtsleeve, and showed me a small tattoo on her left forearm. It was a dead ringer for the winged serpent on the carved chunk of slate she claimed the prospectors had given her. I could tell she'd had the ink for a long time, the way the lines had faded and blurred together and feathered out. It was something she'd brought with her when she'd come to Mars. I looked into her face, beginning to suspect that the urgent glint in her eyes, that edge I'd first glimpsed in my mod the night before, might, in fact, be the hot glow of insanity; I'd been burned in that fire enough times to recognize it. And I understood then that whatever she and her mates were playing at, it was something considerably more deranged than my landlord's suicidal get-rich-quick scheme.

"*Show* her," George said again.

"I'm leaving now," I said, to no one in particular, to everyone there. I sounded scared, and I figured they could hear it, too.

Sang Hee rolled her sleeve back down, buttoned the cuff, and, all but whispering, she said, "I'm sorry, Professor. But not just yet. Soon, but not yet." She took my elbow then and led me over to the isotank, and she pointed out the tattoo on the man's neck. I hadn't noticed it before, half hidden in the stubble of his beard. It was identical to Sang Hee's. Identical to the mark on the stone. And then I listened while she talked of her childhood in the squalor of Phnom Penh and a secret temple hidden on the muddy banks of the Mekong River. She told me about the priest who'd given her the tattoo when she was only ten years old, and the things she had been taught by her mother and her father (because, Earthborn, she'd had one of each), of a god who slept on Mars, waiting until the day when three stars in the constellation Centaurus would align, just like the three rubies in a golden crown that was kept on an altar in the temple by the river. She told me how she'd been chosen from among so many thousands of others all around the world to make the pilgrimage across three and fifty-four million kilometers of space, to be there when her god finally awakened. How the two dead wasters had been privileged to look upon the face of that divine being, and how they'd paid for it with their lives and minds and with their eternal souls. And she told me who the man in the isotank was, and about his part in everything that was to come. I stood there, and I kept my mouth shut.

What the fuck else was I going to do?

4. The Getaway

When she was done, Sang Hee sent me back to my mod above the scrap-yard. I assumed I was followed, likely by George and her rifle. And I also assumed that someone would be watching me from that point onwards. Yet, I could not help but entertain thoughts of running, no matter how impractical those thoughts might have been. I sat at my packing crate, sipping tea and waiting for word from Narmeen, instructions, directions, whatever. Sang Hee said I'd be informed where and when we were to meet, and to keep my mouth shut and my head down until then. But there was a westbound ice freighter, on its way back to civilization from the Athabasca mines, departing Kayne that same evening, and I thought maybe I had enough credits in my account left to bribe a company ship to overlook one stowaway. I even packed the tatty canvas holdall that I'd carried when I first arrived in Kayne. At some point, it had been wadded up and stuffed tightly into a drafty corner, that bag, and its time as a makeshift sealant had taken a toll. A couple of the seams were giving out, the latch was bro-ken, and there was a hole as big around as my thumb in one corner of the fabric. But I stuffed it full with a somewhat random jumble of clothing and toiletries, a couple of books I didn't want to leave behind, some use-less items with only sentimental value, and at the very bottom, a pistol I'd bought the week I came to the dome, but never learned to shoot. I didn't even know if the goddamned thing would fire, but I tucked it beneath a clean undershirt, along with two extra charge clips. I tied the holdall closed with at least a meter or so of twine, then sat alone at my crate, the bag there on the floor beside me, and stared out the dust-streaked window – waiting. It's hard to say which frightened me more, Narmeen's blind determination to find the crashed ship and claim salvage rights or Sang Hee's lunatic devo-tion to some pagan shadow cult.

As the evening wore on and no news came from either one of them, or from anyone else, I began to allow myself to hope that there had been some change in plans. Maybe the local authorities had gotten wind of one plot or the other or the both together. Maybe someone had talked – most likely the two prospectors – and even now that shiny containment tube and its improbable occupant were on their way to Hershel or, more probably, Phobos Station. Maybe I was off the fucking hook. Maybe, even, none of the conspirators would get it in their heads it was somehow my doing, and so none of them would let slip the matter of my being a dodger.

Near dawn, I nodded off and dreamt of Earth, and of cities filled with men, and cloudy skies pregnant with rain. I dreamt of the sea, lapping at a sandy shore, the air above it dotted with white birds. But then the rain became steaming black oil and all the birds lay dead on the tarry sands. I stood in that hydrocarbon downpour, watching as something gigantic passed by, something that might have been flesh and might have been metal, and it peered into the gloom with rows of glowing orange eyes or strips of landing lights. It rumbled and roared and clanked and clattered, drifting over a sea that had begun to boil. There was no place to hide, or I would surely have hidden, for I knew that it was looking for me. And I knew, too, *what* it was, and that it was no single thing. This Titan, this multi-eyed Polyphemus, it was the crime I'd run from in Hershel, and it was also what all humanity had done to Earth and then, in turn, to Mars, and it was the Big Grim and whatever waited for us at the Patera. It was the reborn god of Sang Hee Trinh, the very last thing that the wasters had seen before their suits had been ripped apart. Perhaps I was dreaming their dead dreams for them.

The rain stopped, but the sands had turned sour and tarry, and now the water was covered with a thick iridescent scum, the collective filth of twenty billion human beings.

Sometimes I was alone on the beach, and sometimes there were other women there with me. Narmeen Jericho had come and gone, muttering disappointment and colorful profanities. My swap mother lingered for a bit, and she talked about strawberries and broken dishes and a strange and terrible sort of circus she'd once seen at Sharonov City, out on the Nilokeras Mensae. I asked her when she'd ever traveled to Sharonov, and she promptly dissolved in the sudden Atlantic or Pacific or Antarctic breeze. There was the first girl I'd ever fucked, Ingrid Dickens, and I watched while she took off her shoes and rolled up her trousers and waded in the foulness of the surf. Dreaming, I understood that all these people had one thing in common with each other, and one thing in common with the ocean, as well. All of them, like it, were dead.

When Ingrid was done wading, she came back to me, and she asked if I knew what was coming, what had happened already, and because of that, those things that never would happen. "You were always bound for here," she said. "Here or somewhere worse."

"I'm not the one who killed you," I replied, only willing to carry the weight of those sins that were rightfully mine. And so she left me alone, though her exit was not as simple, nor as abrupt, as my mother's had been.

Far out at sea, I glimpsed the monstrous shape that had come so near before, an indistinct smudge against the horizon. Its eyes opened and closed, shining on and off. It had assumed the form of a many-tiered tower, and as I watched, it submerged, then rose much nearer to shore once more. Its decaying hide rippled and grew taut again, some corroded alloy of fish scales and metal and raw mammalian meat. Parasitic mechanisms and spongy colonies of macroviral symbiotes clung or burrowed or sprouted from its walls. It had a voice, that living tower, and, because of Sang Hee, it knew my name. With great effort, I turned my back on that monstrosity and on the waves, and I looked out across a field of dunes, and beyond that, the sprawling ruins of a scorched city.

I started walking towards those ruins, and it seemed as though I walked for days. But I never reached them. Sometimes, there were people who walked with me, hardly more than shades, but usually I was alone.

When I woke, there was weak sunlight streaming into the module through the closed blinds. My shoulders and kidneys ached from the hours I'd slept hunched over the crate, and somewhere outside but very near there were people shouting. I sat up and rubbed at my eyes, the nightmare still more tangible than anything my waking mind beheld. And then there were gunshots. Three of them, in quick succession. I told myself it was only a series of backfires, minute explosions in some sand-clogged engine's intake manifold, maybe a leaky fuel pump, but nothing out of the ordinary for a town where almost every piece of tech was a jerry-rigged rebuild.

I sat there in my chair, scarcely breathing, listening for a fourth shot that never came, hearing my heartbeat and the shouting down in the scrap-yard, knowing perfectly goddamn well that I hadn't heard backfires, but gunshots. And suddenly someone was hammering at my door, and still I only sat and listened and stared, trying to be sure this was not merely some more realistic turn the dream had taken. Then I heard Sang Hee calling from the other side of the locked panel, and finally that shook me all the way into myself again.

"Professor," she said, somehow shouting and whispering at the same time. "I *know* you're in there. Now I need you to open this fucking door."

"I'm coming," I croaked, that or something near enough. "I was asleep."

"Well, you best wake the hell up. We don't exactly have an excess of time at our disposal."

Never had I wished so hard that the module possessed a rear exit, and it was something that I'd wished very many times before. I stood and ran my fingers through my hair, wondering if I could get to the pistol at the bottom of my holdall before Sang Hee broke down the door. It seemed extremely unlikely, as I'd tied numerous knots in the twine that was holding the bag shut.

"Now would be better than later," Sang Hee growled, and a moment or two after that I was sliding the bolt aside and twisting the door handle. Compared to the murk of my module, the morning sunlight seemed impossibly bright, and I squinted and cursed and shielded my eyes as Sang Hee pushed her way past me. The first thing I noticed was that she was carrying a rifle, a low-frequency boomer identical to the one the woman named George had been so keen to point at me the day before. Maybe it was the very same gun.

"Is that yours?" Sang Hee asked and nodded at the holdall on the floor beside the table. I told her that it was, and I was about to ask what the fuck was going on when she grabbed the bag, shoved it into my arms, and then produced a yellow, plum-sized sphere from inside her vest.

"Go," she said.

"Is that a grenade?" I asked, beginning to think I was not awake, after all.

"I said *go,* Professor," and she gave the yellow ball a hard squeeze; immediately, it began to glow more sickly green than yellow. Sang Hee tossed it towards my bed and then turned and shoved me out the door and down the catwalk, all the while counting aloud, backwards from fifty. When we reached the scrapyard, I saw Narmeen Jericho sprawled facedown in the rusty grime. There wasn't any blood. Not a drop, but I didn't need to see blood to know that she was dead.

"Did you do this?" I asked, but Sang Hee ignored the question and pushed me towards the street, still counting backwards. I think she reached ten when the grenade went off, and, for some scant fraction of a moment, all the world seemed made of fire.

I never found out what was inside Sang Hee's little yellow ball, but the shock wave knocked us both off our feet, sent us tumbling like rag moppets, and shattered windows for several blocks around. I lay there, stunned and beginning to think I was already dead as Narmeen, while the air about me writhed with heat and light. After the blast, there was no sound to be heard but a painful, shrill ringing in my ears. I lay there, waiting for some confirmation that I was, in fact, dead, waiting for the synaptic connections and neural circuitry in my head to get the message and wink out. Surely, there would only be blackness soon. No, not even blackness, but some utter absence of color, just as there would come a merciful absence of consciousness and memory, an end to all perception. The air stunk of burning plastic and hot metal, and then it began to rain. Not oily drops of water, as it had rained in my dream of Earth, but a fine grey powder, the stuff they load into the aluminum bellies of the fire sprayers. Sang Hee Trinh's sprayer bots, clinging like fat spiders to the underside of the dome, built to detect such an explosion within only two or three millionths of a second.

The brominated flame retardant began to blanket the ground like a fine ash or frost, and watching it, I realized that I had not been killed, not yet, and I rolled over onto my right side. The holdall was lying nearby, and despite the broken latch it had not come open when I dropped it. And then someone was tugging at my hand, and when I turned my head I saw it was Sang Hee. Her lips moved, but I could only guess at the words, hidden behind the ringing her bomb had left inside my skull. Still, I was not so stunned that I could not see the urgency on her face, that determination in her eyes I'd first glimpsed in an alley the day before. She was covered with dust and soot and the grey powder, and there was a gash along her chin that would need stitches. Her lips moved again, shaping silent words, and then she was dragging me to my knees and up and onto my feet. She was still holding the rifle. Or she was holding the rifle again.

"I have to get my bag," I said, unable even to hear my own voice. I pulled free of her grip and looked back at the blazing wreck where my mod had been. It was farther away than I'd expected, and I realized the blast had thrown us past the edge of the scrapyard, almost all the way out to the street. There was no sign of Narmeen's corpse; it had been engulfed by the spreading flames and was lost in there, somewhere amid the destruction.

The sprayers didn't seem to be making much headway against the fire, and I wondered how the thin skin of the dome had fared against the explosion. Maybe there had been a breach, high overhead, and even now Kayne City's precious atmo was leaking away as the structure's decrepit robot custodians rushed to patch the rapidly widening perforation. I picked up my holdall, dimly surprised the knots had held, and then Sang Hee was pushing me again, buffeting me towards the street. A crowd had begun to gather – frightened, startled, curious faces, pointing fingers – women shielding their eyes against the glare of the fire, breathing through cupped hands in an effort not to inhale the falling PBB powder.

I remember thinking that it tasted a lot like soap.

There was a busted-up green skid waiting for us at the curb, the passenger-side door standing open, though I didn't remember it being there when I'd first stood up and glanced towards the road. It was a five-seater with a full cargo hutch, and there were already four inside. I leaned against the cab and shook my head, trying futilely to drive the ringing from my throbbing ears. Sang Hee nudged me hard in the ribs, trying to force me into the idling vehicle, and I wheeled on her. From her expression, that might have been the first thing that morning she hadn't expected. She took a step or two back, clutching the rifle to her chest. Blood dripped from her chin to the pavement at our feet.

"No time," she said, speaking very slowly, exaggerating the syllables so that I would be able to read her lips.

I swallowed and tasted copper.

"Fuck you," I replied, speaking just as slowly and with the same absurd care, assuming that she'd been temporarily deafened, too. Sang Hee blinked once or twice, then nodded her head and smiled. Behind her, part of the iron scaffolding that had held up my module collapsed in a brilliant swirl of embers and choking black billows of petrochemical smoke. She said something else then, something I couldn't make out, and an instant later, I felt the faint prick of a hypojet in the small of my back, just above my buttocks. For a while, then, there was nothing at all.

5. Outside (The End)

There isn't much more left to tell. Whatever this will be when I am done, I suspect it won't be a satisfying read or a well-constructed story arc. I am a poor sort of Ishmael, and this is only a coward's confession coming to it's untidy, abrupt conclusion. Then again, as I'd tried to teach the all-too-often witless daughters of farmers and mechanics, literature is only artifice, and plot bears little or no resemblance to the messiness of life. Still, maybe if I'd begun the tale earlier, back before I fled Herschel City and consigned myself to the slow-death purgatory of Kayne, back when there were still things in my life worth living for, this brief narrative would have made for a more rewarding sort of morality tale. At least then, I might not have come off so – what? Deprived of agency? Indecisive? Craven? But the truth of it is, flipping back through these pages, I see so clearly how I was never more than a spectator, at best a bit player – well and truly cocked – stumbling through events that, even now, she hardly comprehends. I suspect that *this* is my sin, the thing that has damned me all along the wretched, winding course of my life – my own dogged passivity. I might have acted, and then it might have gone another way. Fate offered the opportunities. But I was always afraid, wasn't I? Afraid that I'd be exposed by the files that Narmeen brought up to my mod that night. Afraid of prison. Afraid of the fire burning bright in Sang Hee's eyes. Afraid of death.

Get on with it. Make an end. I'm tired of words.

I don't know what was in the needle, but I slept, and it was a deep and perfectly dreamless sleep, as sound as the sleep that comes courtesy those little purple and green pills I mentioned earlier. When I came around, it was to the faint, rheumy growl of a crawler's idling engine. I opened my eyes and stared up at the low ceiling only a dozen or so centimeters above my face, at a patchwork of sloppy, rusting welds and stitch bolts and steel plating. Looking about, I saw that I was in an upper berth, alone in the cramped crew quarters of the machine. Two lines of bunks, six beds, five still neatly made. There was a lot of junk laying about, unstowed luggage and clothing, a miscellany of personal belongings, evidence that I wasn't actually alone on the crawler. The portholes were dialed shut, but there was light from the reading lamps over the beds. I lay there a while, getting my bearings, remembering the blast and everything that had come before it, disoriented and fighting the lingering fog from whatever I'd been dosed with. At least the ringing in my ears was gone.

Where am I? I thought. *Where am I, and how long was I out?*

My mouth was painfully dry and my throat was sore; when I finally decided to get up, it was the thirst that got me moving. Every muscle ached. Every bone felt bruised. My legs were weak, but I could stand. I leaned against the bunks for support, just in case I'd misjudged my strength. I was already on my feet and turning towards the hatchway before I realized that my hands and face had suffered superficial burns from the inferno released by Sang Hee's yellow squeeze ball. In places, my skin had been scalded an angry shade of pink, and there were a few blisters, here and there. I ignored the burns and punched the release toggle on the wall; the hatch door popped and creaked and groaned reluctantly open.

Out in the corridor, I found the first body. It was the woman named George. She'd been shot through the head and her brains and the back of her skull were spattered across the wall behind her corpse. Whoever had killed her, or someone else who'd come along afterwards, had scrawled a message in the gore, five letters traced with a finger, one word that meant nothing to me: DAGON.

Even now, I'm proud to say I surprised myself by not puking. I left her there and headed towards the front of the crawler, towards the cockpit. On the way, I found a second body, a woman I'd never seen before, and she'd also taken a shot to the head. Half her face was missing, and her one remaining eye was open wide, staring blindly up and staring out and staring nowhere at all.

By this point, both my thirst and any discomfort from my flash burns had been duly forgotten.

I opened another hatchway and stepped into the cockpit. The storm shutters were down, and the only light came from the chartreuse glow of the instrument panels and from recessed track lighting set into the floor. There were two more corpses waiting for me, one in the pilot's seat and one at the navigator's station. I'd never seen either of them before. Unlike George and the other woman in the corridor, they hadn't been shot. Near as I could tell, they'd both been bludgeoned to death. Before that day, if someone had talked about the smell of blood, I don't think I'd have known what she meant. But standing there in the abattoir that had been made of that crawler, blood was a *stench,* heady and hot and metallic, and I'll never forget it so long as I live. The four women couldn't have been dead for very long; they were all still warm. Whatever had happened here, I'd just missed it. Maybe only by minutes. Probably, the noise was what had finally roused me from the affects of the narcotic I'd been given back at the dome. I found a clock, and assuming it was correct, saw that I'd been asleep almost thirty hours.

"Where am I?" I said aloud, as if I expected one of the dead women to sit up and politely reply. But it wasn't hard to find the answer for myself. Our position was displayed on a brightly colored elevation map that filled one of the many display screens in the cockpit. We'd hardly even made it halfway across Gusev Crater. The crawler was parked some hundred and sixty kilometers out from Kayne, still a good two hundred klicks south of the rim of Apollinaris Patera. I sat down in the empty copilot's chair, and I searched the controls until I found the lever that opened the storm shutters.

It was just a little past midday out there, and at first the summer sunlight was blinding. I sat squinting and blinking at the low yellow-brown sky and the red plains, waiting for my eyes to adjust to the glare. The vast, all but featureless expanse of Gusev stretched away from me in every direction, a monotonous vista of low, rippled dunes, interrupted here and there by boulders and outcroppings of wind-worn basalt. I think the storm shutters had been up almost a full minute before I spotted Sang Hee Trinh, even though she couldn't have been more than a few dozen meters from the nose of the crawler. She was near enough that I could make out her face through the clear bubble of her EVA helmet. She was kneeling, her head thrown back, her eyes gazing up at the heavens. In her gloved left hand she clutched the carved piece of slate that she'd shown me in that basement two days earlier, and, as I watched, she lifted her arms, and it seemed to me that she was offering that stone to the cloudless sky.

No, not to the sky.

Not to the sky at all.

I think I said her name aloud once, maybe twice, and then I began frantically searching the panels in front of me for comms control, because her suit would have an uplink to the crawler. But the instruments all looked the same to me, a bewildering array of dials and switches and knobs, digital readouts and indicator lights. It was a miracle I'd been able to get the shutters open. And anyway, only a couple of minutes after I spotted her, she took off her helmet. I didn't have the stomach to watch her die. It was quick, though. The unknown force that had prolonged the suffering of the two wasters, at least she was spared that.

And then I heard something, even if I can't recall just what it was. Only some small bump or thud, a sound to mar the perfect, silent stillness of the scene, and I turned to find the man from Earth standing in the hatchway. I let out a breath I hadn't realized I was holding, and I was only surprised that the sight of him didn't surprise me. Somehow, it made sense, him being there, his appearance at exactly that instant, as if on cue. It was simply What Came Next. He was looking at the dead habitat tech, curled up fetal in the dust, and his eyes were a startling pale grey. I'd never before seen anyone with grey eyes, and I never have since. I noticed that he'd shaved. He was wearing a black shirt, unbuttoned, and trousers that were a little too large, and he was barefoot. I find it odd that I can remember so clearly what he was wearing, but I do.

"I sincerely wish she hadn't dragged you into this, Babette Flanagan," he said, not taking those startling grey eyes off Sang Hee. "But she was never really what one would call levelheaded." His accent was German – I recognized it from old movies – and his voice was softer than I'd have expected it to be. He was taller than he'd seemed in the isotank, but not much taller than me.

"Did you kill them?" I asked him and nodded at the two bodies there in the cockpit with us. "And George and the other woman in the corridor?"

"No," he replied. "No, I didn't. But it's probably for the best that they're out of the way, all things considered."

I didn't ask what he meant by that, and he didn't volunteer the information. But he glanced at me then, and the man from Earth smiled a weary sort of half smile.

"Why aren't you sick?" I asked him.

"Ah," he said. "Yes, that. Well, you could say I cheated, I suppose. You see, I was not born a man, not physically. So, like you, I'm immune to the virus."

"Did she know?" I asked, turning back towards the desert and Sang Hee Trinh. When she'd collapsed, she'd fallen over on top of the carved piece of slate, and I found that I was grateful that it was hidden from view.

"Yes, she knew. She was my wife, after all. We met at university in Heidelberg, many years ago. She was an outstanding student. She'd have made quite a fine engineer, had a promising career ahead of her, but…" and he trailed off, leaving the thought unfinished.

I thought about closing the storm shutters again, almost reached for the lever. Then I almost asked the man what his name was. "Are you going to kill me now," I asked him, instead.

"Why, Babette Flanagan? Do you want to die?" And he smiled again. "Is that how it is? Are you also a suicide?"

"No," I said.

"No, I didn't think so." And then, at last, he looked away from Sang Hee. He went to the navigator's station and began examining the elevation map. With an index finger, he traced a path from our present position on Gusev to the red-orange bull's-eye of Apollinaris Mons, and then he said, "And that being the case, if I were to offer you the chance to continue on with me, how would you answer?" He glanced back over his shoulder, and the smile was gone.

"I'm not supposed to be here," I told him.

"No, you aren't. But that wasn't the question, was it?"

"If I say no, are you going to kill me?"

He laughed and turned his attention back to the map. "I'm not going to kill you," he said. "But I also can't take you back to Kayne. There isn't time."

"There isn't time before what?" I asked him, but the man from Earth shook his head.

"In or out?" he replied, offering a question for a question.

Returning to my earlier comments about agency and opportunity, about the ways this story could have gone but didn't, I could very well have said yes. After all, what the fuck did I have to go back to? No one and nothing, and whatever mystery or terror lay ahead, slumbering beneath that extinct caldera, the question mark that had set all this in motion, surely it was the best offer I was ever going to get. It might even have been a chance for redemption. I knew that then, and I still know that now. And still I said no.

He honestly seemed relieved.

So, the man from Earth gave me an EVA suit with forty-eight hours worth of oxygen and water, plus a flimsy foldout emergency shelter constructed of aluminum struts and mylar. He activated the distress beacon sewn up inside one of my boots, and I helped him load Sang Hee's body back onto the crawler. He didn't bother to ask if I were sure, if I'd like to reconsider my decision. There was no second chance. He took his wife and all those other dead women, and he also took that graven piece of slate, and he left me there. I didn't lose sight of the vehicle until just after sunset.

He hadn't asked me not to talk about what I'd seen, what I knew. I never promised him I wouldn't.

It was late the next morning before a tinker caravan bound for Kayne picked me up, and I spent the night huddled inside the shelter, with all the dazzling vault of heaven wheeling on its axis overhead. For a while, I tried to keep my mind occupied by tracing the slow paths of familiar stars and of tiny silver Diemos low on the eastern horizon. But as the night wore on, I felt a sort of anxiety I'd never known before, an apprehension of the sky and of the night, and I soon retreated inside the mylar shelter.

Towards dawn, I dozed and dreamt of a ghost story that my mothers had told me when I was a girl, the tale of the wreck of the *Michiko Maru,* an ice freighter on its way back from the south polar mines that blundered off course during a summer dust storm and tried to follow the winding path of the Ma'adim Vallis north to the relative safety of Gusev Crater. The captain had hoped to make an emergency landing there, then sit tight until a recovery team arrived. But almost everything that could go wrong did, and while the ship managed to reach Gusev, it crashed there, killing everyone on board. The salvors and zep breakers who came for the bones of the *Michiko Maru,* and for its valuable load of ice, claimed that at night the spirits of the fallen crew would appear as beautiful bluish wisps who danced across the dunes beyond the wreck's debris field. In my dream, I watched those wisps, cavorting above the sand and basalt, and I heard them singing to me, just as they'd been singing to travelers for the better part of a century. They knew my name. Unlike the stars and the darkness between the stars, the ghosts didn't frighten me, and, in return for their company, I told them a story about a man who'd fallen from the sky, and they were kind and listened.

Written to the music of
Cliff Martinez and Clint Mansell.

THE DANDRIDGE CYCLE

A Redress for Andromeda
(2001)

W here the land ends and the unsleeping, omnivorous Pacific has chewed the edge of the continent ragged, the old house sits alone in the tall grass, waiting for Tara. She parks the rental car at the edge of the sandy dirt road and gets out, stares towards the house and the sea, breathing the salt and the night, the moonlight and all the wine- and apple-crisp October smells. The wind whips the grass, whips it into tall waves and fleeting troughs the way it whips the sea, and Tara watches the house as the house watches her. Mutual curiosity or wary misgiving, one or the other or both, and she decides to leave the car here and walk the rest of the way.

There are a few other cars, parked much closer to the house, though not as many as she expected, and the porch is burning down in a mad conflagration of jack-o'-lanterns, a hundred candle-glowing eyes and mouths and nostrils, or at least that's how it looks to her. Walking along the sandy road as it curves towards the ocean and the tall gabled house with its turrets and lightning rods, that's how it looks; the house besieged by all those carved and flaming pumpkins, and she takes her time, walks slow, listening to the wind and to the sea slamming itself against the headland. The wind is colder than she expected, and all she's wearing is a white dress, one of her simple shirtwaist dresses fashionable forty or forty-five years ago, a dress her mother might have worn when she was a girl; the white dress with its sensible cuffs and collars, and black espadrilles on her feet, shoes as simple as the dress because that's what Darren said. *It isn't a masquerade, nothing like that at all. Just be yourself.* But she wishes she'd remembered her coat. It's lying on the passenger seat of the rental car, and she thinks about going back for it, then decides she can stand the chill as far as the front door.

She knows a little about this house, but only because Darren told her about it; never much of a geek for architecture herself, even old houses with stories like this one has. The Dandridge House, because the man who built it in 1890 was named Dandridge, and back in the sixties it was one of those places that hippies and occultists liked to haunt, someplace remote enough and out of sight and nobody to notice if you sacrificed a farm animal now and then. Darren told her ghost stories, too, because a house like this has to have ghost stories, but she took two Xanax on the drive up from Monterey, and they've all run together in her head.

Not much farther before a sandy walkway turns off the sandy road, a rusted mailbox on a post that's fallen over and no one's bothered to set it right again, and Tara follows the path towards the wide, pumpkin-crowded porch that seems to wrap itself all the way around the house. Her shoes are already full of sand, sand getting in between her toes, and she stops and looks back towards her car, all by itself at the edge of the road, and now it seems a long way back.

There's a black-haired woman sitting on the porch steps, smoking a cigarette and watching her, and when Tara smiles the woman smiles back at her. "You must be Tara," the woman says and holds out her hand. "Darren said that you would be late. I thought someone should wait out here for you. A friendly face in the wilderness, you know."

Tara says thank you and shakes the woman's hand, and this close the jack-o'-lanterns seem very, very bright; they hurt her eyes after the night, and she squints at them and nods for the woman on the steps of the house.

"You didn't have any trouble finding us?" the woman asks, and "No," Tara says. "No trouble at all. Darren gives good directions."

"Well, it's not as if there's much of anything else out here," and she releases Tara's hand and glances past all the jack-o'-lanterns towards the cliffs and the sea. "Just keep going until there's nowhere left to go."

"Who carved all these things? There must be a hundred of them," Tara says, pointing at one of the jack-o'-lanterns, and the woman on the steps smiles again and takes another drag off her brown cigarette, exhales smoke that smells like cloves and cinnamon.

"One hundred and eleven, actually," she says. "They're like birthday candles. One for every year since the house was built. We've been carving them for a week."

"Oh," Tara says because she doesn't know what else to say. "I see."

"You should go on inside, Tara," the woman says. "I expect they'll be waiting. It's getting late," and Tara says nice to meet you, we'll talk some more later, something polite and obligatory like that, and then she steps past the woman and towards the front door, past and between the grinning and grimacing and frowning pumpkin faces.

"Yes, she's the one that I was telling you about last week," Darren is saying to them all, "The marine biologist," and he laughs, and Tara shakes someone else's hand, all these pale people in their impeccable black clothes, and she feels like a pigeon dropped down among the crows. Not a masquerade, not a costume party, but she could have at least had the good sense to wear black. A tall, painfully-thin lady with a thick French accent touches the back of Tara's hand, this woman's nails the red-brown color of seaweed, and she smiles as gently as did the woman out on the porch.

"It's always so nice to see a new face," the French woman says. "Especially when it's such a fine and splendid face." The woman kisses the back of Tara's hand, and then Darren's introducing her to a short, fat man wearing an ascot the color of a stormy summer sky.

"Ah," he says, and shakes Tara's hand so forcefully it hurts. "A scientist. That's grand. We've had so few scientists, you know." She isn't sure if his accent is Scots or Irish, but it's heavy, like his face. Jowls and wide, thin lips, and the man looks more than just a little like a frog, she thinks.

"We've had doctors, yes, lots and lots of doctors. Once we had a neurologist, even. But I've never thought doctors were quite the same thing. As scientists, I mean. Doctors aren't really much more than glorified mechanics, are they?"

"I never thought of it that way," Tara says, which isn't true, and she manages to slip free of the fat man's endless, crushing handshake without seeming rude. She glances at Darren, hoping that he can read the discomfort, the unease, in her eyes.

"If you'll all please excuse us for a moment," Darren says, so she knows that he has seen, that he understands, and he puts one of his long arms around her shoulders. "I need to steal her away for just a few minutes," and there's a splash of soft, knowing laughter from the little crowd of people.

He leads her from the front parlor towards what might once have been a dining room, and Tara's beginning to realize how very empty the house is. The way it looked from the outside, she expected the place to be full of antiques, perhaps neglected antiques gone just a bit shabby, a threadbare and discrepant mix of Edwardian and Victorian, but still, she thought that it would be furnished. These rooms are almost empty, not even carpets on the floors or drapes on the tall windows; the velvet wallpaper is faded and torn in places, hanging down in strips here and there like a reptile shedding its skin. And no electricity, as far as she can tell, just candles and old-fashioned gaslight fixtures on the walls, warm and flickering light held inside frosted crystal flowers.

"They can be somewhat intimidating at first, I know that," Darren says. "It's a pretty close-knit group. I should have warned you," and she shakes her head, smiles, and no, it's fine, she says, it's not a problem.

"They were probably as anxious about your being here," he says and rubs his hands together in a nervous way, glances back towards the crows milling about in the parlor, whispering among themselves. *Are they talking about me?* she wonders. *Are they asking each other questions about me?* and then Darren's talking again.

"I trust you didn't have any trouble finding the house? We had someone get lost once," he says, and "No," she says. "Finding the house was easy. With all those jack-o'-lanterns, it's almost like a lighthouse," and she thinks that's probably exactly what it would look like to a ship passing in the night, fishermen or a tanker passing on their way north or south, an unblinking lighthouse perched high on the craggy shore.

"That's one of the traditions," Darren says, brushes his long black bangs away from his face. Not exactly a handsome face, something more honest than handsome, something more secretive, and the reason she finds him attractive buried somewhere inside that contradiction.

"One of the traditions? Are there many others?"

"A few," he says. "I hope all this isn't freaking you out."

"No, it isn't," and she turns her head towards a window, the moonlight shining clean through the glass, shining white off the sea. "Not at all. It's all very dignified, I think. Not like Halloween in the city. All the noisy drunks and drag queens, those gaudy parades. I like this much better than that. I wish you'd told me to wear black, though," and he laughs at her then.

"Well, I don't think it's funny," she says, frowning slightly, still watching the moon riding on the waves, and he puts a hand on her arm. "I must stick out like a sore thumb."

"A bit of contrast isn't a bad thing," Darren says, and she turns away from the window, turns back towards him, his high cheekbones and high forehead, his long aquiline nose and eyes that are neither blue nor green.

"I think you need a drink," he says, and Tara nods and smiles for him.

"I think maybe I need two or three."

"That can be arranged," and now he's leading her back towards the crows. A few of them turn their heads to see, dark eyes watching her, and she half expects them to spread wide black wings and fly away.

"They'll ask you questions," and now Darren's almost whispering, hushed words meant for her and no one else. "But don't ever feel like you have to tell them anything you don't want to tell them. They don't mean to be pushy, Tara. They're just impatient, that's all." And she starts to ask what he means by that exactly, impatient, but then she and Darren are already in the parlor again; the small and murmuring crowd opens momentarily, parts long enough to take them in, and then it closes eagerly around them.

An hour later, after a string quartet, Bach and Chopin and only one piece that she didn't recognize, and now the musicians are carefully returning their sleek instruments to black violin and viola and cello cases, cases lined in aubergine and lavender silk.

"It really isn't very fair of you, Mr. Quince," someone says, and Tara turns around and sees that it's the dapper fat man with the grey-blue ascot, the man who's either Irish or Scottish. "The way you're keeping her all to yourself like this," and he glances past her to Darren, then, coy glance, and the man smiles and rubs at his short salt-and-pepper beard.

"I'm sorry. I wasn't aware," Darren says, and he looks at Tara, checking to be sure it's okay before leaving her in the man's company; but he seems harmless enough, as eccentric as the rest, certainly, but nothing threatening in that eccentricity. He has a walking stick topped with a silver dolphin, and she thinks that he's probably gay.

"Oh, I think we'll be fine," she says, and Darren nods once and disappears into the crowd.

"I am Peterson," the man says, "Ahmed Peterson," and then he kisses the back of her hand the same way that the tall French woman did earlier. The same peculiar antiquated formality about him, about all of them, manners that ought to come across as affected but don't somehow.

"Quince tells us that you're a marine biologist," he says, releases her hand and stands very straight, but he's still a few inches shorter than Tara.

"An ichthyologist, actually," she says. "I do some work at the aquarium in Monterey and teach at Cal State. That's where I met Darren."

"Marvelous," Peterson beams. "You know, my dear, I once came across an oarfish, a great, long, spiny thing, stranded on the shingle at Lyme Regis. The fellow I was with thought for sure we'd found ourselves a sea serpent."

"I saw an oarfish alive off the coast of Oregon about ten years ago, when I was still a graduate student," she tells him, happy to be swapping fish stories with the fat man, starting to relax, feeling less like an outsider. "We estimated it at almost twenty feet."

"Ah, well, mine was smaller," he says, sounding a little disappointed, perhaps, and then there's a jolting, reverberating noise, and Tara turns to see that one of the women is holding up a small brass gong.

"Oh my," the fat man says. "Is it really that late already? I lost track," and then Darren's standing next to her again.

"What's happening?" she asks, and "You'll see," he replies, takes her hand and slips something cold and metallic into her palm, a coin or a token.

"What's this?" and "Just hang onto it," he replies. "Don't lose it. You'll need it later." So, *It's a game,* she thinks. *Yes, it must be some sort of party game.*

And now everyone is starting to leave the parlor. She lets Darren lead her, and they follow the others, file down a narrow hallway to a locked door near the very back of the house; behind the door are stairs winding down and down and down, stone steps that seem to have been cut directly from the native rock, damp stone walls, and some of the guests have candles or oil lanterns. She slips once, and Darren catches her, leans close and whispers in her ear, and his breath is very faintly sour.

"Watch your step," he says, "It's not much farther, but you wouldn't want to fall," and there are cool gusts of salty air rising up from below, not the sort of air she'd expect from a cellar at all; cool air against her skin, but air tainted by an oily, fishy odor, low tide sort of a smell, kelp and dying starfish trapped in stagnant tidal pools.

"Where the hell are we going?" she asks him, not bothering to whisper, and a woman with a conch shell tattooed on her forehead turns around and looks at her with a guarded hint of disapproval, and then she turns away again.

"You'll see," Darren whispers, and she realizes that there's something besides the salty darkness and the light from the candles and lanterns, a softer yellow-green glow coming from somewhere below; chartreuse light that gets a little brighter with every step towards the bottom of the stairway.

And now, if Darren were to ask again whether or not she was getting freaked out, now she might say yes, now she might even tell him she really should be going, that it's late and she needs to get back to the city. Papers to grade or a test to write for her oceanography class, anything that sounds plausible enough to get her out of the house and onto the pumpkin-littered porch, back down the path to her rented car. The stars overhead instead of stone, but he doesn't ask again, and the chartreuse light grows brighter and brighter, and in a few more minutes they've come to the bottom.

"No one ever understands at first," Darren says. He has one hand gripped just a little too tightly around her left wrist, and she's about to tell him that it hurts, about to ask him to let go, when Tara sees the pool and forgets about everything else.

There's a sort of a boardwalk at the bottom of the stairs, short path of warped planks and rails and pilings gone driftwood soft from the always-damp air, from the spray and seawater lapping restless at the wood. The strange light is coming from the water, from the wide pool that entirely fills the cavern at the foot of the stairs, light that rises in dancing fairy shafts to play across the uneven ceiling of the chamber. Tara's stopped moving, and people are having to step around her, all the impatient crows grown quiet and beginning to take their places on the boardwalk, no sound now but the hollow clock, clock, clock of their shoes on the planks and the waves splash-ing against the pier and the limestone walls of the sea cave.

Like they've all done this thing a hundred, hundred times before, and she looks to Darren for an explanation, for a wink or a smile to tell her this really *is* just some odd Halloween game, but his blue-green eyes are fixed on the far end of the boardwalk, and he doesn't seem to notice.

"Take me back now," she says. "I don't want to see this," but if he's heard her it doesn't show on his face, his long, angular face reflecting the light from the pool, and he has the awed and joyous expression of some-one witnessing a miracle. The sort of expression that Hollywood always gives a Joan of Arc or a Bernadette, the eyes of someone who's seen God, she thinks, and then Tara looks towards the end of the boardwalk again. And the crowd parts on cue, steps aside so she can see the rocks jutting up from the middle of the pool, from whatever depths there are beneath her feet, stacked one upon the other as precarious as jackstraws. The rocks and the thing that's chained there, and in a moment she knows that it's seen her, as well.

"When I was five," she says, "When I was five I found a sea turtle dead on the beach near Santa Cruz," and she opens her hand again to stare at the coin that Darren gave her upstairs.

"No, dear," Ahmed Peterson says. "It was an oarfish. Don't you remember?" and she shakes her head, because it wasn't an oarfish that time. That time it was a turtle, and the maggots and the gulls had eaten away its eyes.

"You must be mistaken," the fat man says again, and her coin glints and glimmers in the yellow-green light, glints purest moonlight silver in her palm. She doesn't want to give it away, the way all the others have already done. Maybe the only thing that's left, and she doesn't want to drop it into the water and watch as it spirals down to nowhere, see-saw spiral descent towards the blazing deep, and she quickly closes her hand again. Makes a tight fist, and the fat man huffs and grumbles, and she looks up at the moon instead of the pool.

"You may not have lived much under the sea," he says, and "No, I haven't," Tara confesses. "I haven't."

"Perhaps you were never even introduced to a lobster," he says.

She thinks about that for a moment, about brown claws boiled orange, jointed crustacean legs on china plates, and "I once tasted – " but then she stops herself, because it's something she isn't supposed to say, she's almost certain.

"No, never," Tara whispers.

And the sea slams itself against the cliffs below the house, the angry sea, the cheated sea that wants to drown the world again. Darren is lying in the tall grass, and Tara can hear a train far away in the night, its steam-throat whistle and steel-razor wheels, rolling from there to there, and she traces a line in the dark with the tip of one index finger, horizon to horizon, sea to sky, stitching with her finger.

"She keeps the balance," Darren says, and Tara knows he's talking about the woman on the rocks in the cave below the house. The thing that was a woman once. "She stands between the worlds," he says. "She watches all the gates."

"Did she have a choice?" Tara asks him, and now he's pulling her down into the grass, the sea of grass washed beneath the harvest moon. He smells like fresh hay and pumpkin flesh, nutmeg and candy corn.

"Do saints ever have choices?"

And Tara's trying to remember, if they ever have, when Ahmed and the woman with the conch-shell tattoo lean close and whisper the names of deep-sea things in her ears, rushed and bathypelagic litany of fish and jellies, squid and the translucent larvae of shrimp and crabs.

Saccopharynx, Stylephorus, Pelagothuria, Asteronyx.

"Not so *fast*," she says. "Not so fast, *please*."

"You can really have no notion, how delightful it will be," sings Ahmed Peterson, and then the tattooed woman finishes for him, "When they take us up and throw us, with the lobsters, out to sea."

It's easier to shut her eyes and lie in Darren's arms, hidden by the merciful, undulating grass; "The jack-o'-lanterns?" he says again, because she asked him why all the jack-o'-lanterns, and "You said it yourself, Tara. Remember? A lighthouse. One night a year, they rise, and we want them to know we're watching."

"Beneath the waters of the sea, Are lobsters thick as thick can be — They love to dance with you and me. My own and gentle Salmon."

"It hurts her," Tara says, watching the woman on the rocks, the lady of spines and scales and the squirming podia sprouting from her distended belly.

"Drop the coin, Tara," Darren murmurs, and his voice is urgent, but not unkind. "Drop the coin into the pool. It helps her hold the line."

Drop the coin, the coin, the candy in a plastic pumpkin grinning basket.

"The reason is," says the Gryphon, who was a moment before the woman with the conch on her forehead, "that they *would* go with the lobsters to the dance. So they got thrown out to sea. So they had to fall a long, long way."

Trick or treat.

And the Mock Turtle, who was previously Ahmed Peterson, glares at the Gryphon; "I never went to him," he huffs. "He taught Laughing and Grief, they used to say."

"Someone got lost," Darren whispers. "We had to have another. The number is fixed," and the black-salt breeze blows unseen through the concealing grass; she can't hear the train any longer. And the moon stares down at them with its single, swollen, jaundiced eye, searching and dragging the oceans against the rocks.

It will find me soon, and what then?

"Drop the coin, Tara. There's not much time left. It's almost midnight," and the woman on the rocks strains against her shackles, the rusted chains that hold her there, and cold, corroded iron bites into her pulpy cheese-white skin. The crimson tentacles between her alabaster thighs, the barnacles that have encrusted her legs, and her lips move without making a sound.

"They're rising, Tara," Darren says, and now he sounds scared and stares down into the glowing water, the abyss below the boardwalk that's so much deeper than any ocean has ever been. And there *is* movement down there, she can see that, the coils and lashing fins, and the woman on the rock makes a sound like a dying whale.

"There is another shore, you know, upon the other side."

"Now, goddamn it," Darren says, and the coin slips so easily through her fingers.

"Will you, won't you, will you, won't you, will you join the dance...?"

She watches it sink, taking a living part of her down with it, drowning some speck of her soul. Because it isn't only the woman on the rock that holds back the sea; it's all of them, the crows, and now she's burned as black as the rest, scorched feathers and strangled hearts, falling from the sun into the greedy maelstrom.

And the moon can see her now.

"I told them you were strong," Darren whispers, proud of her, and he wipes the tears from her face; the crows are dancing on the boardwalk, circling them, clomp-clomp-clomp, while the woman on the rock slips silently away into a stinging anemone-choked crevice on her island.

"Will you, won't you, will you, won't you, won't you join the dance?"

Tara wakes up shivering, lying beneath the wide grey sky spitting cold raindrops down at her. Lying in the grass, the wind and the roar of the breakers in her ears, and she lies there for a few more minutes, remembering what she can. No recollection of making her way back up the stairs from the sea cave, from the phosphorescent pool below the house. No memory of leaving the house, either, but here she is, staring up at the leaden sky and the faint glow where the sun is hiding itself safe behind the clouds.

Someone's left her purse nearby, Darren or some other thoughtful crow, and she reaches for it, sits up in the wet grass and stares back towards the house. Those walls and shuttered windows, the spires and gables, no less severe for this wounded daylight; more so, perhaps. The bitter face of anything that has to keep such secrets in its bowels, that has to hide the world's shame beneath its floors. The house is dark, all the other cars have gone, and there's no sign of the one hundred and eleven jack-o'-lanterns.

She stands and looks out to sea for a moment, watches a handful of white birds buffeted by the gales, whitecaps, and *Next year,* she thinks, next year she'll be here a week before Halloween to help carve the lighthouse faces, and next year she'll know to dress in black. She'll know to drop the silver coin quickly and turn quickly away.

One of the gulls dives suddenly and pulls something dark and wriggling from the seething, storm-tossed ocean; Tara looks away, wipes the rain from her eyes, rain that could be tears, and wet bits of grass from her skirt, and then she begins the walk that will carry her past the house and down the sandy road to her car.

Nor the Demons Down Under the Sea
(1957)

The late summer morning like a shattering blue-white gem, crashing, liquid seams of fluorite and topaz thrown against the jagged-rough shale and sandstone breakers, roiling calcite foam beneath the cloudless sky specked with gulls and ravens. And Julia behind the wheel of the big green Bel Air, chasing the coast road north, the top down so the Pacific wind roars wild through her hair. Salt smell to fill her head, intoxicating and delicious scent to drown her city-dulled senses and Anna's alone in the backseat, ignoring her again, silent, reading one of her textbooks or monographs on malacology. Hardly a word from her since they left the motel in Anchor Bay more than an hour ago, hardly a word at breakfast, for that matter, and her silence is starting to annoy Julia.

"It was a bad dream, that's all," Anna said, the two of them alone in the diner next door to the motel, sitting across from one another in a Naugahyde booth with a view of the bay, Haven's Anchorage dotted with the bobbing hulls of fishing boats. "You know that I don't like to talk about my dreams," and then she pushed her uneaten grapefruit aside and lit a cigarette. "God knows I've told you enough times."

"We don't have to go on to the house," Julia said hopefully. "We could always see it another time, and we could go back to the city today, instead."

Anna only shrugged her shoulders and stared through the glass at the water, took another drag off her cigarette and exhaled smoke the color of the horizon.

"If you're afraid to go to the house, you should just say so."

Julia steals a glance at her in the rearview mirror, wind-rumpled girl with shiny sunburned cheeks, cheeks like ripening plums and her short blonde hair twisted into a bun and tied up in a scarf. And Julia's own reflection stares back at her from the glass, reproachful, desperate, almost fifteen years older than Anna, so close to thirty-five now that it frightens her; her drab hazel eyes hidden safely behind dark sunglasses that also conceal nascent crow's feet, and the wind whips unhindered through her own hair, hair that would be mouse brown if she didn't use peroxide. The first, tentative wrinkles beginning to show at the corners of her mouth, and she notices that her lipstick is smudged, then, licks the tip of one index finger and wipes the candy-pink stain off her skin.

"You really should come up for air," Julia shouts, shouting just to be heard above the wind, and Anna looks slowly up from her book. She squints and blinks at the back of Julia's head, an irritated, uncomprehending sort of expression and a frown that draws creases across her forehead.

"You're missing all the scenery, dear."

Anna sits up, sighs loudly and stares out at a narrow, deserted stretch of beach rushing past, the ocean beyond, and "Scenery's for the tourists," she says. "I'm not a tourist." And she slumps down into the seat again, turns a page and goes back to reading.

"You could at least tell me what I've done," Julia says, trying hard not to sound angry or impatient, sounding only a little bit confused, instead, but this time Anna doesn't reply, pretending not to hear or maybe just choosing to ignore her altogether.

"Well, then, whenever you're ready to talk about it," Julia says, but that isn't what she *wants* to say; she wants to tell Anna she's getting sick of her pouting about like a high-school girl, sick of these long, brooding silences and more than sick of always feeling guilty because she doesn't ever know what to say to make things better. Always feeling like it's her fault, somehow, and if she weren't a coward she would never have become involved with a girl like Anna Foley in the first place.

But you are a coward, Julia reminds herself, the father-cruel voice crouched somewhere behind her sunglasses, behind her eyes. *Don't ever forget that, not even for a second,* and she almost misses her exit, the turnoff that would carry them east to Boonville if she stayed on the main road. Julia takes the exit, following the crude map Anna drew for her on a paper napkin; the road dips and curves sharply away from the shoreline, and the ocean is suddenly lost behind a dense wall of redwoods and blooming rhododendrons, the morning sun traded for the rapid flicker of forest shadows. Only a few hundred yards from the highway there's another road – unpaved, unnamed – leading deeper into the trees, and she slows down, and the Chevrolet bounces off the blacktop onto the rutted, pockmarked logging trail.

The drive up the coast from San Francisco to Anchor Bay was Anna's idea, even though they both knew it was a poor choice for summertime shelling. But still a chance to get out of the laboratory, she said, to get away from the city, from the heat and all the people, and Julia knew what she really meant. A chance to be alone, away from suspicious, disapproving eyes, and besides, there had been an interesting limpet collected very near there a decade or so ago, a single, unusually large shell cataloged and tucked away in the vast Berkeley collections and then all but forgotten. The new species, *Diodora thespesius,* was described by one of Julia Winter's male predecessors in the department and a second specimen would surely be a small feather in her cap.

So, the last two days spent picking their way meticulously over the boulders, kelp- and algae-slick rocks and through shallow tide pools constantly buried and unburied by the shifting sand flats; hardly an ideal place for limpets or much of anything else to take hold. Thick-soled rubber boots and aluminum pails, sun hats and gloves, knives to pry mollusks from the rocks, and nothing much for their troubles but scallops and mussels. A few nice sea urchins and sand dollars, *Strongylocentrotus purpuratus* and *Dendraster excentricus,* and the second afternoon Anna had spotted a baby octopus, but it had gotten away from them.

"If we only had more time," Anna said. "I'm sure we would have found it if we had more time." She was sitting on a boulder smoking, her dungarees soaked through to the thighs, staring north and west towards the headland and the dark silhouette of Fish Rocks jutting up from the sea like the scabby backs of twin leviathans.

"Well, it hasn't been a total loss, has it?" Julia asked and smiled, remembering the long night before, Anna in her arms, Anna whispering things that had kept Julia awake until almost dawn. "It wasn't a *complete* waste."

And Anna Foley turned and watched her from her seat on the boulder, sloe-eyed girl, slate-grey irises to hide more than they would ever give away; *She's taunting me,* Julia thought, feeling ashamed of herself for thinking such a thing, but thinking it anyway. *It's all some kind of a game to her, playing naughty games with Dr. Winter. She's sitting there watching me squirm.*

"You want to see a haunted house?" Anna said, finally, and whatever Julia had expected her to say, it certainly wasn't that.

"Excuse me?"

"A haunted house. A *real* haunted house," and Anna raised an arm and pointed northeast, inland, past the shoreline. "It isn't very far from here. We could drive up tomorrow morning."

This is a challenge, Julia thought. *She's trying to challenge me, some new convolution in the game meant to throw me off balance.*

"I'm sorry, Anna. That doesn't really sound like my cup of tea," she said, tired and just wanting to climb back up the bluff to the motel for a hot shower and an early dinner.

"No, really. I'm serious. I read about this place last month in *Argosy*. It was built in 1890 by a man named Machen Dandridge who supposedly worshipped Poseidon and – "

"Since when do you read *Argosy?*"

"I read everything, Julia," Anna said. "It's what I do," and she turned her head to watch a ragged flock of sea gulls flying by, ash and charcoal wings skimming just above the surface of the water.

"And an article in *Argosy* magazine *really* said that this house was haunted?" Julia asked skeptically, watching Anna watch the gulls as they rose and wheeled high over the Anchorage.

"Yes, it did. It was written by Dr. John Montague, an anthropologist, I think. He studies haunted houses."

"Anthropologists aren't generally in the business of ghost-hunting, dear," Julia said, smiling, and Anna glared at her from her rock, her storm-cloud eyes narrowing the slightest bit.

"Well, this one seems to be, *dear.*"

And then neither of them said anything for a few minutes, no sound but the wind and the surf and the raucous gulls, all the soothing, lonely ocean noises. Finally the incongruent, mechanical rumble of a truck up on the highway to break the spell, the taut, wordless space between them.

"I think we should be heading back now," Julia said finally. "The tide will be coming in soon."

"You go on ahead," Anna whispered and chewed at her lower lip. "I'll catch up."

Julia hesitated, glanced down at the cold saltwater lapping against the boulders, each breaking and withdrawing wave tumbling the cobbles imperceptibly smoother. Waves to wash the green-brown mats of seaweed one inch forward and one inch back; *Like the hair of drowned women,* she thought and then pushed the thought away.

"I'll wait for you at the top, then," she said. "In case you need help."

"Sure, Dr. Winter. You do that," and Anna turned away again and flicked the butt of her cigarette at the sea.

Almost an hour of hairpin curves and this road getting narrower and narrower still, strangling dirt road with no place to turn around, before Julia finally comes to the edge of the forest and the fern thickets and giant redwoods release her to rolling, open fields. Tall yellow-brown pampas grass that sways gently in the breeze, air that smells like sun and salt again, and she takes a deep breath. A relief to breathe air like this after the stifling closeness of the forest, all those old trees with their shaggy, shrouding limbs, and this clear blue sky is better, she thinks.

"There," Anna says, and Julia gazes past the dazzling green hood of the Chevy, across the restless grass, and there's something dark and far away silhouetted against the western sky.

"That's it," Anna says. "Yeah, that *must* be it," and now she's sounding like a kid on Christmas morning, little girl at an amusement park excitement; she climbs over the seat and sits down close to Julia.

I could always turn back now, Julia thinks, her hands so tight around the steering wheel that her knuckles have gone a waxy white. *I could turn this car right around and go back to the highway. We could be home in a few hours. We could be home before dark.*

"What are you *waiting* for?" Anna asks anxiously, and she points at the squat rectangular smudge in the distance. "That's it. We've found it."

"I'm beginning to think this is what you wanted all along," Julia says, speaking low, and she can hardly hear herself over the Bel Air's idling engine. "Anchor Bay, spending time together, that was all just a trick to get me to bring you out here, wasn't it?"

Anna looks reluctantly away from the house. "No," she says. "That's not true. I only remembered the house later, when we were on the beach."

Julia looks towards the distant house again, if it *is* a house. It might be almost anything, sitting out there in the tall grass, waiting. It might be almost anything at all.

"You're the one who's always telling me to get my nose out of books," and Anna's starting to sound angry, cultivated indignation gathering itself protectively about her like a caul, and she slides away from Julia, slides across the vinyl car seat until she's pressed against the passenger door.

"I don't think this was what I had in mind."

Anna begins kicking lightly at the floorboard, then, the toe of a sneaker tapping out the rhythm of her impatience like a Morse code signal, and "Jesus," she says, "It's only an old house. What the hell are you so afraid of, anyway?"

"I never said I was afraid, Anna. I never said anything of the sort."

"You're *acting* like it, though. You're acting like you're scared to death."

"Well, I'm not going to sit here and argue with you," Julia says and tells herself that just this once it doesn't matter if she sounds more like Anna's mother than her lover. "It's my car, and we never should have driven all the way out here alone. I would have turned around half an hour ago, if there'd been enough room on that road." And then she puts the Bel Air into reverse and backs off the dirt road, raising an alarmed and fluttering cloud of grasshoppers, frantic insect wings beating all about them as she shifts into drive and cuts the wheel sharply in the direction of the trees.

"I thought you'd understand," Anna says. "I thought you were different," and she's out of the car before Julia can try to stop her, slams her door shut and walks quickly away, following the path that leads between the high and whispering grass towards the house.

Julia sits in the Chevy and watches her go, watches helplessly as Anna seems to grows smaller with every step, the grass and the brilliant day swallowing her alive, wrapping her up tight in golden stalks and sunbeam teeth. And she imagines driving away alone, simply taking her foot off the brake pedal and retracing that twisting, tree-shadowed path to the safety of paved roads. How easy that would be, how perfectly satisfying, and then Julia watches Anna for a few more minutes before she turns the car to face the house and tries to pretend that she never had any choice at all.

The house like a grim and untimely joke, like something better off in a Charles Addams cartoon than perched on the high, sheer cliffs at the end of the road. This ramshackle grotesquerie of boards gone the silver grey of old oyster shells, the splinterskin walls with their broken windows and crooked shutters, steep gables and turrets missing half their slate shingles, and there are places where the roof beams and struts show straight through the house's weathered hide. One black lightning rod still standing guard against the sky, a rusting garland of wrought iron filigree along the eaves, and the uppermost part of the chimney has collapsed in a red-green scatter of bricks gnawed back to soft clay by moss and the corrosive sea air. Thick weeds where there might once have been a yard and flower beds, and the way the entire structure has begun to list perceptibly leaves Julia with the disconcerting impression that the house is cringing, or that it has actually begun to pull itself free of the earth and is preparing to crawl, inch by crumbling inch, away from the ocean.

"Anna, wait," but she's already halfway up the steps to the wide front porch, and Julia's still sitting behind the wheel of the Chevy. She closes her eyes for a moment, better to sit listening to the wind and the waves crashing against the cliffs and the smaller, hollow sound of Anna's feet on the porch, than to let the house think that she can't look away. Some dim instinct to tell her that's how this works, the sight of it to leave you dumbstruck and vulnerable.

My God, she thinks. *It's only an ugly, old house. An ugly, old house that no one wants anymore,* and then she laughs out loud, like it can hear.

After she caught up with Anna and made her get back into the car, and after Julia agreed to drive her the rest of the way out to the house, Anna Foley started talking about Dr. Montague's article in *Argosy* again, talked as though there'd never been an argument. The tension between them forgotten or discarded in a flood of words, words that came faster and faster as they neared the house, almost piling atop each other towards the end.

"There were stories that Dandridge murdered his daughter as a sacrifice, sometime after his wife died in 1914. But no one ever actually found her body. No, she just vanished one day, and no one ever saw her again. The daughter, I mean. The daughter vanished, not the wife. His wife is buried behind the house, though I'm not sure…"

Only an ugly, old house sitting forgotten beside the sea.

"…to Poseidon, or maybe even Dagon, who was a sort of Mesopotamian corn king, half man and half fish. Dandridge traveled all over Iraq and Persia before he came back and settled in California. He had a fascination with Persian and Hindu antiquities."

Then open your eyes and get this over with, and she does open her eyes, then, staring back at the house, and Julia relaxes her grip on the steering wheel. Anna's standing on the porch now, standing on tip-toes and peering in through a small shattered window near the door.

"Anna, wait on me. I'm coming," and Anna turns and smiles, waving to her, then goes back to staring into the house through the broken window.

Julia leaves the keys dangling in the ignition and picks her way towards the house, past lupine and wild white roses and a patch of poppies the color of tangerines, three or four orange-and-black monarch butterflies flitting from blossom to blossom, and there's a line of stepping stones almost lost in the weeds. The stones lead straight to the house, though the weedy patch seems much wider than it did from the car.

I should be there by now, she thinks, looking over her shoulder at the convertible and then ahead, at Anna standing on the porch, standing at the door of the Dandridge house, wrestling with the knob. *No. I'm so anxious, it only seems that way,* but five, seven, ten more steps, and the porch seems almost as far away as it did when she got out of the car.

"Wait on me," she shouts at Anna, who doesn't seem to have heard. Julia stops and wipes the sweat from her forehead before it runs down into her eyes. She glances up at the sun, directly overhead and hot against her face and bare arms, and she realizes that the wind has died. The blustery day grown suddenly so still, and she can't hear the breakers anymore, either. Only the faint and oddly muted cries of the gulls and grasshoppers.

She turns towards the sea, and there's a brittle noise from the sky that makes her think of eggshells cracking against the edge of a china mixing bowl, and on the porch Anna's opening the door. And the shimmering, sticky-wet darkness that flows out and over and *through* Anna Foley makes another sound, and Julia shuts her eyes so she won't have to watch whatever comes next.

The angle of the light falling velvet-soft across the dusty floor, the angle and the honey color of the sun, so she knows that it's late afternoon, and somehow she's lost everything in between. That last moment in the yard before this place without even unconsciousness to bridge the gap, then and now, and she understands it's as simple as that. Her head aches and her stomach rolls when she tries to sit up to get a better look at the room, and Julia decides that maybe it's best to lie still a little while longer. Just lie here and stare out that window at the blue sky framed in glass-jagged mouths. There might have been someone there a moment ago, a scarecrow face looking in at her through the broken window, watching, waiting, and there might have been nothing but the partitioned swatches of the fading day.

She can hear the breakers again, now only slightly muffled by the walls, and the wind around the corners of the house; these sounds through air filled with the oily stench of rotting fish and the neglected smell of any very old and empty house. A barren, fish-stinking room and a wall with one tall arched window just a few feet away from her, sun-bleached and peeling wallpaper strips, and she knows that it must be a western wall, the sunlight through the broken window panes proof enough of that.

Unless it's morning light, she thinks. *Unless it's morning light, and this is another day entirely, and the sun is rising now, instead of setting.* Julia wonders why she ever assumed it was afternoon, how she can ever again assume anything. And there's a sound, then, from somewhere behind her, inside the room with her or very close to it; the crisp sound of a ripe melon splitting open, scarlet flesh and black teardrop seeds, sweet red juice, and now the air smells even worse. Fish putrefying under a baking summer sun, beaches strewn with bloated fish-silver bodies as far as the eye can see, beaches littered with everything in the sea heaved up onto the shore, an inexplicable, abyssal vomit, and she closes her eyes again.

"Are you here, Anna?" she says. "Can you hear me?"

And something quivers at the edge of her vision, a fluttering darkness deeper than the long shadows in the room, and she ignores the pain and the nausea and rolls over onto her back to see it more clearly. But the thing on the ceiling sees her too, and it moves quickly towards the sanctuary of a corner; all feathery, trembling gills and swimmerets, and its jointed lobster carapace almost as pale as toadstools, chitin soft and pale, and it scuttles backwards on raw and bleeding human hands. It drips and leaves a spattered trail of itself on the floor as it goes.

She can see the door now, the absolute blackness waiting in the hall through the doorway, and there's laughter from that direction, a woman's high, hysterical laugh, but so faint that it can't possibly be coming from anywhere inside the house.

"Anna," she calls out again, and the laughter stops, and the thing on the ceiling clicks its needle teeth together.

"She's gone down, *that* one," it whispers. "She's gone all the way down to Mother Hydra and won't hear you in a hundred, hundred million years."

And the laughing begins again, seeping slyly up through the floorboards, through every crack on these moldering plaster walls.

"'I saw a something in the Sky,'" the ceiling crawler whispers from its corner, "'No bigger than my fist.'"

And the room writhes and spins around her like a kaleidoscope, that tumbling gyre of colored shards, remaking the world, and it wouldn't matter if there were anything for her to hold onto. She would still fall; no way not to fall with this void devouring even the morning, or the afternoon, whichever, even the colors of the day sliding down that slick gullet.

"I can't *see* you," Anna says, definitely Anna's voice but Julia's never heard her sound this way before. So afraid, so insignificant. "I can't see you *anywhere,*" and Julia reaches out (or down or up) into the furious storm that was the house, the maelstrom edges of a collapsing universe, and her arm sinks in up to the elbow. Sinks through into dead-star cold, the cold ooze of the deepest seafloor trench, and "Open your eyes," Anna says, and she's crying now. "Please, god, open your *eyes,* Julia."

But her eyes *are* open, and she's standing somewhere far below the house, standing before the woman on the rock, the thing that was a woman once, and part of it can still recall that lost humanity. The part that watches Julia with one eye, the pale green and desperate, hate-filled eye that hasn't been lost to the seething ivory crust of barnacles and sea lice that covers half its face. The woman on the great rock in the center of the phosphorescent pool, and then the sea rushes madly into the cavern, surges up and foams around the rusted chains and scales and all the squirming pink-white anemones sprouting from her thighs.

Alone, alone, all, all alone,

And the woman on the rock raises an arm, her ruined and shell-studded arm, and reaches across the pool towards Julia.

Alone on the wide, wide Sea.

Her long fingers and the webbing grown between them, and Julia leans out across the frothing pool, ice water wrapping itself around her ankles, filling her shoes, and she strains to take the woman's hand. Straining to reach as the jealous sea rises and falls, rises and falls, threatening her with the bottomless voices of sperm whales and typhoons. But the distance between their fingertips doubles, triples, origami space unfolding itself, and the woman's lips move silently, yellow teeth and pleading, gill-slit lips as mute as the cavern walls.

– murdered his daughter, sacrificed her –

Nothing from those lips but the small and startled creatures nesting in her mouth, not *words* but a sudden flow of surprised and scuttling legs, the claws and twitching antennae, and a scream that rises from somewhere deeper than the chained woman's throat, deeper than simple flesh, soul-scream spilling out and swelling to fill the cave from wall to wall. This howl that is every moment that she's spent down here, every damned and salt-raw hour made aural, and Julia feels it in her bones, in the silver amalgam fillings of her teeth.

Will you, won't you, will you, won't you, will you join the dance?

And the little girl sits by the fire in a rocking chair, alone in the front parlor of her father's big house by the sea, and she reads fairy tales to herself while her father rages somewhere overhead, in the sky or only upstairs but it makes no difference, in the end. Father of black rags and sour, scowling faces, and she tries not to hear the chanting or the sounds her mother is making again, tries to think of nothing but the Mock Turtle and Alice, the Lobster Quadrille by unsteady lantern light. *Don't look at the windows,* she thinks, or Julia tries to warn her. Don't look at the windows ever again.

Well, there was mystery. Mystery, ancient and modern, with Seaography: then Drawling – the Drawling-Master was an old conger-eel...

An old *conjure* eel –

Don't ever look at the windows even when the scarecrow fingers, the dry-grass bundled fingers, are tap-tap-tapping their song upon the glass. And she has seen the women dancing naked by the autumn moon, dancing in the tall moon-washed sheaves, bare feet where her father's scythe has fallen again and again, every reaping stroke to kill and call the ones that live at the bottom of the pool deep below the house. Calling them up and taunting them and then sending them hungrily back down to Hell again. Hell or the deep, fire or ice-dark water, and it makes no difference whatsoever in the end.

Would not, could not, would not, could not, would not join the dance.

Julia's still standing at the wave-smoothed edge of the absinthe pool, or she's only a whispering, insubstantial ghost afraid of parlor windows, smoke-grey ghost muttering from nowhen, from hasn't-been or never-will-be, and the child turns slowly towards her voice as the hurting thing chained to the rock begins to tear and stretches itself across the widening gulf.

"Julia, *please.*"

"You will be their queen, in the cities beneath the sea," the old man says. "When I am not even a *memory*, child, you will hold them to the depths."

And they all dead did lie, And a million million slimy things Liv'd on – and so did I...

"Open your eyes," Anna says, and this time Julia does. All these sights and sounds flickering past like the last frames of a movie, and she's lying in

Anna's arms, lying on her back in the weedy patch between the car and the brooding, spiteful house.

"I thought you were dead," Anna says, holding onto her so tight she can hardly breathe, and Anna sounds relieved and frightened and angry all at once, the tears rolling down her sunburned face and dripping off her chin onto Julia's cheeks.

"You were so goddamn cold. I thought you were dead. I thought I was alone."

Alone, alone, all, all alone...

"I smell flowers," Julia says, "I smell roses," because she does and she can think of nothing else to say, no mere words to ever make her forget, and she stares up past Anna, past the endless, sea-hued sky, at the summer-warm sun staring back down at her like the blind and blazing eye of Heaven.

Study for *The Witch House* (2013)

"I'm a busy woman," says the woman who owns the gallery at the corner of Elizabeth and Broome. "You have proof of authentication, and I don't have all evening to sit here debating the issue." She knows that's pushing, but she's spent two hours coddling the man who is still only a prospective buyer. And she does have somewhere to be, a date for the opening of the Hammons exhibit at L&M. The man's hemming and hawing and doubt is getting on her nerves. But he's come all the way from LA, and she doesn't want to lose the commission. The owners of the painting might be angry enough to pull it from the gallery if the man in the White Stripes T-shirt and banana yellow slacks and yellow fedora backs out because she put pleasure before business.

He chews at a thumbnail and squints at the Perrault.

The man's name is O'Hara, and he already owns three pieces by the dead painter. Indeed, he owns the most famous Perrault of all, *Fecunda ratis*. Or perhaps it's more accurate to think of that painting as infamous. Before the man in the yellow fedora acquired it, its two previous owners had both committed suicide. And both had killed themselves on the anniversary of the painting's completion. But that sort of shit only increases value, adding an air of risk to possessing a "cursed" object. A bad reputation draws the wealthy and morbid like flies to honey. Giovanni Bragolin's *The Crying Boy,* Diego Velasquez' *Venus With Mirror,* Bill Stoneham's *Hands Resist Him.* As do lost paintings. Or paintings no one has even suspected existed. Paintings like the one cradled on the easel in front of them. Personally, she feels the same way about *Study for "The Witch House"* that she feels about the rest of Albert Perrault's oeuvre. It's hideous, no matter how accomplished it might be. Curse or no curse, she wouldn't have it in her home for love or money.

"There's no record of it," says the man from LA. "He was fastidious about entering everything he finished in his Commonplace Book. But this one isn't there."

"Have you considered that might be because it's only a study?"

The man scratches at his scraggly goatee. The beard gives him a bit of a goatish appearance, and she thinks that, considering his stubbornness, the impression is not altogether inappropriate.

"You have the report from Freemanart right there in front of you. They've authenticated van Goghs and Picassos. Everything's right. The brushstrokes, the signature. Everything checks out."

"The fingerprint," O'Hara says.

"Yes, the fingerprint. It's hard to imagine anything more convincing than the fingerprint analysis."

"I might say the fingerprint's just a little too convenient, you know? There are ways to forge even a fingerprint. For that matter, proving Perrault touched the paint while it was still wet, it doesn't necessarily prove he did the painting."

She pictures herself driving an icepick through the man's face and out the back of his skull. She pictures a couple of other ways she might murder him and end this goddamn dithering.

"Any possibility you'd be willing to get a second opinion, another investigation to compare with the first?" he asks. "Corroboration."

She manages not to roll her eyes, but only just.

"I'm fairly certain the owners wouldn't be willing to pay for that. Perhaps if you were willing to cover the cost yourself, possibly then."

He frowns and scratches at his goatee. "You'd think, given the asking price, they'd be more reasonable. Wouldn't you agree?"

"I'm only an intermediary in the transaction," she says. "It's not my place to judge a client's decisions."

"Even though a forgery would be a disaster for your gallery? Even though it's possible you could be named as an accessory in a criminal conspiracy, or, at best, an accessory after the fact?"

You fucking dickbag, she thinks. *An icepick would be letting you off easy.*

She sighs. "I'm afraid we're coming to an impasse, Mr. O'Hara. I don't know what else I can possibly – "

"Charlie," he says.

"Charlie, I don't know what else I can say to persuade you this is, in fact, a genuine Perrault."

"Why didn't it go to auction?"

"I can't say."

He takes his eyes off the painting just long enough to shoot her a skeptical glare.

"Yes, but surely you've asked yourself the same question. They could get twice what they're asking at auction. Maybe the owners are afraid there's a greater chance that a fraud would be exposed if they went that route."

She almost looks at her watch. Instead, she looks down at the iPad in her lap, just to have anything to look at that isn't O'Hara or the wretched fucking painting.

"I wouldn't be so reticent if there were any mention of it – or plans to do a canvas titled *The Witch House* – anywhere in the Commonplace Book or any of his extant journals or correspondence. That makes it suspect, obviously."

"Which," she says, "is precisely why the owners paid for such a professional and thorough authentication process."

"I have quite a lot of his letters, you know," the man reminds her. He's already told her this twice, and never mind that she knew it before he even arrived. "And his 1987 journal. Given that this painting is *dated* '87, but isn't mentioned in the journal, you have to understand my apprehension."

"Perhaps he didn't mention it because he was dissatisfied. Perhaps he never went ahead with the actual painting because he lost interest in the subject matter." She didn't look up from the tablet.

"You are aware that Perrault discusses a lot of what he considered failures. Several projects he abandoned are discussed, two or three in detail." He doesn't even try to hide the condescension in his voice.

"You know the man better than I do, Charlie."

"I'm considered an authority," he says. "A few have said I'm the foremost authority on Albert Perrault."

"I suppose someone had to be," she says, hardly above a whisper. Still, she immediately wishes she had kept the thought to herself. O'Hara turns and glares at her. He clears his throat.

"You don't agree Perrault is worthy of my attention?"

She hesitates, but there's only so much backpedaling she can do without making a fool of herself. And commission or no commission, she's too tired of this man to give him the satisfaction. She settles for a middle ground.

"Perrault simply isn't to my taste, that's all. I will say that I'm glad he didn't become an architect." She means that. The crooked, ramshackle house in the painting, clinging to the edge of a towering sea cliff, it's a hideous thing. It strikes her, even, as a malignant thing, as it seems not to have been built, but to somehow have sprouted or been accreted from the stone and tall yellow grass.

"Oh, he didn't invent the house," O'Hara tells her. "It's a very real place. It's in California, somewhere north of Anchor Bay. Well, actually, there was a fire back in 2003, and not much of the house survived."

Now it's her turn to glare at him.

"You had no idea this painting even existed, and you still doubt its authenticity, but you know that's a real house? You even know where it is?"

"You could show me a painting of a house or a field in Arles, and you could claim it to be a genuine van Gogh – since you invoked his name a few minutes ago, van Gogh – and it may well be counterfeit, but that does not mean the forger didn't have a real house or field in mind."

"Point taken," she whispers. The two words feel sour in her mouth, just as the painting strikes her eyes as sour. She's just familiar enough with Perrault to know that this piece is typical of his earlier efforts, when he was still in his twenties. The style is more realistic, as if he might have intended a career as an illustrator. He'd already turned his back on contemporary schools of art, though he hadn't yet taken up what critics would eventually describe as a retro symbolist-impressionist fusion. He hadn't yet succumbed to his obsession with fairy tales and mythology, a fascination that would dominate his work until his death. The words feel sour in her mouth, almost as sour as the wicked old house on that wicked spit of land at the edge of the Pacific. She thinks that the house seems almost to writhe. That's nothing she'd ever say aloud, but that's how it strikes her. The gables and turrets seem, she thinks, to claw at the sky. Ugly, sour, wicked, hardly more than a stark silhouette.

"When you sent the photographs, that note pasted to the back – "

"Also authenticated as Perrault's handwriting."

" – I did some research."

The note – faded ink scribbled on a scrap of paper, then pasted to the back of the canvas – reads simply: Study 1 for 'The Witch House.' S. of Pt. Arena, Cal.

"I googled 'witch house' and 'Point Arena, California.' And found it. It was built in 1890 by a man named Machen Dandridge, supposedly some sort of wizard, right. In the sixties, hippies and occultist types treated it as a sort of mecca, and the locals talk about a cult that supposedly met there every Halloween until the fire."

"A cult," she says. She wants a cigarette; she's trying to stop smoking, but there's half a stale pack of Camels in her purse.

"Some pretty far-out stuff. This Dandridge fellow is supposed to have worshipped a bunch of obscure gods and goddesses of the ocean. Poseidon and some Semitic god of fishing and grain called Dagon. A couple of really fucking weird deities, Mother Hydra and Father Kraken, that I suspect he invented. Guy was a nutcase. Died around 1917 or 1918. Committed suicide, after accusations that he'd murdered his family, sacrificed them one by one to his pantheon."

O'Hara is in his element, lecturing the ignorant, holding court.

She looks away from the hideous, sour house. She looks at the floor, instead.

"You found all this online?"

"Some of it," he says, leaning nearer the painting. He takes a loupe from a shirt pocket and is inspecting the signature again. "There was also an article in the April 1957 issue of *Argosy* magazine. I scored a copy off eBay. There are a couple of photos, though they were taken from the seaward side, looking west. Supposedly there's another article in an issue of *Fate,* but I haven't tracked that one down yet."

She's never heard of either *Argosy* or *Fate,* but she doesn't say so.

"It all sounds like urban legend to me," she says.

"Oh, I'm sure a lot of it is. But Machen Dandridge, he was real enough. If this *is* a Perrault, I'm sure he went to the house after hearing about its unsavory reputation. Have you noticed this?" he asks, so she has to look up to see what he's talking about. "Right there," he says, pointing to a darker blotch near the base of the cliffs, where the waves are battering the stone. It might be a cave. There would be caves in rocks like that, hollowed out over centuries. If it is a cave and not just a murky patch where Perrault failed to capture the texture of the rock, it lies directly below the house.

"Listen, Charlie. If you want it, I'm authorized to offer a five-percent discount."

He puts the loupe away and rubs his goatish goatee.

Just take the damned thing. I don't want it here anymore.

She's having trouble taking her eyes off the maybe sea cave. She thinks it looks like a mouth.

"Five percent. Why didn't you tell me that to start with?"

"That's the best I can do," she says, ignoring the question.

A hungry mouth, a mouth that drinks in the tide and pukes up the world's secrets. And she thinks, *It's not the house Perrault was trying to capture. It was that goddamned hole.*

"Take it or leave it, Charlie."

He sighs and nods his head, the ridiculous yellow fedora bobbing up and down.

"Fine. Yeah," he sighs. "I'm not saying, mind you, that I'm totally, completely convinced it's the real McCoy. But if it is, I'll spend the rest of my life kicking myself if I let it slip through my fingers."

"You won't regret it," she says, her voice sounding odd and far away.

"Well, I'm going to pay for my own authentication."

"In twenty years, we've never once sold a forgery, Mr. O'Hara."

"Charlie," he says, frowning slightly. "Not that you know of. And there's a first time for everything. And if you *have* and *know* that you have, not like you'd sit there and own up to a felony, now would you?"

"No. I guess not," she says, perfectly aware she should be offended, should be furious that he'd have the nerve to make insinuations like that to her face. But she's having difficulty concentrating on anything but the cave, half hidden in the violence of white-capped breakers and spray. She's confident now that it *is* a cave, there beneath the house. And the longer she stares, the more it seems there's something else, something not quite human, peering out.

It's trapped. It's trapped there, and it's hurting. It's in agony.

"It should be in the Commonplace Book," O'Hara says again.

…after accusations that he'd murdered his family, sacrificed them one by one…

Ovid was a liar, and Perrault saw that.

"Trust me, he wrote everything down. He was obsessive in that regard."

In the weeks to come, the woman who owns the gallery will dream of the sour, wicked house and the maw of that cave. She'll dream she's steering a tiny storm-tossed dory that can find no safe harbor, of a secret, shimmering green pool below the witch house, and an island in the center of that pool, of the daughter of Cepheus and Cassiopeia stripped naked and chained to the ragged shore of Aethiopia, waiting for a rescue that will never come.

Andromeda Among the Stones

I cannot think of the deep sea without shuddering...

H.P. Lovecraft

October 1914

Is she really and truly dead, Father?" the girl asked, and Machen Dandridge, already an old man at fifty-one, looked up at the low buttermilk sky again and closed the black book clutched in his hands. He'd carved the tall headstone himself, the marker for his wife's grave there by the relentless Pacific, black shale obelisk with its hasty death's-head. His daughter stepped gingerly around the raw earth and pressed her fingers against the monument.

"Why did you not give her to the sea?" she asked. "She always wanted to go down to the sea at the end. She often told me so."

"I've given her back to the earth, instead," Machen told her and rubbed at his eyes. The cold sunlight through thin clouds was enough to make his head ache, his daughter's voice like thunder, and he shut his aching eyes for a moment. Just a little comfort in the almost blackness trapped behind his lids, parchment skin too insubstantial to bring the balm of genuine darkness, void to match the shades of his soul, and Machen whispered one of the prayers from the heavy black book and then looked at the grave again.

"Well, that's what she always said," the girl said again, running her fingertips across the rough-hewn stone.

"Things changed at the end, child. The sea wouldn't have taken her. I had to give her back to the earth."

"She said it was a sacrilege, planting people in the ground like wheat, like kernels of corn."

"She did?" He glanced anxiously over his left shoulder, looking back across the waves the wind was making in the high and yellow-brown grass, the narrow trail leading back down to the tall and brooding house that he'd built for his wife twenty-four years ago, back towards the cliffs and the place where the sea and sky blurred seamlessly together.

"Yes, she did. She said only barbarians and heathens stick their dead in the ground like turnips."

"I had no choice," Machen replied, wondering if that was exactly the truth or only something he'd like to believe. "The sea wouldn't take her, and I couldn't bring myself to burn her."

"Only heathens burn their dead," his daughter said disapprovingly and leaned close to the obelisk, setting her ear against the charcoal shale.

"Do you hear anything?"

"No, Father. Of course not. She's dead. You just said so."

"Yes," Machen whispered. "She is." And the wind whipping across the hillside made a hungry, waiting sound that told him it was time for them to head back to the house.

This is where I stand, at the bottom gate, and I hold the key to the abyss…

"But it's better that way," the girl said, her ear still pressed tight against the obelisk. "She couldn't stand the pain any longer. It was cutting her up inside."

"She told you that?"

"She didn't have to tell me that. I saw it in her eyes."

The ebony key to the first day and the last, the key to the moment when the stars wink out, one by one, and the sea heaves its rotting belly at the empty, sagging sky.

"You're only a child," he said. "You shouldn't have had to see such things. Not yet."

"It can't very well be helped now," she answered and stepped away from her mother's grave, one hand cupping her ear like maybe it had begun to hurt. "You know that, old man."

"I do," and he almost said her name then, Meredith, his mother's name, but the wind was too close, the listening wind and the salt-and-semen stink of the breakers crashing against the cliffs. "But I can wish it were otherwise."

"If wishes were horses, beggars would ride."

And Machen watched silently as Meredith Dandridge knelt in the grass and placed her handful of wilting wildflowers on the freshly turned soil. If it were spring instead of autumn, he thought, there would be dande-lions and poppies. If it were spring instead of autumn, the woman wrapped in a quilt and nailed up inside a pine-board casket would still be breathing. If it were spring, they would not be alone now, he and his daughter, at the edge of the world. The wind teased the girl's long yellow hair, and the sun glittered dimly in her warm green eyes.

The key I have accepted full in the knowledge of its weight.

"Remember me," Meredith whispered, either to her dead mother or something else, and he didn't ask which.

"We should be heading back now," he said and glanced over his shoulder again.

"So soon? Is that all you're going to read from the book? Is that all of it?"

"Yes, that's all of it, for now," though there would be more, later, when the harvest moon swelled orange-red and bloated and hung itself in the wide California night. When the women came to dance, then there would be other words to say, to keep his wife in the ground and the gate shut for at least another year.

The weight that is the weight of all salvation, the weight that holds the line against the last, unending night.

"It's better this way," his daughter said again, standing up, brushing the dirt off her stockings, from the hem of her black dress. "There was so little left of her."

"Don't talk of that here," Machen replied, more sternly than he'd intended. But Meredith didn't seem to have noticed or, if she'd noticed, not to have minded the tone of her father's voice.

"I will remember her the way she was before, when she was still beautiful."

"That's what she would want," he said and took his daughter's hand. "That's the way I'll remember her, as well," but he knew that was a lie, as false as any lie any living man ever uttered. He knew that he would always see his wife as the writhing, twisted thing she'd become at the last, the way she was after the gates were almost thrown open, and she placed herself on the threshold.

The frozen weight of the sea, the burning weight of starlight and my final breath. I hold the line. I hold the ebony key against the last day of all.

And Machen Dandridge turned his back on his wife's grave and led his daughter down the dirt and gravel path, back to the house waiting for them like a curse.

November 1914

Meredith Dandridge lay very still in her big bed, her big room with its high ceiling and no pictures hung on the walls, and she listened to the tireless sea slamming itself against the rocks. The sea there to take the entire world apart one gritty speck at a time, the sea that was here first and would be here long after the continents had finally been weathered down to so much slime and sand. She knew this because her father had read to her from his heavy black book, the book that had no name, the book that she couldn't ever read for herself or the demons would come for her in the night. And she knew, too, because of the books he had *given* her, her books – *Atlantis: The Antediluvian World, The World Before the Deluge,* and *Atlantis and Lost Lemuria*. Everything above the waves on borrowed time, her father had said again and again, waiting for the day when the sea rose once more and drowned the land beneath its smothering, salty bosom, and the highest mountains and deepest valleys will become a playground for sea serpents and octopuses and schools of herring. Forests to become Poseidon's orchards, her father said, though she knew Poseidon wasn't the true name of the god-thing at the bottom of the ocean, just a name some dead man gave it thousands of years ago.

"Should I read you a story tonight, Merry?" her dead mother asked, sitting right there in the chair beside the bed. She smelled like fish and mud, even though they'd buried her in the dry ground at the top of the hill behind the house. Meredith didn't look at her, because she'd spent so much time already trying to remember her mother's face the way it was *before* and didn't want to see the ruined face the ghost was wearing like a mask. As bad as the face her brother now wore, worse than that, and Meredith shrugged and pushed the blankets back a little.

"If you can't sleep, it might help," her mother said with a voice like kelp stalks swaying slowly in deep water.

"It might," Meredith replied, staring at a place where the wallpaper had begun to peel free of one of the walls, wishing there were a candle in the room or an oil lamp so the ghost would leave her alone. "And it might not."

"I could read to you from Hans Christian Andersen, or one of Grimm's tales," her mother sighed. "'The Little Mermaid' or 'The Fisherman and his Wife'?"

"You could tell me what it's like in Hell," the girl replied.

"Dear, I don't have to tell you that," her ghost mother whispered in a voice gone suddenly regretful and sad. "I know I don't have to ever tell you that."

"There might be different hells," Meredith said. "This one, and the one father sent you away to, and the one Avery is lost inside. No one ever said there could only be one, did they? Maybe it has many regions. A hell for the dead Prussian soldiers and another for the French, a hell for Christians and another for the Jews. And maybe another for all the pagans."

"Your father didn't send me anywhere, child. I crossed the threshold of my own accord."

"So I would be alone in *this* hell."

The ghost clicked its sharp teeth together, and Meredith could hear the anemone tendrils between its iridescent fish eyes quickly withdrawing into the hollow places in her mother's decaying skull.

"I could read you a poem," her mother said hopefully. "I could sing you a song."

"It isn't all fire and brimstone, is it? Not the region of hell where you are? It's blacker than night and cold as ice, isn't it, mother?"

"Did he think it would save me to put me in the earth? Does the old fool think it will bring me back across, like Persephone?"

Too many questions, hers and her mother's, and for a moment Meredith Dandridge didn't answer the ghost, kept her eyes on the shadowy wallpaper strips, the pinstripe wall, wishing the sun would rise and pour warm and gold as honey through the drapes.

"I crossed the threshold of my *own* accord," the ghost said again, and Meredith wondered if it thought she didn't hear the first time. Or maybe it was something her mother needed to believe and might stop believing if she stopped repeating it. "Someone had to do it."

"It didn't have to be you."

The wind whistled wild and shrill around the eaves of the house, invisible lips pressed to a vast, invisible instrument, and Meredith shivered and pulled the covers up to her chin again.

"There was no one else. It wouldn't take your brother. The one who wields the key cannot be a man. You know that, Merry. Avery knew that, too."

"There are other women," Meredith said, speaking through gritted teeth, not wanting to start crying but the tears already hot in her eyes. "It could have been someone else. It didn't have to be my mother."

"Some other child's mother, then?" the ghost asked. "Some other mother's daughter?"

"Go back to your hell," Meredith said, still looking at the wall, spitting out the words like poison. "Go back to your hole in the ground and tell your fairy tales to the worms. Tell *them* 'The Fisherman and his Wife.'"

"You have to be strong now, Merry. You have to listen to your father, and you have to be ready. I wasn't strong enough."

And finally she did turn to face her mother, what was left of her mother's face, the scuttling things nesting in her tangled hair, the silver scales and barnacles, the stinging anemone crown, and Meredith Dandridge didn't flinch or look away.

"One day," she said, "I'll take that damned black book of his, and I'll toss it into the stove. I'll take it, Mother, and toss it into the hearth, and then they can come out of the sea and drag us both away."

Her mother cried out and came apart like a breaking wave against the shingle, water poured from the tin pail that had given it shape, her flesh gone suddenly as clear and shimmering as glass, before she drained away and leaked through the cracks between the floorboards. The girl reached out and dipped her fingers into the shallow pool left behind in the wicker seat of the chair. The water was cold and smelled unclean. And then she lay awake until dawn, listening to the ocean, to all the unthinking noises a house makes in the small hours of a night.

May 1914

Avery Dandridge had his father's eyes, but someone else's soul to peer out through them, and to his sister he was hope that there might be a life somewhere beyond the rambling house beside the sea. Five years her senior, he'd gone away to school in San Francisco for a while, almost a year, because their mother wished him to. But there had been an incident, and he was sent home again, transgressions only spoken of in whispers and nothing anyone ever bothered to explain to Meredith, but that was fine with her. She only cared that he was back, and she was that much less alone.

"Tell me about the earthquake," she said to him, one day not long after he'd returned, the two of them strolling together along the narrow beach below the cliffs, sand the color of coal dust, noisy gulls and driftwood like titan bones washed in by the tide. "Tell me all about the fire."

"The earthquake? Merry, that was eight years ago. You were still just a baby, that was such a long time ago," and then he picked up a shell and turned it over in his hand, brushing away some of the dark sand stuck to it. "People don't like to talk about the earthquake anymore. I never heard them say much about it."

"Oh," she said, not sure what to say next but still full of questions. "Father says it was a sign, a sign from – "

"Maybe you shouldn't believe everything he says, Merry. It was an earthquake." And she felt a thrill then, like a tiny jolt of electricity rising up her spine and spreading out across her scalp, that anyone, much less Avery, would question their father and suggest she do likewise.

"Have you stopped believing in the signs?" she asked, breathless. "Is that what you learned in school?"

"I didn't learn much of anything important in school," he replied and showed her the shell in his palm. Hardly as big around as a nickel, but peaked in the center like a Chinaman's hat, radial lines of chestnut brown. "It's pretty," she said as he placed it in her palm.

"What's it called?"

"It's a limpet," he replied, because Avery knew all about shells and fish and the fossils in the cliffs, things he'd learned from their father's books and not from school. "It's a shield limpet. The jack mackerel carry them into battle when they fight the eels."

Meredith laughed out loud at that last part, and he laughed, too, then sat down on a rock at the edge of a wide tide pool. She stood there beside him, still inspecting the shell in her hand, turning it over and over again. The concave underside of the limpet was smoother than silk and would be white if not for the faintest iridescent hint of blue.

"That's not true," she said. "Everyone knows the jack mackerel and the eels are friends."

"Sure they are," Avery said. "Everyone knows that." But he was staring out to sea now and didn't turn to look at her. In a moment, she slipped the shell into a pocket of her sweater and sat down on the rock next to him.

"Do you see something out there?" she asked, and he nodded his head, but didn't speak. The wind rushed cold and damp across the beach and painted ripples on the surface of the pool at their feet. The wind and the waves seemed louder than usual, and Meredith wondered if that meant a storm was coming.

"Not a storm," Avery said, and that didn't surprise her because he often knew what she was thinking before she said it. "A war's coming, Merry."

"Oh yes, the jack mackerel and the eels," Merry laughed and squinted towards the horizon, trying to see whatever it was that had attracted her brother's attention. "The squid and the mussels."

"Don't be silly. Everyone knows that the squid and the mussels are great friends," and that made her laugh again. But Avery didn't laugh, looked away from the sea and stared down instead at the scuffed toes of his boots dangling a few inches above the water.

"There's never been a war like the one that's coming," he said after a while. "All the nations of the earth at each other's throats, Merry, and when we're done with all the killing, no one will be left to stand against the sea."

She took a very deep breath, the clean, salty air to clear her head, and began to pick at a barnacle on the rock.

"If that were true," she said, "Father would have told us. He would have shown us the signs."

"He doesn't see them. He doesn't dream the way I do."

"But you told him?"

"I tried. But he thinks it's something they put in my head at school. He thinks it's some kind of trick to make him look away."

Merry stopped picking at the barnacle, because it was making her fingers sore and they'd be bleeding soon if she kept it up. She decided it was better to watch the things trapped in the tide pool, the little garden stranded there until the sea came back to claim it. Periwinkle snails and hermit crabs wearing stolen shells, crimson starfish and starfish the shape and color of sunflowers.

"He thinks they're using me to make him look the other way, to catch him off his guard," Avery whispered, his voice almost lost in the rising wind. "He thinks I'm being set against him."

"Avery, I don't believe Father would say that about you."

"He didn't have to say it," and her brother's dark and shining eyes gazed out at the sea and sky again.

"We should be heading back soon, shouldn't we? The tide will be coming in before long," Meredith said, noticing how much higher up the beach the waves were reaching than the last time she'd looked. Another half hour and the insatiable ocean would be battering itself against the rough shale cliffs at their backs.

"'Wave after wave, each mightier than the last,'" Avery whispered, closing his eyes tightly, and the words coming from his pale, thin lips sounded like someone else, someone old and tired that Meredith had never loved.

"'Till last, a ninth one, gathering half the deep and full of voices, slowly rose and plunged roaring, and all the wave was in a flame – '"

"What's that?" she asked, interrupting because she didn't want to hear anymore. "Is it from Father's book?"

"No, it's not," he replied, sounding more like himself again, more like her brother. He opened his eyes, and a tear rolled slowly down his wind-chapped cheek. "It's just something they taught me at school."

"How can a wave be in flame? Is it supposed to be a riddle?" she asked, and he shook his head.

"No," he said and wiped at his face with his hands. "It's nothing at all, just a silly bit of poetry they made us memorize. School is full of silly poetry."

"Is that why you came home?"

"We ought to start back," he said, glancing quickly over his shoulder at the high cliffs, the steep trail leading back up towards the house. "Can't have the tide catching us with our trousers down, now can we?"

"I don't even wear trousers," Merry said glumly, still busy thinking about that ninth wave, the fire and the water. Avery put an arm around her and held her close to him for a moment while the advancing sea dragged itself eagerly back and forth across the wrack-scabbed rocks.

January 1915

Meredith sat alone on the floor at the end of the hallway, the narrow hall connecting the foyer to the kitchen and a bathroom, and then farther along, leading all the way back to the very rear of the house and this tall door that was always locked. The tarnished brass key always hung on its ring upon her father's belt. She pressed her ear against the wood and strained to hear anything at all. The wood was damp and very cold, and the smell of saltwater and mildew seeped freely through the space between the bottom of the door and the floor, between the door and the jamb. Once-solid redwood that had long since begun to rot from the continual moisture, the ocean's corrosive breath to rust the hinges so the door cried out like a stepped-on cat every time it was opened or closed. Even as a very small child, Meredith had feared this door, even in the days before she'd started to understand what lay in the deep place beneath her father's house.

Outside, the icy winter wind howled, and she shivered and pulled her grey wool shawl tighter about her shoulders; the very last thing her mother had made for her, that shawl. Almost as much hatred in Merry for the wind as for the sea, but at least it smothered the awful thumps and moans that came, day and night, from the attic room where her father had locked Avery away last June.

"There are breaches between the worlds, Merry," Avery had said, a few days before he picked the lock on the hallway door with the sharpened tip-end of a buttonhook and went down to the deep place by himself. "Rifts, fractures, ruptures. If they can't be closed, they have to be guarded against the things on the other side that don't belong here."

"Father says it's a portal," she'd replied, closing the book she'd been reading, a dusty, dog-eared copy of Franz Unger's *Primitive World.*

Her brother had laughed a dry, humourless laugh and shaken his head, nervously watching the fading day through the parlour windows. "Portals are built on purpose, to be used. These things are accidents, at best, casualties of happenstance, tears in space when one world passes much too near another."

"Well, that's not what Father says."

"Read your book, Merry. One day you'll understand. One day soon, when you're not a child anymore, and he loses his hold on you."

And she'd frowned, sighed, and opened her book again, opening it at random to one of the strangely melancholy lithographs – *The Period of the Muschelkalk [Middle Trias].* A violent seascape, and in the foreground a reef jutted above the waves, crowded with algae-draped driftwood branches and the shells of stranded mollusca and crinoidea. There was something like a crocodile, a beast the author called *Nothosaurus giganteus,* clinging to the reef so it wouldn't be swept back into the storm-tossed depths. Overhead, the night sky was a turbulent mass of clouds with the small white moon, full or near enough to full, peeking through to illuminate the ancient scene.

"You mean planets?" she'd asked Avery. "You mean moons and stars?"

"No, I mean *worlds.* Now, read your book, and don't ask so many questions."

Meredith thought she heard creaking wood, her father's heavy foot-steps, the dry ruffling of cloth rubbing against cloth, and she stood quickly, not wanting to be caught listening at the door again, was still busy straightening her rumpled dress when she realized that he was standing there in the hall behind her, instead. Her mistake, thinking he'd gone to the deep place, when he was somewhere else all along, in his library or the attic room with Avery or outside braving the cold to visit her mother's grave on the hill.

"What are you doing, child?" he asked her gruffly and tugged at his beard. There were streaks of silver-grey that weren't there only a couple of months before, scars from the night they lost her mother, his wife, the night the demons tried to squeeze in through the tear, and Ellen Dandridge had tried to block their way. His face grown years older in the space of weeks, dark crescents beneath his eyes like bruises and deep creases in his forehead. He brushed his daughter's blonde hair from her eyes.

"Would it have been different, if you'd believed Avery from the start?"

For a moment he didn't reply, and his silence, his face set as hard and perfectly unreadable as stone, made her want to strike him, made her wish she could kick open the rotting, sea-damp door and hurl him screaming down the stairs to whatever was waiting for them both in the deep place.

"I don't know, Meredith. But I had to trust the book, and I had to believe the signs in the heavens."

"You were too arrogant, old man. You almost gave away the whole wide world because you couldn't admit you might be wrong."

"You should be thankful that your mother can't hear you, young lady, using that tone of voice with your own father."

Meredith turned and looked at the tall, rotten door again, the symbols drawn on the wood in whitewash and blood.

"She can hear me," Meredith told him. "She talks to me almost every night. She hasn't gone as far away as you think."

"I'm still your father, and you're still a child who can't even begin to understand what's at stake, what's always pushing at the other side of – "

" – the gate?" she asked, interrupting and finishing for him, and she put one hand flat against the door, the upper of its two big panels, and leaned all her weight against it. "What happens next time? Do you even know, Father? How much longer do we have left, or haven't the constellations gotten around to telling you that yet?"

"Don't mock me, Meredith."

"Why not?" and she stared back at him over her shoulder, without taking her hand off the door. "Will it damn me faster? Will it cause more men to die in the trenches? Will it cause Avery more pain than he's in now?"

"*I* was given the book," he growled at her, his stony face flashing to bitter anger, and at least that gave Meredith some mean scrap of satisfaction.

"I was shown the way to this place. They entrusted the gate to me, child. The gods – "

" – must be even bigger fools than you, old man. Now shut up, and leave me alone."

Machen Dandridge raised his right hand to strike her, his big-knuckled hand like a hammer of flesh and bone, iron-meat hammer and anvil to beat her as thin and friable as the veil between Siamese universes.

"You'll need me," she said, not recoiling from the fire in his dark eyes, standing her ground. "You can't take my place. Even if you weren't a coward, you couldn't take my place."

"You've become a willful, wicked child," he said, slowly lowering his hand until it hung useless at his side.

"Yes, Father, I have. I've become a *very* wicked child. You'd best pray that I've become wicked enough."

And he didn't reply, no words left in him, but walked quickly away down the long hall towards the foyer and his library, his footsteps loud as distant gunshots, loud as the beating of her heart, and Meredith removed her hand from the door. It burned very slightly, pain like a healing bee sting, and when she looked at her palm there was something new there, a fat and shiny swelling as black and round and smooth as the soulless eye of a shark.

February 1915

In his dreams, Machen Dandridge stands at the edge of the sea and watches the firelight reflected in the roiling grey clouds above Russia and Austria and East Prussia, smells the coppery stink of Turkish and German blood, the life leaking from the bullet holes left in the Serbian Archduke and his wife. Machen would look away if he knew how, wouldn't see what he can only see too late to make any difference. One small man set adrift and then cast up on the shingle of the cosmos, filled to bursting with knowledge and knowing nothing at all. Cannon fire and thunder, the breakers against the cliff side and the death rattle of soldiers beyond counting.

This is where I stand, at the bottom gate, and I hold the key to the abyss…

"A *world* war, father," Avery says. "Something without precedent. I can't even find words to describe the things I've seen."

"A world war, without precedent?" Machen replies skeptically and raises one eyebrow, then goes back to reading his star charts. "Napoleon just might disagree with you there, young man, and Alexander, as well."

"No, you don't understand what I'm saying – "

And the fire in the sky grows brighter, coalescing into a whip of red-gold scales and ebony spines, the dragon's tail to lash the damned. *Every one of us is damned,* Machen thinks. *Every one of us, from the bloody start of time.*

"I have the texts, Avery, and the aegis of the seven, and all the old ways. I cannot very well set that all aside because you've been having nightmares, now can I?"

"I know these things, Father. I know them like I know my own heart, like I know the number of steps down to the deep place."

"There is a trouble brewing in Coma Berenices," his wife whispers, her eye pressed to the eyepiece of the big telescope in his library. "Something like a shadow."

"She says that later," Avery tells him. "That hasn't happened yet, but it will. But you won't listen to her, either."

And Machen Dandridge turns his back on the sea and the dragon, on the battlefields and the burning cities, looking back towards the house he built twenty-five years ago. The air in the library seems suddenly very close, too warm, too thick. He loosens his paper collar and stares at his son sitting across the wide mahogany desk from him.

"I'm not sure I know what you mean, boy," he says, and Avery sighs loudly and runs his fingers through his brown hair.

"Mother isn't even at the window now. That's still two weeks from now," and it's true that no one's standing at the telescope. Machen rubs his eyes and reaches for his spectacles. "By then, it'll be too late. It may be too late already," Avery says.

"Listen to him, Father," Meredith begs with her mother's voice, and then she lays a small, wilted bouquet of autumn wildflowers on Ellen Dandridge's grave. The smell of the broken earth at the top of the hill is not so different from the smell of the French trenches.

"I did listen to him, Merry."

"You let him talk. You know the difference."

"Did I ever tell you about the lights in the sky the night that you were born?"

"Yes, Father. A hundred times."

"There were no lights at your brother's birth."

Behind him, the sea makes a sound like a giant rolling over in its sleep, and Machen looks away from the house again, stares out across the surging black Pacific. There are the carcasses of whales and sea lions and a billion fish and the bloated carcasses of things even he doesn't know the names for, floating in the surf. Scarlet-eyed night birds swoop down to eat their fill of carrion. The water is so thick with dead things and maggots and blood that soon there will be no water left at all.

"The gate chooses the key," his wife says sternly, sadly, standing at the open door leading down to the deep place beneath the house, the bottom-less, phosphorescent pool at the foot of the winding, rickety steps. The short pier and the rock rising up from those depths, the little island with its cave and shackles. "You can't change that part, no matter what the seven have given you."

"It wasn't me sent Avery down there, Ellen."

"It wasn't either one of us. But neither of us listened to him, so maybe it's the same as if we both did."

The sea as thick as buttermilk, buttermilk and blood beneath a rotten moon, and the dragon's tail flicks through the stars.

"Writing the history of the end of the world," Meredith says, standing at the telescope, peering into the eyepiece, turning first this knob, then that one, trying to bring something in the night sky into sharper focus. "That's what he kept saying, anyway. 'I am writing the history of the end of the world. I'm writing the history of the future.' Father, did you know that there's trouble in Coma Berenices?"

"Was that you?" he asks her. "Was that you said that or was that your mother?"

"Is there any difference? And if so, do you know the difference?"

"Are these visions, Merry? Are these terrible visions that I may yet hope to affect?"

"Will you keep him locked in that room forever?" she asks, not answering his questions, not even taking her eye from the telescope.

Before his wife leaves the hallway, before she steps onto the unsteady landing at the top of the stairs, she kisses Meredith on the top of her head and then glares at her husband, her eyes like judgment on the last day of all, the eyes of seraphim and burning swords. The diseased sea slams against the cliffs, dislodging chunks of shale, silt gone to stone when the great reptiles roamed the planet and the gods still had countless revolutions and upheavals to attend to before the beginning of the tragedy of mankind.

"Machen," his wife says. "If you had listened, had you allowed me to listen, everything might have been different. The war, what's been done to Avery, all of it. If you'd but *listened.*"

And the dream rolls on and on and on behind his eyes, down the stairs and to the glowing water, his wife alone in the tiny boat, rowing across the pool to the rocky island far beneath the house. The hemorrhaging, pus-colored sea throwing itself furiously against the walls of the cavern, wanting in, and it's always been only a matter of time. Meredith standing on the pier behind him, chanting the prayers he's taught her, the prayers to keep the gate from opening before Ellen reaches that other shore.

The yellow-green light beneath the pool below the house wavers, then grows brighter by degrees.

The dragon's tail flicks at the suicidal world.

In his attic, Avery screams with the new mouth the gate gave him before it spit the boy, twisted and insane, back out into this place and this time.

The oars dipping again and again into the brilliant, glowing water, the creak of the rusted oarlocks, old nails grown loose in decaying wood; shafts of light from the pool playing across the uneven walls of the cavern.

The dragon opens one blistered eye.

And Ellen Dandridge steps out of the boat onto the island. She doesn't look back at her husband and daughter.

"Something like a shadow," Meredith says, taking her right eye from the telescope and looking across the room at her brother, who isn't sitting in the chair across from Machen.

"It's not a shadow," Avery doesn't tell her, and goes back to the things he has to write down in his journals before there's no time left.

On the island, the gate tears itself open, the dragon's eye, angel eye, and the unspeakable face of the titanic alien sleeper in an unnamed, sunken city, tearing itself wide to see if she's the one it's called down or if it's some other. The summoned or the trespasser. The invited or the interloper. And Machen knows from the way the air has begun to shimmer and sing that the sleeper doesn't like what it sees.

"I stand at the gate and hold the key," she says. "You know my name, and I have come to hold the line. I have come only that you might not pass."

"Don't look, Merry. Close your eyes," and Machen holds his daughter close to him as the air stops singing, as it begins to sizzle and pop and burn.

The waves against the shore.

The dragon's tail across the sky.

The empty boat pulled down into the shimmering pool.

Something glimpsed through a telescope.

The ribsy, omnivorous dogs of war.

And then Machen woke in his bed, a storm lashing fiercely at the windows, the lightning exploding out there like mortar shells, and the distant *thump thump thump* of his lost son from the attic. He didn't close his eyes again, but lay very still, sweating and listening to the rain and the thumping, until the sun rose somewhere behind the clouds to turn the black to cheerless, leaden grey.

August 1889

After his travels, after Baghdad and the ruins of Nineveh and Babylon, after the hidden mosque in Reza'lyah and the peculiar artefacts he'd collected on the southernmost shore of Lake Urmia, Machen Dandridge went west to California. In the summer of 1889, he married Ellen Douglas-Winslow, black-sheep daughter of a fine old Boston family, and together they traveled by train, the smoking iron horses and steel rails that his own father had made his fortune from, riding all the way to the bustling squalor and Nob Hill sanctuaries of San Francisco. For a time they took up residence in a modest house on Russian Hill, while Machen taught his wife the things that he'd learned in the East – archaeology and astrology, Hebrew and Islamic mysticism, the Talmud and Qur'an, the secrets of the terrible black book that had been given to him by a blind and leprous mullah. Ellen had disgraced her family at an early age by claiming the abilities of a medium and then backing up her claims with extravagant séances and spectacular ectoplasmic displays. Machen found in her an eager pupil.

"Why would he have given the book to you?" Ellen asked skeptically, the first time Machen had shown it to her, the first time he'd taken it from its iron and leather case in her presence. "If it's what you say it is, why would he have given it to anyone?"

"Because, my dear, I had a pistol pressed against his rotten skull," Machen had replied, unwrapping the book, slowly peeling back the layers of lambskin it was wrapped in. "That and knowledge he'd been searching for his entire life. Trust me. It was a fair trade."

And just as the book had led him back from Asia to America and on to California, the brittle, parchment compass of its pages had shown him the way north along the coast to the high cliffs north of Anchor Bay. That first trip, he left Ellen behind, traveling with only the company of a Miwok Indian guide who claimed knowledge of "a hole in the world." But when they finally left the shelter of the redwood forest and stood at the edge of a vast and undulating sea of grass stretching away towards the Pacific, the Miwok had refused to go any farther. No amount of money or talk could persuade him to approach the cliffs waiting beyond the grass, and so Machen continued on alone.

Beneath the hot summer sun, the low, rolling hills seemed to go on forever. The gulls and a pair of red-tailed hawks screamed like harpies warning him away, screeching threats or alarum from the endless cornflower sky. But he found it, finally, the "hole in the world," right where the Miwok guide had said that he would, maybe fifty yards from the cliffs.

From what he'd taught himself of geology, Machen guessed it to be the collapsed roof of a cavern, an opening no more than five or six feet across, granting access to an almost vertical chimney eroded through tilted beds of limestone and shale and probably connecting to the sea somewhere in the darkness below. He dropped a large pebble into the hole and listened and counted as it fell, ticking off the seconds until it splashed faintly, confirming his belief that the cavern must be connected to the sea. A musty, briny smell wafted up from the hole, uninviting, sickly, and though there was climbing equipment in his pack, and he was competent with ropes and knots and had, more than once, descended treacherous, crumbling shafts into ancient tombs and wells, Machen Dandridge only stood there at the entrance, dropping stones and listening to the eventual splashes. He stared into the hole and, after a while, could discern a faint but unmistakable light, not the fading sunlight getting in from some cleft in the cliff face, but light like a glass of absinthe, the sort of light he'd imagined abyssal creatures that never saw the sun might make to shine their way through the murk.

It wasn't what he'd expected, from what was written in the black book, no towering gate of horn and ivory, no arch of gold and silver guarded by angels or demons or beings men had never fashioned names for, just this unassuming hole in the ground. He sat in the grass, watching the sunset burning day to night, wondering if the Miwok had deserted him. Wondering if the quest had been a fool's errand from the very start, and he'd wasted so many years of his life, and so much of his inheritance, chasing connections and truths that only existed because he wished to see them.

By dark, the light shone up through the hole like some unearthly torch, taunting or reassuring but beckoning him forward. Promising there was more to come.

"What is it you think you will find?" the old priest had asked after he'd handed over the book. "More to the point, what is it you think will find *you?*"

Not a question he could answer then and not one he could answer sitting there with the roar of the surf in his ears and the stars speckling the sky overhead. The question that Ellen had asked him again and again, and always he'd found some way to deflect her asking. But he *knew* the answer, sewn up somewhere deep within his soul, even if he'd never been able to find the words. Proof that the world did not end at his fingertips or with the unreliable data of his eyes and ears or the lies and half-truths men had written down in science and history books, that everything he'd ever seen was merely a tattered curtain waiting to be drawn back so that some more indisputable light might, at last, shine through.

"Is that what you were seeking, Mr. Dandridge?" and Machen had turned quickly, his heart pounding as he reached for the pistol at his hip, only to find the Indian watching him from the tall, rustling grass a few feet away. "Is *this* the end of your journey?" and the guide pointed at the hole.

"I thought you were afraid to come here?" Machen asked, annoyed at the interruption, sitting back down beside the hole, looking again into the unsteady yellow-green light spilling out of the earth.

"I was," the Miwok replied. "But the ghost of my grandfather came to me and told me he was ashamed of me, that I was a coward for allowing you to come to this evil place alone. He has promised to protect me from the demons."

"The ghost of your grandfather?" Machen laughed and shook his head, then dropped another pebble into the hole.

"Yes. He is watching us both now, but he also wishes we would leave soon. I can show you the way back to the trail."

The key I have accepted full in the knowledge of its weight.

"You're a brave man," Machen said. "Or another lunatic."

"All brave men are lunatics," the Indian said and glanced nervously at the hole, the starry indigo sky, the cliff and the invisible ocean, each in its turn. "Sane men do not go looking for their deaths."

"Is that all I've found here? My death?"

There was a long moment of anxious silence from the guide, broken only by the ceaseless interwoven roar of the waves and the wind, and then he took a step back away from the hole, deeper into the sheltering grass.

"I cannot say what you have found in this place, Mr. Dandridge. My grandfather says I should not speak its name."

"Is that so? Well, then," and Machen stood, rubbing his aching eyes. He brushed the dust from his pants. "You show me the way back and forget you ever brought me out here. Tell your grandfather's poor ghost that I will not hold you responsible for whatever it is I'm meant to find at the bottom of that pit."

"My grandfather hears you," the Miwok said. "He says you are a brave man and a lunatic, and that I should kill you now, before you do the things you will do in the days to come. Before you set the world against itself."

Machen drew his Colt, cocked the hammer with his thumb, and stood staring into the gloom at the Indian.

"But I will not kill you," the Miwok said. "That is *my* choice, and I have chosen not to take your life. But I will pray it is not a decision I will regret later. We should go now."

"After you," Machen said, smiling through the quaver in his voice that he hoped the guide couldn't hear, his heart racing and cold sweat starting to drip from his face despite the night air. And, without another word, the Indian turned and disappeared into the arms of the whispering grass and the August night.

July 1914

When she was very sure that her father had shut the double doors to his study and that her mother was asleep, when the only sounds were the sea and the wind, the inconstant, shifting noises that all houses make after dark, the mice in the walls, Meredith slipped out of bed and into her flannel dressing gown. The floor was cool against her bare feet, cool but not cold. She lit a candle, and then eased the heavy bedroom door shut behind her and went as quickly and quietly as she could to the cramped stairwell leading from the second story to the attic door. At the top, she sat down on the landing and held her breath, listening, praying that no one had heard her, that neither her father nor mother, nor the both of them together, were already trying to find her.

There were no sounds at all from the other side of the narrow attic door. She set the candlestick down and leaned close to it, pressing her lips against the wood, feeling the rough grain through the varnish against her flesh.

"Avery?" she whispered. "Avery, can you hear me?"

At first there was no reply from the attic, and she took a deep breath and waited a while, waiting for her parents' angry or worried footsteps, waiting for one of them to begin shouting her name from the house below.

But there were no footsteps, and no one called her name.

"Avery? Can you hear me? It's *me*, Merry."

That time there was a sudden thumping and a heavy dragging sort of a sound from the other side of the attic door. A body pulling itself roughly, painfully across the pine-board floor towards her, and she closed her eyes and waited for it. Finally, there was a loud thud against the door, and she opened her eyes again. Avery was trying to talk, trying to answer her, but there was nothing familiar or coherent in his ruined voice.

"Hold on," she whispered to him. "I brought a writing pad." She took it out of a pocket of her gown, the pad and a pencil. "Don't try to talk any more. I'll pass this beneath the door to you, and you can write what you want to say. Knock once if you understand what I'm telling you, Avery."

Nothing for almost a full minute and then a single knock so violent that the door shivered on its hinges, so loud she was sure it would bring her parents running to investigate.

"Not so *loud,* Avery," she whispered. "They'll hear us," and now Meredith had begun to notice the odor on the landing, the odor leaking from the attic. Either she'd been much too nervous to notice it at first or her brother had brought it with him when he'd crawled over to the door. Dead fish and boiling cabbage, soured milk and strawberry jam, the time she'd come across the carcass of a grey whale calf, half buried in the sand and decomposing beneath the sun. She swallowed, took another deep breath, and tried not to think about the awful smell.

"I'm going to pass the pencil and a page from the pad to you now. I'm going to slide it under the door to you."

Avery made a wet, strangling sound, and she told him again not to try to talk, just write if he could, write the answers to her questions and anything else that he needed to say.

"Are you in pain? Is there any way I can help?" she asked, and in a moment the tip of the pencil began scritching loudly across the sheet of writing paper. "Not so hard, Avery. If the lead breaks, I'll have to try to find another."

He slid the piece of paper back to her, and it was damp and something dark and sticky was smudged across the bottom. She held it close to her face, never mind the smell so strong it made her gag, made her want to retch, so that she could read what he'd scrawled there. It was nothing like Avery's careful hand, his tight, precise cursive she'd always admired and had tried to imitate, but sweeping, crooked letters, blocky print, and seeing that made her want to cry so badly that she almost forgot about the dead-whale-and-cabbages smell.

HURTSS ME MERY MORE THAN CAN NO

NO HELP NO HELLP ME

She laid down the sheet of paper and tore another from her pad, the pad she used for her afternoon lessons, spelling and arithmetic, and she slid it beneath the door to Avery.

"Avery, you *knew* you couldn't bear the key. You knew it had to be me or mother, *didn't* you? That it had to be a woman?"

Again the scritching, and the paper came back to her even stickier than before.

HAD TO TRY MOTER WOULD NOT LISSEN SO

I HAD TOO TRIE

"Oh, Avery," Meredith said. "I'm sorry," speaking so quietly that she prayed he would not hear, and there were tears in her eyes, hot and bitter. A kind of anger and a kind of sorrow in her heart that she'd never known before, anger and sorrow blooming in her to be fused through some alchemy of the soul, and by that fusion be transformed into a pure and golden hate.

She tore another page from the pad and slipped it through the crack between the floor and the attic door.

"I need to know what to *do,* Avery. I'm reading the newspapers, but I don't understand it all. Everyone seems to think war is coming soon, because of the assassination in Sarajevo, because of the Kaiser, but I don't *understand* it all."

It was a long time before the paper came back to her, smeared with slime and stinking of corruption, maybe five minutes of Avery's scritching and his silent pauses between the scritching. This time the page was covered from top to bottom with his clumsy scrawl.

TO LATE ~~IF~~ TO STOP WAR TOO LATE NOW

WAR IS COMING NOW CANT STP THAT MERRY
<u>ALL</u> SET IN MOTION NINTH WAVE REMEMBER?
BUT MERY YOU CAN DONT LISSEN TO FADER
YOU <u>CAN</u> HOLD ~~NINE~~ THEE LINE STILL TYME
YOU OR MOTHER KIN HOLD THEE LIN STILL
IT DOEZ NOT HALF TO BE THE <u>LADST</u> WAR

When she finished reading and then re-reading twice again everything Avery had written, Meredith lay the sheet of paper down on top of the other two and wiped her hand on the floor until it didn't feel quite so slimy anymore. By the yellow-white light of the candle, her hand shimmered as though she'd been carrying around one of the big banana slugs that lived in the forest. She quickly ripped another page from the writing pad and passed it under the door. This time she felt it snatched from her fingers, and the scritching began immediately. It came back to her only a few seconds later and the pencil with it, the tip ground away to nothing.

DUNT <u>EVER</u> COME BAK HERE AGIN MERRY
I LOVE YOU ALWAYTS AND WONT FERGET YOU
<u>PROMISS</u> ME YOU WILL KNOT COME BACK
<u>HOLD THEE LINE HOLD THE LINE</u>

"I can't promise you that, Avery," she replied, sobbing and leaning close to the door, despite the smell so strong that it had begun to burn her nose and the back of her throat. "You're my brother, and I can't ever promise you that."

There was another violent thud against the door then, so hard that her father was sure to have heard, so sudden that it scared her, and Meredith jumped back and reached for the candlestick.

"I remember the ninth wave, Avery. I remember what you said – the ninth wave, greater than the last, all in flame. I *do* remember."

And because she thought that perhaps she heard footsteps from somewhere below, and because she couldn't stand to hear the frantic strangling sounds that Avery had begun making again, Meredith hastily gathered up the sticky, scribbled-on pages from the pad and then crept down the attic stairs and back to her bedroom. She fell asleep just before dawn and dreamt of flames among the breakers, an inferno crashing against the rocks.

March 1915

"This is where it ends, Merry," her mother's ghost said. "But this is where it begins, as well. You need to understand that if you understand nothing else."

Meredith knew that this time she was not dreaming, no matter how much it might *feel* like a dream, this dazzling, tumbling nightmare wide-awake that began when she reached the foot of the rickety spiraling staircase leading her down into the deep place beneath the house. Following her mother's ghost, the dim glow of a spectre to be her Virgil, her Beatrice, her guiding lantern until the light from the pool was so bright it outshone Ellen Dandridge's flickering radiance. Meredith stood on the pier, holding her dead mother's barnacle- and algae-encrusted hand, and stared in fear and wonder towards the island in the pool.

"The infinite lines of causation," the ghost said. "What has brought you here. That is important, as well."

"I'm here because my father is a fool," Meredith replied, unable to look away from the yellow-green light dancing across the stone, shining up from the depths beneath her bare feet.

"No, dear. He is only a man trying to do the work of gods. That never turns out well."

The black eye set deep into the flesh of Meredith's palm itched painfully and then rolled back to show its dead-white sclera. She knew exactly what it was seeing, because it always told her; she knew how close they were to the veil, how little time was left before the breach tore itself open once and for all.

"Try to forget your father, child. Concentrate on time and space, the aether, on the history that has brought you here. All the strands of the web."

Meredith squeezed the ghost's soft hand, and the dates and names and places spilled through her like the sea spilling across the shore, a flood of obvious and obscure connections, and she gritted her teeth and let them come.

On December 2, 1870, Bismark sends a letter to Wilhelm of Prussia urging him to become Kaiser. In 1874, all Jesuits are ordered to leave Italy, and on January 8th, 1877, Crazy Horse is defeated by the U.S. cavalry at Wolf Mountain in Montana. In June 1881, Austria signs a secret treaty with the Serbs, establishing an economic and political protectorate, and Milan is crowned King of Serbia —

"It hurts," she whispered; her mother frowned and nodded her head as the light from the pool began to pulse and spin, casting counterclockwise glare and shadow across the towering rock walls.

"It will always hurt, dear. It will be pain beyond imagining. You cannot be lied to about that. You cannot be led to bear this weight in ignorance of the pain that comes with the key."

Meredith took another hesitant step towards the end of the short pier, and then another, and the light swelled angrily and spun hurricane fury below and about her.

"They are rising, Merry. They have teeth and claws sharp as steel and will devour you if you don't hurry. You must go to the island now. The breach is opening."

"I am afraid, mother. I'm so sorry, but I *am* afraid."

"Then the fear will lead you where I can't. Make the fear your shield. Make the fear your lance."

Standing at the very end of the pier, Meredith didn't dare look down into the shining pool, kept her eyes on the tiny island only fifteen or twenty feet away.

"They sunk the boat when you crossed over," she said to her mother's ghost. "How am I supposed to reach the gate when they've taken the boat away?"

"You're a strong swimmer, child. Avery taught you well."

A sound like lightning, and *No,* she thought. *I can't do that. I can do anything except step off this pier into that water with them. I can stand the pain, but –*

"If you know another way, Merry, then take it. But there isn't much time left. The lines are converging."

Merry took a deep breath, gulping the cavern's dank and foetid air, hyperventilating, bracing for the breathless cold to come, all the things that her brother had taught her about swimming in the sea. Together they'd swum out past the breakers, to the kelp forest in the deep water farther offshore, the undulating submarine weald where bat rays and harbor seals raced between the gigantic stalks of kelp, where she'd looked up and seen the lead-pale belly of an immense white shark passing silently overhead.

"Time, Merry. It is all in your hands now. See how you stand alone at the center of the web and the strands stretch away from you? See the intersections and interweaves?"

"I see them," she said. "I see them all," and she stepped off into the icy water.

October 30th, 1883, an Austro-German treaty with Roumania is signed, providing Roumania defence against the Russians. November 17th, 1885, the Serbs are defeated at the Battle of Slivnitza and then ultimately saved only by Austrian intervention. 1887, and the Mahdist War with Abyssinia begins. 1889, and a boy named Silas Desvernine sails up the Hudson River and first sees a mountain where a nameless being of moonlight and thunder is held inside a black stone. August 1889, and her father is led to the edge of the Pacific by a Miwok guide. August 27th, 1891, the Franco-Russian Entente –

The strands of the web, the ticking of a clock, the life and death of stars, each step towards Armageddon checked off in her aching head, and the water is liquid ice threatening to freeze her alive. Suddenly, the tiny island seemed miles and miles away.

1895 August, and Kaiser Wilhelm visits England for Queen Victoria's Golden Jubilee. 1896, Charles E. Callwell of the British Army publishes Small Wars – Their Principles and Practice. *February 4th, 1899, the year Aguinaldo leads a Philippine Insurrection against U.S. forces –*

All of these events, all of these men and their actions. Lies and blood and betrayals, links in the chain leading, finally, to this moment, to that ninth wave, mightier than the last, all in flame. Meredith swallowed a mouthful of sea water and struggled to keep her head above the surface.

"Hurry, child!" her mother's ghost shouted from the pier. "They are rising," and Meredith Dandridge began to pray then that she would fail, would surrender in another moment or two and let the deep have her. Imagined sinking down and down for all eternity, pressure to crush her flat and numb, to crush her so small that nothing and no one would ever have any need to harm her again.

Claws swiped at her right ankle, slicing her skin, and her blood mingled with the sea.

And then she was digging her fingers into the mud and pebbles at the edge of the island. She dragged herself quickly from the pool, from the water and the mire, and looked back the way she'd come. There were no demons in the water, and her mother's ghost wasn't watching from the pier. But her father was, Machen Dandridge and his terrible black book, his eyes upturned and arms outstretched to an indifferent Heaven. She cursed him for the last time ever and ignored the blood oozing from the ugly gash in her ankle.

"This is where I stand," she said, getting to her feet and turning towards the small cave at the center of the island, her legs as weak and unsteady as a newborn foal's. "At the bottom gate, and I hold the key to the abyss."

The yellow-green light was almost blinding, and soon the pool would begin to boil.

"The ebony key to the first day and the last, the key to the moment when the stars wink out one by one and the sea heaves its rotting belly at the empty, sagging sky. The blazing key that even angels fear to keep."

For an instant, there was no cave, and no pool, and no cavern beneath a resentful, wicked house. Only the fire, pouring from the cave that was no longer there, to swallow her whole, only the voices of the void, and Meredith Dandridge made her fear a shield and a lance and held the line.

And in the days and weeks that followed, sometimes Machen Dandridge came down the stairs to stand on the pier and gaze across the pool to the place where the thing that had been his daughter nestled in the shadows, in the hollows between the stones. And every day the sea gave her more of its armour, gilding her frail human skin with the calcareous shells and stinging tentacles that other creatures had spent countless cycles of Creation refining from the rawest matter of life, the needle teeth, the scales and poisonous barbs. Where his wife and son had failed, his daughter crouched triumphant as any martyr. And sometimes, late at night, alone with the sound of the surf pounding against the edge of the continent, he sometimes thought of setting fire to the house and letting it burn down around him.

He read the newspapers.

He watched the stars for signs and portents.

When the moon was bright, the women still came to dance beside the sea, but he'd begun to believe they were only bad memories from some time before, and so he rarely paid them any heed.

When the weather was good, he climbed the hills behind the house and sat at the grave of his dead wife and whispered to her, telling her how proud he was of Meredith, reciting snatches of half-remembered poetry for Ellen, telling her the world would come very close to the brink because of what he'd done. Because of his blind pride. But, in the end, it would survive because of what their daughter had done and would do for ages yet.

On a long rainy afternoon in May, he opened the attic door and, with an axe and his old Colt revolver, killed what he found there. Colt revolver. He buried it beside his wife, but left nothing to mark Avery's grave.

He wrote long letters to men he'd once known in England and New York and Rio de Janeiro, but there were never any replies.

And time rolled on, neither malign nor beneficent, settling across the universe like the grey caul of dust settling thick upon the relics he'd brought back from India and Iran and the Sudan a quarter of a century before. The birth and death of stars, light reaching his aging eyes after a billion years racing across the vacuum of space, and sometimes he spent the days gathering fossils from the cliffs and arranging them in precise geometric patterns in the tall grass around the house. He left lines of salt and drew elaborate runes, the meanings of which he'd long since forgotten.

His daughter spoke to him only in his dreams, or hers, no way to ever be sure which was which, and her voice grew stronger and more terrible as the years rushed past. In the end, she was a maelstrom to swallow his withered soul, to rock him to sleep one last time, to show him the way across.

And the house by the sea, weathered and weary and insane, kept its secrets.

Publication History

"Lovecraft and I" 2011 *Lovecraft Annual* (August #5), Hippocampus Press (keynote address, 15th Annual H.P. Lovecraft Film Festival, Portland, Oregon)

"Valentia" 2000 *Dark Terrors 5,* ed. Stephen Jones and David Sutton, Victor Gollancz

"So Runs the World Away" 2001 *The Mammoth Book of Vampire Stories by Women,* ed. Stephen Jones, Carroll & Graf

"From Cabinet 34, Drawer 6" 2005 *Weird Shadows Over Innsmouth,* ed. Stephen Jones, Fedogan & Bremer

"The Drowned Geologist (1898)" 2003 *Shadows Over Baker Street,* ed. Michael Reaves and John Pelan, Delrey

"The Dead and the Moonstruck" 2004 *Gothic! Ten Original Dark Tales,* ed. Deborah Noyes, Candlewick Press

"Houses Under the Sea" 2007 *Thrillers II,* ed. Robert Morrish, Cemetery Dance Publications

"Pickman's Other Model (1929)" 2008 *Sirenia Digest* (Mar. #28), Goat Girl Press; reprinted 2010 *Black Wings: New Tales of Lovecraftian Horror,* ed. S.T. Joshi, PS Publishing

"The Thousand-and-Third Tale of Scheherazade" 2009 *Sirenia Digest* (Jan. #38), Goat Girl Press; reprinted 2012 *Confessions of a Five-Chambered Heart,* Subterranean Press

"The Bone's Prayer" 2009 *Sirenia Digest* (Feb. #39), Goat Girl Press; reprinted 2010 *The Year's Best Dark Fantasy & Horror 2010,* ed. Paula Guran, Prime Books

"The Peril of Liberated Objects, or the Voyeur's Seduction" 2012 *Confessions of a Five-Chambered Heart,* Subterranean Press

"At the Gate of Deeper Slumber" 2012 *Confessions of a Five-Chambered Heart,* Subterranean Press

"Fish Bride (1970)" 2009 *Sirenia Digest* (May #42), Goat Girl Press; reprinted 2011 *The Weird Fiction Review* (#2), ed. S.T. Joshi, Centipede Press

"The Alchemist's Daughter (A Fragment)" 2009 *Sirenia Digest* (June #43), Goat Girl Press (first print publication)

"Houndwife" 2010 *Sirenia Digest* (Mar. #52), Goat Girl Press; reprinted 2012 *Black Wings II,* ed. S.T. Joshi, PS Publishing

"Tidal Forces" 2011 *Sirenia Digest* (June #55), Goat Girl Press; reprinted 2011 *Eclipse Four,* ed. Jonathan Strahan, Night Shade Books

"John Four" 2010 *Sirenia Digest* (Sept. #58), Goat Girl Press; reprinted 2014 *A Mountain Walked,* ed. S.T. Joshi, Centipede Press

"On the Reef" 2010 *Sirenia Digest* (Oct. #59), Goat Girl Press; reprinted 2011 *Halloween,* ed. Paula Guran, Prime Books

"The Transition of Elizabeth Haskings" 2012 *Sirenia Digest* (Jan. #74), Goat Girl Press; reprinted 2013, *Weirder Shadows Over Innsmouth,* ed. Stephen Jones, Fedogan & Bremer

"A Mountain Walked" 2012 *Sirenia Digest* (Sept. #82), Goat Girl Press; reprinted 2014 *The Madness of Cthulhu: Volume 1,* edited S.T. Joshi, Titan Books

"Love Is Forbidden, We Croak & Howl" 2012 *Sirenia Digest* (May #78), Goat Girl Press; reprinted 2014 *Lovecraft's Monsters,* ed. Ellen Datlow, Tachyon Publications

"Pushing the Sky Away (Death of a Blasphemer)" 2013 *Sirenia Digest* (Aug. #91), Goat Girl Press (first print publication)

"Black Ships Seen South of Heaven" 2015 *Black Wings IV,* ed. S.T. Joshi, PS Publishing

"Pickman's Madonna" 2013 *Sirenia Digest* (Oct. #93), Goat Girl Press; reprinted 2015 (revised and in part) *Cherry Bomb: A ~~Siobhan~~ Quinn Novel* (as Kathleen Tierney), Roc/NAL

"The Peddler's Tale, or Isobel's Revenge" 2013 *Sirenia Digest* (Dec. #95), Goat Girl Press; reprinted 2015 *The Mammoth Book of Cthulhu,* ed. Paula Guran, Prime Books

"The Cats of River Street (1925)" 2014 *Sirenia Digest* (Jul. #102), Goat Girl Press; reprinted 2015 *Innsmouth Nightmares,* ed. Lois Gresh, PS Publishing

"A Redress for Andromeda" 2000 *October Dreams: A Celebration of Halloween,* ed. Richard Chizmar and Robert Morrish, Cemetery Dance Publications

"Nor the Demons Down Under the Sea" 2002 *The Children of Cthulhu,* ed. John Pelan and Benjamin Adams, Del Rey

"Study for *The Witch House*" 2013 *Sirenia Digest* (Sept. #92), Goat Girl Press

"Andromeda Among the Stones" 2003 chapbook accompanying *Embrace the Mutation,* ed. William K. Schafer, Subterranean Press

"M Is for Mars" (first publication)

The author wishes to note that the text for each of these stories, as it appears in this collection, will differ, often significantly, from the originally published texts. In some cases, stories were revised for each reprinting (and some have been reprinted numerous times). No story is ever finished. There's only the moment when I force myself to stop and provisionally type THE END.

Originally, "Pædomorphosis," written in 1997, was to have been included in this volume, as it was my first overt use of Lovecraft's "mythos." However, the prose has not aged well, and ultimately the decision was made to exclude the story. Anyone so inclined can find "Pædomorphosis" in my first short-fiction collection, *Tales of Pain and Wonder* (2000, 2008, 2016).

Acknowledgments

Mythos Tales was proposed to me by Jerad Walters in the spring of 2013, though I didn't actually manage to assemble the manuscript until the summer of 2015, and then I didn't finish editing it until February 2016. Without Jerad's interest and encouragement, this book simply would not exist. I would also like to thank S.T. Joshi. William K. Schafer, Michael Cisco, Vince Locke, Richard A. Kirk, Piotr Jabłoński, John Kenn Mortensen, and Christopher Geissler. Special thanks to my partner, Kathryn A. Pollnac, for all her assistance and support with this project and to all my Patreon supporters for sticking with me. The typescript for *Mythos Tales* was proofread entirely at the John Hay Library, Brown University.

Caitlín R. Kiernan
15 February 2016
Providence, Rhode Island

About the Author

The New York Times has called Caitlín R. Kiernan "one of our essential writers of dark fiction" and S. T. Joshi has declared "...hers is now the voice of weird fiction." Her novels include *Silk, Threshold, Low Red Moon, Daughter of Hounds, The Red Tree* (nominated for the Shirley Jackson and World Fantasy awards), and *The Drowning Girl: A Memoir* (winner of the James Tiptree, Jr. and Bram Stoker awards, nominated for the Nebula, World Fantasy, British Fantasy, Mythopoeic, Locus, and Shirley Jackson awards). To date, her short fiction has been collected in thirteen volumes, including *Tales of Pain and Wonder; From Weird and Distant Shores; To Charles Fort, With Love; Alabaster; A is for Alien; The Ammonite Violin & Others; Confessions of a Five-Chambered Heart; Two Worlds and In Between: The Best of Caitlín R. Kiernan (Volume One)* and *Beneath an Oil-Dark Sea: The Best of Caitlín R. Kiernan (Volume Two); Cambrian Tales: Juvenilia;* and the World Fantasy Award-winning *The Ape's Wife and Other Stories.* She has also received the World Fantasy Award for Best Short Fiction for "The Prayer of Ninety Cats." During the 1990s, she wrote *The Dreaming* for DC Comics' Vertigo imprint and has recently completed *Alabaster* for Dark Horse Comics. The first volume, *Alabaster: Wolves,* received the Bram Stoker Award. She lives in Providence, Rhode Island with her partner, Kathryn Pollnac.

But all she ever *wanted* was to be a paleontologist...